Ardistan and Djinnistan

The Collected Works of
KARL MAY

Edited by Erwin J. Haeberle

Series I: Volumes 1 and 2

Volumes 1 and 2

ARDISTAN AND DJINNISTAN

: *A Novel by* :

KARL MAY

Translated by

MICHAEL SHAW

A Continuum Book

THE SEABURY PRESS : NEW YORK

1977 : *The Seabury Press*
815 Second Avenue : New York, New York 10017

The present text is based on the two volumes, *Ardistan* and *Der Mir von Dschinnistan,* published by Karl-May-Verlag, Bamberg. © 1967 Karl-May Verlag, Bamberg.

Library of Congress Cataloging in Publication Data

May, Karl Friedrich, 1842–1912.
Ardistan and Djinnistan.
(The Collected works of Karl May; ser. 1, v. 1 & 2)
Translation of Ardistan and of Der Mir von Djinnistan.
I. May, Karl Friedrich, 1842–1912. Der Mir von Djinnistan.
English. 1977.   II. Title.   III. Title: Djinnistan.
PZ3.M4508Co   1977   ser. 1, v. 1–2   [PT2625.A848]
77–12605
ISBN 0–8164–9316–2   833′.8s [833′.8]

Contents

VOLUME ONE

Kennst du den unergründlich tiefen See,
in dessen Flut ich meine Ruder schlage?
Er heisst seit Anbeginn das Menschheitsweh,
und ich, mein Freund, ich bin die Menschheitsfrage

1 : The Land of the Starflowers

My tale begins in Sitara, the "Land of the Starflowers," which is almost completely unknown in Europe. The Sultana of this realm is Marah Durimeh, a princess whose family has ruled this land for thousands of years. The farflung region of Mardistan with the mysterious forest of Kulub is also part of Sitara. There is a rumor of a spirits' forge in its deepest ravine where souls are refined into spirits through pain and torment. But today, we shall avoid this place and rather wander through the gardens of Ikbal to forget all earthly suffering.

Ikbal is one of the most beautiful residences of Marah Durimeh. Her princely apartment, resembling a temple rather than a castle, rises from the ground like a verse from the Song of Solomon. Wrought of white marble, clear, pure and light, it shines against the dark background of mountains that tower high into the sky. They lie in the northern part of the country, while toward the south there is the blue sea with its silver threads, breathing gently like a sleeeping, happy child that smiles in its dreams. The houses of her subjects sit at the foot of the palace like so many precious, shimmering pearls that an artful fairy has brought back from the depth of the ocean and placed in green gardens along the shore. The sea air lessens the heat of the burning sun. Shaded paths lead from the valley to the mountain, from the mountain down to the valley. Golden fruit beckons in the dark foliage, and every current of air wafts the sweet scent of flowers. Untouched by the filth of ordinary life, the river Ed Din pours forth from the mountains like a revelation, circles Ikbal with its two strong arms, and then pours into the sea to purify its water.

There is no communication between Ikbal and the outside world except by a single, fairly sizable sailboat in its small harbor. It is called "Wilahde," resembles an ark, and is always ready to sail. Age-old, with the form and lines of past millennia, its rigging and sails may have been invented in early Babylon or Egypt, yet it is not deficient in any way. Its fittings admirably suit the purpose for which they are intended.

As her guest and accompanied by Hadji Halef Omar, the sheik of the Haddedihn of the Shammar tribe, I had come to Marah Durimeh to acquaint myself with the land of the starflowers. She had received me like a close relative, indeed as a son. We did not stay in the city but in her palace. My apartment was on the same floor as hers while Halef stayed at ground level in the servants' quarters. She was fond of him, being touched by his almost unrivalled love and devotion, and congratulated me for having found and trained him as my companion. But she faulted him for making no effort to transform his soul into spirit, and judged what others praised, his charm, to be his greatest weakness. Being an incomparable student of human nature, she could consider no one a developed human being who did not have the strength to transcend the demands of his physical anima.

Shakara, who had once saved me from certain death, was a particular favorite of her mistress and would leave her side only when matters of great importance needed attending to. Now she also was in Ikbal, and cared for me in the same sisterly, self-sacrificing way as once before when I had been weak and ill.

Our departure was set for the morrow. Marah Durimeh, Shakara, and I had strolled through the city and its environs once again to visit the sights that had become dear to me. Then we walked to the lush meadow behind the palace where our two horses were grazing. They were the black stallions Assil Ben Rih and Syrr, the most noble animals that ever lived. They had carried us here from a distant country and were to take us back by the same route, or so we thought. But things were to turn out differently.

Later, some time after sunset, the three of us were sitting on a high balcony, eating a simple meal of bread and fruit. Below us, in the court, Halef had joined a number of servants to tell them of his adventures, talking bombastically and greedy for approval, as was his wont. But the interest his tales had aroused elsewhere was absent here. His audience listened quietly but did not praise or applaud him. A tolerant nod or an ironic smile was the only response, and so he got up, raised his arms contemptuously, turned his back on his listeners and walked out of the gate.

We paid no attention to him and his well-deserved defeat. We were absorbed by the magnificence of the divine creation lying before our eyes as it glowed in almost supernatural splendor in the light of the setting sun. Far in the south, where sky and sea merged, there was a small but constantly growing point which now flashed like lightning, now shimmered like gold, sparkled like silver, or flickered in the colors of the rainbow.

"A messenger is coming," Shakara said as she pointed to it.

Marah Durimeh turned her gaze in the direction from which the point was approaching us and then said with greater precision:

"Yes, it is a messenger, but it is one of ours."

"Which one?" Shakara asked.

"The one who is bringing me the response from the Mir of Djinnistan."

Though of an age so advanced that one could no longer determine it, this woman had an extraordinary keenness of vision. Straining with all my might, I could only sense but not clearly see that this iridescent point was actually a white sail. But she saw the boat and presumably the man guiding it. Yet it was not only her eyesight but the name she had mentioned that astonished me. The Mir of Djinnistan! I imagine that none of my readers has ever heard of this famous man, the ruler of a great realm. I also had been ignorant of his existence before making the acquaintance of Marah Durimeh. Then I had gradually learned from her the names of the numerous regions over which her influence extended. The boat was being sped along by a favorable wind and was rapidly approaching the harbor. Its occupant had been sent to the Mir and was returning from him. The message she was expecting seemed of great importance, for she rose from her seat, shaded her eyes, bent over the railing of the balcony, and observed the boat attentively for a minute or so. Then she said:

"Yes, it is he," and added with a deep breath: "Now a decision will be made."

She sat down again, looked thoughtfully at the ground, then raised her eyes toward me, and asked:

"Must you return home, Sidi, or not?"

"I am always my own master," I answered.

"I know that," she said kindly. "Perhaps it is good that you are still here among us."

"Good? For whom?"

"For you, for me, and especially for the Mir of Djinnistan."

I quickly rose to my feet and exclaimed in surprise:

"For us, and for him as well? Your remark is mysterious."

She looked at me with wide open eyes as if to penetrate my inner being, and answered:

"You yourself are the greatest of all mysteries. If you find the answer, you will also solve the mystery of the Mir of Djinnistan. Sit down and wait until I have spoken to the messenger."

What had first been a point had meanwhile become larger and appeared as a white sail. Then one could see that there were actually three of them. I noticed later that the boat had two masts to which the sails were attached in a manner I had never seen before but which was very practical. The foresail pierced the air while the two mainsails could be compared to a plough, coming together in front to form an edge but fanning out in back to catch the wind. The crew consisted of only two men to handle sails and rudder. The captain stood far forward. In white clothing and fluttering turban, drawn up to his full height with one hand proudly planted on his hip, he looked less like an ordinary earthly messenger than one of those supernatural beings in old oriental legends, they that suddenly emerge with their ships from the bottom of the sea to bring to human beings the greeting of eternity and the blessing of heaven.

Now, as the boat was coming close to the harbor, the sun was setting. A transparent shadow of purplish hue flashed through the light shining on the waves. All at once, the serenity of the golden day had become the seriousness of approaching evening. From the nearby mosque, we heard the Muezzin's call to prayer.

That was all we heard, for now the majestic bells joined their voices, harmonizing all other sounds in their glorious evening chimes. Marah Durimeh rose, and so did we. We folded our hands but she pointed to the bell tower and said:

This is the sound that rings through the universe
The only sound that brings happiness and peace
All earthly strife disappears in it
The Lord be praised forever.

At this precise moment, the boat reached the harbor. The messenger saw his mistress on the balcony. Raising both arms, he saluted her. Then he knelt down where he had been standing and folded his hands in prayer.

It is difficult to describe the extraordinary remoteness and isolation of this place, the gradually fading tints flashing across the sky and the earth, the ever more magical and mystical coloration of the sea and, finally, the sound of those bells. Surely no European had ever come here before. But more impressive than all this was the commanding figure of our mistress.

Often, when he had seriously reflected about her, Hadji Halef had said to me:

"She is no ordinary woman, and no ordinary queen. She is a Djini, a soul, a spirit. Indeed, she is more than that. She is not only a soul or a spirit but the mistress of all souls and all spirits. May Allah bless her."

And now, I felt something stronger than a mere intimation that there were thoughts and powers in this incomparable woman which my academic psychology could not hope to understand. The man kneeling in the bow of his ship struck me as an envoy from mankind as it searches for its soul and for deliverance from danger.

The bells fell silent, the prayer was over, dusk was descending from the mountains. The man in the boat rose to his feet and steered his vessel to the shore. He disembarked and then disappeared between the houses as he took the path that would lead him to us. Shortly thereafter, it was announced that he had arrived and requested to see the mistress. She left while I remained with Shakara. In her sisterly, caring way, she wanted to prepare me, and said:

"Perhaps it would have been better had you already left us. I am afraid the mistress will give you a difficult task."

"Something impossible, perhaps?" I asked with a smile.

"No, she would not do that."

"Then put your mind at rest, Shakara. Now that she has mentioned the Mir of Djinnistan, I hope and even wish that I won't have to leave just yet."

"There is no question but that you will leave."

"But where to?"

"To the Mir."

"The Mir?" I was both pleased and surprised.

"Yes. You have never been in Djinnistan. But do you know where it is?"

"Yes."

"And that access to it is difficult?"

"I know that as well. There are only two routes: the first, from the Madaris Lake, which is very long, or through all of Ardistan, which is the shorter but also the more dangerous way."

"Much more dangerous. Do you know the Mir of Ardistan?"

"No, but I have heard about him."

"What?"

"That he is a man of violence, a tyrant—"

"A friend of war, a man who hates peace," she interrupted me in a lively manner. "Every healthy citizen of his country is a soldier. For peaceful endeavors, he uses the sick and the maimed. It is dangerous for Europeans to enter his country. He hates everything that comes from the west, and he especially hates the people living there. Should he find out that you are European—"

She was interrupted by Marah Durimeh's return. Although that woman had an extraordinary control over herself, a trembling in her voice that she could not wholly suppress betrayed her agitation.

"The messenger's report has been broken off only temporarily. There is still much to be told, and he will return. But I had to come back to tell you that the terrible misfortune I wanted to prevent cannot be averted."

Startled, Shakara clapped her hands.

"Will there be war?" she asked.

"Yes."

"Between whom?" I asked.

"Between Ardistan and Djinnistan."

"Has it already been declared?"

"Declared? What an expression! Only among civilized rulers is there such a thing as a declaration of war. The Mir of Ardistan is a barbarian. He attacks whenever he pleases. He doesn't ask questions or make announcements. All I can say is that there will be war but that it has not yet begun. I wanted to prevent it, and so did the Mir of Djinnistan. But all our efforts were futile. Now he and I have to act quickly. I need a man I can rely on, and I need him immediately. He must be someone who is not clever, not tricky, but honest and intelligent. But he must be so intelligent that even the wiliest scoundrel won't be able to beguile him."

She turned to me, and asked:

"Do you know such a person, Sidi?"

"No," I answered.

"Don't you?" she asked with a smile.

"I really do not," I answered seriously and with conviction.

"Oh yes, there is one, and that is you," Shakara said.

"You are mistaken, my dear. I have never seen a person so smart that even the wiliest rascal cannot deceive him, and I probably never will. But there is someone who will try to act as thoughtfully, intelligently, and courageously as possible, and it is true that I am that person. If you, mistress, have none better suited at this moment, I ask that you send me."

The last words had been addressed to Marah Durimeh who did not answer right away. She stepped to the railing of the balcony and looked across the sea and up to the darkening sky where the first stars were beginning to sparkle.

After some moments, she turned to me and said:

"Yes, you shall go, Sidi. I hoped that you would offer to of your own accord, and you did. I have rarely been so pleased. I cannot thank you here and now as I would wish. It will be up to you to ask for that gratitude in Ardistan and Djinnistan where it will be offered you on all your paths. But a kind of thanks will be given you today, for I will let you know why it is you I prefer entrusting with this mission. Come here."

As I did so, she gave me her right hand and pointed to the sky with her left.

"When I was standing here before answering you, I was speaking to the stars. Look up at the firmament. Those are not the stars that shine over your country. They are the stars of the south. There you can see Virgo, Pyxis, and Crux. But those were not the stars I talked to. My astronomy is of a different sort. I do not derive it from the visible sky that is flaming and glowing above us. But as I gaze at the stars, I open my inner eye to the spiritual firmament and behold stars others never see. I also saw yours. Shall I show it to you?"

It was a strange, even a miraculous moment. She stood facing me like one of the famous seers from the time the tower of Babel was built. Her ghostly features looked as if cut from lightly darkened alabaster.

Her eyes were shining in the starlight, her long, heavy, silver-white braids hung almost to the ground, her voice was unearthly. And a lightly scented breath wafted about her, a curious, mysterious aura for which the right word does not exist in any known language. I did not wholly understand what she said but merely had some vague notion.

I asked her:

"Show it to me."

"You will see it," she answered, "but not by my pointing my finger at it and telling you it is there, but by my showing you where and how it must be searched for. For only the star you can find can be yours. If God, our Lord, wishes it, you will see it in Djinnistan the moment it stands above you. You do not yet know that country. Nor have you ever been in Ardistan. I shall take you to the library where I shall give you the books and maps that will instruct you. But before that, I have to tell you something of enormous importance. Let us sit down."

Marah Durimeh began:

"In the West, people would probably laugh at what I am about to tell you. But I am utterly serious. I am thinking of the prophecy of the heavenly hosts: 'Honor to God on high and peace on earth.' That He, the Lord of the universe, is shown the respect that is His due is something He sees to in His omnipotence and wisdom. But it is our task to work for peace here on earth."

"It almost seems as if this peace would never come," Shakara said.

"It will come," the mistress said gravely. "It must come, for such is God's will."

"Thousands of years have passed and it is not here yet."

"But thousands more will not pass."

"There are already some stirrings in the West," I interjected. "The noblest men and women are uniting to pave the way."

"I know. But what good are the proposals of even the most noble of men if the large hints that life itself gives us are disregarded? Even if a hundred empresses and a thousand queens were to join in raising their voices on behalf of so-called eternal peace, that chorus could not prevail against the horrible, unceasing outcry of the blood that has been spilled since the beginning without there ever having been a year of which it might be said that it was a year of peace."

"The rulers and princes are sending envoys to peace conferences," I said.

"Where war, not peace, is being prepared for," Marah Durimeh interrupted me.

"War is being made more humane."

"Which means that killing is becoming quicker and less painful, but there is killing nonetheless. I tell you, my friend, that proud war will never stoop and stretch its hand out to peace. Peace must rise up to it and bring it crashing down, for war will forever resist. If war has an iron hand, let peace have a fist of steel. Only power impresses, real power. And if peace is to make an impact, it must become powerful. Heretofore, all the armaments of the world and all the armaments of the nations have been directed toward war. As if it were impossible to arm for peace in the same way! Do you understand what I mean?"

"I do," I answered. "Whichever is more powerful will rule. But where does war get its power?"

"You will see that in Ardistan."

"And where does peace?"

"That you will discover in Djinnistan. Now is not the time to waste words discussing these questions. In any event, words are not what is needed. Something has to happen. There is the science of war, which has both a theoretical and a practical side. There is the science of peace, which is merely theoretical. Everyone knows how war is waged but no one knows how to wage peace. You have standing armies for war which cost billions each year. But where are your citadels of peace, your strategists of peace, your officers of peace? I will ask no further questions, for all of them will confront you in Ardistan, and the answers will manifest themselves to you in Djinnistan. But only if you keep your eyes open! Your journey to these two countries will be one of training and study and what you will learn there is my repayment for the readiness with which you accept this mission. These two countries will provide you with a fairly faithful image of earth, its inhabitants, and all the relationships nations entertain with each other. And should you encounter mysteries you cannot solve, remember what I am now telling you."

She slowly pointed toward the east, and continued:

"Back there, the yellow race has awakened from a long, profound slumber. It is just beginning to stir, to breathe freely. Woe to us if it should sense its strength and leap from its repose to show us that it has no less right to live than others."

Then she pointed west, and went on:

"Over there, you have America which you falsely call the New World. The Indian lives there and you think he is doomed. But you are mistaken. The Indian will not die. No Portuguese, no Spaniard, no Englishman, and no Yankee has the power to exterminate him. The so-called 'dying' Indian will rise again. The Orient also is beginning to rouse itself. It is stretching its limbs, testing its muscles and joints. Giant Islam, whose powerful figures stand on European, Asian, and African soil, is not afraid of the apparent superiority of the Occident. The Kismet it believes in is irresistible and of infinite endurance. It counterbalances the superiority of European arms. If the Orient has good leaders, it will be victorious. And should it be defeated, its destruction will also be yours. Why? Because the Occident was not great, just, and noble enough to subject its so-called spheres of interest to a humane review and to reconcile itself with the Orient."

"To reconcile itself with the Orient?" I asked. "That is false, for it is not the Occident but the Orient that has been offended, deeply injured, and suppressed. Almost everything the Occident possesses has come from the Orient. Its religion, its art, its science, all its knowledge and morals, its cereals, its fruit, the entire ground of its outer and inner life. And what it did not take from it directly was transmitted as impulse. The gratitude we owe is enormous. And how did we repay it? How, and with what?"

"You are asking the right question," Shakara answered. "How did you reward us, and with what? After we had given you everything we possessed, you came with your cunning and your arms to take from us what we had left. If the Orient had given you no more than the single phrase 'God is love,' you could not repay this gift with all the suns, moons, and stars, however many of them there may be in the sky. But you have never done anything to thank us for what you have received. You repaid us with blood, war, envy, and hatred."

"If you were to say that in the West, people would laugh at you, Shakara," I answered. "There, people maintain the very opposite."

Now Marah Durimeh said:

"The Occident has to learn to love the Orient. There must be peace. The Orient and the Occident must stand by each other's side as unconquerable friends, governing the world and forcing the peoples of the earth to put their swords away and let them rust."

"When will that come about?" I asked. "How soon, or should I say, how late?"

"Go to Djinnistan. There, the hour will strike," she answered. "But I have come to the end of my preamble and will give you my instructions by simply telling you that we human beings will not be given a present of peace. We must deserve it! Peace can only come from above. We must prove that we are worthy of it. Then, when it comes down to us, we have to go toward it with devotion, concern, and hard work so that we may hold on to it forever. And now, it is your mission to go toward it."

"Go toward peace? You are expressing yourself in images."

"Oh, no. These are not images. They will become realities. It was decided that the war which is now breaking out will be the last between Ardistan and Djinnistan. I have done everything I could to prevent it, but I failed. This Mir of Ardistan insists on having his will. And therefore I shall arm mine. If he forces Djinnistan into war, he will force me as well. I will accept the challenge. But my strategy and my tactics are not his. He wants to spill blood; I don't. In spite of all his armies, I will show this man that we will defeat him without firing a single shot. Would it not be foolish to pit the life of even a single man of grace against that of a bloodthirsty man of violence? Am I to drive those I love, and who love me, against lions? Never! My plan is this: beast of prey against beast of prey, panther against panther. I repeat: panther against panther. You don't understand that yet but you will soon learn what I mean. I know you are fearless, Effendi. And yet I ask: Is it not possible that the Mir of Ardistan might arouse feelings of fear in you?"

"No," I answered.

"Would you have the courage to search him out in his capital of Ard as his declared adversary and to deal with him face to face?"

"If my cause is just, I would."

"It is. You will encounter the Mir of Djinnistan in Ard."

"The Mir of Djinnistan? The two of us as adversaries of the Mir of Ardistan?"

"Yes."

"In the enemy's capital?"

"Yes."

"You mean when the war is over and has been won?"

"No. During the war, and utterly unprotected. Without weapons. You will only be accompanied by your Hadji Halef, and he by two or three companions. In the cave of the lion, which is also the cave of the panther of whom I spoke just now."

"You always choose what is right and best. I am ready."

"I thank you. The Mir of Djinnistan will come down from his mountains to bring peace to Ardistan by conquering it without a single stroke of the sword. And you are to come toward him by ascending from the low-lying swamps of the Ussul in order to prepare Ardistan and its ruler for him. Do not be frightened, my friend. Nothing impossible is demanded of you. You will experience strange things. But here, the strange is finally being recognized for what it is, the natural, while what has been considered natural heretofore will become an oddity, a mere whim, a chimera. Are you ready then, Effendi, to undertake this journey for me?"

"Gladly, with all my heart," I answered, for it was true and I felt great joy.

"Then come to the library with me to receive detailed instructions and to see the books, maps, and plans by which you will prepare yourself."

I followed her from the balcony to the library where she gave me more precise orders about the task I would undertake and selected those works which would inform me about the planned journey. She had "Wilahde," the sailboat, prepared for my departure the following morning. She then brought in the messenger who had returned from Djinnistan that day. There was a fairly long discussion which later proved beneficial to me. Finally, toward midnight, I found myself alone and went down once again to the horses, as was my daily custom. They were so used to this that they would not have gone to sleep if I had omitted this visit.

When I returned to my apartment, I found it impossible to fall asleep. The project of visiting the two most mysterious regions in the world would have been intensely interesting at any time. But this was more than a mere idle visit. I had an important mission, and the sense of an extraordinary obligation made me restless and drove me back to the library where I sat studying books and maps until early morning. I wanted to be able to tell myself later that I had neglected nothing to prepare myself for the demands that might be made of me.

Marah Durimeh and Shakara had risen early and found me in the library. From there, we went to the balcony for breakfast. The boat would weigh anchor precisely at noon. Shakara was to accompany us on the voyage to the place of debarkation to answer any questions I might have. Then she would return to Ikbal.

When our equipment was being packed, Marah Durimeh added some objects which she felt might be useful to us. Among them, there was a polished breastplate. It was not a complete piece of armor for the upper body but a thin, lightweight shield for the protection of the heart and lungs, made of a metal or metal alloy unknown to me. It was so flexible that it could be worn under a thin garment without being conspicuous.

"I want you to put on this shield before you enter Ardistan," she said.

"Do you believe that the dangers threatening us there will be so great?"

"There will be considerable danger," she answered. "But I do not worry about you; you will survive them. This shield is meant for your protection and provided with straps so it can be worn over the chest, but it is also an identification by which certain persons you will encounter can recognize you."

"May I know who they are?"

"I shall not tell you now. I want you to be free, not tied to a name."

"But if they recognize me by this shield, how will I recognize them?"

"By the very same shield. It is the shield of the hosts in black armor and of the lancers of Djinnistan. Wear it, but don't talk about it. Should you encounter someone who tells you that he is the owner of such a shield, tell him that you also were given one by Marah Durimeh. Then you can trust and rely on each other in all danger."

2 : Prehistoric Men

When the time for our departure had come, we ourselves led the horses on board, for they were too valuable to be entrusted to anyone else. Marah Durimeh accompanied us to the ship. She was simply and modestly dressed, like any ordinary woman, and greeted by all who saw her with respect and love but without ceremony, in a perfectly natural manner. This is also how we said farewell. She was standing on the shore and raised her hand in greeting as the anchor was weighed. Then she left. A short time later, we saw her on the balcony where she remained until we could no longer see her. Then the palace, the city, the dark mountains, all of Sitara as we had come to know it vanished and there was only the infinite sea to which we had entrusted ourselves.

At any other time, I would certainly have carefully inspected the ship, its equipment, and crew. But here I did not have the chance, having to make use of every available minute to go through the material I had taken along, for it had to go back with Shakara. I spent all my time reading and made notes of everything I considered important. Shakara helped me. After three days, I had compiled a mass of notes of inestimable value. With their aid, I would be able to orient myself in every situation and locality.

During these three days, we had encountered no vessels and were now approaching our destination. We could expect to arrive on the coast of Ardistan at noon on the fourth day. But even there, we did not see a single ship or even a bark for we steered clear of all harbors. Because we had to land in total secrecy, we chose a deserted part of the coast which seemed inaccessible. There was a small, narrow bay where we could land but not cast anchor, for even close to the shore the water was so deep that it would not reach bottom.

Shortly after noon, a dark line emerged before our eyes which we approached under a favorable wind. It was Ardistan, a low-lying coast of swamps and moors.

We slowed down and approached to within half a mile, then heaved to. A rowboat and crew, with the two horses firmly tethered on board, was lowered into the water. A rope ladder was then let down for Halef, Shakara, and me. Shakara steered. Along the bay, close to the shore, some trees allowed us to fasten the boat. The horses were led ashore. Since they had already been saddled, we were ready to ride. Hadji Halef took leave of Shakara with an abundance of words. Then I took her hand. She said nothing, but her lips were trembling and there were tears in her eyes. Then she gave the signal for the boat to be pushed back into the water. Moments later, the profound, mysterious sea had already separated us. As if the same thought had occurred to her, she called out to us:

"Effendi, if you find yourself in a danger you cannot deal with, or if the tears of universal suffering should threaten to drown you, do not lose courage, but believe that Marah Durimeh and Shakara will always be close to you. Farewell."

"Farewell," I answered.

Then the boat sped back toward the ship while we were still standing on the shore, following it with our eyes. In a final greeting, a white flag was raised on the mainmast. Next to me, I heard suppressed sobbing. Halef was crying.

"Don't laugh at me, Sidi," he said. "I don't like Sitara because I was laughed at, but I can't help howling. What are tears for? Surely not always to keep them bottled up. They have to come out. It's true I upbraided the inhabitants of that country occasionally, yet I care for them, especially Marah Durimeh and Shakara. There goes the ship. I am going to sit down to watch until it can no longer be seen. I won't get up until then."

He uttered these sentences disconnectedly, in a whining tone. I knew how attached he had become to Shakara, our young, noble friend, and taking leave of her moved him. And he really did sit down on the damp ground and followed the ship with his eyes until it had disappeared over the horizon. Then he got up and said:

"Now it's over. Leave-taking is painful but we are no children. We are men. More importantly, we know that we are about to enter an unknown country and embark on a life of adventure. So we must pull ourselves together and look bravely ahead, not back at what lies behind us. Have you got all your things, Sidi?"

"Yes."

"And the copies of the maps, plans, and all those thousands of names? Surely you haven't forgotten those?"

"No."

"Where are they?"

I reached into my breast pocket but they weren't there. I went through all my other pockets, but in vain. I had left them on the ship, these copies which I had made with such care and which were of such enormous importance. This sort of thing had never happened to me before. Up to that moment, I would not have believed I could be so thoughtless. Profoundly troubled, I sat down. Without these notes, it might be impossible for me to move about unaided in a strange country, unfamiliar as I was with local conditions and at the mercy of any chance event. Halef had just referred to us as "men." But without this material, we resembled children who make nothing but mistakes when they act on their own. I was extremely angry with myself and more out of sorts than I had ever been before. On top of that, Halef now planted himself in front of me and said:

"Well now! There you sit, just as I was sitting a few moments ago. All we need now is that you start bawling as I did. So you forgot them?"

"Unfortunately I did," I confessed.

"That's what I thought," he went on. "You have always been forgetful. Terribly forgetful. As long as I have known you."

"Oh, no," I contradicted.

"Yes, yes," he maintained. "You also have some other faults, of course, my dear Sidi, but the most serious has always been your forgetfulness. And I don't think that will change. You know as well as I that I have done everything I could to cure you of this flaw, but unfortunately without success. For a rational person like me, that's no cause to be angry with you, let alone disrespect you, for innate shortcomings cannot be cured. But I am saddened that I seem destined to keep discovering them in you. That you left those notes on the ship is utterly incomprehensible."

He placed the butt of his rifle on the ground, supported himself on the barrel, and continued:

"Sidi, you know that we have been sent to Ardistan and Djinnistan where great adventures await us and where we are to accomplish those deeds which are impossible to anyone but the two of us. But since you left your maps and plans on the ship, you will admit that it is I that will have to do what must be done. Before, you were the principal actor and I the supporting cast. Now, the roles have been reversed. I have become the important person, and you are just tagging along. Do you admit that, Effendi?"

"Readily," I answered. "Actually, I am delighted

that I no longer have to think and plan and assume responsibilities. I will simply obey your orders."

"Hm," he mumbled. "Get on your horse then. We are leaving."

Both of us had got dirty on the damp soil, and this enraged Halef, who was much concerned with cleanliness.

"Allah w'Allah. Now the whole swamp is sticking to our clothes," he exclaimed. "That's Ardistan for you, precisely the way it was described to me. In my country, the very desert is so clean that even the faithful wash with sand before they pray if there is no water to be had. But when one enters Ardistan, one becomes mired in filth at the first step and cannot cleanse oneself until one reaches the border of Djinnistan. Let's hurry and get away from this dirt and mud."

He got on his horse, and I mounted mine. He waited for me to ride ahead, but I refused and told him:

"You show the way. I am merely the supporting cast."

"Very well, I shall," he answered in a seemingly confident manner. But then he added: "You don't have to ride behind me. There's no reason why you should not keep alongside me. You know me. Even as the star, I remain affable."

The little rascal wanted me next to him so that he could take his cue from me. But I would not go along with that ruse. He became embarrassed. He was utterly unable to decide on the direction we should take, turned to me a few moments later, and asked:

"Sidi, tell me at least if I am going in the right direction."

"It's the right one," I answered. "Straight ahead."

"But what if there is a swamp?"

"Then we'll change direction."

"Everything seems to be swamp here. I think it's terrible! The horses are sinking into the ground up to their knees."

"It will take us three days to cross this plain."

"Three days? May Allah have mercy on us. What kind of human beings live here?"

"None. We won't come across any people until we

get to the other side of these lowlands."

"And who will they be?"

"The tribe of the Ussul."

"Do you know it?"

"No."

"Then you should be pleased that I am in charge now. Without me, you would be lost once you met them. I know what I shall be dealing with. I've heard about them. Be careful, Effendi! The Ussul are giants. They have legs like elephants, and their arms are as long and as strong as twenty-year-old trees. Their hair resembles a lion's mane, their eyes glow like lanterns, and their voices roar like thunder. When they become angry, the ground trembles under their feet. They live in impregnable citadels which they build only on the water. They murder and pillage for a living and believe neither in Allah nor the devil. Anyone that tangles with them is doomed."

It is not my purpose here to give a complete account of our journey. I merely have to report what is important to my fundamental idea. Suffice it to say that we spent three full days crossing the coastal plain and that during that time nothing of consequence happened. While I saw to it that we took the direction that would get us into the interior, I let Halef believe that he was the leader and that I merely followed him. I was already looking forward to the face he would make when he was disabused of that illusion.

We had enough to eat, for Shakara had supplied us with adequate provisions. The nights were spent at suitable places in the forest where the ground was dry and we were reasonably well protected from the mosquitoes, which were a problem in this low-lying region. On the morning of the fourth day, the aspect of the land changed. It became drier and trees began to appear. Open, green, meadow-like stretches offered good and tasty grass to our horses, and we passed occasional streams and ponds with an abundance of animal life. We also found traces of human activity though they were old and indistinct. But at one point, where they led through tall grass and crisscrossed as if something had been eagerly searched for, they seemed of more recent date, and I therefore thought it advisable to examine them. I stopped.

"Why aren't we going on?" Halef asked.

"Don't you see those tracks?"

"Of course I see them. They must have been made by deer or boars."

"Halef, you should be ashamed of yourself."

"So you think they are human?"

"Of course. That's something one can tell at first glance."

"And that means we have to examine them?"

"Certainly."

"Then you should dismount."

"Me? Why?"

"What a question! Up to now, the examination of tracks has always been your specialty. Why change now?"

"Reading tracks is very difficult and carries considerable responsibility. A mistake may prove fatal. And that's why it is always the head man that does it."

His face became a few centimeters longer. But he jumped from his saddle and began what he hated to do because he had never reached the point where he could infer one thing from another, something that everyone who claims he can read tracks and trails must be able to do. I also got off my horse. I wanted to find a comfortable spot in the grass and watch him.

His helplessness was amusing. He had watched any number of times the care with which I did this work. Tracks must only be looked at, never touched. But he ran back and forth over the impressions and destroyed them without considering that this was an unpardonable mistake. When he was done, he reported:

"Sidi, you are completely mistaken. Those were not human beings."

"What else?"

"Elephants, rhinoceri, hippopotami. Huge, powerful beasts."

"Why do you say that?"

"Because these imprints are huge. Only elephants or hippos have such feet."

"How many legs does an elephant have?"

"Four, of course."

"Then you are wrong. The monsters that ran around here had two, not four, feet."

"I wonder. How can you be so sure? We aren't seeing the animals but merely their tracks. So how can one tell if two or four belong together? You say two, I say four, and surely you know that the majority is always right. It follows that these were elephants."

"Did you also look at the tracks to see if there were spurs on the boots?"

"Spurs on the boots?" He started laughing. "Since when have elephants been wearing boots with spurs on them?"

"Since they have been riding hippopotami," I answered and began laughing myself. "In any event, you aren't done yet. You have decided that these were animals. Now we have to find out where they came from and where they went."

"And you want me to do that?"

"Of course."

"Then I'll have to put down my rifles. They are getting in the way."

He was carrying a long Arabic rifle with a good deal of ivory inlay and the European double-barrelled rifle I had given him as a present. He took them off his shoulder and placed them across the saddle. Then he resumed his investigation. To understand what will follow, it is necessary to have a conception of the area in which we found ourselves.

From where I was sitting in the grass by the two horses, fairly dense bushes extended to the left and the right. Where they left off, the forest began. Directly ahead of me, there was a grassy clearing where Halef was looking at the tracks. It was perhaps two hundred paces long, extending to the edge of the forest in a straight line and then turning left to disappear behind the bushes. The tracks came out of the bushes to my right, were visible along the entire clearing, and turned with it in the far left corner. It looked as if there had been three or four persons. The crisscross pattern of the imprints and the fact that they were layered suggested that flowers, edible roots, or things of that sort had been searched for. Even from a distance, the prints looked very large. In part, this was due to the height of the grass, in part to the type of footwear. There had of course been a perfectly good reason why I had asked about boots and spurs. It is always essential to determine whether the persons one may encounter are on horseback or on foot.

Halef felt it was most important to discover where the tracks led, for that made it unnecessary to find out where they had come from. He therefore followed them along the entire clearing and then disappeared to the left, behind the bushes. I did not think it risky to leave him to his own devices. While he did not have the farsightedness or developed powers of deduction which were indispensable on a journey such as ours, he was intelligent, even cunning, and I did not believe he would run into any natives. While the tracks were relatively fresh, they were not recent enough to suggest that the people who had made them were still nearby. I therefore did not worry about him. He would not stray too far, and would return immediately should he come across something suspicious.

Halef had not been gone long when Syrr gave me a signal. He came close to me, raised his small, delicate head, moved his ears forward and sniffed the air through his red nostrils with that faint, intermittent noise which indicates suspicion. Assil Ben Rih, Halef's horse, immediately started. Both animals were looking to the right where the tracks were coming out of the bushes. Were other persons approaching from that direction? I strained my hearing, but in vain. Then I placed my ear to the ground and listened. I did perceive a noise that seemed to be coming closer, for its loudness increased. It sounded like slow, heavy steps which were accompanied by the rustling of leaves. I returned to a sitting position. Now the noise could be heard more distinctly and was coming closer. It became louder and louder until, finally, I began thinking that Halef had been right when he had mentioned rhinoceri and elephants. The branches rustled and made a slapping sound as they whipped back. Twigs snapped, steps pounded and rumbled, but they were not the movements of a wild animal. They came at regular intervals, rhythmically, and had a snug, placid quality as if a giant in excellent spirits was going for a walk through the woods, paying no attention to the bushes and the ground he was crushing and pulverizing. Now I finally rose and picked up my rifles.

3 : In Search of Early Beginnings

The foliage was parted and I had the living cause of the noise before my eyes. A being or, more correctly, a biform entity was looking at me with as profound astonishment as I looked at it. Or was it two distinct beings, one sitting on the other? Yes, it was a rider, but what a rider! And the animal on which he sat! Was it a misshapen hippopotamus, a degenerate tapir, an antediluvian giant stag without antlers, or an overfed camel with elephantine legs but no humps? What was facing me had something of all of this but as I looked more closely, I found it impossible to reject the idea that this zoölogical curiosity was a horse. It had hooves of a size I had never seen before. The head resembled that of a giant elk, particularly the mouth or, rather, the snout. The mane was so thick and long that it seemed to consist of twine rather than hair. Its color, like the color of the animal generally, was hard to define for it had almost entirely disappeared under a heavy, armor-like layer of filth. I had seen such protective mud on American buffalo, which wallow in it to escape insect bites. The eyes and tail of this extraordinary creature were especially noteworthy. Whether the tail had long hair or merely a tuft at the tip I could not see. There certainly wasn't much hair, and what little there was was covered by a crust of scab and dirt. In spite of its compactness, this tail was in perpetual motion, describing circles most of the time. The eyes were of a similar restlessness. But to call them "eyes" is really an exaggeration, for they were much too small for this colossus whose body had the volume of two grown oxen. The small eyes darted to the left and the right, up and down, here and there, and all of this at the same moment, it seemed. Because the white of the eye was constantly in evidence, this movement made a strange, cunning, almost disquieting impression. It was as if, in an earlier incarnation, this heavy, clumsy, ungainly body had been inhabited by the soul of a magician or a member of the secret police. At the very first sight of these eyes, one realized that this beast had to be treated kindly and that it could not be taken in.

The being that sat on this animal was human but of enormous dimensions. Involuntarily, one was reminded of the Biblical Goliath. It seems unlikely to me that he can have been any larger or stronger than this rider, who was a head and a half taller than I and had the shoulders and muscles to go with that height. The spear in his right fist resembled a warp beam and the knife in his belt was of such form and weight that it could also be used as an axe. On his back hung a heavy bow made of crocodile hide, and below it a quiver of tortoise shell which could not be penetrated by arrows or spears and was large enough to serve as a shield. His feet and legs up to his knees were covered by heavy boot-like bast tubes with wide leather straps wound around them to provide the necessary support. The soles of his feet were long and wide enough to account for the impressions that had been left in the grass. The upper thighs were sheathed in solid leather cylinders and a leather garment also covered his body, a kind of jerkin which was wide open in front and exposed a very hairy chest. One had the feeling that the rest of the body would be equally hairy. His uncovered head was protected by a forest of dark hair which hung down over half his back like a mane. Similarly, only small sections of skin could be seen in a face that was almost totally obscured by a beard which hung down almost further than the mane. The eyes, like those of his horse, were much too small for this giant with his huge head and broad face, his low but powerful forehead. I saw neither saddle nor stirrups, but a strap had been wound around the horse's mouth so that the rider could hold both ends in his hand. That was easy on the animal but inconvenient for the man, who had to rely on the pressure of his thighs to make the horse obey.

I certainly intend no ridicule with this description. On the contrary, I should say that while I was astonished, it was not by the comic but the serious aspect of this apparition. The biform shape confronting me gave the impression of straightforward naturalness, undiminished vigor, total fearlessness, brimming good health and, last but not least, of that insouciant good nature that characterizes all living beings still relatively close to their origin. And "origin" was precisely the right word for what came to mind as I beheld this man and this horse.

The giant looked at me as quietly and searchingly as I looked at him. Then he asked:

"Where do you come from?"

I pointed behind me and answered:

"From there."

"Where are you going?"

"There," I said, pointing ahead.

"Express yourself with more precision! From there, over there, are not answers. You don't seem to know me."

"It's true that I have never seen you."

"Then listen to what I am telling you. I am Amihn, the highest sheik of the unconquerable tribe of the Ussul. Did you understand that?"

"Yes."

"Then conduct yourself accordingly! This entire country from the coast to the point where the desert of the Tshoban begins behind the El Chatar defile is my property. Everything that grows, lives, and walks here belongs to me. It follows that you belong to me. Have you understood?"

"Yes."

"If the man belongs to me, so do his possessions. Do you admit that?"

"Yes."

"I am glad, stranger. Apparently you aren't stupid. No one has understood as quickly as you that I am the legal owner of his property. I am going to have a close look at you and your belongings."

He rode up to me and got down from his primordial horse. It was only now that I could see the size of his feet, thighs, and arms. His hands were almost twice the size of mine, and the width of his shoulders was enormous. Next to him, I was almost a dwarf. He took hold of both my upper arms and turned me around twice. I put up with this but not because I was afraid. This was a confrontation of body and mind, of crude, ungainly strength and disciplined reflection, of muscle and brain, and there could be no doubt which would ultimately gain the upper hand. My apparent docility seemed to please him, for he said:

"I like you. From now on, you'll be my servant. It's true I don't know how you can serve me, or what use you can be, but something will turn up so you can prove to me that you aren't altogether worthless. Let's see what you've got."

He rammed his spear into the ground to free his hands, and reached for my rifles. He didn't waste much time with the carbine before he threw it to the ground. It was too light for him.

"I don't know these things, and I don't like them," he said contemptuously. "Children's toys."

But the exceptional weight of my hunting rifle impressed him. He balanced it in his hand, then grasped the barrels and swung it through the air as if he wanted to club someone with the butt, and finally condescended:

"This one is better. It won't break if one hits the enemy over the head with it."

While this primeval being was inspecting my weapons, the horse took it into its head to have a closer look at me. It simply pushed its master aside with its snout, came up to me, cranked its tail, eyed and sniffed at me, and seemed to conclude that I wasn't such a bad fellow, for it did me the honor of drying its wet snout on my face. I slapped it as hard as I could but far from feeling offended, it raised its ungainly head high in the air, closed its small eyes, opened its mouth wide and— but that was no neighing! It was a sound not wholly

unlike the trumpeting of an elephant, the roaring of a
lion, the foghorn of a steamer, so surprising that I
almost fell to the ground though I cannot say whether
from fright or amusement. Its master turned and
snapped at it:

"Have you gone mad? Roaring like that? Here, on
an open field where there may be other strangers who
mustn't know where we are? Shame on you!"

The animal quickly lowered its head even further
than usual. The tail stopped rotating, the eyes moved
toward each other and looked down the nose in
shame, and a sigh of such length and depth rose from
its heart that one might have thought the poor animal
was about to sink into the ground with remorse. I felt
genuinely touched. No doubt, this horse was a horse of
feeling.

"It's called Smikh," the sheik told me. "We have
many horses. You'll see them."

"When?"

He did not suspect all the information my question
was meant to elicit, and answered:

"Tomorrow, or the day after. Today we are far away
from home, hunting."

"Where?"

"Over there in the forest."

He pointed in the direction Halef had taken.

"How many hunters are there?"

"Twenty, not counting the women. The men hunt,
the women dig for roots which are eaten with the
meat."

To avoid arousing his suspicion, I asked no further
questions. I knew enough. The women had been looking for roots in this clearing and had left the imprints.
The tracks led to the camp and its twenty huge Ussul.
If they resembled their sheik, they were good-natured,
yet a danger to us. Halef was staying away too long. It
was quite possible that he had been seen and taken
prisoner. If the Ussul subscribed to the principle that
every foreigner that entered their country belonged to
them, they had also applied it in Halef's case and I
knew him well enough to be certain that he would not
put up with such treatment. He had resisted, been

overcome, and was now in danger. I had to follow and help him. And I had a weapon which would be more effective than any other, and that was the sheik himself. I had to seize him and use him as a hostage. Presumably, that meant a fight between us but that did not frighten me. My opponent was physically superior but a simpleton, a booby, and it would not require much intellectual effort to give me an even chance.

After he had inspected me, he passed on to our horses but he was obviously no connoisseur. His animal was worth more to him than our two stallions together. He told me that they were much too light to carry him and of no use in this terrain because their small hooves would sink into the swamp at every step, and they would drown or suffocate with their riders. The larger and wider the hooves, the more valuable the horse.

As he explained this to me, Smikh, the chubby one, stealthily came up behind me to bite me affectionately in the back of the neck. I immediately gave him an even more vigorous slap than before. Again, he took it for a sign that I returned his sentiments and raised his head, closed his eyes, and opened his mouth to emit the horrible fundamental sound of his being. The sheik pulled his spear from the ground and beat the singer so badly that he immediately fell silent. Horses among the Ussul were properly disciplined, it seemed, but I made up for the severity of his master by patting the animal. I noticed that the eyes, the corners of the mouth, the nostrils, ears, and other sensitive parts of the body were so full of flies and horseflies that he must be in considerable torment. I felt sorry for chubby Smikh and picked up a small piece of wood to remove the insects which formed veritable clusters at certain points. The animal had never been treated so kindly. He stood still until I had finished and then sighed profoundly to express his gratitude and relief, trying to convey by a show of affection that I had conquered his heart. Later, I often performed this service for him, and he repaid me by a regard which one could almost call tenderness.

It was with a truly childlike naiveté that the sheik examined my things and reacted to them as if they were already his property. My watch pleased him so much that he immediately put it into his pocket. I pointed out to him that it was mine, not his, but he looked at me almost uncomprehendingly, shook his head, and said:

"I don't understand you. Didn't I tell you that all these things are mine, and didn't you agree?"

"You are mistaken," I contradicted him.

"I am not. Out of respect for you, I'll assume that you have a poor memory. If I didn't, I would have to take you for a liar. Yet you will surely admit that that is the worst that can happen to anyone. Or did you perhaps not admit that every man that enters my country is my property?"

"No, I did not admit that."

"But you said so."

"But I did not agree. You asked if I had understood what you had told me, and I said I had. And then you told me that if the man is your property, it follows that everything he owns is also yours. I consented. But does that refer to me? And how can you prove that I am yours, that I am your servant or slave?"

"I told you. That's proof enough."

"And suppose I don't want to be your slave? What if I put up a fight?"

He looked me up and down, laughed, and answered:

"Put up a fight? Dwarf! Look at my hands! One more objection, and I'll crush your stupid skull with my fists so that it will stick to my fingers like mush." And he raised his huge paws threateningly.

"That would do you no good," I warned him. "I am not alone."

"Not alone? I don't see anyone!"

"But you see two horses. Hasn't it occurred to you that one rider is missing?"

"Missing? Why? Where is he?"

That was worse than naive. He was not dissembling; there was no cunning in him. His speech was an accurate reflection of his thinking. He was looking for the man that had disappeared. But I was being less frank, for it was my idea to sound him out and I phrased my answer accordingly. Yet it did not contain a lie but was the complete truth:

"Unfortunately, I don't know where he is at this moment. He noticed the tracks here in the grass and wanted to see who had made them. So he followed them and hasn't come back yet."

"Did he go straight down here and then turn left around the bushes?"

"Yes."

"Then he won't come back at all."

"Why not?"

"We have taken him prisoner."

"You mean your men saw him?"

"They saw and seized him. No question. One can see that far from our camp."

"Then it must be over there, to the left, in the forest beyond the bushes."

"It's not inside the forest but along the edge. Your companion was seen right away when he turned the corner. Is he as small as you?"

"He's smaller."

"Smaller still?" he smiled. "Then he can hardly have been any trouble."

"But suppose he resisted?"

This was the important question. I was curious to know what he would say.

"Then he's dead," he answered. "We don't tolerate resistance. We demand obedience. And a pygmy like that, even smaller than you, we make short shrift of if he dares put up a fight. The world doesn't need dwarfs. They are useless. Everyone who is too small and sick merely stands in the way of the great and the healthy. He has to disappear. If your companion was disobedient, he is dead by now. But that's not our concern. I have to examine what you own. When I am finished, we'll ride to the camp where we will divide your property. But first I have to see if there are things I like so that I get them when they are passed out."

That was all very honest but not particularly reassuring. There was no question that I would enter the camp, though certainly not as a prisoner. That meant that I would first have to subdue this giant. How this could be done was as yet uncertain. Firearms or knives were out of the question. The sheik was a good, dear fellow whom I must not injure, let alone kill. On the contrary, I had to try to gain the affection of the Ussul. This tribe would provide a base for future operations and so I must not hurt its leader. As it turned out, it was unnecessary to spend much time thinking about this problem. He met me halfway and offered me an opportunity I only had to seize.

As he was looking through my belongings, he asked about every single object to get to know its use and value. In the course of that examination, he also saw the long, very carefully made strap that was hanging from Syrr's neck.

"What is that?" he asked, as he looked at and touched it.

"A lasso."

"I have never heard that word. Plaiting is a great art. We also make straps, but short ones. We don't know how to make them this firm, this even, and this long. So that's called a lasso? What is it used for?"

"To catch people."

There was a reason, of course, for my not giving him a correct answer.

"Catch people with this strap?" he asked quickly, and with interest. "Enemies as well?"

"Yes."

"During battle? When they want to escape?"

"Whenever one wants to catch them."

"Can you show me?"

"Of course, if you wish."

"Then do it quickly. Catching one's enemies with a strap like that! Splendid! Look, there is a bunch of them hanging from my belt. They aren't used to catch the enemy, but to tie him up. For that, one first has to capture him. Go on, show me!"

"But whom am I to use?" I asked as I took the lasso from the neck of the horse. "There is no enemy for me to catch."

"No matter," he said. "Just imagine that I am the enemy. Does it take long?"

"Just a few seconds."

"Does it hurt?"

"Not the least little bit."

"Go on, then. What do I do?"

"Mount your horse and try to get away."

"Fine. Which way do you want me to go?"

I pointed back in the direction from which Halef and I had come, for I knew the terrain. It was essential to get the sheik away from this spot, because his camp was relatively close. If his men heard him shout for help, my entire plan would fail. I also needed a concealed tree to which I could tie this giant without having to worry that he would be found too soon.

"Flee in that direction, and as quickly as you can."

"Do you plan to catch up with me?" he asked with a broad smile.

"Yes."

"And then catch me? On horseback? On these dogs which no one would call horses? Listen, I am laughing at you. But go ahead and try. The disgrace will be yours, not mine."

Having no stirrups, he had to climb laboriously on the broad back of his beast.

He settled himself comfortably as one would on a sofa after a hard day's work, nodded contentedly at me, and called to his horse:

"Away from here, Smikh! But hurry, or you'll get a terrible beating."

The nag seemed neither to understand these words nor feel they were addressed to it. It did not act as if someone were sitting on its back. It only had eyes for me. The sheik urged it on, but it remained immobile, gazing at me. He dug his heels into its sides but it continued standing there. And even when he gave it a blow with his fist and hit it with his heavy spear, the results were no better.

"Can't you see that he doesn't want to go? Why don't you give him a good slap?"

"You want me to make him go? But I am not the rider."

"True. But he seems to have taken a fancy to you. He doesn't want to move. So it's your duty to chase him away. After all, he's mine, not yours."

I found it difficult to contain my amusement.

"Is that perhaps the disgrace you spoke of? What

kind of race is it going to be if your horse won't budge? Aren't you the master?"

"Of course I am. When I want him to go, I press my thighs against his body—"

"And off you go?"

"Yes. And when I want to turn right, I pull the right strap."

"And then he turns right?"

"Yes. And when I want to turn left, I pull the left one."

"And he turns left?"

"Yes. And when I want to stop, I pull both straps at the same time."

"And he stops?"

"What else?"

"I don't believe it. Prove it! You are urging him on, but there he stands."

"That's because I forgot the preliminaries. I did not want to dismount to go through them now, and that's why I asked for your assistance. But to prove to you that he obeys, I have to get down. You watch me!"

Cumbersomely, he worked his way down, raised his spear, and began vigorously beating the horse. Smikh lowered his head and put it as far as possible between his forelegs to avoid the blows as best he could. He put up with this treatment as a normal, everyday occurrence to which he had become accustomed. The sheik finally stopped, climbed back up, and said:

"Now you'll see how fast he can run. If he is to really take off, I have to get him excited. There's no way you can catch up with me. I'm off!"

Smikh pulled his head from between his forelegs, raised it high in the air, let his indescribable voice ring out provocatively, and shot forward. "Come and catch me," the sheik called out, and then there was no more talking, for all his efforts were needed to keep from being thrown. The sudden and rapid forward movement of the ungainly, massive beast made so irresistibly amusing an impression that I could not keep from laughing out loud. There was no need for a rapid pursuit. Halef's Ben Rih was more used to lassos than Syrr. I had been riding him for years but Syrr for only a short time, and I wanted to spare my thoroughbred the sudden jolt from the lasso shortly after it is thrown because it puts a strain on the bones. I securely fastened the rifles and the rest of the gear the horses were carrying, tied Syrr's reins to the pommel, looped the lasso, and swung myself on Ben Rih. Syrr followed unbidden, for these intelligent horses understood that it was a question of catching the rider dashing along before us.

Smikh did what he could. When I had got into the saddle, he must have been some four hundred horse lengths ahead, but I did not even make the effort to catch him quickly. The sheik had called the horses "small dogs," and they ran like dogs chasing deer— without first having to be beaten with a spear.

The terrain was reasonably suited for such a race. To the left and the right, there was forest or tall bushes. We were rushing through a sea of scents from two kinds of Oriental genista growing along a narrow, twisting, treeless strip. The flowers were of an intense yellow and a metallic white.

This golden and silvery course made frequent turns and I kept losing sight of the sheik. But every time he reappeared, I had come closer, and hardly two minutes had passed when the distance between us had shrunk to a mere eight or nine lengths.

"Here I am," I called out to him. "Watch out!"

He turned. When he saw how close I was, he shouted:

"That doesn't matter. I am just beginning to gallop."

It was an absurd remark. His horse made a genuine effort but had almost run out of breath. Though he sighed at every movement, the sheik was belaboring him so mercilessly with his feet, his hands, and the spear that compassion alone obliged me to put an end to the pursuit.

"Hold on," I warned him. "I am going to catch you now."

He wasted no time looking behind him and I could not understand his mumbling. I took the lasso into my left hand, raised the loop over my head, carefully calculated the throw, and let go. The moment had been well chosen, for the sheik had just lowered both arms. "Stop," I called out to my horses. There was a final spurt, and they stood still. The untearable leather loop was hovering directly over the sheik's head. A small movement of my hand and a vigorous pull, and it came down over his upper arms. At the same moment, Ben Rih was jerked forward but he had been trained for this. He placed himself at an angle to avoid being pulled down as the sheik was hurled from the horse by the taut lasso. Smikh kept running a short distance and then stood still, his flanks heaving, trying to catch his breath. Then he turned to see where his master had so suddenly disappeared. But the sheik was covered by the fragrant flowers and barely visible. I walked up to him and knelt down by his side. He was unconscious, presumably because his head had hit the ground rather hard.

Had he been an Indian, I would have been wary of a trick, but the Ussul sheik did not have the talent for such playacting. Although I could hear his pulsebeat, it was obvious he had fainted. This put him out of action temporarily. I freed him of the lasso and used the straps in his belt to tie his arms and legs to his body. I then cut some branches, placed them alongside him and tied his body to them, using it like a stretcher which I could place across my two horses. But just as I was making the last knot, he came to. His eyes were quite expressionless at first, but then his memory returned and he recognized me. His first question was:

"Where is Smikh? I don't see him." And without waiting for my answer, he added: "So you did catch me. Unbelievable!"

"And I even took you prisoner."

Only now did he realize that he could not move. After he had tried and failed, he said:

"But that does not change the fact that you entered my country without permission, and that I am therefore your lord whom you must obey. I am ordering you now to untie me."

"I'll be glad to, but not just yet," I answered in my friendliest manner.

"Why not?"

"Because I haven't quite finished taking you prisoner."

"What do you mean?"

"Don't you know that no one is a prisoner until he is in prison? You thought it would be impossible for me to subdue you, and so I had to prove that I could. That means that I now have to take you to a prison."

"Is there one nearby?"

"Yes."

"You are a stranger, yet you know places which I, the owner of this country, have never seen. And now you want to take me to a prison which I don't know to complete your victory?"

"Yes."

"How are you going to do that? I am tied up."

"I'll have my horses carry you. Or I'll tie you to Smikh's tail and have him drag you there."

"You will do nothing of the sort. I will ride."

"And get away? That's out of the question."

"Then I'll walk."

"No."

"Why not?"

"Because then I would have to untie you."

He understood that. He reflected for some time, and then said:

"You are right. I have to go to prison if you are to keep your word. If you untie me, I will escape. But there is something between these two extremes that we can agree on. You untie my feet and not my arms."

"All right," I agreed. "But in exchange, you must not resist being put in prison."

"I don't mind promising that," he laughed. "That prison only exists in your imagination. Untie my feet, and we'll be on our way."

"That means you'll walk and I'll ride."

"I don't mind."

He assumed that I would ride on one of my horses but I led them to one side, tethered them, and told them to lie down. They obeyed immediately and I knew they would stay there and not get up until I returned. When the sheik observed this, he was surprised.

"You are leaving them here? I thought you were going to ride?"

"I will, but not on one of them."

"You mean you'll take my Smikh?"

"Of course."

He burst into roaring laughter and exclaimed:

"He wants to ride my Smikh, the fool! My Smikh who doesn't even obey me! The horse will throw you before you know it."

"We'll see."

I stepped up to him, tossed the reins across his back, took hold of the mane and swung myself astride. Smikh was so startled, both his forelegs went into the air. But then he stood still. No one had ever mounted him so quickly before.

"You watch out! You'll be flying through the air in a moment," the sheik warned me.

But nothing was further from Smikh's mind than fighting me. When he felt that I was taking both ends of the strap into my hands, he raised his head and uttered such a triumphant roar one might have thought he would burst with joy. I pressed his sides, and he began walking. I pulled the right, then the left end of the strap. He obeyed instantly. He trotted and galloped as I increased the pressure of my thighs, and stopped immediately when I pulled. Then I dismounted. Smikh turned his head and snorted genially.

"I don't know what to say. He's never acted like that, never," the sheik honestly admitted. "How do you explain it?"

"We'll discuss that later. We don't have the time now to think about the thoughts and feelings of animals."

"Thoughts and feelings?" he asked. "You think they have them?"

"Of course."

"But they don't concern us. A beast like that has to obey, that's all."

"You are mistaken. But more of that later. Right now, I have to take you to your prison."

I removed the straps from his legs, pushed the branches up along the body so that they wouldn't get in his way, and then helped him get to his feet. He accepted his powerlessness good-naturedly, with amusement and an ingenuousness one would have found nowhere but in the land of the Ussul. I tethered him to one end of the spear, took the other firmly into my hand to direct him, and got back on the broad back of his horse. Then we started out.

When I had mentioned a "prison," I had been thinking of a tree to which I would attach the sheik. Near a bush of tamarix gallica, I saw a tall poplar which suited my purpose. Its trunk was substantial and the nearby bush provided an umbrella which would hide my prisoner from view.

When we came to the spot, I dismounted and led the sheik through the bushes to the tree.

"Lean firmly against the trunk," I told him.

"Why?"

"I have to tie you to it."

"Is that part of it?"

"Yes."

"Go ahead then."

To make things easy for me, he pressed against the poplar and calmly watched me use his straps and the lasso to attach him so firmly to the tree that he would be unable to free himself unaided. He said guilelessly:

"I really don't understand why you are tying me to this old poplar. If you are going to waste all this time here, how long is it going to take until we get to the prison you promised me?"

"It won't take long," I answered. "We are already there."

"What do you mean?"

"This poplar is the prison."

He was securely tied now, and I sat down.

His face took on an increasingly thoughtful expression.

"And I took the whole thing for a joke, although the sheik of the Ussul is not the sort of person one can make fun of with impunity. But remember that I was amusing myself with you, not you with me. So this tree is the prison, and I am its inmate?"

"That's right."

"And for how long? When will I be let go?"

"As soon as you wish."

"That's good. I am glad, and I am telling you to untie me right now. I have to get back to my men, and you have to come along."

"There's no hurry."

"But you just told me I would be free when I chose. I am the sheik of the Ussul, and you are my property."

"By what right?"

"The right of custom and usage."

"Then people have to do what is right and customary in their tribe?"

"Of course."

"Then we are in agreement."

"Of course we are. Among the Ussul, law and custom provide that the person and all of the property of anyone who comes to them without special permission belongs to them. That's why you are mine and have to obey me. Don't you have that custom?"

"Yes, but it works differently."

"How?"

"We don't say: everyone who comes to visit us, but everyone we visit."

"You are a strange people. Shame on you!"

He made a gesture to indicate loathing, and spat on the ground.

"You think that's wrong?"

"It certainly is. But perhaps I misunderstood you. You say that when you come to a foreign country, that country belongs to you, including all its inhabitants and their possessions?"

"Yes."

"Then I repeat, shame on you! You are robbers, rascals, scoundrels."

He spat again, and went on:

"What kind of people are you anyway? What's the name of your tribe?"

"It's called Djerman."*

"I'm surprised. I have heard of it. The Djerman live in the far west of the Occident and are supposed to be very good, intelligent, brave, and reasonable people."

"But they are!"

"How can they be if they are as you describe them? You, a Djerman, come here, and I am yours?"

"Yes."

"Shame on you! What's your religion?"

---

* German.

"We are Christians."

"I believe it. Wherever the Christians come, they steal all they find."

"How do you know that?"

"All the world knows it. In the beginning, the Christians were beggars, totally impoverished individuals who owned nothing and stilled their hunger by eating corn. Isa Ben Marryam,* the founder of their religion, did not even have a place to rest his head. Today, they own most of the countries and nations on earth. That's because they committed wholesale theft and robbery with violence and cunning. And still they are not satisfied but continue to steal and rob and will not stop until they own everything on earth. And you are one of these robbers, murderers, and scoundrels?"

"I am."

"Shame on you, I say again."

He spat. Then he wanted to give me a contemptuous glance but saw me smiling calmly at him. He became agitated and continued angrily:

"And you are so calm when I say you should be ashamed. Have you no conscience?"

"Should you not ask yourself that question?"

"Do you wish to insult me?"

"No. I am simply holding a mirror up to you so you can recognize yourself. Suppose it were true that we take all they own from the people whom we visit, the fact remains that we only take from strangers. But you don't steal from strangers but from people who come to you, who are your guests. Who is the greater robber, rascal, scoundrel?"

He looked very surprised but was honest enough to confess after some hesitation:

"We are, of course. To steal from a guest is the gravest misdeed there is. It had never occurred to me that we are such rascals."

He suddenly interrupted himself, reflected, and then went on:

"But—but—I see that you took me by surprise with your talk. The truth of what you say must first be examined. Do I really rob my guests?"

---

* Jesus Christ.

"Of course."

"Prove it! Are you my guest, perhaps? When I take your property, I take it from someone who is a total stranger to me. And were all those you deprived of their country really total strangers to you? Wasn't there a single case when you were the guests? So I ask you not to brag. One robber is like the next, one rascal like any other. Let's be honest and not lie to each other. The person that falls into someone else's hands is wrong, that's how it has always been. That's the way it is among you, that's the way it is here. And since it is you that fell into my hands, you are in the wrong, and I am in the right. Isn't that so?"

"No. Show me those hands of yours into which you say I fell."

"I can't, since you tied them."

"Then look at mine. They are free. So would you say that I am in your power, or you in mine?"

This went beyond his understanding. He raised his head and opened his mouth almost as wide as his horse could. But he didn't neigh; on the contrary, he quickly closed it again, lowered his head, and said:

"Listen, stranger, you are expressing ideas no one can follow. I am beginning to worry about you. You are not a good but a dangerous man, very dangerous. I suspect you won't obey me. Tell me honestly, what are your thoughts?"

"You'll find out in a moment. But first, let me tell you that I am a free man and not your property, and I will prove it to you. The things I have with me aren't yours either. That's why I am taking back what you took from me."

I put my hand into his pocket and retrieved my watch.

"So it's no longer mine?" he asked naively.

"No."

"It doesn't matter. I'll get it back."

"Go ahead and try. I am riding to your camp now to—"

"Then untie me," he interrupted.

"Patience, patience. I am first going by myself."

"Then you'll be taken prisoner, just like your companion."

"You took me prisoner, and who is the prisoner now?"

"I was a single person, and trusted you, but there are many of them, and they won't trust you."

"It doesn't matter whether they do or not. I only want them to obey me."

"How could you make them?"

"Through you."

"Through me? I won't permit you to use me for that purpose."

"You are talking without thinking. You have already allowed yourself to be used. Now I am riding your chubby Smikh to your camp and—"

"My Smikh?" the sheik broke in. "That'll cost you your life. My warriors will kill you on the spot."

"Why?"

"Because they'll think that you laid hands on me."

"That's exactly what I want. I not only want them to believe it, I'll tell them myself."

"Then you are done for."

"On the contrary. It will save my companion if they have evil intentions."

"You don't know them."

"That isn't necessary. I know you. I'll tell them that you are my prisoner, that you are tied up and will have to die if they commit the slightest act of hostility toward me or my companion."

"Die?" He sounded scared.

"Yes, indeed."

"My wife Taldsha will be shocked."

Taldsha means snowdrop. Was it possible that this man had a wife whose beauty, purity, loveliness, and grace could be compared to a snowdrop? It made me curious to see her.

"So you are going to threaten my men with my death?" he went on.

"Yes."

"They cannot possibly believe that a midget like you could have got the better of me."

"That's the reason I am taking your Smikh. When they see that I took him away from you, they'll be convinced that you are in my power."

"Stranger, you are a devilishly cunning fellow. When are you coming back?"

"It may be just a short while, but it could take hours. It all depends on whether your warriors are reasonable or not."

"And I am supposed to stay here during that entire time?"

"Yes."

"Then I'll call for help. My men will hear me when they get close. They'll untie me, and that will be the end of you."

"You won't be able to shout for help. I am going to gag you."

"Then I'll growl loud enough for them to hear it. That's possible even when one has one's mouth closed."

"Then I'll also tie your nose shut."

"Really? I would suffocate."

"I know, but you leave me no choice. You are threatening that you will shout and growl, and you know I must prevent that. What a pity."

I said these last words regretfully. He scrutinized me, and asked:

"What is a pity?"

"That you are forever forcing me to be severe with you. I don't like inconveniencing you."

"Is that true? You are not only clever, you are also a nice fellow. But wait. Let me think. Perhaps I'll find a way so we can do without the gag."

He wrinkled his brow in the intellectual effort he was making, and blinked at me to show that his native intelligence was beginning to work. Then he suddenly exclaimed:

"I've got it! What will you do if I promise that I will neither growl nor call for help?"

"Then I won't gag you. I know you will keep your promise."

"I will," he agreed. "Have I never told you that the Ussul hate lying? I would keep quiet even if my men were to show up here."

"But you would let them untie you?"

"Not even that if you promise to come back without fail."

"And would you believe my promise?"

He looked at me with surprise, and answered:

"Why shouldn't I? You also believe me. Do you think that I am a worse human being than you?"

What an amazing person he was! I felt obliged to reward this unexampled honesty on the spot, and so I told him:

"I will prove to you how much I trust you. If you promise to stay here by this trunk and to consider it your prison until my return, I'll untie you now."

"I promise. Is that good enough?"

"Yes."

I first loosened the lasso and then the straps. As I was doing this, I told him frankly:

"I am even prepared to release you altogether and to take you along with me to the camp if you give me your word not to treat me or my companion as enemies."

He shook his head and stated:

"That proposal comes from your heart, but I am forbidden to accept."

"By whom?"

"By honesty. We Ussul never make promises if we know that they probably will be broken. I don't know anymore than you where your companion is, what he may have done, or what happened to him. Should he have been captured, he may have resisted. If only a single drop of blood was shed, that will cost him his life. And even if he made no attempt to defend himself, remember that I am not the only one to decide his fate. The Sahahr* also has a voice. So I cannot make you a promise, and prefer to stay here in my prison, for I am an honest man. I don't want to purchase my freedom through deception."

In the meantime, he had been freed of his ties. He sat down and supported himself against the trunk of the poplar, looking like a man determined to stay where he was.

"Then I'll leave alone," I said. "So you are going to wait here until I get back?"

"Yes."

---

* sorcerer, magician.

"I'll hurry. Farewell."

I gave him my hand. He shook it in brotherly fashion and a friendly smile appeared on his bearded face.

"Come back soon. I am looking forward to it. I have come to like you as much as my horse has."

Smikh had begun trampling the ground with joy as he saw that I was about to ride him once more. And when I was sitting on him, he uttered a shout of jubilation which sounded as if the deepest note of a trumpet were competing with the highest tone of a piccolo. He ran off with such speed that one would have thought he wished never to see the sheik of the Ussul again.

4 : Strange People

Our route, the clearing, led straight toward the forest and into it. It was not level but had a downward slope which permitted me a welcome view. Though it was not wholly unobstructed because huge trees were standing on either side, the spaces between them made it possible to survey the situation.

The camp had been set up at the edge of the forest. It consisted of huts made with poles, branches, and foliage. There were several fires. A path led through trees to a kind of lake which had an island in it. A canoe, a huge dugout, made of a single trunk that had been hollowed out with fire, was being paddled toward the island by two men. I could clearly see that there were two passengers who were doing nothing. I could not make out their clothing or features but one of them was significantly smaller than the other. The camp seemed empty. The people I saw were standing by the shore of the lake or on their way back from there toward the camp.

As I came closer, I recognized the clothing of the little fellow in the canoe. It was Halef. He obviously had been captured and was now being taken to the island. Up to this moment, I had not been noticed because attention had been directed to the boat, but now I was seen. The sheik's horse with a stranger as the rider, galloping madly and much faster than ever before! Shouts rang out and people began running toward me from the opposite side of the camp. They were all huge, some even bigger than the sheik. They pulled their weapons from the trunks against which they had been leaning and looked at me threateningly. They believed, of course, that I would stop inside the camp. Smikh seemed willing, for when we were about thirty horse lengths away, he slowed down. It occurred to me that once Halef had been successfully transported to the island, he would be a hostage the Ussul could trade against mine, and my advantage would be gone. I felt certain that the chubby, round horse was a good swimmer. He mustn't come to a halt, but must dash to the lake and into the water. To protect them, I placed my revolvers inside my leather belt and took the rifles in my hand to keep them above the water as we jumped in. We shot past the camp, into the forest, and toward the lake. The men standing there heard the shouting of those that had been on their way back. They saw me and joined in.

Those powerful trees, the snakelike lake shimmering like a lurking disaster, the shouting, these gigantic shapes, the grotesque, ungainly movements that expressed their threats, and finally the strange sight that I offered them as I sat on a loudly groaning Smikh, made for a wild scene. My spurs urged him on, and he obeyed. He seemed totally unafraid of the water. When he had come close, he roared loudly, and took a truly giant leap into the waves. Even today, I cannot understand why the water did not lift me off his broad back. I held the rifles high, but because of the weight of the horse we were submerged so completely that everything got drenched. We resurfaced immediately and luckily only the outside of the rifles had gotten wet. I was still sitting firmly on Smikh and could let him support me instead of having to swim for myself.

He behaved as if he were descended from amphibians, equally at home in the sea and on dry land. He swam not only well but quickly. Even more important, he saw the boat moving toward the island and went in pursuit as if he had understood my plan. I could now see the features of the small man clearly. It really was Halef, and of course he recognized me, too.

"Hamdulillah, Allah be praised that you are coming," he called out to me. "They want to imprison me on that island. They captured me."

He was using his native dialect and it was unlikely that any of the Ussul would understand him.

"Are you tied up?" I called across the water.

"Only my hands on my back."

"Are those in the boat armed?"

"They just have knives. The fellow next to me is the sorcerer."

"Have you told them who we are?"

"Certainly not."

"Did you mention me?"

"I let them believe I was alone."

"Did they ask about your horse?"

"No."

"But you are wearing spurs. They must have concluded you had one."

"They are too stupid. Are you going to overtake the boat?"

"Yes."

"Then I'll make it easier for you."

During this brief exchange, the sorcerer had repeatedly gestured to Halef to stop talking. Halef now turned to him to answer the questions he was being asked. How cleverly he did this the reader will soon see. The sorcerer gave the crew an order and the boat changed direction and came toward me.

"They are going to seize you," Halef called out.

"All the better. Stay where you are and hold on so you won't fall out. The boat is soon going to start rocking. I am going to throw the sorcerer into the water."

"Allah, Wallah, Tallah. Now that you are here, there is a change in tenor."

My chubby friend was moving along vigorously, and the men paddling the canoe were also doing their best. Since we were approaching each other rapidly, the sorcerer though the time had come to address a few words to me. He was a giant, but no longer young, with a white beard and white hair. Since his movements were rather ungainly and his bare chest was also covered by white hair, he looked a little like a polar bear.

"Who are you?" he asked me.

"You'll find out soon enough."

"What do you want here?"

"I want to go to the island."

"That's forbidden! You have to get into the boat."

"I wouldn't dream of it."

"You have to obey, or I'll force you to," he threatened.

"Try!"

"If you refuse, we'll simply beat you to death with the paddles."

Feigning fear, I said timidly:

"Surely you wouldn't do that? You aren't murderers."

"No. We are Ussul, and I am the Sahahr, the priest. We don't murder. But anyone who resists us endangers his life. I'll stretch out my hand and pull you in."

The dear old fellow! He acted so martial, yet he had the kindest face imaginable. He was standing erect in the middle of the canoe and directing it so that it stopped exactly in front of me.

"Come on board," he ordered as he bent down to me and offered his hand. "Take it, I'll help you."

"First, take these rifles and place them inside the canoe."

I handed them over. The clumsy fellow really took them and put them carefully where it was driest. Then he again held out his hand and repeated:

"I'll pull you."

I slipped from my horse, clutched the canoe firmly with my left hand, and stretched out my right to take hold of him, not his hand, but his upper arm. A vigorous pull—a heave—and instead of pulling me inside, he flew out of the boat into the water where he briefly disappeared from view. Only a moment later, I was standing inside the dugout. I pulled my knife and cut Halef's straps. He jumped up, threw his arms into the air, and exclaimed jubilantly:

"Allah be praised! Thanks to you, Effendi, I can use my hands again. You'll see right away what I am going to do with them."

He picked up my heavy hunting rifle, pointed it at one of the men and called out:

"Pull the paddle into the boat and jump or you'll be shot!"

Compared to Halef, the man was a giant. But he merely looked at the barrel, obediently did as he had been told, and jumped overboard. Now Halef pointed the rifle at the man sitting in back, who did not even bother to wait for the command but followed his comrade into the water.

"They are real heroes," Halef laughed as he put down the rifle.

"Let's get away from them," I warned him as I took one of the paddles and gestured to Halef to take the other.

I did not want the three Ussul back in the boat. When the sorcerer had been thrown into the water, the boat had been propelled forward, and we now tried to increase our distance. The Ussul proved to be very skillful swimmers. They also decided to avail themselves of the strength of the horse. The sorcerer was trying to climb on its back while the other two reached for the reins. But Smikh would not let them. He kicked at them, tried to bite them, and splashed vehemently.

"That's quite an animal, that horse," Halef said. "Where did you get it, Sidi?"

"I'd rather hear how you got into this antediluvian vessel," I answered.

"Can't you spare me that recital, Sidi?"

"No."

"Then permit me at least not to look at you as I tell you. I am ashamed."

"Really?"

"Yes."

The three Ussul were still trying to subdue the horse. I was sitting at one end of the canoe, rudder in hand, and Halef at the other. He stared down, threw his head back with determination, and began:

"It's no use. I have to admit that I am an ass, an owl, a goose, a born fool, in short. No one could be a greater simpleton. There are moments when I consider myself the most intelligent and finest human being Allah ever created. And there are others when I could swear that I am the most incompetent person in the world. Do you believe me?"

"I do, for every person that is not completely mature knows such moments. But recognizing one's shortcomings is the first step toward change. And I think it's only natural that you would be thinking of changing for the better at this moment."

"It's very true that I am," he admitted. "Later, I'll be able to tell you what happened in greater detail, but now there isn't time. I followed the tracks like a simpleton without even considering that I could be seen from a considerable distance. They spotted me and I had no idea how close I had come to their camp. They hid on both sides behind some bushes and attacked. Then they dragged me into the camp to decide what to do with me. They wanted to know who I was, where I had come from, what I was doing in their country."

"What did you tell them?"

"Nothing."

"Nothing?" But that's not possible. Surely you had to give some sort of answer."

"No, I didn't. Nothing occurred to me, absolutely nothing."

"I can't believe it. It must have been the first time in your life."

"That's right."

"Was it fear?"

"No, amazement. Allah w'Allah! What people they are, what heads, beards, and manes they have! I am telling you, I was so astonished, my voice failed me. And how foolish! Just think, they thought I was a court jester that had run away, a dwarf, a prankster! And later the sorcerer had the mad notion that I was probably the favorite dwarf of the Mir of Ardistan and that I had not run away but been sent by him to spy on them. If the sheik had been there, I would have been killed on the spot. But because they couldn't do that in his absence, they decided to take me to the island for safekeeping."

"Did you try to resist?"

"No, I couldn't. When they fell on me so unexpectedly, the first thing they did was to take my knife, my pistols, and everything else I had in my belt. How could I have defended myself? Their hands are four times the size of mine. It's a good thing you came when you did. How are you going to get us out of this?"

"What a question! We are out of it now; we have been rescued."

He looked around and laughed happily.

"That's true. You are absolutely right. There's only one boat here. We don't have to return to them but simply cross the lake. We'll get there much sooner than they, for they have to make the detour along the shore. But you know, Sidi, I would prefer not to let them keep what they took from me."

"You won't have to. We have no reason to flee; they will have to do as we say. I am going to compel them to be peaceful. I captured their sheik."

"Hamdulillah! We've got the upper hand. We'll have to tell them right away! Pick up a paddle, and let's get over there."

I had no objection and merely asked where we should look for what had been taken from him. He told me:

"The lady Taldsha has everything. She said that it all belonged to the sheik and that she would keep it. I have the impression that it is she who rules the tribe, not he. Even the sorcerer didn't dare contradict her. He was very polite to her. She seems to be the sheik's wife."

The three Ussul that had been driven from the canoe were now some distance away, swimming toward shore where their people were standing, gesticulating and raising all kinds of noise to convey how incomprehensible they found what had happened. We paddled toward them, but at a leisurely pace. We had no reason to hurry. The sorcerer and his crew reached land much sooner than we, and Smikh no longer paid any attention either to them or to me. He was swimming here and there, occasionally grunting with pleasure. He seemed to enjoy getting clean but had no sooner reached shore than he immediately began wallowing in the deep mud to restore the protective cover to his skin.

Naturally, our attention was directed toward the people on the shore. They had now stopped shouting and were quietly waiting for our arrival. I counted them. There were nineteen men and only one woman. So only the sheik was missing, and of the women it was presumably only his wife who was permitted to participate in such important occurrences. When we had come so close that two more strokes would bring us to the shore, I signalled to Halef to stop. All the Ussul were giants, and all of them had the abundant hair and beard of their chief and were similarly dressed. The sheik's wife made an impression on me which at first I could not account for and only began to understand after some time had passed.

She was dressed entirely in leather but it was more delicate and softer than any I had ever seen. It was blue. It looked as though it were covered by an extremely delicate pollen which had a metallic sheen. Her shoes were of somewhat sturdier leather. They had been skillfully cut from a single piece, and flattered her shapely feet, which seemed almost small and dainty in relation to her height. Her hands were even smaller, relatively speaking, and her hair was fine, thick, and golden. It waved and hung down in back far below her belt. This shimmering abundance was adorned with the feathers of the paradise bird but the effect was one of naturalness and simplicity. Although we were in the midst of a wilderness, there was not the smallest spot, the least trace of dirt anywhere. Pure, fresh, unstained, natural, such was the effect produced at the very first glance. Her eyes were large and of a blue which was certainly rare in this remote corner of the Orient. Later, I noticed that she exuded a delicate, soothing scent, a bouquet of health, vitality, constant rejuvenation, which made one feel an inner compulsion to stay away from everything questionable while in her presence. It was as if I already sensed this fragrance from a distance, for it did me good to see her standing in front of me, quite apart from the fact that the strangeness of her appearance attracted my interest.

She had stepped to that point along the shore toward which our boat had been headed. She was standing by the sorcerer's side. There were five men a few paces behind them, while the rest stood further back and off to both sides. This proved to me that, during the absence of the sheik at least, this woman ruled here, albeit with the aid of the sorcerer. I later discovered that she could also control the sheik and that he undertook nothing without first having consulted her.

When the boat stopped, she and the Sahahr exchanged a few barely audible words which we could not understand. Apparently, she had not wanted to begin the interrogation but had asked him to do so, for he now took a short step forward and asked us:

"Why do you hesitate? You must land and disembark."

"Why?" I asked.

"Because I order you to."

"No one may give me orders. Who are you?"

"I am the sorcerer and priest of the giant people of the Ussul. And here, by my side, is Taldsha, the wife of our sheik."

"And the sheik? Where is he?"

"He isn't here now but soon will be. Well, now, I am ordering you to leave the boat. I am going to interrogate you."

"I have already told you that we owe obedience to no one, and that includes all of you. But it is my custom to be respectful toward priests. In the distant land where I was born, all good men honor women and accede to their wishes, provided they are reasonable. I therefore agree to your interrogation, but before you begin I wish to correct a misapprehension."

"A misapprehension? I don't know of any."

"You believe that you will interrogate me. That is an error. It is I who will interrogate you, not the other way around."

He began laughing, and was joined by the rest.

"He is mad," he exclaimed, and "He is mad, mad," the others echoed as their laughter became a roar.

Taldsha turned and raised her hand. The silence was instantaneous.

The sorcerer, serious once again, continued:

"So you want to interrogate us. Who gives you that right?"

"Your sheik."

"Our sheik?" he asked in surprise. "Do you know him?"

"Yes."

"How long have you known him?"

"For one hour. He is my prisoner."

"Your what?" he said, as if he did not trust his ears. "Did I hear right?"

"You did. Amihn, your sheik, is my prisoner."

I saw that he was making an effort not to burst out laughing. He controlled himself, and asked:

"You have to forgive me, stranger, but what you are telling me sounds like the biggest lie—"

"Then turn around," I interrupted him as I pointed to Smikh who was just getting out of the water and beginning to wallow in the mud. "Look at his horse. You have seen it before, for it carried me to your boat. The fact that I arrived on it should tell you that I subdued Amihn. And the fact that I did not hesitate to rescue my companion, to toss you out of the boat, and to come here instead of fleeing surely proves that I have him in a safe place from which he cannot escape."

"The horse, yes, of course," he said, embarrassed. "I hadn't thought of that. Since you came here on its back, I suppose you did get the better of our sheik in some fashion. But why did you do it?"

"Because I needed a hostage. You had taken my companion prisoner. So I captured your sheik to compel you to release him."

"But how could you dare tackle this man, this giant, this hero, who has never been defeated in his life?"

"I'll show you right away."

Earlier, when I had untied the sheik, I had looped the lasso again and was now carrying it on my shoulder. I took it down, kept one end in my left hand, and threw it at the sorcerer. A vigorous tug—his arms were pulled toward his body, and I jerked him away from where he was standing and toward me. He fell into the water but Halef quickly helped me and a moment later he was lying in the boat, tied so tightly that he could not move. I now took the knife from his belt and raised it threateningly. The Ussul were shouting with fear, and he called out:

"Stop, stop! Do you mean to murder me? I haven't done anything to you."

I put the knife back, straightened up, and answered:

"I wouldn't think of killing you. I am your friend, not your enemy. I only wanted to show you how easy it is to take an Ussul prisoner."

"Then let me go," he asked rather timidly.

"I let you escape once before. Instead of being grateful, you treated me as a prisoner and wanted to interrogate me. This time, you won't get away that easily. You'll stay here until I am certain that you will treat me as a guest and a friend."

"And what if we won't?"

"Then I will plunge this knife into your heart," I answered and Hadji Halef added as he rolled his eyes:

"And if that shouldn't kill you, I'll finish the job, depend on it. I am Hadji Halef Omar Ben Hadji Abul Abbas Ibn Hadji Davuhd al Gossarah, the famous sheik of the Haddedihn of the great Shammar tribe." The long name apparently had its effect, for the sorcerer said quite fearfully:

"You are a famous sheik? You didn't tell us that. And who is the other one?"

"He is the greatest hero and scholar of the Occident. His name, which is known throughout the world, is Emir Hadji Kara Ben Nemsi Ben Emir Hadji Kara Ben Djermani Ibn Emir Hadji Kara Ben Alemani. His sabre is sharp, his bullets never miss, and when he makes a long speech, he always finishes it properly. He has never lost a fight in his life. No enemy can defeat him. And when he shows how learned he is, it is like a whirlwind which never stops before it has circled the globe and pulled down everything in its path."

"I never heard his name or yours," the sorcerer

apologized. "I am as unfamiliar with your country and your tribe as I am with his people and the land where he was born. I am the priest and sorcerer of the Ussul. Religion is my only concern, and I do not have the time for politics, geography, and universal history. So you have to forgive me for knowing nothing of these matters. I seek my glory in my nation's belief in its god and creator. Do you believe in God?"

"Yes."

"That reassures me. Someone who has a God does not murder."

"But you threatened to kill us," Halef reminded him.

"Threatened? Perhaps. But did we do it?"

"Not so far."

"Then wait until it happens."

"Wait?" Halef laughed. "Yes, we'll wait, all right. With pleasure. Up to now, no one has managed to kill us, and I wonder how you would go about it."

Now Taldsha came toward us, stopped at the water's edge, and gave this exchange a different, more propitious turn.

"Is the one who calls himself Hadji Halef Omar an Arab?"

"Yes," Halef answered.

"Is he really a sheik?"

"Yes."

"What country does Emir Kara Ben Nemsi come from?"

"I am from Djermanistan," I answered.

"I don't know it, so it cannot be in our part of the world."

"It is in the Occident, not the Orient."

It had been suggested to me not to mention that I was from the West. But looking at the clear, exceptionally honest eyes I felt incapable of lying. I could tell from a rapid movement of her head that she was not unpleasantly surprised. She went on: "In the West. And where are you going?"

"Through all of Ardistan."

"Then you must be either very reckless or very bold. The Mir of Ardistan would probably have you killed if he found out that you are an Occidental. Fortunately, you will escape that death because you will not get there but stay here. According to the laws of our country, you are our property."

"But not according to the laws of mine," I answered.

"Do you intend resisting us?"

"Yes."

"That will be futile."

"You are mistaken. Up to now, I have been successful. We are not in your power, but free. But your sheik and your priest have fallen into our hands. If we cross the lake in this canoe, we will get to the far shore much more quickly than you. Who can prevent us from first killing the priest and then the sheik, should we be persuaded that you will not keep the peace?"

She did not answer immediately but scrutinized me closely. Then she said:

"I am uncertain and dissatisfied. I like both of you. I would like to hear about the Occident. It would please me to be able to tell you that you are our guests, not our property. But I must abide by the laws of my country, not my wishes. Though it is true that there is a way—"

She did not continue but gestured to indicate that she felt her idea could not be carried out.

"What way?" I asked.

"It's pointless to ask," she answered and repeated her gesture.

Again, she reflected and studied us, looking benevolent but uncertain.

Then she went on:

"There is one way of freeing you from the servitude that threatens you. The law makes you ours, but that same law can set you free by allowing you to fight for your freedom."

When Halef heard this, he threw up both arms and exclaimed:

"Sidi, we'll fight."

But I paid no attention to him for he had proven during the last two hours that he was not man enough to hold his own unaided.

Now the woman said:

"You surely won't deny that you will be defeated by us?"

"Defeated?" I pointed at the sorcerer. "He is tied up.

Do you call that being defeated? So far, it is we that have been victorious, not you."

She looked at me with astonishment, took a deep breath, and admitted:

"That sounds odd, and yet you are right. You are still free and have already taken two of us prisoner."

"And consider who they are," I warned her. "Among you, the sheik represents the secular, the Sahahr the spiritual power. These two are now in our hands. Not you but we are the masters over woe and weal, life and death. Do you understand?"

She turned to her men and asked:

"Do you hear?"

The meaning of the mumbling and grumbling that answered her was not clear to me but she understood it, for she turned back to me and said:

"You seem to be quite different from us. We don't understand you, and yet you compel us to try. Where is the sheik?"

"At a secure place."

"Is he tied?"

"Yes."

"How?"

"By his word."

She made a gesture of surprise, and asked:

"You trusted him?"

"Yes. First, I tied him so that he could not budge. I was even going to gag him, but he promised to stay where he was even if all the Ussul came for him. So I untied him."

"Then you believed him?"

"Why shouldn't I?"

"Did you hear? This stranger loves the truth as much as we do. He believed the word of your sheik. Is that the mentality of a servant, a slave?"

"No," the five standing closest to us answered. "No, no," the rest agreed.

"Only free men act in that fashion," she went on. "So these two strangers deserve that we look on their resistance as the struggle to free themselves."

"You are right," all of them answered.

Turning back to us, she went on:

"I ask you, Emir, to take me to my husband, our

: 61 :

sheik. Are you willing?"

"Gladly. But I must ask you what you plan to do there."

"I have to counsel with him about you."

"Whom else would you have to consult?"

"Only the Sahahr."

"Then I would have to release him?"

"Yes, I am asking you to."

"Do you realize what you are demanding?"

"I do. You have to surrender temporarily the advantage you have."

"Temporarily?"

"Yes. You untie the Sahahr so he can accompany us. If I cannot persuade the sheik to be peaceful, I'll take you back here to this boat and the Sahahr will be tied up again. Do you believe me?"

"I do. Then only four persons will go to the sheik, you, the sorcerer, and the two of us?"

"Yes."

"And the rest of the Ussul will wait here until we get back?"

"Yes."

"Then I'll release him. We can leave."

I untied the Sahahr and threw the lasso back over my shoulder. Then all of us jumped ashore.

"Can we walk, or is it so far that we have to take horses?" the woman asked.

"It's some distance, but we can walk," I said, for I wanted to make use of the time it would take us to explore the woman's mind and soul.

We set out without further delay. I walked with Taldsha, Halef with the sorcerer. The rest followed us only as far as the camp where they remained without having received further orders.

We took the trail I had taken, and while it was noted by Taldsha and the Sahahr, they did not pay anywhere near the same kind of attention that Indians or Bedouins do. It followed that the Ussul were not threatened by the same sort of danger as the peoples of the deserts and the savannas.

Halef and the priest were walking behind us. They soon were conversing with total absorption and great animation. From time to time, they would stop as one does when one is discussing an interesting point, and so dropped back further and further. An old pattern repeated itself here: Halef made friends very quickly. The two of us were walking along quietly, and I noticed for the first time the delicate, inexplicable scent that emanated from Taldsha. It was the scent of a flower, but in spite of my efforts, I could not decide which one. An age-old Oriental fairy tale says that the wings of angels consist of the scent of flowers, and that the human soul can only leave and return to its body in their scent. When I remembered this tale, I thought of Sitara and the valley of the starflowers where I had so often walked with Marah Durimeh. Their pure, chaste fragrance had delighted me, and my old friend and protectress had said: "There is only an infinitely small number of souls that succeed in retaining this fragrance in their bodies. However ugly such a body may be, you can trust the soul inhabiting it, for its home is the light, not the darkness, and it will never mislead you." It suddenly occurred to me that the fragrance I scented was that of the starflowers, and I felt joy, confidence, and a sense of security. There was also Taldsha's unusual manner of speaking. It was without a trace of inquisitiveness or the desire to hear what was merely ordinary. Everything she said was carefully considered. She asked about the Occident and confessed that she longed to go there. She had heard many evil and strange tales about it but had no faith in them. She said: "If everything that is told about you is true, those nations must be nations of liars, thieves, cheats, and evil sorcerers of whom one would have to be extremely wary. If they really do exist, there can be no God. And I see you! You did not lie to us although you certainly had reason to. Do you know God?"

"I am a Christian."

"A Christian? A pagan, in other words."

"A pagan?"

"Yes. Surely the Christians are pagans."

"Why do you say that?"

"Because everyone who does not believe in our religion is a pagan."

"We say the same thing. We call everyone a pagan

that does not believe in the God of the Christians."

"That's only fair. You consider your religion to be as true as we do ours. You have as much right to call us pagans as we do you."

"Then you will permit me to ask you about your belief, as you asked me about mine."

"Our belief? We have none."

"But that's not possible!"

"Oh, yes! We have God. So why should we also have a belief in Him? We don't believe in Him, we have Him. If your father is still alive and lives in your house, you don't believe that you have a father, you know it, and the word 'belief' is meaningless. The Ussul have a religion but no belief. They have God."

That sounded strange and profound, and so unshakable in its conviction that I thought it prudent not to discuss this delicate topic further.

When we came to the spot where our horses had been tethered, I took Taldsha to the left, to the tree where the sheik was still sitting precisely as I had left him. She stopped, and asked him:

"You are a prisoner?"

"Yes," he answered without attempting to get to his feet.

"How is that possible?"

"He outsmarted me." Then he turned to me:

"May I get up now?"

I nodded.

"So I am no longer a prisoner?"

"Yes, you are. I will not let you go until you have become my friend. Did you notice the quince tree we passed not far from here? Get up and follow me. There is something I want to show you."

"Very well. You can take me back here whenever you want."

The quince tree was heavy with small fruit and just as we got to it, Halef and the Sahahr arrived. They were discussing something heatedly and seemed to have become reasonably friendly. Our adventure had clearly taken a favorable turn. I pointed to one of the branches of the tree, and asked the sheik:

"How many quinces do you see there?"

"Twelve," he told me when he had counted them.

"Now I will show you what would have happened to your hunters, had they dared lay hands on me or Halef. I will shoot down six of these fruit, and then the branch."

When I had chosen the proper distance, I turned and aimed.

"Now, now," Halef shouted. "He's starting."

I aimed very carefully, for if I was going to achieve the effect I was after I must not miss. I fired six times in rapid succession, and twice more to bring down the branch. When I saw it fall, I put the carbine down. Halef was jubilant and the Ussul momentarily speechless. After a few moments, the sheik said:

"It's unfortunate we don't have a shot and rifles like that when we go hunting."

His wife nodded.

"And when we battle the Tshoban."

"Now would be a good time," the sorcerer interjected. "We know they are preparing to attack us."

Taldsha explained:

"We are sending all our men hunting to gather the food we will need during the war, which may be lengthy and is always quite bloody."

"Who are these Tshoban?" I asked.

"A wild tribe that lives in the steppes and the desert. They raise horses, camels, cattle, and sheep. They move from place to place; they are nomads. They worship a God they call Allah, and practice blood feuds. Whenever they have a bad year and lose their herds, they invade our country to take ours. We are expecting such an invasion in the near future and are now preparing the meat we will need to survive during the siege."

"Siege?" I asked. "Don't you engage them in battle?"

"No. They are too numerous and our most important job is to protect our animals. We retreat with our herds behind the water and let the Tshoban lay siege to us there. Whoever can last longer is the victor. Your rifles carry very far. I will ask you later if they are enchanted. But that you can shoot so accurately is of the greatest value."

As she said this, she bent down to pick up the branch, looked at it closely, and asked:

"Would you help us against these enemies, Emir?"

"One only has to help one's friends," I answered.

"But you are our friend."

"Prove it!"

"I decided that."

She said that very emphatically and looked both the sheik and the sorcerer in the face. The sheik lost no time telling me:

"Yes, if she has decided, that's the way it will be. I will agree with her."

And the sorcerer added:

"When the sheik's wife makes a decision, a counsel is unnecessary. She makes no mistakes. I gladly give my assent. If you wish, you can become an Ussul the moment we get back to our city tomorrow. That is a sacred ceremony over which I, the priest, will have to preside after you have first proven that you are worthy of becoming one of us."

"How am I to prove that?"

"By fighting one of our men. If he defeats you, you cannot join our tribe."

"And if I win, do I take his place? Is he expelled?"

The question confused him, and it took a few moments before he found an answer:

"No, you can't ask for that. The greatest hero may have a mishap. It's a chance, not a disgrace. So why should we cast him out?"

"We'll fight, Sidi, we'll fight!" Halef cried enthusiastically. "Who will be my adversary?"

"You have the right to choose him," the sorcerer explained.

"Then I'll choose you," Halef said, making a polite bow.

"Me! Why me of all people?"

"Because I have taken a liking to you. And also because I have never had the chance to fight a Sahahr. My fame will grow if I can tell them back home that I defeated and killed you in a duel."

"Kill? You would kill in such a test?"

"Of course. Victory is not complete until the vanquished lies dead on the ground. Who chooses the weapons?"

"The stranger."

"That would be me. Then we'll use firearms."

"Firearms? That would be my death, although I am a giant compared to you."

"That's the point," Halef laughed. "To shoot a giant dead would be a great joy for me. That's the one occasion where it can be shown that it's not size that counts. What weapons will you choose, Effendi?"

"The same," I said, going along with the joke.

"With whom are you going to fight?"

"The sheik."

This startled him. "With me? Why with me?"

"Because I like you. You see, I have precisely the same reasons as my Hadji Halef. He is a sheik, I am an Emir. We could not possibly fight ordinary warriors. That's why we choose you, and we are convinced you will see this choice for what it is, an honor for both of you."

I had been addressing the sheik. Now I turned to his wife, and added:

"We are willing to become Ussul. But that won't be until tomorrow. What are we until then, friends or enemies?"

"Friends," she said. "You need not hesitate to release the sheik and the Sahahr. You are free."

"Only for now, or forever?"

"Forever. I promise you that."

She gave me her hand, and I shook it. The two men also shook hands with me and Halef.

Now that the sheik had been released, he was anxious to get back to camp. His wife kept the quince branch to show to her warriors, and we went to our horses. When they jumped up, Taldsha gave a cry of surprise. She had keener perceptions than her husband.

"What beautiful, magnificent animals," she said, clapping her hands with pleasure. "Much smaller than ours. But incredibly graceful and well shaped. I should like to kiss them."

She put her arms around Ben Rih's neck and kissed him on the forehead. He suffered this without stirring. But when she also kissed Syrr, his nostrils flared as he took in her scent and he neighed delicately and curiously, in a way that I had never heard before. She

quickly stepped back, looked at me oddly and searchingly, and asked:

"Effendi, does the hair of this horse crackle?"

"Yes," I answered.

"All the time?"

"No, only when I comb and stroke him."

"What is his name?"

"Syrr."

"That means mystery, enigma. As I touched his
neck, I felt something pass through my hands. It was
precisely the same feeling I had when the man from
Sitara gave me his hand."

"What is Sitara?" I asked, feigning ignorance.

"A land far away from here of which almost nothing
but its name is known. May I try?"

She was pointing at Syrr. I did not know what she
had in mind, but nodded. Again, she stepped up to the
horse and began stroking his mane. She listened and
gestured for me to approach.

"Do you hear it?" she asked.

"Yes. If it were dark, you would even see it."

"Tiny bright sparks, of a yellowish blue which jump
back and forth between the hair and the hand. Isn't
that it, Emir?"

"So you know?"

"Yes."

"How?"

"From Aacht and Uucht."

Aacht and Uucht means "brother and sister." She
could tell that I was anxious to know more about this
pair, and explained:

"Aacht and Uucht are two dogs that are surely
unique. The Ussul are famous for the size, beauty, and
strength of the dogs they breed. Some years back, we
sent the Mir of Djinnistan a pair, although that is
forbidden here in Ardistan. But he had done us a great
service and we wanted to thank him. Of course, it had
to be done secretly. Just as secretly, a stranger later
came to us. He was from Sitara and on his way back
there. He had been with the Mir of Djinnistan and
was bringing us his return gift, two dogs that were
even more handsome, faster, and more intelligent than
ours, but not as strong. The man from Sitara was the

one I mentioned a while ago. He told us the condition the Mir of Djinnistan attached to his gift. It was strange. It was that the entire offspring that came from the crossbreeding of his dogs and ours would be ours except for one pair, a brother and a sister, which would be turned over to the man who had visited him, and who would come to us with a hidden shield covering his chest, and be very useful to us. The two dogs were called Aacht and Uucht. I maintained that these are the most beautiful, strongest, most intelligent, and fastest dogs there are. Curiously enough, I see small sparks when I fondle them, just as I see them here, coming from your horse. Get in the saddle now; we are returning to camp."

"I am coming along," the sheik said. "I'll ride the horse of his companion."

He walked over to Ben Rih and took his reins. Halef was not enthusiastic about this but I gestured to him not to offend Amihn.

He apparently obeyed for I saw that he gave his horse the sign I have mentioned on former occasions, telling Ben Rih what to do. When the sheik placed his hand on the saddle, Halef warned him:

"I wouldn't do that if I were you, sheik."

"Why not?"

"Because this horse will throw anyone that doesn't belong on it."

"Including me?" the Ussul laughed.

"Including you," Halef answered with a smile I was all too familiar with.

"I am not going to take your word for it. Woe to the horse that thinks it can throw a man such as myself."

He swung himself into the saddle or, rather, he climbed on the horse as if it were Smikh. But before his right leg was over the side, Ben Rih jumped to one side, leaped forward, and then stood still, while the sheik found himself sitting behind him in the fragrant grass. He was so annoyed that he decided to make up for this defeat. He quickly got to his feet, again took the reins, and was about to put his foot in the stirrup.

"Be careful," the Hadji warned him.

"Silence!" the sheik thundered. "This beast will have to obey, it has to, I tell you!"

He thought he knew the horse now and that he would therefore be safe from its tricks. But he did not notice that Halef had given Ben Rih a different signal. The sheik slowly raised himself in the stirrup so that he would be able to jump down without delay, should the horse repeat its antics.

The horse did not move even when he was safely in the saddle.

"Now, can I do it, or can't I?" he asked triumphantly.

"You can't," Halef answered.

"But you see that—"

He could not finish the sentence because Rih suddenly reared up, moved to one side, came down, and then threw his hind legs so far up into the air that the sheik was hurled out of the saddle and catapulted across the horse's head.

". . . you have to get down," Halef completed the sheik's sentence. "I'll show you what you must do to stay on him."

He jumped into the saddle to make it impossible for the sheik to try a third time. The latter was furious for having again made a fool of himself. After two unsuccessful attempts, nothing could have made him try again.

"Your beast is crazy," he said. "No one can ride it."

"Not even me?"

"Not even you. You'll see how quickly you'll be unseated."

He clenched his fist and smashed the horse so violently between the eyes that I thought its forehead would break. For a moment, Ben Rih stood utterly motionless, momentarily dazed. Halef was not yet firmly in the saddle.

"For heaven's sake! Take the reins," I called out to him. "Your horse is about to bolt."

Just in time, he pulled himself together. Ben Rih started to tremble and twitch. He took a huge forward leap, jumped first to one side, then to the other, made a one hundred and eighty degree turn and rushed off as if all the hounds of hell were in pursuit.

"Shame on you," I told the sheik. "Why do you hit

such a noble animal with your fist? That wasn't right, and does you no credit."

I threw my rifles over my shoulder and swung myself on Syrr.

"Where to?" Taldsha asked.

"After him. If the horse's hoof gets caught in one of these plants, both of them might break their necks."

"When are you coming back?"

"I don't know. Perhaps never. We don't like such crude manners!"

"But if I ask you—"

That was all I heard. Syrr flew forward to catch Ben Rih, who had already disappeared behind one of the numerous bends I mentioned before. What I had told the woman was true. Actually, there should have been no reason to fear for Halef. Over the course of the years, he had shown me how excellent a horseman he was and that he could manage without my help. Besides, his stallion was too much of a thoroughbred for the blow to have more than a temporary effect. But the dense, tangled masses of roots and branches through which he was riding made a crash almost inevitable. And considering the speed at which his horse was running, this could be fatal. I soon discovered that my fears were justified, for after I had covered a fair distance at a very fast gallop, I saw Ben Rih, his head lowered, standing still among the flowers. The rider had to be somewhere, probably in the direction the horse's head was pointing.

5 : The "Panther"

When I got to him, Halef was lying on the ground, stiff and immobile, his eyes closed, looking like a corpse. I could tell from the tracks that the horse's legs had got caught and that he had fallen. A tough tendril was still attached to one hoof. If it had not torn, Ben Rih would have broken a leg and would have had to be killed. Halef was alive, though unconscious. He was unhurt and I could move his limbs. That the pain did not wake him reassured me, and so I sat down comfortably by his side to wait until he came to. Ben Rih was not injured in any way.

A considerable time passed before Halef stirred. He opened his eyes, looked at me, closed them again, and said:

"There he sits at his ease, but I have to ride. If Ben Rih gets caught in the bushes, and I fall, I'll break my neck."

He stopped, for he had opened his eyes again.

"You here, Sidi? But didn't I just dash past you? You were sitting still, looking at me expectantly, but the stallion ran on and on, and crashed, and I with him. I landed on my head. It hurts, and you smile."

"Yes," I nodded.

"Why?"

"Because I am delighted that you will be in a position to answer a very important question for me."

"What is the question?"

"I want to know what goes on in a person's soul when he is unconscious."

"Unconscious? Do you mean to say that I—"

He broke off.

"Allah w'Allah! Look, Sidi! Do you see what I see?"

He was pointing at three horsemen who had suddenly appeared at some distance from us and now stopped.

We were still on the narrow strip where I had chased the sheik of the Ussul and taken him prisoner. This strip resembled an aisle and was bordered by trees. The camp of the Ussul lay behind us but was so far away that it would probably have taken more than an hour to walk to it. Before us, this narrow, perfectly straight path continued for a short distance, but then widened and became a clearing. The dense growth of the trees bordering the path concentrated all available light on it, and at the point where it widened I saw three horsemen as through binoculars, with their contours sharply defined. They had come from the clearing and were looking down the path, wondering whether they should follow it. I could tell all this from their movements. It seemed obvious that they did not know the lay of the land, and therefore probably were Ussul who had never been at this particular spot before. But I could not exclude the possibility that they might not be Ussul at all.

When they had finished deliberating, they started toward us. But there was something curious about their approach, for they avoided the center of the path and kept so close to the trees on either side that they could not be seen from a distance.

"Those are not Ussul," Halef said.

"Nor are they friends of theirs," I added. "They don't want to be seen. So their intentions must be hostile."

"Are we going to conceal ourselves?"

"It's too late for that. Sit down here next to me; we'll have the horses lie down."

It required only a single word for the two well-trained animals to lie down where they stood among the bushes. These had the height and color of broom and hid us so completely that we could only be seen from very close up.

The strangers were advancing so slowly that we had sufficient time to scrutinize them before they reached us. Two of them were bearded men of mature years, though not white-haired, while the third was a youth of perhaps twenty-five. Their horses were not as massive as those of the Ussul, tall and bony. Reins and bridle were simple and made of undyed leather. They were armed with bows, arrows, and knives. In addition, each one carried a spear and a rifle, but the latter seemed of the type Bedouins normally own, by which I mean that they were of light, thin steel, poorly made, and used a powder that was so coarse that the weapon easily became more dangerous to its owner than to his target. The colors of their dyed clothes were garish, as is customary among dwellers of the steppe. Each wore pants, a vest, jacket, cape, turban, and leather boots with terrible spurs which had left their bloody marks on the flanks of their poor animals. The two older men looked serious and ill-humored. The younger, whose beard was just beginning to curl, had a more open face in which I later also observed traces of cruelty and cunning. The heads of his companions were apparently shaven but he wore his hair in two carefully plaited pigtails with gold and silver coins in them. There are barbarian and semi-barbarian tribes where such queues indicate high rank or prestige. Halef had been looking at them with considerable curiosity, and now said to me:

"Sidi, I think I'm having a vision. This young man is an enchanted prince, his ungainly, big horse the sorcerer. Both of them are looking for an adventure that will free them of the spell. What do you think?"

"Hm," I answered. "It's true he doesn't look like an ordinary person, but I don't believe he is a prince. If he is, he is undoubtedly one of those rulers where a short, decisive moment determines whether they become the angels or the devils of their people. Watch out, here they come!"

Though very close now, they had not seen us. I got up, and the three halted.

Halef also jumped to his feet. Instead of waiting for me to say something, he asked threateningly:

"What are you doing here?"

One of the men, some distance away from the other two, quickly rode over to them. They exchanged a few words, and then he answered:

"We don't want anything. We are just passing. We are riding to the sea."

"Who are you?"

"Travellers."

"From where?"

"From the interior."

"What tribe?"

The stranger threw an arm in the air, laughed out loud, and said:

"You ask yourself that question, not us."

He reached for his rifle, and the other two followed his example. Three shots rang out, all of them missed, and then they dashed back in the direction from which they had come. It is not difficult to avoid being hit by the shots of such untrained and careless people.

"They have no sense," Halef exclaimed. "Let's go after them!"

"Very well. But don't kill them. They will be no use to us dead."

We rode after them at a distance which left them no time to separate and seek cover in the dense forest. We wanted to wait until we came to the clearing where the horses had room to maneuver. When I had first seen them, it had occurred to me that these men might be Tshoban, the enemies of the Ussul who periodically attacked and pillaged. The behavior of these three confirmed my suspicion.

When they turned and looked back the first time, they did so to express their contempt and to laugh at us. But they soon became aware that we were drawing closer. Now they dug their huge spurs into the bloody flanks of their poor beasts with such force that the horses neighed loudly with pain and tried to run faster. But this only worked for a brief moment. They tired quickly and became breathless. As we entered the wide clearing, I called out to them to stop. Instead, they let a few arrows fly at us.

The clearing was perhaps half an hour's walk wide, and so long that I could not see the far end. It consisted of sandy soil on which only sparse vegetation grew and an occasional bush struggled to survive.

I had assumed that the three would now separate to force us to do likewise, but this did not happen. They stayed together, the two older men keeping somewhat behind the younger to protect him from us. He seemed to be an important person who must not be abandoned, and I therefore decided to make every effort to capture him. As I was still trying to think of a suitable maneuver to separate them, I noticed that the young man continued to hurry along while his companions stopped, turned to face us, and took their spears in their hands.

"Sidi, after him," Halef called out. "I'll deal with these two careless fellows."

He reined in his horse, drew his pistols, and slowly rode toward them as I sped past in pursuit of the other. When they saw this, they turned away from Halef and began pursuing me.

It was impossible for them to catch up with me. Although it had not taken them much time to separate from their companion and to turn to face us, it had been long enough for me to get a considerable head start. When I looked back, I noticed that they had given up their pursuit of me and had once again turned on Halef. The young man was urging his horse on so brutally that I decided to cut matters short, and not to use my lasso but to seize him with my hand. A short, piercing whistle, and Syrr increased his speed. The young man saw us coming closer and closer. He again used his bow to shoot an arrow which was so well aimed that it would have struck me, had I not quickly bent forward. But now I was alongside him. I took him by his belt, and gently kicked Syrr who immediately took a jump to one side. The rider was thrown from his animal by this sudden leap. I held on to him, gave him a heave, and then released him. He flew to the ground in a wide arc. Syrr stopped. I jumped down and walked up to him. He tried to get to his feet, but collapsed.

"Don't move," I ordered him. "You are my prisoner."

"Prisoner!" he laughed. "Don't you see them coming?"

He was pointing at his companions who were dashing toward us.

"They can't do anything to me," I answered. "Away with your weapons."

His spear and rifle had already fallen out of his hands when I had pulled him from the horse. I now also took the quiver and the arrows, which might have poisoned tips, and the knife which he had seized to thrust at me. I hurled all these things away. There was no time to see whether he had suffered injuries, for his two companions were coming close. They probably did not have the skill to reload their rifles in the saddle, and because they could not use their bows either, they attacked with their spears. I easily parried the thrust of the first with my hunting rifle. The attacker shot past me, and reined in his horse to turn around. But with two or three rapid leaps, I was by his side, and pulled the horse down. It was about to straighten up again but I pushed its head down. As it kicked up its hind legs, the rider lost his hold and was thrown out of the saddle. He quickly got to his feet but had not yet recovered his equilibrium when I hit his shoulder so violently with the butt of my rifle that he collapsed with a cry of pain. A moment later, he had been disarmed. Now his companion was coming toward me but Halef was hard on his heels. Thinking only of getting at me, the second attacker was urging his horse toward me, his spear tilted. But he did not have a chance to use it. Halef sped toward him, whirled his rifle over his head, and hit him with the butt. The man let go of his lance and reins and raised both hands to his head. His horse leaped sideways and he tottered out of the saddle. Halef quickly turned his horse and seized the man by the throat.

"Hamdulillah," he shouted merrily. "Now they are all sitting on the ground. Shall we collect them?"

"All right."

The man Halef had knocked down was unconscious. He pulled him up and pushed him toward the young man, who was still unable to move. I went to pick up the third, to whom I had given such a blow that he no longer attempted to resist. When they had all been collected and their weapons stacked nearby, Halef sat down by them with that look on his face which always showed that he was going to have some fun. He eyed them closely one after the other, and said:

"How delightful that we are back together. Won't you tell me what we did to offend you so grievously that you decided not to stay with us?"

"Who are you?" the young man asked in a firm tone, ignoring Halef's politeness.

"How is it that you should ask me that question?" Halef answered. "Why are you saying anything at all? Your companions are older and probably more experienced than you."

"I am of higher rank," the man answered.

"Of higher rank? What do you call higher rank?"

"I am the firstborn."

He pronounced this word as if it were a title and referred to the crown prince.

"So you are the oldest son of the ruler?"

"Yes."

"What ruler?"

"That's no business of yours."

"You are mistaken. If I don't find out from you, I will from the others. But you would be well advised to be open with us."

"I can think of no reason to talk confidentially to people of your sort. You are our enemies. You are Ussul."

"Ussul? Us?" Halef asked and burst out laughing. "Anyone who calls us Ussul must be blind and deaf."

"Are you going to deny it?"

Now one of his companions said very politely:

"They are smaller than the Ussul. We overlooked that. And one of them is addressed as Sidi. That word is used only by the Turkish and Persian Arabs."

"So you are Turks?" the younger man asked.

"No," Halef answered.

"Or Persians?"

"No."

"What then?"

"That's no concern of yours. Those who tell us nothing cannot expect answers from us. But I'll make an exception in your case. I will tell you who we are. We are also firstborn. He is mine, and I am his. I am his father, and he is mine. That makes us even nobler than you."

"Fool," the young man said. "The wag is always the lowest of the tribe. I have nothing but contempt for you. I don't care who you are. Leave us."

"We certainly will leave, but we are taking you along."

"Where?"

"That also doesn't concern you."

"Don't dare lay hands on us again. We are not unbelievers like the Ussul. We are Muslims."

"Do you think that's reason for conceit? I am a Muslim too. You seem to have a remarkably high opinion of yourself, but in truth you are an exceptionally stupid, inexperienced fellow. I'll show you how people like you should be dealt with."

He jumped up, pulled his beloved whip from his belt, and continued:

"First, have a look at your poor beasts. Those holes along both flanks are full of blood and pus. Are you human beings? The horse is also one of God's crea-

: 78 :

tures, a thousand times more beautiful and noble than you. Don't imagine that we will treat you with consideration and gentleness. The language you understand best is a whipping."

"Dog!" the young man shouted. "You dare threaten me with your whip? You'll pay for this with your life. I'll—"

He stopped. He had tried to jump up but had collapsed again with a cry of pain.

"My life?" Halef laughed. "You are just a boy. How pathetic you are! Never in my life have I seen triple stupidity as close up. You stupidly came riding to the place where we took you by surprise. You stupidly tried to escape. You committed the even greater stupidity of keeping together. Your attempt to help this one here get away was of unrivalled stupidity. How stupidly you let yourselves get caught! And how unspeakably stupid to posture now on top of everything and to offend us, who are the masters of your destiny. We'll—"

"You'll do nothing," the firstborn interrupted him with a roar. "Be silent!"

I had remained still up to this point and had been standing between them and their weapons so they would not take it into their heads to leap suddenly to their feet to try to seize them. The third one couldn't move because he had hurt himself. I now walked up to him and asked:

"Are you in pain? I'll see if you broke something. We may have to bandage it."

"Away from here, scurvy jackal! Do you know who we are?" he barked.

"No," I answered calmly.

"Among us, to lay hands on the sheik or his sons is the greatest of crimes. You did it, and that dooms you. If I allowed you to touch me, that would entitle you to pardon, according to our law."

"Thank you for this warning, but I am not looking for pardon. I am telling you this, however: If you refuse to be touched by us, be careful that we don't use the whip on you."

We stared at each other. He was boiling with rage and about to give way to it, but my glance restrained him. He controlled himself, and asked:

"So you also dare mention a whip?"

"Dare? If I feel like whipping you, I shall. Courage isn't involved. And now pay attention to me: If any one of you utters one more word without permission, he will be given a blow for every one he utters. Remember that! I am not joking."

"May Allah curse you," one of the other two said as he tried to rise to his feet. But Halef's whip descended on him, and I took out my two revolvers, showed them the mechanism, and said:

"Have a look at these. You can see for yourselves that each can fire six bullets, so I can shoot twelve times without reloading. Be careful. If the whip won't do the trick, bullets will."

That did it. They could not understand the mechanism but saw the cylinder and were impressed by the mystery of it. No one said another word, although it was quite apparent from their faces what we could look forward to, should we ever have the misfortune of falling into their hands. I stayed with them, the revolvers ready to fire, while Halef tied their horses one behind the other. Then the two older men had to place their companion on the lead horse because we were not allowed to help him into the saddle. They tied his hands on his back and we started off.

It had been a curious experience. It was my impression that capturing these three men would be an important service to the Ussul, but that we had also laid the groundwork for later troubles or even dangers to ourselves. But this was not our fault. If the three strangers had conducted themselves differently, if they had not tried to get away without apparent reason, and had been less abrupt and belligerent, this encounter would have taken a different turn. Even if they should be Tshoban, the archenemies of the Ussul, a way might be found to avoid hostilities. I was wondering if the Ussul knew who they were.

We returned by the same route, but before we reached Amihn's prison, we saw half a dozen horsemen coming toward us on massive Ussul beasts. It was the sheik, Taldsha, and the Sahahr with three Ussul. They were surprised at seeing five of us moving along in single file. They stopped and waited. Although we were still some distance from them, Halef couldn't restrain himself:

"The courageous were successful, the brave victorious. The fight is over. We triumphed."

"You have been fighting?" Amihn asked.

"With three strangers. We don't know them. But they succumbed before our might and were knocked into the dust by our fists. Here they are. Have a look!"

He guided his horse to one side so that the Ussul could see the first of our prisoners.

"Wallahi," Amihn exclaimed. "That is the Palang,* the oldest son of the sheik of the Tshoban."

"Palang, the firstborn," the sorcerer added.

"Where did you find him?" the sheik asked.

Halef was about to launch into one of his self-congratulatory speeches, but I cut him off:

"We saw them back there. When they noticed us, they fled. We pursued them to capture them and bring them to you. You can see we succeeded."

"You have accomplished a difficult and dangerous task. There can be no doubt this is the 'Panther' of the Tshoban. I have seen him before. I don't know his two companions. Whose prisoners are they?"

"Mine."

"Will you turn them over to us?"

The other Ussul immediately and vigorously joined in this request. While it was my intention to do as they asked, I felt it would be best to wait, and so I said:

"I may let you have them but there should be certain conditions."

"Which?" his wife asked. "Name them!"

"You must not let them go without my permission."

"Agreed. Can we take them now?"

The Ussul were already pressing toward the prisoners who had been silent up to now, afraid of Halef's whip. Now the "Panther" asked me:

"May I talk now?"

"You may."

He turned to the sheik and his wife, and said:

* The panther.

"If this stranger turns us over to you, you would be obliged to release us again."

"Why?" Taldsha asked. The men seemed quite willing to let her do the talking.

"Because only enemies, not friends, are taken prisoner."

"But you are enemies."

"No, not this time. I came as a friend. My father sent me to you with a message of peace. Everywhere in the world, such a messenger is inviolable. You know what would happen, should you treat me as an enemy. My father would attack your country and kill every Ussul that fell into his hands."

"Yes, he would," the woman agreed. "We can only consider you an enemy if you came with hostile intentions. But that is certainly the case."

"How can you prove that?"

"No Tshoban ever comes here as a friend."

"This time we did. I was sent to conclude an alliance with you, a long-term alliance, even a permanent one, if possible."

"Now it's my turn to ask for proof."

"The signing will be the proof. But I cannot do that here, and cannot do it today or tomorrow. It will require long days of negotiations. And even if they should have to be broken off, you must not lay hands on me and would have to let me go for I am here as a messenger of peace."

"And was it as a messenger of peace that you shot at us?" I asked.

"At you?" he said condescendingly. "Are you an Ussul?"

"No."

"Then don't talk. I wasn't sent to you."

"That's true. But that's also the reason I don't have to treat you as a friend. You are my prisoner."

"That won't keep me from negotiating with the Ussul, and I am telling you that they will demand that you turn me over to them. Woe to you if you refuse."

"What is your decision? Will you let us have him, or not?" Taldsha asked me.

"I am going to keep him for a little while. As soon as

I have convinced you that he came here with hostile intentions, I will let you have him."

"You won't be able to," he barked at me.

"I'll prove it before the day is out. Now let's get started. We are going back to camp."

I had addressed the three Ussul who now joined the prisoners without saying a word while the sheik, his wife, and the priest followed me. To have their archenemy in their power meant a great deal to them. It gave them a hostage more valuable than any amount of money, but their advantage would boomerang if the "Panther" really had come for peaceful purposes. Otherwise, the law of all the nations and tribes of Ardistan was on the Ussuls' side. They were free to do as they liked with the prisoner.

"It's a great miracle that you are still alive," Amihn remarked as we were riding along. "It's true they are neither as tall nor as strong as we, but the two of you are smaller still. And you were only two against three."

"That simply means that you should remember that it is not physical size or quantity that counts," I told him. "You say yourself that the Tshoban are smaller than you, yet they usually defeat you. Do you think he came with peaceful intentions?"

"No," the sheik answered. "That's quite unlikely. Yet we must enter into negotiations with them the moment you let us have them, at least until his hostile intentions become apparent. Do you really think you can prove that today?"

"I am sure of it."

"Who is going to tell us?"

"He will, or one of his companions."

"Why should they?"

"They will. They'll be overjoyed at the chance to betray their secrets. All we have to do is give them an opportunity to talk freely to each other. If you help me, we'll succeed. Is there a place where these prisoners can be kept during the night and easily guarded?"

"The island or the camp. We'll simply tie them to three trees. A single guard will be enough. The rest of us can go to sleep."

"How easy and simple that sounds. Is that the way you usually do things? No wonder the Tshoban always outsmart you. No one will stay in the camp during the night."

"Why not?"

"Do you really believe that the sheik of the Tshoban would commit the unpardonable error of sending his firstborn and successor into your country with no more than two men for an escort?"

"You are right," the sheik agreed. "I wouldn't do it."

"Do the Tshoban carry sabres?"

"Almost every one of them."

"These three have none. Why? Because they would get in their way. They wanted to proceed quietly, unheard, unseen. And if your territory is to be combed and they want to find out what you are up to and where you are, would three men be enough?"

"You are frightening me."

"I don't mean to. But even if you really were frightened, that would be preferable to a surprise attack. I don't believe that these three men are the only Tshoban reconnoitering here. So I'll be sure not to put them where they can be rescued easily. And that's why I would advise you against spending the night in your camp, which may have been under surveillance for some time. The way the prince approached suggests that he knows where it is."

"It's been in its present location for quite a while."

"That makes it all the worse. And all the more dangerous to move into it at a time when the enemy is nearby."

"What other site do you propose?"

"None at this moment. I don't know this territory but will have a look around before it gets dark. But come what may, there's no doubt you have been very lucky so far today."

When we got back to camp, everybody was surprised to see the three Tshoban. Those who had remained behind were jubilant. Without much ceremony, the "Panther's" two companions were tied to two trees far enough apart so that they could not talk to each other. The "Panther" had to be placed on the ground, for he could not stand up. The inquisitive priest examined him and discovered that his foot was broken and in need of speedy treatment if it was not to remain lame. The Tshoban became frightened when he heard this and asked the Sahahr to bandage him. The priest was also the physician of his tribe and went about his business with the help of two Ussul. How this was done was no concern of mine, for I had more important matters to attend to. First, a more convenient camp site had to be found, and then I had to paddle to the island to find out if it suited our purposes. My plan was to get the prisoners to talk to each other, and to eavesdrop on them. The sheik accompanied me. Halef wanted to join us but had to stay behind to guard the prisoners and to prevent their talking to each other or to anyone else. This was intended to make them more anxious to communicate later.

We soon found a good spot to spend the night, and then went to the island. I had assumed that the large boat I had seen earlier was the only one the Ussul had, but there was a second, a small and light canoe carefully hidden in the bushes. It was covered with leather and could easily be taken apart and transported anywhere. It was this boat we used. Before we set out, the sheik sent one of his men to his "residence" to bring the population the joyful tidings that the "firstborn" of their archenemy had been taken prisoner, and to tell the people to prepare a solemn reception. He was talking of his "capital," his "castle" and his "citadel," and I assumed that he was exaggerating. He also mentioned a "temple" for religious services. I was growing curious.

The island was some fifty paces long and only half that wide, with dense bushes all along the water's edge. There were several trees I could use. One of them was very close to a tiny bay which was just wide enough for our canoe.

"We are going to tie the 'Panther' to this tree," I told the sheik.

"When?"

"During the night."

"So you mean to bring him over here?"

"Yes, and also his two companions. My Hadji Halef

Omar, who is a very smart fellow, will bring them here. But the two of us will come here before they arrive. The tree to which the 'Panther' is to be tied is so close to this little bay that we can practically touch him with our outstretched arm. But he won't see us because we will be hidden by the water plants along the shore. We'll hear every word that is spoken here. The other two will be tied to trees along the far shore, but loosely enough so that they can free themselves. And they certainly will, in order to have a discussion with their superior."

"That's very clever," the sheik praised me. "That's a good plan, but will it work? Will they really be careless enough to talk to each other? Won't they become suspicious, and won't it occur to them that we will eavesdrop on them?"

"No. I'm sure we'll attain our purpose. When they are taken from the camp, they will be sure to see that all of us are there."

"All of us? But the two of us will be gone, and that's precisely what will make them wonder."

"No, because we won't leave before but after them. Besides, they will be taken across in the large, heavy boat, and as slowly as possible. But we will take this one, and get here much earlier. They will be convinced that only Halef and the crew have left camp. And once they have been tied to the trees here, the two companions will notice that the three men in the large boat are really leaving. So they will think they are unobserved and conduct themselves accordingly. Of course, we must not give ourselves away. Can you suppress coughing and sneezing?"

"Certainly. Even if we should have to stand in water all night long, you won't hear the slightest noise from me."

"Then we can go back. I still have to take Halef here, tell him about our plan, and give him the necessary instructions. He must do nothing to arouse their suspicion while he brings them here."

We returned and disembarked without anyone's being aware of it, not because I did not trust the Ussul, but because I did not want anyone to mention the small canoe. I also took care that Halef left camp unnoticed. On our way to the island, I told him our plan. He was delighted.

"Sidi," he assured me, "I'll do my job so well you will have to praise me. I would give a great deal for a chance to listen in on them but I can see that that won't be possible. You will show me to which trees I am to tie the prisoners. I'll do that carefully but see to it that the two rascals will mock me after they have managed to get loose. I won't mind that. I shall have my revenge later."

All I had to do now was to show him the place so that he would know precisely what to expect once it was dark. When we had gone ashore on the island, I showed him the three trees I had picked and he explained all the ruses he would use to deceive the Tshoban. We also rearranged the plants along the shore so that they would hide us and our canoe could disappear among them. Then he went back to the new camp site to which the Ussul had moved in the meantime. Dry wood was being collected, for it was getting dark and fires had to be lit. Taldsha and the women began preparing the evening meal. The men settled around the largest fire and we began a conversation but deliberately refrained from mentioning the three prisoners. Here also, they had been tied to trees that were sufficiently far apart so that they could not see each other. But they could hear everything we said, and therefore the Ussul gave the conversation a turn that would necessarily impress and frighten the Tshoban. The Ussul pretended that Halef and I were their best friends and practically gods. Halef treated our hosts as familiarly as he would old friends and they responded in a way which would make it impossible for them later to treat us as enemies. I remained quiet. Halef did the necessary talking while I studied the Ussul as closely as I could.

We ate game the Ussul had hunted and roasted on the fire, and a supplement of roasted vegetables, wild onions and a kind of Canna indica. It tasted very good.

When it was time to settle down for the night, I had sentries posted. To mislead our prisoners, we then gathered for a mock counsel, pretending to deliberate what to do with them. The sheik proposed to take them to the island to tie them up there because no guard would then be required. We agreed, and Halef offered to take them there if two men would paddle the canoe. All this was said and done so naturally that the Tshoban did not suspect the deception. They were untied and taken to the shore where the large boat lay ready. Then the sheik and I hurried to the place where we had left the smaller boat. Protected by the shadows along the shore and unseen by the prisoners, we made straight for our destination. When we entered the small bay, we had time enough to settle comfortably behind the heavy branches. The tree to which the "Panther" would be tied stood so close that the roots on our side were hanging into the water.

We heard Halef's voice earlier than the movement of his boat. He was intentionally speaking loudly and when he landed on the far side, we could make out every word he said.

During the short trip to the island, he had been talking to the prisoners. He had a cunning way of interrogating people and was no less skillful at letting me know what he had found out from them.

"So the two of you are the teachers of the prince of the Tshoban, nicknamed the 'Panther.' One of you teaches him how to govern, the other how to wage war. One of you is the 'Pen,' the other the 'Sword of the Prince.' All of you will be tied up now. The 'Pen' will be first. Come along, step out of the boat."

He led the "Pen of the Prince" from the boat to the tree and tied him to it with straps, creating the impression that he was careful about what he was doing. While he was busy with this, he said:

"Now that I have heard how important a person you are, it grieves my soul from head to toe to be obliged to tie you to this trunk which is ignorant of your elevated station in life. But when I leave here, it will console you that I will return early tomorrow to hear if you spent a pleasant night."

Then he got the "Sword of the Prince" and tied him to the second trunk, making some ironic remarks to him as well. The crew then had to carry the "Panther" to the third tree. The two counselors had been attached in an upright position, but because the "Panther" had a broken foot he was allowed to sit down and only his back was tied to the trunk. As Halef was seeing to this, he said:

"I love you, prince. You have conquered my heart. It's true that you did it secretly when you told me a while back that you would give me a whole saddlebag full of gold coins if I took you to your horses and fled with you. And because you whispered it to me, I am now saying it out loud. Your gold coins are not yours, but belong to your friends, the Ussul. When I get back to them, I will tell them and the sheik how ready you are to pay. Sleep well! May Allah send you a dozen happy dreams from his seventh paradise."

He left and got back into the boat with the two Ussul. We continued hearing the paddles and Halef's voice for some time because he again spoke loudly. Then all became quiet. Everything had proceeded so naturally and matter-of-factly that it did not occur to the three Tshoban that they might not be alone, or that Halef was perhaps secretly returning to eavesdrop on them.

We waited. The sheik was anxiously wondering if my prediction would turn out to be correct, but I did not have the slightest doubt that the prisoners would not wait long before they began talking to each other. And that's precisely what happened. Halef's voice had barely faded when the "Pen of the Prince" called out to the other two:

"Listen! Can you hear me?"

"Yes, yes," he was answered from both sides of the island.

"We are alone."

"Are you absolutely certain?" the prince asked.

"Yes. From where I am standing, I could see the boat until it disappeared. There is no one that could hear us. How stupid these people are!"

"Are you tied securely?"

"It looks that way, but I'll see."

'So will I," the "Sword of the Prince" joined in. "I think I may be able to free myself."

It was quiet for a little while, and then we heard shouts of joy. Both had managed to loosen the straps but this did not strike them as suspicious. They were jubilant and hurried over to the "Panther" to untie him as well. Then they discussed how they might get away. It now became clear how great is the influence of birth and upbringing on men that are otherwise of almost equal rank. The prince was more nobly born, and in spite of the fact that his counselors were older and more experienced, he proved to be the more circumspect.

"Stop! Don't untie me," he ordered. "We don't know whether we might not have to tie ourselves up again. Should that become necessary, we will be unable to make the same loops they did, and they will know what we have been up to."

"Tie ourselves up again? Why should we?"

"Can you swim?"

"No. We are not fish or frogs. If Allah had given us fins or webbed feet, he might have wanted us to. You know how, but your foot is injured."

"Yes, this miserable foot," the "Panther" wailed. "I won't soon forget that this dog of a stranger pulled me from my horse and lamed me. But the time will come when I shall settle accounts with him. I'll show no mercy."

He gritted his teeth, and continued:

"Well, then, since it's impossible to swim ashore, we have to stay where we are. Leave me as I am, so they don't notice tomorrow morning how poorly they fastened you. They'll pay more attention to me than to you."

"Are we going to abandon any attempt to get away?" the "Sword" asked.

The "Panther" reflected for a few moments.

"I have to submit because of my foot. But you don't. You could flee the moment an opportunity offers itself. But for my sake it would be more intelligent not to. They take their anger out on me. Your escape would disprove my claim that we came with peaceful intentions and as my father's envoys."

"But we cannot stay until they discover that that is a lie. Even now, the two strangers don't believe us. Consider that our army will cross the Chatar defile one week from today. If we are still prisoners at that time, we are done for. The moment they find out that we don't want peace but are invading their country with a large army, they will kill us."

"Certainly," the "Panther" agreed. "But there is no danger as yet. If we act convincingly, they will let us go soon. We will conclude a treaty with them which my father will have to examine before he puts his seal to it. We will say that we must bring it to him, and that we therefore have to leave."

"But suppose they reject the treaty?"

"Impossible. We know that we won't keep it and therefore can make things so attractive that they cannot turn it down. These Ussul are fools. And the most stupid is the sheik. If he did not have a wife who tried to preserve the small measure of intelligence he has, there would be no greater simpleton on earth. During the next victorious battle, I'll take him prisoner and exhibit him all over the country so that people finally discover how a person looks that—"

"This is what he looks like," a roaring voice interrupted him, and at the same moment he was given a slap in the face which I must admit reverberated more loudly than those I had given Smikh when he had become too insistent for my liking. The moment it had become clear that the peaceful mission of these men was a ruse, the sheik had lost all self-control. His breath had become audible. I took him by the arm to calm him down, and this might have had the desired effect, except for the insulting remark. He became furious, stood up, thrust the branches hiding us aside, hit the prince in the face and jumped ashore. I followed him.

"Allah w'Allah," the "Sword" exclaimed in terror.

"And the stranger, too," the "Pen" added.

The "Panther" said nothing. The slap was probably absorbing his attention so completely that he was momentarily incapable of speech.

"Yes, the sheik and the stranger," Amihn roared on. "The sheik whom you are going to exhibit all across your country. The sheik, the greatest of all fools. But your heads have been so crammed full of cleverness since you were children that one only has to tie you to the nearest tree to find out all your secrets. Away with you! Back to the trees."

Using one hand for each, the sheik took them by their necks and dragged them away. They did not dare put up a fight which they probably would have had occasion to regret. We tied them firmly to the trees and then returned to the "Panther" to examine his straps. They were so tight that no adjustment was required.

"Scoundrel," he said venomously.

"I only came here to keep my word," I told him.

"What word?"

"You challenged me to prove that you are the Ussuls' enemy, and I promised to do so before this evening was over. It's still some time before midnight. Farewell. We'll see each other tomorrow morning."

We got into the canoe and left the island. When we were too far away to be heard, the sheik said:

"You were right. How wise that we eavesdropped on them!"

"And how wrong that you acted so prematurely," I reproached him. "Who knows what we would have found out if you had remained still."

"Forgive me, but I couldn't stand it any longer. It's not amusing, being called a fool when that isn't true. And I think we heard enough. Now we know what to expect, and that's all we need. We even know the day the army of the Tshoban will ride through the Chatar defile."

"Where is that defile, and what is it like?"

"It lies along the edge of the desert which separates the steppes of the Tshoban from my fertile country. It consists entirely of rock, and is so long that one needs almost half a day to ride from one end to the other. At its widest point, it can be crossed in a quarter hour. But there are spots where it is so narrow that I can hear every word someone standing on the other side calls out to me."

"What's to the right and the left? Mountains?"

"No, water."

"What water?"

"The sea."

"The sea?" I asked in surprise. "Then your country is like the delta of the Nile, alluvial soil? A peninsula that is connected to the mainland the way the Gulf of Corinth connects the Greek Peloponnese with Hellas?"

Scratching his beard in a gesture of embarrassment, he answered:

"I don't know about Corinth, Hellas, or the Peloponnese. All I can tell you is that wise men are supposed to have said that the land of the Tshoban was once a huge lake, and that south of it, where we are now, there was the sea. Both the lake and the sea were separated by a massive wall of rock. There was a large river which fed the lake until so much pressure built up that the rocks could no longer withstand it. It rushed out into the sea and tore the rocks along, piling them up high on both sides in the sea. This is how the Chatar defile was allegedly created. When the lake had emptied, it turned out that the bottom along its southern part consisted of rocks. That is the desert of the Tshoban which I mentioned before. The northern part was more useful. Gradually, grass and shrubs grew there, though no trees. That is the steppe of the Tshoban. The river passed through both the northern and the southern parts. After a time, bushes and trees grew along its banks but only there. For the fertile soil which the river carried down from higher regions and out into the sea was deposited there and grew ever deeper and wider. The river divided into countless arms and branches, all of which contributed to the creation of this new land. It's probably the same sort of thing you called Corinth or Hellas or delta just now. The water and the winds brought seeds which found fertile soil. Forests developed whose size increased with the land. That is Ussul country where you are now."

"And the river?" I asked. "Where do I find that?"

"It disappeared. It's gone, never to return."

"Gone where?"

"Hm. Where! There is an old legend which is too long for me to tell you now. We'll soon have reached shore. Since the river has disappeared, there hasn't been a drop of flowing water in the steppe or the desert of the Tshoban, and all the trees and bushes that once stood on the banks of the river have vanished. But the country of the Ussul is like a sponge which sucks up the water of the sea, purifies it, and makes it fit to drink. Look at this water here, which comes from the sea, yet does not contain any salt. And tomorrow, when we get to the capital, you will see that no one suffers from thirst there, that all have more than they need of what the Tshoban desire for themselves, but in vain."

Our conversation had to be broken off, for we had reached the shore. What I had heard was very interesting, and not merely interesting, for the sheik had spoken in a way which was unlike his customary manner. It seemed one only had to descend charitably to the level of Ussul intelligence to awaken and raise it. I was already looking forward to hearing the legend about the river that had disappeared.

6 : The River of Paradise

After arriving at the new camp, we first sent two Ussul to the island to guard the prisoners. While I did not consider this essential, it was nonetheless true that, after what we had discovered, the three Tshoban had become so important to us that no precaution could be considered excessive. Then we told the men what had happened, and that was exciting news. The Ussul had heard that the Tshoban were preparing an invasion, but had neither known it for certain, nor suspected that it was imminent. They had been hunting to provision themselves, and told me that other groups had been sent into the forests for the same purpose. It had become necessary to obtain more game than during previous invasions because the losses their herds had suffered during the last Tshoban foray had not yet been made up. The sheik and Taldsha both told me that their entire tribe would be threatened by starvation unless they could prevent new losses.

"What are your plans?" I asked.

"The same as always."

"You mean a siege?"

"Yes," he nodded. "If we find out about the attack in time, we bring our herds to the capital. All the warriors also gather there. The women and children go into hiding until the danger has passed. The enemy surrounds us, but we are protected by the water. He can't cross, and has to leave again."

"How long does all this usually take?"

"Several weeks."

"And during that time, the enemy pillages while you sit behind the water that protects you, do nothing, and not only have to feed all those men but also your herds. That can only harm you, even if the enemy is ultimately forced to pull back. Isn't that so?"

"Yes," Taldsha answered. "Even when the Tshoban have to lift the siege without having taken everything we own, they still have all the booty they captured everywhere else. And due to hunger and confinement, our herds are almost always decimated."

"So your defense has always been to allow yourselves to be surrounded and besieged?"

"Yes."

"Why?"

"Because such is the custom. Our forefathers always did it that way, and so we did, too."

"And it never occurred to you to become the attackers instead of being the attacked?"

"Never."

"How strange."

Halef said:

"The Tshoban attack you by invading your country. What prevents you from taking the same course and invading theirs? Their law, Islam, commands that you return like for like. So you would be honoring and respecting their law if you did to them what they have so often done to you."

"Invade their country?" the woman asked, as if to suggest that this was something altogether implausible, and all the others echoed her.

"Why not?" Halef asked. "Surely you can do what the Tshoban can?"

"I should think so," the sheik said confidently.

"If you know that, why don't you do it? Is it lack of courage?"

"No," the sheik insisted, and again his answer was echoed by everyone.

"Or is it lack of skill, speed, intelligence?"

"It isn't that, either."

"Then I don't understand. There is only one reason I can think of."

"What is that?" the sheik asked.

"That you are too lazy."

"Too lazy?" the sheik protested angrily. "I'll kill anyone that says that," and he raised both his fists.

"But what would we be doing over there?" the priest asked.

"Exactly what they are doing here."

"So you are saying that we should steal, pillage, burn?"

"Precisely. What they think they can do to you cannot be something that you are not allowed to do to them."

"Oh, yes," Taldsha said in a serious tone. "No thief will persuade me to steal, and no robber to rob."

I said:

"The sheik of the Haddedihn does not mean it so literally. He is not interested in persuading you to invade the country of your enemies without any reason, and to pillage and murder there. But if they could be compelled to run away from you, and you pursued them into their territory, that surely would not go against your feelings."

"No, certainly not," she admitted. "I would even advise such action."

"Really?" I asked.

"Yes."

"Why don't you, then? Drive them out of your country and back into theirs. Or, better still, don't wait for them but attack at your borders and force them to retreat."

"A lot of blood would be spilled."

"No," I answered. "Perhaps not even a single drop."

"Impossible! It's impossible to drive back an entire army without spilling blood."

"I agree," the sheik said. "But that shouldn't prevent

us from taking their advice. I like what they are saying. A few dead is better than being called cowards by the Tshoban and the rest of mankind. Please tell us your plan, Effendi. If we can follow it and it will accomplish something useful, we will do as you say. I am sure Taldsha will give her consent."

The woman nodded, and I said:

"I cannot outline a plan right now; I don't have one. I still don't know your country or the region we are talking about. I do have an idea which may work. But to develop it, I need the answers to some questions I cannot ask today. There will be time for that tomorrow. It may well be possible to defeat the Tshoban and to drive them out so that they will never return, and all that without a single casualty. If you want, I shall tell you tomorrow. But it is past midnight now, and I am going to sleep."

"Me, too," Halef said. He had understood that I wanted to break off the conversation.

We went to our horses and lay down, using their necks as pillows. Both we and the animals were used to that. But the Ussul stayed where they were to pursue the totally incomprehensible but absolutely vital subject I had brought up. They could not get it into their indolent heads that it might be possible to defeat the Tshoban so thoroughly that they would never return, for up to now, all they had done was to run away and hide; then, when the enemy was leaving again, they had whined and cursed. The description of the Chatar defile had given me an idea. What came to my mind was one of my adventures among the Haddedihn Arabs whose sheik Halef was. I had succeeded in herding all their enemies into the "Valley of the Steps." A description of this encounter may be found in the first volume of my travel books.* Perhaps the Chatar defile was even better suited to such a maneuver than the "Valley," for the enemy had had to be lured into the latter while the Tshoban could not avoid passing through the defile. I was convinced that their passage might easily become a disaster for them.

When I made a brief comment about this to Halef,

---

* In the Desert.

he was immediately wide awake. He half raised himself, and said: "Sidi, it would be delightful if we could repeat that adventure. How did you get that wonderful idea?"

"Through the sheik. He described the place to me. It's true that what that dear fellow said cannot be taken as geological fact. One would first have to investigate. But it undoubtedly contains some element of truth and a good deal of bloodshed could be avoided if we could persuade the Ussul to confront the Tshoban in that narrow pass a week from today."

I then repeated what the sheik had told me in the canoe. When I had finished, Halef mentioned that during our absence, the Ussul had also discussed the vanished river. And at his request, the Sahahr had told him the legend.

"So you know it?"

"Yes. Do you want to hear it?"

"Very much."

As was his custom when he was about to launch into such a tale, Halef paused for a few moments to collect his thoughts. Then he began:

"Far, far from here, high up in the mountains beyond Djinnistan, there lies what was once paradise. Its gates are closed. Those looking for it see it shining from afar, but no one can enter and the walls are much too high to see over them. Above it, in letters of golden sunlight during the day, and in the flaming script of the stars at night, one sees the divine call: IF THERE IS PEACE ON EARTH, YOU MAY COME. Whenever a century ends, all the doors and gates of paradise open, and an unending abundance of light floods the earth and all living on it. Whatever happened, and still happens today, stands revealed. The archangels post themselves in front of the gates. Thousands and tens of thousands appear on the walls. They look down to see if peace has finally come, but all they ever see is quarrels and disputes, war and murder. They raise their voices in a cry of woe which descends to earth. The light vanishes, and paradise with it. But this cry is not heard by the powerful, the rich, the victors, but only by the weak, the poor, the oppressed, and the enslaved. Wringing their hands, imploring help, they pray in their poverty and their solitude that God the Lord will deliver them from their suffering and torment.

"These prayers are more powerful than the most powerful among men. They accomplish what no mortal can. Invisible, they rise to paradise, gather under its walls, and swell until there are untold millions of them. They assist each other, help each other across the walls, enter paradise, and cling to the angels. They attach themselves to the wings of mercy and compassion soaring above paradise and are carried by them to the Most Merciful. They enter His heart until it overflows. 'Give us peace,' they wail on earth; 'give us peace,' they lament in paradise; 'give us peace,' God's own soul prays. Now He sends the most severe of His spirits, Moses, down to Sinai. He chisels this command into stone: THOU SHALT NOT KILL. WHOEVER SPILLS HUMAN BLOOD SHALL ALSO HAVE HIS BLOOD SPILLED. NO sooner has this been heard by those to whom it is addressed than they leave Mount Sinai, break in upon the land of the Canaanites, and sacrifice streams of human blood to that same god. These rivers of blood flow through the centuries and the blood streams to heaven. Once again, the wail for peace is heard all over earth, and once again, it is echoed in paradise and in God's own soul. Now He sends the most loving of all his spirits to earth. He is called Jesus. He teaches and exhorts and is heard in all the lands on earth: LOVE YOUR ENEMIES. BLESS THOSE THAT CURSE YOU. DO GOOD AT THOSE THAT HATE YOU. AND PRAY FOR THOSE THAT SLANDER AND PERSECUTE YOU. FOR WHOSOEVER TAKES UP THE SWORD SHALL PERISH BY THE SWORD.

"This sacred call for neighborly love has never gone unheard, and it is still heard today, but no one heeds it. Once more, the wail for peace is heard on earth. It echoes in an empty paradise. God's own soul still begs for it. Now He sends the most earthly of all His spirits, Mohammed, who still speaks almost like a mortal being and can therefore be easily understood. But he loses his way between paradise and earth and vainly tries to find the path that would lead deep into the hearts of men. And the Lord says: 'If no one can bring peace, I shall go.' In human shape, He descends to the fountain of Suhl* in paradise. That source becomes a wide river as it flows to Djinnistan and from there through Ardistan, bringing fertility and abundance to both banks. At its mouth, it creates new land and a new people. Following the river, God walks to Djinnistan to announce the will of heaven. But no sooner has He begun the work of peace than He is recognized and the people hurry to worship Him. He blesses all those before Him, but permits only the Mir to see the distant future, to behold a time when not the sword or the cannon but only sheer spirit and flaming thought will do battle. Then He continues downstream to Ardistan. He believes He will arrive in time. Wherever He comes, the trumpets of war are blaring. The Mir of Ardistan is setting out to conquer Djinnistan and secretly preparing a sudden attack. In many places, the Lord tries to raise His voice to avert the disaster, but in vain. When, in the large city of the Mir which lies on the river like a dream image from a fairy land, He speaks out against a violation of the peace, He is arrested as a traitor and taken to the Mir. The Mir sits in judgment and pronounces this sentence: 'He is to be taken to the bridge and thrown into the water because he is afraid of the blood of war.' The Lord asks: 'Is there someone who can change this sentence?' 'No one,' the Mir answers. 'Not even God?' 'No, Allah is God, and he has ordered us to spread his reign by fire and the sword. Let there be war.' Now the Lord raises His hand and calls out: 'The peace will be kept! High above Him whom you have made into a god, there stands One who is compassionate. I am saying to you: Not a drop of blood must be spilled.' The Mir jumps up from his throne and thunders: 'And I, I say to you, coward and seducer of my warriors: Just as the river in which you will drown will not reverse its course, before it comes to our bridge, to spare you, so the sword I have drawn for battle will not be returned to its sheath.' For the second time, the Lord raises His hand, and says: 'It will be as you say. Judgment has been rendered, and will be carried out. If God can no

---

* Peace.

: 100 :

longer teach by His word, He will preach by His deeds. The river came to you for works of peace, not the destruction of life. It will be taken from you. Not a single puddle large enough to drown even one human being will remain. And woe to you, should you attempt to compel it through force of arms to return to you. For all that lives would then perish.' Mocking laughter greets these words. He is taken to the bridge, the Mir riding in the lead. When they come to the deepest spot, he gives the order to seize the prisoner and to throw him down. The Lord now raises His hand for the third time. But He remains silent. Immediately, the sky darkens. Lightning flashes, threatening thunder rolls. Downstream from the bridge, the water continues to flow, but on the other side it stops. It surges, it rises higher and higher and forms a wall stretching toward heaven. Howling with terror, the people rush back to the banks. Only the prisoner remains. His face shining, He stands on the bridge which the rising waves have torn loose and raised into the air until it disappears. The waves subside, the water begins to flow again, not downstream, but upstream, back to its source. It becomes light once more but the riverbed is empty and the horrified population flees. The city's waterless ruins even today stare out into the steppe through which the dried-up riverbed wends its way in countless turns, twisted by hunger and thirst, finally disappearing in the forests of the Ussul."

When Halef had come to this point, he stopped to reflect, and then said:

"Isn't it touching how friendly the Ussul conceive their god to be?"

"But isn't He?" I asked.

He did not answer right away. Then he said:

"Sidi, you have told me that every legend contains some truth which one must search for. What is the truth in this legend?"

"It is probably a two-fold truth, one that lies at the surface, a geographical one, and another that is less apparent and is philosophical and social in nature."

"I don't understand."

"The geographical element is that there really was a major river here at one time, and that it disappeared, probably as the result of some natural event which no one understood. So the legend was invented to account for it."

"But large rivers do not suddenly disappear."

"That's true. But they can leave their original bed, change their course, and even gradually disappear as a result of the deforestation of mountains. After we have been in this country for some time, we will discover what happened in this particular case."

"And what about the inner truth of the legend?"

"That refers to the fact that the development of mankind must proceed along peaceful, conciliatory paths, not those of war. The name of the source and of the river was Sulh, which means peace, and the source is in paradise. Peace is a gift from heaven. Where it flows, it not only blesses what already exists but also what it creates, visible and invisible lands, commerce and trade, art and science. And all of that declines when the river of peace dries up and armaments devour all it has brought forth. Or if in a single brutal gesture, war sweeps from the table all the gifts peace laid out there. Peace will then withdraw to its source in paradise, or at least in Djinnistan, and though this may not last forever, it will be for a very long time. If it finally does return, it will be slowly, fearfully, hesitantly. It cannot be forced. Therefore the words the legend puts into God's mouth are important when He says: 'Woe to you if you compel it through force of arms to return to you, for all that lives would then perish.' The peace among nations which we seek can only develop very gradually. If its roots encircle the entire globe, if a fibril takes root in every human heart, it will grow beyond this earth and wear the eternal stars in its crown as its fruit. But universal peace that is not rooted in the heart of mankind but suddenly and violently enforced would destroy rather than create and bring life. And here, there is something in the legend of the river that returned to its source that I do not see, a secret I do not understand. It almost sounds as if it were possible to bring peace by arms, suddenly and without preparation, and that would be an even more horrible catastrophe than its disappearance. A legend as clearly structured as this one never tells us anything useless. Like a terrible threat for Ardistan, it hovers high above Djinnistan. And if, in this tale that the visionary soul of the people invented, no less a being than God warns of this cloud, the danger exists not only in the poetry, but in fact."

"You think so? Then you believe in legends?"

"In their real content, yes."

"So do I. I am glad we agree. But now I shall lie down again. Allah does not give sleep so that it has to be watched. Good night, Sidi."

He fell asleep in a few moments, but I didn't. After such important events, there is the obligation to try to understand what has happened so that it may serve as a foundation for what is in store. I lay still, and meditated. Above me, the dark tops of the trees hid the starry heavens. But when I turned to the side where the clearing began, I could see two stars between the trunks which attracted my attention because they were the only visible ones. They were part of Cetus. As I kept gazing at them, it looked as if a shining path as wide as their distance from each other stretched from me to them. Along it, the thoughts preoccupying me appeared to come and go. The two stars lay before the physical eye but, in my inner vision where those two radiant worlds were glowing, I saw the gate through which the archangels came and the walls on which their hosts appeared to look for peace. Then I also saw God Himself come to Djinnistan and the ruler of that land sink down before Him on his knees in adoration. And then I saw Him walking to Ardistan, in the capital, and on the bridge. The water rose like a wall and returned to its source when the Lord was gone. The city withered and decayed. Then I was standing among its ruins, trying to find the royal palace where God had been judged and sentenced to death. I discovered the way, which led up a hill through an immensely tall and wide stone gate whose pillars supported an old Babylonian sun dial. The palace was only a short distance further, and surrounded by walls. The gate was closed. I knocked. The gatekeeper came. I asked him to open and to let me enter. But he shook his head, and answered: "Not today but later, perhaps." "Why not now?" I asked him. "Because now you are sleeping," he explained to me. "Here, we can only use spirits and souls that are awake." Then he suddenly took on the figure and face of my little Hadji who had taken me by the arm, and was shaking me and calling out: "Wake up, Sidi, wake up! All of us are already up and about, and breakfast is being prepared. When we have eaten, we will be leaving."

I jumped up. Everything I had seen was a dream, but that dream was so curious and inspired such confidence that I felt the need to cling to it.

The sheik had gone to the island personally to pick up the three prisoners. They did not look dejected when he brought them back. Quite the contrary. Their expression and manner were those of men eager for revenge. After they had been given ample food and been tied to their horses, we set out for the capital.

7 : The Djirbani

The terrain through which we rode was level and consisted of alluvial deposits. We saw many canals which looked like rivers that had suddenly frozen over. Their water was stagnant, yet must have been pure, for the horses readily drank it. We came through extensive, mostly deciduous forests. Between them lay pastures for cattle and other domestic animals.

All the small, narrow channels flowed into a very wide and deep one which seemed to have some fall, for the leaves swimming on it were moving slowly.

"That is Es Ssul," the Sahahr said.

"The one that comes from Djinnistan and Ardistan?" I asked. I was anxious to hear more about it.

"Yes," he said.

"Then it is the same that also flows through the Chatar defile?"

"Yes. You can follow it all the way up there."

"And is it completely dry there?"

"Yes."

"I imagine your capital lies on its banks?"

"It does. We have no mountains, no rocks. We cannot build walls to protect ourselves. Only our temple and the sheik's palace are of stone. A long time ago, the building material was brought from Ardistan. In those days, every Ussul that wanted to travel there was given that permission only if he agreed to bring back as large a stone as his horse could carry. In that way, we got enough of them together to put up those two buildings. I suppose that makes you laugh?"

"No. I am familiar with that procedure."

"Then they also do it in your country?"

"Yes, but in a different way. Every science, every art, derives its foundation and structure from a more highly developed field. The same is true of every individual work of the intellect. It is a universal law that the Ussul obtains what he needs but does not have from an Ardistan or even a Djinnistan. But you were going to tell me about the site of your capital. What is its name?"

"It is called Ussula, and it is quite a large city. Because we could not protect it by walls, we had to use water, and therefore built it on the banks of the stream. We excavated for many years to force the river not to pass through but around it. Every householder also surrounds his land with deep ditches. You might say that every building is a fortress which the Tshoban must take to conquer the city. There are also two large lakes, one to the East, the other to the West, which were included within the town. Many dwellings were put up there, partly along the shore, partly on the water. Contact between those living there is maintained either by barges or by swimming. If the barges were to be hidden or taken away, even the occupation of the entire city would be useless to the Tshoban because they don't know how to swim."

Nothing of consequence happened that day. The Ussul avoided straying from their route, just as they avoided all excitement, and I began to realize that they cherished their comfort above all else. But once such people have been shaken out of their indolence, they find it much more difficult than others to return to a state of quiescence.

The only noteworthy event during that entire day was their attempt to describe the city for me. They talked about the temple, the palace, the thoroughfares and streets, the squares, and the most important buildings. Among them, they mentioned a prison. At that time, the most dangerous inmate was a madman who also suffered from a skin disease and had to be isolated from all others because of the danger of contagion. I was sympathetic when I heard about this madness but did not know what to make of the disease, which was not leprosy. I therefore inquired about this prisoner in some detail.

"Do you have a physician who knows how to treat such a disease?" I asked disingenuously.

"Of course," the Sahahr answered proudly. "I am that physician."

"Do you think you can cure him?"

"No. This Djirbani cannot be helped. He will die of his disease. And his madness also is incurable. As he grows, his disease devours him. All that can be done is to isolate him so that no one else catches it."

"How does his madness express itself?"

"He does everything differently from the way we do it."

"Hm," I mumbled, and Halef smiled. It seemed obvious that one did not have to be mad to do a great many things differently.

"And the way he thinks is also not the same as ours," the Sahahr went on. "He doesn't say so, but one can tell that he imagines he is more intelligent than others. He has his own views about religion, geography, universal history, art, and government. He doesn't discuss these views, but teaches them by living and acting in accordance with them. That's the most dangerous thing there is, and that's the reason we keep him locked up. For if someone were to observe him, he would be misled, feel affection for him, and then begin imitating him. And that's the worst kind of madness because it infects others."

"Do you know where he gets his ideas? Does he have a teacher?"

He seemed embarrassed.

"Not really a teacher," he answered. "Do you know what a hamail is?"

"Yes. It is a copy of the Koran which comes from Mecca and is worn by a string around the neck as a souvenir of the pilgrimage to that holy city." I did not tell him that I had one myself.

"That's right," he said. "The Djirbani has such a hamail. But the book hanging from his neck is no Koran. I once asked him for permission to look at it, and he allowed me to. There was this sentence in it: 'Become a human being, for you aren't one yet.' Isn't that insane? When I asked him in what sense we were not yet human, he tried to tell me that each person is born with an animal inside him which he must starve to death or kill in some way. What remains is a free, good, noble human being. If that isn't madness, I don't know what is."

"Could there not be some other explanation?" Halef asked.

"Impossible. The Djirbani is mad. But that isn't all. There is also the fact that it is difficult to detain him. He has been in every kind of prison and always managed to escape. So we finally took him to a place where escape is impossible. He is fenced in by thorn hedges and guarded by huge dogs. If he should try to get out, or someone should attempt to rescue him, he would be torn to pieces."

I shuddered when I heard this and began to feel that this alleged madness must be of a very special kind. I asked:

"How old is this man?"

"Not much over twenty."

"So young, and yet so unhappy. That is terribly sad. Who gave him the book you mentioned?"

"His father."

"And who was he? An Ussul, I imagine."

"Certainly not! It was a stranger but—but—his mother was an Ussul."

He had said that hesitantly and seemed to have difficulty admitting it. His bearded face had become animal-like and he was gritting his teeth as he went on:

"Why shouldn't I tell you since you will hear about it in any event? She was my daughter."

"Then he is your grandson," I exclaimed. "And you keep him locked up?"

"Yes, I do," he answered in an incredibly venomous tone.

"And guarded by dogs that will tear him apart if he attempts escape?"

His eyes shining with anger, he turned to me and shouted as if he meant his answer to be heard far and wide:

"Let them! Just as anger, wrath, and grief tore me when I vainly tried to persuade his father to save my child from him and his madness. I have nothing in common with this creature. He was the son of my daughter, flesh of my flesh, blood of my blood. But that flesh has died, that blood has dried up, and so he is a stranger to me, more alien than any other human being. Let the dogs tear him apart."

And he whipped his startled horse, which took fright and rushed ahead. He did not even try to rein it in. As he was galloping away and our eyes followed him, the sheik said:

"Now he is furious again, but he is right. Religion must be preserved from mad and erroneous ideas. You shouldn't think that this skin disease is a physical thing, Effendi. The rash for which this young man is being called the Djirbani does not attack his body but his soul, his thoughts and feelings. He inherited the disease from his father, and it is incredibly contagious. He has already infected hundreds who are now as incurable as he, and that's the reason he has to be locked up. If religion means that we have animals within ourselves that must be killed, the entire earth will soon become one gigantic insane asylum."

Now Taldsha raised her arm in one of her imperious gestures to demand silence, and said:

"From her earliest youth, his mother was my friend, and she remained my friend until she died. She was younger than I and I looked up to her as a protectress. I loved her very dearly and looked after her when she was exiled. She died from longing and grief, and now that she is dead, I have transferred that love to the person she left us. Does this sort of thing interest you, Effendi?"

"Very much," I answered. "I would like you to tell me more about this Djirbani."

"There isn't much to tell; the matter is very simple. A stranger came to our country. He was from Djinnistan, and a descendant of the ancient mythical family, the Erdjani. He had no intention of remaining among us. But he met my friend and came to love her as she did him. Because of her, he decided to stay. As you know, he had to fight and defeat an Ussul to become one himself. He won easily, for although he was physically smaller than we are, he was so strong and nimble that the crude strength of his adversary was of no avail. As soon as he had become an Ussul, he asked my friend's father for his consent to the marriage. But it was refused, for the Sahahr did not agree with the philosophical ideas of the Djinnistani, who maintained that humanity could only progress through peace, conciliation, love, and kindness. The Sahahr hated all that, and still hates it today. For him, those beliefs are nothing but cowardice, stupidity, and softness, and he thinks that the Ussul would inevitably perish if love of one's fellow man became a common thing. Whenever he had the chance, he attacked the Djinnistani, treating him not only as a public but also as a personal enemy, a man intent on stealing his daughter from him. He stated that he would rather die than give his child to the Djinnistani in marriage. As a result, the dispute was taken to the great council of the elders of the tribe whose decision was precisely what it had to be according to Ussul law: The Djinnistani and the Sahahr must fight each other. The Sahahr was so furious and so certain of victory that he demanded that this be a fight to the finish. But it did not turn out as he had expected. He was defeated, but the Djinnistani spared him. The marriage was exceptionally happy despite the Sahahr's decision to renounce his daughter. A son was born whose physical appearance became that of an Ussul but whose nature was that of a Djinnistani. He was the pride and joy of his parents. From his mother, he inherited the enormously powerful physique and the pure, engaging soul. But his father passed on to him the spirit of Djinnistan and became his mentor, his model, and the ideal which the son tried to emulate. I was often present when this spirit and this intelligence expressed themselves in conversations with his wife and child. What I heard on such occasions made so profound an impression on me that it will never leave me. I am unlike the rest of the Ussul women and care about this Erdjani, whom I consider neither mad nor ill, let alone dangerous. That abusive term, Djirbani, was given currency by the Sahahr who did not even want to leave the Djinnistani his good name."

"I took the Sahahr for a very good-natured person," I said.

"He is," she answered. "But his daughter would have become the high priestess and his plans for her went far beyond what he told us. Those plans came to naught because of the Djinnistani, and that is something he cannot forget or forgive. The Sahahr is incapable of killing even a worm. He has never hated anyone. But he hates the Djinnistani with a passion, and has transferred that hatred to his son, his own grandson. He persecutes him remorselessly and no one dares protest because he is the chief sorcerer and the highest male priest in the land. Whenever that poor unfortunate said something that did not please him, he had him locked up. And now he is even guarded by bloodhounds. He will never get out as long as he lives."

"Oho," little Halef exclaimed.

"What do you mean by that?" she asked.

"I don't believe there is such a thing as a hopeless situation."

"Who could help him?"

"My Effendi. He is not afraid of any dog, however big or vicious. If he wants to get the Djirbani out, he will, depend on it."

"Really?"

"Yes, really. Besides, my Sidi is not alone; I will help him."

In his wrath, the Sahahr had ridden far ahead and the sheik had spurred his horse to follow him. The two of us were alone with Taldsha and could exchange a few words without Amihn's hearing them.

"I will confess to you that I have always taken the Erdjani's side, and still do today," she said. "But in this case, the Sahahr has the upper hand because he was smart enough to make this affair a religious issue. It is not advisable to have him for an enemy. I would be deeply grateful to you if you could help—both me and the Erdjani."

"We'll help you," Halef said. "Even if my Effendi should not give his consent, you could depend on me. I could get the Djirbani out of that prison by myself, and defend him against all his enemies."

He gave that assurance in his most persuasive manner. She looked down on the little fellow smilingly, and said:

"All by yourself? You will fight the dogs, and go against the will of the sheik and the power of the Sahahr? And against the many that believe in him?"

Halef laughed, and answered:

"My business is neither with the dogs nor the sheik or those Ussul who have faith in their sorcerer. I will only deal with the Sahahr. Tell me, does he despise death?"

"Certainly not. On the contrary, he loves life."

"Ah! Did you see his reaction when I told him that I would only fight him, and no one else?"

"Yes."

"That didn't seem to please him, right?"

"No, it didn't. He has never been heroic, and ever since he was defeated by the Djinnistani in spite of his superior physical strength he has become even more cautious. He knows how good your weapons are, and he certainly noticed that you do everything better than he does. I have no doubt he is afraid of a duel with you."

"And that is unavoidable?"

"Actually, it is. Although there has been some talk about exempting you since you have amply demonstrated that you are worthy of being friends and allies of the Ussul."

"How kind, how friendly," Halef mocked. "But for us, things are different. We insist on the same rights as you do. That means that the Sahahr has to prove that he is worthy of being our friend and ally. If he is so fearful that he wants to spare us the duel, we are courageous enough to fight it."

"What an idea," she said. "But you are really right."

"And listen to this: Allah commands that man be punished in exactly the same way he has sinned. When the Sahahr engaged the Djinnistani in a duel he dared make it a fight to the death. He knew he was stronger than his adversary but was so stupid that he did not consider the powers of the soul and the spirit, and that's why he was defeated. That was a simple result, not a punishment. The real punishment will be inflicted on him now when he has to fight a similar duel. For I also shall demand that this be a fight to the finish. You can imagine what the outcome will be."

"What?" she asked curiously.

Halef told her:

"Either the Sahahr will ask me not to stipulate such a condition, and I will accede to that request only at the price of the Erdjani's freedom. Or he will be ashamed of his cowardice and yield to my demand. Then we will have the kind of fight he once asked for, and my Effendi will be happy to assure you that there can be only one issue, and that is the death of the Sahahr. With him out of the way, no one else will wish to torment the Erdjani."

"Your idea is good," she said, "but what you said just now is untrue. Even after the death of the Sahahr, it would be felt that the Erdjani suffers from an inner sickness. That's what people believe, and once people have gotten such an idea into their heads, it is almost impossible to rid them of it. I will discuss this with you further. But now we have to join the sheik. He is waiting for us."

"There is one other thing I would like to know," Halef said.

"What is that?"

"What became of the Djinnistani, the Erdjani's father?"

She told him as we rode on.

"Once a year, at the time of the summer solstice, he would ride up to Djinnistan to visit those who loved him. He went there for books which he read and used to instruct his wife and child. And over a period of time, he also brought with him those white stones with the mysterious inscriptions which today can be seen and read on the Island of the Heathens. The Sahahr opposed the erection of these stones. He said that the inscriptions were the greatest madness imaginable, but because the island had become the Djinnistani's property, and still belongs to his son today, he had the right to do as he pleased there. He placed the stones near his lotus pond and in the shade of some magnolia trees."

"Why did you call this place the Island of the Heathens?"

"Because it is an island, and because, judging by our standards, the Djinnistani lived there as a heathen. Anyone who does not believe in the god of the Ussul is a heathen."

"Then his son is also a heathen, in your view?"

"Yes."

"And yet you love him."

"Certainly. Is it different where you come from? Do you hate and persecute heathens? But you wanted to know what became of the Djinnistani, and I told you that once a year he rode back home. But there came a time when he did not return, and was never seen again. All inquiries led nowhere. We assumed that he had fallen into the hands of the Tshoban and been murdered. His widow died of a broken heart, and her son buried her on the island. If you wish, I can take you there and show you the grave. But let's stop talking about this for now; the sheik doesn't like to hear about it."

We had caught up with Amihn, and soon also overtook the Sahahr, who had calmed down and seemed embarrassed about his outburst. Our conversation did not touch on this topic again, and I hardly participated. I was preoccupied by what I had heard about the Erdjani. I was beginning to feel that a rather alien world would open up for me during my stay among the Ussul.

Sometime past noon, a large number of horsemen came to meet us. They had been sent out from the city to welcome us, and were the elders and officials or men occupying high positions who had received the message the sheik had sent the day before. The fact that the "firstborn" of the Tshoban had been taken prisoner was important news and they wanted to see him. Equally great was their interest in the two strangers who had captured the prince. They looked at us as if we were fabled beasts. I maintained my reserve; my interest at this moment was general, scientific. All of them were of unusual size and dressed and armed like the sheik. The entire group of more than forty persons had no more than five bad rifles. Their horses resembled Smikh, although I must confess that he was more handsome than any of the others.

Little Halef reacted differently, and quickly established rapport. He was pleased by the respect they showed him in spite of his small size, and when they expressed their desire to see the three Tshoban, he immediately declared his willingness to wait with them, to show them the prisoners, and to tell them how we had defeated and captured them. I did not prevent this, for I knew he would do what he could to increase their respect for us. Except for the oldest among them, the others stayed with him to await the arrival of the rest of the Ussul and the prisoners.

Up to this time, we had been riding through uninhabited country. Now, groups of individuals occasionally appeared and we also saw small herds of horses, cattle, sheep, and even goats and goatherds. Something like fields made their appearance, and the forest was becoming less dense. The trees were either what remained of a former wooded area or had been recently planted for later use as timber. We came to a network of canals along whose banks we saw an occasional cottage. Some houses had been built on piles in the water and consisted entirely of trunks and sticks that had somehow been attached to each other. The windows and doors seemed almost absurdly small and narrow, considering the size of their inhabitants. These pile dwellings first lay far apart and only gradually became more numerous as we approached the capital's outskirts. We stopped to wait for the troops and the prisoners, for it had been decided to enter the city in a body.

Finally, they caught up with us. Halef nodded to me when he was still some distance away, smiling and in good spirits, looking pleased with himself. When we started off again, we were riding side by side, and he said:

"Sidi, everything is in good shape. I have prepared everything."

"Prepared what?"

"The expedition to the Chatar defile. I told them what happened in the Valley of the Steps, and what you did and accomplished there, all by yourself. They are amazed about your cleverness and caution, your courage and strength. They are ready to take orders from you and do everything you ask of them."

That sounded quite satisfactory, but unfortunately I knew little Hadji Halef Omar well enough to take everything he said with a grain of salt. When he said "your" cleverness and "your" courage, he had really been talking about his own. Quiet, meditative people like the Ussul usually have an acute awareness of exaggeration and I took care not to bask in Halef's enthusiasm but acted as if our surroundings demanded my entire attention.

The city lay on totally level ground. Countless canals and ditches divided it into squares and occasional triangles or other geometric patterns where a number of ditches came together. Along the periphery of the city, every such plot of land only carried a single building, but further toward the center, the dwellings stood closer together. But all were of identical material and construction. There were neither walls nor fences between them. The ditches sufficed. Those who wanted to protect themselves from the curiosity of their neighbors had planted bushes or shrubs. Trees were rare, and I saw nothing that looked like European fruit trees. What fruit there was had grown naturally, and not as the result of cultivation. Because intercourse between the inhabitants was possible only by boat, we saw any number of them, ranging all the way from large dugouts to small rafts consisting of willow branches that had been tied together and were lying in the shallower ditches. There were surprisingly few bridges. Apparently, the population didn't care for them. Waterways too wide to be jumped over were crossed by boat or swimming. Not only the children but the adults swam and dived like fish. That their rather scanty clothing got soaked in the process did not seem to disturb them.

We headed toward the so-called "castle" or "palace," which lay in the center of the town, directly on the river. The approach to it was one of the few stretches that could be called a road. The population stood ready to welcome us and had been joined by large numbers living in sections we would not pass through. All of them were very quiet. There was none of the cheering customary on such occasions elsewhere. Even the children were silent. Wherever we went, they shrank back fearfully, with wide open mouths. I do not wish to seem ungrateful, however, and should mention that there were several attempts to receive us with some pomp. This always happened when we passed someone who owned a rifle. These weapons were fired but it was done with such seriousness, one might have thought it was an extraordinary, politically significant act. When the smoke had cleared, the returning silence was felt all the more keenly. But every time a shot had been fired, the sheik, riding at the head, turned back to look at us to observe the effect. This made Halef smile. Perhaps he was thinking of the reception that would have awaited us, had we come to visit his tribe, the Haddedihn. At such times, thousands of rifles were fired, the shouting and enthusiasm deafening, the amount of powder expended enormous. But gradually, the smile disappeared from his face. He was turning serious.

"Sidi," he said. "What poor people they are! They have so few rifles, and powder seems terribly expensive here. But that is not the only reason. The real cause lies in their souls; I can tell by looking at them. They don't have the right spirit. In the country of their souls, there are no rifles either. What can possibly become of such a nation?"

"Hm. Didn't you just assure me that they would glady obey me and do everything I asked of them?"

"But that's what I believed. Yet now it seems as if I had to reconsider. The people I was talking to were the most important, the most intelligent, and therefore also the liveliest among them. I could instill some enthusiasm in them, if only for a while. But those of lesser standing, those that are staring at us now in total silence—it will be difficult to get them to ride to the Chatar defile to defeat their enemies. Don't you agree?"

"Let's wait and see. One should not waver between hope and fear as you are doing, but learn to take things as they are. You mustn't measure these people by your standards, but by theirs. It's in their nature, this immobility and indolence. But once they are aroused, you may be certain that nothing will easily bring them to a halt."

Taldsha had stopped to wait for me. When I reached her, she said:

"We will soon pass the rear section of the prison. The other part borders on the river."

"You mean the thorn hedges?"

"Yes."

"Will I be able to see something when we ride by?"

"You will see the hedges but not the Erdjani unless he has come to the gate to see what is going on."

"Do you think he will have noticed that something extraordinary is happening?"

"Certainly. He heard the shooting, and that's rare here, and he will also hear the horses. I should think he would come up to the bars to see what is causing all the commotion."

"Do you want us to free him?" Halef asked.

"Yes, I do," she admitted.

"All right. We will get him out of there right now," Halef promised in his good-natured but unthinking way.

"Don't!" she warned him. "The dogs would kill both you and him. We have to choose some different way, perhaps by cunning. But not by fighting the dogs. They are trained."

"Who trained them?"

"The Sahahr. Because they are so dangerous, they are also kept away from everybody by the only man-made fence in this city. Just seeing them from outside is enough to keep one away. Anyone who would dare

: 117 :

climb that fence would be as quickly and certainly killed as the Erdjani, should he be reckless enough to try to cross it. You can see the two fences over there."

To understand what was about to happen, one has to visualize the place we were looking at. Our procession consisted of cavalry and a crowd of pedestrians running behind us. We were moving along a road which resembled a dike and which was bordered on both sides by canals too wide for a horse to jump across. An Ussul nag such as Smikh might have managed half that distance, but certainly not more. On the other side of the water, there was a grassy area which was perhaps twenty paces wide and surrounded by a fence somewhat higher than a man. Through the spaces between the bars, it was possible to see what lay on the far side. There was a second barrier behind the first. It consisted of dense and tall thorn hedges and other prickly plants. It was impossible to see either through or over them and their needles were so sharp and pointed that special tools would have been required to cut one's way through. As is well known, the Orient has such vegetation in great abundance. This impenetrable enclosure surrounded the area which the sheik's wife had called the prison. There was just one small opening which served as entrance and exit and was closed off by a wooden gate more than two meters high. The bolt, on the outside, was inaccessible to the prisoner. But even if he could have pushed it aside, escape would have been impossible because the dogs roamed the area between the two fences and could therefore seize the Erdjani at any point.

We had now come close enough to see these animals. There were three of them, of a size and a strength I had never encountered. With thick, shaggy hair and a broad, powerful skull, they looked something like bears, although they were considerably taller. And their short, split snout and small, mean eyes were also reminiscent of that animal although their large, drooping and continuously slavering chaps had nothing bearlike about them. Their chests were wide, their thighs exceptionally muscular, and their feet armed with sharp claws and a strongly developed webbing. It seemed likely, however, that they excelled in strength and endurance rather than speed or the ability to jump. A single glance at them was warning enough. In addition to an impression of exceptionally brutal physical strength, one also had a sense that they were cunning, and I have never had as clear a perception of the meaning of the word "beast" as I did then.

They had heard us approach and had sat down close enough to the bars so that we could have a good look at them. Two of them were considerably more muscular, rugged, and heavy than the third, which was somewhat more slender and certainly the youngest and most nimble of the three. It seemed important to me whether the fence was too high for this third dog to jump. If such a bloodthirsty animal, trained to attack humans, took it into its head to leap over the fence and then across the water, there was no telling what damage it might do. But that was the Sahahr's worry. He must know how far his control over these beasts extended. I heard later that he had bred and trained these giant dogs, and had instilled in them the hatred of human beings through incessant torture and pain, unceasing blows and punishment. How curious, this combination of priest, sorcerer, and dog tamer! But now I understood his cruelty toward his daughter and grandson. A person capable of torturing a faithful, obedient, and grateful dog that needs affection, until it becomes a bloodthirsty hater of humans, was probably equally capable of behaving toward his fellow creatures as the Sahahr had. I began to have my doubts about his good nature, to see it as a deception, a mere mask. And he had already demonstrated that he had a violent temper and lacked self-control.

Just as I was thinking about all this, the Sahahr turned to me. He had seen that Halef and I were attentively looking at the thorn hedges, and also remembered his anger about our conversation. That anger now returned. He pointed across the water, and said:

"There is a person locked up over there about whom you probably talked a good deal after our conversation. Do you wish to see him?"

"Yes," Halef answered immediately, although he

was quite aware that the question had been meant sarcastically.

"Then why don't you ride over there?" the sorcerer laughed.

"Across the water?"

"Yes."

"Are you serious?"

"Perfectly," the Sahahr insisted, feeling sure no one would have the courage to try.

"Very well, if that is your pleasure."

A moment later, Halef flew through the air on his magnificent Assil Ben Rih and landed on firm soil on the far side. The hooves of his horse had not touched a drop of water. A shout of horror rose, and was followed by one of admiration. The three giant dogs had got up on their hind legs and begun barking and howling threateningly.

"Here I am," Halef laughed. "What do you want me to do now?"

"Get back here, get back this very moment," the Sahahr ordered.

"I wouldn't dream of it. You sent me over here to see the Erdjani, and that's precisely what I am going to do."

"No, you won't. That's forbidden."

"By whom?"

"By me."

"Nonsense. You are the very person who suggested it. Or do you think you can play games with me?"

He turned his horse toward the fence.

"For heaven's sake, be careful of the dogs," the sheik's wife warned fearfully.

"I hope they devour him," the Sahahr said. "But he will not see him, he must not see him, for he would talk to him, and I don't want him to."

In her anxiety, the sheik's wife took my hand, and asked:

"Call him back. He will obey you. Otherwise he's doomed."

But I told her:

"You need not worry about him. He will do nothing dangerous or harmful. He knows I am here."

Meanwhile, the sorcerer was angrily shouting at the little Hadji:

"That's not allowed. It will cost you your life. If you don't turn back this very moment, I am going to come over."

"Come on, then. Or are you too much of a coward?"

Halef had turned his horse to look at him, and the Sahahr had to carry out his threat. He felt that he could do so without danger, for wasn't he the master of the dogs? And hadn't they been taught obedience by hunger and blows? Now that they were unchained, he expected them to be grateful to him. But he was too cautious to try jumping across on his fat, clumsy nag, for he would never have made it. He drove the horse slowly into the water, swam across and emerged on the other side. Halef observed him with a smile on his face, and asked:

"All right, now you are here. And how are you going to keep me from seeing and talking to the Erdjani?"

He turned his horse back toward the entrance of the prison as the Sahahr drew his knife and called:

"You are staying! Otherwise I am going to thrust this blade into your chest."

No sooner had he said this than Halef had a pistol in his hand, pointed it at him, and said:

"You go ahead. But remember that my bullet is faster than your knife."

This loud, angry exchange had been accompanied by the furious, uninterrupted howling of the dogs. As Halef had come closer, they had jumped up against the fence. When the Sahahr, their tormentor, followed Halef, their fury intensified and they attempted vainly to jump the fence. They were too heavy and kept falling back. This increased their rage. But the third was not only more agile but also more intelligent. When he saw that he could not negotiate the fence, he tried climbing. When that also failed, he decided on a combination of the two. He dashed toward the fence and leaped, but only got three-quarters of the way up and then slid down again, unable to support himself on the cross bar. If he managed this the second time, he would be able to clear the fence and be as dangerous as a panther or a tiger. The second try was more successful, and I called out to Halef:

"Get back! Protect your horse from that beast!"

He had just pulled out his pistol, determined to have his way, and probably would not have heeded my shout, had it not been for his love of Ben Rih. For himself, he did not fear the dogs but he was not so rash as to expose his horse to their teeth. He glanced briefly at the fence where the dog was just about to make his third attempt, and then quickly followed my order. Just as Rih and his rider landed back on our side, the dog came flying through the air. To prevent a misfortune, I quickly seized my carbine, but wasn't fast enough. The animal had barely landed on the ground outside the fence when he seized his master by the thigh and pulled him down. He would certainly have sunk his teeth into the Sahahr's throat if I had not quickly gotten a bullet into him. Because my aim had not been careful, I did not succeed in killing the animal with my first shot. Afraid of hitting the master, I could not aim at the chest or the head and therefore fired at the body to get him away from the priest. The moment he had been hit, the dog let go of the Sahahr and looked around for his new enemy. I was still aiming. With two leaps, he had reached the water's edge and was jumping across when my second bullet struck him. He collapsed as he hit the ground on our side and did not get up again. A short, convulsive twitching passed through the huge body; then he stretched out and lay still.

The other two dogs were still howling and the sorcerer, lying between the fence and the water, was screaming with pain. Shouting loudly, the Ussul were meanwhile expressing their satisfaction with my aim. Apparently, unusual occurrences could shake them out of their lethargy. But this was not the time to bother with their applause; it was essential to go to the Sahahr's aid. It looked as if only his thigh had been injured, but if a large vein had been ripped his life would be in danger. Halef jumped back across the canal and I followed him on my Syrr, who took the obstacle with such elegant ease that the bystanders burst into shouts of admiration. As Halef dismounted to inspect the sorcerer's wound, he shouted at him venomously:

"Get away from me! Don't touch me! I don't want to see you! It's your fault I have been maimed. If you had obeyed me, I would have stayed on the other side. Get away, I say!"

I called across to the Ussul to send some men, and they executed this order in the same leisurely way in which the Sahahr had crossed the water before. They slowly went into it, swam across, dismounted and did what they could for the priest. The cavalry and the crowd that had been accompanying us watched the proceedings.

Halef swung himself back into the saddle, assuming that he would immediately join the others, but I hesitated for I was rather interested in seeing the Erdjani. Perhaps this was an opportune moment that might not return. I therefore rode to the gate of the outer fence behind which the two bloodthirsty monsters were still waiting. Halef followed me. He took his rifle from his shoulder, and said:

"It's true they can't get out. But with beasts like that, one has to be prepared. If they become dangerous, I won't dillydally."

The Sahahr saw this, and in spite of his wound, he shouted at the Hadji:

"Don't you dare shoot! Anyone who kills one of the dogs will have me to deal with. Be gone, you have no business here!"

But we paid no attention to him since he was the only one to object to our approaching the prison. All the rest, including the sheik and the elders, had nothing against it and were eagerly awaiting developments. We did not ride all the way up to the fence so as not to infuriate the dogs further. They were no longer merely barking and howling but roaring and seemed ready to tear the fence apart. Even Halef, normally courageous and even reckless, was intimidated and stayed somewhat behind me.

"This is awful. I can barely stand it," he shouted to make himself heard. "These monsters are not of this earth, they've come straight from hell."

"It isn't all that bad," I answered. "Look at our horses. Are they afraid?"

"No, they are perfectly calm. I wonder why."

"It's not because they are thoroughbreds. Even the most noble animal is afraid of brutes, but they don't seem to feel that that's what they are. And look at the dogs. Do you see a trace of slaver or foam?"

"No."

"You can be sure that these animals aren't nearly as vicious as they seem. I also overestimated them, but now that I see them close up, I would say that it is only because of their training, not their nature, that they rage like this. They mislead you, just as their master does. One thinks they are monsters, yet good nature is probably their real, natural character. He pretends to be good-natured and—"

"Look, Sidi, someone is coming over there," Halef interrupted.

He was pointing across the fence. I mentioned before that there was only a single gap in the thorn hedges, and that was blocked by a gate. But because we were sitting on our horses, we could see a large part of the inside of the prison, an open, grass-covered area, and someone slowly crossing it on his way toward the gate. It seemed as if this person had not taken any notice of the noise up to this moment. He was exceptionally tall and imposing. His slow walk betrayed a curious pride. He was dressed in an ample, comfortable haik which a thin leather belt pulled close to his hips. His head was bare, and an abundance of hair hung down over his back. His noble features were of a curious, almost striking beauty. He wore no beard, surely a rarity here in the country of the Ussul, who were proud of their hair and viewed every beard-less person as a mere boy, or even as contemptible. I was to find out later that they had a law which punished dishonorable acts by shaving the beard and prohibited growing it again. Perhaps the Erdjani had been subjected to that punishment. As he was approaching the gate, it seemed that, with every step, his figure increased in size and became more impressive. I did not ask myself whether this was simply a question of perspective or somehow related to the man himself, taking note of the effect without inquiring into its causes. Having arrived at the gate, he looked us over. There was no surprise in his face. His large, dark eyes scrutinized us, and when I raised my hand to my chest and forehead in greeting, he answered in the same manner. Then I asked in a loud voice:

"Are you the Erdjani?"

I had to shout because of the dogs, and he answered as loudly: "Yes, I am."

Little Halef was as affected by the extraordinary appearance of this man as I was. He had the inclination to give in to such feelings and so he spoke up without hesitation:

"Are you the Sahahr's grandson?"

The Erdjani nodded.

"Do you wish to be freed?"

The man raised his hands to his face, clapped them, and called out:

"With all my heart!"

"Then we will get you out. Immediately. We will shoot the dogs."

The sorcerer and those with him had heard these words. He wanted to repeat his prohibition and raised himself as much as he could to call out to us. He only managed to utter some inarticulate sounds and then fell back again. His wound seemed to be more dangerous than I had thought. The Ussul around him were talking to him. They were his close friends and disciples. Then one of them came toward us and said:

"You are strangers, and strangers are not allowed to interfere in our affairs. Even if you had already been accepted among the Ussul, you would not have the right to concern yourselves with this prisoner. Only the Sahahr has that right. According to the laws of our people, not even the sheik may take any action. But because you have rendered the Ussul an important service and are willing to assist us further, and because the Sahahr has become your friend and wants to demonstrate that friendship, he has decided to do as you wish and to release the Djirbani, provided you meet one condition."

"What is that?" Halef asked.

"You have to subdue the dogs without injuring them."

"The dogs?"

"Yes, they must be neither hurt nor killed. You are strictly forbidden to harm them in any way. So, before you fight them, you have to lay aside all your arms and rely entirely on your hands. Further, you may not enter together. Instead, the Emir from Djermanistan will be first and only after he has been torn to pieces may the sheik of the Haddedihn follow him."

"Would you keep your promise to release the son of the Djinnistani if I were to succeed in subduing the dogs without using my weapons, and without hurting them?" I asked.

"Yes," the sorcerer answered. Momentarily, the expectation that I would be torn to shreds by the dogs made him forget his pain.

I turned to the Erdjani.

"I will need witnesses to this agreement. Did you hear what he promised?"

"Yes," he said. "But surely you won't be so reckless as to—"

I did not let him finish but turned to our companions and the crowd:

"Did you hear, and will you testify that you did?"

"Yes, yes," they all shouted with a single voice, but there were also some that were warning me against such an unusual and uneven fight.

I paid no attention, dismounted, and told Halef to hold the reins of my horse. He looked at me with wide open eyes.

"May Allah have mercy on us. Are you really prepared to do this, Sidi?"

"Yes."

"In spite of the danger of being dismembered and devoured?"

'Yes. But that danger isn't nearly as great as you imagine."

"I hope you are right," he sighed.

"I am. Did you see the dog I shot attack his own master?"

"I did, but only when the Sahahr was already lying on the ground."

"That was too late. What I mean was already over at that moment. I paid close attention to the way these dogs have been trained. They first pull down the person they attack and only start biting afterwards. So the main thing is not to let them throw me, and to keep them away from my neck and throat. And the Erdjani will help me."

"Him? But how?"

"He has to keep one of the dogs busy so they don't attack at the same time."

"Allah be praised! That's a good idea! I am beginning to be less worried about you. And yet I am telling you that I will keep your carbine in my hand. Should one of them manage to pull you down, he will get so many bullets into his devilish body, he won't have a chance to count them."

I handed my weapons over to Halef and then wrapped my belt around my neck.

"He's going to do it! He has the courage, he's going ahead," the Ussul commented when they noticed my preparations.

There were repeated warnings, and the Erdjani also cautioned me, but I answered him:

"Don't be afraid. If you help me, I will succeed."

The Erdjani stepped close to the gate and asked:

"I should like to help you, but how?"

"By shaking and rattling the gate as if you wanted to get out. If you do that, I hope that one of the dogs will turn on you so I will have only one of them to deal with."

"I will, but you have to tell me when."

"Right now. You can start right away."

I was standing a few feet away from the gate in the outer fence. As the Erdjani began shaking the gate in the hedge, the two animals turned their backs to me. They were howling very loudly. This was the right moment. I jumped to the outer gate, pulled back the bolt, and opened it. There was a loud shout of terror and then, abruptly, total silence. The decision had come. I carefully avoided passing through the open door. It was not wide enough for both of these large, strong dogs to rush through at the same time. By not advancing beyond the opening, I made it impossible for them to attack me simultaneously. But just then, they were not heeding me but had directed their attention to the inner gate the Erdjani was shaking. They did not notice that I had opened the outer one until I loudly called out to them.

What I was doing was not so very dangerous. Hundreds had done it before me, in North America, when they still had slaves in the southern and central states of the Union. Large numbers of those poor wretches had run away from their pitiless, cruel masters and many of them had been hunted by specially trained bloodhounds. Normally, the blacks had been unarmed. Their only defense against these dangerous animals was the trick of quickly wrapping their arms around their necks and choking them as they were about to go for the throat. Of course, the pressure of the arms had to be carefully timed, or the runaway was doomed. Every slave who considered escape practiced this hold and pressure. Any dog trader would sell some old, otherwise useless animal that could serve to practice choking an attacking bloodhound with one's bare hands. What I proposed to do was thus nothing extraordinary. The only difference here was that there were two dogs and that these monsters were considerably bigger and stronger than their American counterparts. But this disadvantage was compensated for by the Erdjani's help. He had the intelligence necessary for his role.

I have already mentioned that he had drawn the attention of the dogs to himself. Then, when I was standing in the open gate, shouting loudly to make the dogs aware of me, the Erdjani had to keep one of them busy where he was. He succeeded. The moment the two beasts saw me, they wanted to rush at me but he went on rattling the gate so vigorously that one turned back to him as the other came running toward me without allowing himself to be distracted. Ordinarily, the enormous impact would have sent me crashing to the ground. But I used the half-closed door to sustain it, and then attacked. The animal caught one of his hind feet between the bars. In his haste and nervousness to get free, he only added to his difficulty, and I could effortlessly and almost without danger wrap my arms around his neck and press him so tightly against my body that the dog's breathing became labored. I pulled him away from the gate. With his back turned to me, he was hanging with his throat in my arms, howling with the fear of death, vainly trying to thrust his claws into me. When the second dog heard this, he turned away from the Erdjani and ran toward me to help his companion and to seize me. What happened now was extremely interesting. He was getting ready to jump as he saw the other dog, half dead and twitching, hanging in my arms, trying to get air. He became terrified. I stepped through the gate and toward him. If he attacked, he would not hurtle against me but against the monster hanging from my arms. He pulled back. I continued advancing, he continued retreating. I followed him and now this huge bloodhound began wailing with fear, pulling in his tail, ready to run. I therefore hurled the dog I was holding away from me so that the outstretched body fell on him. Feeling the impact, he howled with terror and ran off, coming to a stop only at a safe distance. He sat down, looked back, moaned and sighed and gave me to understand that he felt he had escaped danger momentarily but was terribly concerned about his motionless mate who was lying there with only his chest gently heaving, his mouth wide open, his tongue hanging out. The dog had nearly suffocated, and I was standing by him, ready to renew my hold. When the air again entered his lungs, the powerful body stretched, the glassy eyes refocussed. Slowly and heavily, he tried to raise himself but his legs wouldn't obey. This was the critical moment. I was spreading my arms to wrap them around him once more, should he rush toward me. He saw me standing before him, and he saw the threatening arms. At the same time, he heard the fearful whining of the second dog, and slowly turned his head toward him. The whining now turned into howling, that curious, long-drawn-out howl in a high-pitched voice that one normally only hears when there is a fire. The animal lying at my feet joined in. Instead of attacking me, he put his neck and head on the ground, closed his eyes and uttered sounds of grief which at first seemed inarticulate but gradually became clearer. Whenever he paused, he looked at me as if to ask: "Did you hear that?" I began talking to him. He fell silent and looked at me, and then answered by resuming the howling. When he was done, I started again, and he answered. In this way, we talked to each other. He howled, and I tried to calm him. He did not understand my language, nor I his, but there was something in those sounds which could not be expressed in words. I knelt down by him and dared stroke his head. He put up with it. I stroked his back and he accepted this caress with considerable pleasure. When I got up again, he followed suit and pushed his snout into my hand, asking to be caressed some more. When the other saw this, he stopped whining and came toward me, slowly and hesitantly, like a good-natured boy who has been punished and then tries to make up with his father. I went along, continuing to stroke his companion, walking toward the second dog with him. I was successful for I finally found myself standing between the two, patting and tousling their shaggy hair so that they sighed with delight. I now started walking back and forth, and they accompanied me. When I turned, so did they. I began circling the entire prison, and they followed. They looked at me with friendly eyes, their entire earlier hostility having disappeared without a trace. When I came to the gate behind which the Erdjani was standing, they were so indifferent, they seemed to have forgotten what had been their duty before. I pulled back the bolt and opened the gate.

"Can you chance that?" the Erdjani asked.

"Yes, come along," I answered, stepping back to let him out.

The dogs were flanking me, pressed close to me. I took the precaution of taking each by one ear.

"I'll do it on your advice, sahib," he said.

He pushed open the gate and came out. I noticed that he was wearing leather garments under his haik, and his boots also were made of leather, not of bast, as among the Ussul. The dogs looked at him without hatred or anger, and I also looked at him or, rather, up at him. He was stronger, taller, and broader in the shoulders than I.

What a person! What nobility, pride, and beauty! I felt as if his soul were standing behind him without his being aware of it, calling out to me: "Look at this man, and love him! He is of royal lineage."

His first glance was long, expectant, scrutinizing. Then something like a warm ray of sunlight passed over his face, and he said:

"You are not a native of this country, but a foreigner. You are noble, good, and brave. When you stopped before this infamous prison, before you had dismounted, I saw that your horse is much smaller than ours but infinitely finer and nobler. You also are much smaller than I, but you more than make up for that by the way you sit in the saddle and by the intelligence you bring to everything you do. You seemed like a heaven-sent vision. Do you know what a vision is?"

"Yes."

"And do you know that I am called the madman?"

"Yes."

"A person who has visions has been blessed by God. As long as he is aware of that, he brings blessings to mankind, whether they believe him or not. But the moment he forgets it, he has lost his sanity and merely resembles a vision that will not materialize."

"How do you know that?" I asked in surprise.

"From this book here."

He pointed at his chest, somewhat below his neck, where the hamail is normally worn. I assumed that the book was hanging from his neck and covered by his haik. He continued:

"When I saw you, it was as if you, the seemingly smaller person, were coming down from the stars to me, the seemingly larger one. I knew immediately that you had come to free me and that what was impossible for others would be child's play for you. When the vision was over and I had returned to reality, I only saw you as a human being and began to fear for your safety. You succeeded. And how easily! Without any weapons, without any brutality, and quickly! Sahib, please tell me how all this could have happened."

"Think about it," I said. "It's easy. I would like you

to find the answer without help from me."

For a few moments, he looked into my face as if he wanted to read there the reasons for my answer. Then he said:

"I thank you. You are acting correctly. What someone can discover by his own thought should not be given him by others. I will not ask you who you are or where you come from. But there is one thing I would like to know: Where will you be staying?"

"Probably in the house of the sheik. I am his guest."

"Then we will separate for now. Do you want to see me again?"

"Yes."

"I want to see you also. Can you visit me on my Island of the Heathens?"

"Yes, I'll be pleased to come. But when?"

"Tomorrow morning, I shall be waiting for you."

"Must I come by myself, or may I bring my companion with me?"

"The little fellow over there who is holding your horse?"

"Yes. He is my confidant, and I am very fond of him."

"Then bring him along, but don't bring anyone else. I'll go now."

We turned toward the outer fence. I was going to leave the dogs and then bolt the gate. But when they saw what I had in mind, they forcefully pushed their way out. This should have been cause for worry, for being set free, their wildness might cause havoc. But no trace of danger was apparent, and they showed so little desire to leave my side that I felt I would be able to control them. As a precaution, I merely took them by their ears, as I had before, and they did not object. Now the Erdjani also tried to caress them, and they not merely suffered it but looked up at him gratefully. Their eyes took on a gentle expression which did not even remotely resemble their earlier fierceness. Then he said:

"People go to such trouble to ruin animals. Who stands on a higher level, a person who will do that, or these dogs? Come, sahib."

We first went back to Halef and the horses. He had

dismounted. The Erdjani stopped to look him in the face, and said:

"Yes, bring him along tomorrow."

Then he looked at the horses attentively and admiringly for some time. Halef could not keep silent for that long, and asked: "Do you like them?"

The Erdjani smiled at this question, and answered:

"They are not from some crude and primitive country. They are part of the vision. How lucky we would be, were it to become reality."

We walked on, toward the canal. The men standing around the Sahahr had not yet succeeded in staunching the flow of blood. The Erdjani walked toward him and I joined him. The men jumped up and stepped back to avoid being close to the "leper." The Sahahr's garment had been cut open and we could see what looked like a dangerous wound. The lower part of the thigh had been mangled and the kneecap smashed. The Erdjani pulled a package out from under his haik, and said:

"If this wound is not carefully treated, he will die. I shall bandage him."

"Do you know how?" I asked.

"My father was the most famous physician in the world. I am his student."

He was about to bend down when the Sahahr opened his eyes, raised himself to a sitting position, stretched both hands with the fingers wide apart toward him, and said in a tone of the greatest loathing:

"Get back! Don't touch me! You are cursed."

The Erdjani straightened up and, disregarding the insult, told him very quietly:

"Except for me, there is no one here who knows how to treat such a wound. If you are bandaged improperly, infection will develop, the wound will suppurate, and you will die."

"Then I'll die," the Sahahr shouted. "Get away! Don't touch me. You are leprous and mad, and I will have nothing to do with you."

The Erdjani put the packet back in his pocket, and we walked to the canal. A raft was brought. It had been lying nearby, ordered by the sheik to take the

wounded sorcerer to his house. When the man bringing it saw the Erdjani get on, he uttered a cry of
horror and jumped on land to avoid being touched.
But the Erdjani disregarded this and said to me:

"I will not thank you now, sahib. One does not
thank a person who acted as you did, one lives one's
obligation to him. Nor will I take your hand, for your
sake. The others would shy away from you."

He gave the raft a vigorous kick to move it across
the canal, got off and walked slowly and quietly away,
like a ruler, without looking right or left. Those he
approached quickly jumped aside as if he were contagious, but he ignored them. Now and then, I had the
impression that there were those who moved aside not
from fear or aversion but from respect.

The general silence greeting his rescue was no less
striking. Their master's wound showed how dangerous
the dogs had been. Anywhere else, my bare-handed
victory would have been loudly cheered. Here, no one
said a word. The silence contrasted conspicuously with
the many loud and well-meant shouts with which they
had warned me earlier. It was not difficult to see why
they reacted like this. Now that the Erdjani had been
freed, the entire population felt oppressed once again
and since they were afraid of being infected, they did
not feel I had done them a service. Having been so
welcome before, I had forced something profoundly
disturbing on them just as I was entering their city.

My little Halef seemed to be thinking similar
thoughts. Holding the reins in his hands, he was standing next to me, looking after the disappearing Erdjani
with glowing eyes. When he no longer saw him, he
mumbled almost wrathfully to himself:

"Ungrateful bunch! You gambled your life and now
that you won, they don't say a word. But no one could
have done as well. See how they are looking at us?
You made an impression on them. Take your horse
and your weapons. We have to get across."

The sheik's wife had waited for us. The only one
prepared to applaud us, she was about to express her
appreciation when she pointed at the canal and called
out in terror:

"Those monsters. They are following you! Shoot them!"

The two dogs had entered the water behind us and were swimming across. The people were fearfully pushing ahead or back, not being able to move aside because of the water. This cleared a space for the dogs to clamber on dry land where I was standing with Taldsha. Everyone nearby picked up whatever weapon was at hand, but I raised my arm to warn them:

"Don't under any circumstances attack or injure them! That would make them as wild as they were before. I promise you they will do no harm."

"Then I'll stay with you," the sheik's wife said courageously.

I dismounted and stepped up to the water to caress the dogs. One of them licked the hand I had stretched out and the other immediately followed his example. I waited until they had shaken the water out of their fur and then used two straps to tie them to my stirrups. They not only put up with this but whined with pleasure. They took this as proof that they now belonged to me. It's what they had wanted and as I mounted again and moved on, they barked loudly and happily. The sheik's wife looked at me with amazement.

"What a miracle," she exclaimed. "You seem to be a much greater and more skillful magician than the Sahahr."

"To repair through reason and love what unreason and hatred have wrought merely requires good will, not a miracle or magic," I answered. "The miracle is that you should take something perfectly natural for a miracle. Considering everything that has been happening here, I just wonder if what I did was useless, or not."

"Useless? What do you mean?"

"Is the Erdjani really a free man now?"

"Certainly," she assured me.

"He cannot be locked up again?"

"Not as a madman or leper. The Sahahr released him under conditions which you fulfilled. From now until the day he dies, he is a free man and safe from interference by anyone, provided he does not violate some other Ussul law. I wanted his freedom and asked you for it. I should like to express my gratitude, but I heard him say that one can only live one's obligations, not talk about them. I think that is wise and will act accordingly by remaining silent now. Your wishes will be no less important to me than mine was for you. I only ask that I may consider myself your friend."

"You not only may, I want you to with all my heart. I feel profoundly reassured when you say that the Erdjani is now permanently free. I have not been able to test the accuracy of the accusation that he is mad, but I will tell you frankly that the Sahahr's hatred suggests madness much more strongly than the kind and totally forgiving behavior of his grandson."

"How strange. Even his own wife occasionally thinks he is mad."

"Whose wife?"

"The sorcerer's. Haven't we discussed her yet?"

"No. This is the first time I have learned that he has a wife."

"She is a much more highly developed human being. I would say that she is the soul, he the body. I see a great deal of her. You will make her acquaintance, perhaps even today. But why do you look so surprised?"

We had entered the inner city. The road had become much wider. Occasionally, there were open areas where the residences of the rich had been built and where there were no canals. Many more people had gathered here, and among them I noticed a strikingly large number of injured and cripples who, although they had not all collected in one place, had attracted my attention because of their curious clothes. All of them wore tall leather cavalry boots and huge spurs with gigantic rowels which clanged loudly at every step and of which these poor wretches seemed inordinately proud. Everyone of them had a full knapsack of dog fur strapped to his back. On their shoulders they had insignia, small replicas of cannon barrels. Because they projected somewhat, they gave these men an appearance of exceptional physical development and strength. They were really epaulets and carried the inscription: "We die for" on the left, and "The Mir of Ardistan" on the right. Later, I noticed that these cannon barrels were not all of iron, but sometimes of silver or gold, and indicated rank. All those I saw standing about seemed in need of help. Yet I did not think of them as cripples but as invalids who deserved respect. I had therefore looked at them closely as we rode past, and the sheik's wife had noticed this and asked me why I was curious.

"Our soldiers seem to attract your attention," she went on.

"Soldiers?" I asked. "You mean veterans, sick and injured men that have been discharged."

"Oh no, they are real soldiers."

"So they aren't invalids? They are still on active duty?"

"Yes, whenever war breaks out. That's what they are there for. And they are the ones that will fight in the army when we move against the Tshoban."

"Then they must also be the soldiers that defended you when the Tshoban besieged you?"

"Of course. They are no good for anything else."

"Hm. Then the people you use as soldiers are persons that can perform no other kind of service?"

"Of course. Isn't that the way it is in your country?"

"No. There, they take precisely the best, the strongest, the healthiest."

"What a terrible pity! I thought everything in your country was done intelligently, and now I hear the very opposite."

"Can you prove that you act more wisely in this respect?"

"Yes. You know there is war, and there is peace. Which of the two is the natural condition, the one both God and we want?"

"Peace."

"Then you admit that war is an unfortunate exception, peace the normal and happy state?"

"Yes."

"All right, then. But there are also useful and useless and even harmful individuals. Which of the two is the normal, desirable condition: usefulness or the reverse?"

"The former."

"What would you call someone who mixes the good and the bad, the harmful and the beneficial? Would you consider him wise?"

"No."

"But that means that the useful, the healthy, those capable of work, belong with peace, while the rest are for war. It is an unpardonable stupidity and sin to send the providers of the nation against the enemy so that he can destroy them. We do the opposite. We keep them at home."

"And are therefore regularly defeated?" I asked.

"Not regularly, but most of the time. But you must remember that the Tshoban only come to steal our herds. Suppose they attack and take a thousand oxen. I can prevent that by sacrificing two or three hundred strong young men who would be killed in battle. But I am saying to you that I don't find it difficult to choose between a thousand oxen and three hundred young men. I'll gladly let the oxen go to save the men. We wouldn't think of sending the Mir of Ardistan the pick of our youth, particularly because the other tribute he demands is really excessive."

"Do you pay tribute?"

"Don't you? What else do you call it?"

"Taxes."

"That's one and the same thing. Taxes are compulsory tribute. No one likes to pay them. If they are used for works of peace, they bring blessings, but if they are demanded for war, they are a curse. The taxes we pay the Mir of Ardistan are only for war. We have to pay for the upkeep of his bodyguard, which consists entirely of tall Ussul whom he uses for display and who are feared everywhere. And it goes without saying that we have to equip those men as well. So we figure this way: We have to furnish the bodyguard and everything they require. Consequently, we only send those men we want to get rid of or whom we would have to support here without benefit to us. I mean the sick in body or mind, the indolent, the reckless, the unreliable, the liars, the thieves. In that way, we eliminate crime and need spend no money for prisons. That was the only reason we could tell you that no Ussul would lie to you, for the scoundrels are with the Mir and no longer among us."

"But do those men submit to this custom? Do they agree to become soldiers?"

"With no hesitation."

"And you also send the Mir men that are physically ill?"

"Yes. Provided they have the necessary height. They almost always benefit from this arrangement. The moment they get out of our low-lying, damp forests and up into the mountains and the sun, they recover. The same holds true of those that are morally sick. The discipline the Mir of Ardistan imposes is severe. Rebels perish. That's why all those members of the bodyguard whom he returns home at their request have become very useful persons who take pride in gaining our respect. We thought it advantageous to form a small, standing army from them and I am convinced that you will soon approve of this way of doing things. You will get to see an entire company of them which is standing ready to salute us. We will have reached the palace in another few minutes. Permit me to join the sheik."

The sheik, and now his wife, were riding at the head, followed by half of the elders. Then came Halef and me with the second half of the elders behind us. A number of curious onlookers were bringing up the rear. Those ahead of us were anxious to get as far away from the dogs as possible, and since those behind felt the same way, Halef and I had a great deal of room to ourselves and could be studied at leisure by the population. The impression we made was anything but favorable. We and our horses were both too small for their taste; their gestures expressed their disappointment. News of our arrival had preceded us and Halef's tales were probably already widely known. And these people, who were used to judge by physical size, could not reconcile the reports they had heard with our small, apparently fragile physique.

8 : In Ussula

Two towerlike structures now came into view, and the road we had been riding on came to an end. It led into a large square. The side facing us was bordered by the river and seemed to be the principal landing area. To the right and the left stood the towers which were identical in appearance except that only one of them had windows. They had an outside diameter of perhaps one hundred and fifty paces and the walls were about twenty meters high, but the height of the towers was considerably greater, for many wooden pillars which supported the roof rose above the walls. The roof looked like a huge umbrella with a pole of very thick trunks at the precise center inside the towers. Wooden stairs led along this pole to a small platform with a railing which lay high above, on the top of the umbrella. The pillars supporting the roof had no connecting walls and thus allowed such an abundance of light to fall inside that windows were unnecessary. Because the roof projected beyond the walls, the interior was protected from rain. The two very high, wide gates also were identical. They were framed very simply by stones and totally devoid of artistic conception or ornamentation of any kind.

The tower to our right, which only showed us its naked walls and not a single window, was the so-called "temple"; the one to the left was the "palace." The latter had four rows of window openings circling it but they were small, looked like firing slits, and had neither glass nor frames. Inside, the walls were of wood. The rooms or chambers directly in back of the walls had two or more windows each. There were also some larger rooms that served as halls. But these rooms did not fill all of the interior space. In the center, around the umbrella pole, there was a kind of inner court with two very large fireplaces. The mats and pillows lying on the floor suggested that, during bad weather, this area was used as a place where councils and gatherings were held.

The Ussul had been satisfied with two stone buildings of this size, and had not troubled with architectural refinements. And yet these towers were impressive precisely because of their lack of expressiveness and spirit. One could see that this nation had wanted to show itself for what it was through its architecture but had been unable to go beyond this one tremendous shout, this inarticulate cry. Then it had relapsed into its original silence and remained mute. Yet that muteness was not total. A second attempt had been made, although this was not architectonic but sculptural. For between these two massive structures and precisely in the center of the square, there stood the not unaccomplished statue of a saddled horse. It consisted of solid pieces of wood and had been painted to protect it from the destructive effects of the weather.

Massive, heavy, and of considerable girth, this horse was standing on a pedestal. That it was meant to represent a horse was evident because a rider sat on it. He was the size of the Ussul while the horse was more than lifesize so that the rider seemed much too small for this exceptionally fat animal. I asked myself why the artist had created something so lacking in proportion. A second question suggested itself as one looked at the monument, and that concerned the material from which the rider had been made. The horse was of wood, but it was impossible to determine what the figure was made of, for it was completely covered by real clothing. Nor did the face give any hint because it was obscured by a huge beard. On his head, the rider wore a brightly colored tall Indian turban topped by a cluster of heron's feathers. The figure was wrapped in a kind of mantel of red cloth with white fur along the collar and the hem at the bottom. Because of the exceptional length and width of this garment, it not only covered the entire body of the rider but also the rear portion of the horse. One could not even see the stirrups or feet.

"A monument," Halef said, surprised. "Here, among the Ussul! So they have some notion of art. Who would have thought that? I'll come back for another look at the rider. What a pity if it rains on that beautiful red coat and the white turban with its feathers. Too bad we don't have the time now to inspect it."

He was right, for the moment the towers had emerged before us, the sheik had begun trotting, and we had to follow at the pace he set. He wanted us to make an impression on the crowd that was so densely packed in the large square and the adjoining area that there was barely room for us and the elders to pass. Those who had been following us had to remain behind.

The silence was total, though not reassuring, but had something disappointing, even alarming about it. Only the two of us were struck by it. For the natives, it was the normal thing. Nor did the press of the crowd hamper our progress. Because of the dogs, people stayed as far away as they could.

As we drew close to the gate of the "palace," we saw a cannon on either side with a crew of four soldiers of the sort I have described. One of them was holding a burning fuse, the second an implement for cleaning the barrel, the third and fourth a sack filled with powder and the primer. Along one side, the "entire company" the sheik's wife had mentioned had lined up. We stopped directly in front of it to enjoy the military display intended for us while the sheik and his wife stayed at our side to answer whatever questions we might have. The company consisted of forty soldiers equipped with cavalry sabres and flintlocks. The men had formed a single line; being longer than two ranks would have been, this arrangement was felt to be more impressive. All of them were bareheaded, wore the previously mentioned high boots with huge spurs and the very large, crammed knapsacks on their backs. Evidence of wounds and injuries was abundant. Any number of them had lost an arm or a leg, or even a leg and a half. Indeed, there was hardly a limb or an organ that had not either been mutilated or lost in one or more cases. But they were all well nourished and standing at attention, and when they began to drill, their movements were vigorous and it was obvious that they were serious about what they were doing. Two had stepped out front. They did not carry rifles but held their sabres in their hands.

"Those are the lieutenants," the sheik explained. "You can see that the gun barrels on their shoulders are not black, but silvered."

A third man was standing still further forward. He also held a sabre and his insignia were bright red.

"Who is that?" I asked.

"The colonel."

"Then you don't have lieutenant colonels, captains, or majors?"

"We don't," he admitted. "It would be too expensive."

"I was only told about iron, silver, and gold insignia, but not about red ones."

"Yes, that's true. Being a colonel, he should have gold ones, but I didn't want to spend the money, so I had them painted red. I think they look all right. You know, having soldiers isn't so bad. One can show how important a person one is. But the moment it stops being profitable and starts costing money, I'd rather dispense with them. There is no point in spending large sums of money to maintain men whose only purpose is to kill others. Pay attention now! The shooting is going to begin. The cannons will fire first. It's all in your honor."

"Fire!" the colonel shouted.

The man with the fuse touched the cannon once—twice—even four or five times, but nothing happened.

"What's this?" the commanding officer wanted to know.

"They won't fire," one of the soldiers answered.

"Why not?"

"Because the powder is damp," one of them answered, and the other added: "Then I was right. Didn't I tell you that it wouldn't ignite? You didn't believe me."

The sheik turned to me:

"You are aware that the shots were only going to be fired in your honor. And you hear that the powder won't ignite. If you insist on the salvo of ten rounds that I promised you, we have to dry it first."

"How long would that take?"

"Three or four days."

"Then I ask that you do not inconvenience your brave artillery needlessly. The powder would only get damp again."

"That's true. Then you are willing to forego it?"

"Of course. Tell your troops that I am delighted with them."

"And you?" the sheik asked Halef.

"I also admire them. Tell your men that we think they are invincible."

The commanding officers returned to the men to tell them how deeply appreciative we were while I thanked the sheik and his wife for the unusual honor they had shown me. Then we were asked to dismount and to enter the palace to celebrate our arrival with a banquet. I ordered the dogs to remain with the horses. They understood, sat down, and remained in place until we returned.

The inside of the "palace" looked something like a circus where one can move only in the circular arena in the center because the stands have been completely closed off by boards. The chambers and rooms I mentioned earlier lay behind these boards; narrow wooden stairs led to those on the upper floors. The central space to which we were taken received its light entirely from above. Huge wood fires were burning on the hearths. Hindquarters of cattle and smaller pieces of meat were being broiled, and large clay pots were used for boiling. They were also baking slender, long, thin loaves.

Taldsha said:

"It is because of the bread that we brought you here. The welcoming meal consists of bread and salt. Permit me to serve you."

She walked up to the hearth where the fragrant warm loaves were lying, salted one, and then broke it into four pieces. The customary words referring to the duties and obligations of the host and his guest were exchanged, and then each one of us ate his share.

"I'd like another piece, but a whole loaf this time," Halef said.

Taldsha was pleased, looked at me smilingly, and asked:

"Would you also like another one, Effendi?"

"Please."

She got the bread for us and Halef sat down and started eating.

"Come, Sidi," he said, moving a little to one side. "Sit down by me. I am not getting up again until I have finished."

This was acting unceremoniously, but the sheik and his wife were delighted and later my little Hadji was told that the informal sincerity with which we had honored their baking skills had won everyone's heart.

Taldsha now left for a short time. When she returned, she was holding a large stone vessel in one hand and four small Chinese porcelain cups in the other. The cups were certainly among her most valuable possessions.

"When we welcome guests, we not only eat, we also drink in their honor," she said. "So here I am bringing you the Simmsemm which is customary on such occasions."

Both "simm" and "semm" mean poison, so that Simmsemm means double poison, and that did not sound inviting. The liquid she poured was light, transparent, and smelled strongly of ethyl alcohol. The sheik said some welcoming words and emptied his cup in a single swallow. Halef politely responded and imitated him. A violent coughing fit was the consequence. Taldsha also emptied her cup in a single gulp but I saw she had not taken much. Unfortunately, I could not pour this brew out. This was a ceremonial occasion; it must be drunk. I did it as slowly as possible and must confess that I had never before tasted anything as acid and repellent.

"Now the ceremony is over," the sheik said, "and I will take you to your apartment. It is not here in the castle but some distance away on the river."

"We did this for your convenience," the wife added, not wanting us to think that we were not properly esteemed guests. "The constant noise here in the palace would be disturbing to you. And you would not be able to have your horses near you. So we are taking you to a quieter, more comfortable place which you will like better. I'll come along."

We returned to our horses. The crowd had almost

entirely disappeared. Only small groups were still standing about, eager to have a look at us before nightfall. As our eyes travelled across the square, Halef suddenly exclaimed:

"Mashallah! What do I see! Miracles happen here."

He was pointing at the equestrian statue. As I looked in the direction he indicated, I saw that the rider was beginning to move. He was slowly opening his coat and let it drop on the pedestal. He then looked back, to the right and the left. Up to this moment, he had been immobile, staring straight ahead. Having convinced himself that the square was empty, he felt it was superfluous to remain where he was. He raised his right leg, swung it across the horse and climbed down on the brick pedestal.

"He's alive," Halef shouted. Then he began to laugh. "A living rider on a wooden horse!"

"What is there to be surprised about?" the sheik asked, half offended, half surprised. "Which is the greater art, to make monuments of human beings or of wood?"

His question baffled Halef, and he understood that his laughter had been tactless. Ashamed of himself, he lowered his eyes. But then he looked up again and answered in his frank, open manner:

"Forgive me, O sheik. But I have never seen anything like this."

"So you customarily laugh when you see something new? In that case, I won't be able to show you anything here, for you would probably see so many strange things, you wouldn't stop laughing."

That comment struck home, but Halef was much too proud to show it. He asked:

"But what is the purpose of this curious arrangement?"

"The man simply acted prematurely, that's all," Taldsha answered. "Whenever strangers visited us or an Ussul returned home from abroad, we heard that other nations honor their famous and deserving men by building them a monument. I hear that sometimes monuments are even put up for people who are neither. The Ussul began to feel ashamed, because they believed that many great and praiseworthy men had lived among them but no monument had ever been erected for any of them. The elders deliberated and decided to adopt this splendid custom by putting up an equestrian statue for every famous and meritorious person, whether he was a good or a bad horseman. For what counts is not riding a horse but the act one wishes to honor. It goes without saying that the sheiks had to be first. The others had to wait. Two committees were set up, the first for the construction of the monument, the second to determine the sequence of the men to be portrayed, for we felt that the fame and the desserts of the person had to be scrupulously weighed and compared to assure that everyone would occupy the place he had earned. We therefore had to decide first which sheik had been the greatest, the most famous, and the most worthy, for he had to come first. While the second committee took up the problem of a just and accurate choice, the first began work by building the base for the first pillar. When this was done, the second committee had not yet come to an agreement about the rider but only about the horse. Construction continued. By the time the horse was finished, the other committee had decided that the most famous sheik was precisely the man who should not be honored because he had done absolutely nothing of merit and brought his nation to the brink of ruin. There were some Ussul who had not been sheiks but ranked far above them in fame and good works. Now factions arose which finally divided the entire tribe. One wanted monuments only for warriors, the other only for men of peace. The third was for both, while the fourth insisted on horses and the fifth wouldn't hear of them. The sixth demanded one sequence, the seventh another. In short, ever since the horse has been standing here, there has been no one who has not believed that either he or one of his ancestors should sit on it, though only after his death, of course. There was more quarreling and dispute, hatred and anger than we had ever had before. We women could no longer recognize our sons and husbands. They had turned into maniacs and fools. Now the women got together and also formed two committees. The first had to show how all these famous and worthy men had looked to their wives and children. The second demanded that instead of these unmasked celebrities, only decent and deserving women should be honored by a monument. It also attempted to identify such women. It soon became apparent that there were thousands who deserved being placed on such a pedestal, and work to determine the sequence was quickly started. Now the men began to understand. The stupidity of their women opened their eyes to their own, and they declared their willingness to reëstablish peace between the sexes. The two female and the two male committees got together and deliberated with whatever rationality and kindness they could muster and discovered that among the Ussul, there had never been either a male or a female that deserved to be honored above the rest. Since this permitted the inference that in the future no one worthy of that distinction would ever appear, it was concluded not to erect any monuments in the country of the Ussul for all time to come."

"But there is a horse standing there, and someone was sitting on it today," Halef said.

"Yes," she smiled. "The horse still stands. Do you think we should have pulled it down and burned it?"

"Yes, it no longer serves a purpose."

"But it does! We let it stand to remind us of our foolishness. Surely that's a purpose, and even a good one. And a second purpose was soon found. A short time after we had understood our mistake, the then Mir of Ardistan demanded that all countries and provinces ruled by or tributary to him must put up a monument. We also had that obligation. We deliberated and decided not to build an ordinary monument but an equestrian statue. We already had the horse, so we would save money. And we also decided not to create an artifact but to use a living human being. Sculptures are very expensive, but you can get people anywhere, and for next to nothing. So we abandoned the idea of having artists and stones brought from afar, and gave the tallest and broadest Ussul the job of representing the Mir of Ardistan. He was given a red coat with white hems and a large turban with heron's feathers. He demands no payment, but does it for the honor. Whenever there is an occasion such as today, for example, when you arrived in the city, and we need to show off our Mir of Ardistan, this man puts on the turban, wraps himself in his coat and mounts the horse. He stays there until the celebration is over, and then dismounts again. If he does well and avoids all movement, so that one really believes he is a lifeless figure, he is especially rewarded by being invited to the banquet. But if he makes mistakes, that distinction is denied him. You see! He has dismounted, and is now standing there, waiting to see whether he will be invited, or not."

"What are you going to do?" Halef asked.

"Well, he sat remarkably still today. He himself found the enormous sabre hanging from his side, saying that this went with the dignity of his office. He has learned to embody what he represents to such a degree that he believes that dignity is really his. He acts the Mir of Ardistan even when he is not sitting on the horse. People therefore say that he has lost his wits. The various insignia he wears on his chest seem to have given him the mad notion that he has all the virtues for which they are awarded."

"Are those insignia genuine?" Halef asked. He liked to be well informed.

"Of course. Actually, they are meant as incentives, not as tokens of recognition. The rulers of Ardistan have always believed that certain merits and services should be rewarded before rather than after the fact. The Ussul sheiks also received medals of honor which gradually accumulated. The Mir of Ardistan, not the real one but this one here, puts them on whenever he displays himself. We permit that, and he may even wear them during the banquet. Then days will pass until he finally deigns to speak to someone. The fact that the coat hides the shining decorations is a real torment for him. That's why he throws it off while he is still sitting on the horse so that they appear at the earliest possible moment. Would you like him to show them to you?"

"Please," Halef said.

Taldsha gestured to the man to approach. He slowly came toward us in what he took to be a princely manner.

"I am the Mir of Ardistan," he told us condescendingly.

"And I," Halef said, "I am—"

"Silence!" the man interrupted him with a commanding gesture. "I already know what you want to tell me, and I don't have the time now to listen to it all over again."

Halef looked at me as if he meant to give a stinging reply but I gestured to him to remain silent. Taldsha identified the various decorations and the names of the sheiks that had received them. All of them had been bestowed by the Mir of Ardistan and not one was of real metal. Since the stones on them were also imitation, this did nothing to increase my respect for this important personage. When we had inspected the decorations, Taldsha told the man:

"You did well today; you may eat with us."

By a condescending gesture, he indicated his gracious acceptance.

"You may go," she added.

The man cast a withering glance at the two of us and majestically strode toward the gate of the "palace" to await the start of the banquet while we went to the house that had been set aside for us. The horses and the dogs followed.

The house lay behind the palace, and, like it, on the banks of a river. It was really a hut that had been divided into four rooms and had a shed next to it where we stabled our horses. By local standards, the house was furnished and there was a fire burning in one of the rooms. Two men received us. They had been assigned to us and instructed to be as attentive as if they were serving the sheik. The fire was not merely decorative. Everything was damp, and dry warmth was necessary to prevent mildew. It would have been impossible for human beings to spend much time here without becoming ill. Taldsha inspected the house carefully. We discovered the reason after she had left with her husband, when some time later cushions, blankets, containers, and a number of other objects and utensils arrived to make our stay more comfortable.

When we found ourselves alone, we first attended to the horses. Everything necessary for them was there, and a good deal of meat and bones had been sent from the palace for the dogs. Then we had a look outside. The house lay in the large vegetable gardens that belonged to the sheik. Unfortunately, it was already getting dark. Dusk is of very short duration in those regions, and we therefore did not have much time for a careful inspection. There were some steps on the bank which led down to the river. We noticed several small rafts, boats, and a leather canoe similar to the one we had used to paddle across the lake out in the jungle. I indicated to the two servants that I wished this boat reserved for our exclusive use.

Some time later, the sheik came to take us to the banquet. He expressed his concern about the dogs. Would they not insist on following us and endangering his guests? But I reassured him. The dogs were lying behind a bolted door, busy with their bones.

The banquet was served in two rooms. The less important guests sat in the central area of the palace, near the hearth. The "Mir of Ardistan," in the splendor of his glittering decorations, was at the head of the table. Although we had to pass him, he felt so superior that he did not deign to notice us. Guests of some consequence had also gathered on the first floor, but in the largest room, which had four windows and might be called a hall. The floor consisted of firmly tamped earth. Poles had been rammed into it and the boards that had been nailed to them served as tables, benches, and chairs. People here were thus eating at fairly high tables, as in Europe. Sitting or lying in the Oriental manner was impossible for the prevailing dampness made the ground uncomfortable.

The food was served on a long table without table cloth or similar refinements. Two large candelabra made of antlers, and containing large candles, gave ample light. Those gathered here included the elders, the colonel, the two lieutenants, and several other important personages whom we had not previously met. Except for the sheik's wife, there were no women present. She was sitting at the head of the table and presided over the animated conversation in a manner which increased our respect for her.

What we ate, how the food was prepared, and in what order it was served are unimportant details. I shall merely mention that the huge portions of meat cut individually for every one of the guests disappeared in such short order that Halef kept wondering about the miraculous speed with which they were devoured. The abundance of vegetables was even greater, and not a single leaf or stalk remained.

I had been seated at Taldsha's right, Halef on her left. The sheik was sitting on my other side. I recognized more and more than though uncultivated, he was an extremely good-natured individual and that with only a measure of care, all quarreling could be avoided. It also became increasingly apparent that his wife was the real ruler of the tribe, and that there would be occasions when she would put considerably more store in the Sahahr's judgment than that of her husband. But that respect was all she felt for the sorcerer. Being a friend of the Erdjani, it was impossible for her to be really fond of him.

No one smoked, and I should mention here that the Ussul don't smoke at all. They consider tobacco a very harmful poison, and smoke offensive. This imposed an unpleasant restraint on two such confirmed smokers as Halef and myself, but there was another poison which they could not do without. That was their Simmsemm, two large containers of which were standing on the table and had been completely emptied by the time the meal was over. The sheik's wife did not drink, nor did Halef or I. The sheik, who enjoyed tippling, therefore felt he owed us an explanation, saying that one had to drink this brew to counteract the dampness of the country.

"You will start drinking it, too, once you have been here awhile," he added. "It's a well known fact that the drier the country, the less poison one needs."

"But there are people who maintain the precise opposite," I contradicted him. "The drier the country, they say, the more one has to drink."

"Let them go ahead," he laughed. "Every person

finds a reason for defending the poison he cannot do without."

It must be said, however, that the Ussul could absorb large quantities. A fourth or a fifth of what the most moderate among them drank would have been enough to intoxicate me, but these sturdy men only became loquacious and good-humored, and that effect was welcome. By making the conversation much more animated than it would otherwise have been, it spared us a conference which had originally been set for later but could be held during the meal because they were in a mood for talk.

This conference dealt with our acceptance into the Ussul tribe, and the campaign against the Tshoban. I had imagined that the discussion would be complicated, excited, and long, but it took much less time than I would have thought possible. All this was due to female ingenuity and cleverness which here, as so often elsewhere, proved superior to my thinking. The Ussul had heard that, in Europe, someone often gets up during such a banquet with a glass in his hand and delivers a speech. I was asked if that was true and what the purpose of it was. I explained it to them and then raised my full Simmsemm cup to toast the Ussul, their sheik, and his wife. Everybody immediately began imitating me. I had barely finished when Taldsha rose to answer. She was pleased that I had praised her people and concluded that I would therefore be delighted to be able to become one of them. She mentioned the law according to which every new member had to fight an Ussul to show himself worthy of that honor by a display of courage. She pointed out that I had even fought the bloodhounds of the tribe and overcome them unarmed, which was more than the law demanded. And she emphasized that Halef and I had defeated and captured the firstborn of the Tshoban and his two companions. This really made further proof of our courage and worth unnecessary, and a council and vote about this matter would thus no longer be required. She was therefore receiving us into the tribe and asking us to swear loyalty to the sheik and the leaders. This was the first toast she had ever proposed, she said. She was proud of having learned this custom from us, and hoped that in the future she would learn other and even more important things.

How quickly those clumsy fellows jumped from their seats, emptied their cups, and came toward us with outstretched arms to shake our hands! There was an enormous amount of cheering which was echoed by those of lesser rank sitting at the other table when someone told them the good news. When I had pressed the hands of the sheik and the elders, Taldsha took mine and held it for a few moments without saying a word, looking at me with a triumphant smile which had a touch of irony in it. Then she said:

"It went faster than you thought, didn't it? Are you angry with me?"

"Not at all," I answered. "I thank you."

Halef was quite happy to have become an Ussul but later, when we were back in our hut, he admitted that he had been upset about the trick the sheik's wife had played on us, for now the legally prescribed duel would not take place.

Deliberations concerning our campaign against the Tshoban were also considered unnecessary. The elders took a very favorable view of my plan and merely asked Taldsha if she felt the campaign was desirable. When they were given an affirmative answer, they said that war now had been decided upon and would no longer be their affair, but the colonel's. Since he was the commander of the army, it was his problem now, and when Taldsha suggested that I should be consulted, I asked the colonel first to take up the plan with the brave Hadji Halef Omar, the famous sheik of the Haddedihn. I told him that he was a soldier of considerable experience and certainly ready to give him whatever hints might be required to insure victory.

I had no sooner said this than Halef jumped from his seat, reacting instantly, and asked the colonel and the two lieutenants to sit down with him at another, smaller table, where they would continue their meal and he could immediately give them the instructions I had mentioned. They proudly complied and when later in the evening I once referred to their table as the "table of the generals," I so completely won their hearts that they promised all imaginable feats of bravery.

I had recognized that Taldsha was the only person whose decisions carried weight. She was one of those profound and noble natures who pass from the level of ordinary humanity to a transfigured spiritual plane without suffering repellent torment, and instill in those who long for perfection the desire to follow them.

She told me that the captured Tshoban were being kept incommunicado in locked rooms in the palace and that they were so strictly guarded that escape was impossible. They were still my property but I had promised to turn them over to the Ussul as soon as I had shown that they had come with hostile rather than peaceful intentions. That fact had been demonstrated, but I had not yet been asked to give them up and still felt that they were under my control. She also told me that the Sahahr had been taken to his home without further mishap and was behaving strangely. His wife had expressed the desire to see me, today, if possible, but her husband must not know about it. I should therefore tell her if I would agree to a meeting in the temple, and when I stated my willingness, Taldsha said that she also would be present, and would accompany me there.

"When are we leaving?" I asked.

"When the banquet is over. I will let her know, and she will wait for us."

"You told me that she was the soul, and he the body. I would rather not let such a woman wait, nor would I wish the other guests to have to leave because I do. How long will they be celebrating?"

"At least until midnight. But you may leave whenever you wish. No one will resent it."

"But you have to stay?"

"Oh, no. Why should I not have the same freedom as you or anyone else? I always remain only as long as it is important for me. All substantive matters have been discussed; what remains is just eating, drinking, and trivial talk. I am only staying on your account. Would you like to go?"

"Yes."

"You are being sincere. I ask that you always be

frank with me, just as I am with you. Be patient for another quarter hour, for I must first let my friend know."

She sent a messenger. Although it was noticed that we were about to leave, this did not cause the slightest disturbance. No one felt that he should follow our example, and even Halef said to me:

"You are leaving, Sidi? But I absolutely must stay."

"There is no reason why you shouldn't. I am not going home yet. Are you discussing important matters?"

"Very," he said, with the expression of a man almost crushed by the quantity and burden of his duties. "Consider that a major campaign is being prepared, and the life and death of thousands of men is at stake. Once we are victorious, we will continue defeating our enemies. We won't stop after our first victory. We just decided to invade the territory of the Tshoban and to depose their sheik. But further conquests remain; other rulers must be deposed. There will be additional deliberations. This one today is the first, but certainly not the last."

When the quarter hour was up, we took our leave. As we passed through the large central area where the other guests were sitting, we noticed that the Simm-semm had caused considerable havoc among them. In spite of the general inebriation, all of them rose from their seats to show their respect. There was only a single exception, and that was the man who had sat on the monument. Drunkenness had had a singular effect on him. He was sitting there stiffly, staring in front of him, and repeating over and over: "I am not only the Mir of Ardistan, but even the Mir of Djinnistan."

The night was dark. The stars were shining and the thin sliver of the new moon lay directly above the road by which we had entered the city. We crossed the square and walked directly into the temple. There was a servant at the open gate who entered with us and immediately locked it again.

9 : Flames in the Heavens

We were standing in a seemingly endless expanse. Only if one looked up could one see the stars between the pillars supporting the roof, shining into the impenetrable darkness as though from another world. Now a candle was lit in the center. It looked so tiny that one hardly noticed it in this apparently infinite obscurity. It was the beginning of the history of this temple, the beginning among the Ussul of the belief in God. One sensed, one felt certain that where that tiny light had originated, something living, something kind, something that was striving for illumination, was moving. Then a second, a third, a fourth light was lit, gradually pushing back the darkness. In the half-light which they spread, the being responsible for it became visible. It was a female, the priestess. She was clothed in a white garment and a shining white veil fell from her head to her knees. It enveloped her completely, making a seemingly unfathomable mystery of her. But from this mystery that had become light, there now came a kindly voice:

"Come toward me."

It sounded ghostly in this large space where there was no trace of an echo, this summons apparently meant to be carried into infinite distances. A curious emotion which did not seem to originate within me but somewhere outside overcame me. I felt I was in a sacred place, that ordinary matters could not be discussed here. We walked up to her. She was as tall and her bearing was as proud as Taldsha's. As she raised her veil, however, I saw that she was much older, with the face of a thinker. From the depth of her eyes there shone a benevolence which was not just innate but, more significantly, the fruit of contemplation.

"I salute you," she said. "You are our guest, and since you are here in God's house, you are also mine."

I bowed. I could not help myself. Was this show of respect due to the fact that we were in a temple, or was it simply the effect of her personality, the feeling that I was now standing in the atmosphere her being had created?

"He has just become an Ussul," the sheik's wife announced.

"Then you are doubly welcome," the priestess said, and a fine delicate hand slipped out of her veil and was stretched toward me. I kissed it.

The priestess said:

"Today, my duties are especially burdensome. But the Sahahr took some opium to be able to sleep, and that gave me the time to come here."

She made a circular gesture:

"You are now in the center of our belief, our religion. As you can see, it offers you only a few small, more than modest lights which are vainly trying to penetrate the darkness. That is the beginning. It is the longing to escape darkness, the first step toward God. I called you here to tell you honestly that we are not presumptuous enough to believe that we have attained clarity. But now I also want you to ascend to our heaven. Have you ever seen it?"

"No."

"Will you come with us?"

"Gladly."

"Then you must help me with the lights. We need them to walk up."

She gestured to the servant who had remained by the gate. We heard the noise of a candelabra with many candles in it being lowered. We lit them. When this had been done, we began mounting the stairs. As we climbed, the servant raised the candelabra at exactly our speed so that that section of the stairs on which we found ourselves was always illumined. When we came to the last step below the platform, the priestess had the candelabra lowered again. She said:

"We are surrounded by symbols. From near heaven, our light descends into the depth, just as revelation leaves its home in its effort to reach earth. The closer it comes, the smaller, poorer, and weaker it seems until it finally almost entirely disappears in darkness. Look down!"

The candelabra had reached its lowest point. One could no longer distinguish the individual candles and their glow was barely visible as it formed a small misty area in the general darkness. Looking down created a certain anxiety. The priestess seemed familiar with this feeling, for she said:

"When one looks down there, one may think that God must occasionally fear for the love He sends to earth. Now we shall see our heaven."

We walked up the final step and came to a platform with a railing. There were several seats and the area was covered by a small but adequate roof. We sat down and looked around.

How clear the firmament was and how pure its lights, and this in spite of the fact that we were in a region where damp vapors obstruct the force of the rays. I was looking north, toward Ardistan, and toward Djinnistan above it. The southern cross stood directly behind my head. Above me, to my left, was Centaurus, and further away Libra and Virgo with far-shining Spica. I would have liked to try to identify more stars, and to ask the women for their local names but the priestess called my attention to a point lying far north. Raising her arm toward it, she said:

"Pay attention! It seems to be beginning. I think we came at the right moment."

"What is going to begin?" I asked.

But there was no need for an answer; the sky itself provided it. A rapid, lightning-like glow flashed across it at precisely the point the priestess had indicated. But this glow did not seem to originate above, in the sky, but below, on earth. Some time later, though not at the same place but further toward the right, there was another flash of lightning. Far to the left, there was a second repetition. Then the stars disappeared abruptly. It became dark in the north. For a while, this darkness remained and then slowly sank toward earth. This recurred several times. I was quiet and asked no questions as I tried to remember things I had once learned in school. But I could find no explanation for these phenomena. It was not a northern light. It came from earth and was thrown upward with great force. Perhaps it was—here it came again but not as it had been before. First, it was in the center. It rose, not like lightning but slowly and powerfully. Purple at first, though fiery and shining, it turned blue, dark red, blood-red, glowing red, orange, yellow and finally became a clear pure light radiating toward the sky. It formed a gigantic pillar which shone in all these hues, being purple at the bottom, running through all the colors of the rainbow as it became ever brighter toward the top, flashing like a kind of living, pure crown of flames as if it meant to embrace and pull down the sky. Just as slowly as this pillar had come into being, it disappeared again. But hardly had this occurred and, overwhelmed by the spectacle, we were taking a deep breath, when the identical phenomenon was repeated in identical fashion, first to the right, then to the left of the original location. This fiery pillar consisted of a flood of flames which became purer and purer the higher they rose. Once they had fully developed, they resembled lighthouses burning from their base all the way to their top, or the fervent prayers of men in need of help as they unite in a heaven-storming beacon, being purified in their upward thrust, and immaculate as they reach God. As they surged at one place, they fell at another, growing and blazing now here, now there, as the intervals became shorter and shorter until finally solid, immobile rainbow-colored walls with thousands of flaming torches on their battlements had formed.

I was deeply moved. I had never seen anything remotely resembling this. It was something unknown to physics, not to be found in any book. I did not see or hear but sensed that the women were praying. The day will come when prayers can be felt. The glowing and shining, the flickering and flaming rising to heaven up there in the north was a prayer earth offered, and when the mother prays, all her children tremble with the desire to join her. We were standing on the roof of the temple, an enormous structure where giants gathered to serve God. And yet, this seemingly huge yet pathetically small house was as nothing alongside the sacred dome of the firmament in whose unfathomable depth the heart of the earth was breaking, calling out to the world that even seemingly dead matter, that much misunderstood substance, has strength, life and a soul.

Absorbed in this incomparable spectacle, we sat for a long time. Then I broke the silence:

"An indescribable splendor and magnificence! And it is not fading."

"It will go on all through the night," the priestess answered, "And even all day long though then it will not be visible. You will see it tomorrow, the day after, and again and again until its time is over. It has been announcing itself for several nights and will not disappear until the question it asks has been answered."

"What question?"

"The question whether there is peace on earth. You don't know that question. You probably have never heard the legend of the river that reversed its course—"

"I have. I heard it yesterday," I broke in.

"And also the legend of the opening of paradise, of the throngs of angels on its walls, the archangels before its gates?"

"Yes."

"Know then that the day for these signal events has come. It is not an earthly but a heavenly day, and therefore longer than twenty-four hours. It is beginning today, now, at this very moment. It was announced to earth. A deep, subterranean rolling which can only be heard in the stillness of the night passed through the land. There is lightning in the north, but no thunderstorms or rain. Those are the signs that paradise is about to open. Raise your eyes and look north! What you see is the gate of paradise. You can clearly distinguish its columns, walls, towers, corners, and lines. I do not know whether it will open, for sometimes it becomes visible but remains closed. But in those cases, it soon disappears again. Do you believe what I am telling you?"

"I do believe that natural phenomena have an esemplary quality. But—"

"Be silent! No 'buts' now," she begged me. "You are mentioning natural phenomena. I know what that means. Up there in the north where we see this supernatural illumination, there are rows of powerful volcanoes which once emitted flames every day and are not even extinct now. They awaken at one-hundred-year intervals and for longer and longer periods at a time to show that they have merely fallen asleep but are not dead. When they begin to stir, the earth trembles. The subterranean forces which gather in the course of these hundred years have now become strong enough to free themselves of the pressures holding them down. They rise and break forth, they change into light and pull along everything that obstructs them. 'What of it?' man asks, for his heart is not strong enough to believe that there are connections between things and the creator's plan. 'A perfectly ordinary eruption which was preceded by a minor, barely noticeable earthquake. The flames pouring out of the earth originate in the fire raging in its interior. The various hues, the shadows and lines which can only be seen from a distance are due to the smoke, mud, and dust being pulled upward.' That's what scientists or unbelievers say. We who are not learned and not lost souls know perfectly well that those statements are correct but their correctness is of a coldness which makes us tremble inside. For we know with an even greater certainty that all that is visible serves the creator to reveal the mysteries of that invisible existence whose laws we must take into account in our spiritual life. For the enemy of God, the earth out there has opened up to eject filth and slag with flaming fists. But for us, who pass from what is visible to what is hidden, from what is below to what is above, the gates of paradise will burst open so that in the truth and clarity of its light, the angels may see whether peace has finally come to earth or is unhappily still remote."

I was amazed at what I heard. Where had this woman come into contact with such ideas, such knowledge and views? Was she an Ussul or not? She had risen while she was talking and was now standing at the northern railing of the platform, while I was sitting along its southern side. Her towering white figure before me was bathed in the glow which the high-lying mountain country was sending down to us. Framed by this sacred light, she seemed a being not of this earth but holy, knowing. An indescribable feeling rose from the depth of my soul. It was not love, admiration, respect, or confidence, yet it was all of these, and much more besides. There was also compassion. She turned as if she had felt this thought, and said:

"Effendi, do not be surprised about what I say or the way I speak. My home is Sitara, the land of God's mountains, which you probably do not know. I was not born there, nor were my parents or grandparents. But my ancestors came from there. They were sent into this low-lying, damp Ussul country to instruct these poor people about God, their Lord, and the tasks of mankind. I think Europeans call that missionary work. Sitara is ruled by a woman, and that principle was brought here by my ancestors. The traditions of my native country are passed on as an inheritance from one generation to the next, and always to the oldest daughter. The man she chooses becomes a priest, but the knowledge, the dignity, the capacity are hers. This is how things have been down to the present but unfortunately it can no longer continue."

She had said the final words hesitantly and sat down again as if she had suddenly become tired. Then she went on:

"The descendants of my ancestors have disappeared, have become Ussul, have been absorbed by that people. But that was the purpose of their mission. I also have become an Ussula. But I have preserved what I inherited from them, I guard it as jewels are guarded. God gave me a child, a dear, intelligent, daughter animated by a love of all that is noble. She was to succeed me. I instilled in her spirit and soul all the treasure whose custodian she was destined to become. As she grew older, I bestowed jewel upon jewel on her and it was a delight and joy to me to see that she would surpass in insight, inwardness, and depth all those that had gone before her. Her father, the Sahahr, has never stopped loving and honoring me and was no less happy than I. This child was the object of all his hopes and desires. His belief in God changed. It turned from heaven to earth. His hope for the future of his child became his religion. He was an Ussul, but an Ussul who strove sincerely and nobly. Anyone who stretched out his hand toward his daughter was attacking his faith, and should this daughter die, that faith, his religion, his God would, also. Can you understand that, sahib?"

"Yes," I answered, for now the Sahahr's hatred was no longer a painful mystery to me.

"Then the Djinnistani came," she continued. "Famous as a physician all over the earth as it is known to us, he was a handsome man with a great soul and superior to us all in intelligence, yet at the same time so simple and modest that he won all hearts, including my child's."

She broke off, pointed north, and said:

"Take heed! I think the gate is beginning to move."

And it really was moving, trembling. Like a light approaching from inside and shining through, a bright point was piercing the lower, purple, blue, and dark red sections of the flaming wall. As it penetrated it, a crack developed and extended toward the base. Upon reaching it, it became ever wider and longer, turning into a huge gate between fiery pillars which gave off a purplish, blue, and dark red light and came together at the top in a blood-red, radiant point. Driven by irresistible, elemental powers, a star of the brightest, purest light broke forth from this gate. The moment it had passed it, it widened in all directions so that even we were flooded and illumined by it. The night around us changed to dawn. The firmament seemed to recede and certain figures who were just emerging from the palace and moving toward the square where the monument stood could be seen so clearly that one could distinguish their movements. What an eruption! What an abundance of radiant force and glowing matter was streaming from the interior of the mountains which had to be crossed on the way to Djinnistan! I began to feel fearful and was supporting myself on the railing. But the priestess bent far forward and called out loudly, as if she wanted her voice to carry to the shining gate of paradise:

"The moment has come. The open gate of the lost paradise. If we had immortal eyes, we could see the angelic hosts. And if we had the hearing of immortals, the voice of the commander of these hosts would ring in our ears as the earth reverberates with the question: 'Is there peace on earth?'"

In her enthusiasm, she called out this phrase four times, turning north and south, east and west in succession. "There is no peace yet, but God has promised it. The entire earth asks for it, and therefore it will come," was the answer my conviction prompted me to give with equal enthusiasm. But I restrained myself and remained silent, and that was a good thing. For just as on earth evil forever accompanies good, and there is no light without shadow, so the sublime and the ridiculous are never far apart. The sound of the priestess' voice had barely faded when that of my little Hadji Halef reached us from below where the men were standing in front of the palace gate:

"Not on your life! Drill and exercises start tomorrow. Our plan has been decided on. Can you see me, Sidi?"

"Yes," I answered, utterly dumbfounded.

"I see you, too. Probably better than you can see me. Why is it so bright?"

"The volcanoes are erupting."

"Does that have to be at night? Can't they wait? I have to sleep. This Simmsemm is pressing my eyes shut. The colonel and the two lieutenants are taking me home. Good night, Sidi. Join me soon!"

"Who was this man?" the priestess asked in something close to wrath. For she also felt as if she had been torn from heaven.

Taldsha told her about the little fellow and his accomplishments and the old woman's anger quickly faded. She said:

"There you have the contrast between heaven and earth. But do not worry! The war the Simmsemm decided on today will quickly be ended by you, and a good peace will follow it."

She planted one arm on the railing and looked far out to where her thoughts dwelled.

"I feel that peace must come. Indeed, I am certain of it. I come from Sitara where war is unknown and every word is a word of love and reconciliation. Oh, my country, my splendid, beloved country! I never saw you. But the last glance my ancestors cast on you as they departed they bequeathed as a sacred legacy. From one family to the next, it was passed on to me. I already see you with their eyes but will only see you with my own when I am dead, you country of souls, of love, of—"

"Starflowers," I quickly said.

She abruptly turned to me, raised herself to her full height, and asked:

"How is it you know them, you, a foreigner, a European?"

"From Marah Durimeh."

"Marah Durimeh?" she almost shouted. "Then you know her as well?"

"I know her better than you or Taldsha or anyone here. She is my friend, my counselor, my protectress."

"You have seen her, talked to her—really?"

"Quite often. And in various places. Even in Sitara."

"You were—" She broke off, took my hand, pulled me toward her, looked into my eyes, and went on: "You were in Sitara?"

"Yes."

"Listen, I am going to test you. What you are saying is impossible."

"Go ahead and test me."

"I shall. Listen, and answer me. It is said that there is a forge there, a very curious, famous old forge. It lies in a deep forest. It isn't iron that is forged there, but something altogether different. If you know Marah Durimeh, you cannot but know this forge. It lies in Sitara."

"No, on the border of Sitara, in Mardistan. Only those who have been hardened there may enter Sitara."

"But you said that you had been in that country."

"I have."

"Then you also were in the forge?"

"Yes."

"In the fire, on the anvil, in the vise?"

"I suffered all the tortures that are inflicted there."

She was almost beside herself, breathing deeply and laboriously.

"Then you know the words?" she asked.

"I have known them for a long time."

"Then recite them, at least the beginning!"

I obeyed:

At Märdistan, in the forest of Kulub
hidden in its depth at a secluded place, there lies
the spirits' forge
but not the spirits do the forging, no, they
are being forged.
The storm, at midnight, sweeps them there,
When lightning streaks across the sky, and
floods of tears pour forth
Then hatred thrusts itself on them in fiercest joy.
And envy digs its claws into their flesh.
Repentance sweats and wails at the bellows.
And pain, with staring eyes in its sooty face
stands at the block, a hammer in its hand——

Up to now, the priestess had let me recite but her
excitement made it impossible for her to remain silent.
She interrupted me and continued herself:

Now, now, oh man, the tongues seize hold of you.
You are thrust into the fire: the bellows creak
The tongues of flame shoot up and out through
the roof.
And everything that you are and own,
Your body, spirit, soul, and all your bones,
Your sinews, fibers, flesh and blood,
Your thoughts and feelings, everything,
everything,
Is burned, tormented and tortured
Until they have burned to a white heat—

Now she was interrupted in turn. The mistress of
Ussul went on with the description of what happened
in the spirits' forge:

And now the tongues pull you from the fire,
You are thrown on the anvil, and held fast there.
The blood crackles and bursts in every pore,
Pain begins its work, the smith, the master,
He spits into his fists and stretches out his arms,
And raises the gigantic hammer in both hands
And unfeelingly brings it crashing down on you.
The blows rain down, each one a murder,

A murder committed against you. You think you
are being crushed,
Hot pieces of flesh fly in all directions,
Your self becomes thinner and smaller and smaller
Yet you must go back into the fire—
Again and again, until the smith
Recognizes the spirit that calmly, gratefully
smiles at you
From this hellish torment, from the clouds of
soot and hammer blows.
The smith now fastens the spirit to the
wooden frame, picks up his file
Which screeches, grates, and gnaws and grinds
What still—

"Stop!" the priestess exclaimed. "That is neither
legend nor fairy tale but the truth. That really is the
forge where everyone who wishes to enter Sitara must
be heated, hammered, refined, and forged by pain and
its huge, remorseless apprentices so that, having been
a man of violence, he may be transformed into a man
of grace. Only he who has become one knows what
suffering, torment, and tortures he had to suffer. Yet
all those who live with or near him know nothing of it.
Are you surprised, sahib, that I know that forge?"

"No. Didn't you tell me that your ancestors came
from Sitara? But I would not have thought that
Taldsha knew of it."

"She heard about it from me. I had to tell her about
it, for she cannot experience it. She is one of those
whom God permits to be ennobled by happiness
rather than suffering. But I am asking you now if you
can guess a request I should like to make, and which
deeply concerns me."

"That is very easy."

"Tell me, then."

"You want me to tell you when, where, and how I
came to know Marah Durimeh."

"Yes. Are you willing to tell me?"

"Gladly, if you have the time to listen."

"I do. When the Sahahr has taken opium, he does
not wake up again before early morning. And neither
Taldsha nor I are tired. If we can hear about Marah

Durimeh, night turns into day. And look into the clear, open eyes of this night. It also is not sleeping but awake. Does not everything below, above, and around us call on us to talk of the great, miracle-working mistress of Sitara? Below us, there is the dark space of the Ussul temple which signifies to me the beginning of all paths that lead to God. Above us, the radiant worlds of the stars draw our eyes to show us the direction of those paths. And all around us shines the richly colored mystical light into which the heavy, solid, and rigid earthly envelope dissolves, revealing to us that it once came from on high and must be led back there on a path of transformations and purifications. This light touches us. It creates a sacred disposition and makes us receptive to all messages which come to us from the country of love and kindness. You also are a messenger for us, sahib, and what you will say is sacred. Sit down. Sit down in front of us and speak of her."

I complied. My report of my relationship with Marah Durimeh was not so much an account but rather an answering of the hundreds of questions these two enraptured women asked. We sat for hours in that silent night, on the battlements of the dark temple but in the flaming glow of the light and warmth of the erupting volcanoes.

When the first pale greeting of day merged with their light, the two friends understood that it was necessary to content themselves for now with what they had heard thus far. We left the platform to descend. Although the servant's patience had been put to a severe test, he was still there. He was told to raise the candelabra again. By the light from the candles that had now almost entirely burned down, we left the temple. The women thanked me. The priestess had a special request which was of great importance to her. In the course of our talk, I had alluded to my coming visit to the Erdjani on his Island of the Heathens. She came back to this now, and asked when I would make that visit.

"He asked me to come in the late morning."

"Would you be kind enough to carry a message from me?"

"Gladly."

"He is my grandson, the son of my daughter, and yet I am not permitted to have anything to do with him. But now the Sahahr is so seriously wounded that only the skill of his grandson can preserve him from death. I therefore feel not only entitled but obliged to disregard for once the promise I have given the Sahahr. I ask that you tell my daughter's son that I shall be in the temple at noon to talk to him. And there is one more thing I ask of you, and that concerns the Sahahr. Since he was brought home, strange ideas have taken hold of him. He seems to be fantasizing, and yet he is completely conscious. At first, I thought it was a traumatic fever that was making an early appearance, but his pulse convinced me that this was not the case. I don't know what will come of those ideas. They also involve you. But whatever turn they may take, I ask you to believe me that the Sahahr deserves your respect and is a man who only wants the happiness and well-being of his people. He only hates his grandson because he is the son of the Djinnistani who put an end to the line of priestesses. But he loves him secretly and all the more dearly as the son of his child. It is this inner conflict which makes him hard and cruel in his acts."

"But could your daughter not also have become your successor as the wife of the Djinnistani?" I asked. "After all, he had become an Ussul."

"Only outwardly. His belief differed from ours, and he changed her way of thinking. Had she remained faithful to the belief of her fathers and mothers, she could have become the priestess even as the wife of this man, but it would have been necessary for him to become my husband's successor, and that was something the Djinnistani utterly rejected."

"Was his belief so different from yours?"

"Yes. He never gave verbal expression to it but always professed it in a manner which is more profound and enduring than words. You will discover that for yourself when you go to the Island of the Heathens. Will you grant me my wish concerning the Sahahr?"

"It is already granted. I respect him, and therefore am deeply sorry that his wound will prevent him from presiding over the ceremony admitting us to the Ussul tribe."

Taldsha laughed and said:

"I spared both you and him that sacred ceremony by having you admitted during the banquet. It is valid nonetheless. You are an Ussul now and will remain one in spite of the fact that the ceremony was not a solemn occasion as the Sahahr had conceived of it yesterday."

We accompanied the priestess to her nearby house. I then took Taldsha to the palace and returned to our hut.

10 : The "Leper"

In the morning, I attended to our horses. They had been fed and watered. I led them out of the stable and tethered them to a long thin rope to assure them freedom of movement. The dogs were also let out. Their first greeting was for the Hadji, who seemed to have won their affection. They were male and female, and had very short names, being called Hu and Hi, as the two servants told us.

They accompanied us to the quay and wanted to come into the boat with us but it was too small. I ordered the servants to tether them during our absence but the moment we pushed off, they jumped into the water to follow us. I was about to turn to get them back ashore when I noticed how they swam. Their webbing was so developed and elastic, it looked like light bladders between their toes and displaced so much water that not just their heads but also their backs rose above the surface. Their thick but light, bushy tails functioned like rudders, and their long hair would not let any moisture through. Swimming was no effort but a pleasure for these animals. They barked loudly and chased each other, and I therefore agreed to Halef's request that we take them along.

The banks were studded with houses which not infrequently were built far out into the water and were sometimes entirely surrounded by it. From time to time, the river divided, forming large inhabited islands, and this gave us an opportunity to study the pile dwellings of the Ussul. As we reached the Island of the Heathens, we saw a very simple raft which had clearly just been made. We landed and tied the canoe to a stake. The island was quite large and at first glance we saw nothing but uncut, neglected bushes and grass, for no one had taken care of this property in the owner's absence. We followed a trail, leading first through tall grass, which then continued under trees obviously planted by someone for their esthetic effect. Under tall limes with gigantic leaves there lay a low but handsomely conceived and constructed cottage. It was made of wood which had been lying in marshy water for centuries and become hard and heavy like stone. It had been used not only for the pillars and beams but also the smaller parts and even the ornamentation. The Djinnistani had done an enormous amount of work here. He had loved the Sahahr's daughter so much that only the handsomest and most salubrious house I had seen anywhere in the country had been good enough for her.

The door was closed and the blinds were down. I saw no one. I called, but received no answer. Tracks led into the house but not out again. We went further, past some blooming and fragrant clusters of bushes, and saw the pond of which I had heard. We were delighted with what we saw.

We were standing at the southern shore of the lake which was almost entirely covered by lotus blossoms. Between them, we saw other flowers of miraculous color whose names I did not know.

To the right and the left, groups and clusters of trees and shrubs had been planted close to the shore. They functioned like stage sets and compelled one to look straight ahead at a structure about two meters in width and more than four meters high, of white marble, which was covered with shining inscriptions of a deep black on all four sides. It was surrounded by a number of smaller pillars which also bore inscriptions. We read them. The quotations on the pillars came from the four Vedas, the Zend Avesta, the five ching of the Chinese, the Bible and the Koran, but those on the larger structure seemed to have been taken from elsewhere. As we looked at them, we first noticed four headings constituting two corresponding pairs. Toward the south, we read CREATION; toward the north, SALVATION. Toward the east it was SIN, and toward the west, PUNISHMENT. Under the heading CREATION, we saw the following lines:

> No soul ever came to earth
> Unless it was first spirit in heaven.

On the north side, there were these lines under the heading SALVATION:

> No spirit ever rose to heaven
> Unless it was first a soul on earth.

SIN had this mysterious pronouncement below it:

> Only a single one refused to become a soul.

And facing it, on the west side, we read under PUNISHMENT:

> Therefore he cannot return to heaven.
> That is the devil.

I must admit that I was amazed, but not because I saw anything extraordinary about the monument or its inscriptions. The Djinnistani had brought these marble slabs back from his travels piece by piece and put them together here. But that these four verses, each of which seemed to convey an altogether insoluble problem, all said what our Christian revelation tells anyone who will listen when they were taken in conjunction made me wonder if the Djinnistani had understood their real meaning when he had placed them here.

Beyond the pond was the grave of the Erdjani's mother and from it, a wide, perfectly straight strip of meadow led down to the river. It was bordered by dense, dark green. The opposite bank had no houses on it. All one saw were gardens and fields and then a wide, long tract of low, newly grown shrubs where the Ussul had cleared away the trees for use as timber. It was an extraordinary perspective that opened up before us. Directly at our feet was the transparent but brown and musty-smelling water from whose processes of decay and disintegration the lotus flowers received their live and brilliant colors. At the far shore, and framed by aromatic flowers, stood the grave of the deceased human lotus blossom and behind it, the dark water of the river and that narrowing strip of new shrubs bordered by woods. Beyond the woods lay the alluvial land of the Ussul, stretching across both lower and upper Ardistan and all the way up to those high mountains which were even at this moment giving off flames suggesting an open paradise. We could not see that because the morning mist of the lowlands still enveloped us.

While this sight not only riveted our eyes but our thoughts, we heard a noise behind us. As we turned, we saw the monument open and the Erdjani emerge from it.

"Mashallah!" Halef exclaimed. "This is one of Allah's miracles. The monument is hollow."

I also was surprised. The work of art was not solid, nor did it consist of cubes as I had thought, but was made of strong, firmly joined slabs between which some stairs led below ground. Some of these slabs functioned as a door which could be opened from either side though someone standing in front of the monument would not have noticed the mechanism.

The Erdjani was dressed as on the previous day. He wanted to greet us but the dogs prevented him. Their joy at once again seeing the man they had been trained to tear to pieces was touching. They jumped up at him, anxious for his caresses.

"What has become of the hatred men forced on them?" he asked. "It has turned into love. I greet you and thank you for having come."

He bowed. I offered my hand but he did not take it. Instead, he stroked the dogs.

"Do you realize the danger you are exposing yourself to, sahib?" he asked.

"I don't think there is any, and I feel it is my obligation to combat that error. Give me your hand, and do so also in the future and in the presence of others."

As he shook and pressed my hand, he said:

"This is deliverance, truly, and I shall not forget it."

It goes without saying that he also shook hands with Halef. Then I conveyed the priestess' message.

"She is asking me to come precisely at noon. To the temple?" he asked thoughtfully. "Then you talked to her?"

"Yes."

"Briefly, or at some length?"

"Almost all night. After the banquet, we walked to the top of the temple to observe the eruption of the volcanoes. We did not separate until dawn. The sheik's wife was also there."

"Then you know a great deal, and I—"

"We spoke mostly about Marah Durimeh," I interrupted him to prevent any misunderstandings on his part.

"Marah Durimeh?" he exclaimed. "The ruler of Sitara? Why did the sheik's wife and the priestess talk to you about this mysterious woman?"

"Because they heard that I am a friend of hers, and that I was her guest a short time ago, in Sitara. I stayed at her castle in Ikbal."

He stepped back and looked at me with the greatest amazement. But gradually this yielded to an expression of considerable satisfaction. His eyes began to sparkle, his voice sounded almost exultant.

"What a joy, what happiness! How is it possible? Yesterday, I immediately recognized you for a man sent by God. Yet I did not feel that you could only have come from Sitara, and from nowhere else. Now that I hear this, I am delighted that those two women spoke of me. You know all about me; there is no need to repeat. I also know about you, not in detail, but certain things which are quite important. Nothing about you personally or your circumstances, but that you came here on your journey to Djinnistan. I am asking you to be frank and to answer a question which my father and mother left me."

"What is it?"

"Do you carry a breastplate which Marah Durimeh gave you?"

"Yes," I answered, feeling that it was my duty to be open.

"What metal is it made of, gold, silver, copper, or bronze?"

"None of those. I don't know what it is, however."

"That's right. Wait!"

He said that in a tone of the greatest joy and delight, hurried down the steps of the monument, and disappeared.

"Sidi, isn't that marvellous?" Halef asked. "Doesn't that sound as if our arrival had been prepared?"

"Nothing is marvellous," I answered, "at least not here, in this country. I am convinced that we will experience other things that will seem ten or twenty times more marvellous to you than this unexpected question about my shield or this marble monument which opens to let people emerge from the earth."

"He said that the question came from his father and mother. That means that they already knew we would come here."

"We? Certainly not. They knew that someone would come from Sitara and that he would have a breastplate given him by Marah Durimeh. That it would be I only became known later."

"He is coming back. What will he bring with him?"

The Erdjani returned, holding a rather large leather case in his hand. He opened it and showed us what was inside.

"That is your shield, Sidi," Halef exclaimed. "Precisely the same. It's of the same metal and shape."

He was right. The leather case contained a precise duplicate of my shield. I pulled mine out from under my vest to show that both were alike. There wasn't the slightest difference between them.

"It is as I thought," the Erdjani exulted. "Walk on ahead until you see light. I shall follow the moment I have locked the door."

He was pointing toward the steps. I tied the dogs to two pillars and told them to wait for me. They understood, and lay down. Then Halef and I descended the steps. I forgot to count them but there were certainly more than ten, for the subterranean room to which they led had a ceiling of earth that was at least six feet high. The Erdjani, who was considerably taller than I, could move about without having to stoop. We first came into a small, square room which was formed by the base of the marble pillar. Some baskets and chests were standing about, but that was all I could make out. A narrow, straight corridor led on from there. It was dark but we could see light at its end. As we went toward it, we first came into a small and then a considerably larger room and then again into a small one, all three being brightly lit by burning sesame oil lamps. It was immediately apparent that the smaller two served as storage areas while the larger room resembled a scholar's study. I saw books, maps, plans, writing utensils, and all manner of implements, some of them unfamiliar, many medical and other instruments, and even Oriental and European weapons. The latter were only a double-barrelled rifle and two revolvers but, although not of modern design, well made and, given local conditions, good enough to assure anyone who knew how to use them a considerable advantage. Where did all these things come from? I need hardly say that I was quite astonished.

When the Erdjani joined us, he said:

"Don't be surprised at these mysterious rooms, or my willingness to show them to you. My father instructed me to act in precisely this way, but I do not know why or for what purpose. He disappeared; allegedly, he was murdered, but I don't believe it. He was not the sort of person that can be stalked, taken unawares, and murdered. Then my mother died, presumably from grief. I don't believe that, either. She never said that she had lost him. I know for certain that she was convinced she would see him again. She merely grieved over the hatred of her father and the separation from her mother. When, shortly before her death, I left her for a week to visit an Ussul relation, she once again impressed upon me all my father's instructions referring to these two breastplates, and was so emphatic that she must have known what would happen. She died shortly after I left and was already buried when I returned. As of today, it is my duty to wear this shield, as you must wear yours."

He hung it around his neck and I noticed that he was carrying a book on his chest, as I had been told.

He explained:

"My father wrote some books for me which are my guides. I cannot bear being separated from them and always carry one on my heart. A sublime, noble, and farseeing mind lives in them and I often visit him to kneel humbly at his feet and listen to his words."

He put some surgical instruments and a package of bandages into his pockets, gave each of us a light, extinguished the lamps, and asked us to follow him. He led us through a similar but longer corridor to a second chamber where he stopped only briefly to take a small object from a cupboard. All of these corridors and rooms were constructed of the petrified wood I mentioned before, and therefore free of all dampness. The object he had taken was a container of cut glass, from which he let a single drop fall into a tiny bottle and then closed it again. Although the vial had been open for only a moment, an indescribably fine, vivifying scent began pervading the air. It was unknown to me, and I felt certain that no register would contain its name. And yet I had the feeling that I had scented it before, and perhaps often, but from an enormous distance. Halef took a deep breath, made an enthusiastic face, and called out:

"What a fragrance! A little more, and I will turn into a poet and have visions. What is it called?"

"Don't you know?" the Erdjani asked as he carefully wrapped the small bottle and put it into his pocket.

"No," the Hadji insisted.

"But you have often smelled it," the Erdjani said.

"Impossible."

"But it stinks. You held your nose."

"No. Tell me its name."

"Very well, but don't be frightened. It is death."

"Death?" Halef asked, and said nothing more. I also remained silent.

"Yes, death," the son of the Djinnistani went on. "Look at the country we live in. What is there except rot, decay, putrefaction, mildew, and stench? And what do you find other than life, beauty, strength, immortality, and fragrance? Today, I say: Life has a fragrance, but death stinks. And tomorrow I'll say: Death has a fragrance, but life stinks. Which of the two is correct? Both! Life and death are one. Life is a continuous dying. And it is impossible to die without life being renewed in the process. Remember, Hadji Halef Omar, that you do not die of your last, but of your first breath. You live by constantly decaying. You must turn the stench of that decay into fragrance, just as happened in that vial and this tiny bottle. If you do that, you are the master over life and death, just as I will be holding both in my hand when I open this bottle at the Sahahr's bedside to kill him for a short time, to anesthetize him to the pain of life. Come along."

The corridor we now followed was even longer and again widened into a small room similar to the one lying under the monument. Here also there were steps. The Erdjani went up first. At the top, he raised the hand holding the light and pushed a trapdoor with the other. We found ourselves in a remote corner of the cottage. When he had opened the blinds, I looked at the trapdoor. It consisted of two layers of beams of petrified wood and had been made so solid and thick that even if one walked over it, no echo would reveal the hollow space below. It must easily have weighed more than a hundred pounds, but the Erdjani had raised it with one hand, and effortlessly. That was the reason I had examined it. I felt almost ashamed of always having considered myself strong.

When he had lowered the door, he also closed the windows and led the way out into the open where we had stood earlier when we had called his name. He locked the house with a key which looked very much like those temple keys of antiquity, of which only a small number have been found. Their shape is known only from their depiction on ancient containers.

We now returned to the marble pillar to untie the dogs. They had been lying quietly and had behaved well. As we walked around the pond and toward the grave, the Erdjani explained the reasons for his actions that day:

"The subterranean chambers you saw were built by my father in utmost secrecy. No one knows of them, and no one knows the things that are kept on this island. Even today, I am not quite clear about his reasons for doing all this but they were certainly commendable. His knowledge made him the superior of any Ussul, including the sorcerer, and he cannot have intended to place tools at their disposal which might become dangerous to them. There is an advantage in being able to get from the house to the monument without being seen. My father could hear everything that was said there. Particularly during sieges when the Tshoban surrounded the house, it was advantageous to be able to leave it at any time. Many of the things there, such as the rifle, the revolvers, and a good deal of ammunition were intended for me, although at that time I was still a boy. That was to be the equipment for the task he passed on to me."

"May I ask what that task is?"

"You may. You are entitled to know, for you will probably be my companion. Both you and I want to journey to the Mir of Djinnistan. I will not ask you for your reasons, for you stand far above me and owe me no explanations. And I know you will tell me of your own accord when the time has come. But as regards myself, I shall tell you frankly if under the seal of secrecy that the time of my departure for Djinnistan has been fixed precisely. The moment I hear that the Mir of Ardistan is preparing war against the Mir of Djinnistan, I only have to wait for a stranger who has the same breastplate as I. I will ride with this stranger; he will be my friend and protector whom I should obey, although I may also refuse, if I so choose. But if I do resist, I will suffer and a heavy penance will be imposed on me."

"Do you know Ardistan?"

"I have never been there, but I have very detailed maps and plans which could not be found anywhere else, not even in that country. They come from Djinnistan."

"I am delighted to hear this. Do these maps show all the five countries that make up Ardistan?"

"Yes, and not only those. I also have one of the

country of the Ussul and one of the country of the Tshoban which both are not really part of Ardistan but merely have to pay tribute to it. Ardistan consists of Ardistan proper with the capital of Ard which once lay on the river Ssul, the one that reversed its course. In the north lies Shimalistan, in the east Sharkistan, in the west Gharbistan, and in the south Djunubistan which is closest to us, for it borders on the country of the Tshoban. Would you like to see the maps?"

"Of course."

"Then wait. I shall go get them. You may take them with you and study them but you must not show them to anyone."

He left and soon returned with the maps. Although I only had time for a quick glance, I could tell that they were masterpieces. The map of Ussul country showed every canal, even the smallest and least significant.

"There are probably other things I should tell you," the Erdjani continued. "You came sooner than I expected. It is almost a miracle that my father's prophecy should have been fulfilled so promptly. No sooner had I heard that Ardistan is preparing to attack Djinnistan than the stranger with the shield appeared. I must collect myself and try to recall everything I have been told about our journey to Djinnistan. It is impossible to remember everything at once."

"Did you mention your shield to anyone?"

"No."

"Not even to your grandfather or grandmother?"

"Not with a single word. You know the Sahahr, my grandfather?"

"Of course. Wasn't your mother his daughter?"

"Yes, he was my mother's father, but that's all. No fibre of my body, no breath of my soul, no movement of my mind comes from him. The two of us have nothing in common. It is not the fact that we are related but only love that could bring us together. But there is none."

"And yet they say that while he persecutes you, he secretly loves you."

"Perhaps. But that love does not exist for me. He never gave me any reason to suspect its existence. All I saw was hatred. And what about my grandmother, you will ask. I love her, but she only greets me from a distance, and doesn't even mention that to him."

As we were talking, we had been slowly walking back and forth near the grave. Now he stopped in front of the mound, and went on:

"The Sahahr is in danger of dying, and now she calls me and begs me to save him. I will. I do not wish her to be lonely, as I am. But I obey her wish without benevolence, without love, without joy. I am only body and mind. My soul has died, it was buried here in this swamp, in this dampness and putrefaction."

He folded his arms over his chest, looked at the grave as if he wished to see through it, lowered his head, and said:

"I ask that you not smile about what I will confess to you. Whenever I stand here, I feel as if my eyes had the power to penetrate the earth and the coffin, and when I look inside it, it is always empty. Isn't that madness? It has been tormenting me for years, and still does. Now, at this moment where I am mentioning it to you, the feeling is so strong and distinct that I have to restrain myself not to scrape the earth with my hands to prove to you that the coffin is empty."

"But that would be a terrible deception."

"Yes, it would. I feel like scraping and scraping to uncover this deception and to throw the boards of the empty coffin into the faces of my mother's parents. But that would be something so monstrous that the mere idea frightens me. And, of course, I ask myself where my mother could be, if not here? Besides, I loved and still love her too much to commit the sin of opening and desecrating her grave."

At that moment, we heard a strong, deep, drawn-out sound. It was almost like a horn, and came from the river. More of the same timbre followed but their pitch was higher and lower than the first. It seemed to be a signal or a fanfare.

"That is the signal of the Hukara," the Erdjani said. "I informed them yesterday that you would be here at this hour. They have deliberated and are now coming to tell me their decision."

"Who and what are these Hukara?" I asked.

"They are the slighted, the despised," he answered. "Sahib, you will discover now that I am not the foolish, indolent boy I must appear. My imprisonment was not wholly involuntary. It aroused indignation, and I knew and wanted that. All those who consider our cowardice toward the Tshoban a disgrace are Hukara. They protest loudly and as often as they can about the way things have been done heretofore. They chose me as their leader, and that prompted the Sahahr to proclaim once again that I was mad and a moral leper, and to have me put behind the thorn hedges. Because I, their leader, was persecuted and despised, they were relegated to the same status and called Hukara. That merely amused them. Then it was learned that the Tshoban were again planning an invasion, and that the two strangers who had captured the firstborn of the Tshoban would arrive. It was said that you had performed superhuman and heroic acts, and everyone believed this. Yesterday, you came yourself, and your very first act was consonant with those reports. You rescued me and I told the Hukara that our time had come. I spoke to their leaders. They had heard that you had offered to capture the Tshoban in the Chatar defile without shedding a drop of blood. Immediately, messengers were sent out and a council was held this morning. They are coming here now to tell me what they decided. Permit me to go and receive them. I shall be back soon."

The Erdjani left. While he was gone, I looked at the map of the country of the Ussul. I was particularly anxious to study the region around the Chatar defile. It was clearly marked. As I looked at it and reflected about it, I thought of the palace at Ikbal and the ship "Wilahde" where I had studied this defile and the surrounding terrain with considerable interest. It is true that I had forgotten the notes on board ship, but now I remembered what they had said. I saw them as clearly before my mind's eye as if I had just finished my studies and not yet taken down anything. As if to confirm that this clear and detailed recollection had come at precisely the right moment, the Erdjani also returned, and said:

"Sahib, this is an hour of enormous import. A complete transformation seems under way. Tell me frankly whether it is really possible to defeat the Tshoban at the defile without losing even one of our men."

I had sat down, but quickly got up again when he asked this question. Its significance seemed to descend almost palpably on my shoulders. The young, noble Ussul also was serious, but it was a joyful, enraptured seriousness that sounded in his voice, and my answer was confident:

"Yes, it is possible. But first certain conditions have to be met."

"Tell me what they are."

"To begin with, there must be no more than four times as many Tshoban as—"

"What are you saying?" he interrupted. "We need not be numerically superior, and can still be victorious?"

"Yes, we only have to be one-fourth their strength. I also demand unquestioning obedience to our leaders."

"Of course. You will be the leader."

"No."

"Who else?"

"You."

"I?"

"Of course. You are the man in charge. We will be your advisors, your friends, that's all."

"How is that possible?" he exclaimed. "No one like you has ever been here before. Come with me to my Hukara. They must see and hear you. But there is one thing you should know about these splendid people before I take you to them. The Ussul have a law according to which people guilty of certain crimes are not allowed to wear a beard. I was punished in that way. And just think, sahib: A moment ago, when I went to see them, all of them had cut off their beards. That is a more eloquent gesture than long speeches. I shall never forget this demonstration of their love and loyalty. Let's go now."

He took me to the open area in front of his house where I saw a densely packed crowd of three or four hundred men. More were still arriving. They were all tall, broad shouldered, impressive men, dressed with extreme simplicity and armed only with long knives, spears, and bows. The number of rifles I saw was negligible. I was jubilant. Almost anything could be accomplished with such men, such muscles, such strength. Their faces were weatherbeaten, honest and open, with keen eyes. And these were supposed to be despised outcasts. I saw that the Erdjani had been right. While all of them wore their hair long, not one of them was bearded. One could tell that they all had shaved that morning, and their broad, somewhat blunt-nosed Ussul faces shone with satisfaction about this show of solidarity and the pleasure at seeing the two protectors of their leader.

The Erdjani asked me to address them. I told them how I conceived of the impending battle with the Tshoban, pointing out that it would not be a battle at all but the perfectly easy and wholly safe setting of a trap. I cautioned them that this briefing was not to be discussed with anyone, not even their friends and relatives, for a single word might suffice to foil the plan. I said that this short battle would usher in a long peace, that a lasting advantage was to be derived from a quick, lightning-like victory. It was essential to impress the Tshoban for once, to show them that the Ussul were at the very least a match for them so that they would put an end to hostilities and conclude an alliance which would lend both tribes the strength to free themselves of the chains of the Mir of Ardistan.

As I expressed these ideas, they cheered loudly. That the Mir of Ardistan had a bodyguard of Ussul, and that the two sons of the sheik had to live at his court, was something they did not judge an honor but a disgrace. They had long felt it to be their duty to shake off this yoke but had not known how. For that reason, they consented to my proposal to bring about a peaceful alliance with the Tshoban, though this would have to be imposed by force of arms, and declared their wholehearted dedication to that end. They asked if I would agree to go with them to the defile, and whether I would lend them the articulate sheik of the Haddedihn for a few hours so that they might take him to their assembly area where he could drill them. When I agreed, they gathered around the little Hadji and his two dogs and marched off to the bank, where they got into their boats and rafts and left. With the dogs at his side, Halef stood on one of the larger rafts and waved to us. He felt important, and that was always a source of satisfaction to him.

My stay on the Island of the Heathens had thus come to an end. It had brought an unforeseen decision and was to have further consequences, though I was not aware of them at that time. The Erdjani also had to leave, for the time of his meeting with the priestess was approaching. We left the island separately, he on his small raft, I in the canoe. As we passed one of the islands in the river, we heard loud smacks and the whistling whine of dogs being punished by a whipping.

"Those are Aacht and Uucht," the Erdjani said.

"Those two noble animals?" I asked as I pulled in the paddles.

"Yes. They are being trained. They don't seem to want to obey, and therefore they are being whipped."

"I don't want their trainer to do that," I exclaimed angrily and turned toward the bank. The Erdjani followed.

The small island served as a kind of kennel for the two dogs. An impenetrable, high wall of live thorns surrounded it to prevent their escape. There was a narrow gate which stood open. After we had passed through it, we found ourselves on a grassy area where two strong poles had been rammed into the ground. The dogs were hanging on these two poles, their heads firmly tied to the ground as in certain regions of the world big oxen are still tied for slaughter. The heaviest slab of a stone floor has an iron ring in its center. The rope on which the animal hangs is pulled through that ring so that its head rests firmly against the slab below. With a dull roar and fear in its eyes, the animal squints up at the butcher as he raises his axe to give it the lethal blow on the forehead. But he does not always kill the animal with the first strike, and it is horrible to have to see and hear an ox, maddened by pain and with the strength that only the fear of death can instill, tear the heavy slab from the floor and yet be unable to get away because a stone weighing hundreds of pounds smashes its legs. The ox roars, the butcher roars like the ox, and keeps slashing away at the pitiful victim until it collapses in a sea of blood.

This is precisely the way the dogs were tied here, their heads hanging down so that they could not defend themselves. In addition, the trainer had stuck their snouts into muzzles so that they could neither bark nor bite but merely whine. He was beating them mercilessly with a whip. I jumped at him, pulled him back, and asked angrily:

"Why are you beating my dogs? Who gave you that permission?"

"Your dogs?" he asked in surprise. He was considerably taller, broader in the shoulders, and stronger than I, and his face was so bearded that one could just see his eyes and the tip of his nose.

"Yes, they belong to me," I answered.

"That isn't true. They are now the property of the sheik and his wife. They are being set aside for a stranger who is wearing a breastplate, and I am their real master. I punish them if they refuse to learn, and no one is allowed to interfere, not even you. I'll soon show you."

He raised his whip again and hit both dogs twice. He was about to deal them another blow when I tore the whip from his hand and quickly lashed him a few times. For a moment, his pain and fear made him forget to defend himself, but then he stretched out his huge fists to seize me. Before he could lay a hand on me, I gave him such a push in the armpit that he was raised into the air and hurled on the ground. He picked himself up, shouted with fury, and was about to throw himself at me. But just as he got ready to jump he stopped, because now the Erdjani stretched out his arm to keep him away from me. The moment the man saw his new adversary, he turned, shouting, "The Djirbani, the leper, run, run," and dashed through the narrow opening.

I untied the two animals and freed them of the constricting muzzle. In their joy, they jumped up, chased three or four times around the grass, came back to me, lay down, and licked my hand. I was their savior and they looked at me with their large, beautiful eyes to ask for permission to show their gratitude.

They got up on their hind legs and I pressed them toward me. They were very beautiful, of great nobility and strength. One might almost have called them royal animals.

"These splendid offspring of the dogs of Djinnistan are even better at finding water than the most famous and best dogs bred by the Ussul," the Erdjani said.

"Finding water?" I asked. "That's something I have never heard of."

"We are accustomed to the constant and considerable dampness of this country, so the dry deserts beyond our borders seem unbearable to us. We cannot stand thirst. As soon as we cross into that region, we are afraid we won't find water, and our horses and dogs feel the same way. But the dogs' noses are fine enough to find even minimal traces of moisture. Where they scrap the earth, one may be certain of finding water at some depth."

"Then there is water in those dried-out areas?"

"Yes, but quite far down. And who has the tools to dig for it? And even if one did, one would die of thirst before getting to it. And yet there have been cases where dogs saved their masters from dying of thirst. So there must be spots where the water rises close to the surface. Once every year, my father travelled to Djinnistan. He never set out without taking a dependable dog along, and marked all the places where he found moisture with the help of these animals. But Aacht and Uucht have the finest noses and are the most dependable of them all. That has been tested. What is more important, they can put up with thirst easily, but that is not true of the rest."

"Do you still have those notes your father made?"

"Yes. They are in a small book crammed with descriptions of all the places he passed between here and Djinnistan."

"That will be of considerable value to us. Be sure you take it with you."

"I shall. There are any number of things I must not forget."

"How well do Aacht and Uucht swim?"

"Like otters, even better than Halef's Hu and Hi.

Why don't you take them with you now? They will swim as fast as we can paddle."

We went back to the river and the dogs followed without hesitation. As we got into the canoe, they jumped into the water, barking joyously, as if it were a settled matter that they now belonged to me. One to the left, the other to the right, they continued swimming alongside the boat, keeping level with it at any speed I set. And from that moment on, that is what they have always done. They have always been at my side, the brother on the right, the sister on the left, as if it had to be that way. At the wharf, I got out and the dogs followed me here as well. They did not make the slightest attempt to stay with the Erdjani who went on somewhere behind the palace to avoid being seen. When we separated, it was exactly noon.

Since there was nothing for me to do, I decided to sleep until dinner to make up for what I had missed during the night. Aacht and Uucht shook the water from their fur and followed me into the house. They flanked me again after I lay down. I quickly fell asleep but woke up again shortly before two. I turned the dogs over to the servants and ordered them to feed them well. Then I went to the palace to dine.

11 : Portents

There were more guests than on the previous day. The elders of the tribe and all persons of some standing had been invited. I again sat between the sheik and his wife. There was a good deal of animation. Neither Halef nor any of the officers with whom he had been planning the campaign were there. I heard that the officers were still sleeping. The Simmsemm had shown what it could do the previous evening, and did so again today. People were growing cheerful. But then something happened that quickly turned the high spirits into seriousness. Ten giants, armed with spears, bows, and long knives entered and announced that they were the officers of five hundred Hukara and had been authorized to speak to the sheik and the elders. Their leader was huge and also, as I discovered later, a man of considerably higher intelligence than the ordinary Ussul. His name was Irahd and he was one of the wealthiest men in the city. He was the skillful and energetic spokesman for the group.

He described the traditional cowardice of the Ussul and emphasized that this deprived them of the justification for looking down on the Hukara, who were courageous warriors. This would have to change, and to change immediately. The Hukara had therefore decided on an expedition to the Chatar defile to give the Tshoban the reception they deserved. Their leader would be the Erdjani who was now in the assembly area to train his five hundred men. Hadji Halef Omar, the famous sheik of the Haddedihn, was assisting him. They would dispense with the help of the old and invalid veterans. To play at war with such men would be childish and would lead nowhere. Ten healthy and strong Hukara could accomplish more than a large band of these old men who had worn themselves out in the service of the Mir of Ardistan. The Hukara were determined to take on the enemy by themselves and to act without help from anyone. But there were certain conditions which had to be agreed upon if victory was to be achieved, and this should be done immediately in a council with the elders. Not a minute was to be lost in this highly important matter.

Not only the sheik but the rest of those present were surprised by this turn of events. While the Hukara had been threatening for a long time to take matters into their own hands, no one had expected that they actually would. Now they were here, energetic and in a hurry. The elders were clearly at a loss.

Everyone was looking at the sheik who, not being a self-reliant person, was turning to his wife as he always did. He spoke softly, but because I was sitting between them, I could hear their exchange.

"What do you say to this?" he asked. "We have been taken by surprise. I don't know what to tell them. But I think it would be a sign of weakness if I gave in to their demands."

"On the contrary, it would be a sign of strength. You have to grant their wish," she answered.

"But they are impure, despised, beneath us. They are rabble."

"Precisely for that reason."

"Why? And who is going to be in command? The madman, the leper! What a disgrace for us! We will become an object of ridicule for having entrusted our honor to an ignoble lunatic."

"Precisely for that reason," she repeated.

"I don't understand. What do you mean?"

Being an intelligent woman, she knew how to deal with her husband and did not make a long speech: "Precisely because neither the Hukara nor the Erdjani are any good, you have to do what they want. Send them against the enemy, and you'll be rid of them."

This had not occurred to the sheik. He looked at her admiringly, and said:

"How intelligent you are! And how right! It's so simple. We grant their request and we'll be rid of them for good. That's exactly what we will do."

He now turned to the leader of the Hukara and told him that nothing stood in the way of a council. They would finish their meal quickly and begin immediately afterwards. The ten Hukara sat down to wait.

"Sidi, did you know that your Halef is drilling the Hukara?" Taldsha asked me.

"No. I only know that they took him along. But you can be sure that what he is doing is not directed against you."

"I know that. I am going to leave when the council begins."

"So will I."

"Then let's stay together, if you like. I should enjoy seeing the exercises. Will you accompany me?"

"Gladly."

"But let's ride your horses, not mine. Or did Halef take his horse with him?"

"No."

"Is it strong enough to carry me?"

"Certainly. Ben Rih is not as strong as your marvellous Smikh, but certainly strong enough for even the heaviest Ussul."

"And may I take my dogs?"

"Which ones?"

"Aacht and Uucht. I mentioned them to you. I should like to find out if they or your horses are faster and have more endurance. You have never seen them; I will show them to you."

"Yes, do take them," I said, but did not mention that they were already at my house.

"But first, I want to find out how the Sahahr is getting on. So I shall leave before you."

At home, I saw a touching picture. Syrr, my magnificent black stallion, had lain down. Aacht and Uucht were lying near him, licking him eagerly as if they were performing this service to earn their keep. It was obvious that the horse was pleased with this show of affection. Why was it that I found the dogs with Syrr rather than with Ben Rih? It was as if they knew that they belonged to him and to me rather than to Rih and Halef. As I caressed them, I felt and heard quite clearly the countless tiny electric sparks passing from their fur to my hand. This also happened when I stroked Syrr, and was probably what constituted the bond between them.

I saddled the horses. When the sheik's wife arrived, she was surprised to see the dogs. She had wanted to ride with me to the opposite bank and call them from there. She approved my having taken them along, but expressed her regret that I could only keep them for the time being since they were meant for the mysterious stranger. We mounted and set out to circle the entire city.

We also went around the two large lakes to the east and the west of Ussula. All who saw us saluted us in a way which made it clear that my companion was loved and respected. She had heard about the incomparable horses of the Arabs and their phenomenal speed, had always wanted to see such a horse, and was happy now that her wish was being fulfilled. Whenever the terrain permitted, we let the stallions run as fast as they wanted to, and Taldsha confessed to me that she had not believed such speed possible. She herself became winded, but not the horses. Ben Rih, who was used to the small and skinny Hadji and had to carry more than twice his normal burden, held up splendidly, never lagged behind my Syrr and did not foam at the mouth or show any fatigue from his heavier rider. All I can say about the dogs is that I could not stop admiring them. Their power and elegance, their endurance and suppleness were extraordinary. Nor did they gasp or pant, huff or puff when we halted. Their hearts beat calmly and their lungs worked as evenly as if we had merely been going for a quiet walk. These magnificent animals would be invaluable on our journey to Djinnistan. To test her reaction, I expressed this idea. Taldsha looked at me in surprise, and asked:

"Then there is more involved than just the battle at the Chatar defile?"

"Yes."

"And you intend to take these dogs along?"

"Yes."

"Then you still don't understand me. Didn't I tell you that a stranger will come—"

I quickly interrupted her:

"Who only has to show you this, and you will give him the dogs the Mir of Djinnistan expressly set aside for him."

As I said this, I opened my upper garment and showed her the breastplate. She stopped, threw up her arms, and exclaimed:

"Thank God! Once again, belief has conquered doubt. Marah Durimeh keeps the word she gave us. How blind I have been! It should have occurred to us that you were the stranger we have been waiting for. I was rather chagrined, since I would not willingly give these dogs to anyone but you, and yet I was to keep them for someone else. Now it turns out that you are that 'someone else.' You can't imagine how pleased I am."

She was very quiet as we rode on, and only after some time did she express her thoughts.

"If you promise me to keep it, I will tell you a secret. Don't be alarmed about what I am going to say. Did you see the grave of the Erdjani's mother?"

"Yes."

"I want you to know that it is empty."

I was dumbfounded, but said nothing and merely looked at her silently.

"You are startled," she said.

"Not startled," I answered, "only amazed that his intuition is correct."

"What do you mean? Does he suspect it?"

"Yes. He does not believe that his mother died. There are moments, he told me, when he feels like scraping away the earth to prove that the coffin is empty."

"It is not empty. Instead of the body, it contains a well-preserved document which reports everything that happened at that time. The son had left on a journey to distant relatives. So his mother, whom all of us thought of as a widow, was alone. You know that she lived on the Island of the Heathens. One evening, her husband, the Djinnistani, appeared. No one saw him. We had believed him dead. Instead, he was living in Djinnistan and had come to take her there. But only his wife, not the boy. He would have to stay behind. And yet it is true that both loved him as only a father and a mother can. Do you understand, Sidi?"

"Perfectly. There are higher considerations which one must obey. And these considerations had prevented the Djinnistani from returning before that time, or from sending news. And on that evening, they prohibited his taking his son along or even letting him know that his father had been there to get his mother. She came to you to tell you all this, to say farewell, and to ask you to take care of her son. Before that, she had seen her parents. The Sahahr had parted from her in anger. He drove her away because he was not sufficiently developed spiritually to understand the reasons for her action. But her mother understood her, and even gave her her blessing and left her with the hope of a happy reunion."

Taldsha reined up.

"How do you know all this?" she asked. "And in such detail? It's impossible for you to know, and yet you do! It's a miracle."

"Oh, no! It is perfectly natural. That's the only way one can reconstruct what happened because it is the simplest explanation. After she had left, the Sahahr felt it was impossible to admit publicly that his daughter, the future Ussul priestess, had left her country and her people for the love of her husband, and gone to Djinnistan. Nor could he understand that a mother would act in such fashion without taking her child, indeed without even seeing him before leaving. For him, his daughter was a criminal. He buried her in his heart, and also buried her on the Island of the Heathens so as to keep secret what he felt to be a disgrace. But just as the burial on the island was a lie, so was the burial in his heart. He believed he could deceive the Ussul, yet was more deceived than anyone. Just as he knows that his daughter did not die physically, he also knows that she lives in his heart. That torments and grieves him. He cannot rid himself of the lie. Every lie tends toward the truth, by which I mean that the Sahahr will not find rest until it has been revealed that far from containing the traces of death, that grave actually contains the proofs of life."

"Did he talk to you about this?"

"No."

"But how do you know all this? I am his wife's only confidant, and therefore you know that she told you nothing. You say that all this is simple and obvious, but I don't see how."

"Look around you, and look into yourself. Then, not only this mystery but many another will become easily comprehensible. There is an inner and an outward life. The former is more important, for it is part of eternity. The outward is incidental; it is made up of ephemeral things. It is there so that what is inward may reveal itself. It is a sign by which to discover the inner. Those who direct all their attention to what is bodily or external may accomplish much in that sphere but they will remain poor, pathetic, and blind as regards the real, the higher life. But the person who accustoms himself to pass in everything he feels, thinks, and does from the lower to the higher, from the physical to the spiritual, will have thousands upon thousands of miracles revealed to him, whereas the other becomes blind. Most important, one has to look at our present life as a form of instruction and training which heaven gives to earth so that when death closes the school, the new, resplendent divine world one will enter will already have been prepared for in this old world which now no longer exists. As one strives and explores in this way, one learns to pass back and forth between appearance and substance, and thereby arrives at insights which are not even suspected by others. What you wanted to keep secret concerning the Djinnistani, his wife, and his son because you believed it would compromise you in the eyes of the Ussul is repeated every hour of every day, and quite publicly. It is only the blind I spoke of that do not see it."

"Then I also am still blind?" she asked. "I see nothing."

"Yes," I answered. "You think you see. But what enters your eye is merely a first, hesitant, hardly noticeable reflection of the radiant light to which your eyes should slowly and gradually open themselves. Your eye already knows the faint light, the promise of a full and bright day, and that is the reason you believe me when I speak of this radiance, this light of day. A blind man would probably doubt, would shake his head, and perhaps even laugh."

"You are right," she said very seriously. "A blind person would laugh. But I won't. The glimmer which my eyes have been permitted to see comes from paradise whose earthly image we saw flaming during the night. What you have said seems to increase my understanding. And when you ride from here to Djinnistan, I will accompany you on the path of my soul. Now, let us go to the assembly area where the Hukara are drilling. On the way there, I will tell you that the Erdjani succeeded in removing the inadequate bandage from his grandfather's wound and put on a new one without his noticing it. I think the life of the sorcerer has been saved."

The assembly area was a large, square clearing. As we arrived, more than five hundred men were going through their exercises on horseback. Women and children had come to watch them. The Erdjani was there but his role was somewhat passive. It was Halef who was really in charge.

After we had been observing the drill for some time,

we were ready to leave again but the Erdjani happened to glance in our direction and noticed us. We had to come out from under the trees. Everyone was pleased to see us, and Halef did his best to impress us. We dismounted and settled down near the Erdjani so that we might use this opportunity alone with him for a talk. For what had to be done, which might well determine the Ussuls' entire future, depended on just two persons, and they were the ones with whom I was sitting. However important the choices that had been made in the palace might seem, the real decision would be made by the three of us.

We sat for more than an hour, discussing what we had to do. There is no need for me to report our conversation here for its results will become apparent in the course of this story. I demanded that the three captured Tshoban be taken along under escort because they were bargaining chips for us. I also mentioned that neither Halef nor I would come to supper because I felt that the impending conflict between the old and the new views would be more quickly and peacefully resolved if no strangers were present. Taldsha agreed. Speaking more generally, I should say that she was a reasonable, courageous, and dedicated ally.

Since the Hukara intended to continue their maneuvers until dark, the two of us got back on our horses and took leave of Halef and the Erdjani. The latter asked me if I would be present at midnight when his warriors would be consecrated, and I agreed. Then he asked me to come one hour earlier and to wait for him on the battlements of the temple so that he might report to me on the events of the evening. I told him I would, and left with the sheik's wife to return to the city.

Along the way, we encountered the ten delegates of the Hukara who were going to the assembly area to report to their commanding officers. They had accomplished their purpose, not, it appeared, because the Ussul felt they were right, but simply because they had wanted to get rid of them. But that evening, they said, the Erdjani himself would be there and use a different tone to speak to the elders. Having told us this, they went on their way.

Back home, I spent the time until dusk inspecting our saddles and harness, cleaning my rifles and revolvers, and repairing my garments. Then Halef arrived. He was in extremely good spirits and overwhelmed me with such a flood of tactical and strategical plans that it would have required two armies of no less than a million soldiers to carry out half of them. He had worked hard all afternoon and I did not begrudge him this kind of satisfaction. Gradually, as he noticed that I was paying attention but making no comment, he became hesitant:

"What is it, Sidi? You aren't saying anything. Why not?"

"Because you are doing all the talking. When two people converse, good manners demand that one be silent while the other speaks."

"Did I go on without interruption?"

"Yes."

"And I didn't give you a chance?"

"No."

"Then I ask your pardon. But my heart is so full, and my head is like a book where thousands of strategists and tens of thousands of heroes registered their experiences and knowledge. Sidi, I demand war! I must have war upon war to show you what an exceptional, incomparable, and famous fellow I am. Do you understand?"

"I do. I have had those feelings myself."

"You have?"

"And I have seen them in others. I also was what you still are today."

"What?"

"A boy, a foolish boy."

"Oho! What do you mean by that?" he asked angrily.

"When I was a boy, I often played soldier with other stupid boys. Almost invariably, the game became serious. Look at universal history. There have been so many boys that have fought other, better, and finer boys instead of allowing them to develop peacefully and as their nature demanded. And in the end, who was to pay the damages, to heal the wounds, to

make good the losses, to clean up? The so-called hero?
Never!"

"Then you are against war?"

"Not against a holy war which God has blessed, and
will always bless. That is the war where the soul of
mankind takes up the sword to protect the development of mortal man. But I always oppose war between boys who are tearing each other's coats and
pants to pieces for the sake of an unripe apple. Ask
those nations that suffered the cruel fate of century-
long hunger and grief because God's 'Peace on earth'
was sinned against and they had to do penance for
what boys did. But I am especially against every war
which originates in that silly, pathetic chatter I heard
from you a moment ago: 'Sidi, I must have war, for it
is only through war upon war that I can show what
an exceptional, incomparable, and famous fellow I am.'
Luckily for you, I know another side of you. For if this
blasphemy really came from your heart, I would send
you to the devil right here and now!"

"You really would?" he asked sheepishly.

"Yes, immediately."

"Then I am lucky that they are bringing supper. Sit
down, Sidi, and eat! I shall serve you. I shall cut everything for you so you can see how much I love you,
how willingly I obey you, and that we are really at
bottom one heart and one soul. We won't discuss this
war any further. I don't need it. I am famous without
it. And what you don't want, I don't, either. So come
and join me. I am already chewing."

The servants were bringing the food because I had
said that I would not go to the palace to eat. This was
grist for Halef's mill. He quickly took everything from
them and pushed them back out again so that he could
serve me himself and improve the atmosphere. But in
spite of his efforts, we ate almost silently. It was not
that I was angry with him, but he needed time and
silence to think about himself. Besides, that day would
be important for him, although he did not suspect it. It
was going to be the last time he would be his former
self. It was my wish that his ride to Djinnistan would
also be the time his purification and moral development would begin. If I wanted to bring that about, I

had to treat him differently. His will was good, but he required unwavering, constant support which only I could provide.

When he asked me after supper how I intended to spend the rest of the evening, I told him that I would go to the temple to watch the "fire from the mountains." As I had foreseen, he asked to be allowed to come along. I agreed, for it was precisely this request I had counted on. The impression I expected that spectacle to make on him was meant to open a gate which, once it had closed behind him, would never permit him to return to his earlier nature. The door of the temple was open, and new candles were being lit for the consecration. The tall staircase was thus fairly well illuminated and Halef could follow me without having to grope his way up. As we emerged at the top, he exclaimed:

"Mashallah—what a miracle! Look, Sidi, the earth is in flames."

Toward the north, five or six huge flames were burning high in the sky. Seen from where we stood, it looked as if they were reaching the firmament and darkening the light of the stars, although this was of course an optical illusion. A strong air current was whipping them back and forth. As they burned, their giant shapes became first low and wide, then elongated and thin so that they seemed to reach the clouds. A dark color muted their glow, which could not break through the darkness of the night, as it had done yesterday evening.

Suddenly, the flames collapsed and vanished and even where they had been burning a moment ago, dark night returned. There, as elsewhere, the stars reappeared. But the power which was at work below the earth did not rest. It was quaking faintly. We could sense and hear a grinding, rolling noise and had the feeling that the battlements of the temple were beginning to waver. We sat down. Suddenly, there was a jolt and immediately thereafter a loud noise as if many cannons of varying size had suddenly been fired. A stream of fire rose from the earth, but this only lasted a moment. Nothing followed it. At first, it resembled a tall, round pillar and then took on the shape of a pear. Slowly, it became circular, contracted, and gradually disappeared.

"Allah is great," Halef exclaimed. "Sidi, I have never seen anything like this."

He folded his hands. He was deeply touched. Now there was a second, loud bang. A cloud of burning gas shot up and immediately dispersed. It was followed by a darkly glowing, heavy, thick mass which seemed to be boiling. It rose sluggishly, like a half-liquid, oozing mass which was slowly being replenished. As it ascended, it darkened, lost its fire, and became more stable and defined in its contours. Then it stood still, immobile, a colossal rock with ornaments in relief along the edges, illumined from inside. It looked like a gigantic altar where invisible giants were offering a fiery, nocturnal sacrifice. And fire did appear. The altar opened and from it came a huge sea of flame that devoured the altar, flowed far in all directions, and turned the night into day. But this day was not bright and clear but of a dark, orange yellow, and in the center of the eruption, a mass of smoke and slag drifted upward. Large quantities of impure ash streamed forth from it. As it spread, the sky to the north became wholly invisible and made us feel as if man and animal had to hide in terror. I was gripped by dread, and Halef was even more profoundly shaken. He slid from his seat, knelt down, folded his hands, and prayed:

"In the Name of Allah, the Compassionate, the Merciful. The Disaster! What is the Disaster? Would that you knew what the Disaster is! On that day men shall become like scattered moths and the mountains like tufts of carded wool. Then he whose scales are heavy shall dwell in bliss; but he whose scales are light, the Abyss shall be his home. Would that you knew what this is like! It is a scorching fire."

It was the one hundred and first Sura of the Koran. However detached a man may be in his later years from the sentiments of his youth, he will always return to those early images, expressions, and comforts when he is profoundly agitated. And this was Halef's experience at this moment. He came from western North Africa where it is customary to pray this Sura when man fears death and damnation. In his present, profound agitation, he was returning to the prayer of his childhood because that childhood had given him the belief which teaches prayer. My little Hadji was not prompted by more elevated considerations, but by his nature and temperament. His soul was still the physical soul, not yet the spiritual one. It strove primarily for physical rather than spiritual well-being. And with respect to the relationship between body and mind, it took the slave for the master, the tool for the creative hand, the effect for the cause. It had not yet taken the step from body to spirit, from the ephemeral to the eternal, and was therefore more profoundly affected by the purely physical spectacle before our eyes than by a much more miraculous phenomenon of a purely spiritual nature. But I hoped that the turn toward a higher plane would be prepared by the sight of this gripping natural event and therefore carefully avoided interfering with this process. I neither could nor wanted to shut out the effect of this extraordinary spectacle.

Halef was silent. He was looking north, trying to absorb as much as he could, and did not speak for some time. Then he said:

"Believe me, Sidi, there is much more yearning for God here on earth than you imagine. But there is no natural way to know Him except through the Koran or the Sahahr."

"But there is," I said.

"How?"

"From this temple. It is the way we will have to ride tomorrow. The way from the land of the Ussul toward Djinnistan."

To show the direction, I raised my arm and pointed north where the fire burning on earth was flaming toward the sky as if to symbolize the longing Halef had spoken of.

It became dark up there for a moment, and then the events I had witnessed the night before were reënacted precisely as I have described them.

"That is paradise," Halef exclaimed when the fiery wall built up and the large gate opened. "That is the Ussul legend, the legend about the angels asking if there is peace on earth, and of God who comes down from paradise to—be still, and don't disturb me."

I had said nothing, nor intended to. He again sank down on his knees, put his arms on the railing, folded his hands and fixed his wide-open eyes so firmly on the developing spectacle that it would have been a serious mistake if I had distracted him. He continued kneeling until paradise had disappeared, and for some time thereafter. He took in the sight like a man who has almost died of thirst and is being given water. In an indescribable state of excitement, he slid back and forth on his knees. Repeatedly, he jumped up, and immediately sank down again. He uttered any number of exclamations, and finally, when he felt too overcome, he raised both arms and recited the hundred names of God.

Having recited the long Muslim prayer, he had not yet returned to his normal level, but had come far enough to take notice of me again.

"Sidi," he said. "Don't laugh at me. I have a great, powerful wish but unfortunately it cannot be fulfilled."

"Why not?"

"It's impossible! I should like to be an angel."

He said this in all earnestness. Anybody else might have laughed, but I remained serious and was even gladdened.

"If you would like to be an angel," I said, "go ahead and be one."

"Be one? Surely that doesn't depend on me."

"On whom else?"

"Sidi, you are joking. But let me tell you: If I were an angel, I certainly would not be one of those that wait one hundred years and then look out of the gate once to see if peace has finally come to earth. I would go to the Almighty and tell him frankly: 'Let me go and talk to mankind. This eternal wailing is not getting us anywhere. And that bit of light, once every hundred years, hardly lasts until the following week. Men don't do anything of their own accord. They demand that one go to some trouble for them. So I ask that you send me down there to talk to them seriously. They are not as stubborn as they seem; they long for peace, for happiness. But they must be told in the right way, and that means by the right person, at the right time. That has never been done. As soon as I get down there, things will change. I'll give them a serious talking-to. Of course, it won't happen quickly, and you can't expect me back right away. But I'll be back before the hundred years are up, depend on it!' That's how I would talk to him, Sidi, and I am convinced He would agree. Angels aren't there to live a hundred years by themselves and then devote a few brief days or hours to mankind. Surely you know what an angel is?"

"Yes," I answered.

"And you believe in them?"

"Of course."

"But there are people who deny their existence."

"That's true, and yet I should also say no, there are no such people. Some maintain that God created legions of heavenly, invisible, pure beings who stand high above sinful, fallen man and yet are there to serve him. There are others who say that that is impossible because it goes counter to God's wisdom and justice, since earth would be a veritable hell for angels and there is no reason why men should be served by beings that are so much more valuable than they. Holy Scripture does speak of angels, but that is no more than the Oriental, symbolic mode of expression. The term 'angels' simply refers to good human beings who place their higher insight, their kindness, and love at the disposal of those who need them without expecting a reward."

"And which of those two opinions do you hold, Sidi?"

"I believe what the Bible says, and also what my heart tells me. And my heart says that in time every human being that truly wishes it may well become the protector, helper, and angel of his fellow man. Therefore—"

I had to break off because the Erdjani had arrived. Halef moved to the far end of the bench. The young, serious Ussul seemed a physical giant to him. He greeted us briefly in a friendly fashion and then stepped up to the railing. He looked straight into the high flames on the mountains which had just begun to burn again. His huge figure seemed surrounded by them. He said:

"And we want to travel up there. Right through that fire. It will be difficult. And dangerous. When my father spoke of his native country, he said that only a person who has a tutelary spirit, a guiding angel, can get to Djinnistan."

Then he sat down by my side and told me about the discussion of his demands that had taken place after supper. None of his requests had been denied. But he admitted cheerfully that this had not been the result of his intelligence and negotiating skill but entirely due to the influence of the sheik's wife.

At a considerable distance, we could see a long torchlight procession coming toward the temple.

"Those are my Hukara. It is almost midnight," the Erdjani said. "Do you see that crowd in the square?"

Only now that my attention had been called to it did I notice a large number of people collected in front of the temple. No one made the slightest sound. How strange half-primitive people are!

"They came to witness the consecration," my young friend told me. "But they may not enter until the bells ring."

"Bells?" I asked. "I didn't know there were bells here."

"No. We use horns."

"Like the ones I saw and heard earlier today?"

"Yes."

Below us, we heard the mechanism of the large candelabra. It was being lit. The torchlight procession reached the square, marched around it, and then disappeared inside the temple with the torches still burning. Then the ringing began. At first, there was a single, deep, very loud and drawn-out note. It was succeeded by three others of a different pitch. Sustained at first, they were then sounded individually, like bells, or like a broken chord. The battlement on which we were standing felt like a small boat being tossed about on a roaring sea of sounds and chords while the dominant note kept repeating its yearning call. It drew us toward the temple with irresistible force.

Not just these sounds, however, but also the smoke of the more than six hundred torches burning inside the temple built up below. As these noxious, thick fumes escaped between the wooden pillars that supported the roof, they formed an almost suffocating ring around us which obscured the view of the mountains and the sky. The most stubborn and foul-smelling clouds piled up directly at our feet and it was no cheerful prospect that we had to work our way through them to get to where we were expected.

"That's unpleasant," the Erdjani smiled. "I hope we won't choke. When God leaves paradise to go to Ardistan, He must feel as we do now."

As we started down the stairs, the horrible odor of soot, pitch, and tar wafted toward us. But we had to get through. We took each other by the hand and made our way down.

12 : Danger at the Pass

When I recollected the events of the last few days, they crowded in upon me with a surprising vividness. It had been a Monday when Halef had been seized by the Ussul and I had captured their sheik. On Tuesday, we had gone to Ussula and during that night, I had stood on the roof of the temple with the priestess and Taldsha. Wednesday, yesterday, the campaign against the Tshoban, with our participation, had been settled on. And today, Thursday, Halef and I were already on our way toward the field of action. This quickening of the pace of events gave me food for thought.

Important obligations and responsibilities had suddenly crystallized, but my attitude was quite matter-of-fact. In a manner of speaking, I had become impersonal. I was in a mood that I had not experienced before, and felt as if what impended did not really concern me, that I had to take part in it only because it would be a blessing, not only for the participants but for me as well. It was like a training course in the difficult art of discerning God's guiding hand in life, and of thereby becoming capable of taking the reins oneself. There are people who do not live but are lived because they have not yet learned what living means. Once, I also had been such a person. I had been lived, and had had to pay for this with many years of great and bitter pain. But then I had freed myself of those who had lived me. A difficult, even arduous apprenticeship with many disappointments had followed. Today, I finally saw myself compelled to prove that I was no longer a slave but my own master.

That is all I have to say about my spiritual state at the beginning of our long journey. Halef was in a serious, gentle mood. He only spoke when something essential had to be discussed. Because of what he had seen and felt the previous evening on the battlements of the temple, he was looking deep into his soul today, and tried to hide that fact by seemingly occupying himself animatedly with his two dogs, Hu and Hi. Before our departure, he had learned all he could about their training and was now trying to put them through their paces. I was pleased that they were so useful. But in this respect also, my two giants, Aacht and Uucht, stood far above them. They attacked every human being and animal in any and every situation. They would pull a rider from a galloping horse and were unhesitatingly and totally obedient. But what they did was not the result of training. They acted from insight and understanding. With an almost human intelligence, they could clearly tell what were the right, what the wrong means, and the course of events will demonstrate that they sometimes acted more correctly and intelligently than I.

Each of the four dogs wore a harness and a kind of saddle on which they carried their own rations and a skin with water for use in the regions lying beyond the Tshoban frontiers. The weight was carefully calculated so that it would not become burdensome, and they were actually pleased whenever the saddles were put on their backs. This pleasure never expressed itself in loud and pointless barking, however, but only in their faces. Indeed, the silence they always observed was one of their most admirable qualities. We often found ourselves in situations where loud noises had to be avoided. But occasionally, when there was no harm in it, I gave these well-bred animals permission to bark to their hearts' content.

Both Halef and I were riding excellent horses, and our equipment was the finest imaginable. Our weapons also were first rate, mine really invaluable. Both of us were in excellent health and spirits, full of enterprise and optimism.

We had been riding almost all day long and only stopped for an hour around noon. Now that evening was approaching, we were looking for a suitable camp site. We found ourselves in a very old cedrela forest which edged the river bank along which we were riding. Unfortunately, this variety of tree exuded a marked, garlic-like odor. It was therefore advisable not to spend the night under them but to wait until we came to different vegetation with a less pronounced smell. Not until dusk began to settle were these trees succeeded by a forest of shorea with occasional groups of sissoo trees.

We stopped, and so did the dogs. Hu and Hi were acting normally but Aacht and Uucht looked at me questioningly as if they wanted to say: "Why are we stopping here? Why aren't you going on?" There had to be a reason for this. Uucht advanced a few steps, raised her right foreleg, sniffed the air, gently wagged her tail, and then looked at me again.

"There is something up there," Halef said.

"Yes, human beings."

"Shall I stay here with the horses and dogs?"

"Yes, and I'll go and see who it is. Be sure there is no noise."

We dismounted and had the horses lie down. They knew that they must not snort. The dogs sat down by them and were told to stay there and remain quiet. I then put down both my rifles because they would get in my way, and entered the forest. Along the river, under the open sky, it had still been light but here, where the tops of the trees formed an impenetrable roof, it was already almost dark. In spite of this, I did not neglect to seek cover behind thick trunks as I advanced. If I walked parallel to the river and did not lose sight of the water shimmering through the bushes, I would detect anything that did not belong here. There was not a breath of air but my sense of smell, the most highly developed of all senses, told me what neither my eyes nor my hearing could perceive as yet: There was a fire. I scented a faint smell of pine wood, then burning resin, and finally meat being roasted. As is well known, the shorea tree yields a valuable resin which is even exported to Europe. But to roast meat on a fire of resinous wood whose odor and taste it will absorb would not occur to anyone who had some experience with life outdoors, and this single circumstance told me that the individuals who were preparing their supper here could be neither Ussul nor Tshoban. They must be people who had long since left the pile-dwelling, hunting, fishing, and nomadic stages behind them and no longer knew how a juicy, pure-tasting roast must be prepared under the open sky.

Finally, after having walked nearly a kilometer, I also saw the fire. The reader can easily imagine how lucky I felt, being the owner of two dogs with such admirably developed sense organs. I was all the more struck by the carelessness of these people. The fire they had lit on the bank was large enough to roast an ox. At this point, the river was quite wide and the view of it unobstructed, so that a fire burning here could be seen from a considerable distance. Had it not been for a bend in the river, we would have noticed the flames an hour earlier. But perhaps these people did not think that concealment was required. If so, it was all the more necessary to stalk them and to determine who they might be. I therefore had to walk back toward the river.

In the meantime, it had become dark. The fire blinded me and I could no longer see the river when I was still some distance away. When I had come close enough and was standing behind one of the last trees, however, it became possible to survey the camp site. I counted six men, six horses, and six camels. Beasts and men seemed to have been camping here for some hours. The camels were heavy pack animals and were lying on the ground, unburdened and untethered, chewing their cud. They had been carrying a fair number of skins and some packages which were now lying next to them, stacked in a pile. The horses weren't bad, a cross of a Persian and an Indian strain, but only the former was of true nobility. Anyone riding a white horse that can be spotted at a considerable distance either has no evil intentions or is stupid and inexperienced. I could tell at first glance that four of the men were servants. They were attending to the animals and roasting antelope meat which had already been ruined by the dense smoke of the resin. The other two were the masters. They were some distance away, leaning against the heavy trunk of an age-old sissoo tree and so far from the fire, their servants, and the animals as to suggest they feared contamination by contact with them. Such separation is only found among the castes of India. But then, who were these two? They carried curved sabres in leather scabbards but the rings, buckles, and other metal parts of these weapons were pure gold. Their belts and the handles of their pistols sparkled with semi-precious stones, and on their fingers, they wore large diamonds, rubies, and emeralds. Their turbans, which were wound in the Indian manner, were decorated with strings of pearls and one of them, who wore glasses, had even managed to have a diamond twice the size of a lentil mounted on either hinge of the frame. He seemed the higher-ranking of the two. What was the object of such a display in the middle of the jungle? Both men were dressed in garments of that incredibly fine, yellowish-white weave which is praised in Hindustani poems as "woven hair." I did not know what to make of all this.

These men came from the north, not from Tshoban territory, but from further away. They were riding south, to the Ussul. Who were they and what did they want? Beyond the pastures of the Tshoban lies Djunubistan, and then Ardistan proper. Could something good come from there, particularly at this moment when the Tshoban planned their invasion, and did these men perhaps have something to do with it? Why, in these swampy, smoky lowlands were they as exquisitely dressed as they would be on a street or a sunny square in front of a temple in Delhi or Benares?

The only purpose could be to make such an impression on the simple and modest Ussul at their first meeting that they would be sure of attaining whatever they had come for. But what was that? It was my hope that I would find an answer to at least some of these questions if I eavesdropped on them.

The sissoo tree against which the two men were leaning was flanked by dense fern behind which I could easily hide. I crawled up to the trunk without having been seen and then stretched out on the soft ground which was as comfortable as a sofa. Only the tree separated me from the two men. They did not speak loudly but I could hear everything they said. Just when I had reached my hiding place, one of the servants cut two pieces of meat from the roast and put them on a sparkling metal dish which was certainly gold. He added two small cakes and carried the platter to his masters. One of them seemed to be hungry for he pulled his knife from his belt and immediately began eating. But the other, with the diamond glasses, restrained him:

"Not like that! I forbid it. You must not forget that you are the highest minister of the sheik of Djunubistan, and a member of the highest caste. You are not allowed to eat food that has been touched by someone of a lower caste unless it has first been consecrated by the hand of a priest."

"I am aware of that," the other answered. "But surely it is allowed on a journey."

"Only if no priest is there. But I am not only a priest but the highest of all priests. I am the Maha-Lama of Djunubistan, and even more. I am God. When my body dies, I shall be reborn again and again as a god. You would therefore be sinning a hundred times over, were you to partake in my presence of something that comes from a person inferior to you. Pass your food to me so that I may cleanse it of its impurity and render it edible for us."

The "minister" held the dish out to him and the Maha-Lama blessed it with a gesture. Then they began to eat loudly, smacking their lips, observing an etiquette to be found among certain peoples. They devoured the meat and the pastry almost without chewing and asked for two more helpings which were blessed like the first. They did not say a single word while they ate. There was so much clicking of tongues, smacking of lips, snorting, and belching that there was no time for speech. Now the servants also started eating. They were the lowly, the despised, contact with whom defiled their betters, but they ate quietly and decently and made a much better impression than their masters.

For me, there is no such thing as chance, and that is the reason I cannot say I was lucky to have discovered so quickly who these people were. One of them referred to himself as the Maha-Lama of Djunubistan. Maha-Lama means something like grand priest. But that wasn't all. He called himself the "highest of all priests." The other was the "highest" minister of the sheik of Djunubistan. Such elevated personages had probably never visited the land of the Ussul before. What did they want there? Their journey could not be official, for their rank would have called for a much larger, more splendid retinue. Why were they travelling in secret? Who was to be kept in ignorance of their undertaking? The Ussul or the Tshoban? Presumably the latter. Yet this caravan of six men, six horses, and six camels had had to cross Tshoban territory. Had they managed to do so unobserved? The inhabitants of Djunubistan are called Djunub. There was enmity between them and the Tshoban. When the sheik of the Djunub sends a message to the Ussul, and the messengers are obliged to cross Tshoban territory secretly, there must be a weighty reason. And if he entrusts that message to his highest-ranking cleric and his highest minister, its importance has to be extraordinary. I must admit that I was anxious to hear something about this, but it did not look as if these two men would discuss the matter. When they had eaten, they continued their silence for some time, and then spoke monosyllabically about perfectly ordinary things of no interest to me. The servants, however, who had now finished their work and their supper and were sitting together, smoking, were carrying on a conversation which had begun softly but gradually became loud enough for me to hear a good deal of what they said.

They were talking about their journey so far. They seemed ignorant of its purpose but did know that it had to be kept secret from the Tshoban. They were also aware that the Tshoban were planning an invasion of Ussul territory and had concentrated their army in the middle of the country, leaving the rest exposed. This was the reason the Djunub had been able to pass through the western part, along the seacoast, without having been seen once. They owed this success in part to an ample supply of water. Not having been obliged to look for any, they had not been caught doing so. Two days ago, they had reached the Chatar defile and spent the night there. Early yesterday, they had left and followed the river up to this place to spend the night and then to continue the following morning on their way to Ussula.

As the servants reached this point in their conversation, the two masters finally began making some comments, but not loud enough for their inferiors to hear them. The "minister" began:

"I only hope our good luck will hold up. The Tshoban did not see us. I wonder if the Ussul will."

"They will see our bodies because that's what we want, and that will be all."

"You mean they may see, but not see through, us?"

"Precisely."

"That's easily done. The sheik is a fool, and while his wife is more intelligent, she suspects nothing and would believe anything. So she will also believe that we want the happiness of her people. But what about the priestess? She is said to have a great deal of influence."

"I don't think so," the Maha-Lama answered disdainfully. "How can a priestess be an influential person?"

"But perhaps her husband, the sorcerer, the Sahahr?"

"He doesn't have any influence, either. He is merely his wife's shadow. And what a religion they have! A god that remains invisible, that never shows himself, is never born as I am born and forever reborn. Anyone seeing me sees God. Anyone talking to me is talking to God. It follows that whoever has me has God. But whom do the Ussul have? Nothing, zero, a vapor, a ghost whom they call God. The Sahahr is the only man in that ignorant nation with whom it may be possible to talk. But what is he compared to me who appeared as the true God and Lord of the world in human shape? Should he dare open his mouth, I will demolish him with two or three words, and he will never open it again. I came down from heaven and will be reborn time and again until I have freed mankind of the suffering of earthly existence. That will happen when everything living on earth sinks into Nirvana. Once that has occurred, my earthly mission is complete, and I rise to the stars to continue there. In this, my mission of salvation, I have now come to Djunubistan. It is my present intent to annex the territories of the Tshoban and the Ussul. Our sheik has understood me. He joins his worldly to my spiritual power. By so doing, he will conquer all the land south of us. We will conclude an alliance with the Ussul, telling them that we will drive the Tshoban toward them. Squeezing the Tshoban between us, we will smash and destroy them. We will then invade the country of the Ussul, seeing to it that they are crushed by the Tshoban in turn. This invasion will be tantamount to conquering thier country, for we will never leave it."

"Provided that we can persuade them," the minister interrupted him.

The Maha-Lama glanced at him with enormous astonishment and indignation. He seemed to wish to annihilate him. He observed a silence of several minutes' duration, and then answered, stressing every word:

"As if these were people who would not believe me when I personally speak to them! I am the Maha-Lama of Djunubistan, the highest of all priests. Remember that! Our outward splendor will immediately win the Ussul over to our side. They will obey us just as speedily when I appear and let my voice ring out. Consider the enormous honor our arrival will be for them."

"If we had come with a large and magnificent escort, the impression would be greater."

"That's very true. Regardless of the degree of one's

superiority, outward appearance should never be neglected. Even God, who is spirit, needs the physical world to be worshipped. But we had to dispense with that this time. The Tshoban had to be kept in the dark. The strictest secrecy was called for. But that also has advantages of some consequence, provided we exploit them. What we lack in pomp and splendor we gain tenfold, for the atmosphere will be more intimate. This inferior humanity may believe in love, compassion, and peace on earth. But it lacks the requisite maturity. It would be horrified if it knew the truth. Love is the greatest lie there is; only hatred is the truth. Every living being strives only for its advantage. And that includes God. The greater a being, the more powerful its egoism. God is the greatest and highest, and therefore his egoism is unparalleled. It is madness to call him Father. He only brings ruin. He does not bestow life but death, not peace but struggle, dispute, destruction. When He created the universe, He destroyed Himself. Spirit having been transformed into matter, the creator became the creature. To become God again, He must destroy His creation, step by step, reversing the order by which it came into existence. That is not love and life but hatred and death, destruction, eternal, endless, universal murder. The greater God becomes, the smaller becomes His creature. When what is left of the universe disappears, God will be greatest. To be intelligent and blessed means not to strive for worldly happiness and the well-being of mankind but for God's greatness. Such a person will shrink more and more until his existence comes to an end and he disappears entirely in God. This cessation of being, this total absorption in God so that no trace of recollection remains, is our bliss, our only and our highest goal—Nirvana."

As he was speaking, he had shifted to one side, and I could therefore see his profile, but when he turned toward the minister, I had almost a full-face view. It was a handsome, almost venerable, intelligent face with a silver beard but it had one flaw which nullified all its beauty and dignity. He was so markedly cross-eyed that anyone seeing him could not fail to be struck by it, and this would be true even of those who do not have the habit of focussing their attention on the shortcomings of their fellow men. As his outward appearance indicated that he was no ordinary individual, his words showed that intellectually, also, he did not walk the paths of ordinary men. He even seemed to have dared go beyond the limits imposed on the thought of mortals. I am convinced that many would have felt that the speech I had just heard was pure madness, but I was inclined tentatively to view it as the very curious exaggeration of a fundamentally healthy idea which one encounters everywhere in the spiritual life of nations without finding it particularly remarkable. While this idea does not seem central to the educated European, it was the atmosphere in which the Maha-Lama had grown up and been taught. It was the air he breathed, and responsible for the religious extravagance from which he suffered. That is the reason it did not occur to me to be startled, let alone to smile at what he had said. I did not see him as the head of a sect but as a powerful, intensely interesting enemy of my friends, come to outsmart and enslave them. And that precisely at a moment when they were vulnerable to the attack of a sophisticated adversary! My task was clear. I had attained what I had come for. I knew with whom I was dealing, and even knew the intentions these two men pursued. The question now was whether I should withdraw or remain to hear more. The Lama had turned to his servants and was saying in a commanding tone:

"The time has come for the evening prayer."

One of them got up and brought a gong. Stepping to one side, he bowed in all the cardinal directions, striking the gong as he made each bow. Then he knelt down to pray. The others also folded their hands and mumbled the prescribed text. Only the Maha-Lama did not pray. He was God, and considered it pointless to pray to Himself. But to believe in his own divinity did not seem madness to him. The prayer lasted for only a few moments but it touched me profoundly. Before me, I had the slowly moving water of the river which emerged from the darkness of the jungle with a phosphorescent shimmer and then flowed through the light of the burning fire. I could see the fantastically illuminated shapes of the horses and camels, the five men kneeling in prayer and the sixth who did not join in but stood proud and erect, his face turned toward the stars as if he were up there, hearing the prayers addressed to him. The sounds of the twelve strokes had travelled beyond the river and created an echo along the dense wall of the jungle which was now coming back to us. It introduced a sudden rattling, thundering, and roaring into the previous silence, as if all the battles these men intended to bring to the peaceful country of the Ussul had already erupted. Involuntarily, I glanced behind me. I was seized by a kind of fear, though not for my own safety. Rather, it was a feeling of dread as I looked at this continually reborn god who had caused all this din without being affected by it. It is characteristic of such natures that they remain utterly calm amidst the misery they so often cause. They feel no responsibility for it. Such was the pose of the Maha-Lama. His beard was shining and his face reflected the glow of the flickering flames. He seemed deeply absorbed in his own divinity, as though in a trance. I would not hear anything further, and so I carefully retreated from my post and returned along the trail by which I had come.

Meanwhile, it had also become dark over the river and therefore unnecessary to remain inside the forest to avoid detection. I stayed under the trees until I could no longer see the fire. Then I walked toward the open strip along the bank and made my way back without constantly bumping into trees.

During my absence, Halef had not stirred. I sat down by his side and reported. At an earlier time he would probably have interrupted me any number of times, but now he listened to me quietly. When I had finished, he laughed briefly.

"So God has come! Allah, the omnipotent and omniscient master and creator of heaven and earth! And it is He whom we will take prisoner. We will bind his hands and feet, and tie him to his horse. Who has ever accomplished anything like that?"

"You certainly haven't."

"Not yet, but I soon shall."

"No. Our mission is to get to the Chatar defile as

quickly as we can and to make whatever preparations are necessary. Do you think we can haul prisoners around with us?"

"Hm," he grumbled. "Of course. There are six of them and only two of us. But we can't let them get away."

"Why not?"

"If we could only be sure that they will fall into the Erdjani's hands, and that he will treat them as we would."

"I am sure he will."

"I'm not."

"Then there is nothing we can do. He is his own master and can do as he pleases."

"Then it is my hope that he will catch this Maha-Lama and bring him to the pass where we can make it clear to him that he will immediately lock him up in his Nirvana if he doesn't do as we say. But at least I will see him. We have to pass by there tomorrow morning."

"No. We'll do that tonight."

"In this darkness?"

"Yes. And we won't move along the river but through the forest and around them."

"That's rather awkward. We are going to bump into trees."

"We would if we went on foot and led our horses. But we will ride. You know that the horses have better night vision than we do. Farther into the forest, the trees are more widely spaced. It will be easier than you think."

We mounted and began riding slowly, describing a semi-circle around the camp of the strangers. For our horses and dogs, the simple command "Be silent" was enough; they did not make a sound. Although the eyes of our horses did not fail us, it took us a fairly long time until we got back to the bank of the river above the Djunub camp. We rode a few kilometers further to make absolutely certain that we would not be seen. Then we stopped and settled down for the night. We did not light a fire.

It is not my task to describe the topography of the country we rode through. Because nothing of interest happened along the way, I shall pass over the time it took us to reach our destination, and resume my account at the point where the gradual dwindling of the water made us aware that we were approaching the border. The river became increasingly shallow. Though still as wide as it once had been when it had come from the higher-lying regions in the north, its waters were disappearing in the porous, sponge-like soil. The river bottom could now be seen. Islands of gradually increasing size and frequency had formed, to be succeeded by extensive sandbanks which were separated only by narrow streaks of water and later by puddles. And finally, these streaks and puddles became isolated sloughs whose water tasted worse and worse and then was no longer drinkable at all. Halef made a thoughtful face, and said:

"Sidi, you made a great mistake."

"What is that?"

"You should have stopped where the water still tasted good, and filled our skins."

"Who? Me?"

"Yes, you."

"And not you?"

"No. Why should I be responsible for the mistakes that are made? Surely it's not my business to think of everything. I leave that up to you."

He stopped because he had seen a bright spot in the old, dark, marshy soil of the riverbed. I said nothing and merely smiled. When he looked at me again and noticed that, he lowered his eyes and confessed in his charming, sincere way:

"Sidi, I am an ox, a donkey, an ass, a miserable wretch. That light spot over there is sand, isn't it?"

"I imagine. Let's have a look. We are getting close to the defile. I hope we will be there long before evening."

We dismounted and walked over. It was sand which was dry to a depth of a few centimeters but then became damp, and this dampness increased with the depth. Whenever Halef understood a mistake he had made, he corrected it with real enthusiasm. He ran back to the horses and returned with his two metal, Arabic stirrups. Because of their shape, they made excellent digging tools. We each took one, and in a very short time, we had dug a hole in which clear, good-tasting water collected. We drank our fill and then the dogs were given as much as they needed. We enlarged the hole and watered our horses. More water seeped in so rapidly that we could wait for it to clear and then fill our skins. All of this did not take much more than half an hour. We got back on our horses and continued on our way. Halef felt ashamed, and said:

"That was quick! I would have needed more than twelve hours to find water and to catch up with you. Do you suppose we'll also find it beyond the defile?"

"I hope so."

"But the desert there is famous. It is supposed to be the driest in the world."

"I don't think so. I am convinced it is better than its reputation. It is bordered by mountains in the north, and behind and above them, there are the mountains of Djinnistan. That should provide enough pressure to bring water into the land of the Tshoban. Besides, on the map the Erdjani gave me, I found markings which must indicate watering places. They were entered by his father who often crossed the desert and knew it well. I was told that he owed the success of his journeys wholly to the scent of his dogs. It would seem to me that his own knowledge was more important than the noses of his four-footed companions. I don't think you realize how important that may also become to us."

"What do you mean?"

"We want to defeat the Tshoban, isn't that so?"

"Yes. But not just to defeat but also to conquer them and occupy their land."

"That's right. But what do we need for such a victory?"

"Courage."

"Is that all?"

"There is more, of course. Bravery, cunning, intelligence, training, persistence, skill, and much more. Sidi, you are smiling. Admit that you are making fun of me."

"A little. Your list applies to any fight between two

parties. But as of last night, we know that there will not only be war between the Ussul and the Tshoban, but that the Djunub will also be participants. I already know who the victor will be."

"We, of course."

"Not so fast! The real victor has a different name."

"Do I know him?"

"Yes."

"Who is it?"

"Skins filled with water."

"What?"

He looked uncomprehendingly at me but then seemed to understand. He closed his mouth, nodded, made a roguish face, and said:

"You are absolutely correct. Skins with water in them. The one who has enough water will survive longest and those who have none will die, however strong or clever they may be. So that's why you ordered all those countless skins. That was intuition, wasn't it?"

"Perhaps it's not altogether false to call it that."

"But where are you going to get the water to fill all those containers?"

"You mean for all those human beings and animals. They are what count, not the containers."

"Just thinking about it troubles me."

"I am not worried."

"But it will be from you that they'll demand it. You will be responsible. Can you produce it?"

"Probably. I have three allies who won't abandon me."

"Listen, Sidi, what a face you are making. I know that expression. Whenever I see that look, I know you have an idea. Am I perhaps one of these three allies?"

"No, my dear Halef, unfortunately not. I'm afraid you won't be able to find all the water I will need."

"Of course not. But even you don't have a rod, like Moses, with which you need merely smite rock for water to gush forth from it."

"I have three rods like that."

"You must be speaking figuratively."

"Of course. I am referring to our three allies. The first is the Erdjani's map, which I have here in my pocket. I think it will prove extraordinarily useful."

"I hope you're right."

"We'll see before evening. But if I am not mistaken, this map is of truly inestimable value."

"Does the Erdjani know that?"

"No. I am talking about a mysterious sign the Djinnistani made on it. If I interpret it correctly, we will never have to suffer from thirst."

"And the second ally?"

"It's the fact that I doubt that the desert of the Tshoban is completely without water. The law of hydraulics—"

"May Allah have mercy on us!" he quickly interrupted. "Leave me in peace with your hydraulics. Tell me who your third ally is."

"The volcanoes of Djinnistan."

"The fire-spewing mountains?"

"Yes."

"I don't understand."

"Remember that they not only glow and flame every evening but constantly, all day and all night, except that during the day you cannot see them as clearly as when it is dark. As Taldsha and the priestess told us, these volcanic eruptions recur at intervals of about one hundred years, and now I remember having read in Marah Durimeh's library that Ssul, the river which dried out because it had to return to its source, tries once every century to come back from paradise. In the book I saw, it said: 'Then its course becomes moist from tears of longing, and nightingales drink the morning dew where at other times even the rock dies of thirst.' Those two legends, the one about the volcanoes, the other about the river, must be connected. The one seems to be the cause or the consequence of the other."

"You mean that the volcanoes spit when there is water in the riverbed?" Halef asked seriously.

"No," I laughed. "The other way around. There is water in the river when the volcanoes are active. Consider the masses of eternal ice lying high up there in the mountains. This ice, which some compare to death, actually conceals an infinite abundance of life, but that is something that has to be pointed out to shortsighted men. And now consider a period of several weeks or months of volcanic eruptions which generate a heat that no cold can withstand. Huge masses of ice melt and turn into water. They rush and flow down. The greater the heat, and the longer it lasts, the more the low-lying regions will be drenched. It will not just fill brooks and rivers but also be absorbed by the thirsty ground as though by a dry sponge. It will even seep into the desert where it comes to the surface in the deep gulleys of old, dried-up riverbeds. I feel that we are extremely fortunate that such a period has begun just now. It will be our ally, for even in the driest parts of the Tshoban desert, it will give us all the water we need. All we have to do is choose the region through which we travel according to the laws of the Wasf ul arz or the Ilmi tabakat-i-arz.* If we do that—."

"That's enough, that's enough," he interrupted again. "What we need is water, and not Wasf ul arz or Ilmi tabakat-i-arz. Don't bother me with those sciences which can neither be put into skins nor heated in coffee pots."

"Very well, Halef. I simply wanted to suggest that it is not so difficult to judge in what part of a region water may be hidden. We will find some, of that I am firmly convinced. And that will be like the fulfilment of a prophecy, like the revelation of a fundamental coherence. Up there in Djinnistan, the gates of paradise open during a night of flashing fires, and in the heat of those flames, the glaciers melt and even bring water into the desert to help man impose by the sword the peace which all the world denies him."

A ray of happiness flashed across Halef's face. He exclaimed:

"Sidi, you know that I hate cowardice and love valor, and am afraid of no enemy. An honest fight for a good purpose is a delight to me. But I understand as well as you that peace is better than war. Both of us have earned more than our share of glory and I should think that would entitle us how to strive for peace without being taken for cowards. We can retreat from a world which is never at peace, we can build homes

---

* Geology.

where we shall be safe from hatred and quarrels. I shall return to my Hanneh, the most splendid flower on earth, and bring her ten camels carrying rugs, blankets, scarves, and linen, and build her the most beautiful tent that has ever been seen. But look, Sidi, there was a fire here."

We stopped. We were still near the riverbed, which was now completely dry. Today also, we had forest on our right but due to the lack of moisture, it was less dense than yesterday. There was a puddle of murky water down in the riverbed. We could tell from the tracks that horses and camels had been watered there. The riders had camped along the edge of the forest, and eaten. They could only have been the Djunub. We did not even dismount. I looked the place over, but Halef was restless. After we had moved on again, he turned around repeatedly and looked back.

"What's wrong?" I asked him.

"Nothing actually, nothing at all. But I have a funny feeling."

"What kind of feeling?"

"That we should have stayed."

"Something like a bad conscience? Or like a fear that we neglected something?"

"Yes, a fear. That's exactly what it is."

"I know the feeling. We will turn back and look the place over carefully. I am convinced we will find something of importance."

We turned back, dismounted, and searched, but in vain. We searched some more with no better result. While the tracks had been made the day before, they were still fairly distinct because the Djunub had had no reason to be cautious. Two servants had taken the horses and camels to the puddle while the other two sat on the bank and watched. Their masters had settled some distance away on some dark-brown, velvety moss. Pieces of skin and muscle showed that meat had been eaten. But despite all our efforts, we could find nothing else. As I was going back to my horse, Halef warned me:

"Sidi, I am going to stay. I have a curious feeling of fear when I see you wanting to leave. There must be something here that we have to know about, there must be! I've never felt such fear before. Look at me!"

He came closer so that I could see him better. I noticed that his cheeks were flushed and perspiration glistened on his forehead.

"That's the sweat of fear," he said as he wiped it away. "I have never been this uneasy. I can hear my heart pounding. Please, let's try once more."

"You are almost frightening me. There is always a reason for such anxiety. We'll be more thorough this time. So far, we have been standing. Let's get down on our knees. If there is something important, it should be near the place where the two masters sat."

We turned back and knelt down, using not only our eyes but also our hands, and had barely started when Halef exclaimed: "Hamdulillah, I've got it!" and I said at the same moment: "Here it is, here in the moss." We pulled out a knife. Only its handle had been protruding; the blade had been buried in the ground. The handle was of metal, but so discolored, old, rusted, or covered with patina that it was the very same color as the moss, and that had made it almost impossible to see. The blade was shiny and sharp as if it had just come from the cutler, yet was of the best old Indian steel, and sharp enough to cut a single floating hair. As I looked more closely, I saw engraved lines and points on the handle but they could not be made out clearly. At this moment, we did not have the time to try to puzzle them out. What did catch our attention, however, was the strong, curious back of the blade which had grooves of varying depth and width running across it. I cannot make this clearer than by comparing the instrument to those suitcase keys which have recently come into use and consist of a wide bit whose notches mesh with those in the pin inside the lock. This odd blade was not fixed but attached to the handle by a hinge and could therefore be moved.

"A knife, a pocket knife," Halef said. "Either the 'first minister' or the 'highest priest' stuck it into the moss here while they were eating and then forgot it. Should it belong to the priest, we have found the knife God uses to eat. Take it, Sidi. And here is something else."

He gave me the knife, and kissed me at the same

time. When I looked at him questioningly, he apologized:

"Forgive me, Sidi, but I could not help myself. I am grateful that you let me go back here and look. There is something within me that is not me. And that something is enormously pleased that we found this knife. It is meant for us. Its owner was compelled to stick it into the moss here, and leave it. This inner something tells me that this knife has a value of which we have no inkling as yet. I am so glad, so happy we found it. Can you understand that? I can't. But what is the purpose of those grooves on the back of the blade? I have never seen that on any other knife. Can you guess what they are for?"

"This knife was once used to kill small sacrificial animals and also served as the key to the temple where the sacrifice was held."

"A key? How?"

"Look! You pull the blade out and insert it in the keyhole. Then you press down on the handle so that blade and handle form a right angle. You then have a crank, and the blade functions as a key which you turn until the lock has been opened."

By pushing the blade down, opening it again, and returning it to a point halfway between these two positions and then turning the handle, I demonstrated how this old Indian knife key could be used. He watched, shook his head slowly, and said:

"That's very interesting, but does not look promising. We have a key, but no lock to go with it. And even if we had one, where would we find the temple to which it belongs? Is it still standing and, if so, where? Having this key is the same thing as having spurs but no horse. It's even less useful, for a horse can be found more easily than some old Hindustani temple which probably has long since fallen into ruin. I am enormously pleased that my intuition did not deceive me, but I would like it better if we had found the temple instead of the key, and only needed the key to open it."

"You ask for too much. I am satisfied with what I have."

"The key?"

"No. We don't just have a key but much more."

"What?"

"Not what, but whom. And by that I mean the person who brought it here and then forgot it. Whether that was the Maha-Lama or the minister is of no importance. Until and unless the opposite is proven, I will assume that it was not the minister but the priest that was the owner. The knife probably has some connection with his office, and it is not impossible that he knows what building the key will open. If that is so, we will find out from him, for we will see him again, and then we will discover whether this find will be of some use to us."

He was utterly silent as we rode on, and so was I, although I was thinking about something different. It was the terrain we were passing through that absorbed my attention. The soil was changing. The moss became sand. Obviously, this also affected the vegetation. Our path lay between two extremes, jungle and desert, taking us from the one to the other. It was as if we were covering the distance from the Indian jungle to the West African desert in a few hours. Finally, the forest disappeared entirely as we were riding over a steppe which resembled the Kalahari. Only at those places where the sand still had some moss in it did I see single trees, or groups of them, but they were similar to the albizia which provides no shade and does not ameliorate but intensifies the desert atmosphere.

Halef did not seem to notice any of this. His eyes wandered over the terrain but absorbed nothing, and even the movements of his arms and legs were purely mechanical. He was brooding, and occasionally he uttered a joyful or peevish exclamation. But finally, he became aware of what lay before us, and called out:

"Mashallah—a divine miracle! Ever since I have been contemplating my inner being and have stopped looking around me, the terrain has completely changed. It's become much more beautiful."

"Beautiful? Really?"

"Yes, more beautiful. The forest is gone, the river is gone, the trees, shrubs and other vegetation, are all gone! And so is the fertile earth. There is nothing left but sand, and more sand."

"And you call that beautiful?"

"Of course! Where I was born, in the West African desert, it looks exactly like this. And one finds everything beautiful that reminds one of one's country, one's youth, the happiness of childhood. Look, our horses are breathing altogether differently. How their muscles are swelling, their tails flowing, their hooves playing! That's because of the sunshine, the light, the open air. There is no stagnant, smelly water, no rotting wood, no poisonous fungus to get in our way. The purest sand all around, as though it had been strained through a fine-meshed sieve. It has a bluish shimmer, like mother-of-pearl. That's the desert I love. Let's give our horses their heads and let them run to their hearts' content."

He spurred his horse, and I gladly did as he asked. We flew over the utterly barren plain. Ben Rih was snorting with delight; the dogs barked joyously. My noble Syrr remained silent but his every jump was a beautiful, eloquent expression of joy.

"Look, Sidi," Halef said, pointing ahead. "Do you see?"

"Magnificent. What could it be?"

Before us, there was something that dazzled, flashed, sparkled, and glowed as if a lighthouse were standing in the middle of the desert but the signals were not just coming from the top; its entire structure consisted of flames. Yet the fire was not blazing. It sparkled in brief, crisscross patterns which seemed to be coming from closely spaced facets. It looked like a giant diamond which millions of workers had been polishing for centuries, imparting to its entire huge surface the capacity to break up the eternal light of the sun into countless minutes and seconds. After the long darkness of the jungle, this glitter over a seemingly endless expanse was an unforgettable sight.

"What can it be?" Halef asked as he reined in his horse to be able to enjoy the spectacle longer.

"Are you asking about the poetry of belief? Or is it a scientific question?" I answered. "The former would call this dialogue between the apparently dead stone and the sun a miracle. As everywhere and always, the scientific explanation of the miracle reduces it to the sober everyday. It tells us that what we see here is a piece of micaceous rock whose glass-like particles sparkle in the rays of the sun."

"So that is a scientific explanation? Tell your science that I won't permit it to minimize the miracle I see in front of me. I don't know what 'micaceous' means, and I don't care. Whether that has something to do with plants or elephants is a matter of indifference to me. I don't want to know. But I do see that it sparkles much more beautifully and delightfully than all your dismal science, and that sparkling is a delight. I would rather ask you how this tall rock got here."

"Well, we probably aren't in the desert any longer. We are drawing close to the isthmus which we know consists of rock, the debris from a gigantic natural event. This micaceous rock is probably that part of it which was pushed furthest during that period . . . but look! It is getting dark. Do you see the figure?"

From the damp terrain behind us, a cloud had risen and blocked the sun so that its shadow fell toward us. It darkened the rock for a few moments. Its contours emerged and the figure it formed could be seen with great clarity.

"An angel, a real angel," Halef exclaimed. "With the olive branch in his hand. It has two wings and stands on a pedestal of several pieces of rock."

Halef was right. The stone colossus had the form he described. When I saw that, I stopped to take out the map the Erdjani had given me.

"What are you doing? Why are you stopping?"

"To consult the map. Didn't I tell you that we would know before evening whether or not it was accurate? That time has come."

"But the map doesn't tell us anything about this sparkling rock, but about water."

"That's precisely what we are interested in.'"

I rode up to him, unfolded the map, showed it to him and went on:

"Here you have the defile, the border between the land of the Ussul and the territory of the Tshoban. The latter is largely desert, and here you can see a series of dots in that desert which stretch from south to north and are all marked with a Mim and a Hahr.* Do you recognize them?"

"Yes. What are those dots, those places?"

"I don't know."

"But you seem to have some idea."

"Of course. The dots go right through the desert; they must refer to something that is important here. And what would you call the most important thing?"

"Water?"

"Yes. I assume that these are places where water can be found, and I don't mean salt water but drinking water."

"And what is the meaning of those two letters M and H?"

"Moje hilwe.† That seems to be the only possibility, don't you think?"

"I agree. These dots certainly lie along the route the Djinnistani followed whenever he went home. He did not need those markings for himself. They are meant for his son to whom he dedicated the map."

"If that is correct, victory is ours, for we have the most important thing."

"But what does that have to do with today? You said that we would see before evening whether the map is correct?"

"Look! Here is the defile. Very close, south of it, there is a dot which is marked 'El Melek,' the angel we see ahead of us. Below it, there are the same two letters, M and H. If we find water near that angel, that means that wherever we have the letters M and H, we will also find water, and that includes the desert of the Tshoban. Do you understand now how important this rock is for us?"

"Certainly. But permit me some doubts, Sidi. Where is the water here supposed to come from? Look at this sand. It is drifting sand, and almost as fine as flour. The wind carried it from the Tshoban desert across the isthmus. And it is very deep. I don't see a blade of

---

* Arabic letters M and H.
† Drinking water.

grass anywhere. I don't believe we will find a single drop of water."

"Let's wait and see. When one looks for water, one must not judge by the sand on the surface. What is important are the rock formations below."

"Ah. Now we are back to your famous Ilmi tabakat-i-arz. I wish you would let that go; I don't want to hear about it. I'll be pleased if we find water, for that's what I want, not the Ilmi."

"Come along, then. We'll find it."

We rode on. The cloud had disappeared, and therefore the angel was sparkling again, but not for long, for the closer we came to the rock, the more the angle at which it received the light shifted relative to our position, and soon there were no more reflections although the sun was still shining. And then we saw something that filled me with delight. For although the rock on which the angel stood lay in the midst of barren sand, it was surrounded by shrubs and even some trees with leafy crowns. The grass growing all around the figure became healthier and lusher the closer to the angel it grew.

"Sidi, you were right after all. There really is water here," Halef said as he spurred his horse to cover the remaining distance quickly. But I did not increase my speed. I knew what he had in mind. He wanted to get to the rock ahead of me so that he would be the one that discovered the water. But whenever he meant to outdo me, his efforts never had the intended result, and that's what happened now. When I reached the angel, Halef had long since dismounted and was crawling all around the rock without finding a trace of water. I waited patiently until he finally admitted:

"I can't find any, Sidi, none at all. We are mistaken."

"I don't think so."

"Oh, yes! If there were water here, I wouldn't have missed it."

"Why you, of all people? Are you smart enough?"

"I should think so," he flared up.

"Really? Did you think before you started looking?"

"No. I looked for it, isn't that enough?"

"I have not even dismounted yet. Perhaps I won't do

any searching, but stay in the saddle, and find it even so. I think instead of blindly rushing ahead."

"May I think along with you?"

"Why not? Two always accomplish more than one."

"Let's start, then. Who is going to begin, you or me?"

"You, of course. Didn't you get here before I did?"

"Thank you, Sidi. But it is always better when you start thinking and I join you later to confirm your results. You must realize that confirmation is what really counts."

"Very true. Let's begin, then. You will see how quickly we will get to the water without having to waste a lot of time looking for it. Tell me first where you think it is."

"Don't make fun of me. Down there, of course, but what good is that? We need it up here."

"I know that as well as you do. There must be a place which will take us down."

"But where?"

"I don't know. You should look for it."

"Look? Me? Listen, Sidi, I don't understand you. First you laugh at me for having looked without thinking, and now you interfere with my deep thoughts and ask me to look. I am telling you, my thinking is so deep that I had almost got down to where the water is. Why did you interrupt? Now, if I don't find anything, you alone will be to blame."

"I didn't mean that you should only think. You must also use your eyes. Look at this rock of the angel. Do you imagine that that form is natural, purely accidental? The longer I look at it, the more probable it seems that humans worked on it. Water is like a saving angel in the desert. This stone, in the middle of it, has a form from which an angel could be hewn without too much trouble. And that was done, although in the rather crude way you have before your eyes. We are probably standing by an age-old well, but one that was only meant for friends. The way to the water was kept secret."

"And you propose finding it? So quickly? After such a long time?"

"Perhaps I already have."

"Oho!"

"Yes. The way to the water must be close by, and it is hidden. There is a hole with a lid which leads down to it. If this hole has been dug in sand or grass, it would leave a mark in spite of the lid, for the moisture would be coming in contact with it. Do you see such a spot?"

"No."

"Neither do I."

"Then that spot is not in the sand or the grass but must be in the bushes."

"No. There aren't enough bushes here for a water-hole to be hidden among them. And it would be a mistake to assume that it would have been covered by earth on which bushes had then been planted because every time someone walked to the water, the bushes would be damaged and the secret would stop being one. So all that remains is the rock itself."

"What? You mean the rock itself is the way down to the water?"

"Of course."

"Then I'll have to look right away."

"That would be a waste of time. The hole is up there."

"Mashallah! Are you omniscient?"

"No. But I keep my eyes open, and reflect. Had the hole been hewn into the side of the rock, its cover would give it away. So it was made at a place one does not see, and that is up on the pedestal on which the angel stands. It looks as if one couldn't get up there, but some steps have been cut into the left edge in back. Do you think you can climb up there?"

"Certainly, just watch me."

He easily climbed up along the edge, looked around when he had got to the top, and said:

"There is nothing here, least of all a hole."

"That's precisely what I expected. Or do you think these people were foolish enough to leave the hole to a hidden well uncovered?"

"But I don't see any lid either."

"If the lid were so thoughtlessly placed that one would see it immediately, they might as well have left the hole uncovered. Probably the surface on which you are standing is covered by drifting sand."

"Yes."

"Is it very deep?"

Halef bent down and then answered:

"Almost a finger high."

"And is that sand untouched?"

"Yes, there are the tracks of some birds, but that's all."

"Then no one has probably been there since the Djinnistani came for his wife and supplied himself with water here. The opening should be along one of the sides of the rock, not in the center. It should be either to the left or the right."

"Why not the center? That's what I would have assumed."

"Because this is certainly not a draw well. One must climb down into it, so there must be steps, and steps require space. They don't descend vertically but at an angle. If they go from the right to the left, the hole should be looked for on the right; if the other way around, look for it on the left. It would only be in the middle if the steps led down vertically, but I think that's quite unlikely. In that case, it would not be a staircase but a ladder, and that would be completely contrary to the customs of the people that built this well centuries ago."

"So then you think I should be looking along the sides?"

"Yes."

"Very well. I'll go to the left first."

Halef had climbed the left side of the rock and was still standing there. He folded his scarf and began dusting the spot where he was. After he had cleared a fairly large area, he said:

"There is nothing here. So I'll go over to the other side and try there."

The Hadji had been mistaken when, seeing it from a distance, he had thought that the angel stood on several large rocks. Actually, it was a single, compact, huge boulder. Nor had the figure first been hewn and then placed atop it; instead, it actually formed its upper part. The lower part, the boulder, was wider. When I climbed it myself, I saw that tools had been used to create a level surface which supported the ample, folded garment of the angel, whose feet were not visible. Halef had just begun to remove the layer of sand near the extreme right fold of the garment when he stopped, bent down, looked at the ground, and called out:

"There is something here, Sidi, that was made by men, not nature."

"What?"

"A figure with three points."

I walked over to have a closer look. It was a recessed triangle whose inside had been treated as a relief. The indentation was filled with very fine, drifting sand. The nightly dew had gradually turned this into a crust which one could not remove by simply blowing it away. I had to use the point of my knife, and as I did so, what was inside the triangle became more clearly visible. It was an eye such as is used as the symbol of God the Father, except that here the eyelashes had been added. The work was so carefully done that the man who had chiselled this symbol must have been an artist.

"An eye," Halef exclaimed. "A real eye. What is that supposed to mean?"

"I learned in Sitara that this eye is the sign and seal of the Mir of Djinnistan," I answered. "So we know that this angel was made neither by the Ussul nor the Tshoban but at the behest of Djinnistan. When, how, and why this was done is nothing we need inquire into now. The question we must answer is why this eye is located precisely here."

"But that's easy enough. It is there to tell you who made the well."

"Oh, no! If that were its only purpose, it would have been placed elsewhere. Here, it cannot be seen from below and the place is so asymmetrically and clumsily chosen that I would be surprised if that were the reason. I am convinced that this symbol is intended to call attention to the spot where it has been placed. That is important, but important in what way?"

"Do you think it indicates the entrance to the well, Sidi?"

"I do. The eye is the sign for the lid. I assume that it

was not placed along the edge but in the center of it. So we have to search around the eye until we see the edge of the lid."

"That won't take long," Halef said as he knelt down beside me to help me look.

But it did not go as fast as he had expected. We could see no trace of a crack or line. The stone seemed compact and nothing suggested how it might be possible to remove part of it.

"Sidi, we are not getting anywhere," Halef said. "You were mistaken. All your thinking has been for nothing. But not mine! If you had not disturbed me when my thoughts had almost reached the water below, this pointless searching could have been avoided."

"And what about the eye we found?"

"That's true; the eye is something."

Near it, I knocked on the stone, and repeated that some distance away.

"The sound varies," Halef admitted.

"Not only the sound. It also looks different. Come over here."

Because I had touched and knocked on it, the place some distance away from the eye had been cleared of drifting sand. The rock became visible and I was immediately struck by the fact that it seemed different, and of a different color. This difference was not considerable, yet it did not escape me. I examined, touched, and compared until I could tell Halef the result of my investigation:

"This Djinnistani is an exceptionally intelligent and careful person. He takes account of things someone else would not think of. He poured water on the lid of the well and then scattered sand over it. Under the crust that developed, the outline of the lid has disappeared so completely that no one can see it. Then, the wind did its share and destroyed the contours. Go get some water, Halef. Climb down and attach one of the skins to the lasso. I'll pull it up and then you'll see how quickly we'll uncover the secret of this angel and its well."

He did what I asked, and then rejoined me. I moistened the stone around the eye and he scraped away the quickly dissolving crust. My expectation was confirmed. The contours of the lid appeared. And I had also been right in my guess that the eye had been placed in the very center of the lid. Judging by the contours, the lid was approximately one and one-half meters long, and equally wide. It bordered on the last, right fold of the stone garment of the figure. But how were we going to remove it? I estimated its weight to be far in excess of a hundred pounds; it lay in deep, tight grooves and had neither a hole nor a handle that would have allowed us to get hold of it. I pondered the problem for some time, but vainly. The crack between the lid and the stone was so tight that not even the thinnest knife blade could have been inserted between them. And even if that had been possible, it was inconceivable that so great a weight could be raised by such a blade. Halef vented his peevishness:

"We are sitting here like camels, chewing their cud, looking at each other. I am at my wits' ends and so are you, it seems."

"Not quite yet. It's much too early to give up. We simply must not allow our thoughts to get on the wrong track. Here we have a stone slab that must be raised. That can only be done by mechanical power. But what is the precise nature of that power? It cannot be tools, for there is neither a hole nor anything else where a tool could be applied. That means that this slab can only be moved through itself. But how? Does it run on tracks or wheels? No. Can it be pushed? No. What we probably have to do is shift the center of gravity slightly, and that requires neither strength nor effort. The person who knows would laugh at us if he could see us trying to find a solution, and not succeeding."

"I'll lash him across the face if I ever run into the fellow and he starts laughing," Halef raged in his funny way. Then he added ironically: "Why not turn to your science that you think so much of? Can't that get you out of this impasse?"

"Of course it can. But I have to avoid the mistake of asking the wrong questions. So far, we know that what is involved here is an easy and effortless shift of the center of gravity. And that means that we must find where that center is, and where we must shift it to."

"Then let us divide this task. You try to find it, and I will do the shifting. What a pity that this angel at those feet we are breaking our heads is made of stone. If it were a real guardian angel, I would ask him for help and—"

"He is one, he is," I interrupted the Hadji. "Pay attention, he'll help us."

"What? This angel here?"

"Yes, precisely. The moment you mentioned him, I had an idea which is probably the right one. And when I started looking for confirmation of that idea, I saw something that we have overlooked although we should have seen it. Halef, we are stupid, really stupid."

"You mean you and your science? But look at me, Sidi. The moment I open my mouth to talk about the angel, the right idea immediately strikes you. So that idea comes from me. I hope you will see now how superior I am. Your learning always leaves you in the lurch when you really need it. But tell me, what is it that you didn't see until a moment ago?"

"What is the form of the stone slab that is the lid of the well?"

"It is square."

"How many sides does a square have?"

"Four. What else?"

"Show them to me!"

The square lay before us, but only three of its sides were visible. The fourth abutted the fold in the garment of the angel, and there was neither a crack nor the thinnest of lines separating the slab from the fold. Both formed a whole, they belonged together, and that was what I had only noticed then. But there was something more. Halef counted the sides of the square by pointing to the visible outlines:

"Here is the first, here the second, here the third, and here—"

He stopped, for now he also noticed that the slab did not end where it reached the fold but formed part of it.

"Sidi, it has only three, the fourth is missing," he went on.

"It's not! It's merely in a different place, probably further up, and runs across the fold," I answered. "Up to now, we paid no attention to the fact that the hem of this fold is also covered by this man-made crust which we had to remove from the slab."

"Mashallah!" he exclaimed after he had taken a careful look and run his fingers over the place. "You are right! Let's get some water so we can make sure."

He picked up the skin, moistened the fold and then scraped away the crust. The previously hidden outlines now appeared and one could see clearly that the slab did not form a level surface but a right angle. Half of it was part of the ground, the other part of the fold of the garment which rested on it vertically. Where it formed the angle, it probably sat on an axis on which it moved. Its upright section was precisely as high as the length or width of its horizontal part. It could therefore be assumed that the two balanced each other and that it would merely require a small amount of pressure to shift the center of gravity and to move the slab by pushing the upright part into the hollow fold, thereby raising the horizontal section. I thought it might be amusing to have Halef do this. He was standing in front of the fold, looking at it, and said:

"Sidi, perhaps your science isn't as pointless as I thought. But it was only through me that you got the idea that part of the garment of this angel belongs to the lid. What's going to happen now?"

"Push the section of the lid that is part of the fold into the fold," I told him.

He tried, but couldn't manage because he was standing on the other half of the lid.

"It won't work, Sidi," he said. "Where do you get this idea that something can be pushed into an opening here?"

"Get off the lid and try again," I answered.

He did, and almost shouted with amazement when the part of the stone garment he was touching receded while the horizontal half of the lid was raised, uncovering the hole we had been looking for. I had never seen him make such an astonished face as at that moment. He stared at me, at the square opening in the fold, and the hole leading into the well, stood for a while open-mouthed, and then exulted:

"Hamdulillah! The hole has been found! Sidi, you are a magician, a sorcerer! Your science is no good, but happily you occasionally have a bright idea and then we can be sure of success, especially when I make my contribution. And that's exactly what happened here. Do I push the fold all the way in?"

"Yes."

By pushing the square section of the fold into it, the other part, the lid proper, was raised high enough so that the hole of the well was completely open. We looked in. Solid, stone steps led down from the right to the left. They had been hewn into the hard rock. There was almost no dampness and the cool air rising from inside did not carry the faintest odor of rot. Halef wanted to climb down immediately but I restrained him to call his attention to the loud, joyous barking of our dogs as they jumped up against the pedestal.

"Look, they are scenting the water," I said.

"So it seems. But why not test them?"

"For what reason?"

"Because their barking and jumping may merely mean that they want to be with their masters."

"Very well. Let's go back down."

But once we were on the ground, they paid no attention to us. Instead, their eagerness to climb the rock increased, but that was impossible. There was no way for them to get up on the pedestal. Besides, they would interfere with the investigation of the well which was probably quite deep. We therefore made them understand that we knew what they wanted. They quickly quieted down and returned to their place next to the horses.

We climbed up again and then descended into the well. There were several superimposed levels or floors. Twenty steps took us to the uppermost one and at that distance, we found ourselves in semidarkness. Once we had accustomed ourselves to this obscurity, we saw to our right a large stone cube with a thin slab covering it. When we had pushed back this lid somewhat, we saw that the cube was hollow and resembled a drawer or chest with all kinds of tools inside. At the top, there were sturdy leather rolls tied at both ends to protect their contents from dampness. We opened one. It contained a very well preserved candle of unprocessed bees' wax. We took another one, and lit them both. They had thick, easily burning wicks and provided enough light for our purpose. In addition to the candles, there were also string, ropes, skins, and similar objects which had some connection with the functioning of the well, and long, wide straps of firm cowhide intended for use in the repair of the mechanism by which the water was drawn.

In the center of this fairly sizeable, subterranean chamber there stood a long, wide trough of rock which had one wheel in front, one in back. When one of them was turned, the other also moved. A leather strap ran across these two wheels and at certain intervals, containers were hanging from it which, filled with water, came up from below on one side, emptied their contents as they passed, and then returned on the other. I felt certain the replacement straps had been there for centuries. Time had been no element in the vision of the man that had built this structure. Who could he have been? High above the stairs which we had descended, I saw the sign of the Mir of Djinnistan and, below it, the single word "Build" in the old, Bramavarta dialect. This word constituted the beginning of a sentence whose continuation we found as we went further down.

On the next lower floor, we saw the very same machinery and also the same objects. At the corresponding place above the stairs, the words "for victory" had been chiselled into the wall in the same dialect and under the same sign as on the level above. On the following floor, the area was identical in all respects to the two higher ones, and here I saw the words "in the struggle." And at the very bottom, there stood a very wide, very deep basin whose contents would have sufficed for many hundreds of men and animals. It seemed that the water perpetually replenishing it was filtered through glacial drift. From here, the mechanism transported the water to the trough on the next higher level. As it was raised from trough to trough, its contact with the air saturated it with carbon dioxide. It thus became not only thirst-quenching but also refreshing. "For peace" were the words I saw here, so that the entire sentence read: BUILT FOR VICTORY IN THE STRUGGLE FOR PEACE.

I was deeply moved. Halef also became very serious when I explained the inscription to him. We were in the interior of the earth, for we had come down eighty steps, and the depth was considerable. Above us, there was the stone angel right in the middle of the desert which had sun, but no water. Here, there was water in abundance, but not a ray of sunlight penetrated. To irrigate the desert, the water had to rise toward the sun. There was a clear analogy between the depth at which this water collected and the remoteness of the past when this well had been built. And just like the water, the past also had to rise to the surface, the present, if it was to bear fruit. God, the omniscient and benevolent Mir of Djinnistan, had, for the benefit of the present, constructed an angel that towered far above this desert in its splendor. We have to descend into the innermost depth of that angel if we wish to irrigate the present and the future with the life-giving water of the past. It is hardly necessary to ask who this angel may be.

We tasted the water in the basin. It was fresh and pure and without any aftertaste, but dead. We began turning the wheels. I had expected that after such a long period of disuse, the mechanism would creak noisily, but this did not happen. The spindles lay in a heavy, fatty substance which, though dry, immediately returned to its original, resilient condition due to the heat caused by the friction. When the water had passed from trough to trough and been raised all the way to the top, it was no longer dead but tasted almost like spring water. It was much better than what we carried in our skins, which we emptied and refilled. We also gave the dogs and horses as much as they could drink. We then closed the hole, returning the lid to its proper position.

"Are we going to sprinkle some sand on water to hide the cracks?" Halef asked.

"No, that precaution is unnecessary. There is no

enemy about that will discover this well. Besides, we must not hide it from our friends but let them know it is here. I tell you, Halef, that this well seems a veritable angel to me, and for more than one reason. First, it allays all my fears over crossing the desert of the Tshoban, for I am sure the Djinnistani's map will be as reliable elsewhere as it was here. We can be certain we won't die of thirst. Besides, this well is a welcome aid to us, for it will help us achieve victory at the isthmus. We will have to starve the Tshoban into submission, and we must also cut them off from all sources of water. But that means that we will have to be amply supplied with both food and water, and water is the most important of the two. It would have taken a string of horsemen to transport the large amount we need from the river to the isthmus. The section of the river nearest to us that could supply that quantity is at least one and a half days' ride away. That's how long the line of horsemen would have to be, and you can imagine how many men and horses, how much work and time this well saves us, for it is close to the isthmus."

"Do you really think that we are already that near? I don't see any signs of it."

"But there is a sign."

"Of what?"

"Of the sea."

"Allah w'Allah! You see it?"

"Yes, to the right, due east. Look over there."

"I see nothing but the sand of the desert that is tinged by the light of the setting sun."

"And then, beyond that?"

"Then there is the sky which has a silvery coloration where it rests on the earth."

"That silver is not the sky but the sea. If the sun were in the east that strip would look dark, but because the sun is in the west we see it in a silver light. But if the sea is so close that we can see it, we can assume that we won't have far to go to the isthmus."

As we rode on, the strip we had seen from the pedestal became broader and lost its silvery sheen. One could see that it was water and soon we also noticed that this water was moving. It seemed to be breathing.

The soil also changed. The sand was succeeded by debris and gravel and gradually rocks of ever increasing size began to appear. Boulders, widely scattered at first, became more frequent and began heaping up. What had once been the riverbed emerged more clearly. It was precipitous and deep, and covered with rocks whose smooth edges showed that water had once flowed over and around them. Ever higher walls of rock ran along the banks. Staggered, they formed hills and even mountains and blocked the view on either side. Although we still could not see the sea, the vegetation on these rocky chains suggested it was close. There were no trees, but even these salt bushes and shrubs could not have grown and survived without moisture.

13 : Messengers from Djinnistan

We had been riding between these heights for perhaps a quarter of an hour when they came very close together to form a configuration which looked as if, millennia ago, giants had taken huge, unhewn rocks to build a tunnel across the isthmus to block it, allowing the water of the river to flow on. Into one of the largest of these boulders, the words "Fum es Ssachr" had been chiselled. This means "rock hole" or "orifice." The diameter of this opening was at most five or six paces longer than the width of the river. On both sides, the rocks rose precipitously and there was only a single place where they could be climbed, which is what we did after dismounting. Our purpose in having come here made it incumbent on us to familiarize ourselves as thoroughly as possible with this most important part of the terrain. Halef's dogs stayed with the horses but when mine saw that there was going to be some climbing, they expressed the wish to join us, and I let them. Our destination lay high up in the mountainous terrain, and I was curious to see how well they could manage. The moment they were released, they dashed ahead of us, leaping from edge to edge, but silently, looking ahead to see where it might be easiest to gain a foothold. They seemed to have assumed the task of finding the best way for us, and as we followed them, we could see that we could not have chosen better. Although they were carrying their full pack saddles on their backs, we had not even come a quarter of the way when they were already on the highest ledge, vertically above the "Fum es Ssachr," next to each other, wagging their tails, asking us to join them quickly. Other dogs would have barked but they remained silent, being thoroughbreds, and beautifully trained.

On the heights, a surprise awaited us. We were on the eastern side, and had not yet reached the very top, when we came to a gap between the rocks and saw the blue expanse of the sea, much closer than we had realized. Having climbed to the highest point where our dogs were waiting for us, Halef shouted with surprise, for on the other side also, the sea had appeared. Flowing into a deep inlet, it came so close that it lay directly at our feet.

"The sea, the ocean!" Halef exclaimed, clapping his hands. "Would you have thought that possible, Sidi? The magnificent blue miracle is here! And what is that far to the north? It looks like a tree of such immense height that it seems to be towering into the sky. I see the trunk and the crown. It looks as if it were moving."

"That is a column of smoke coming from the volcanoes of Djinnistan," I answered.

"Which becomes a flaming pillar at night, just as it says in Holy Scripture. The Lord walked ahead of His people in a pillar of smoke during the day, a pillar of fire during the night. And look at this gate directly ahead of us. Like the barrier on top of which we are standing, it also straddles the entire width of the isthmus. We can't go further in either direction. We'll have to climb down to where we started."

The "gate" he was speaking of lay due north of us, perhaps half an hour's ride away. It was unquestionably a natural formation but looked as if it had been created by men or, rather, by giants. A tall, compact wall stretched across the isthmus from coast to coast. In the very center of this wall, a single gap ran from top to bottom. It was wide enough for the river to have flowed through it once upon a time, and a narrow path ran alongside it. A stone slab lay across the top on which I saw some bushes and what looked like a small elevation, perhaps a pile of rocks. If this wall had no opening other than this gap in the center, the stretch between it and where we were standing was the best imaginable trap for the Tshoban. When I pointed this out to the Hadji, he agreed. Unfortunately, it was too late in the day to walk to it. The sun was about to set and night comes so quickly in those regions that even if we had hurried and reached it, there would not have been enough time for a closer look. We therefore merely confirmed that on our side, at the "rock hole," there was no other passage. Then we climbed down to examine it at greater leisure.

It was so narrow that, if the river bed had not been dry, only a path of a width of some three meters would have remained to get from one side to the other. This path was some fifty feet in length and could be swept by rifle fire, for the scattered, large boulders in the river bed afforded scant protection.

We mounted our horses and rode through the "orifice." On its far side, the rocks could not be climbed anywhere. It would take about half an hour to walk the distance from end to end, and if I was correct in my belief that this was the place where the Tshoban would be trapped, we first had to determine whether the rock walls which formed the sides of the defile offered a possibility of escape. The defile was called "Chatar," which means "danger." This suggested that it would not be without risk to pass through it, and we could therefore assume that the nature of the terrain would favor us and put the Tshoban at a disadvantage. We rode slowly to inspect both sides of the pass. We covered perhaps three-quarters of the way, and came fairly close to the "rock gate" we had seen from a distance, without finding a single place where the abrupt, irregular, sometimes overhanging rock walls could be scaled. If we could lure the Tshoban here, they would not get away.

As regards water, our situation was equally favorable. We had naturally assumed that there would be no drinking water and were therefore rather surprised when we noticed a somewhat deeper sandy place in the river bed that was damp. We immediately examined it but were reassured to discover that while prolonged digging yielded some water, it was so salty and contained so many foul tasting particles that it was unfit for man or beast. The layer which carried good drinking water, came from the distant mountains, and opened inside the well angel was inaccessible below the ocean floor.

Before darkness fell, we looked for a suitable camping site. While there was no grass, we did find some soft ground where drifting sand had collected and formed a small, closed-off nook in the rock. We settled down. The dogs were given meat, the horses their first ration of dried grain. We did not light a fire, for it was not absolutely certain that we were completely safe and could not be spotted. Though the region was deserted, anyone travelling from one country to the other had to pass here. The prince of the Tshoban had come this way, and so had the Maha-Lama and the highest ranking minister from Djunubistan. Others might therefore come by, and we could not let them discover us. We decided to let the dogs stand guard so that both of us could get some sleep.

Night fell, but its darkness did not last long, for the moon rose. There was profound silence all around, and yet this silence was not total. I was uncertain whether it was the movement of the sea that I heard, whether it was something outside or within me. It seemed to be in the air, yet also in the ground on which we lay. The moon was of a curious, golden yellow. When one looked directly at its friendly profile, its rays seemed to have a bluish tinge, perhaps the result of the dampness of the air. A faint inhalation and exhalation were perceivable in the otherwise quiet surroundings. Was this caused by the sea? Both Halef and I were praying, and I had just silently said 'Amen' when we suddenly heard a loud voice ringing through the still night:

"Ja Kudah, ja Kudah . . . God, I am calling on You."

Apparently come from above, it was a beautiful, resonant, pure alto floating down as though from heaven. Another, deeper voice, a far-reaching baritone, joined in when the invocation was repeated.

"What's that, Sidi? Who is that? Where does it come from?" Halef asked as he sat up.

"Be still. Let's listen some more."

Now the two voices sang in unison:

"Ja Kudah . . . Ja Kudah."

It sounded unearthly, supernatural. Spirits seemed to be hovering above us and their voices to want to seize us, to lift us. After a brief silence, these introductory invocations were followed by something for which we have no name in our occidental music. There were two voices, a magnificent, youthful, bright alto or mezzo-soprano and an equally splendid, deeply moving baritone which seemed so far apart and yet so close that one could have thought that all the heavenly and earthly songs of praise sounded in this single "Ja Kudah." What we now heard high above us was a duel, and yet it wasn't. Nor was it a song, but singing in its highest, simplest form; it was that perfect language which will not be heard on this earth until art no longer reigns but strives to serve, and goodness and compassion inform the grammar of a single, great, humanized mankind.

It was certainly a man and a woman who must be standing high above us, on the slab stretching across the "rock gate." Although we could not see them, they had probably seen us. That they should nonetheless be singing, that they did not hide from us, proved them to be peaceful and harmless. They were also devout, for a person who believes nothing and does not feel the need for elevation lacks the words and sounds which were floating up there in the moonlight as though on angels' wings. They faded in a slow, solemn melody which was sung by the alto and accompanied by the baritone and concluded with the same exclamation with which the song had begun.

Now that silence had returned, Halef launched into all sorts of questions and suppositions, as was his habit, but I wanted to cling to the profound impression these voices had made on me, and answered him so curtly that he understood, and stopped. I fell asleep but when I woke up again, I could still hear the voices, although they were no longer as close as yesterday evening. I looked up and could clearly recognize the two singers. They were standing on the slab that had been placed across the "rock gate," far out in front, on a projection. They had to be utterly free from vertigo to dare step that far forward. It was a man and a woman but the distance made it impossible to determine their ages. Their bright, ample garments were fluttering in the wind of the early day. Suffused in the light of the dawn, and with the folds of their garments billowing, they looked as if they were in motion themselves and about to float down from the rock.

"Sidi, they are going to jump down," Halef exclaimed. He was more fully awake than I but had remained lying on the ground so that he would not disturb my sleep. Now he jumped to his feet, threw up his arms and shouted up to the rock, telling the two to be careful.

The singing stopped. They were listening, for while they had seen and heard Halef, they had not understood him. Now both stepped back from the dangerous spot and disappeared. Halef breathed a sigh of relief.

"Allah be praised! I couldn't stand looking on any longer. During the whole time, they seemed about to come crashing down. May I finally talk about them? Last night, that was forbidden."

"Because such sacred and profound emotions must be respected, dear Halef. Even now, it would have been better not to have interrupted them. We shall ride toward them."

We quickly washed, saddled our horses, mounted, and turned toward the gate, which we reached in a few moments. Here also, there was no place on either side of the river bed where the rocks could have been climbed. The trap was perfect, from our point of view. The only possible ascent had to lie on the other, the northern side of the gate. We rode through it, went a few steps further, and stopped.

Some minutes passed, and no one came. Halef became impatient and rode slowly back and forth. Then

I saw him make a gesture of surprise, raise his hand to his face, and look up.

"What is it?" I asked.

"A small stone fell down," he answered.

A few moments later, he made the same movement, and then repeated it.

"Sidi, someone is throwing them," he said as he looked up again. "The aim is quite accurate. The target is my head! Someone is up there."

"Hardly. No one could get up there and down again."

"And yet someone must be able to, for those small rocks came from there. Who could it be that dares make fun of me?"

"A girl. A charming, lively girl of less than seventeen."

"Can you see her?"

"No."

"Then how do you know she is charming and less than seventeen?"

"Because a girl who is older and not charming would not frolic like that."

"That's true. Perhaps you already know what she looks like?"

"Pretty much."

"How?"

"I judge by the vigor, fullness, and exceptional softness of her voice, for I assume it is the singer. She is used to taking deep breaths, she climbs well, she never feels dizzy. You tell me what can be inferred from all that."

"Hm," he answered, embarrassed. "Wouldn't you rather tell me, Sidi?"

"No, I want to hear it from you."

"Very well. I infer that she has good eyesight, a boldly jutting nose, a strong, wide mouth, a thick, heavy neck from which those loud and full sounds come, well developed shoulders and two iron-hard hips for climbing—"

He was interrupted. Someone was laughing gaily. Halef looked up again, and asked:

"Did you hear that, Sidi? She is laughing about her own hips. That's like—"

He broke off, touched his face, and went on:

"She threw another stone. I am going to get off this horse and catch her."

He jumped from the saddle and closely examined the immense pillar of the gate. He really believed that the imp was hidden up there. But whenever he had been struck, I had been able to tell from what direction those well-aimed little missiles had come. It had not been from above, but from below, from near the pillar where large boulders lay scattered. Behind them, a completely vertical wall rose so smoothly that not even a squirrel or monkey could have climbed it. The singer could not possibly have come down there, and therefore I had paid no attention to that spot. But now I guided my horse there.

"Sidi!" someone was calling softly.

"Where are you? Come out!"

But no one came. I decided to go along with the joke and dismounted to have a look.

"Sidi!" the voice came again, from the left, but when I got there, I was facing the smooth wall and no one could be seen. "Effendi!" the voice came from the right. I now turned in that direction, passed among some stones, and again found myself facing the wall. "Sidi, Effendi," and "Effendi, Sidi," it now came from one point, now from another, but the prankster remained invisible. Halef began to realize that he had looked in the wrong place. He joined me in my search but was equally unsuccessful.

"She is invisible," he laughed, but I could tell he was chagrined.

"No, only barefoot," I answered. "If she wore shoes, we would hear her."

"But a man like you should not allow himself to be led by the nose by a girl that isn't seventeen yet," he said.

"That's true. So I'll catch her inside two minutes."

Now I heard a suppressed, provocative laugh from my left, but only a few moments later, the voice came from the right:

"Sidi, in two minutes."

"Probably in one. Watch out!"

Up to this moment, I had played her game standing

up. But now, where I had to demonstrate that I was as good as my word, I quickly moved between the stones and then lay down, crawling forward. I felt I knew the spot I had to find. There had to be a hiding place here somewhere, but one that could not easily be discovered. It could not be between the various boulders for I had been there and seen nothing. It therefore had to be in the wall itself and hidden from view by a projecting rock. And there was such a place. Both Halef and I had passed it when we had been searching. There was a rock, perhaps five meters in width, whose base was separated from the wall but whose top leaned against it, giving it the appearance of a slanting roof. The space was narrow and not high enough to stand. One had to sit or kneel. It was open at both ends but there had to be a passage from it into the wall, and that was the hiding place where our goblin quickly retreated after she had thrown something or called out.

I crawled close to the boulder, pressed against it so I would take up as little space as possible, and waited. And there she was, flitting past me on my left to disappear among the stones. The movement was so rapid that I only saw something white. I quickly crawled to the center of the space where I found an opening that was almost two meters high and wide enough to allow a grown person to pass through. To my surprise, it did not lead into the rock wall but quickly back out into the open. It was only its front that was solid. Its far side was full of gaps and cracks which formed an ascending zigzag path that could not be seen from the outside. The opening which now lay behind me had certainly at one time been covered; it had given on the river valley. But later, there had been reasons to conceal this access to the top of the "rock gate." The stone had been placed out front to mark the spot so that one would not see it at a cursory glance. I straightened up, quickly scanning the surroundings. Then I sat down on a stone lying next to the opening through which I had just come and through which the singer also had to rush to hide again while we were vainly looking for her outside.

And she did come a few moments later, crawling

just as I had. Then she stood up but with her back toward me.

She laughed, and this one sound was enough to make one love her. She took a step back, and touched me. Abruptly, she turned, and I rose at the same moment.

"Sidi, Effendi," she exclaimed, startled, as her beautiful, noble face was suffused by a glowing red.

"In one minute. Did I keep my word?" I asked.

"Yes," she answered, while her eyes seemed to grow bigger to take me in. "I suppose you always keep your word."

"How do you know?"

"From looking at you. I had the courage to throw something at the other one but not at you. What's his name?"

"Hadji Halef Omar."

"So he is a Hadji, a devout person? That pleases me. Had I known, I would not have played tricks on him. But when I saw him, I felt one had to play games with him."

"He enjoys jokes, but not games. He is very brave, loyal, widely travelled, and the sheik of a famous tribe."

"What tribe?"

"An Arabic one."

"From beyond the sea?"

"Yes."

"Are you also an Arab?"

"No, I am European."

"European? From what country? Forgive me for asking, Effendi."

"Do you know the countries of Europe?"

"And also their peoples. My father taught me. He knows a great deal, almost everything."

"I am Alemani."*

She clapped her small, beautifully formed hands, and exclaimed:

"An Alemani! That will please him. What am I going to tell him when he asks me your name?"

"I am called Kara Ben Nemsi."

---

* German.

"Nemsi means the same as Alemani. My father's name is Abd el Fadl,* and I am Merhameh."†

"Was it you that sang last night and this morning?"

"Yes. Do you know what we sang"?

"No."

"It is the morning and evening prayer of Djinnistan. We sing both of them every day."

"Do you know Djinnistan?"

"It is the country of my birth. The Fadl line is as old as mankind. My father is a loyal servant of the ruler. He was sent by him to—"

She broke off as if she had said something she shouldn't have, and then went on:

"We are now living here on the 'rock gate,' awaiting the fulfillment of what has been promised."

The tone of her words prompted me to ask:

"Do you mean the promise from Sitara?"

She raised her head and asked tensely:

"Do you know Sitara, Effendi? Do you know it?"

"I do."

"But not the woman that rules it?"

"I know her as well."

"By name?"

"Personally."

"You have seen her?"

She asked slowly, seriously. Her long, heavy lashes were shadowing a look that was full of astonishment, curiosity, and contained joy.

"I not only saw her but also talked to her. I was her guest."

"In Ikbal?"

"Yes. I lived in her house."

"You lived there?"

"Yes."

"Are you perhaps coming from her? Did she send you?"

"Why do you ask?"

She had been almost ecstatic. When she heard my answer, she restrained herself and continued more calmly:

---

* Servant of kindness.
† Compassion

"Forgive me, Sidi. I realize that I am too young to be asking such questions. But please allow me to touch you."

"Go ahead."

I assumed that she wanted to take my hand but instead, she approached me, raised hers and tapped my chest with her index and middle fingers, while she bent her head to listen.

"He has it, he has it!" she exulted. "I had a feeling! He has it!"

"What do I have?"

"The breastplate. I can feel it, or is the foil which protects your heart not a shield which the lady of Sitara gave you?"

"It is. Do you know her name?"

"Marah Durimeh. I have to go. I have to go to my father, and tell him that—"

She could not finish her sentence because at that moment Halef, who had followed me, made his appearance. And now something so surprising, rare and deeply moving happened that even today I cannot report it without emotion. He looked at her, took half a step back, and looked again. His face changed. It became serious but softer and softer. His eyes misted over and took on the mildest, most tender expression of which they were capable. And yet they also radiated enthusiasm. He seemed to be dreaming. Then he took the sleeve of her white linen garment, kissed the hem, and said as he turned to me:

"She is very beautiful, Sidi."

The girl did not blush, nor did she answer like some other girl might have, but said just as seriously and sincerely: "He does not see me, he only sees my soul; that's why he talks as he does."

"Your soul?" Halef asked. "Yes, that too. But what I really meant was your form. Marah Durimeh, the soul of mankind, must have looked precisely as you do to those who were fortunate enough to see her when she was still young."

The girl answered:

"You kissed my garment. But that kiss was for her, not for me. What you two find beautiful, what makes you happy and elates you, comes from her. I send her the sacred kiss that was really intended for her by giving it to the person who knows her."

She quickly stepped up to me and pressed her lips on the cuff of my sleeve. Then she continued:

"Father asks if he should come down here or if you prefer climbing up to where he is."

"We will climb up there," I answered. "But we don't want to leave our horses where someone might see them."

"I know a good hiding place," she said. "It's very close, and I will show it to Halef. It's enough if he accompanies me. You go on, Effendi. You cannot miss the way. We will catch up with you."

I nodded, saw Halef bend down and again disappear through the opening, and then turned to do as she had suggested.

The path zigzagged, as I already said, and led through narrow clefts to the heights. As I followed it slowly, I thought about the young, beautiful, immensely appealing person I had just met. Her name was Merhameh, "compassion," and she was of the age-old, famous family of the Fadl, which means "kindness." Many members of that family had been enlightened rulers, great scholars, and famous artists. Those who know the history of mankind realize how great has been the number of important and influential men who were called Fadl, ben Fadl or Abd el Fadl. And I was suddenly to meet an Abd el Fadl, who was an emissary of the Mir of Djinnistan and was living here at this time, above the "rock gate." What were the purposes, the reasons behind this?

I would not dream of attempting to describe Merhameh's beauty, for it is precisely the characteristic of true beauty that it cannot be described. I shall merely mention that she was not dressed like a wealthy, but a poor person. She was barefoot, as I had thought. And because the ground was not sandy but covered with debris, I had not been able to find her tracks when we had been playing hide and seek. Her simple oriental garment was held together at the waist by a leather belt. It was made of perfectly ordinary cheap linen but was white and completely spotless, something I must mention because water was so scarce in this region. Her

heavy, dark, wavy hair was not braided but held together at the neck by a string with flowers, from which
it fell to a considerable length. Whatever else should
be said about her will be mentioned in the further
course of this story.

I had not progressed far when I heard a noise behind me. As I turned, I saw Aacht and Uucht, my two
dogs. Halef had permitted them to follow me. When
they had caught up with me, they asked if they might
rush ahead but I had them stay at my side.

The path had taken me first to the left, then to the
right. It was once again turning left when I heard
voices. Merhameh and Halef were coming.

"Effendi, can you see me? Here I am."

I looked back. The girl had just turned the last corner, and while I could see her, Halef could not. I
stopped to wait for her. Her face was radiant with
satisfaction, and in her eyes there shone an excessive
spiritual force which had been in danger of withering
in her lonely circumstances. She was like that great
friend of mankind whose name she bore, compassion:
If it cannot be active, it loses its power.

"I have only spent ten minutes with your Hadji," she
said, "but I already know his fame, and all his qualities. And I also know Hanneh, that loveliest of all
flowers, and Kara ben Halef, his son, who some day
will be even more renowned than his father. Effendi, I
ran away from him because he meant to praise me. He
was going to compare me to everything between
heaven and earth. But it is not I that deserve such
praise, but he. His love for you is as tender, as limitless, as the love of the body for the soul. It won my
heart."

At many points, the path was so precipitous or narrow that Merhameh had to precede me, and it was
therefore difficult to converse. Even without words,
however, she absorbed my entire attention. Every one
of her vigorously beautiful, harmonious movements
cast a spell. She seemed like a poem that God had
created in flesh and blood to match the beauty of her
name with a corresponding physical beauty.

Shortly before we reached the heights, Halef caught
up with us. He had been hurrying because he wanted

to be there when I met Abd el Fadl. I could tell that a jocular remark about the daughter was on the tip of his tongue, but the seriousness and sublimity of the moment restrained him. Just then, as we were reaching the top, we were standing on the western pillar of the gate, and had only to climb the slab lying across it to see the unending sea on either side, and the desert behind and in front of us. No ship, no boat, broke the utter stillness of the ocean. The long billows of the day before had become dark green, foam-crested breakers. The foam looked as though it were made of pearls, the visible sign of a mysterious life breathing in the depths that longed to rise to the surface and could find no other release. Looking back, toward the desert, we saw nothing in that sandy desolation but a tiny rise at its edge which could barely be recognized. That was the well with the angel. And looking forward, the eye travelled over the boundless, seemingly bleak desert solitude with the volcanic smoke from Djinnistan on the distant horizon. In the midst of this isolation and emptiness, there was the narrow, stony Chatar defile which might be devoured at any moment by the two oceans unceasingly gnawing at it. On the narrow gate of this defile, we were pathetically weak creatures, but with large designs nonetheless. Because of an optical illusion, it seemed as if the isthmus were floating on the water and being tossed back and forth, in danger of suddenly capsizing and being submerged in the flood.

"Sidi, I am becoming dizzy. I have to sit down, otherwise I'll fall. Don't you feel it?" Halef asked.

"A little, but I hope it will pass."

"Not with me. I feel that I cannot stay here but must climb down. The sea is opening both jaws, one to the left, one to the right, ready to devour me."

Merhameh said:

"Then permit me to lead you."

"You? Hm. Perhaps that will work. But are you really going to hold on to me?"

"Yes, so you won't stagger. Look, there is my father, waiting for us. Come along."

I mentioned before that there was a pile of rock up here, surrounded by bushes which had their roots in the slab. It was mysterious to me how they could survive. Now I saw that this pile of stones was actually a hut. Abd el Fadl was just leaving it. He was barefoot like his daughter, and also dressed in white. His simple garment was held together at the hips by a string, and he had wound a white piece of inexpensive linen around his head so that two corners were hanging down on his shoulders in an arrangement I had never seen before. In front, a pin whose head was an ordinary rifle bullet had been stuck into the cloth.

Abd el Fadl was a tall man of noble bearing whose calm, sure movements revealed strength of character and clarity about himself. His face seemed that of someone of more than sixty but inwardly he was still young. His features were like his beautiful daughter's but more developed, mature, and firm. They, his voice, and his entire manner expressed kindness, a tolerant moderation and benevolent chivalry which immediately captivated me, not just at that moment, but enduringly.

Our greeting did not take the form we had imagined, and certainly was not what Halef expected. The moment Abd el Fadl appeared, he had risen and held out his hand for Merhameh to guide him. But the sight of the sea far below made him stagger like a drunk person. He stretched out his free arm, swinging it back and forth as if he were carrying a balancing pole. The dogs and I slowly walked behind him, and thus we approached the father of our young guide who was looking at us expectantly. Halef found it impossible to remain silent. He was about to launch into a speech when he lost his balance, pitched forward, turned around and sat down.

I felt somewhat foolish that we should present ourselves so gracelessly. But Merhameh burst out laughing and on the face of her father there shone so cordial and frank a lightheartedness that I forgot all about my embarrassment. Abl el Fadl excused Halef kindly, saying:

"He isn't the first. Not everyone can face both the depth and the heights at one and the same time without losing his hold."

This form of expression was as ambiguous as his

daughter's had been earlier. As he was speaking, it was the dogs rather than Halef or I that absorbed his attention. They seemed to interest him greatly. But then he quickly added:

"Your companion was not born in the mountains."

"No," I answered. "His home is the desert; he loses his balance up here on your heights."

"He is an Arab," Merhameh added, "the sheik of a famous tribe, and his name is Hadji Halef Omar ben Hadji Abul Abbas Ibn Hadji Davuhd el Gossarah."

But her father was not listening to this lengthy name. He was still looking at the dogs.

"Forgive me for being so impolite, and for paying attention to these animals rather than to the two of you," he said. "But they are very important to me. I have seen a pair, not these here, which were sent north as a present. And I saw a second pair which also were sent as a present, but from the north to the south."

"The first went to Djinnistan, the second to the country of the Ussul," I broke in.

"And these here?" he asked.

"They are brother and sister, a cross between the two breeds."

He took a step back, looked at me, and asked:

"Are they yours?"

"Yes, they were a present."

"Present?" he exclaimed happily. "Then you are the—?"

He did not dare complete his sentence, but his daughter quickly said:

"He is, father, he is. He has the shield, do you hear?"

She walked up to me and tapped my chest so that the sound of the metal could be heard. Then she also tapped on his, and I heard the identical sound. A radiant smile of happiness passed over his face, but, taking me by the hand, he merely said:

"You are welcome. Come to the place that is yours."

He led me to some soft green grass by the hut and asked me to sit down. I did and, immediately, Aacht and Uucht took their places on either side of me.

"Please excuse us for a moment; then we will be at your service. Come, my child."

He took his daughter by the hand and walked to the

edge of the stone slab. That was the place where they stood when they sang. As they walked, Merhameh was talking to her father. She seemed to be giving him a brief report about what Halef and I had told her. Now they were standing close to each other, her head leaning against his shoulder, almost immobile, looking out into the distance and up to heaven, communing silently.

"Sidi, I think they are praying," Halef said.

I did not answer. This seemed a sacred place and I felt that invisible mysteries were all around me, and that their solution only seemed to lie out there over the sea or in the desert, but must really be found within me. When father and daughter returned, their eyes were moist, and there was something like an anxious question on their faces. He sat at my feet while his daughter modestly looked for a place somewhat further away, yet close enough to hear what we were saying. Abd el Fadl began:

"My daughter has told me that you are from the country of the Alemani and are called Effendi or Sidi. Will you permit me to use those titles also?"

I nodded, and he went on:

"You have a shield, and I also have one. We do not have to know each other, and yet we do. What you are in your country, what I am in mine, is of no importance at this hour and place. We shall not go into those things. But please tell me who gave you that shield, and whether it really was Marah Durimeh."

"It was. She gave it to me in Ikbal when I and my Hadji Halef were her guests. She gave it to me when she asked me to travel to Djinnistan."

"Then you are the one I expected, but there is also another person who has a shield."

"He will be here in a few days."

"Who is he?"

"A young man from the country of the Ussul. He is called the Djirbani there."

"The leper? Do they also believe he is mad?"

"Yes."

"Allah be praised! And I also thank you for this message."

Looking at his daughter, he nodded to her and continued: "It is he. There probably is not a single great idea on earth which was not considered madness in the beginning. The hour of fulfillment seems to be approaching. The mountains are burning, and the ice of the north is trying to make its way south. The desert is being filled with food and drink. The 'madness' which will bring us peace is about to appear. But how?"

These last words were again directed to me. But I did not have a chance to answer because Halef broke in in his usual, bragging manner: "He will not appear alone but at the head of an army, not as someone with a request, but as a commander whom all the world must obey."

"At the head of an army?" Abd el Fadl asked.

"Yes."

"To be led against whom?"

"The Tshoban. They are making ready to attack and despoil the Ussul. But the courageous ones among the Ussul who are called Hukara are setting out to meet them under the leadership of the Erdjani. Both armies will clash here in this defile."

"When?"

"In a few days. We rode ahead of the army to inspect the defile and to spy on the Tshoban as they approach."

"So there is going to be war?" the "servant of compassion" exclaimed as he clapped his hands in considerable agitation. "War and bloodshed. Is it because peace can only be won through blood?"

"No, no bloodshed," Halef contradicted him. "We intend to win through cunning and kindness, not through hatred and blood."

"Impossible," Abd el Fadl exclaimed, but perhaps only to test us.

"What do you mean, impossible? We have experience in winning such battles. Let me tell you about them."

He told about the "Valley of the Steps," and of various experiences we had had which proved that intelligence wins out over violence, kindness over injustice. Then he recounted how we had become acquainted with Marah Durimeh and then met her a second time.

He finally mentioned Sitara, and then the Ussul. He spoke concisely, his report being a complete change from his usual way of expressing himself. What he had never been able to do before, he managed this time: He avoided all indiscretions, made no ill-considered statements, and omitted all praise or blame which was not directly relevant to the matter at hand. He gave a complete account of our adventures among the Ussul and our ride to the defile, so that when he had finished, Abd el Fadl was fully informed.

Father and daughter had listened with considerable interest, and the effect on Abd el Fadl was extraordinary. He said nothing but got up and slowly walked to the spot where he and Merhameh had been standing a while ago. She said:

"Forgive him for leaving you without saying anything. He is deeply moved. Some time ago, we asked God that the man we were expecting not be a man of violence but a hero of kindness. And now that we have heard that this wish will be granted, father is leaving to thank Allah. He always does it; he cannot help himself. We have long yearned for you, and I cannot tell you how much we looked forward to your arrival. But the carpet on which you are sitting will tell you."

She pointed at the grass. I looked at the soft, green surface which the weight of my body was pressing down, and suddenly realized something that had not occurred to me when I had sat down before. I quickly got up.

"This carpet," I exclaimed. "That is a treasure in this region. Do you have water?"

"We collect the dew of the night and drink the juice of the naras fruit," she answered.

"But this grass wasn't here originally. Did you sow it?"

"Yes, we brought the seed from far away."

"And how did you water it?"

"We used the dew we did not drink to make it grow."

"And for whom was it intended?"

"For—"

She did not answer right away, looking around anxiously, as if she were not permitted to discuss the matter.

"I am not allowed to talk about it. It is a secret. I will tell you, but only you. Father isn't looking over here, and your Halef won't hear me if I speak softly. But please, do **not** mention it to anyone, anyone at all."

She stepped close to me, placed her hands around her mouth, and whispered:

"For—the new Mir of Djinnistan."

"Is the old one dead?" I asked.

"Oh no! God forbid!"

"And yet there is a new one?"

"We hope so."

"How strange. And this magnificent carpet is for him?"

"Yes."

"Is he coming here, then?"

"When the prophecy is fulfilled, he will come across this isthmus."

"Then why did I have to sit down on this grass which was destined for him? I am not he."

"How can you be sure?"

"How?" I asked, startled. "A European cannot possibly become Mir of Djinnistan."

"Why not? Suppose he is the one that was chosen?"

"I don't understand what you mean."

"You will. Father is coming back. Please, do not mention anything to him."

This caused me some embarrassment, for I could not possibly go back to my old seat. I did not belong there. After Abd el Fadl had repeatedly asked me to sit down again, and I finally chose a spot near the grass, he looked at me and his daughter and noticed that she blushed.

"Why is the Effendi not sitting where he sat before?" he asked her.

"Because I told him," she confessed, joining her hands.

"What did you tell him?"

"That this grass is for the new Mir of Djinnistan."

He merely raised his index finger; there was no other sort of chiding. Turning to me, he said:

"And you presumably did not believe that you were that new Mir?"

"Neither the new nor the old one," I smiled.

"We know who the latter is but no one can say who the former will be."

"It's certainly not me."

"Are you quite sure?"

"Yes."

"But you can't be. For the new Mir is never born or raised in Djinnistan."

"But probably not in Europe either."

"Oh, yes. He may even come from America. The laws of Djinnistan are rather curious. In this particular case, I happen to know that you are not the new Mir but your coming here is closely tied to his, and I shall be frank and tell you that when I first saw you, the effect was such that I asked you to sit down on the seat that is really meant for him. It is your idea to capture the Tshoban here. And only you had the kind intention to avoid all bloodshed. Should you need our help, I want you to ask for it if you feel we might be useful."

"I do not reject your help, I request it. But there is one condition which you must meet."

"Which one?"

"Silence! It must appear as if the Erdjani were in complete command. And I do not want people to talk of us, but of him. I want him to garner the honor and glory, and no one should even think of praising me."

Then I told him everything about our journey and stay among the Ussul, and added some reflections that had occurred to me yesterday after our arrival. He wholeheartedly agreed with everything I said, and found nothing to change or criticize in what I had decided on.

"I am infinitely grateful to you, Sidi, for having considered us worthy of hearing all this from you. Now we see that we may contribute our share to a successful conclusion. We will help you as regards the defile, and also the steppe and desert of the Tshoban through which I have travelled so often that I probably know it better than anyone. Both of us know this defile very well. We have had time enough to explore its every

: 265 :

nook and cranny. May I make a suggestion?"

"Please do."

"Today, you won't ride on but stay with us. This defile is of such importance to you that you must not neglect it. You have to get to know it, and I will show it to you. We have to do that on foot, so your horses will have a day of rest. In the morning, we will look over one half of the isthmus, in the afternoon the other. Merhameh will stay behind to prepare the evening meal."

"I have meat and other provisions she can use," I said.

"Thank you, but I do not want to take anything from you. We won't go hungry. The sea provides us with delicious fish, we obtain manna in the desert, and along the coast we grow tasty apples which I am sure you will enjoy. Tomorrow, the sheik of the Haddedihn will stay with Merhameh because you only have two horses. You and I will ride north to reconnoiter. I know the region so that we will probably be more successful than if you went with Halef whose presence is required here, should something unforeseen occur during our absence."

Halef and I agreed to his proposal, and we climbed down, taking Abd el Fadl with us.

14 : On the Rocky Heights

When we had come down, Merhameh took me to the place where the horses had been hidden. We unsaddled them and the dogs, for the latter were to accompany us and should therefore be free of all burdens. We turned our water, provisions, and rifles, except for my carbine, over to Merhameh. We needed the morning to explore that part of the defile through which we had come yesterday. In the afternoon, we would turn to that section through which the Tshoban would come. There is no reason for a detailed description of that narrow strip of rock which led from one country into the other. There were some spots where it was so narrow that one could call from one bank to the other and be clearly understood. At its widest point, a mere quarter hour was needed to cross it. Along both sides, the coastline was so precipitous that it was not possible to climb down. When Abd el Fadl wanted to fish, he went to the southern end of the isthmus where it bordered on Ussul territory. He had a raft hidden there between the rocks which served well enough for this purpose when the sea was calm. He had also constructed a small, well-concealed basin where the fish were kept. On the same side, though not directly on the water, there was a half natural, half man-made plantation of a species of tree he called naras.

It was the fruit of this tree that Merhameh served us at noon. We also had fish and a kind of manna bread that is made of the starchy thallus of a species of lecanora which occurs in great abundance in desert regions. These small thallus pieces resemble grains of wheat but are so light that the wind carries them over considerable distances. When they collect in depressions in the desert, people say that manna has rained from heaven. There are holes in those deserts which, were they filled with water, would be called ponds or lakes. They do not contain water, however, but lecanora grains which have been blown there by the wind and deposited so far below the surface that they cannot be picked up again and carried further. When the wind then covers them with a layer of sand so that the spot becomes indistinguishable from the surrounding area, a hidden storage depot is created. A single one of these is enough to save a caravan from starvation. Abd el Fadl told me that such a storage area lay half an hour's ride away, northeast of the isthmus, and that he had discovered it only by chance, since he had no dog.

"Are there dogs which will find manna?" I asked.

"Yes, didn't you know that?"

"No. What breed can do this?"

His face took on an entirely different expression. He nodded to himself, and asked:

"But you know that the dogs of the Ussul can find water?"

"Yes."

"And the dogs of the Djinnistani find bread. No Ussul dog will stop when he runs across a place where manna lies hidden in the ground. But Djinnistani dogs let one know immediately, provided the animal is a thoroughbred. There aren't many of those, and they are very expensive."

When he said that, something suddenly occurred to me.

"So that's the reason for the crossbreeding. Dogs that can scent both manna and water. How farsighted of the Mir. And the first pair of these dogs was given to me who—"

"The first pair?" he asked. "Oh, no! The Mir of Djinnistan was the first to be given a pair of dogs by the sheik of the Ussul. He immediately experimented with crossbreeding them, and when this proved a success, he returned the present with two of his noble Djinnistan breed. So that he was the first one to have animals of this new strain."

"What is his name? I have never heard it. He is always referred to as the 'Mir of Djinnistan,' but no one says his name."

"Because he doesn't have one."

"No name?" Halef asked. "But the name is the main thing."

"That is the custom in your country, but not in mine. In any event, names and character frequently don't match, and it can happen that the most wretched person is called Felix. You don't have that in Djinnistan. There, the name is true, for it defines the character, the activity, the profession. I am called Abd el Fadl, and it is really my profession to be a 'servant of kindness.' My daughter's name is Merhameh, and you will soon discover that she is only guided by compassion which helps others carry their burdens even when they are self-imposed. The ruler is therefore simply and briefly referred to as Mir, but he is what the word means. Mir is an abbreviation of Emir, which signifies prince, master, ruler. And that he is, in the fullest meaning of the term. So what would be the point of additional designations or names? We do not have those registers that list hundreds of important personages which one has to learn by heart. We only have the Mir. You want to go to him, and you will see him, and perhaps get to know him. So it is unnecessary for me to make long speeches about him, or us, which wouldn't convey the way things are."

When, toward evening, we had finished reconnoitering and I assumed that I had come to know all that was necessary about the defile, I told Abd el Fadl how satisfactory I found its topography. A locale better suited to our purpose was difficult to imagine. If we succeeded in luring the Tshoban into the stretch between the "orifice" and the "rock gate," we could not but be successful. I only wished that there might be a path on the heights that would connect those two points. If there was such a path up there by which one could move back and forth between our troops without being seen by the imprisoned Tshoban below, this would assure us an inestimable advantage. When I mentioned this to Abd el Fadl, he expressed considerable satisfaction, and said:

"There is such a path, but you did not see it because it is never used. I and my daughter only take the one below."

"Is there a trail that leads directly down?"

"Not all the way. We tried, but could not get beyond the last ledge."

"Is it far from there to the bottom?"

"No. The ledge is about four meters above the river bank."

"That isn't much. Have you never tried to extend it all the way?"

"No, the rock is too hard and we do not have the necessary tools. Do you want to see it?"

"Yes. I should like you to show me the entire path up there. Then we can determine whether the trail leading down from it will be of use to us, or not."

We were standing in the place where the horses had been hidden. They were eating the manna grains and I was very pleased to notice that they liked this unfamiliar fodder. This settled the important problem of feeding them in the desert.

We climbed up to the gate. Only because it was never used and therefore showed no tracks had we failed to notice the path the day before. Now that I saw it by moonlight, I felt certain that I could pass it even at night, and this might prove useful to us. We had walked its entire length and Abd el Fadl had not shown us the spot where the trail branched off and led down. But now, as we came back and approached it, we turned around a projection which we had disregarded before and saw a series of weathered natural steps that made it possible to descend to the ledge Abd el Fadl had mentioned. It was about four meters above the path which ran along the river bank and was large enough to make it impossible to see someone lying on it. Fortunately, the steps leading to the ledge were not exposed but formed a channel. A person using them would not be seen from below. This was an important advantage, and for what I had in mind— an unobserved infiltration of the enemy—the height of the ledge was no obstacle. My lasso was long enough to reach all the way down and there were enough cracks and holes to attach it. I did not mention this. There would be time for that later, should it prove necessary.

When we got back to the "rock gate" the sun was about to set, but I was curious to see how good a horseman Abd el Fadl was, and also wanted to pick up some fresh water for our ride the following day. I therefore suggested that he accompany me to the well angel before nightfall. He knew of it but was unaware that it contained a basin filled with water. We had told him about it, and he was anxious to get to know the interior of this interesting, age-old waterwork. We emptied all our skins and then took our four dogs along to bring back all the water they could carry.

Abd el Fadl was not a bad horseman but out of practice. We quickly reached the angel and spent some considerable time inside it. He told me that an identical figure stood in the "City of the Dead," yet no one knew what purpose it might have served when people were still living there. When I asked him what he meant by the "City of the Dead," he told me that it was the former capital of Ardistan which had had to be abandoned when the "river of peace" had suddenly reversed its course and had returned to Djinnistan and paradise. He said that it was the most magnificent of all ruins and suggested that we visit it in spite of the fact that it did not lie along the direct route. We would never again have a chance to see anything approaching it.

Upon our return, we had our supper on the heights with his daughter, but Halef came to get his and then climbed down again, saying that he wanted to sleep near the horses. Actually, however, he felt that the danger of falling was even greater during the night and had therefore decided to remain below where it was safe. But I preferred the heights, not only for themselves, but also because I wanted to spend the evening with these two highly interesting persons and get to know them better. There was also the volcanic fire which was invisible from below but which would probably be seen even more clearly from here, high up on the rocks, than from the top of the Ussul temple which was framed by treetops.

During our ride to the well angel, Halef had been alone with Merhameh and used that opportunity to tell her as much as he could about the two of us. In her ingenuousness, she repeated everything to her father. When he heard that I was a writer and had written more than one book, he became more interested in me. At first, he merely asked about the purpose and content of these books. When I had told him, Merhameh clapped her small hands and exclaimed joyfully:

"Then you write about the very same sort of thing my father has also written so much about. You will be a welcome guest in our palace in Djinnistan, where you will see the library and all the books he has written."

In the course of our conversation, I discovered more and more appealing qualities in the highly educated father of beautiful, charming Merhameh. He was a statesman, a scholar, and a poet. He was also a warrior of great skill, as the reader will discover. Ordinarily, he seemed taciturn, but he enjoyed talking that evening, and I enjoyed listening to him. It was an unexpected enrichment for me, and I learned more about the psychology of the Orient in that one evening than

I had previously learned in months, even years. Gradually, the smoke clouds in the north again changed to glowing flames, as if the mountains wanted to add their great, radiant, eternal words to our conversation. It is impossible for me to do justice to this evening. During the entire time, Merhameh sat silently, with folded hands. What happiness to be the child of such a father, to have been privileged to live in such a pure, sublime atmosphere from childhood on!

I called Abd el Fadl a statesman. He was also a skillful diplomat. It was actually the kindness of his manner that made it impossible to refuse telling him everything he wished to know. Although I did not talk a great deal, he soon knew all about my literary activity and goals and about what was still an uncommon way of trying to attain them. It goes without saying that he was especially interested in learning whether I would also describe the present journey. When I told him I would, he asked:

"Where will you begin? I imagine with a description of the Ussul. They are the fertile soil from which your work will rise to bring forth flowers and fruit."

"You are right," I answered.

"Then the first part of your book will be boring."

"Unfortunately, that is unavoidable."

"The soil from which something grows is never interesting to the reader. And even if you do your duty and enliven it by showing how future events are rooted in it, you still won't be understood. You will be reproached for being a mystic, for all seed is planted in mystical darkness. You will be criticized and perhaps even suspected. But don't allow that to deter you. You must plow, fertilize, plant, and make the roots grow, whether those who are not gardeners like it, or not. Then, when the earth opens up and the first, healthy, fresh buds appear, from which the stem will develop, people will change their minds and grant you your rights. Do you know where those buds will show themselves?"

"Yes, here, among you. You two, kindness and compassion, are the first signs of life as my tree rises from Ussul earth. From them, the strength of the trunk will come."

"The Erdjani?" he interrupted.

"Yes. For it is only through him and with him that the rest of us can grow."

"You understand, you understand," he exclaimed with sincere pleasure. "Let them blame you as much as they like. Just as the land of the Ussul lies behind you, so all their carping soon will. First, you had to write in the oppressive, close lowlands and the dark forests of the swampland. The only light there came from the volcanoes. So it is not surprising that you also should be considered dark and mystical while actually you are merely reporting real, everyday, though unknown, events. The isthmus on which we find ourselves here not only leads you but also your pen from the land of a necessary and natural opacity into the land of unobstructed sunlight where life is not lived in obscurity but in the full light of God's eye and the eye of mankind. As early as tomorrow morning, we will enter that land. And from tomorrow on, thousands of shapes and hundreds of deeds and events will rise from the desert of the Tshoban and the fields of the Djunub, just as your readers desire it, so that those who doubt your book will be shown that you did right when you described the Ussul, that there was no other way. I know this country, and I also know that the desert may be filled with a surprising life. And we also know what lies ahead. The Tshoban and the Ussul are both coming here to pit their uncouth strength against each other. And the Djunub are gathering far from here to attack both of them. The Mir of Ardistan is preparing war against the Mir of Djinnistan. And here we stand, four poor, weak humans, but humans who are inspired by kindness and a great trust in God, and firmly resolved to accept battle against all these armies, and to reconcile them through love. Effendi, you were not born in that part of the world that you want to describe. But I come from Djinnistan and know what will happen. There is much we will experience and there will be much for you to tell. Your readers will be satisfied with you."

He took my hand as if he were giving me a firm promise. Then the time had come to go to sleep, for it was after midnight and we wanted to set out early in

: 273 :

the morning. When I lay down, golden, flashing rays illuminated the northern sky, striving south as if on angels' wings. And when I awoke, it was dawning and Merhameh had already prepared breakfast. We ate and then went down to Halef who was expecting us. The horses and my two dogs were saddled. I believed that we would be gone for two days, but we would probably have to do four days' riding during that time. That was not too much to ask of my horses but it remained to be seen if the strain would not be excessive for my companion.

As I gave Halef some necessary instructions, Merhameh listened attentively. There was such an openness and such calm understanding in her eyes that I felt I could rely on her almost as much as on the Hadji. Today, Abd el Fadl was not barefoot but had put on light, leather riding socks. Instead of the customary string he wore around his hips, he had put on a wide linen belt and stuck a knife and two pistols in it. As I glanced at these weapons, he said apologetically:

"They are not meant for attack but defense, and won't be used unless there is no other way."

As we set out, the sun was rising from the sea. We had said a brief farewell, for we did not believe that we would run into danger. The skins were filled with water and we had ample provisions. While we had been sleeping, Merhameh had baked manna bread for us and broiled our meat so that it would keep until tomorrow evening. She always had ample wood for fires, for the daily tide carried it here from the forests along the Ussul coast.

During the first quarter hour of our ride, the dogs gave me a pleasant surprise which I must mention here because it relates to something important that happened later. Riding north, we had not left the defile far behind when Aacht and Uucht suddenly stopped and barked. They were asking for permission to move to the left. Abd el Fadl smiled:

"Let them," he said. "They want to show you what they are capable of. This is the first time for them, yet they seem quite sure of themselves."

We followed the dogs, who stopped after a few

moments and began to sniff and then scrape at the ground at a spot where visible tracks showed that someone had been there before us and had dug at the same place.

"What is it?" I asked. "Would it be manna?"

"Yes," my companion answered. "That is the manna storage point we discovered and have been using ever since. I was curious to see if they would find the place and show it to us. I feel reassured now. As long as we have these dogs, we won't go hungry. We can move on."

But first I dismounted to praise my dogs. I dug a handful of grains from the sand, held them out to them and stroked and caressed them, repeating the word "manna" often enough to make clear to them that I was referring to the grains they had found. They wagged their tails and jumped about to show me they understood. Only then did I get back on my horse to follow Abd el Fadl.

I need not mention that he was riding Halef's stallion, Ben Rih, for I would not have surrendered my Syrr. Nor is it necessary to describe the terrain at this time, for I shall return to that later. But I do want to remind the reader that the southern part of Tshoban territory was desert, the northern part steppe. Both were traversed by the empty bed of the dried-out river which divided the country into an eastern and a western half. According to the Djinnistani's map, water could only be found in the west, but because the Tshoban believed there was more moisture in the east, it could be taken for granted that they would march through that part on their way toward the land of the Ussul. We could therefore ignore the west and concentrate on the east. Until the middle of the afternoon, we rode due north, keeping close to the old river because there was no chance that the Tshoban army would stray west of it. But it seemed probable that they had chosen a more easterly route which began at the southernmost oasis where their animals would have their last opportunity to graze. We therefore changed direction now by turning due east. Should the Tshoban already have passed, we would see their tracks and act accordingly. If we didn't, it meant that they had not yet set out and we need merely wait for them.

We had stopped only once, during the most intense heat shortly before noon, and had decided not to rest again before evening unless compelled to do so. The horses had stood up well, and so had Abd el Fadl. They showed no sign of fatigue although by now we had covered a distance for which the Tshoban army would probably require two days. We rode on for another few hours until the previously level, monotonous plain began to show those elevations which the Arabic-speaking Bedouin calls "Shiwahn el Handal." This means "tent of bitter gourds" and the term was chosen because these rises in the ground usually have the form of a tent of sometimes enormous size, and owe their existence to gourds or similar desert vegetation. As they break the force of the daily winds, they are covered with sand. In its attempt to thrust its way above it, the plant grows new lateral and upward shoots. This struggle between wind and vegetation gradually forms a hill which usually has the form of a round, but sometimes of a polygonal, tent which may be quite tall. A person finding himself between these sandy structures is seized by a feeling of uncertainty. At any moment, an enemy or some other surprise may confront him.

For that reason, I was against spending the night amidst these elevations but they extended as far as the eye could see, and the sun had almost set. We had no choice but to bow to circumstance. We looked for a place that would be surrounded by sand hills and offer the necessary shelter. Soon, we found such a spot and dismounted. I then circled the area to make sure that no one else was close. I could see no traces of any living being and we therefore unsaddled and made ourselves and our horses and dogs as comfortable as we could.

Being tired, we soon fell asleep. That we could safely rely on the acute senses and intelligence of the dogs instead of standing guard ourselves was proven this very first evening. Judging by the stars, it was not yet midnight when they woke me. I sat up and listened. There was nothing to be heard or seen. But a curious, acrid, and nauseating odor I had never scented before was perceptible, though it was so faint that it required a keen sense of smell to notice it. Its source could therefore not be so close as to make us fear discovery. I could not doubt that there were human beings nearby. I would have to reconnoiter and see who and where they were. I roused Abd el Fadl to let him know what was going on, and then walked off in the direction from which the odor came. I had left the dogs behind, for I would not need them.

After only a short time, I recognized the smell. It was the unpleasant bitter principle of the coloquint. Dead, withered roots had been dug from the sand and were being used for a fire. That wasn't intelligent, and I concluded that the people I was dealing with were neither cautious nor experienced. I had to thread my way through a large number of sand tents until I reached the spot I was looking for: three men, three horses, and three camels. The fire was small, its stench more powerful than the illumination it provided. I saw and smelled immediately that it had been lit to brew freshly made coffee. At this moment, the fire was being allowed to die. It seemed curious to me that the smelly wood of these plants should have been used to brew aromatic coffee, but I had every reason to be pleased, for there is no telling what might have happened if this imprudence had not betrayed these people's presence.

Hills of sand provide excellent cover. The moon, which had been just a narrow sickle the first night we had spent among the Ussul, had by now become a semi-circle and its light was sufficient to show me all I needed to see. What I could not make out at this moment I saw all the more clearly the following morning, and I can therefore describe our new acquaintances in greater detail than I could observe that evening. The camels were one-humped and their long, slender bodies meant that they were not pack animals but riding camels, perhaps even racers. But they were being used to carry things, for saddles were lying nearby. They had been carrying skins, provisions, a few articles of clothing, and blankets. That these animals should have been chosen meant that the men were in a hurry. Two of the horses had the same bony structure as those of the three captured Tshoban mounts, which I have described before. While not racers, they were of good quality and certainly had endurance. The third horse was of a nobler breed and of the same Persian strain as the white horses of the Maha-Lama and his minister. One of the three men seemed a perfectly ordinary individual. He was dressed in a shirt-like haik and had a piece of cloth on his head. He was sitting off to one side and had been taken along as a guide, as I found out the next day. The other two were by the fire. One of them had made the coffee and was pouring it rather clumsily from a can into small cups. Unlike the guide, he was dressed like a well-to-do nomad. The green color of his turban meant that he was considered a descendant of Mohammed and therefore held the title "sayyid." He was an older man but treated his much younger companion with a love and deference which showed that the latter was of higher rank. I felt I had seen this younger man before. He was about thirty, and wore a white turban, pants, a vest, a jacket, a many-colored cape, and leather boots and spurs with very large rowels. He had an appealing face although the two braids framing it made him look alien, almost like a Hun. The men were armed with lances and rifles, arrows, bows, and knives. As I observed the young man, I began to feel that he was one of those people whom one cannot help loving.

It was his two braids which had made him look familiar. Our prisoner, the "Panther," the firstborn of the Tshoban, also wore them. The man who was facing me was some years older but resembled him so closely that it seemed likely they were related. I found him much more attractive than the "Panther." Because of this resemblance and the boniness of the horses, I was reasonably certain that they were Tshoban. If this was true, they might be an advance party, but I was not altogether convinced. The time wasn't right. I knew on what day the Tshoban intended to move through the Chatar defile. If they kept to this schedule, they had to be further along than these three men, for I had calculated that I would be behind them on that day so that I might read their tracks and find out whatever we needed to know. Since our horses were fleet, it would not be difficult for us to pass them again.

The two were now drinking the coffee and almost simultaneously, they spat it out again.

"Awful," the sayyid exclaimed. "May Allah curse bitterness. Who can drink this?"

With a gesture of disgust, he threw the cup into the sand.

"I warned you," the young man said, laughing. He also put down his cup, but more calmly. "This is the first time you have made coffee."

"And I had to use that wood," the sayyid said angrily. "Why is coffee so unreasonable as to take on the stench and taste of the coloquints? I am annoyed. Not for my sake, but for yours. Forgive me, prince."

I was struck by this form of address. The "Panther" also was called "prince," and he even referred to himself as the firstborn. He did not recognize his older brother because, while they had the same father, the older brother's mother was not a Muslim but a Christian. It was known that the "Panther" did everything in his power to usurp his brother's place and, should this fail, to establish himself as ruler elsewhere. This strife with his father and brother was the reason the "Panther" was almost never at home. He spent most of his time with the Mir of Ardistan and it was said that he was the favorite of this warlike ruler and had won his complete confidence. That the "Panther" had preceded the Tshoban army in its invasion of Ussul territory was not to be judged as a proof of loyalty but rather meant that he had plans which differed from those of the present sheik and his successor, and that might well be directed against them.

This brother, the real Ilkewlad, the actual "firstborn," was highly thought of by everyone. He was popular and better liked than the younger man. Was it he whom I had encountered here, in the middle of the desert? Should that be the case, it would be a great stroke of luck for us, provided we exploited the situation intelligently.

The sayyid wanted to pour out the coffee left in the can, but the guide asked for it. The two masters then lit their pipes so that the aroma of the tobacco would drive away the odor of the coloquints.

"Just a few puffs, then we shall have to sleep," the prince said. "We must set out before sunrise. Do you think we'll reach the defile before nightfall tomorrow?"

"Yes," the sayyid answered.

"But then we cannot stop and rest during the day," the guide remarked. "It takes our soldiers two days to get there from here. I think that we can do it in one because our horses and camels are good, but by the time we arrive, they will be too exhausted to go a step further."

"And when would we have caught up with our thousand men if we had followed them along the route they took instead of riding directly to the defile?" the prince asked.

"Not until day after tomorrow," the sayyid said.

"Then we did the right thing, choosing the direct route although our animals can find nothing to eat. My only hope is that our men will have enough food. Otherwise, they'll be delayed and we'll be too late to rescue my brother. It's lucky that those from whom he separated before he was taken prisoner with his two companions decided to follow him nonetheless because they had begun to fear for his safety. And it was even smarter that they did not waste their time trying to rescue him but turned back to report to my father right away. My brother wanted to lead the expedition. Now he is a prisoner and my father has taken command while I, who am peaceful, had to stay behind to take his place. Unfortunately, this is no ordinary foray but a campaign to conquer all of Ussulistan. How much I should have liked to be there, to temper as much as possible the brutality of war, to accomplish through love what costs so many victims when there is hatred. I pity the Ussul, should we be victorious, and I have no doubt we shall be. I would forgive them. I find it perfectly natural and right that they should have taken my brother prisoner. But he knows no mercy; he will impose a bloody punishment, and will not shrink from sacrificing the lives of his own men to be able to revenge himself on the Ussul. There will be battles which will also cost us many casualties. And yet we need men now more than at any other time—"

"The Djunub, the Djunub," the sayyid interrupted.

"Yes, the Djunub. Who would have thought that war with them would suddenly break out? And precisely at this moment when a thousand of our best soldiers are marching south, with my father in command. He knows nothing about this danger. But it would have been a mistake to send him a messenger."

"That's right."

"It's too important. I must bring him that information myself and hear his decision and then execute it. It would be best if we tried to take Ussula by a surprise attack instead of dillydallying making pointless speeches, or entering into useless negotiations as we have in the past. We have to attack the city like a thief in the night. I am convinced it will surrender without offering resistance and that will give us the chance to act humanely. It will also free my brother more speedily so that he can complete the conquest of Ussulistan while my father quickly returns home to confront the Djunub. My friend, I feel that a difficult time is approaching, but it will also be a decisive historical moment. It is essential that we understand this era. Believe me, it is no longer the sword that decides. At an earlier period, conflicts between nations were settled by brute force, and later through the use of intelligence. Today, even that intelligence is not strong enough to win on its own. There is a new element which up to now has been ignored in the history of war, and that is humanity, kindness, and compassion. Without these virtues, every battle will be lost, even if one wins it."

He had jumped up and continued speaking enthusiastically, walking back and forth. Because he repeatedly came very close to my hiding place, I thought it best to withdraw. I had heard enough, and what I did not know I could figure out for myself. I had already decided that I would speak to this splendid young man. When I returned to the camp site, Abed el Fadl was waiting for me.

He was amazed when he heard whom I had seen

and what had been discussed. When I had finished my report, he said:

"So there were more Tshoban spies in Ussulistan than we had thought. I did not see them. People with hostile intentions usually move through the defile at night. They know that the 'Panther' is a prisoner, so the old sheik himself assumed command. And then the older prince, who had remained behind in Tshobistan, heard that the Djunub plan to do to the Tshoban what the Tshoban propose doing to the Ussul. He follows his father as quickly as he can to warn him about this impending danger. He is intelligent enough to ride directly to the defile while the troops keep further east because there are a few places along that route where they can pick up provisions. But that will merely delay them. So they aren't well supplied. They must expect to start pillaging the moment they have passed the defile, as they always have in the past. What do you think of their plan, Effendi?"

"They are making a mistake," I said.

"I agree. So what have you decided?"

"Right now, we can safely go to sleep."

"Without bothering further about the prince?"

"Yes."

"You don't think he will discover us?"

"No. This is not his direction. He is riding south, and we are west of him. He wants to start out before sunrise, so he won't have the time to look around."

"You propose letting him go without having talked to him?"

"Yes."

"And will you look for the tracks of the Tshoban?"

"No. This prince has told me more than any number of tracks. We will stop looking; we have found more than enough. We will turn back and follow him."

"To capture him?"

"Why? Only a bad policeman bothers with someone that is running to prison of his own free will. Only if absolutely necessary will I use force, only if events I cannot now foresee compel me to. There is no reason we should not go to sleep now."

"But when we wake up he will be gone."

"All the better."

"And perhaps not where you think. He may change his mind."

"Then we will simply follow him. Now that I am on his trail, I won't let him get away."

"Are you so certain that you will be able to do that without seeing him?"

"Yes. Under these conditions, his trail is like a firm thread that cannot break or slip out of my hands. Good night, my friend."

"Good night, Effendi," he answered, taking a deep breath. "If you think there is reason for confidence, I am satisfied. May Allah grant us peace, and not only for this night."

I soon fell asleep and slept so profoundly that Abd el Fadl had to wake me.

"Get up, Effendi! The prince is long since gone."

"How do you know?"

"The sun rose some time ago and he wanted to leave before then. Do you want to make sure?"

"Right away."

I got up and cautiously advanced to the Tshoban camp site. They had left. Their tracks were so obvious, it seemed they had made them intentionally. When we set out after them a quarter hour later, it was child's play to follow their trail. It really was the firm thread I had spoken of.

Without urging, our horses ran more rapidly than theirs, and before long, we saw them in the distance. We stopped. Because this happened repeatedly, we decided to pass them without their seeing us, and once we had them behind us, we kept increasing the distance so that we would be sure to reach the defile before them. Abd el Fadl could not praise our incomparable horses warmly enough. He had become fond of them and caressed them constantly.

It was about two hours after we had stopped for a rest when I saw cavalry on the horizon to our right. When they had come close enough to be seen clearly, I counted eight of them. They had been moving south in a line which would eventually have converged with ours, but when they noticed us, they came toward us. Behind them, a second troop soon appeared. It consisted of a great many camels and enough horsemen to control them. They carried the water for the eight, seven of whom rode very good, dark Persian horses. Only one of them sat on a white horse that was a real thoroughbred. He was at the head, a long-legged figure but with so short a body that his feet almost touched under the belly of his animal. Nature and art had attempted to compensate for this flaw by lending his face a particularly marked martial expression. He also wore a long beard and an exceptionally tall military fur cap, which was topped by an equally tall bunch of heron feathers. His seven companions also wore such caps but the feathers decreased in size so that the sixth only had a single, small one, and the seventh none at all.

All of these men looked extremely warlike. They were dressed identically, in comfortable, Oriental clothes of the same color and cut, which meant that they were uniforms, and they carried the weapons customary in that part of the world. The man at the head wore a costly sabre and a pistol in his belt, but no other arms. When he had reached us, he uttered a loud command. His men halted instantly. The two of us continued riding.

"Stop!" he called to us.

We pretended not to have heard.

"Stop," he repeated, roaring this time. We kept moving, however, and he came after us.

"Why don't you obey?" he thundered at us. "Stop I say, stop!"

When this had no effect, he came closer and continued:

"If you are deaf, tell me. Can you hear me, or not?"

"We aren't deaf. We hear you."

"Why don't you obey?"

"Who are you that we should obey you?"

"Tell me first who you are."

"I am an Ussul."

This was true, for I had become one.

"Ussul?" he asked as he looked at me. "I imagined the Ussul differently. I am on my way to them. I come from Djunubistan. Do you know that, some days ago, two very important gentlemen from there came to you for a visit?"

"I do."

"Have you heard who they are?"

"The highest minister and the Maha-Lama, the highest priest."

"That's right. How were they received?"

"As befits their high station and their intentions."

His face became friendlier, and his voice lost its anger.

"I am glad to hear it. But of course you don't know what they want from you."

"Why shouldn't I? They want to conclude an alliance with us against the Tshoban."

"Allah!" he exclaimed. "Right again! Who told you?"

"They did."

"They did? Is that so?"

He was scrutinizing me even more closely than before.

"Why should I say something that isn't so?" I asked sharply.

"Forgive me. The two dignitaries would not discuss their business with an ordinary Ussul."

"Did I say I was an ordinary one?"

"No. And your horses—Mashallah! What thoroughbreds! I thought you Ussul only had fat, malformed monsters which look like rhinoceri."

"You'll find out many surprising things about us."

As we continued riding, he kept looking at us and our horses. He clearly understood their great value, but my appearance, which did not resemble that of the local inhabitants, and the shabby clothes of my companion confused him. He said:

"Only a noble and rich Ussul could own such horses. Please tell me who you are."

"Among us, it is the custom to first find out with whom one is speaking."

"I was not supposed to tell, but since I hear that you know of the secret visit, I may tell you what you want to know. I am the Tertib we Tabrik Kuwweti Harbie Feninde Mahir Kimesne of Djunubistan."

I reined up and asked:

"You will excuse me for interrupting you, should your title be longer still. Look at your men. They are waiting for permission to proceed. If you do not give it, we will have disappeared before you have finished with your title."

The men were actually still at the very spot where they had stopped, looking at us. The commander did not perceive the irony in my words, and shouted back:

"Move on, I permit it."

They did, and we also started off again while he told us who they were.

"You know now who I am, the highest ranking officer in all of Djunubistan. On journeys such as this, all ranks of the army must escort me. That's why you see a general, a colonel, a major, a captain, a lieutenant, a non-commissioned officer and a private."

"Then your purpose is military or strategic?"

For his entire long title meant nothing more than "strategist." He was probably the chief of staff of the sheik of Djunubistan.

"Very much so," he answered, slapping his sabre and forcing his horse into a fast trot. "You already know that the Tshoban are attacking you?"

"Yes."

"And do you also know that we will help you defeat them?"

"Yes."

"Such alliances are normally kept secret. But our sheik has his own reasons for dispensing with such secrecy. Our best spies surround the sheik of the Tshoban, and they informed us that he sent his son, the 'Panther,' to reconnoiter in Ussula. This 'Panther' will direct the conquest of Ussulistan. He has an older brother, an exceptionaly intelligent man whose advice may cause us problems. As long as he and his father stay home, we have to maintain two armies, one to observe these two, the other to fight at your side. So we tried to find a way to oblige the sheik and the older prince to take part in the expedition to Ussulistan, for then it would be easy for us to deal with the leaderless Tshoban that would remain behind. But nothing occurred to us. Then, one of our spies suddenly sent a messenger with the news that the 'Panther' had been captured by the Ussul and that the old sheik would personally assume command of his men, move through the Chatar defile, and rescue the prisoner. You can imagine that we were overjoyed. What we have to do now is to remove the older prince as well. If he were to hear that we are coming to your aid, he would have to let his father know. But such important messages cannot be entrusted to others. One conveys them oneself, particularly when the son and the father must decide how to beat us back in the north and in the south, where the Ussul are. We therefore sent a messenger back to Sef el Berinz' son and instructed him to tell the prince about our alliance with you. We also suggested that he convey this information personally, and not through a messenger."

"Did he?" I asked.

"I don't know. I did not have the time to wait. But I am convinced that the prince is already on his way. But so am I. Because both the sheik of the Tshoban and his older son are moving south, we need no troops for observation in the north. Our army could stay together, and it immediately left for the south, for the Chatar defile, to join up with your soldiers. I rushed ahead to conclude your negotiations with our Maha-Lama and our minister, should they have led to no result so far. Perhaps it is a good thing that I encountered you along the way. What is your opinion?"

I pretended that I was carefully weighing and reflecting, and remained silent for the moment. I wanted to gain time. Unforeseen facts and complications were crowding in upon us. It was as if a powerful hand high up in the north were pushing events toward us like balls in a bowling game. All we had to do down here was to set up the pins at the right time and in the right place.

More importantly, this "strategist" had unwittingly committed an extraordinary, unpardonable mistake. In his eagerness, he had mentioned a name he should have kept secret, and had thereby revealed that the person who was betraying the Tshoban to the Djunub was the son of the "Sword of the Prince," our prisoner. This allowed inferences which I could not fully develop at this moment.

Because the Djunub would not attack the Tshoban in the north, along their common border, but here in the south, we had to act so quickly that there was hardly time to think. Today was Sunday. On Monday, the Tshoban would arrive at the defile, if they stuck to the plan which the Sef el Berinz had revealed on the island while the sheik of the Ussul and I eavesdropped on him. A great deal remained to be done before that. Would the Erdjani and his Hukara arrive in time? This most important question and many others were rushing in upon me but I did not have a chance to consider them, for the "strategist" was claiming all my attention Now he was saying:

"I have told you who we are, and expect the same politeness from you. I am asking you first."

These words had been addressed to Abd el Fadl who answered by stating his name.

"Are you also from Ussula?"

"No."

"From where, then?"

"I come from Djinnistan."

When he heard this, the "strategist" rose as high in the saddle as his short body permitted, and asked distrustfully:

"A Djinnistani? An enemy of ours? And you pretend to be an Ussul?"

"When did he do that?" I asked. "You two haven't exchanged a single word so far."

"Since you are an Ussul, it was natural for me to assume that he was one as well. Now I am asking you for your name."

"I am called Kara ben Nemsi."

I had hardly finished when he quickly reined in his horse, seized the bridle of mine, and asked severely:

"Ben Nemsi? Then you aren't an Ussul either?"

"Yes, I am."

"But your name points to a different origin. Where were you born?"

"In Djermanistan."

"Then you are no Ussul. You lied to me."

In any other situation, I would have protested vigorously, but in this case I answered with utmost calm:

"I was not born an Ussul, but did not lie to you. I became an Ussul because that's what the Ussul wanted."

"Someone who is not born an Ussul can never become one. I don't believe you. The Ussul are not as small as you, and do not have such horses. Besides, you are not coming from there, but are going in that direction. Which means that you are coming from the land of the Tshoban. That's most suspicious. You are either Tshoban or friends and allies of theirs. Perhaps the older prince stayed back home after all, and you are the messengers he is sending to his father to inform him about our alliance with the Ussul."

"But consider that I knew that your highest minister and the Maha-Lama rode to Ussulistan. It follows that I must be a citizen of that country."

"Oh, no! For the son of—" he broke off, and then went on: Our spy among the Tshoban knew that we were going to send those two men. He also told the prince, and it is from him that you heard it. Oh, I see through you. I have to guard against surprises, and must take you prisoner. I hope you won't resist; you would fare badly. I am the ranking strategist of the Djunubistan empire. Do you understand?"

"That doesn't impress me," I answered.

"But there are eight of us, and only two of you. Remember that."

"Even that would not prevent me from putting up a fight if I decided to. But it would be foolish. We are riding to the Ussul, and so are you. Once we get there, we will see how things stand. So there is no need for me to resist."

"I agree. Apart from your being suspect, you seem a decent and cautious man. There is no need to treat you like a scoundrel. Normally, I should take your weapons but I will let you keep them if you promise to consider yourself our prisoner and won't attempt to escape."

"Very well."

"And your companion also agrees?"

"Yes," Abd el Fadl answered.

"That satisfies me," the strategist decided. "You can see that a man of my rank must have no contact with prisoners. I shall therefore leave you. We will form two sections. Four of us will ride in front of you, four of us behind. So take your places."

We did as he had ordered. With the general, the

colonel, and the major he took the lead and the others fell in behind us. We started off. No one spoke but I noticed that Abd el Fadl kept glancing at me. Finally, he asked:

"Do you really propose riding on like this? As a prisoner?"

"Yes."

"What is Halef going to say to that? Judging by the way he described you to me and my daughter, I would have expected something altogether different."

"Then his account was inaccurate."

"But what would you do if you really were no Ussul but a friend of the Tshoban?"

"I would laugh at the man with that unending title and at the others. But under these circumstances, I have no reason to. If I were to resist now, he would spoil the fun we will have at the defile."

"What fun?"

"The reunion of all the prisoners, for I already consider prisoners those we have not taken yet."

"Including these eight?"

"Yes. It will be amusing to see the two Tshoban princes encounter each other, and to be there when our escort here and the Maha-Lama and his minister admit to each other that their alleged intelligence, rank, and dignity notwithstanding, they acted so foolishly."

"And when you confront the two, the Tshoban and the Djunub, who first wanted to outsmart and murder the Ussul and then each other, and now have to admit to their shame how completely they were taken in," Abd el Fadl quickly interjected. "Yes, you are right, Sidi. Very interesting moments await us, perhaps as early as today. We are quite close to the defile. We'll be there in one hour. But what is that out there?"

He was pointing out to the plain where a fat animal with someone riding it had appeared. It was making straight toward us, at a trot. The reader can imagine my surprise when I recognized Smikh and Halef.

These two strange creatures first provoked the astonishment and then the amusement of the Djunub. They stopped and began laughing. This rider on this horse, or this horse with his rider, looked comical, especially when Halef wanted to stop but Smikh would not obey. My chubby friend had lowered his head, was staring straight ahead and running on and on in a perfectly straight line. He was not paying the slightest attention to the requests, the threats, the pounding and pummelling of his rider, who was holding onto the reins but finding it impossible to make the obstinate monster change course. Only I could help. I rode forward, jumped down, and placed myself in the way of the runaway with outstretched arms. Now the Hadji recognized me:

"Hamdulillah! So it's you, Sidi! Save me!"

"Smikh, Smikh," I called out.

He recognized my voice and raised his head. But his momentum was such that he found it impossible to stop. I had to jump aside as he rushed past me, uttering so horrible a shriek of joy that one might have thought that seeing me again was rending his very soul. Finally, he managed to come to a halt. He turned, stood still as if nailed to the ground, threw up his head, opened his mouth wide and began bellowing and howling with pleasure. The laughter of the Djunub became a roar.

I have heard many people laugh in the course of my life, but never with the explosive force and perseverance of these officers. Only one of us did not join in, and that was the target of this Homeric laughter, my little Halef Omar, who was beginning to realize how funny he looked. And while he did not resent our amusement, he merely smiled faintly, waiting patiently until the noise died down. Then he said to me:

"Thank you, Sidi. That animal jumped into the water with you. With me, it wanted to circle the globe in five minutes. Who are these strange people?"

I brought my hands close together which, in the sign language of the Haddedihn, is a command to be careful, and then pointed to the strategist:

"This one here is the Tertib we Tabrik Kuwweti Harbie Feninde Mahir Kimesne of the sheik of Djunubistan, and the others are his staff."

Halef must have been surprised but did not appear so. He glanced at the short body of the man, and shrugged:

"His title is longer than he is. If he sat on Smikh, he would hardly look more royal than I did. Shall I trade places with him? I like the looks of his horse."

"Be silent!" I said, pretending to be angry. "I ask you to show this hero the proper respect. We are his prisoners."

"His prisoners? The prisoners of this bunch?"

As he surveyed them, he first seemed astonished but gradually began looking amused. When the small folds around the corners of his mouth and eyes began to twitch as they did at this moment, I knew that he was preparing a prank. The strategist asked:

"Who is that little fellow that is brazen enough to want to trade places with me?"

"Who am I?" Halef asked. "An admirer of your horse, as I said. Let me have it. I'll show you how quickly my Effendi will be a free man."

He quickly jumped from Smikh's back. With a second jump, he moved toward the strategist, and with a third he swung himself into a kneeling position behind him, pulled the rider from the stirrups, threw him down, and took his place in the saddle. He then seized the reins and rode off, calling out to me:

"The trade has been made! Let him ride Smikh!"

He galloped back in the direction from which he had come, toward the defile. The strategist rose from the ground and did something very foolish.

"After him, after him!" he called out to his men. "Catch him. Shoot him down, and bring back my horse."

They obeyed and rode off, exactly in the order of their rank, the general in the lead, the private in the rear. Each of them had waited until the man directly above him in rank had begun the pursuit, and then followed him. They looked silly, and their procedure was no better, for it gave Halef a head start which kept increasing because the strategist's horse was the best and fleetest of the lot. When the private finally took off behind his non-commissioned officer, the little Hadji had almost disappeared over the horizon, and the man with the long title was wailing:

"They won't catch him! My horse is lost. I must pursue him. Get off your stallion, get off right now!"

This order was not addressed to me but to Abd el Fadl, who looked at me questioningly. But I pointed at Smikh and told the strategist:

"These horses are ours. Take the nag."

"I don't like it."

"Then you'll have to stay here."

We started off but he seized the reins from Abd el Fadl, and shouted:

"Give me that stallion! You are my prisoners and have to obey!"

But Abd el Fadl pulled the reins away from him, and we rode off. When Smikh saw this, he threw up his head and began to whine. He did not want to come along. At the same time, the strategist, growing fearful, rushed up to him and climbed him. Smikh immediately changed his mind. The moment he felt the unknown rider on his back, he screamed angrily and ran after us. He could not keep up, of course, and roared with increasing frenzy to vent his annoyance.

When I looked back a few moments later, I saw that in spite of his long legs, the strategist was having trouble staying on top of Smikh's broad back. He was no longer sitting but lying, clutching on to the mane with both hands, and was invisible except for his headgear, so that it looked as if the tall, waving plume of feathers were crowning Smikh's head. To pass the Djunub more quickly, we spurred our horses, flying along, "the hooves devouring the earth," as the Bedouin says.

The order of rank prohibited the Djunub from passing a superior. As we overtook them, they were still in the same positions in which they had started and amazed to see us rushing past them like the wind. Now only Halef was still ahead.

Although the encounter with Smikh had been absurd, we had to take it seriously. Behind us, the armies of our enemies, the Tshoban and the Djunub, were drawing near but at that moment, that did not worry us. I was much more unsettled by the sudden appearance of Halef and Smikh, for where Smikh was, his master, the Ussul sheik, could not be far behind. Why had he come, and what did he want? Had the Erdjani already arrived? Something of considerable importance must have happened, otherwise Halef would not have left the defile and Merhameh to ride out into the desert to meet us. I felt that we were rushing toward unforeseen events and we will soon see that this feeling did not deceive me.

15 : The Trap in the Defile

When we passed the Djunub, Halef was a small dog on the horizon. As the distance decreased, I saw that he was no longer galloping and when he became aware that we were catching up with him, he stopped. He was laughing.

"Did he get the chubby one?" he asked when we were still some distance away.

"Yes."

"May Allah have mercy on him! What it means to ride that monster, only my bones know. Unfortunately, I am the only one that hears what they are saying. How did you run into those people, and what do they want? Why did they take you prisoner or, rather, why did you let yourselves be taken?"

"I shall tell you later, Halef. Right now, I have to know why you rode out to meet us, and on Smikh, at that. He should be in the capital."

"He should be where his master is."

"That's right. The moment I saw him, I told myself that Sheik Amihn must have followed us."

"Not only he, but his wife as well."

"What happened?"

"Something rather important. You'll hear right away."

But with him, "right away" could never be taken literally. It was his wont to deal with matters he considered weighty as circumstantially as he could. He made a short pause to heighten the tension and then began with something that apparently had no connection whatever with my question.

"Sidi, you know that Ardistan has a coast but no harbors and therefore no maritime traffic?"

"Yes. Only occasionally, an enterprising Indochinese

sails his skiff to that inhospitable coast to trade with the few people living there."

"That's right, Sidi. And it is on such a skiff that the servant came."

"What servant?"

"Ah, yes, you haven't heard. Well, the Mir of Ardistan has finally declared war on the Mir of Djinnistan. It's official. And I suppose you know that the two sons of the sheik are in the bodyguard of the Mir of Ardistan?"

"Yes. But it seems that in spite of that position, they are really prisoners. They don't command, they are hostages, and the Mir uses them to exact obedience."

"Apparently so. The two sons of the sheik have suddenly disappeared. The Mir demanded that the sheik send him a thousand Ussul warriors to assist him against Djinnistan. The sons refused to go along and stated that the Ussul had no reason whatever for fighting the Mir of Djinnistan. So they were arrested in the middle of the night and secretly taken away with one of their servants. They were not told their destination. But the servant claims that it was probably the 'City of the Dead' because that has always been the place where people that have fallen into disfavor were taken and disposed of. They were tied to their horses, and the ride was long. The second evening, the servant managed to escape. He made his way to the coast and was picked up by a skipper who took him across the bay and up the river, almost all the way to Ussula. He came to the city just after the Erdjani had left with his Hukara. The elders were quickly called together for a council and decided to follow the Erdjani to discuss with him and you what should be done. The parents were fearful, and made such haste that they arrived here yesterday morning."

"And the Erdjani?"

"He got here last night."

"But not with all his Hukara? How is that possible?"

"He only brought some with him. The rest came during the night, as quickly as their horses permitted. He did not sleep but immediately made preparations which you will probably approve. Between the defile and the capital, a chain of outposts has been set up, and other soldiers are hauling water from the river. I also took the Erdjani to the well of the angel. He was impressed. Then, he made a careful inspection of the stretch between the 'orifice' and the 'rock gate'—"

"Including the hidden path?" I interrupted.

"Yes. He said that it was an ideal trap. His Hukara have already been assigned their places. I don't think there is anything further for you to do. You will be satisfied."

"Where is the 'Panther' and his two companions?"

"They have been put into a cave. They can't escape and are being guarded by Hu."

"And the highest minister and the highest priest of Djunubistan?"

"They are being kept elsewhere and guarded by Hi. They had run into the Erdjani and he told them that they should come with him since he was the one that would deal with their proposal. He thought they were honest men and treated them as their high rank demands. But when I told him what their real intentions were, he had them put under guard."

"Did the Tshoban and the Djunub see each other?"

"That could not be avoided."

"And why did you come to meet us? Is that what the Erdjani wanted?"

"No, he didn't. But the sheik and his wife drove me to it. They fear for the lives of their sons and have more confidence in you than in the Erdjani. They are impatiently waiting for your advice and asked me to ride out to meet you and to ask you to hurry back. When the Erdjani told them that that was superfluous and perhaps even dangerous, they made me do it without his knowledge. I had to give in and would have preferred one of the Tshoban or Djunub horses but then the Erdjani would have found out. So I had to take Smikh and ride off secretly. And Smikh was smarter than I. I wanted to go north, but he bolted and ran northwest, and that's how we met."

The sea and the defile were now coming into view. As I told Halef of our experiences, we reached the isthmus, and after a few moments, the first Ussul detachment that had been standing guard here left their cover behind a rock and showed themselves. It was

Irahd and eight of his men. He had personally taken charge of this important post to make sure that no mistakes would be made. As we were talking to him, the Erdjani with a dozen of his men came along to inspect this sector of the battleground. We shook hands, but I was struck by the fact that he bowed deeply before Abd el Fadl as before a person of the highest rank. A short exchange was all that was needed to trade whatever news there was, and then he asked if he might show me the disposition of his troops. I agreed although I should have liked to witness the capture of the Djunub who could be expected at any moment. I instructed Irahd how to proceed and he assured me that he would stay to assure a proper reception for these important gentlemen.

The Erdjani was riding the thoroughbred of the Maha-Lama. Because this was a fast horse, we would not need much time for our inspection. This was important, for I was convinced that the older Tshoban prince would make every effort to reach the isthmus before nightfall, and I wanted to be present when he was taken prisoner. Thus, there was no time to be lost.

We first rode to the "rock gate" where I greeted Merhameh. The thirty soldiers posted there would withdraw when the enemy approached. Then, we went to the other end of the defile where a unit of equal size had been stationed. This was the point where the first onrush of the Tshoban would have to be sustained and repulsed. For the time being, however, the small number sufficed. The main body of the Hukara had been placed further back at a point where the southern part of the isthmus began. What we saw here was a camp in the truest and most romantic sense of the term.

The huge shapes of the Ussul, their equally over-dimensional mounts, their weapons, and the peculiar massiveness and weight of their movements and gestures are things only a Homer could describe. When it had become known that the two sons of the sheik had disappeared, a great many had joined the Erdjani's army which now consisted of twelve hundred men. He had rejected no one that had offered his services, for soldiers were not only needed at the isthmus, and those who could not fight found useful employment elsewhere. Two chains had been set up, one of which went to the river and from there to the capital to transport the daily supplies of fodder and water for the horses. The other connected the defile and the well of the angel from which drinking water for the troops was brought.

It was here in the camp that we met the sheik and his wife, and while our greeting was cordial, it was also brief, for we had to return to the northern extension of the defile since that was the direction from which the enemy would approach. But first I had a look at the two places where the "Panther" and his two companions and the two high-ranking Djunub were kept. I convinced myself that escape was impossible. There were any number of recesses in the rocks, and we picked out one for the older prince of the Tshoban. We did not want him to have any contact with his younger brother, in part for humane, in part for diplomatic reasons. We did not want the "Panther" to know that his older brother was also our prisoner.

We rode back through the pass and were pleased to see that Halef and Irahd had done their duty with a sense of humor. For as we turned back on our way toward the northern end of the defile, a soldier sitting on the horse of the Djunub general was coming toward us. The general was running alongside him with one hand tied to the stirrup. He was being taken to the Maha-Lama and the minister. We rode past, looking very serious and pretending not to see him. Later, a second Ussul brought in the colonel, tethered in the same manner, and the major, the captain, the lieutenant, and the non-commissioned officer followed.

"Are you satisfied, Sidi?" Halef asked. "That takes care of them. And now look over there, at the last two, one behind the other."

He pointed in the direction from which we had approached the defile. First, we saw Smikh, his head lowered, trotting toward the isthmus and far behind him, the strategist, who was running as quickly as his long legs would carry his short body. He was holding his headgear in his right hand, the sabre in his left.

"Look at him," Halef said to the Hukara. "That's the Tertib we Tabrik Kuwweti Herbie Feninde Maher Kimesne of the brave Sheik of Djunubistan, and—"

He broke off, having spotted three horsemen further to the right on the northern horizon.

"Who could they be?" he asked.

"The older prince of the Tshoban with his friend and guide," I said.

"Hamdulillah! Then our work is done. It's a good thing he is getting here before evening. How is he to be treated?"

He did not address this question to me but to the Erdjani. I had instructed him to treat the Erdjani as the commanding officer. He told him:

"The way a decent person should be, even if he is an enemy. I do not wish to destroy the Tshoban but to make them my friends. And it is especially this prince whose support I will need. Of course, true victory means the total destruction of the enemy. In past, cruel times people tried to annihilate their opponents. But today, and even more in times to come, victory can be achieved much more dependably and humanely by transforming hatred into love, by making one's adversaries one's allies. That is the course we shall take. I want to win my battles through love, not through death."

Smikh arrived, and the strategist shortly thereafter. Though completely out of breath, he started thundering away the moment he saw me and Halef. But two sturdy Hukara soon seized him and dragged him off.

The sun was about to set as the prince of the Tshoban approached. We had dismounted, hidden our horses, and sought cover. The three riders had felt perfectly safe, and were stunned when we suddenly emerged from our hiding place and formed a tight circle around them.

"Ussul!" the prince exclaimed. "Who are you?"

This question was addressed to the Erdjani who had stepped up to the prince's horse to seize the reins.

"I am called the Erdjani."

"Then you are the man that your people call the Djirbani?" the prince asked. "Though I have never seen you, I did not share the foolish thoughts people have about you. I like the way you look. But what do you want from us? Why are you crowding in on us?"

"To take you prisoner."

"For what reason? You have no right to attack us. The Chatar defile lies between your territory and ours. Only its southern end belongs to you, the northern part is ours. That's where we are now. How can you seize us in our own territory?"

"Because you are coming to the isthmus to cross it and then attack us."

"Do you know who I am?"

"Yes. I will be as sincere as you were. I respect you. But we captured your brother when he was spying in our country, and know everything. You will soon understand that I am neither your enemy nor the enemy of your tribe, but for the time being, you are my prisoner."

"Why yours, of all people?"

"I am the leader of the Ussul."

"You? When did the Ussul begin to think?"

Now Irahd walked up to him and answered in the Erdjani's place:

"When they decided to attack rather than to defend themselves. You are the firstborn prince of the Tshoban and I am Irahd, the second-in-command of the Ussul. Nothing will happen to you. You will be our prisoner for only one day. Come with me, and don't resist."

The prince and his companions were so hemmed in by the huge Ussul that they had no choice but to let themselves be taken away. After the necessary instructions for possible action during the night had been given, we rode back through the defile toward the camp. A tent had been put up there for the sheik where supper had been prepared for us. Abd el Fadl, Merhameh, the Erdjani, Hadji Halef and I had been invited. The Erdjani assumed that I had long known Abd el Fadl, and only as we were going to supper had he learned that that was not the case. He asked:

"When did you see Abd el Fadl for the first time?"

"A few days ago."

"Do you know who he is?"

"No."

"Then you will be surprised when I tell you that he is the prince of Halihm, and the wealthiest man in all of Ardistan. Yet you see that he is more simply dressed and more modest than many a beggar. He has made a vow though I don't know exactly of what kind. He never discusses it. It is a secret he shares only with Merhameh, who is his favorite daughter."

"Then she is not his only child?"

"No. There are others, both sons and daughters, who are close to the throne. It means a great deal that he is championing our cause."

This time, we had no Simmsemm but only water with our meal. The invitation had been cordial; it also gave the sheik and his wife the chance to plead with us that we free their two sons. Amihn had been firmly resolved to accompany us and to force the Mir of Ardistan to surrender his prisoners. Although with difficulty, we finally convinced him, with the help of his intelligent wife, that he would be more hindrance than help. She had only come along to dissuade him from carrying out his plan. She was no less fond of her sons than he, but she knew that he was a perfectly ordinary Ussul and could expect neither obedience nor success beyond the borders of his country. In the end, he consented to return home, but stipulated that he would remain until victory at the defile had been achieved.

I was pleased that, after these few days, the sheik's behavior toward the Erdjani had already changed considerably. Now where it was no longer matter but spirit that ruled, matter deigned to acknowledge its rights.

Because events of such great importance impended, this may be the place to give a short and clear picture of the locale.

The isthmus connected the Tshoban desert in the north with Ussul territory in the south. There was water in the south but none in the north. It was reasonable to expect that the Tshoban and their horses would be parched when they arrived, and they certainly counted on a quick passage through the defile so that they might reach the river on the other side. Our plan was to make this impossible. They had to be stopped on the isthmus. Thirst was going to be our ally, and we hoped that it would be great enough to force them to surrender unconditionally. To achieve this, their confinement had to be so severe and painful that they would abandon hope. Fortunately, nature favored our plan. The defile was made up of three sections of almost equal length. Because two high rock formations stretched across it from one sea to the other, there was a northern, a middle, and a southern section which would have been completely isolated from each other, had it not been for a narrow passage leading through each of these walls of rock. They were the "rock gate" and the "orifice." The final, southern third extended from the country of the Ussul to the "orifice," the northern third from the Tshoban desert to the "rock gate." The middle third, which would be the trap proper, thus lay between the "gate" and the "orifice." If I was correct, the Tshoban would enter this trap without any hesitation. I did not believe that they would take the time to explore the area. Being eager for water, they would want to get through the defile as rapidly as possible. Once they had passed the "rock gate," that avenue of escape would be closed off. And having come to the "orifice," they would not be allowed to advance any further. Being unable to advance or retreat, all of them would be prisoners.

I wanted no blood to be spilled, but as I thought carefully about the situation, it seemed very likely that a struggle at either end of the trap might well be unavoidable, for it could be assumed that the Tshoban would try to force their way through. It goes without saying that such efforts would be futile and bloody. When I mentioned this to the Erdjani, he said:

"There is no need for concern. No blood will be spilled. You haven't yet seen the precautions we have taken. After we have eaten, I will show you what we have done. The four elements will be our allies."

"You mean earth and air, fire and water?"

"Yes. And these four friends of ours will give us all the help we need."

As he said this, he looked out toward the two seas and then up at the sky.

"I admit that you are right about two of them," I said. "The earth has constructed this gigantic trap from its most solid rock, and the water along both sides makes it impossible for the Tshoban to break out. But what do you mean when you talk about fire and air?"

"Look up at the sky! The moon is shining, but there are no stars. Yet there should be thousands of them up there. The firmament is like the ceiling of a room that has been painted a thick yellow. Only the moon penetrates this atmosphere. It's only because you are a stranger that that doesn't strike you. But we know our country and our sky. There will be a storm tomorrow, and then you will see that the air is in league with us."

"And the fire?"

"That will save us powder," he said. "The moment I arrived here, Halef and Merhameh took me up to the 'rock gate.' When I looked over the trap from there, it occurred to me to guard the two entrances by fire rather than by men with rifles, and I acted accordingly. A troop of my Hukara was sent back to the point where the forest begins. Wood was cut and brought here. We already have an ample supply, and more is still being made ready. Tonight, they will haul whatever we need to the 'orifice' and light it the moment it becomes dark tomorrow."

"That's an excellent idea," I interrupted. "Of course, you will do the same thing at the 'gate?' Except there it cannot be piled up. The Tshoban would see it."

"That wood will be rafted to the northern end of the isthmus and hidden there. The Tshoban won't see it when they pass. You know how well the Ussul handle rafts."

"I do. It's a well-thought-out plan. It would be even better if we could block the entire passage by fire. Unfortunately, the 'orifice' is more than an opening, and wider than the path. There is also the former river bed. I don't see how you can collect enough wood to light and maintain a fire that will stretch across that entire width."

"That's where the water comes in," he smiled. "When it is as stormy as I expect it to be tomorrow, the river will quickly fill with water. The waves will be lashed against the rocks, enter the cracks and channels and run down into the dry bed. When both storm and tide coincide, there may be such an abundance of water that the river will flood its banks and rise several additional feet. You would have noticed traces of such flooding along the path if you had looked for them. You didn't because you didn't believe it could happen."

"And you expect such a storm tomorrow, the very day the Tshoban arrive here? Is that chance?"

"Chance?" he answered. "I know that you don't believe in chance events, sahib. When man obeys those natural laws which God lays down for him, all of earthly nature comes to his aid. Then, miracles occur. But how they are connected with our wishes and desires, only God could explain if we were intelligent and devout enough to understand Him. But let's not philosophize but be practical. Let us gratefully accept the help heaven sends us, even if we dare not presume it is intended for us. And yet we know it is."

After we had taken leave of our host and hostess, he took me to the sea where I saw the rafts being constructed and floated down the coast. Then Halef and I rode to the "rock gate." We wanted to sleep at the same spot where we had spent the night of our arrival, in the soft sand between the rocks which would protect us from the storm, should it come during the night. Contrary to his usual manner, Halef was conspicuously quiet that evening. He felt that I was aware of this, and explained:

"We have had many experiences together, Sidi, but never anything of such consequence. Even our adventure in the 'Valley of the Steps,' which seems so similar to what is happening here, did not affect me like this. And do you know what is most curious about it all?"

"Tell me."

"I have complete confidence in the Erdjani. At an earlier time, I would not have involved myself in something unless you and I held all the threads in our hands. Here, things are different. I am perfectly happy to take second place. I do not begrudge the Erdjani the courage and strength he needs to go his own dangerous way. I am glad that we are not in command. We can stand behind him and protect and help him. And therefore I am pleased that he is asserting his independence. He was very polite toward the sheik, and considerate toward his wife. And yet he energetically rejected every attempt to tell him what to do. He said that there was only one person in command, and that he was that person; that it was the sheik's task to provision the army, and that that was so demanding that he could not also find time to bother with tactics and strategy. And the sheik's wife agreed with him. He is beginning to develop."

It was quiet all around us when we lay down, and we slept until daybreak. Although we found ourselves between precipitous rocks and could see only a small part of the sky, we could tell that the Erdjani had been correct when he had predicted a storm. We heard a sound as of very deep organ notes, occasionally broken by the high-pitched, shrill whistling of a clarinet. And this whistling and rustling continued unbroken. The sky seemed to be pressing down on the earth. Its heavy, dark clouds did not form a compact mass, however, but scudded across the isthmus like torn rugs and pieces of cloth. Because the storm was coming from the east, it swept the entire length of the defile. It stirred up the waters of the sea, raised them to a considerable height and then forced them against the rocks where they filled those cracks and channels I have mentioned. From them, the flood poured into the old river bed. Everywhere, the water was coming down in countless cascades, but not continuously, because it gusted only intermittently. A large quantity of sea water was whipped against the outer side of the rocks and then driven into the defile. It had already covered the entire bottom of the riverbed and was still rising. For centuries, winds from the north had forced desert sand along the entire length of the defile as through a blowpipe. It had collected on the other side, in the south. As a result, the river no longer had any appreciable fall; its water did not flow, at least not yet. Even now, it was already several feet high. If the tide continued at this rate, the bed would be completely impassable in a few hours, and we would be able to block by fire the two points which alone permitted passage.

Just as we had risen, Merhameh came. She had known where we had passed the night and prepared a breakfast. While we ate, the Erdjani came by. He was on his way to keep a look-out for the approaching Tshoban. I accompanied him. He pointed at the river, and said:

"You can see that the storm has come. I think it may turn into a real tempest. And the water is also here. In another two hours, not only we but the elements will be ready to receive the Tshoban."

"And I see no reason why they should hesitate to move into the trap," I said.

"Not only thirst but also the storm will drive them into it."

"But that keeps me and Halef from riding out into the desert to watch them."

"Had you intended to?"

"Yes. As it is, we cannot be certain when they will be here. But now we have to give up that plan. It will be much rougher out there than here where the rocks protect us. And it just occurs to me that the waves are too high now for the rafts. Do we have enough wood on this side?"

"I hope so. We'll soon see. Water transport is no longer possible. If we need more, it must be moved along the hidden trail which connects the 'orifice' and the 'gate.' Come along."

Halef and I had slept so soundly that we had heard nothing of the preparations that had been made. Because there had been the possibility that the Tshoban would come during the night rather than today, the Erdjani had sent enough Hukara north to close the trap behind them. A number of his men had even had to ride out into the open desert to keep a lookout and report a possible approach. In spite of the storm and the enormous quantities of sand whirling about, which made it almost impossible to see into the distance, these men were still out there.

The Hukara that had been posted outside the "rock gate" came to about one third of our army, i.e. some four hundred men. Yet no trace of them was to be seen, and the wood also had been carefully hidden.

Here, along the northern third of the defile, Irahd was in command. When he saw us, he left his hiding place and accompanied us. The water in the riverbed was rising, and out here the howling of the storm was much more audible than inside. The further we came, the more keenly we felt the movement of air. The storm had become almost strong enough to knock me down. And when we had reached the end of the tall protective rock wall, we saw the sea of desert sand, churning, whirling in huge clouds, a flying desert which the spirit of the air was lashing with a thousand thongs.

Nothing would have pleased me more than to take my dogs and ride out into this tempest to await the arrival of the Tshoban. I did not have much confidence in the training and stamina of the few Ussul that had been sent out there. But my Syrr meant too much to me to have his nostrils, eyes, and ears filled with sand. He was too valuable to have him die of pneumonia in the performance of such a routine task. I therefore returned to the "rock gate" with the Erdjani and Irahd, and then rode to the "orifice" with Halef where another four hundred Hukara had been stationed to sustain the attack. Meanwhile, the river had risen more than a meter and water was also beginning to come in from what had been the lee of the isthmus. Now that the channel was being filled from both sides, passage through the "orifice" was possible only on the narrow trail along the bank, and this had been blocked by an enormous pile of wood. Once lit, any attempt to remove it would be futile. Close by, there were four hundred armed men who would keep the fire going and repel the enemy.

We now rode to the southern end of the defile where our command post had been set up. I inquired about our prisoners and was told that the "Panther" wanted to see me urgently. I decided to talk to him in the course of the day. First, a shelter for our horses had to be found, for they could no longer be used. We found a place between some rocks where they would be protected from the storm and not be bothered by anyone.

The moment the arrival of the Tshoban was reported, the following action would be taken. Because he was in charge, it was agreed that the Erdjani would be at a central location. He chose a spot along the upper, hidden trail almost halfway between the "gate" and the "orifice." There, a hollowed-out, projecting rock offered space for about a dozen people and protection from even the heaviest rain. Equidistant from the two points where the fires would be lit, it also had the advantage that reports and orders could pass back and forth without the Tshoban being aware of it. The Erdjani asked me and Halef to keep him company there, but I wanted him to have a completely free hand and therefore obtained his consent to move about at will.

Around eleven o'clock, the outposts that had been sent into the desert came back and reported that the enemy was approaching. These brave Hukara had suffered much from the sand and the storm, and had done their job well. They had not been seen, and looked exhausted. Clearly, the Tshoban would be in even worse condition. The Erdjani immediately went to his post and Halef and I strapped whatever provisions and water we would need that day on the backs of our dogs. This made us completely mobile. We then walked along the still rising river to the "rock gate." We were reassured to notice that along the entire distance, the Hukara had effaced all signs of our presence. From the "rock gate," we climbed up by the same trail we had taken with Merhameh. Up on top, the storm was raging so fiercely that we had to support ourselves to avoid being swept away. It proved impossible to get to Abd el Fadl's stone hut. Luckily, we found a cleft which faced north and was therefore shielded from the east wind. We settled down, and did not have long to wait until we saw the enemy. It was a thin, frequently broken, very long line of tired, hungry, and thirsty men and animals. Even at this distance, one could tell that they could barely stay on their feet. Since they might also be able to see us, we quickly withdrew to observe their arrival inside the trap.

We walked along the hidden upper trail until we

reached the Erdjani and his staff, who had made themselves as comfortable as possible. The steps that did not lead all the way to the bottom but only to the exposed ledge were nearby. Merhameh and her father were sitting at a well-placed spot somewhat above this ledge from where one could survey almost the entire trap without being seen. We joined them and unloaded our dogs. There were enough provisions to last us until tomorrow. We had even taken our blankets along.

From our vantage point, the passage through the gate could be seen if we looked to the left. It took quite some time until the first Tshoban made his appearance. I assumed that they had stopped on the other side to await the sheik's orders, and indeed, he was the first man to come through the gate. He was riding a sturdy horse of the same breed that the "Panther," his son, had ridden. Now, of course, the animal seemed so tired that it could only walk slowly and when it had come level with us, it tottered, stopped, and refused to go on. He neither beat or mistreated it. Nor did he wear those large, horrible instruments of torture I had seen on his son. His spurs were small. He caressed the horse, stroked its neck, and tried to persuade it to go on. This was appealing, but he had no success. The horse was willing but unable. He dismounted, and the moment it was free of its rider, it lost whatever energy it had left, began to tremble, and collapsed. He sat down by its side, took its head in his lap, and looked around to see if one of the men passing him still had some water in his skin.

"Sidi, this is a decent man," Halef said. "He loves his horse. Nothing must happen to him. Do you agree?"

I nodded. My entire attention was being taken up by the men who, driven by thirst, were literally crowding through the fatal gate without suspecting that they were about to lose their freedom. And they continued pushing and jostling once they had passed it. Their uniforms, faces, and horses looked pitiful. Every fold, every opening was filled with sand and both men and beasts could barely see out of their eyes. Coughing, panting and moaning, they drove their nearly collapsing mounts with whips and spurs. Occasionally, someone stopped to say an encouraging word to the sheik, but no one had any water to give him. We heard later that these men had been jubilant when they had reached the river but their joy had turned to fear when they tasted its water. And this fear had become horror when they began to realize that this sea water would pour from the upper, dried-out river into the one below, from which they had expected their salvation. Nonetheless, they were pushing vehemently. The riverbed was not yet so full that the sea water could drain. They saw that it was still stagnant, and so they kept hastening on.

Now the van, camel riders with empty skins and exhausted animals, tired horsemen who had dismounted and were pulling their animals behind them, followed.

Just then, some shots were fired near the "orifice." Out in the desert, the tempest would have drowned out the noise but here, where the storm's force was broken by the rocks, it was distinctly audible. This was the signal that the Tshoban had reached the gap but could not advance because our Hukara had lit the fire. Down below, men began shouting. The forward impetus faltered and came to a halt. Only a few more Tshoban still came from the "rock gate" and finally even the last was inside the trap. Shots were now also fired up there.

The sheik jumped to his feet and shouted into the air:

"Silence, silence! What happened? Why did you stop?"

The tumult was so considerable that I could not hear everything he said, but it was clear he was asking questions and people were answering him. This increased the hubbub and only a few, isolated words such as "Ussul," "trapped," "water," "fire," could be made out. The sheik repeated his questions but in vain. Now Merhameh rose to her feet. No one had asked her to; she was simply obeying her own intuition. She took one of our skins, stepped down to the ledge, placed it there and then walked up to the edge, raising her arm, ordering all to be silent. I use the word "order" intentionally. The way she was standing there with outstretched arm, her stance royal, exceeds my powers of description. The sheik was the first to see her. He made a gesture of surprise, stepped back to look at her, pointed, and commanded silence. These words also were lost in the general uproar but everyone's eyes turned toward him, and those who saw Merhameh fell silent. Her appearance had that power which can only be understood by those who have themselves experienced the irresistible force of a being that is pure in soul. In spite of the tempest, one could clearly hear her voice as she called out to the sheik below:

"Throw me your skin. I will give you water for your poor horse."

His horse was more tired and thirsty than any other. He had worn it out, keeping his men together in the storm like a dog that constantly circles the flock so that no sheep may be lost.

"Water? For my horse?" he asked. "May Allah bless you for your compassion. Tell me who you are."

"I am Merhameh," she answered simply.

"Then you are what I am speaking of, compassion, which Allah may bless."

He took his skin from the saddle and threw it toward her. She filled it and, kneeling down, reached far enough for him to catch it. He immediately went to his horse to water it. As he did so, Merhameh smiled down on him while all the Tshoban stopped to look up at her. Yet there was really nothing unusual in what was happening. A girl was giving a rider water for his thirsty horse, something that had been seen a thousand times before. How was it that the sight of this girl had so calming an effect and so suddenly transformed the earlier clamor into total silence?

Now the skin was empty. The sheik straightened up as his horse jumped to its feet. He looked at Merhameh, nodded to her to thank her, and asked:

"Has heavenly compassion clothed itself in an earthly form? Or is Merhameh the name of a human being?"

"I am what I seem," she answered. "It is the name my father gave me."

"Who is your father?"

"Abd el Fadl."

The sheik stepped back a few paces further, and asked:

"Is he Abd el Fadl, the prince of Halihm who made the famous vow?"

"Yes."

"Is he here?"

"Yes."

"May I speak to him?"

"No. His name expresses what he is and what he desires. He knows no ruler other than kindness, but kindness may have no traffic with men who pillage, murder, and want to spill blood. There are only two that may speak to you, severity and compassion."

"You are compassion. And who is severity? Who is in command here? Why are we being stopped? It seems that the gap in the rock has been occupied and that we are not to be permitted to pass. Who is doing that?"

"I am," a voice near Merhameh rang out.

The Erdjani had come down from the heights and stopped alongside Merhameh. In his noble bearing, his aristocratic movements, his leather garment, he looked like a giant savage. His long hair gave him something of the appearance of an untamed lion.

"You?" the sheik of the Tshoban asked. "I don't know you; I have never seen you before."

The Erdjani had no need to answer, for some and then more and more of the Tshoban called out:

"The Djirbani! The madman! The leper!"

And someone else added:

"The one who was locked up by the Ussul and always came fleeing to our country to run to Djinnistan. But we did not let him pass."

"Is that true?" the sheik asked.

Ignoring the slander, the Erdjani answered calmly:

"It is true that I am called the Djirbani. Whether or not I am mad or leprous you will soon be able to judge for yourself. Your son, the false Ilkewlad, who is not the firstborn, fell into our hands. He revealed your plans. So we set a trap for you. There are more than a thousand of us, and we have manned the gap in the rock down there to block your passage."

"A trap?" the sheik interrupted. "It does seem that we cannot move forward. But who is going to keep us from turning back where we came from?"

"Hunger, thirst, and fire. Look!"

He pointed to the "gate." The few minutes that had passed had sufficed to gather the necessary wood and to light it. Because the fire was burning beyond the gate, it could not be seen but the wind blew the smoke inside, prevented it from rising, and forced it to follow the bank of the river. It looked like a snake slithering along. The sheik uttered a cry of terror.

"And your other son, the real firstborn, also fell into our hands," the Erdjani went on. "We seized him yesterday when—"

"My son Sadik?" the sheik interrupted again.

"Yes."

"That's a lie!"

"Very well, if that's what you want to believe."

"He cannot be here. I don't believe it. He is back home."

"I can only repeat what I have said. I don't mind if you prefer to believe I am lying. But then you should also be too proud to continue talking to me, a liar."

He turned away and slowly climbed back to his post. Merhameh also left the ledge and rejoined us. I found that correct. The Erdjani's conduct would assure respect. The sheik called out to him several more times, but was given no answer. He now ordered some of his men, probably elders, to come to him. They sat down in a circle to deliberate. Such a council of elders is called a Djemmah, as is well known. This Djemmah took place directly before our eyes. Men were sent to both ends of the defile to bring back reports. Naturally, we could not hear what they said when they returned. Because of the tempest, we had barely been able to understand the earlier shouting. By now, the initial excitement of the Tshoban had subsided somewhat. Those who had not yet dismounted did so and settled down to await the outcome of the deliberations.

I should mention that the river was still rising. The storm that was raging north of the "rock gate" and south of the "orifice" was driving the smoke from the two gigantic fires into the trap so that the acrid clouds met at the place where the council was being held. Occasionally, it became so dense that it hid the Tshoban from view. Then, we had to wait until a whistling wind blew through the pass and whirled the smoke upward. This gave the scene something curiously elemental and primordial. The Tshoban seemed a lost host of pygmies about to be crushed and destroyed by gigantic, irresistible forces. Not yet fully realizing their predicament, they began looking for paths leading up to the heights, but without success. Now some crossed the river, but on their horses, for the Tshoban are afraid of water and cannot swim. Animals still strong enough were chosen, but there were very few of them. These men were supposed to search on the other side, but returned without having accomplished anything. Now a second, longer deliberation was held, and then two sections mounted their horses, one going south, the other north. When the horses were finally forced into the water, they refused to swim. The riders quickly returned to the safe bank because they came under fire. The Tshoban understood that there was no getting out of the trap and went back to their Djemmah. Soon, the second section also returned, having had no better success.

One could tell from the faces of the elders that they were at their wits' end, but this did not mean that they had decided to surrender. They were inveterate fatalists. They had tried to find a way out, but in vain, and felt they had done their duty. Now, things must be left to Allah who knew what was best for his Tshoban. This fatalism would not perhaps have made itself felt so directly, had it not been for their fatigue. Many sat down and put their hands in their laps while others wrapped themselves in their blankets and fell asleep. They lacked the energy to realize that sleeping merely postponed a decision. We could also see that the members of the Djemmah could not agree, and while we did not hear what they said to each other, their very expressive gestures showed that they were divided into several factions. Only after some time, it seemed, had they agreed on a course of action. The sheik rose from his seat. Significantly, he called for

Merhameh, not the Erdjani. She came down. He was very polite and admitted that he and his Tshoban were trapped. But he also maintained that a vigorous attack would free them and that they could even get through the fire since there was water in abundance to extinguish it. He then asked for a truthful statement concerning the situation and the intentions of the Ussul.

I asked myself how such questions could be addressed to a young, inexperienced girl. But Merhameh's answer was as adequate as any we could have given. She was perfectly truthful, yet cautious and diplomatic. She spoke like a lawyer who has prepared for any and every objection and gives his adversary no opening. But she was also gentle and friendly, like someone more concerned with forgiving than conquering. And sometimes, she sounded like a natural, ingenuous child who cannot grasp how someone could conduct himself as the enemy had. There was something irresistible in the words she chose and the deeply felt, persuasive force she gave them. Halef was sitting next to me and I happened to look at his face. I saw how surprised he was. When she had finished, he breathed deeply, and said:

"Did you hear her, Sidi? I thought I was a first-rate orator, but do you know what I am?"

"What?"

"A bleating sheep, a screeching crow, a yawning camel! What a voice, what sounds!"

He stopped to be able to hear the sheik who was calling out to Merhameh:

"I believe everything you say, for all the world knows that Abd el Fadl and Merhameh never lie. So you confirm that Sadik, my older son, is your prisoner?"

"Yes."

"Then I ask the Djirbani for two hours so that we can evaluate our situation. When that time is up, I shall return here to continue our discussion. Please convey that message to him."

Followed by his elders, he left to see with his own eyes if his men had reported accurately. During this time, I intended to see the "Panther," who had demanded to talk to me. I took Halef along because his dogs were guarding the prisoner, and they would obey no one but him. On our way, we could see the sheik of the Tshoban going from one group of warriors to the next, talking to them. Whenever we could be seen from below, the soldiers pointed at us, but it was a good thing that the men down there should be aware that we could move about up here and that they could not prevent it. The four hundred Hukara stationed near the "orifice" were in good spirits. They knew as well as we did that the Tshoban had no choice but surrender.

16 : Across the Border

The cleft which served as the temporary prison of the "Panther" was still further down. Natural causes had created an opening between two huge boulders that was large enough to accommodate a dozen men. Because there was only one entrance in front, it was light there but dark further back. Inside, Hu, the Hadji's dog, was guarding the prince and his two companions. I entered the prison by myself. The palang lay on the ground; the other two were sitting next to him. They got up when they saw me and remained standing during the entire discussion because I stood and did not ask them to sit down again. I greeted them, and asked:

"You wanted to speak to me. Go ahead. I am listening."

That was rather abrupt, and he looked at me for some time, uncertainly, before he answered:

"Others call you Effendi. May I do the same?"

"You may."

"And may I speak as sincerely as one only talks to a man to whom truth is more important than anything else? I have heard that you are such a man."

"You may. You have to. You would find it difficult to lie to me."

An expression of sneering cruelty passed over his handsome face. He said:

"Then let me tell you first that I hate you as I have never hated anyone. And it is only natural that you should return that feeling."

"Oh, no. One doesn't hate people one is indifferent to. Besides, I am a Christian."

"Yes, Christian," he exclaimed, and spat. "I know all about that. And are you really indifferent to me? I am a prince, you understand?"

"And I am not. That's all the difference there is. Go on."

"Like all princes, I spent some time at the court of the Mir of Ardistan. I was his particular favorite, and still am."

"Why should I care about that? Go on, go on, I don't have much time."

"Be patient, noble Christian! You will learn soon enough to take an interest in what I say. At that court, I made the acquaintance of the man who is now the commander-in-chief of the Ussul army."

"You are mistaken. The Erdjani is the commander. But you must mean that old, wounded colonel whose powder is never dry, and who only commands invalids."

"Don't mock! He repeatedly visited me here and talked to us for hours. He also talked about you."

Now I pricked up my ears, although I did not let him see my interest. Could this curious hero have committed treacheries? But I was reassured, for I soon discovered that that was not the case. There had been small talk, and that was all. The prince continued:

"Don't think that he said more than he should have. He did not mention your campaign here, but he warned me. He claimed that we would be destroyed if we came to bring war instead of peace. Since your arrival, the Ussul have been animated by a new spirit; that was all he would say. I have been able to observe what kind of spirit he meant. Are you aware what sort of day this is?"

"I am."

He supported himself on one arm, raised the upper part of his body, and asked:

"Do you know who is going to come here today?"

"I do. All the Ussul do."

"Then you found out and told them. You claim to be a Christian, but you are a devil. And tell me: Did they come?"

"Yes."

"Here to the isthmus?"

"Yes. Exactly the way they planned to."

"And what did you do? I heard shots and screams."

"We let them advance no further than the midpoint of the defile. Now they are stuck. The sea has filled the river and fires have been lit at both ends. No one can get out. Because of the tempest, the Tshoban almost died of hunger and thirst on their march here. Your father's horse collapsed from exhaustion—"

"My father?" he interrupted. "My father is here?"

"Yes."

"Then my brother stayed at home, which means that the country and the people have been turned over to a mere boy, and I am a prisoner. My father is in danger of being captured. Then things will take an entirely different course from—"

He forgot that his foot was injured and wanted to jump up but collapsed with a cry of pain. He clenched his fist, shook it at me threateningly, and gritted his teeth.

"All that is your fault, cursed Christian dog!" As he said this, his face became ugly, even repellent. "What do you plan to do with the Tshoban?" he roared at me. "What are you going to do? Let's hear!"

I did not have to answer him and could simply have left. But I had a curious compassion for this young, gifted, but utterly miseducated young man and therefore answered all his questions:

"We intend to defeat you without spilling a drop of blood. If the Tshoban surrender, we are ready to make a peace with them which will be equally advantageous to both sides. But if they don't, they will be trapped here without water and food until they die."

"All of them?"

"From the first to the last."

"Dog! And you call yourself a Christian. I must talk to my father. Take me to him."

"You are staying here," I said.

"Then bring him to me. But before peace is con

: 318 :

cluded, you understand? I am ordering you."

"Worm!"

I only said this one word, but it sufficed. Unbridled as he was, he had been about to burst out even more angrily, but his companions were beginning to fear for him, themselves, and the fate of the army whose situation called for the utmost restraint. They told him that, spoke soothingly to him, and beseeched him to control himself. In their present predicament, they said, good manners would have better results than insults and spite. He listened to them, his head lowered so that I could not see his face. Suddenly, he looked up. His expression had completely changed; it was beaming benevolence. And his voice sounded gentle and winning when he said:

"You are right. I was a fool. I am too quick to anger. Please help me up. I want to talk to the Effendi standing on my feet. My rank and the respect he is entitled to demand that."

There had been good reason to nickname him the "Panther," snarling, threatening, gnashing and baring his teeth one moment, and smooth as velvet the next. Supported by his two companions, he raised himself. He could use only one foot and therefore placed his arms on the shoulder of one and his injured leg on the shoulder of the other, who had to kneel. Meanwhile, I looked more closely at the space I was standing in. I had my back turned toward the entrance and thus had the dark section of the cleft in front of me, and although I had been standing here for only a few minutes, my eyes had already become accustomed to the darkness. I noticed that the two adjoining boulders did not completely come together but that there were a few narrow openings. And there was excrement on the floor which bats must have left there. I inferred that the cleft continued beyond this space but that the three prisoners did not suspect this. At this moment, I could not consider this further, for the "Panther" had raised himself and continued speaking:

"I ask that you listen to me as calmly as I am now speaking to you, Effendi. You agree that I need not hesitate to speak the truth. But the most important truth we are dealing with here is that everything that has happened recently and also everything that will happen in the near future depends on only two persons. Do you know who they are?"

"Perhaps you will tell me."

"It's you and me."

"How so?"

"Don't pretend! You know that I am right. Hide behind your Djirbani as much as you like. But the person standing in back of him is the one that is in control. I am talking about you. You may think about me as you please but the moment you open your eyes wider than you have up to now, you will recognize the man to whose tune the Tshoban march, and that is myself. We are the real commanders. Do you admit that?"

"Go on."

"I have heard that you want peace. So do I. You are a Christian; I am a Muslim. So our ways of attaining peace are not the same. One of us must be in error, either you or I. History tells us who is mistaken. Islam began with struggle and war, Christianity began with peace. Wherever you look, Islam is peaceful but everywhere on earth, Christianity engages in conquests, sheds blood, and wages war. All countries and nations know this; Christianity starts off peacefully, but inevitably brings war. But Islam begins with wars and inevitably leads to peace. Is that true?"

I answered:

"The Christianity and the Islam you are speaking of are completely unknown to me. Please go on."

His words had been friendly and heartfelt and it was almost impossible to believe that this was the same person that had been so vindictive a moment ago. And he continued in that same polite and persuasive manner:

"Don't be modest and say that you don't know. Both that modesty and that ignorance are lies. But I am telling the truth. I am neither European nor Christian, but an Asian and a believer in the Prophet. More importantly, my father is no servant, my mother no maid, and I am a prince. Do you realize what that means? My father has four wives. My mother is a Muslim from Sahrima, which means she is orthodox. I am her

: 320 :

son. The mother of my older brother is a Christian. May Allah curse her! Secretly, he inclines toward her faith, not the belief of his father, and therefore we have always hated each other. He stayed at home, for his mother would not let him leave. But I went to the sheik of Ardistan and learned the art of war from him. But don't believe that that has made me a servant of war. I am prince and will govern some day."

He gestured with his arms as if he meant to suggest that one day he would rule the earth. Becoming gradually more animated, he went on:

"For me, war is merely a means to a sacred end. And this end is peace. Do you understand?"

"I do."

"Then talk!"

"Your mother is a Muslim, anxious for glory and honor for herself and you, but she is not an ordinary but a noble woman. She conceives of glory and honor as a means to a much higher end. And that end is the happiness of all those whom you mean to govern some day, in other words, it is peace."

"What are you saying? Those are almost her own words. For me, war is not its own end but exists for the sake of entirely different things. For the Christians, bliss lies in heaven, beyond this world. You seek peace with God, eternal peace. But Islam is primarily concerned with worldly bliss, the peace of all nations which can be found here on earth. And one cannot attain that peace by benevolence and prayer, nor through God's mercy and compassion. One has to fight for it. One has to compel those who want no part of it to keep the peace. For me, war is the greatest work of peace on earth. Your Christianity is almost two thousand years old, but has never given a single nation peace, although peace was its first word. But I, a Muslim, will not talk about peace. Instead, I shall make a fist of my hand and smash and destroy war with it. 'An eye for an eye, and blood for blood' is the hard and just law of Islam. 'The murderer must be murdered.' War, the most horrible of all murderers, is subject to the same law as any other murderer. And because it is suicide when mankind slaughters itself, divine justice demands that war should also perish

: 321 :

through itself, through suicide. Do you understand, Effendi?"

I was astonished. This young man had thought a great deal, and profoundly. His cheeks were glowing, his eyes flaming. It seemed that his features had changed; they looked transfigured. Earlier, he had nauseated me, but now I felt like pressing his hand.

"I understand. Those are the thoughts that claimed my allegiance before I attained clarity."

"Clarity? But I see and understand perfectly clearly, and that is the reason these thoughts have found a permanent dwelling place within me but not in you, for even today you do not see. Your Christianity does not permit—"

The entrance darkened, and a voice behind me called, "Sahib!" As I turned, I saw the Erdjani standing before the cleft. He told me he wanted to see me. I said a few brief words to the prince and then followed the commander. When we were out of earshot, he gave me an important and surprising piece of news:

"The Djunub are coming."

"Which Djunub?"

"The entire army."

"When?"

"In a few hours."

"Thank God!"

"Thank God? I didn't think I was bringing you good news."

"But you are."

"Really? But we aren't done with the Tshoban. And that has to be finished if we are to succeed in overwhelming the Djunub."

"Then we should hurry. You spoke of a few hours. That is ample time for someone who has learned how to use it. Who told you that they were coming, and when they would get here?"

"The storm made it impossible for them to stay out in the desert. The sand would have engulfed their camp. Only by hurrying could they escape the wind and they therefore caught up with their officers much sooner than planned. But the ride was horrible and they were overcome with fatigue. Repeatedly, they had to stop and finally spent half a day resting to gather the strength necessary for the rest of the way. Some men on good horses were sent ahead to see how things stood at the defile. They came all the way up to the "rock gate" and I went there to interrogate them."

"How did you receive them?"

"As enemies, although they pretended to be friends. We have no time for lengthy diplomatic maneuvering. We have to act, and so I threatened them that I would have them shot on the spot unless they admitted they were deceiving us. It was probably not so much because of that threat but because they were physically and psychologically at the end of their strength that they admitted it and told me something of great importance. I'll let you know later. Right now, I want to hear what you have to say to this unexpectedly rapid development."

"I say that we should welcome it."

"But the Tshoban?"

"Rest assured that we can deal with them as rapidly as you may wish. What about their older prince?"

"I talked to him briefly. I don't believe he will create difficulties."

"Then tell me one more thing. Are you familiar with the cleft where the 'Panther' is being kept?"

"Yes."

"I mean the section in back."

"Is there one?"

"I am not certain, but I believe so."

I told him the simple reasons that led me to this conclusion. He shook his head and said:

"I don't understand. Suppose the cleft does run further back. What of it?"

"That might be very important."

"Why?"

"To show that we know what the Djunub are up to. We might hide with the Tshoban in back. I expect it would be possible to see from there what goes on up front. And perhaps one could also hear everything being said. As we wait with the Tshoban, the officers of the Djunub, the minister and the Maha-Lama, could be brought to the front section and told that this is the place they will have to stay. Then our guards leave. As soon as they believe no one can hear them,

: 323 :

they will discuss the reasons other quarters were assigned to them and I would be very much mistaken if they did not also make some remarks which would reveal that they merely came to deceive us and the Tshoban."

"It sounds like a good plan."

"Of course, important men such as the Lama, the minister, and the general may not discuss their secrets in front of ordinary people such as the non-commissioned officer or the soldier. I would therefore suggest you leave the lower-ranking personnel where it is and move only the others, from major on up."

"A good idea. But how do we get behind the crack, supposing there really is an opening there?"

"I hope we will find out quickly enough. I'll climb up and see if I am right or not."

As I said this, I pointed to the apex of the two boulders. They were approximately eighteen feet tall, and it was therefore impossible to tell from below whether they actually came close together. There were some indentations and ledges which made it possible for me to climb them, and when I got to the top I was delighted to discover that I had been right. The forward portion of the cleft where the "Panther" was kept was closed at the top, but it was open in back and so much sand had been blown into it that one could easily get down inside. When I had done this, I immediately noticed the openings I had observed before. Where I now was, the crack was so wide that I could readily look through them. But from the other side, that could not be done because it narrowed at that point. This meant that one could look in from the outside, but not the other way around. When I pressed my ear against one of the holes, I not only heard the prince talking to his companions but understood every word. In the remote corner where I was standing, the silence was total. The howling of the storm could not be heard. In short, a more suitable place for our purpose could not have been found, and I asked the Erdjani to join me so that he might see for himself where we would have to stand with the Tshoban to eavesdrop on the Djunub. Halef was told of our plan, and then the Erdjani and I climbed out again, for the two hours were almost up and the sheik of the Tshoban would soon demand that negotiations between him and our commander begin.

When we rejoined Abd el Fadl, the sheik had just begun talking to Merhameh. As we arrived, he was asking for permission to see and talk to his two sons before coming to a decision. This was precisely what we had counted on. We agreed, and told him to join us atop the ledge. He mounted a camel, rode it up to the boulder, and was then hoisted up with my lasso. He looked at all of us in turn and then let his eye travel over his fatigued men. He said:

"The man that had the idea of having us run into this trap is either a very dangerous or a very useful person. Honesty obliges me to admit that we are completely in the Ussuls' power, but only for the moment. Allah is kind and omnipotent. He can give our fate a different turn. What are your demands?"

This question had been addressed to the Erdjani.

"Surrender," was the laconic answer.

"What does that involve?"

"You will find out as soon as you have talked to those you want to talk to. Follow us."

When we came to the "Panther's" prison, I stepped inside and told him:

"You wanted to see your father."

"Yes, and you wouldn't allow it."

"I am bringing him nonetheless, and before peace has been concluded, as you demanded."

The Erdjani added:

"You may talk, but make it short. I will allow you ten minutes, not more."

We stepped out. Halef was now told to bring two strong Ussul who were given the job of taking the "Panther" and his father across the boulder to the rear section I had discovered. The "Panther" could not walk, much less climb, but I wanted him to be there when we overheard the Djunub. When the ten minutes were up, we walked back in.

"We aren't finished yet," the "Panther" said. "We demand a full hour to—"

"Impossible," the Erdjani interrupted. "Talking gets you nowhere. You have more important things to do.

We have captured Djunub here who—"

"Djunub!" the "Panther" exclaimed. "Who took them prisoner? When, where?"

He sounded almost frightened, and he looked worried. It occurred to me that the son of one of his fellow prisoners had plotted with the Djunub, and I wondered if he knew about this, or was involved in it. In spite of his behavior so far, I did not think him capable of betraying his own tribe. But he was planning conquest, and it was not inconceivable that he might scheme and plot behind his father's back and thus appear to be guilty of treason. Since the Djunub intended to deceive both the Ussul and the Tshoban, there was the chance that a young man such as this prince might have thought of allying himself with them and would laugh in their faces, once he had attained his objective.

I considered these things when I heard his hasty questions and saw the concern he could not hide. The Erdjani noticed none of this, and answered:

"We first captured the Maha-Lama and the highest minister, and then the strategist with five officers, a non-commissioned officer, and a soldier."

The "Panther" was startled when he heard this, but no one else noticed. His father was profoundly astonished, and asked:

"Allah w'Allah! Did these high-ranking officers come to see you?"

"Yes."

"And you took them prisoner? Why? Did they come as enemies?"

"No, as friends, and that's precisely the reason we seized them. We mean you no harm."

"Us?"

"Yes, you. They came to us to ally themselves with us against you."

The prince interrupted:

"Is that a fact?"

"I don't lie."

"Can you prove it?"

"That's why we are here. You are going to leave now. Behind this area, there is another one from which you can look in and see and hear what goes on here.

We are taking you and your father there. But the Djunub will be brought here so that you can eavesdrop on them and convince yourselves that everything we tell you is true, and that we are being honest with you. Here are the men that will carry you."

The two Ussul now took the "Panther" out and across the boulder into the rear section where they placed him in front of the lowest of the openings so that he could easily see through. They then took away his two companions, whom we did not need, and we joined the prince.

He was sitting behind one of the openings, his father behind another. The Erdjani and I would use the remaining two. The "Panther" was in a state of considerable excitement, and that could have only one cause. He saw now that everything that went on on the other side could be seen and heard from here, and he did not know that I had only recently discovered this listening post. He therefore had to assume that he and his two companions had also been overheard, and since he had spoken to them about any number of matters, he had reason to fear that we had discovered all their secrets. While he said nothing, I could tell from his restlessness that these thoughts were going through his mind.

It was not long before Halef brought the Djunub, from the Maha-Lama on down to the major. We could see them clearly. At first, they remained silent, distributing the space according to rank and standing. The Maha-Lama was shown more respect than anyone else, being the highest-ranking person among them. They then carefully explored the area but did not discover the openings because it was dark there. When they had settled down, they began to converse, but about wholly indifferent matters. This may have been due to excessive reverence or respect for the Lama. Nothing could be touched upon that he did not make a topic of conversation. Temporarily thwarted, we could do nothing but wait. After a while, the sheik of the Tshoban said softly:

"These people believe in the Lama. They are slow, mindless, torpid. We will have to wait for hours if we want to hear them say something."

"They will talk right away," the Erdjani answered. "Effendi, go in there and help them get started."

"Are you giving me any specific instructions?"

"No. It will be much easier for you to think of the right thing."

I left our hiding place and joined the prisoners. Initially, the Maha-Lama had been treated as a friend by the Erdjani. He had also heard about me, but neither he nor his minister had seen me as yet. The officers had, however, and had even considered me their captive, although they had not known who I was. Now, they had been together for a while, spoken of their experiences and probably also mentioned me. I was received accordingly. When the strategist saw me, he exclaimed:

"There is the disobedient fellow whom I shall have to punish."

"The owner of the most beautiful horse I have ever seen," the general added. It seemed Syrr had made more of an impression on him than I had.

"So that must be the Christian the Djirbani told us about when he still took us to be his allies."

I bowed, then made another bow before the Maha-Lama, and said to him:

"Circumstances oblige me to importune you. The commander-in-chief of the Ussul sends me here."

He frowned, being used to deeper bows and a more humble manner.

"Who are you?" he asked.

"I am called Kara ben Nemsi."

"So you really are the Christian," he interrupted, turning to the minister.

"Yes, the Christian. I was sent to you to inform you of the reason you were given a different prison. We would like—"

"What you would like is of no consequence," he interrupted a second time. "It is not your wishes but mine that are to be complied with. Not only do you treat us as enemies, but also as lower human beings. Yet I am the Maha-Lama of Djunubistan, the highest of all priests."

"Have you finished your sentence?"

"Yes. I always finish my sentences. Why are you asking?"

"Because I also am not used to being interrupted. I allowed you to finish because I have learned to be polite. But you interrupted me twice in less than a minute. If you continue, I shall be obliged to consider you a very rude person, and I won't have a chance to tell you what I came here to say."

When he heard this, his eyes doubled in size and his face expressed the highest degree of divine amazement. But I went on:

"Just now, the highest minister of the sheik of Djunubistan mentioned that you had been considered allies of the Ussul. Was that your intention?"

"Of course," the minister answered. "You were referred to as the confidant of the Djirbani, but you don't seem to be that, for if you were, you wouldn't ask that question. Didn't he tell you that we came to conclude an alliance with the Ussul?"

"An alliance against whom?"

"The Tshoban."

"Why? Are the Tshoban enemies of yours?"

"As long as there have been Tshoban and Djunub, they have never been our friends. And during all that time, they have also been the enemies of the Ussul. It therefore appeared both natural and necessary to us that the Ussul and the Djunub should become allies to destroy their common enemy. The best opportunity arose when we heard that the Tshoban planned to move through the Chatar defile to attack the Ussul. We immediately called our warriors together to come to the aid of the Ussul. Our sheik sent the two highest-ranking men of the country, the Maha-Lama and me, to conclude a pact with them. Then the most famous strategist of our army set out with his staff to let the Ussul know that we would drive the Tshoban through the narrow defile and into their arms. They would be unable to escape to the right or the left, and would be squeezed, crushed, and destroyed as between two fists."

"So that's what you wanted. Is that what you did?" I asked, pretending to be surprised.

"Of course. Didn't you know that?"

"I know something altogether different. If I am to believe you, I must ask you to have the Maha-Lama confirm your words. It seems that the Ussul were to be misled concerning your honesty and good will. So it is most desirable that we state the truth as clearly as possible, and exclude all possibility of error. I therefore ask the highest priest of Djunubistan if he will affirm what the highest minister has just maintained."

Because there was the possibility that the three eavesdroppers had not heard every word, I decided to trick the Maha-Lama into repeating the important points. I had called him the "highest priest of Djunubistan," and this mollified him somewhat. His face became less sombre, and he said:

"I affirm it."

"That the Tshoban are your mortal enemies?"

I asked him this and the following questions so slowly and clearly that the eavesdroppers could not possibly fail to hear them and his answers.

"Yes."

"That you want to annihilate them?"

"Yes, with the help of the Ussul."

"That you came here for the purpose of concluding a pact with the Ussul?"

"That's correct. With the Ussul, and against the Tshoban."

"Is your army already on its way?"

"Yes, three thousand strong."

"And the Tshoban are to be squeezed to death and exterminated by you and the Ussul here on the isthmus?"

"Yes. That's the right word: exterminated. No one will be allowed to survive. Now, do you believe that we came as your friends? Do you understand now that you were unintelligent and ungrateful? We are your liberators, yet you lock us up like criminals and have us guarded by dogs."

"I believe neither the one thing nor the other. It's you who were ungrateful and unintelligent, not the Ussul."

"We? Prove it!" the minister flared up.

"Prove it!" the Maha-Lama chimed in.

"Prove it, prove it," all the rest echoed.

"That's easily done. You have admitted that the Tshoban are your mortal enemies and that the Ussul were to help you get rid of them. So gratitude alone obliged you to be honest with us. But you will hear in a moment that you were ungrateful. And just as any ungratefulness and dishonesty is also unintelligent, you abandoned all intelligence when you camped one evening down by the river and talked about things which no Ussul should have heard. I was coming along that route, in the opposite direction. I saw your fire. I dismounted and stalked your camp. I was lying on the other side of the tree against whose trunk you were leaning, and heard every word you said."

"You eavesdropped on us?" the minister asked.

"Eavesdropped?" the priest joined in. "On me, the Maha-Lama of Djunubistan?"

"Yes. I will prove it to you by repeating everything you said."

And that's exactly what I did. I described the entire situation and repeated every word that had been spoken while I had been there. They sat utterly motionless and looked as if they did not dare breathe. To deny, to contradict, to make excuses did not occur to them. They were too dismayed. Then, suddenly, we heard a curiously muffled voice which sounded as if it were coming down from the clouds or the interior of the earth:

"Effendi, don't say another word to these liars, these traitors, these scoundrels. Spit in their faces, and then come back to honest people, to us."

The Djunub were violently startled. They jumped up and began shouting in confusion. I walked out, past Halef and his dogs, to the two Ussul who had earlier carried the prince to the hiding place, and told them to bring him back. It was he who had called out those muffled words. When they raised him from the cleft and he saw me, he called out:

"Effendi, you win. I'll do whatever you want. I agree to everything you decide. All I ask is that, being a dog, I be allowed to sit down there by yours to guard those miserable wretches."

The Erdjani answered:

: 331 :

"You may." And, turning to the two Ussul, he told them: "Put him down there where he wants to be. He has the right to demand that place from us."

The "Panther" was so much a slave to his wrath, he could think only of those by whom he felt betrayed. Temporarily, it had slipped his mind that the fate of his tribe would be decided in a few moments. However gifted he might be, this lack of circumspection proved that he could never be a great man. His temperament ruled him like a wild animal. Like himself, it also was a "panther." When I had been talking to him earlier, I had not told him everything that was on my mind. There had been something of importance that I had wanted to add. Only I sensed this weakness in his character. I was beginning to wonder if he had the capacity to grow like an organic being, or at least to crystallize like an inorganic one, a diamond. Or did he only grow by holding fast to the moment's inspiration whatever that might be?

Characteristically, his father did not say a word to either encourage or restrain him in his desire for revenge. What he had heard had much less effect on him than on his son. He did not think of himself, or vengeance, but of his tribe that was in danger of losing its most valuable possession, its independence, its freedom, and its identity. He was willing to enter into negotiations, but the Erdjani would not consent:

"Not now. You have a second son whom you must see and talk to. Come with me."

We went to the older prince's prison which also lay between some rocks. A Ussul stood guard there.

"Go in and talk to him," the Erdjani told the sheik. "I will give you ten minutes. We will wait here."

When the sheik had disappeared inside, we sat down next to each other on a boulder to await his return.

We did not speak a single word. The Erdjani stared at the ground, and I looked at him without his noticing it. He did not appear to have aged, and yet it struck me how mature his face had become during the last few days. The greatness that lay in him had begun to manifest itself.

When the ten minutes were up, the sheik returned

with his son. Both were serious, and one could see that they had come to a firm resolve. As he pointed at the prince, the father asked:

"I brought him along. Is he still your prisoner?"

"Yes," the Erdjani answered.

"For how long?"

"Until peace has been concluded between you and me, between the Tshoban and the Ussul."

"That peace will be concluded," the son said. "And it is my wish that it be done without delay. Who could have anticipated that this would be the result of our campaign? But I sense God's hand in everything that has happened and we will go where He is pointing. My father will speak to our Tshoban to that effect. Will you permit it?"

"Gladly."

"And may I do the same?"

"Of course. Come with me."

All of us climbed back to the heights and followed the trail to the ledge to return the sheik to his men. As we were walking along, the sheik asked about the conditions of the peace.

"Choose," the Erdjani said.

The sheik stopped and looked at him with wide-open eyes.

"Did I hear right?"

"Yes."

"You will not impose them? I am to choose?"

"Certainly. Does that astonish you? We will make each other the gift of peace. We will not purchase or sell it dearly. I wish to become your brother, and your nation to become the sister of mine. Even the smallest price is too high for an imposed, untenable peace. But the highest price is too small if I can win the lasting love and loyalty which will unite your tribe and mine in brotherly love. I make no demands. I want to give. Do you understand?"

The sheik held out both hands, and answered:

"I understand very well, and will act as your magnanimity demands. You are great in what you give, and I will be no smaller in what I receive. As I am holding your hands in mine, so our nations will henceforth be united as if they were one. Your friends shall be ours, your enemies our enemies. Am I right?"

"Yes. As of today, the Ussul and the Tshoban shall be like brother and sister, honestly and loyally helping each other. And we will put this alliance to the test this very day. Are you willing to ally yourself with me against the Djunub?"

"Immediately."

"And to forgive them as I now forgive you, should we be victorious?"

The sheik wanted to consider, but his son entreated him:

"Consent, father! We are standing here on storm-swept heights. We must act with greater freedom, greater purity, and greater nobility than those down there in the valley. I know that my mother taught not only me but also you to think thoughts that outrun this indolent, hard, and irrational age. Allah decreed that today we should meet men who not only think as nobly but much more nobly than we do. What they want is nothing ordinary but something truly great. The highest, finest thought of my soul could rise from depth and obscurity and become incarnate in the Erdjani. This makes me very happy, and I ask that you consent, father."

The sheik pulled his son toward him, kissed his cheek, mouth, and forehead, and said:

"So be it! If you forgive them, so will I."

Now the Erdjani said very seriously:

"Thank your wife, and thank this son of yours. Up to this moment, your fate was still hanging in the balance. Only now that you are ready to forgive will you also be forgiven. You are free, all of you are free. There will be no punishment, no sacrifice, no atonement of any kind. I shall accompany you to the Djemmah to plead for a sincere, lasting peace. All of you will be given food and water for yourselves and your animals. A half hour from now, no Tshoban should be visible here, for all that happened here must be kept secret from the Djunub."

"You are going to too much trouble on their account," the sheik said disdainfully, almost contemptuously. "They are not men but puppets in the shadow plays of the Mir of Ardistan. He makes them believe that they govern themselves. Actually, they are his slaves. He arms them as if they were heroes, and yet they are the greatest cowards imaginable. For them, life is a kef, an afternoon nap. They are even too lazy to pray. They use prayer wheels which turn in the wind and the water and really believe that Allah is so stupid as to be pleased by that. When they get here, they will be well armed and sit on fine horses, but you won't see them perform great deeds."

This was not the first time I heard the Djunub characterized in this manner, and what the sheik said was perfectly correct. Compared to the desert of the Tshoban, their land was immensely fertile. To survive, they barely had to lift a finger; everything they needed fell into their laps. That had drained them of their vigor, and made them arrogant and cowardly.

Because the sheik had gone with us, his men had bunched together close to the ledge, expecting that a decision would be announced upon his return. They were so astonished by what they heard that there was no cheering when he finished. Then the Erdjani addressed them. He was a better orator than the sheik, and had the gift of persuasion. He briefly set forth all the advantages of the alliance and suggested that they could avail themselves of them without really having deserved them. He showed them their past, their present, their hard, barren life in the desert. And he developed for them an image of their future that would result from an alliance with the Ussul. They warmed to him, and their trust and joy expressed themselves in loud acclamations. When he had finished, the applause was thunderous.

Now the prince stepped to the edge of the ledge and was greeted jubilantly. One could tell from their reception that it was he and not his brother who was the tribe's favorite son, and when he raised his hand to signal that he wanted to speak, the silence was instantaneous. He elaborated what the Erdjani had said and showed why it was so. From now on, there would be peace among those who had warred against each other so incessantly. But it would not be the kind of peace that already looks toward war as it is being concluded. Instead, it would be the true, sacred peace the angels call for as they come out of an open paradise and see the mountains glow. This peace, he said, was now descending from those mountains, and was about to arrive. Embodied in the Erdjani, it was standing before them, stretching out its hand. He himself had seized that hand and was holding onto it, and as he said this, he took it and embraced the Erdjani. Then he could not go on for the burst of applause mingled with the wind, and the enthusiasm of these joyful men was carried up from the narrow valley far out into the limitless distance. The soldiers were pushing close to the rock, raising their hands as if they wanted to seize the prince, and calling on him to come down. When he shook his head to convey that it was too high, they threw up ropes which I tied together to let him down. Below, he disappeared like a drop of water in the sea. I also let down the sheik and the Erdjani, and then joined Abd el Fadl and Merhameh to await further developments.

They came more quickly than anticipated. The Djemmah renounced all further deliberations. Because the enthusiasm was general, what had to be done was accomplished with miraculous speed. The fire at the "orifice" was put out and water from the river poured over the hot ground so that the Tshoban might leave the defile through this passage. When they had done so, the fire was lit again. And at the other exit where all traces of the earlier fire had been removed, a new one was started so that the trap soon became again what it had been before the Tshoban had moved into it.

Up to this time, there had been a storm but no rain. Now, a fine drizzle began to fall. Abd el Fadl told us that before, when the prince of the Tshoban had been speaking and it had been utterly calm, the storm had only been catching its breath, and that it would now return and be accompanied by flooding. To prepare against this, we had blankets brought from the camp and barricaded ourselves between some rocks so that even the most violent downpour would not reach us.

We had barely finished when the first Djunub appeared by the "rock gate."

Irahd, who was in command there, welcomed them and told them they should ride on to where a warm fire was burning, that their Maha-Lama, minister, and officers had already arrived, and that everything had been attended to.

They entered slowly, exhausted, on horses that stumbled from fatigue. They were well armed, almost all of them carrying the same make rifle. And their dress also was really a uniform. These units looked well cared for. Yet the impression they made at that moment was depressing. I did not see a single upturned face. Their heads were hanging down, their bodies shaking. They were not riding so much as being pushed by the man behind. The drifting sand covering them and even hanging from their beards made them look like corpses that had returned from their graves as they dragged themselves across the "bridge of death." Off to one side, someone was saying:

"You can see everything from here. Put him down and make a stone hut to protect him from the rain. I understand it will fall all night long."

It was Halef, talking to some Ussul who were carrying the "Panther." Because he had his two dogs with him, I asked where the captured Djunub were, and whether they no longer needed to be guarded.

"No," he answered with a slightly malicious smile. "They are being taken along the upper trail now and down to the 'rock gate.' Once the army is inside the trap, we will push them in behind it."

"Very good. That saves us a lot of talking and negotiating. Who had that idea?"

"One of the smartest people I know," he said, pointing at himself. Then he went on: "I did it to have some fun. When I heard that there would be cloudbursts all night long, and that the Djunub down there would really get drenched, I felt there was no reason why the Maha-Lama, the highest minister, the strategist with the long name, and all the rest of them should not share that pleasure with their poor, half-starved troops. I told the Erdjani, and he agreed. Then I invited the prince, who wanted to watch the capture of the Djunub, to come here where we have the best view. I'll have to stay with him rather than with you, Sidi, for until tomorrow we have to make ourselves as comfortable as we can."

He was right. Where I was, there was not enough space for him and the prince, especially because he had his large dogs with him. As the Ussul were putting up a stone hut for Halef and the "Panther," the latter was observing the "gate" through which the Djunub were hastily squeezing and pushing their way to escape the tempest raging outside. The expression of malice on his face made him look ugly, and whenever Merhameh glanced at him, she quickly turned away. But he kept staring at the beautiful girl and made no effort to hide his interest. He knew who she was but was not aware that his older brother was also here. His father had not told him because of the hostility between the two.

Having come to the "rock gate," the Djunub could advance no further, but from the other end, they were still pushing forward when the last stragglers finally came through the passage. Then some shots were fired and everyone looked at the gate. A final group was coming through there on foot. They were the already captured Djunub whom Irahd had pushed inside before lighting the fire. The Maha-Lama and the minister were at the head. When Halef saw the strategist directly behind them, he rubbed his hands gleefully, and said:

"There is my strategist who has become so fond of us all. May Allah grant him sunshine tomorrow and an umbrella full of a thousand holes for tonight."

As he said this, the wind was already driving the smoke through the gate and we knew that the trap was closed now.

"They are all there, from the first to the last," the "Panther" exulted. His eyes were sparkling. "No one can get away. May Allah curse them and send them to his deepest hell for having deceived me."

That curse had barely been uttered when Merhameh's voice rang out beside me:

"May Allah take pity on them so that they do not

fall into the hands of a man who does not think like a human being, but like a panther."

This had a curious effect on the prince. It seemed at first that he would clench his fists and jump up but his injured foot prevented him. Then he stared at her with wide-open eyes. Suddenly, an almost naive, childlike good nature came into his face. In a melodious voice, he said:

"Quite right, quite right. May Allah take pity on these dear fellows and lead them out of this cursed trap and into his best heaven."

With a radiant smile, he nodded at Merhameh and turned back to the river and what was going on there. At that moment, lightning flashed across the sky, a peal of thunder followed as if all the rocks of the defile were crashing down, and immediately the floodgates of heaven opened. What came down was not drops of rain but a single, impenetrable, compact mass of water. The scene before our eyes disappeared. All we saw was the incessant flood crashing down, roaring, surging, and foaming around us, and then tumbling past into the depth in its greedy fury. This must have gone on for an hour. Then more lightning streaked across the sky and the noise of the thunder became so vehement that my ears began to hurt. In the flashing light, we could see that the river and the valley were no longer distinct, but that the river had flooded its banks and reached the rocks. As if the water coming down from the heavens to the accompaniment of the closely spaced lightning and claps of thunder had exhausted itself, there was a sudden pause when not a single drop fell. But it lasted half a minute at most. Then a rain began to fall which lasted all evening and all night, and did not stop until early the following morning. It reduced visibility until we could only see a few steps in front of us, and that only as long as there was daylight. We were surrounded by flowing water and a single, solid, heavy, immobile darkness. But during that short interval between cloudburst and rain, we had seen that horses and men were sitting and lying in the water and could thus slake their thirst more easily than they cared for.

Fortunately, the stone hut had been finished when it

had begun to pour. Halef and the prince sat inside, as dry as we were, but talking was out of the question. It would have required too much effort for what we had to say.

I passed a tolerable evening and night. Occasionally, I woke up, thinking of the poor Djunub down by the river or, rather, inside it, for the entire valley had become one streaming flood. There were also the Tshoban and the Ussul, of course, but the latter were water rats and such a downpour would do them no harm. Then it seemed as if someone were calling for help. Others joined in, and the calls were repeated, sometimes nearby, sometimes further away. But I thought I was dreaming and slept on until I heard Halef's voice:

"Sidi, don't you hear anything? Are you dead?"

I woke up, rubbed my eyes, and looked around. I was the only one left in our shelter. Outside, the sun was shining brightly, and Halef and our four dogs were standing before me. I stepped outside. It was utterly calm, the rain had stopped. The river was still full but no longer flooded its banks. The trap was empty. There was no one about. Halef laughed.

"You don't look terribly intelligent, Sidi."

"I believe it. I am amazed. And I slept while all this went on."

"I didn't wake up myself until just now, when the prince asked to be taken to his father. This curious rain and this marvellous air were like an irresistible sleeping potion."

"But where is everybody?"

"Down below. Come along, I'll tell you all about it."

What Halef told me overturned all the plans I had made concerning the Djunub. The Erdjani and his staff had spent a difficult night and could have used our help but had not wanted to burden us with a task only he could accomplish. The cries of help I had heard had been real. The water of the river had risen to such a height that it had threatened to engulf the horses and men below. The Djunub had feared for their lives and had been shouting for help until far beyond midnight. Because of the masses of water that had come down, the two fires had almost gone out, and the Djunub had been able to approach the guards to request that the Erdjani negotiate with them. He had exploited their fear, and had moved back and forth between the two exits, negotiating with the Maha-Lama and the strategist in turn. The minister and the generals were also dealt with individually, for everyone was pursuing some private objective and making confessions or revelations which would exonerate him and incriminate the others. Finally, the Erdjani had called all the men together and interrogated them in the streaming rain where they stood in chest-high water and under the watchful eyes of a hundred huge Ussul armed with spears. Convinced that they were doomed unless they confessed, they had told everything they knew.

"What they knew? From whom?" I asked Halef.

"From their sheik. But especially from the Mir of Ardistan."

"And what happened then?"

"They did not achieve the results they expected. The Erdjani left them without a word. A short time later, the gate was opened and the Djunub permitted to move out, in single file. Everyone had to surrender his horse and weapons. Now all of them are camped in the sand in the southern part of the isthmus and are being guarded by our men."

"So they are prisoners of war."

"No, they are like the children of Israel in Babel. The Erdjani won't let them go but will send them to the jungles of the Ussul where they will have to turn the wilderness into fertile land."

"All of them?"

"Yes, including the strategist, the Maha-Lama, and the minister. But what's the matter?"

"Come with me. I have to see the Erdjani."

I rushed along the trail and then down to the opening in the rocks. When I got to the end of the defile, I saw thousands of horses far off to the right. On the left, and equally far away, were their riders. Everywhere Ussul and Tshoban were milling about. Directly ahead of me, the tent of the Ussul sheik, which had been taken down because of the storm, was being put up again. Men were forming a tight circle around it and something important seemed to be going on. Halef and I pushed our way through the crowd and saw Amihn and Taldsha, the Erdjani, the sheik of the Tshoban, and Sadik, his older son, standing together in a group. Abd el Fadl and Merhameh were also there. Facing them stood three horses, bridled and harnessed to take the "Panther" and his two friends and advisers on a long journey.

When the "Panther" saw me, he called out:

"There he is. Ask him! He knows how to eavesdrop, interrogate, explore, and discover. He showed us how to listen in on the officers of the Djunub. And before that, I sat in that very same room with my two companions. There can be no doubt he also eavesdropped on us. Go and ask him! He will tell you why I have to leave immediately after having met my brother."

He was pointing at Sadik, of whose presence he had only heard that morning. Then he rode close to Abd el Fadl and asked him:

"You are Abd el Fadl, the prince of Halihm?"

"Yes."

"And this is Merhameh, your daughter?"

"Yes."

"Then I am warning you. Don't ever give her in marriage to anyone except me. Yesterday, she dared bless where I had cursed. And she is beautiful. She is mine, and I shall come back for her."

He moved his horse in a tight circle, to look all in the face those standing there, and then called out loudly:

"Listen, you Tshoban! And you Ussul, listen as well! There you see Merhameh, Abd el Fadl's child. And here I am. Now, I am only a prince of the Tshoban, but soon I shall be much more. I say that Merhameh is my bride. Woe to her father, should he dare prefer another to me. Woe to her, should she not remain faithful. And woe to the wretch at her side when I return. He will die a death that will weigh more heavily than a thousand others. Farewell! May Allah protect you! You need it!"

Accompanied by his two counselors, he rode off. I stood there looking after him with no comprehension of what he had said or was doing. The Erdjani came up to me, took me by the hand, and said:

"Come with me, Effendi. There is something of great importance that I must tell you. What happened here yesterday and what is happening now is not the end. It seems we will be going north to Djinnistan."

VOLUME TWO

1 : The Mir of Djinnistan

It was a little more than two months later. Djunubistan had been compelled to submit. With his greatly enlarged army, the Erdjani now stood on the border of
Gharbistan which, like Sharkistan, did not have a ruler
of its own but was governed by the Mir of Ardistan.
Halef and I were far ahead of the troops; the reader
will soon discover why. We had travelled across
Gharbistan and advised the Mir of Ardistan that we
were envoys of the Erdjani. He had sent a cavalry unit
to meet us and to take us to Ard, his residence. These
soldiers claimed that it was their task to protect us.
Actually, however, we had to consider ourselves their
prisoners, for they had been given strict orders to turn
us over to the feared tyrant. They were commanded
by a colonel who tried to make us believe that we
were in no danger. We were riding our own horses but
had left our rifles, pistols, and revolvers with the Erdjani for two reasons. In the first place, we wished to be
considered envoys and therefore must not be armed.
Besides, I did not want to risk having my valuable
rifles fall into the hands of the Mir. We were thus
completely unarmed, for the knives everyone always
carries were utensils, not weapons. Nor did we have

our dogs with us. It had been impossible to take them along to Ardistan where they might be a hindrance. We therefore had entrusted them to Abd el Fadl, Merhameh, and the Erdjani.

For a day and a half, our escort had been taking us through terrain which became increasingly fertile as we drew closer to the capital. But we noticed that the routes along which we travelled were deserted and had been chosen to avoid encounters. The country had become mountainous, and the mountains were partly densely wooded, partly covered with vines and fruit trees. On some fairly extensive plains, we saw houses, gardens, and fields, and there was flowing water in the depth of the passes. Compared to the desert of the Tshoban, which fortunately lay behind us, this was a pleasing sight.

Half of the afternoon was already over when signs increased that the residence was near. On all roads, we saw people either journeying there or returning from it, and it was no longer possible to avoid all contact. We were particularly struck by the large number of military personnel. Like the Djunub two months ago, they were dressed almost identically and wore insignia on their garments.

As we reached the crest of an extended ridge, we involuntarily stopped our horses. The sight before us was surprisingly beautiful. A wide basin had come into view, entirely enclosed by mountains, with four rivers which joined directly below us. As far as the eye could see, houses and gardens were strung out along them. The houses were built in widely varying architectural styles, and the large number of houses of worship represented all historical periods. Among the temples, pagodas, and minarets, we noticed an occasional modest building with a cross on its roof.

But most striking was a marvellously fashioned and articulated stone structure in the center of the city. It riveted our attention. Its center element, a large, bold dome, was flanked at the four cardinal points by four powerful towers of identical appearance, massive at the bottom but becoming increasingly delicate. Their spires seemed to turn to ether and wholly disappear in it. Smaller domes had been constructed next to these four principal towers. Along the northern, the southern, the eastern, and the western sides, descending sets of towers and domes followed so that the entire complex seemed to return to the earth from which it had originally risen. I wondered if this might be a cathedral.

"A magnificent city, isn't it?" the colonel asked as he glanced at us to see what impression all this was making. "This is the site of paradise. Do you see those four rivers? They are called Pison, Gibon, Tigris, and Phrat, names which you find in the Koran, the Bible, or the Vedic texts, but that's of no interest to me. I don't believe in any of those books. The towers are the castle of the Mir. God himself laid the foundation stone when paradise still existed, and placed it in its very center. He ordered the Assyra and Babyla, who were giants, to begin building what he had decreed would be the residence of the Mir of Ardistan. The giants did as he asked. But later, the Christians came and claimed that all this belonged to them. They drove off the Assyra and Babyla and continued building. When they were done, they placed a cross on every spire and in every corner. The Mir who governed in those days permitted this. It amused him that they should believe they might live in his house. When the last cross had been put in place, he had all of them taken down, and he moved into the house in which his descendents have lived to the present day. But the Christians were severely punished for their arrogance. Even today, they are despised and hated, and the Mir has shown great mercy in not destroying or banishing them but allowing them to live in the smallest, most remote houses of the city. They have to put crosses on them as a warning to others not to defile themselves by entering them. But we must move on. The Mir ordered me to have you there this evening because the audience you desire is to take place tonight."

"Where are you taking us?" I asked him.

"To the castle, of course. You are his guests, so you will stay there."

"Guests?" I asked, and looked at him closely.

He seemed uneasy, but repeated:

"Yes, guests."

"Did he tell you to use that word?"

"That very word! Certainly." Having given me this assurance, his tone became more confidential.

"He is anxious to see you. He already knows you."

"From where?"

"I am not permitted to say. Perhaps he will tell you himself."

We continued down the slope toward town. During the hour we must have spent riding up and down streets and thoroughfares and crossing a number of bridges, the variety and contrasts everywhere made us feel that we were in a cosmopolitan center containing everything the world has to offer. Halef felt almost discouraged.

"I am beginning to be afraid, Sidi," he said. "This is not at all the same thing as the forest, the open fields, or the freedom of the desert where one can do as one pleases. Here, one is no longer the master of one's own destiny, and courage and intelligence are useless. One can't avoid being squeezed to death. Why are you smiling?"

"Do you really believe Allah remained outside the gates? Or did we lose our courage and cunning out there? Are we fools that have lost their belief in God and are riding toward certain destruction?"

The castle was so large that it remained visible during the entire time we rode through the city, and we were taken by surprise when we abruptly stopped by a gate and the colonel told us that we had arrived. The gate did not lead into a building but a courtyard two sides of which consisted of stables. We were told that the horses belonging to guests of the Mir were kept there. As soon as we had dismounted, the colonel wanted to take us into the building but we refused. In the situation in which we found ourselves, our horses were as important to us as our own well being. The officer had to wait until they had been stabled, cleaned, washed, watered, and fed. When he became impatient and told us that he could not wait any longer but must report to the Mir at once, Halef answered in his characteristic, succinct way:

"But we are not asking you to stay. Let the Mir wait

if you can't. My horse is more important to me than he is."

The officer gave in, and when we were done, he took us to one of the smaller towers where our quarters lay. He turned us over to a polite but monosyllabic servant who brought us food and drink and then sat down outside the door. Since he carried pistols in his belt, he seemed more of a guard than a domestic. After we had eaten, we spent some time enjoying the view from our window and then went down into the yard because we wanted to see if we would be allowed to move freely. The servant did not prevent us from leaving our room, but he followed us. When we walked toward the gate, he told us that it was locked. It would be opened if we wished to take a walk in the city. First, though, the guard would have to be called to accompany us, since the Mir did not wish anything to happen to us. This told us what our situation was. No one had said so specifically, but it was obvious we were prisoners, and that was precisely what we had expected. As we returned to our quarters, it was growing dark, and the servant brought candles. An hour later, the colonel came to tell us that he had been ordered to take us to the Mir. He also said that the Mir would not speak to us, that we had to show the proper humility and to answer truthfully all questions he would have others address to us.

"I can see what is coming," Halef whispered to me. "My Sidi will hardly submit to this sort of treatment."

The Mir of Ardistan is an important oriental prince, a despot who knows no law but his will. He stood in bad repute. It was said that even the wealthiest, greatest, best, and most intelligent person was, to him, a mere mosquito that one grinds to powder between one's finger tips. But I knew that, both in the good and the evil he does, a human being always remains human. No one is a pure angel. Nor is anyone so utterly rejected by God that he is wholly a devil. Not even the Mir of Ardistan would be an angel or a devil, and it was doubtful that he was as much of a fiend as rumor had it. If human life meant nothing to him, it was probably because those he dealt with year after year

: 351 :

were vile, submissive toadies, parasites, and sycophants. And that was a reason to pity rather than to fear or hate him.

We were taken through long corridors and up and down a number of stairs. Everywhere, the light was just sufficient to see where we were putting our feet. The walls were covered with mats and rugs which muffled the sound of our steps. As on our journey here, the attempt had been made to isolate us from all contact with others. We saw no one, not even servants to open the doors we passed through. All this was done by the colonel. Finally, he led the way into a long, narrow room which was so dark that we had to grope our way. This was intentional, as we soon discovered, for the abundance of light which suddenly flooded in on us was meant to overwhelm and blind us after the preceding darkness.

For a clearer understanding of what now took place, I have to mention that when I spoke of the colonel opening doors, I did not mean to suggest that there were real wooden doors. Indeed, we did not know if any existed in that palace. With the exception of the gate leading from the street into the courtyard, all openings through which we had passed up to this moment had been covered by rugs or curtains which had to be thrown to one side. As the colonel parted the heavy curtains which closed off the darkness in which we found ourselves and called on us to enter, we were assailed by a profusion of fragrances and an abundance of light refracted from colored glass, lanterns, and lamps hanging from the ceiling and attached to the walls. The candles and the burning sesame oil were scented. Momentarily, we were blinded and our senses benumbed.

We had come into a large room, the throne room of the Mir of Ardistan, and yet it wasn't really that but something altogether different. Architecturally, this hall had something sacred, church-like about it, but this effect could not wholly assert itself because it was marred by worldly splendor.

I shall not describe the precious throne or the person sitting on it, for all I saw were the garments he wore and the white veil which hid his face and had only a narrow slit for the eyes. All of this shone with gold and sparkled with diamonds and other precious stones. Courtiers and high-ranking officers, all of them dressed in shimmering garments or uniforms, were standing on either side of the throne. At a greater distance, a crowd of lesser dignitaries had gathered. They were so abundantly armed that their weapons could have equipped six times their number. The impression to be conveyed was thus not simply one of opulence and splendor but also of warlike power. Poor devils that we were, the two of us felt like valueless copper coins in a pile of gold pieces.

Why such a display on our account, we asked ourselves. But there was no time to search for an answer to this question. We could not remain where we were. With all eyes turned toward us and everybody wondering what we might do or say, we advanced to the center of the hall and stood facing the throne. We stopped and looked at the ruler, or rather, his spread out, layered garments underneath which he completely disappeared except for his eyes. He did not move, and neither did we.

"Why don't you salute?" I heard a voice I recognized immediately.

"Whom should we salute?" I asked.

"The ruler."

"Where is he? Why doesn't he show himself?"

"He is sitting right there. Are you blind?"

Up to this moment, the speaker had been standing behind the Mir. Now, he moved to one side. It was the "Panther." I did not allow his presence to startle me, however, but answered:

"We are hardly blind. But my eyes must be deceiving me. I came to speak to the Mir of Ardistan. Instead, I only see a perfectly ordinary Tshoban who abandoned his father, his people, and his country, and betrayed them to the enemy."

I spat and turned to leave.

"Stop, you must stay here," he thundered.

"Who can keep me?"

"I will; all of us."

"Try it."

I began walking, and the courageous Halef followed.

"Stop, stop," the "Panther" called again.

"Stop, stop," everyone echoed.

Those close by hurried after us. Some were stretching out their arms and one of them who had put his left hand on my shoulder even drew his curved sabre. I tore it from his hand, hurled the man against the others, and shouted:

"Get back! Take care! If anyone is anxious to be sent to the devil right here and now, let him approach."

For a moment, all was quiet. Their horror had immobilized them. Such a desecration of the throne, of the sacred place in which it was standing, was unprecedented, a crime that must be punished by death. A moment later, they attacked. I had decided to withdraw to the narrow corridor where the darkness would help me to keep them away. Perhaps we could reach the courtyard and the stables. What would happen then was beyond our power. As it turned out, things didn't develop to that point. A huge noise was heard outside, a confusion of fearfully shouting voices. The curtain over the main entrance was pulled aside, and someone roared:

"Help, help! Save yourselves! Four mad dogs, the size of camels!"

"Where?" our attackers wanted to know.

"They were howling down by the gate, wanting to be let in. Then they dashed to the main gate and are now running and searching through the corridors and rooms. There they are! Save yourselves!"

The shouting was now drowned out by the voices of dogs. It was not a barking or howling but the far-reaching, yearning, seeking, and asking which will not cease until the animal has found its master. It was coming closer and about to pass. The dogs had not picked up our scent, since we had come from the other side. We saw all four of them rushing past. They had almost disappeared when Uucht turned and looked into the room. She no sooner saw us than she roared like a lioness and the others rushed in. They would have knocked us down, had we not quickly stepped back against the wall. All those still in the hall were shouting, bellowing, and screaming with fright and terror, scurrying away as quickly as they could.

It had obviously been impossible to keep these faithful animals where we had left them. We later heard that all efforts, all tenderness, had achieved nothing. We knew that they would have stayed, had they not been treated incorrectly. We had ordered them to, and they had understood us. Their four-day journey was a considerable achievement, and they had also come through an unfamiliar, bustling city and roamed an entire palace to find us. They were about to drop from thirst and hunger, and looked miserable and worn out. Now, they were whimpering and whining with joy. We caressed them, speaking to them in words they could understand. Somewhere, we had to get water and meat for them.

"Yes, water is most important, and then lots of meat," Halef said. "Even if that means taking the kitchen by storm. They really deserve it."

"You won't have to take it by storm," we heard a deep, resonant voice. "Magnificent dogs, splendid dogs. I'll give the order myself. You can go back to your rooms. Nothing will happen to you as long as you are in this house. You are my guests. I shall send you the castellan. Immediately."

We were dumbfounded, for we had felt certain that everyone had left and our entire attention had been taken up by the dogs. And now, as he spoke and we looked at him, we realized that the principal actor, the Mir, had calmly remained seated and was observing us as we caressed the exhausted animals. He rose, gathered up his garments, raised them so as to be able to walk, and left. He stopped at the door, turned his veiled face toward us, and repeated:

"I shall send the castellan to bring meat. Farewell."

"Mashallah," Halef said when the Mir had gone. "Would you have believed that possible, Sidi?"

"Hardly."

"First, I thought we'd be beheaded because we used the sabre to—it's still lying there. And now the Mir seems perfectly content and is even having meat sent. What do you think?"

"It's the dogs that saved us."

"Who sent them?"

"Don't ask. Come along."

"Right away, Sidi. But let me—there is no wall here, only a large thin veil, and small stars moving behind it. What could that be?"

He went to have a look. There was a balustrade such as normally runs along a choir. It had been closed off all the way up to the ceiling by two vertical strips of the finest Bukhara wool. When one pushed them aside, one could see into the room lying behind the balustrade. It was quite large but utterly dark. The stars Halef had mentioned were burning lamps which, though numerous, did not illumine anything. Only a misty light like a comet's tail fell from the room in which we were standing. I assumed that we were directly under the highest dome of the cathedral, but could not be certain.

The unexpectedly kind manner of the Mir encouraged us to look more calmly at what lay ahead. Because his voice was deep and pure and did not have the disagreeable quality one might expect from an evil tyrant or despot, Halef and I felt that this man's heart could not be made of stone. Just then, the colonel came rushing up to us. He told us that the Mir had personally ordered him to take us back to our quarters. When I thought of the noise and confusion our dogs had created in the castle, the greatest imaginable wrath on the part of the prince would have been understandable. Miraculously, the precise opposite had happened. Back in our rooms, we felt much more at ease than before, particularly since the servant seemed to have been instructed to behave as one, rather than as a guard.

He first brought water for the dogs, and then three pipes and tobacco. He informed us that the third was intended for the castellan who would shortly make his appearance, but that we should not wait for his arrival to begin smoking. The tobacco was of that exceptionally rare sort which is called Bachuhr* and is offered only by princes and other privileged individuals.

---

* Fragrance.

The castellan was not the man we had expected. Involuntarily, we made a much deeper bow and answered him much more politely than local custom prescribed. He was middle-aged, tall and slender, but strongly built, and wore a splendid black beard, which hung down over his chest and made his virile, handsome face look almost deathly pale. The expression in his eyes was enigmatic and had to be studied before it could be described. He was dressed in perfectly ordinary simple white cloth, and wore no rings or ornaments. After greeting us, he immediately stated the purpose of his visit. He sat down by the dogs, stroked them, and gestured to the servant who brought in a basket filled with meat, and a knife. He began cutting the meat into small pieces and feeding it to the dogs. At first, they refused. In spite of their great hunger, they would not have taken anything without our permission. That touched our visitor. He gave each one the same amount, talking to them as if they were human. When one of them understood him he was pleased, but it pleased him even more to have them rub against him or lick his hand gratefully. His voice sounded tender, childlike, devoted, trusting. It also inspired trust.

When he was done, he pushed the basket aside but the dogs had to stay near him. He filled his pipe and lit it himself, for the servant had left. Then he began:

"Don't be surprised that I love dogs. They are better than human beings. Has a dog ever deceived you?"

"No," I agreed, because he had looked at me.

"Does a dog pretend to love you when he actually hates you?"

"Certainly not."

"And when a dog, a horse, or some other domestic animal turns out badly, becomes suspicious and begins to bite, whose fault is it? It is always the human being's fault who does not act humanely but like a beast. I love dogs and horses. They are honest, and don't lie. But I hate human beings, and despise them. I have never found one worthy of receiving a single piece of meat from me."

"Poor fellow," Halef said.

"Poor? Is that all?" the Ardistani asked. "It's worse

than being poor. Even the dogs I keep because occasionally I want honest affection cannot always be with me, and are regularly spoilt by their keepers. The love and loyalty of these animals is taken away from me. How I envy you! And how pleased I am about the faithfulness of these beautiful animals and your intelligence for not punishing them, but for being grateful to them. I am telling you that the moment your dogs came and almost died with love for you was much more important to me than you probably suspect. It was the first time since the death of my mother that I felt that there were other human beings who might be worthy of being loved, not just by dogs, but by men."

"Were you there when the dogs arrived?"

"Yes, but I wore different clothes, and so you don't recognize me. Why didn't you salute the Mir?"

"We aren't tailors that study cloth and costumes. We came here as men, to see and talk to a man. Where we are from, we salute the person, not his garment."

"How proud you are!"

This exclamation sounded half admiring, half offended, with a touch of anger which he could not entirely suppress. In a gesture of warning, the hint of a threat, he raised his finger and went on:

"This pride could have cost you your life."

"Hardly," I answered.

"Oh, yes! Certainly. The sabres would have slashed you to pieces. Only your dogs saved you."

"Perhaps, perhaps not. We were armed with knives, and I got hold of a sabre quickly enough. And we had a shield which certainly would have protected us from any bullet or knife."

"A shield?" he asked. "I didn't see any."

"It was sitting on the throne. I am referring to the Mir."

"What do you mean, the Mir?"

"We would have jumped up to him and protected ourselves with his body. If only because of his cumbersome garments, he would have been helpless. And no one would have dared injure him."

"But what if someone had?"

"Then we would not have died without first thrusting our knives into his heart."

He jumped up from his seat.

"Is that true?"

"Certainly. Depend on it."

The Ardistani walked to the window, looked out, and reflected for a long time. Then he turned and said:

"I am telling you that the Mir will never again dress in such unwieldy clothes. And I also tell you that it would have been a great pity if you had been killed. Finally, I am seeing human beings, men, real men. Of course, you would hardly dare tell the Mir what you just said to me."

"Why not?" I interrupted.

"He is a tyrant, a despot, who remorselessly—"

I interrupted again:

"If he were a tyrant in my eyes, I would not have come here. Do you think I am afraid of him? Didn't I refuse to salute him? Didn't I tell him that I wasn't really seeing him? And didn't that compel him to get out of that ridiculous, lifeless outfit which resembles a coffin and to show me a human being, a man, the true Mir, and not the slave of his mummery and his servants?"

"You compelled him?" he asked in surprise. "And when did he step out of his garments?"

"Now, right here."

As I said this, I got up, crossed my arms over my chest and made a polite bow. Halef did likewise. The Ardistani took a step back and asked:

"Then you know who I am. You recognized me. How?"

"By your enunciation."

A smile passed over his face, and he exclaimed:

"Will you believe me when I tell you that except for my mother, my father, and my tutor, you are the first to dare speak to me of this flaw? Oh, these toadies, these worms, lice, and fleas! My foot twitches with eagerness to kick them whenever they appear." He moved his foot to give emphasis to his words, sat down, filled his pipe, offered us the tobacco, and continued:

"My identity was to be kept secret but now that you know who I am, we shall have to let that pass. I shall speak to you first as a prince, but only briefly. As a prince, I consider you my enemies. I know who you are. You are the Effendi from Djermanistan, and your companion is an Arab sheik who told the Ussul all your adventures. The Prince of the Tshoban heard all this from them, and reported it to me. So now you know why I am treating you as I have treated no other human beings and as I will treat none in the future. We are enemies, but men. We are too proud to lie to each other, and I therefore request that you only ask about things I may tell you, for otherwise I must either remain silent or tell untruths. Why did you come? Be honest! That will be no more dangerous for you than lies. Above all, be assured that you are enjoying the hospitality of my house and my city and will only be treated as outlaws beyond its limits."

"Thank you," I answered. "I agree. Let's act like men and only speak the truth. We aren't your enemies but your friends, probably the best you have. But to see that, you have to know more about us than the Palang told you. There is war. The Erdjani is on the border of Gharbistan and ready to cross it when he hears from us. Just as I do not inquire into your plans and ask about your troops, you will not ask about mine. We only came to you because of the hostages, that's all. We wish to free them and—"

"The two of you?" he asked quickly.

"Yes, the two of us."

"That's just like you. And you tell me this so frankly?"

"Why shouldn't I? We came precisely to tell you this and to hear from you what we must know to be able to rescue them."

He didn't know whether to consider me impudent, or sincere but mad. He clapped his hands, looked at me as if I were something unbelievable, and said:

"You want me to tell you what you must know to steal my prisoners? Anyone who dares make such a demand must be—but tell me, what do you want to know?"

"If the hostages, the Ussul princes, are still alive."

"They are."

"Where are they?"

"In the City of Ghosts, which is also called the 'City of Death' or of the Dead.'"

"Is their death inevitable?"

"Yes."

"When?"

"The moment your troops cross the border of Ardistan. That is irrevocable."

"Thank you. We have no further questions. That's all we wanted to know."

"Then I could dismiss you immediately, and your mission would be completed?"

"Yes."

He jumped up, walked back and forth, and marvelled:

"What people you are! I have never seen anything like you. I can heardly believe it."

He walked back to the window, pushed his head far out as if he felt the need to cool his forehead, returned to his seat, and announced:

"Our conversation as enemies, officers, and diplomats is over. For tomorrow morning, the Mir of Ardistan is granting you a second audience when he will give you his answer. And now, we will be men and human beings, nothing else. For as long as I have been prince and ruler, this is the first time I have felt no nausea or contempt. My soul wants to breathe. Allow it to drink of the love of life that entered with you. Speak freely and without fear, be honest and open, don't be frightened of the tyrant. I know that that is what I am, an oppressor, a man of violence and terror, arrogant, presumptuous, remorseless. But it is not that despot that is sitting here before you. That person was so scared of these four 'mad dogs' that he could not get out of his official dress. And when he saw that all the scoundrels and toadies were fleeing before those beasts, and that it did not occur to a single man to raise his hand in defense of his prince to protect him from the venomous bites of those monsters, the depth of their ingratitude and of his loneliness terrified him, and he crept even further into the splendor and majesty of his dress. There he remains, and will not interfere with us now. Only my soul came here. Do not begrudge it a little light, a little warmth so that it may forget for a brief hour that it is only the yearning of a ruler whom God created to love his neighbor, but whom fate sentenced to violence."

We gladly granted his wish. First, we talked as men who gradually want to become acquainted with each other, and then as human beings searching for the fundamental and final causes and purposes of their existence, who are called upon to be humane and peace loving, who endeavor to uplift and raise others to a higher level. And finally we talked like persons who have an inner affinity, and are obliged to act in concert. The Mir was deeply involved, and continued to be as the hours passed. He seemed to feel newborn. He became serene and more than once laughed happily. He even pressed our hands now and then. Of course, there also were moments when the ruler and man of power awoke in him. Then he looked around with amazement, about to thrust us back into the nothingness from which we had come. But the soul always quickly regained the upper hand and restored the threatened balance.

At one point during our talk, when the audience hall was mentioned, Halef asked about the many small flames that could be seen through the thin material.

"That is the sky of Bet Lahem.* There is an old law according to which they must now shine during the night as they await the great, sacred 'star of the redeemer.' Have you never heard about that?"

"No," I answered.

"But you know the legend of the river that returned to its source? And you also know that it is said that paradise opens its gates once every hundred years and that the angels and archangels call across earth, asking if peace has finally come?"

"Yes, the Ussul told us."

"That is just a legend, of course. But the people believe it and think it is true. And that belief must be respected unless one wants to run the risk of losing power over the minds of the credulous. There are mountains up in Djinnistan that spew fire, but no paradise. Nor did God ever come down or the river

---

* Bethlehem.

ever reverse direction. Its course was changed by a geological catastrophe, and now it no longer flows down this side of the mountain but the other. That obliged the inhabitants of Ardistan to abandon their capital, which is now called the 'City of Ghosts' or the 'City of the Dead,' and to build another residence. They did this here, in this region, where the very wealthy Christians of those days had built their church between four smaller rivers which do not get their water from the large stream. In order not to make these people too indignant, they were not completely expelled from the church but allowed a share in it, although that share was purely nominal and did not interfere with those in command. A kind of prophetic promise was added to the old legend which will never be fulfilled, of course, because it does not come from above, in spite of what the Christians believe. It is said that this church is a symbol of the coming salvation, and that world historical events will be symbolically represented under its central dome before they become reality. This dome was left to the Christians, not for use at all times, but for important events. For ordinary gatherings, they use the small houses of worship which are designated by a cross. But once every hundred years, when the mountains burn and paradise opens, and the question about peace is asked, Bet Lahem must be ready for the star of the redeemer. Then the Christians are allowed into the church every evening and may remain until early morning. At those times, countless small lamps hang down from the high dome. They represent the sky of Bet Lahem, and directly above the always heavily shrouded altar the great star awaits the spark which will rise from earth and ignite it."

"What kind of star, and what kind of spark?" I asked.

"All those many flames can of course only be lit by a fuse. For ordinary use, there are two fuses on the right side of the altar. On its left is the one which ignites the large star, and in the center the fuse for the altar itself. As long as princes have lived here, however, that altar has never been unveiled, and never will be. But the Christians think differently. Here's what they maintain: When the time has finally come for redemption to come from heaven, and peace is about to descend on earth, all the forces that suppress peace will unite. There will be war not only between Ardistan and Djinnistan, but also civil war among the states of Ardistan. For that reason, peace will not come down but up the river. It will be wholly unsuspected, and unrecognizable. The person bringing it will not have an army or any sort of earthly weapons. But he will ally himself with the inhabitants of the 'City of Ghosts and the Dead' and come with them to the residence to conquer it without a shot being fired or a sword being raised. There will be no bloodshed. The Mir who will be ruling Ardistan at that time will be an enemy of Christianity, and will suppress it as much as he can. But he will be forced, with his own hand, to light the star that must appear over Bet Lahem. The moment he does this, what lies in store can no longer be arrested. To begin with, he will unveil the altar. As soon as that is done, the voices of compassion and kindness will resound from the heights of the firmament and heavenly sounds such as have never been heard in Ardistan will ring out. They will be loud, like the roar of the storm, lovely like the voices of angels, and gentle, like the breathing of the souls in Abraham's bosom."

He paused briefly, and then went on with a deprecatory gesture:

"You can see, Effendi, that much could be promised to these foolish people because it was known that none of it would be kept. At intervals of one hundred years, the lamps and candles for the altar and for the 'Star of Bet Lahem' are prepared, and while the mountains glow, we have to put up with the nightly visit of the Christians, that is all. No Mir of Ardistan, particularly if he hates Christianity, will light the 'Star of Redemption.' Who is going to represent 'compassion' and 'kindness' and sing from the heights of the firmament? And what human being could produce heavenly sounds such as have never been heard here? Surely you, too, must find this laughable?"

"No," I answered. "For me, legends are sacred."

"But this one was manufactured to beguile the Christians."

"You would find it difficult to prove that. Suppose those who made up this legend were themselves mistaken? Is it not possible that they believed they were serving their own ends, yet unconsciously obeyed a higher will? Did you say that the sacred hall is open to the Christians at this time?"

"Yes, throughout the night."

"And are they coming?"

"Long processions of pilgrims are arriving from far and wide. Today, a group from Sharkistan came, and they are holding a celebration."

"At what hour?"

"From midnight till morning. Which means that it has already begun."

"You know that I am a Christian. As your guest, am I permitted to go down and attend the closing moments of this celebration when you have left us?"

He looked at me for a while, smiling with amusement. Something seemed to have occurred to him.

"Unfortunately, you are a Christian. But a well-educated one, not an unreasonable, blind fanatic. All this talking and babbling won't edify you, but will seem as absurd to you as it does to me. I have no objections to your going. Indeed, you may go this very moment, and I will accompany you. I frequently walk about the streets at night, in disguise. Why shouldn't I attend the nighttime service of the Christians, for once? I have never seen it. We can go now, if you wish, and return here afterwards."

He got up, closed the buttons of his outer garment over his long beard, and covered his forehead and eyes with a corner of his turban. This made him unrecognizable, and we left.

Again, we walked up and down dimly lit stairs and along corridors until we reached ground level. The main portal of the tall, magnificent dome was open but we entered by a side door. What we saw did indeed look like the night sky. The stars seemed quite small and appeared only along one half of the dome. The man in charge here must be a thrifty person to think that half a sky was enough for the Christians. Where we were standing, there was a sort of half light which made everything appear mysterious and shadowy.

A great many persons had come. Some were arriving, some leaving, and others were quietly crossing the extensive space which was sacred to them. Everywhere, people were kneeling and praying. Those who had come from other parts of the country stood together in groups and were listening to sermons. Observing everything, stopping occasionally, we walked to the altar which was completed covered by a solid wooden structure to which thick felt pieces had been nailed, but which had some holes in them at eye level. Something, perhaps the "star of Bet Lahem" of the legend which the Mir had told me, was floating high above the altar.

Many people were close by, listening to a preacher who was addressing them from a pulpit. He was recounting the legend, but treating it as prophecy. He was a venerable old priest whose admirable enthusiasm entranced his audience. I would have liked to stay and listen but the Mir, who had decided to show me everything, directed my attention toward the dark area of the extensive space where something I could not recognize was rising into the air.

"That is the place for the singer and the organ," he said.

"There is an organ here?" I asked in surprise. "In this country?"

"Why not? Or did you think organs exist only where you come from? I have heard that they were invented in the Orient. In the beginning, there was only a very small, very old one. But then, precisely one hundred years ago when the mountains were glowing as they are today, Abd el Fadl, who was then prince of Halihm, made a gift of one to the Christians here. It is said that it was built in Anglistan and sent here through India. I have not been able to discover what obliged the Mir at that time to permit this, and even my father could not tell me. Foreigners brought and assembled it. Then they left again."

"How curious," I said. "And what a pity one cannot see it. It is quite dark."

"Would you like to?"

"Yes, very much."

"Then wait. Today, only some of the lamps and lights have been lit. I don't know why. Over there you see the fuse for the rest. It will be lighter right away."

He walked up to one of the openings in the covering of the altar and reached inside. It took him some time to find what he was looking for. Meanwhile, I turned my attention back to the orator, who was now facing in my direction so that I could hear his words clearly:

"The time of peace will come, it must come, because everything we have been promised will be fulfilled. *Peace on earth* rang out on the field of Bethlehem when the star stood in the sky and the redeemer was born. *Peace on earth* will be heard again when the star, the star of the legend, becomes visible here, in this house, the star for which all of us—"

He broke off and looked upward. The eyes of his audience also turned to the ceiling.

At the same moment, the Mir quickly rejoined me, and asked:

"Can you see the organ now? It's very well lit; it almost seems as if—"

He did not go on and again looked up.

"The star, the star of Bethlehem," the priest exulted. "There it is. Who lit it?"

The Mir was terribly startled. "I lit the star, not the lamps and lights," he shouted. "We are on the wrong side. I have to put it out again—"

He rushed to the altar but his effort was futile. It had been possible to light the flames; now, they could not be put out again. They had to be allowed to continue burning until they went out by themselves. The Mir was beside himself. Because he had moved his arm, his garment had opened and his beard became visible. But he did not notice that. In order to see more clearly, he pushed the turban out of his face. Now the priest recognized him, and exclaimed:

"The Mir of Ardistan did it, with his own hand. The prophecy is about to be fulfilled."

The Mir took me and Halef by the hand and tried to hide between us.

"Away from here, quickly. Otherwise, there'll be an incredible uproar."

We rushed off as quickly as we could, but all eyes were turned toward us and some people even came running after us. Then fifty, a hundred voices called out:

"The star has appeared. It was lit by the Mir himself. The Mir did it, the enemy of the Christians, just as it was prophesied."

There was turmoil behind us. Then we could no longer distinguish the voices or words. We only heard what sounded like the excited buzzing of a swarm of angry bees, but that also faded. We encountered no one on the stairs and in the corridors, and reached our rooms without having been seen by anyone else.

"That's good," the Mir said in great excitement. "Nothing can be proven, and I shall of course deny everything. It wasn't I. And you, you will testify that I didn't do it because—"

"We will testify that it was you," I interrupted. "You called on us to speak the truth."

"Yes, when you talk to me. But I did not ask you tell this low, contemptuous Christian rabble the truth."

"I owe the truth to everyone, God, myself, all living things. And I particularly owe it to those you call contemptuous rabble. Remember that I also am a Christian."

Suddenly, he seemed transformed. He raised himself to his full height. His forehead narrowed, his eyes became slits, his brows contracted. The despot was emerging in him.

"What you will say is not your decision but mine," he thundered at me. "I know that this Hadji of yours said that his horse is more important to him than I, but that doesn't mean you don't owe me obedience. If you are asked, you will say that I was not the person who was in church with you, that it was not I that made that careless blunder. That is an order I am giving you."

"You may issue orders if you wish," I answered calmly. "But we are neither your subjects nor in your employ. And even if we were, we would refuse to lie."

"You will have to," he snapped. "You are in my power. A single gesture, and you are done for."

"You are mistaken," I answered with a smile. "Our life is in God's hands, not yours. You speak of a gesture. I only have to signal, and my dogs will tear you to pieces. Look at them, and take care! They will not tolerate someone talking to us in this tone."

Although he had fed them, all four dogs were now baring their teeth at him menacingly. Hu and Hi were directly in front of him, directing their attention exclusively at him, ready to attack at a moment's notice. But Aacht and Uucht were more intelligent and sensitive. They were eying the door as if someone were standing outside, eavesdropping. The Mir also noticed this. He quickly stepped into the corridor and called out, but there was no answer. As he came back in, he said:

"This is suspicious. If your dogs belonged to me, I would send them out there and—"

I did not wait until he had finished, but gestured to them, and they immediately left the room. A moment later, there was a howl. It was Uucht. She had been wounded. Then we heard Aacht's angry growls, and hers. Bones were cracking, voices were calling for help. Now Hu and Hi rushed out. There was more shouting, and the breaking and splintering of bones. Then all became quiet. We rushed into the corridor. At some distance from our apartment, four people, each guarded by one of the dogs, were lying on the floor. Uucht had been stabbed in the throat but the wound was inconsequential. None of the four men was still alive. Their throats had been bitten through, and the forearms they had raised to protect themselves were completely crushed.

"Do you know these people?" I asked the Mir as I let light fall on their faces.

He looked down, and then said in surprise:

"The lieutenant of the guard and three of his soldiers. What was he doing here where he had no business? And why didn't he answer when I called out?

: 369 :

Whom was he spying on, you or me? You can see they were armed."

I immediately thought of the "Panther," but said nothing. Instead, I told him:

"It doesn't matter about the three soldiers. Do you know the family of the lieutenant?"

"Yes."

"Who and what is his father?"

"He is dead. He was an officer; I had him shot for disobeying orders."

"And in spite of that, his son could become an officer?"

"Such a thing might be impossible in your country, but not here in Ardistan. I am going to the guardroom now to investigate this personally."

"I wouldn't do that. Where does this lieutenant live?"

"Near the castle, with his mother."

"The widow of the man you had shot?"

"Yes."

"Who else lives in that house?"

"The brother of the older man, that's all."

"Then you can find out more from the mother and the uncle than at the guardroom. But you should go now. It is important that you do this personally."

He quietly looked at me for a few moments, and then he said:

"Why does your advice seem so obvious to me although it contravenes all rules and customs? Is it because the prince of the Tshoban told me about you? Or is it also something about you? I shall follow your suggestion. Return to your rooms and bandage Uucht. I'll have a servant bring what you need."

We left the Mir and returned to the apartment. A little later, we heard the muffled steps of people who must have come to remove the bodies and clean up. Then it was quiet. Only the servant came to bring us bandages for the injured dog.

Because we found it impossible to go to sleep, we sat down in my room and discussed the events of the day. The dogs were lying near us, apparently asleep. Suddenly, Uucht raised her head, pricked up her ears, remained in that position for a moment or two, and then drew back her upper lip, showing the tips of her magnificent white teeth. Directly, Aacht also became alert.

"There is someone outside," Halef whispered.

I merely nodded, got up, and carried the burning candle into Halef's room so that we could not be seen from outside. Carefully, we pulled the curtain aside and looked out. A male figure, holding a lantern in his right hand, was tiptoeing along the corridor. The lantern illumined only one side. When the man came to the spot where the four dead had lain, he stopped and bent down. He noticed the damp blood and we could see that he was startled. He touched the carpet and had a closer look. Then he straightened up and stood still, as if considering. Having apparently come to a decision, he advanced toward my room. We stepped back and gestured to the dogs to remain quiet.

The man stopped outside the curtain, the light from his lantern shining through it. Had this been an experienced evildoer, he would not have made such a mistake. He was just placing his lantern against the opposite wall and advancing stealthily toward Halef's curtain to pull it aside when I quickly slipped up to him, seized him by the throat, and pushed him into the room. Halef laughed, made a deep bow, and greeted him with these words:

"Welcome, creeping lantern. Sit down. Believe me, you will not just make our acquaintance, but you'll get to know these dogs as well."

I pressed the man to the floor where he sat down without offering the slightest resistance. The dogs surrounded him. He was staring at us with open mouth, too terrified to speak. I went outside for his lantern, placed it so that its light fell directly on him, and then sat down facing him. It seemed as if this illumination not only restored his presence of mind but also freed him of all embarrassment. The dazed expression disappeared from his face. He smiled, and this smile reflected the consciousness of a man who knows he is in control. I could tell at the first glance that he was no ordinary individual. He looked intelligent, I would almost say intellectual, with the well-defined features of a man of thought. Yet there was also gentleness and even a touch of exaltation in them. He might be capable of fanaticism, but his fundamental traits were benevolence and a sense of justice.

"I was deeply troubled," he said. "That's why I went on this nocturnal prowl which is really beneath my dignity. Do you know who I am?"

"No," I answered.

"I am the Bash Islami of Ardistan and live here in the castle. Or perhaps I should say that this is my official residence. My own house is outside of town."

Bash means head, the person of highest rank. He was a Moslem, and apparently had the same spiritual office as the Sheik ul Islam in Turkey. I did not ask, and he went on:

"I know you very well, much better than you think."

"How?" Halef asked.

"Permit me to tell you about that later. Before I can give such information, I must make certain that you really are the men I take you for. Above all, I ask you not to think you took me by surprise. I came here to talk to you and—"

"Here? At night?"

"Yes," he nodded. "Tonight. Of course, my secret visit also had another purpose. Something was supposed to happen but apparently didn't. It was a matter of some consequence. I waited for news, but in vain, and therefore decided to look for myself. I noticed the bloodstains and came here to ask you what happened. It is only from you that I can now get reliable information."

Convinced that this conversation would be of considerable importance to us and that I would have to be extremely careful, I asked:

"What is it you want to know?"

I noticed that Uucht had turned her head toward the corridor but then rested it again on her forepaws, apparently reassured. Immediately thereafter, Aacht squinted at the door connecting our rooms and waggled the tip of his tail. Unaware of this, the Bash Islami continued talking. But Halef had also noticed, and was smiling. The behavior of the two dogs meant that someone had first stood at the curtain and then quietly entered my room and stayed there. It was someone the dogs knew, and could therefore only be the Mir. For some reason, he had returned, but quietly, as the late hour demanded. Having realized that someone was with us, he was now sitting next door, where he could hear every word that was said. This made our situation more difficult. The other two dogs had also sensed the presence of the Mir, but the Bash Islami unsuspectingly answered my question:

"What I want to find out from you is not really a great deal, and yet of some consequence. I know that the Mir came here to feed your dogs. I also know that he took you inside the church and inadvertently lit the star of Bet Lahem. Then he left the church with you. Where is he now?"

"I admit he was here, that he took us to the church, lit the star, and then accompanied us back here. But how can I know where he is at this moment? Do you suppose he would allow us to spy on him?"

"No. But there are fresh bloodstains in the corridor. Did you know that?"

"Yes."

"Whose blood is it?"

"Human blood."

"Whose?"

"The blood of soldiers."

"Who spilled it?"

"Our dogs."

He jumped up with an exclamation of terror, and shouted:

"These dogs, these huge, horrible monsters did that? Why? Was the Mir present?"

"Of course."

"And did he know that he alone was the intended victim?"

"No one else?"

"No one."

"That's not true. We were also the target."

"You are mistaken. I know. I am—"

He stopped in mid-sentence, looked at me, Halef, and the four dogs, and went on:

"I must be honest and tell you. Yet it isn't easy. For it may ruin me and all the others. I shall pray before I begin."

He knelt down, folded his hands, raised his eyes, and prayed the first Sura of the Koran.

To see this man kneeling and praying was a deeply moving sight. My feelings went out to him; I was ready to take his side. Within me, two men were struggling with each other, the Bash Islami and the Mir. Who would be victorious? It was not impossible that Halef and I would perish in this struggle. Now the Basch Islami got up, sat down again, and went on:

"I hope by Allah that the path I am taking now is the right one. I heard a voice within me, urging me to trust you, for otherwise all of us will die, although our cause is honest and just. Effendi, I ask you to swear to me that you will not betray to the Mir what I am about to tell you."

"I never swear an oath," I answered. "But my word is as sacred as one."

"Very well. Will you promise not to tell him?"

"Yes. If you don't tell him yourself, we will say nothing."

It may seem that this promise was a ruse. But it will be seen shortly that it was meant sincerely. The Basch Islami continued:

"What I have to say is enormously important. If you reveal it, it may cost me and many others our lives. Will you give me your word that it will be as if I had told you nothing?"

"Yes," I answered.

I was quite conscious of what I was saying. I promised not only for myself and Halef, but also for the Mir who was sitting next door, hearing everything.

The Bash Islami seemed to have some idea of the responsibility I was assuming, for he looked at me almost admiringly, and said:

"You are a courageous man, Effendi. Do you realize what you are promising?"

"I do."

"Then I can have confidence in you and tell you

everything. Listen, for this will dumbfound you: The ruler of Ardistan will be deposed."

He gave each word such weight that it seemed as though he was underlining it with a colored pencil. I asked him very calmly:

"By whom?"

"By the Bash Islami himself, by me. Do you understand?"

I pretended to be astonished.

"By you, really?" I asked in an incredulous tone.

"Yes, by me," he answered proudly.

"Are you man enough to accomplish something so weighty and difficult?"

I looked at him searchingly as I said this. In answer, he struck his chest with his hand:

"I am. I am the Bash Islami. It is my duty to see that there is faith in the country, that Allah is the First and the Highest in life and death. I must make justice and humanity prevail wherever the dignity of my office extends. But what are conditions in Ardistan under the government of this our ruler? He believes neither in God nor the devil. He mocks heaven and hell, salvation and damnation. He never prays. He oppresses the country. He sucks his subjects dry. He steals from widows and orphans. No one is safe. He hates peace. Blood flows wherever you look. We addressed our requests to him, and he laughed at us. We warned him, and he mocked us. We threatened him, and he taunted us. His severity grew, his cruelty went beyond all bounds. We submitted, for we had sworn loyalty. And we hoped that Allah would have mercy on us and finally touch the tyrant's heart. But this wish was not granted. The opposite happened. The Mir began intriguing against the Mir of Djinnistan, the kindest and wisest ruler anywhere. He declared war on him. This is mad presumptuousness. We are facing certain destruction. We have to save ourselves and can only do so by removing him from the position he occupies."

The Bash Islami paused, and I asked:

"Who are these 'we' you keep mentioning? You are not just talking about yourself?"

"No. I represent the Moslems of the country. But the heads of other religions are with me."

"The Christians also?"

"No. The Christians are like dogs that even lick the hands of their tormentor. They maintain that God installed the Mir, and therefore they remain loyal to him. But there are millions of us, and there are even more Buddhists and Lamaists, not to mention those who have other beliefs. We have joined against the Mir to depose him and to choose another ruler. Events favor us. He has sent his best troops north, against the Mir of Djinnistan, and the hosts of the Ussul and Tshoban are approaching from the south to storm the capital. The army of the Djunub which he counted on was destroyed by you, and is scattered. The two of you did not fear to come here. This seemed the propitious moment to take the steps long since decided on. We discovered that the Mir had visited you here, and ordered the guard, which is on our side, to take him prisoner."

"You mean here?" I interrupted him. "You intended to kill him?"

"For the time being, we only wanted to put him away."

"And what about us? What was going to happen to us?"

"That still had to be decided."

"No. It was a settled matter. The Mir was to be attacked here in our rooms, and killed. And we were going to be called his murderers. It would have gone badly with us then, yet we are perfectly honest and innocent. But God prevented this. When the murderers came, they only found dogs here. We were in church with the Mir. The divine service of the Christians saved his life and his throne. Your plan was not carefully thought out. You failed to take the dogs into consideration. And even if your entire guard were to come back again, I would have all of them torn to shreds. But there were only four, not to attack us, but to see how things stood. They paid for it with their lives. And what is going to happen to you?"

He looked at me with surprising openness and honesty, and said:

"Nothing will happen to me. I believe you. You will tell the Mir nothing."

"I won't, because it isn't necessary. He knows everything."

"He knows? From whom?"

"From you. He heard everything you said. He is in the room next door."

I had hardly said this when the curtain was pulled aside and the Mir entered. His face was of a deathly pallor. His eyes were flashing, his lips trembling, his hands shaking.

"How did you know I was here?" he asked. He was so excited that his voice sounded rough and hoarse.

"The dogs scented you. Even before you entered the room, the gentle movement of their tails told me that the person who had fed them was near."

"And still you promised something you cannot keep?"

"How so? It is not my custom to make such promises. I said that I would not tell anything."

"Don't joke. That was your first promise. But you made another one. You said that everything would be as if this dog, this rebel, this traitor and murderer here had said nothing. And yet you know that I was here and heard everything. Did you only speak for yourself?"

"No, I spoke for you as well."

"So you expect me to conduct myself as if I knew nothing?"

"Yes."

"Do you want this scoundrel to go free?"

"Yes."

We had risen when the Mir had entered. The Bash Islami was so frightened he did not know what to do, and chose to hide behind me. But I looked the ruler calmly in his dangerously flickering eyes.

"Are you mad?" His voice had lost its resonance and become a threatening hiss.

"No," I answered. "What may seem madness to you is more carefully considered than you realize. I ask you to trust me, and to keep the word I gave for you as I also shall keep it."

"And what if I refuse the accede to this madness?"

"Then I'll force you to."

"Force me!" he thundered, raising himself to his full height. "How?"

"With my fist or my knife. My word commits you, and you are obliged to keep it. If you don't, only one of us will leave this room. I was fully aware of what I promised and intend to stick to it. I will die before I become a liar."

He stepped back, showed me his glistening teeth, and clenched his fists. I also stood erect. Now Halef raised his hand in warning:

"Do what he asks. It is in your best interest. My Sidi always knows what he is saying. If you and he were alone, he would talk differently. But here, he can't."

In his mortal fear, the Bash Islami had sunk down on his knees and began to pray. He sounded so helpless and powerless that the Mir unclenched his fists. His face changed. Still looking at me darkly, though no longer threateningly, he exclaimed:

"What a person you are! I never saw anyone like you. But I will do what you demand. I feel a need to believe in you as this Hadji Halef believes in you." He pointed at the Moslem and went on:

"You want me to let him go?"

"Yes," I answered. "Exactly as if you knew and had heard nothing."

"And I am not to remove him from office, or punish him?"

"No."

He burst out laughing. He sounded grim, but also amused. Then he picked up the lantern, returned it to the Basch Islami, and ordered:

"Get out of here, you scoundrel, and don't ever forget that it was not a Moslem but a Christian that saved you."

The Bash Islami did not hesitate. I went to the door and followed him with my eyes until his light had disappeared at the far end of the corridor. When I turned back, the Mir was standing expectantly in the middle of the room.

"I have done the impossible. Now justify yourself! I expect you to give me immediate proof that I acted correctly."

"You won't have long to wait," Halef said confidently.

I asked the Mir:

"Do you believe that the Bash Islami was telling the truth? That all your subjects except the Christians have joined together to depose you?"

"I do," he answered. "I not only believe his claim, but am convinced that your suspicions are correct. I was not only to disappear or be taken prisoner; I was to be murdered here. And you would have been accused of that crime. That way, both you and I would have been eliminated. I should have had the Bash Islami arrested, and have had his house and those of his fellow conspirators searched to discover what is going on. I should have them executed. I have—"

"You are mistaken," I broke in. "All that would have been a mistake."

"Why?"

"Because the Bash Islami is right. You really are the tyrant he described. Everything he said is true. Indeed, he didn't say all that could be said. One has the impression that you are deliberately goading your subjects into rebellion. It's a miracle that you weren't deposed or even murdered long ago."

"Silence!" he interrupted. "I indulged you, but that's no reason to believe that I shall now acquiesce in everything you may say. I'll crush you!"

He stretched out both arms as if to seize me.

"Try," I answered. "It's you that will be crushed. The army of the Erdjani is at your borders. Should he cross them and make common cause with the rebels, you are done for. They will receive him jubilantly. I am far from telling you only things that must offend you. You are a tyrant. But you are also much more than that: a human being. You only have to will it, and the tormentor will become the benefactor. Let the Bash Islami go, and don't inquire who his fellow conspirators may be, or what their intentions. Things won't turn out as they expect. Up to this moment, they are in the right. Teach them to feel that they are wrong, that you are magnanimous, and their resistance will collapse. That you did not have the Bash Islami arrested was the first step toward a new future for your people. And that step will be a greater blessing for you than you realize. It is not your task to drive one nation against the other in hatred, but to be a prince of love and peace. If I was able today to make you change your ways, to turn to the good, I am also prepared to direct the consequences of that act toward a beneficial issue. If the rebellion we discovered really does break out, the Erdjani will immediately place his army at your disposal, and you can suppress it with a single blow."

The Mir had long since lowered his arms and was listening attentively. Now he quickly asked:

"Is it really true that the man who is leading his army against me would be ready to help me in such a case?"

"I guarantee it."

"And what does he demand for his help?"

"Nothing."

"Nothing?"

"Nothing at all. He is coming as your friend, to help you quell the rebellion. Then, he will return and once again become your adversary."

"Is that really true?"

"Yes. He demands no reward; he does it because he is interested in you and respects you. But there is a request of mine which I want to present to you before you come to a decision. I am not asking anything for myself but really for you, for your own well-being."

"What is it?"

"Today is the fifteenth of December. On the twenty-fifth of this month, the Christians celebrate their most important holiday which is called Christmas. Permit them to proceed in their fashion, in the church, where we were a while ago. Do not do it for their sake only, but also for yours. You have heard that they are the only ones that are loyal, although everyone knows that you hate and persecute them. Teach them to respect and love you. Then they will become an irresistible weapon in your hands, a wedge you can drive between your enemies. What I am asking is little, the permission to celebrate the birth of the redeemer whom the Moslems also worship. Thus you will not be showing the Christians preferential treatment. In exchange, they will become helpers on whom you can rely in every difficult situation, and also in the present danger."

There was no answer. Halef smiled. The Mir again walked to the open window and looked out into the night. For a long time, he was struggling with himself. It was a fight against his own base anima which had not yet become a soul. Several minutes passed. When he turned back to us, his pale face was glowing. He was smiling, and his voice sounded a heartfelt kindness:

"Sidi, I willingly admit that you conquered me. That will make me the victor. I have made my decision and won't waste time with speeches. Are you willing to do without sleep tonight?"

"Gladly," Halef answered.

"I will have three horses saddled. Once we are on our way, you will hear where we are going. I am leaving you now but will be back shortly. May I take one or two of your dogs with me to protect me out there in the dark corridor?"

Halef ordered Hu and Hi to accompany him. We did not know where our nocturnal journey would take us, and therefore had to await developments calmly. Hardly half an hour had passed when the Mir returned with the two dogs. He was simply dressed but had thrown a coat with a hood over his shoulders. He took us down into the courtyard where we had dismounted on our arrival. Three saddled horses were waiting for us. When we had examined the harness and found everything in order, we mounted and followed the Mir out of the gate, which was closed behind us. Our four dogs were with us.

It was a dark night. There was a new moon, and though the sky was full of stars, their light could not penetrate the atmosphere of the large city. Some time after we had left the castle behind us, we came through a narrow alley where the Mir pointed out a small house.

"This is where the dead lieutenant lived with his mother and her brother-in-law. I had her arrested but will release her today. It would be unjust to punish them more severely than the Bash Islami, who is the

: 381 :

principal culprit. The brother denied everything and claimed to be ignorant. But because she was nervous about her son, the mother made a confession. She said I was not only to be taken prisoner but also killed. The new Mir apparently gave that order."

"Is there already a new Mir?" I asked.

"That's what she said."

"Did she mention a name?"

"Yes. But she must be insane. Seeing her husband beheaded made her lose her mind. She has been conspiring against me ever since. In her mad desire for revenge, she even gambled the life of her son, and when she heard of his death, she wanted to pay me back by accusing the only man I have ever loved, saying that he was the new Mir, the scoundrel that ordered me to be killed. She is out of her senses."

"May I hear who this man is?"

"My confidant and disciple, the 'Panther,' the second prince of the Tshoban. It's obvious she is raving."

"Hardly," I answered. "The Moslems are heading the conspiracy, and he is a devout believer."

"But that doesn't prevent him from loving me sincerely, from being loyal and grateful. I say it is madness to believe that he of all people should be capable of such an act. I would not even hesitate to call you incurably insane, should you express such suspicions."

"Then I'll keep silent."

"What do you mean? Did you intend—"

"Yes," I admitted.

"Then I suggest you remain silent. You could easily ruin everything you have accomplished."

That sounded so abrupt and threatening that I said nothing and resolved not to mention this matter again unless he himself asked me to.

We passed from the labyrinthine part of the city into a section where the streets widened. He stopped in front of a fairly large house whose carefully locked gate had a sounding board attached to it. These boards have the same function as our bells. They are quite thin and equipped with a wooden hammer. Everyone knows the sound of his board and comes when he hears its tone. The Mir ordered us to dismount and to tether our horses some distance away.

We then walked up to the gate and the Mir knocked. He had not told us who lived there. It was nearly morning, people were still sleeping, and he had to knock repeatedly until someone came to ask what he wanted.

"Is this the house where the Bash Nasrani from Sharkistan is staying?" he asked.

"Yes," the servant answered from behind the gate.

"Is he at home?"

He is asleep. He only returned from church a short time ago. Allow him to rest."

"I must talk to him."

"Why? Is it so important that I must wake him? Who are you? You must be an important and wealthy person, otherwise you wouldn't dare deprive the highest Christian official of Sharkistan of his sleep."

"I am a poor man, a beggar, and can't pay. But I have sinned and must save my soul. I wish to confess. Tell him that."

"Wait, then."

The servant went back inside, and the Mir explained:

"Now you know whom I want to see, the bishop of Sharkistan who spoke in the church and recognized me when the star began to shine. I am testing him. And by testing him, I test all of Christianity and the teachings about Christian love. Everything depends on his willingness to be disturbed in his sleep. If he comes, I will grant your wish and permit the Christians to celebrate Christmas in their way. Let's wait and see."

The reader can well imagine how tensely I awaited the result of this test. A short time later, we heard steps and another voice asked from inside:

"Are you still there?"

"Yes," the Mir answered as he moved up to the gate so that he alone would be seen.

"I will open right away."

"May I speak to him?"

"Of course. I am not the servant but the priest."

"And you got out of bed?"

"Immediately," the Bash Nasrani said as he stepped outside. "Your soul is in distress. That is the

: 383 :

most severe stress there is. You wish to confess. Confessing means speaking to the Redeemer. What kind of savior, what kind of redeemer, would he be if he slept when he should be saving souls?"

"But I am a poor beggar."

"We are all beggars before God. Perhaps I beg more than you. Before God, a beggar may be richer than a rich man. If your repentance is great, so will his mercy be, and this repentance makes you richer than the prince who repents nothing. You are welcome. Enter."

The Mir obeyed, and the two of us came in behind him. When the Bash Nasrani saw us, he asked:

"You are not alone?"

"No, there are two more. They have not sinned as greatly as I but are the greatest beggars there are. They even beg for you. Come along."

The bishop of Sharkistan bolted the gate and led the way toward the house. That there should suddenly be three visitors instead of one may have disquieted him. When he came to the house, he picked up a lamp that was standing behind the door and lighted our way into a room that seemed to serve as a parlor. Then he asked us to sit down.

"No, we won't sit down," the Mir told him. "We don't have the time."

Only now did the light of the lamp fall on our faces. As he recognized us, the priest became frightened.

"The Mir, the Mir," he exclaimed, quickly putting down the lamp. "And his companions from the church?"

"Yes, I am the Mir, and these are my companions," he answered. "At first, it had been my intention to deny that I was inside the church. That is the sin I wish to confess, and I hope you will forgive it. And this is Kara Ben Nemsi Effendi, a Christian pilgrim from Djermanistan. He told me that an important holiday will be celebrated in ten days, the birth of the Savior. He wishes to celebrate this holiday with the Christians of my lands, and has asked me to place the large dome of the cathedral at your disposal. I have decided to grant his wish. I did not care for the Christians, and that's the reason there was only one bishop in Sharkistan, yourself, the Basch Nasrani. You are only an occasional guest in this country of mine, in this town, as you are today. Just now, I tested you, and, through you, Christianity itself. I am appointing you Bash Narsani of Ardistan and Gharbistan, which makes you the highest priest in all the countries I govern. I request that you come to the castle this afternoon, at the third hour, to thank this Effendi here and to discuss preparations for the holidays. He can be found easily. His apartment is directly next to mine. Sleep well."

Having said this, he took the lamp and quickly walked out. We followed without looking back, hurried to the gate, put the lamp down, pulled back the bolt and went out into the street. It was not until we were back in the saddle that the clergyman overcame his surprise and came running after us. As we rode off, we heard his voice but could not understand what he was saying. It can hardly have been something unpleasant.

2 : The Conspiracy

As we rode along, we heard the Mir laughing to himself several times. He seemed in good spirits and pleased with the way he had tested the bishop, and the way the latter had passed the test. He rode ahead of us by a horse's length, presumably to indicate that he did not wish to converse with us just then but needed time to reflect. His silver-white stallion wore a harness of inestimable value and shone before us like a fairy tale horse which we had to follow. We continued on until we had left the city. It seemed extensive, for although we were moving rapidly, it took us over an hour to get from its center where the castle lay to its outskirts.

The few houses still to be seen now lay further back from the road. It was dawning, and what we could make out in the early light was pleasing. We were coming through orchards and vineyards, and later through a splendid, dense forest of firs which was all the more welcome because that tree is rare in these regions. I was telling Halef that Christmas was always celebrated with lighted fir trees in the country of my birth. The Mir heard this remark and asked:

"Why do you burn them?"

"We don't burn them. We use them to decorate churches and houses. Everyone buys one, and puts fruit, angels, colored stars, and candles on its branches."

"Why candles?"

This question gave me a welcome opportunity to describe our Christmas to him, and to explain the profound symbolic import of the tree. I could see that all this interested him.

I was beginning to feel that the celebration might be a great help to us. For a long time, the Mir remained silent, busy with his own thoughts. Repeatedly, his glance moved along the edge of the forest as if he were estimating or calculating. Suddenly he nodded to himself. An idea had come to him. He slowed his horse, and when we had reached his side, he asked:

"Where do so many people in Djermanistan get all the trees they need?"

"From the government and the owners of forests."

"I am the government. No one else owns forests."

Then he turned to Halef:

"You will be in charge of the men that will exhibit trees in all the streets of the city and its environs to see how the population responds. And you will announce that Christmas is coming."

"In that case, we should take some trees with us today and decorate them so that no time will be lost."

"Take as many as you like. My Ussul will assist you."

"Your Ussul? Which ones?"

"I am surprised you should ask. Haven't you visited Amihn, the Ussul sheik, and didn't he tell you that I have a personal bodyguard which consists of five hundred of the tallest Ussul? The colonel who commands them has two adjutants, sons of Amihn and Taldsha. When I declared war on the Mir of Djinnistan, those three, the colonel and the princes, refused to obey because their father is on friendly terms with the ruler of Djinnistan and would never fight him. So I sent them to the 'City of the Dead' where they were either to reconsider, or die. Then I exiled the five hundred soldiers. They have been put up in ancient buildings which date back to the time of my ancestors and are used as penal barracks. That's where we are riding now. They have always been loyal. But the guard with which I replaced them wanted to kill me today. The exiles will be pleased to see me appear in person to lead them back to the city. By returning them to duty as palace guard, I accomplish two things: I make up for my mistakes and unintelligent behavior, and replace the murderers with honest, dependable men. I let the Bash Islami go and therefore must not lay hands on any of his followers. But you will see how rapidly the conspirators will disappear from the city. And if they don't do so voluntarily, I'll help them along. The return of the Ussul will be a signal and a warning to them."

"And what about the colonel and the two princes?" He stopped.

"Yes, those three. I haven't thought about that yet. If I am going to take back the soldiers, I cannot put their commanding officers into prison. They didn't do anything to—"

He broke off in mid sentence, made a face that expressed his confusion, and shook his head.

"You two are giving me trouble. You beat me at every turn, and I am constantly obliged to accommodate you. First, I had to tell you that these prisoners are still alive. Now, I have no choice but to free them myself. There is an unknown power at work which stands by your side, and I feel that it will come to mine the moment I decide to act as you would wish me to."

As he said this, the sun was rising above the dark forest, greeting us with its friendly light. This was a perfectly ordinary event, but the Mir felt deeply moved by it. The flood of light had barely enveloped him when he threw an arm into the air and exclaimed:

"And I will make that decision. The sun has risen to

tell me to. I shall go ahead, whatever the consequences."

He spurred his horse and galloped on. We were
riding directly toward the sun, straight into that
splendor of light and color, as if we meant to disappear in it. Was the Mir of Ardistan really a tyrant?
Or was he merely the last in a line of despots who had
to appear as severe as his predecessors, although he
was of a nobler and gentler mold?

Soon, we saw a group of ancient buildings surrounded by forest on three sides and a drill ground
and riding course on the fourth. Riderless horses were
running about the low barracks and stables and soldiers were sitting outdoors, preparing their morning
brew. Although we were still at least two hundred
horses' lengths away when they first noticed us, our
arrival caused considerable stir, for they recognized
the stallion of the Mir. They had never before been
visited by their master. They dropped what they were
doing and ran to their horses. The relationship between officers and men in this unit was patriarchal.
The men were children, the officers fathers; they all
belonged together. They also were all in one place so
that no time was lost looking for the officers. Because
the Mir had slowed down, the unit had time to line
up.

The Mir addressed them in a concise, commanding
manner, telling them that he had come to share their
morning coffee and to take them back to the city. He
ordered them to dismount and to continue preparing
breakfast. The men were enthusiastic.

A few minutes later, the two of us, the Mir, an old
major and two captains were sitting on an old rug that
had quickly been spread out, each of us holding a
heavy clay container from which the fragrance of what
they called coffee rose to our faces. The Mir was in
good humor, and even beaming, although he looked
occasionally as if he were puzzled by his affability.

Later, I asked for permission to go into the forest to
choose suitable trees. So that the population would
understand quickly what we had in mind, they would
have to be shown at a number of different places

throughout the city, and I was wondering how many we might need.

"Why count?" the Mir asked. "Ard is large, and what we don't use today, we can save for tomorrow. Let's take a hundred trees. We have time and men enough to fell them."

I taught the Ussul how to use long, thin branches as ropes so that the twigs could be pulled close to the trunk and the trees be transported more easily. Then, the order was given to return to the city.

There, the unexpected return of the Ussul guard did not go unnoticed, for it was known that the Mir had banished them from the capital.

Upon our arrival at the castle, we first stored the trees in a courtyard. Then the guard was relieved of its duties and its nearby barracks surrounded. This entire, unreliable unit had to surrender its weapons and march out to the penal barracks, where the men were interned by the Ussul. In addition, all troops of questionable loyalty were sent out of the city. I did not involve myself in this because the preparations for the Christmas celebration required my entire attention. The military and diplomatic maneuvering was a superficial event. But Halef and I had the task of rousing the sleeping soul of the people, of initiating the most important, most sublime movement that can occur in the lives of nations and individuals, the movement toward God which begins in the depths of the soul and rises toward the eternal heights of heaven. Ard was a large city with a population of several hundred thousand, not only craftsmen and laborers but scientists and artists as well. It was also an important trade center with a Muslim, a Buddhist, and a Confucian university, and large numbers of schools. Everything I needed for my purposes could be found there.

I should mention here that we did not return to our two small rooms, but were given a suite of much more comfortable and splendid chambers adjoining the Mir's apartment. Our horses also were more adequately stabled. This was a good sign. I heard that the "Panther" had been living in the quarters that had been assigned to me, but that he had suddenly and unexpectedly left the night before. While the Mir was having the horses saddled for the ride to the penal barracks, he had gone directly to the "Panther" to inform him of the planned conspiracy. He had ordered him to join immediately the troops that were marching against the Mir of Djinnistan. He was to assume their command because the officer in charge was a fanatic Moslem and therefore no longer to be trusted. The "Panther" had been given ten minutes to make his preparations. The Mir had accompanied him to the stables and been present when he had mounted his horse and ridden away. He himself told me all this and when I asked him why this had been done in such haste, he said:

"When my throne and my life are at stake, delays are inadmissible. Did I act incorrectly? You don't seem to like the 'Panther'?"

I merely said:

"What you did was right. The only question is whether he also will do the right thing."

That evening, when I had already gone to bed, I had another surprise. Aacht and Uucht had stretched out by my bed. The candles had been put out and I was just falling asleep when both dogs leaped toward the door of the adjoining room. There was a suppressed outcry, then silence. I got up and lit a candle. A man had tried to slip into my rooms. The dogs had pulled him down and were lying on top of him but had done him no harm. As I moved the candle close to the man's face, I saw that it was the "Panther." I ordered him to get up. The dogs moved back toward the door to foil any escape. His glance traveled across the rug as if he were looking for something. Then he turned to me with an expression of the fiercest hatred and said contemptuously:

"Of course you'll run and tell the Mir I am here."

"Oh, no," I answered. "If I am to talk of someone, he must have some importance. You don't. I am thinking of your father and brother and feeling sorry for the disgrace you are bringing on them. You may go. I shall even accompany you to the gate so that no one else will arrest you. But I am telling you this: Should I once more see you inside the city while the Mir believes you are with the army, I will not remain silent. Go into the antechamber and wait there."

He obeyed. The dogs accompanied him. I dressed and, looking against the light, glanced at the place where he had lain on the floor. I saw what he had lost. It was a small, iron object, square, pointed, and elbow-shaped. It must be a key he had wanted to use to get something he had been unable to put away when he had left so hurriedly, and which must be both important and incriminating. Otherwise, he would hardly have taken the considerable risk of returning for it. I pocketed the tool and took him downstairs.

The next morning, we began our preparations for the Christmas celebration. Contracts were made with the manufacturers, suppliers, and workers. I supervised all this while Halef, who had a special talent for this sort of thing, dealt directly with the individuals concerned. The bishop helped by sending messengers to Gharbistan and Sharkistan to announce that pilgrimages to Ard should be undertaken.

We also had to arrange for quarters and provisions for the large numbers of strangers we expected, and a corps of voluntary Christian policemen had to be organized because demonstrations or worse might be staged by rebels and adherents of other religions. All this was troublesome and complicated, yet we managed, for behind all our work there stood the will of the Mir, whose sudden change of heart had a miraculous effect. Beyond this, a heavenly influence guided all our hopes and expectations, for its eternal love, wisdom, and justice look to the remotest future, and know when the time for the salvation of individuals and peoples has come.

I was in good spirits, for I knew we would accomplish our purpose. How the people of Ardistan might react to our concerns had become a secondary consideration with me. They might resist, even rebel, but this did not alarm us. If we succeeded in stirring the soul of the nation, we would have achieved our goal. Then an event occurred which conferred the appropriate solemnity and a more profound consecration on our labors.

I should mention here that we were no longer

treated as prisoners but could come and go as we pleased. Anyone could visit us, and the most welcome visitor was the bishop. Our fondness for him increased, perhaps in part because he had a special talent for always bringing us good news. On the first day he came to see us, he was accompanied by two people, a man and a woman, who had pulled the hoods of their coats so far forward that their faces were almost entirely hidden.

"I am bringing you two dear friends," the Basch Nasrani said. "They are not from here but are frequent visitors. Like myself, they always stay in the house of my host where you came to see me with the Mir. Just now, they happen to be here in town and would like to speak to you. Will you permit it?"

I nodded. They threw back their hoods and I saw Abd el Fadl, the prince of Halihm, and Merhameh, his daughter. This was no accidental meeting but the work of providence. The moment I saw them, an idea occurred to me. What was the prophecy we had been told about? "Kindness" and "compassion" will raise their voices in the cathedral. And sounds never heard in Ardistan will ring out. Didn't Fadl mean "kindness," and Merhameh "compassion"? And had I not heard their magnificent "morning and evening prayer of Djinnistan"? If their two incomparable voices were to sing in the cathedral, the effect would be overwhelming. And wasn't there an organ though it had never been played? I am not an accomplished player, and certainly no virtuoso, but I felt my musical skill might satisfy the demands of the local population. Wasn't it possible that my playing would be taken for those sounds which had never been heard in Ardistan? Can only invisible angels fulfill prophecies? Might this not also be possible for visible human beings?

The joy we felt at their arrival was both great and sincere. The real reason they had come was that the dogs had run away, and the Erdjani had been especially disquieted about this. He had felt that their arrival in Ard might create great danger for us and had therefore considered it necessary to send someone after us who might secretly inquire what had happened, and take the measures necessary to insure our safety. Should this prove impossible, it was his intention to march his army here and free us by force. Abd el Fadl had declared his willingness to go to Ard with Merhameh. He knew the country and the city because he had often been there, though secretly, since the Mir disliked him and would not permit him in his residence. He therefore went disguised as a teller of tales. To avoid attracting attention, he and his daughter had not come on horseback but chosen fast mules. They had arrived the previous evening. The Erdjani had sent with them a trustworthy friend who would immediately set out on the return journey to report to him.

Fortunately, the situation had improved beyond all expectation. I gave the messenger both oral and written instructions which would enable the Erdjani to take appropriate measures. When I told the prince and princess of Halihm of my plan to have them sing to the accompaniment of the organ, they immediately and cheerfully agreed. Then I pointed out to the bishop that, because of the names of the two singers, and the organ music, the old, widely known prophecy would be literally fulfilled. In his enthusiasm, he would have preferred to proclaim this news to all the world, but I cautioned him not to say anything for the moment, since it was essential that the Mir not be told about this as yet. Unless he was presented with a fait accompli, there was reason to fear that all our plans would be ruined. I therefore insisted that no one be informed of the impending fulfillment of the prophecy and that I be the one to tell the Mir.

3: The Feast of the Savior

The celebration of the birth of the Savior was to begin at midnight on the twenty-fourth of December. The Mir had promised a salvo of twelve cannon at exactly that time. Hundreds of thousands of pilgrims had come from the rest of Ardistan, Gharbistan, and Sharkistan.

Only a small fraction of them could be put up inside the city. Because there were also many strangers there who had not come for religious reasons but out of curiosity, it was feared that quarrels or worse might develop, and the Mir had therefore issued a proclamation that anyone interfering with the sanctity of the holiday by creating a disturbance would be shot, regardless of rank. People knew him well enough not to have any doubts that he would carry out this threat, and I am therefore happy to be able to say that the peace was preserved.

Our central concern was the altar. It had been covered since time immemorial and the reader already knows the myths and hopes tied to its unveiling. But when the bishop had timidly suggested this possibility to the Mir, he had lost his temper and had forbidden the matter to be brought up again.

The ugly felt and wood hiding it had the same effect a large grey spot would have in an artistically perfect painting. When, some time before the beginning of the celebration, the Mir had entered the church in the company of his wife and children, he had walked up to me and asked:

"Wouldn't the gown in which you first saw me be appropriate in this setting?"

"Certainly not," I had told him. And then, seizing the opportunity for restating our request, I had added: "That would disfigure you as much as this felt covering does this beautiful and sacred object."

"Why would it disfigure me?"

"Because you are the Mir, and are held responsible for everything the unreason of the rebels should be blamed for."

"The rebels?"

"Yes. Aren't those who persuaded you to cover this altar the same people who now want to depose you and make you a figure of felt and wood?"

"Allah w'Allah," he agreed. "What should I do?"

"This entire celebration is a present we are making you. You are not a petty but a great man, and it is my hope that you will not spoil it."

"There is no need for your praise. If you do not wish

the altar to be covered, remove the wooden frame."

When we had done so, it turned out that the altar was quite different and much more beautiful than I had imagined. Carved from a very hard wood of a golden-brown color, its decorative sculpture represented a two-storied temple whose architecture showed old Indian, Buddhist, and modern Oriental motifs, and the wood exuded the clearly perceptible fragrance of violets.

As the hour of the service approached, all the Christians tried to crowd into the church, which was still only sparsely lit by a few candles. Those who could not enter had to console themselves with the fact that the celebration would also be held during the following two days. The Mir, his wife and children, and the bishop, Halef, and myself then took up positions at the head of the long, solemn procession of officers and officials, marching slowly to the stand that had been especially built for him, his family, and the court dignitaries.

A short time later, as I was about to sit down at the organ and begin to play, Abd el Fadl came to me and asked:

"Do you see those four strangers there under the Christmas trees, Effendi?"

"Yes."

"That is the Sheik el Beled of El Hadd with his three companions."

When I had begun to play and looked at them, I noticed that they were moving away from the trees and coming toward the organ. They did not seem at all surprised that there should be an organ here, or that I should be playing it, but I could tell that the effect pleased them. They struck me as so interesting that I repeatedly glanced at them. This interest was reciprocated. All of them were dressed in closely fitting leather which was tanned but not dyed, and was cut into diagonal straps which ran across the body and were so closely spaced that no skin was visible. They wore sandals, and light, white turbans which they had taken off and were holding in their hands, for they were Christians. Long, thin coats with hoods were hanging from their shoulders. They were handsome men, not as large in stature as the Ussul but of a tall, noble, and well-proportioned physique rarely found among ordinary men. Their features also were handsome, but of a beauty difficult to describe. Especially the large, sincere eyes of the Sheik el Beled attracted my attention. Why were they shining so curiously? Did this light come from within or without? Was it the joy of Christmas or merely the reflection of the innumerable candles that now were burning in the church. El Hadd is a small, mountainous, quite inaccessible country on the southern border of Djinnistan. Because it lies high up, and is isolated and rocky, its inhabitants are said to be very poor. But in spite of their simple clothing, these four men did not look as if they were suffering from an oppressive poverty. I am deliberately describing them in some detail. There are reasons for this which I will not mention now. They will become apparent later.

Because of the unusual conditions that obtained, the bishop had kept the service as simple as possible. He was reading from the Bible, and had just come to the words "Praise to God on High and peace—" when he broke off. Outside, in front of the open gate, a hubbub had arisen. Whips were being snapped and the closely pressed crowd was parted. With loud calls and threatening gestures, some heralds entered to create a path for three sedan chairs the size of small buildings, each of which were carried by eight Lama servants. They pushed their way inside. Although the worshippers were so densely packed that it seemed not even a single additional person would have found room to stand, they recklessly thrust their way through the angry crowd until they arrived at the altar where they deposited the chairs. The Maha-Lama of Ardistan, dressed in precious ritual robes and decked out with the insignia of his elevated "spiritual" office, climbed out of the first one. Two ministrants crept out of the others. They were holding prayer wheels, musical instruments, and other "spiritual" weapons in their hands. The wheels and other paraphernalia were made of the skull bones of deceased Lamas and abundantly decorated with gold and silver. With the two lower officials preceding him, the Maha-Lama walked up to the stand where the Mir was sitting with his retinue while the twenty-four porters stayed with their chairs. On the stand also, every place had been taken except along the railing, directly in front of the Mir and his family, where some space had been left unoccupied to give the ruler room to move about. It was here that the three went. They greeted the Mir with a barely perceptible nod and gestured to their servants to bring them pillows from the sedan chairs. They were stacked directly in front of the Mir to make three high seats on which these illustrious personages slowly sank down. It began to look as if our Christian celebration were being held merely to honor these three Lamas, or that they felt it necessary to supervise it. That the placement of their pillows made it impossible for the Mir to see anything whatever did not seem to trouble these gentlemen.

Because I knew the man, I did not think he would tolerate such behavior, and was therefore surprised when he did nothing to put an end to the offensive conduct of these inconsiderate intruders. But when they had settled comfortably on their seats and were looking about triumphantly, he and his family got up and joined us in the organ loft where the best seats were immediately turned over to them.

Up to this moment, the bishop had been unable to continue reading from the Bible and, like him, the entire assembly had had to wait. This was an unprecedented disturbance and its effect was intensified by the brutal manner in which it had been carried out. Everyone had quietly put up with the arrival of the men. But when they had obliged the ruler to yield his seat and to look for another one, the previous silence became an initially subdued, then increasingly loud, murmuring and whispering. The sacred devotion of the worshippers had been callously disrupted, and they felt indignant. Voices, at first indistinct, but soon quite clear, were being raised.

"Throw them out," someone called down from the balustrade.

"Out with them," others joined in.

"The servants first, and then their masters. Grab them!" another was shouting from near the altar.

I noticed that an attempt was being made to seize the porters and the chairs. In another minute, there would be a tumult whose outcome could not be predicted. But the bishop had not lost his presence of mind, and called out: "Stop, stop!"

Those who had been ready to rush in desisted, and all eyes were turned toward the Bash Nasrani as he raised the Bible in both hands and continued:

"For the sake of the Holy Bible, let there be peace on earth, and peace here among us. Woe to those that disturb that peace. It behooves Christians to be patient. We shall begin again."

As he said this, he looked up at me and I understood that he felt it was impossible to continue reading without some transition. I went back to the organ and played until the widespread anger had subsided.

Then the Bash Nasrani resumed reading from the Bible, and this was followed by a duet, a song of praise, sung by Abd el Fadl and Merhameh. They used an Arabic text, an almost literal translation of some verses from the one hundred and third psalm.

After the sermon, the Mir, clearly pleased, thanked Abd el Fadl and Merhameh. He could not speak to the Bash Nasrani who was busy elsewhere. Then he saw the men from El Hadd. He hesitated, for he did not know them, but their exceptionally becoming dress had struck him. When Abd el Fadl told him who they were, the Mir addressed the sheik with obvious cordiality:

"You are from El Hadd? I love that small, beautiful country, although I have never visited it and do not know its people. But I do know that their attitude toward me is friendly. Their land borders on Djinnistan, yet there have never been any hostilities between us. Are you the Sheik el Beled?"

"I am," the sheik answered.

"Then it is especially to you that I am grateful. What is your religion? You are inside a church and are holding your turban in your hand."

"We are Christians."

"Where are you staying?"

"In a caravanserai, as one always does when one is in a strange country."

"And your horses?"

"We have none. We are poor. We came on foot."

"You are no longer strangers in a strange country. I know you now and bid you welcome. You will be my guests. There is always room for people such as yourselves. An hour from now, there will be a Christmas dinner at the castle. Please come."

We had known nothing of this dinner because it had been meant as a special surprise and therefore kept secret. The sheik's bow of acceptance was polite but not deferential, the gesture of a free man. As the Mir left with his family, Abd el Fadl and Merhameh, I walked to the balustrade of the choir to watch the crowd leave the church quietly and with dignity. An expression of satisfaction, even of enthusiasm, could be seen on the faces of the congregation. I felt justified in believing that from this day forward, the relations between the Christians and the rest of the population, and their role in the public life of Ardistan, would take on a wholly different complexion. It is true that the Mir had not made a single comment on the behavior of the Maha-Lama, but I was certain that Lamaism, so powerful heretofore, would now lose much of its influence. If one also considered how much the Christians had gained in prestige, the combined result would be a considerable difference in their standing.

To prevent possible acts of hostility, the sedan chairs had been surrounded by calm, cautious men, so that the Lamas had to wait until the church had emptied completely. Then they left, unnoticed, as soldiers disperse after a lost battle. Suddenly, a cannon shot was fired. Others followed. The Mir must have ordered this salvo only moments earlier. The effect the celebration had had on him must have been profound. I felt it had won him to our side. A similar reaction was apparent out in the streets, where shouts of jubilation could be heard. I walked about for a time, taking pleasure in the Christmas bustle. Lanterns and lights had been lit everywhere. The houses were illumined; it was almost as bright as during daylight hours.

The work of the previous days had exhausted me. I therefore excused myself before the Christmas dinner was over and returned to my apartment. The men from El Hadd had sat near me but not close enough for a conversation to develop. Only a few questions and answers had passed back and forth, yet I had had an undefinable sense that I knew the Sheik el Beled, although I was sure that I had never seen him before. Was there perhaps someone in the circle of my acquaintances who resembled him? I thought about this but found no answer.

On that day, we had been in our rooms only a few times and were therefore expected eagerly by our dogs. They had long since become too serious to play, but when Halef and I entered my room, we saw that Aacht and Uucht had been busy with the wall covering, which consisted of a thin material that had been nailed to the walls and arranged in folds to form decorative arches. This material had been removed so thoroughly that the walls were almost completely bare.

At first, I was rather startled. Normally, the dogs were reasonable animals and the prank they had played was not something I could approve of. But their behavior was odd. They did not show the slightest trace of remorse but received us in high spirits, as though convinced that they had accomplished something commendable. I had hardly entered when Uucht jumped toward a wall, raised herself to her full height, and began scratching it. When Aacht saw this, he attacked a different spot. As I moved closer to inspect the damage, I noticed that the walls were not of brick but wood, and inside this wood I saw small, vertical, narrow openings which could only be keyholes. There were a number of them, all at a convenient height, and invariably at a place where the folds of the material had hidden them from view. That the dogs knew perfectly well that there were hollow and suspicious spaces hardly needs mentioning. It was unimportant how they had made this discovery. They had stood on top of the Prince of the Tshoban and scented his odor, which clung to these hiding places. That had been sufficient for their delicate noses, and explained everything.

It is only natural that I immediately thought of the tiny key the prince had lost when he had tried to sneak into this room. I had laid it aside in a safe place but had not had the time for a closer look. I went to get it and tried to insert it in the keyholes. It fitted. I turned it and pulled out some small boxes. There were five of them. They contained written documents of such importance that I immediately left to get the Mir, and told Halef not to let anyone come inside while I was gone.

The Mir was still in the dining room. He followed me, although I had not been able to tell him why I had come in front of others. But on the way back, I made an allusion to my discovery. We spent the entire night sorting, deciphering, and reading the documents. We had been tired, but all our fatigue disappeared. What we had found were papers relating to the previously mentioned conspiracy. Its spiritual head was the Bash Islami, who wanted to become the father-in-law of the new Mir of Ardistan. But its guiding spirit was the Maha-Lama who had behaved so brazenly that day. And that man's right hand was the "Panther" who had taken it into his head to become ruler. At daybreak, we finally knew what there was to know. I derived satisfaction from the fact that Halef and I were the only persons with whom the Mir discussed the measures to be taken. He decided to proceed with the greatest possible secrecy and to avoid bloodshed as much as possible. First, the leaders had to disappear quickly. They would not be executed, however, but put in prison. This was easy in the case of the Maha-Lama of Ardistan, but the Bash Islami and the "Panther" had already grown suspicious and left town. The lists of the conspirators contained the names of so many officers that the Mir began to doubt the loyalty and reliability of all his troops. I did not share this estimate, but was careful not to tell him so, because I was anxious to have him attach the highest possible value to the support of the Christians. I merely pointed out to him that the Christmas celebration would win him support, and that no other party would dare incur the considerable risk of disturbing the peace of these days. For any unanticipated contingencies, I once again placed the Erdjani and his troops at the Mir's disposal. This reassured him. He told me that even if these lists had not been found, the Maha-Lama would have been removed from office since he, the Mir, was unwilling to forgive the insult inflicted on him in church. He had only remained quiet because he had not wanted to disturb the festivities, which had made a profound impression on him. He gave orders for the repair of the walls and had the documents taken to his apartment. Then he asked in a wholly different, reflective tone: "Do you know what happened today, and during the last few days, Effendi?"

"I think so," I answered.

"The fulfillment of the old prophecies?"

"Yes."

"Of the star of Bet Lahem?"

"Yes."

"Now, if the voices of kindness and compassion were to ring out in the church, and God were to come from Djinnistan to Ardistan as he did before the river reversed its course, all the prophecies the Christians believe in would be fulfilled and the angels could report that peace had finally come to earth. You are smiling, Effendi?"

"Oh, no. This is an extremely serious matter."

"It is serious for me as well. Up to now, it merely seemed absurd to me, but yesterday changed my mind."

He raised his hand to his forehead, almost staggering with fatigue.

"I also am tired, as you are, and weak besides," he went on. "Too much has rushed in on me during these last few days. Am I still the Mir of Ardistan? Or am I someone else that is being blown here and there, like a weightless feather, or a man without a will of his own? I must sleep, rest, collect myself."

Another thought struck him.

"What do you think of the men from El Hadd, Effendi?"

"I like them."

"So do I. Especially the Sheik el Beled. What a pity he is such an inconsequential person and not an important ruler. Then one could love and honor him, and be friends with him. But we have talked long enough. Is there something you would like?"

"No."

"Consider what I owe you. Don't you want my gratitude?"

"No."

"Or my thanks to the Christians?"

"No. They have fulfilled their obligations, and will continue doing so. You are in no position to render thanks; only Heaven can."

He looked at me uncomprehendingly, shook his head, and said:

"I don't understand. Sleep well."

And with that, he left.

4 : Betrayed

The Christmas celebration had an enormous effect. Those who had come to Ardistan did not want to leave it again, and the daily arrival of pilgrims inspired the old Bash Nasrani and prompted him to ever new efforts. What had originally been planned as a three-day festivity continued for an entire week, and then the old man could not go on and had to rest. The prestige of the formerly despised Christians had suddenly risen to such an extent that they were greeted when they were seen in the streets. This had never happened before. People realized that they had not understood them and had been unaware of their numbers and their character. No one had believed that there were so many of them. They had been hesitant to make their beliefs known, fearing oppression. Now, when they learned that the Mir regarded them with benevolence, they arrived in such numbers that the population of the city seemed entirely made up of them. And these throngs were so modest, calm, and well mannered that the ruler could claim that public order had never been greater, even though the city was overflowing with people.

I made it my task to get to know the country and people as thoroughly as possible. I began exploring the city and its environs and then went on more extended expeditions. Halef was always with me.

These excursions were easy, since we had become well known during the celebration. The Christians liked us and were eager to inform and assist us, while those who may well have hated us did not dare show their sentiments.

The objectives which had taken me to the capital of Ardistan could be considered accomplished. We had come here to learn whatever we could of local conditions so that the Erdjani might derive the greatest possible benefit from such information. We had known how dangerous this would be but luck had been with us. The Mir had quickly become fond of us and felt grateful. For this reason alone, he no longer looked upon the Erdjani as his enemy. There were, besides, the events inside his country and capital. He had declared war on the Mir of Djinnistan and already ordered his best troops into action when he made the disturbing discovery that he was to be deposed and could no longer rely on the officer corps of his army. It was in this extremely dangerous situation that I promised him the Erdjani's help against the rebels. This proved to him that the Erdjani was a noble adversary and caused him to set aside temporarily the disputes between them. He asked me if I would do him the service of arranging an armistice with the Erdjani. This was not only in our own interest, but would provide a welcome respite after the long and strenuous march through the desert, giving the Erdjani and his troops time to recuperate and reorganize. I was therefore certain that even if he were to hesitate initially, he would finally agree. However, I did not wish to undertake this journey myself. I wanted to become acquainted with Ardistan and not keep travelling back and forth along the same route, and therefore persuaded the Mir to entrust someone else with this mission. He sent one of his officers, carrying a letter written by me and signed by the Mir. He was thus an official representative to the Erdjani with suitable recommendations.

This was the situation when the Mir sent a servant to me early one morning to ask if he could see me. I had barely awakened, but we were both early risers, so the hour did not surprise me. I advised him that I was at his disposal. That he did not order me to him but visited me himself was a sure sign that whatever preoccupied him was urgent and claimed his entire attention. When he entered my apartment, he was wearing boots and spurs and did not look as if he wanted to go for a short excursion. Even before he let the curtain drop behind him, he said hastily:

"He is here. He came during the night, but in spite of the considerable importance of the matter, he did not have me wakened."

"Who?" I asked.

"The Bimbashi."

"Bimbashi" means major, and was the rank of the officer he had sent to the Erdjani. Although it was not a high rank, he had chosen this man because he considered him loyal, skillful, and circumspect.

"He was received very politely and was successful," the Mir continued. "The Erdjani is willing to agree to an armistice and has assured me that he will not insist on difficult conditions."

"He won't? That means they haven't been stipulated yet. He did not convey them to you through the Bimbashi?"

"No. It is his view that both his and my position are rather precarious, and that our agreement must be kept secret. Therefore negotiations also have to be conducted secretly. Nothing must be written down, everything has to be done face to face and not through an intermediary. He is right, I see that. Do you agree?"

"Yes. I see that you are dressed for a journey. Is there some connection?"

"There is. He says we should meet halfway."

"Where?"

"Along the same road by which you came here, by an old, dilapidated mosque with a well. You must have seen it when you rode past."

"We even camped there."

"That's to be the meeting place. What do you think?"

"It's certainly suitable. Did the Erdjani communicate this to you orally or in writing?"

"Orally. Although the Bimbashi is loyal and de-

: 405 :

pendable, a letter might have been lost, or might have fallen into the hands of people for whom it was not intended. I think the Erdjani is perfectly right to be cautious. He also thinks that no one should know that we are to meet or what our intentions are. Our escorts are therefore to be as small as possible, and should look peaceful. The Erdjani will be accompanied by only four men and asks that I bring no more. Can you guess who he suggested?"

"Only two of them, Halef and myself."

"That's right. He insists that you be there. And the other two?"

"Why don't you tell me?"

"The two Ussul princes."

"I'm glad."

"So am I. I mistreated them, although they were innocent, and I owe them some restitution. They know the Erdjani and are of the same age. Their mother, Taldsha, has always been his friend and protectress. I have already let them know about our trip and asked them to keep themselves in readiness. They are very pleased to be joining us and look forward to seeing their friend again."

"When are we leaving?"

"I should like to leave now, but since I shall be gone for several days, there are some matters I must attend to, and this will take a few hours. I hope I shall be ready before noon. Do you think it is right that there are only five of us?"

"Yes. That's what the Erdjani apparently wants. The greater the number, the more conspicuous we'll be."

"Then we won't take servants?"

"Certainly not for me or Halef. We are used to serving ourselves. And I should think that the two Ussul will also feel that the presence of servants will only be a burden and perhaps make it impossible to proceed in secrecy. As regards you, I'll admit—"

"There is nothing to admit," he interrupted. "Am I any different?"

"Yes."

He smiled.

"Well, well. But at least I do not wish to appear different, so I am riding incognito, and we'll do without servants. We are allowed two pack animals to carry whatever food and other supplies I consider essential. We don't need guides. I know the route, and so do you and Halef. I had ordered the colonel who brought you here to travel through the most sparsely populated areas. We have every reason to do likewise, to follow the same trails. This time, at least, the two Ussul will have to do without their giant nags. I'll give them better and faster horses from my stables. Unless I am mistaken, we should reach our destination by tomorrow evening. So get ready, and wait until I send for you."

"Is no one to be told of this?"

"No one. Or are there persons whom you must inform that you will be gone for a few days?"

"Yes."

"Who?"

"The priest and the two singers, the father and the daughter."

"Go ahead. You owe them that. They are true, sincere friends. They would be concerned about you if you left without letting them know. Tell them, but don't tell anyone else."

He left, and Halef and I made our preparations for the journey.

We left before noon, but individually. The Mir was the first; the two Ussul followed, choosing a different route through the town, and taking the pack animals with them. Then it was our turn by yet another route. We rendezvoused outside town.

We reached our meeting place by the evening of the following day. We had taken our dogs along. The Mir was riding a very valuable white stallion with Indian harness, and the Ussul had two strong, unflagging geldings who enjoyed galloping in spite of their riders' size.

The dilapidated mosque lay in a completely open, steppe-like, level area which could be surveyed as far as the horizon. There was no reason for special care, and we rode around the old, crumbling walls to inspect them before entering the building simply out of curiosity. As far as one could see, no one was visible, and the building was empty. There were neither tracks nor footprints. It appeared that the Erdjani had not yet arrived.

We dismounted, attended to our horses, and settled by the well, which provided drinking water. While we were eating, night fell, but we did not light a fire. We had been riding strenuously all day and were tired. We slept so profoundly that none of us woke until we were roused by Ben Rih. He had suddenly jumped up, and was neighing so loudly and persistently that it was obvious he wanted to draw our attention to something. Syrr also got up but stayed quiet. The dogs were stretching their necks, pricking their ears, but not barking. The time was early morning.

"They are coming, Sidi," Halef shouted as he got up. "Let's hurry out to greet them."

He rushed outside. At the same moment, a horse was neighing in answer to our Ben Rih. But it wasn't just one. There must have been as many as eight. It sounded as if this were not a group of five horsemen but a larger mounted troop, already so close that we could hear the hooves of the horses. They were coming at a gallop. Halef yelled, and as we followed him out of the building, we saw some thousand men, an entire regiment of cavalry just about to surround the mosque.

"What are they doing here?" the Mir asked, half angrily, half in surprise. "Without orders from me! I'll show them—"

He broke off, and we saw why. Part of the regiment had not swerved off to one side but was coming directly toward us. The officers were in the lead and the "Panther," the second prince of the Tshoban, was riding out in front of them.

"Arm yourselves," Halef shouted. "We have been betrayed."

But this was a vain exhortation. Halef himself had no weapons, and neither did I. We carried knives, but that was all. The sabre and the two pistols of the Mir were valuable, but decorative rather than useful weapons. Both the Ussul were armed with a sabre and a rifle but the latter was for hunting, not for defense. And we were faced by a thousand well-armed men, rebels, who did not hesitate to confront their ruler. It would have been madness to offer resistance. I quickly said as much to the Mir. He was rational enough to see that, for the moment, there was no choice but to give in. He said nothing and merely nodded in agreement, but his eyes were glowing and he pressed his lips together and clenched his hands. He was boiling with anger.

Now the troop had reached us. The "Panther" had given his men precise instructions. They jumped off their horses and pressed forward, obviously intent on separating us. The Mir called out:

"Stay together. Draw your knives. I'll stab anyone who touches me."

We obeyed his command, and the soldiers stepped back. The knives would have been useless in a serious fight but, as there was no intention to kill us, we were allowed to stay together. As we were being herded into the ruin our giant dogs were standing near the horses, their heads raised high, their eyes sparkling, ready to defend us. But this was not the time to test the courage of these noble animals. We ordered them to lie down, and they obeyed instantly.

Almost the entire squadron had pushed its way inside. We were so completely surrounded and hemmed in, it would have been reckless to jump on our horses and try to escape. The Mir did not look at anyone. He sat down by the water, his knife in his hand. Immediately, the two Ussul princes posted themselves to his right and his left to defend him, should that become necessary. Halef and I sat down opposite them. Anyone who knows my little Hadji must realize that he was not the sort of person to be intimidated by any surprise attack, even when staged by an entire regiment. He acted as if no one else were there, picked up the food that had been left from the night before, and said:

"We slept, and slept well. Now we are going to breakfast, and then we'll ride on."

"Where to?" the "Panther" asked.

With the officers behind him, he had stepped up to us but Halef ignored him. He opened the packages and cut up the meat to distribute it to us. We took what he offered and began eating. Only the Mir refused. He was so agitated that he could not manage to swallow a single bite. Quite suddenly, his face had become a dirty yellow. From one moment to the next, it had taken on a repellent ugliness.

"Get up! I have to talk to you," the "Panther" began. We did not stir.

"Get up! That's an order," he repeated.

We stayed where we were. Now he took Halef by the neck to pull him up, and began screaming:

"Dog, get up! I'll—"

He could not complete his threat because the four dogs had jumped up, seized him, and pulled him down, baring their teeth. He realized that he would be torn to pieces, should he make a move to defend himself. Two or three officers quickly pulled their pistols to shoot at the dogs, but he called out to them:

"Put away your arms. Don't shoot, or they'll tear me apart."

Now Halef turned to them, and said:

"That fellow isn't as stupid as I had thought. He knows quite well what to expect. The moment you aim a pistol or rifle at us, they'll tear his throat out, and he'll be done for. I know this fellow, the greatest scoundrel alive. But who are you?"

The officer wearing the most insignia thundered at Halef:

"Be silent! He is the new Mir of Ardistan. Heretofore, I was the colonel of this regiment. Now, I am general."

Quite amiably, Halef laughed in his face, and answered:

"You are a general? But then you are as big a rascal as he is. You and he belong together. Hu! Hi!"

As Halef called his two dogs, he pointed first at the new general and then at the place where he wanted him taken. The order was obeyed instantly. A moment later, the officer was lying alongside the "Panther" and none of his subordinates dared increase his danger by attempting to free him. Halef warned them:

"Sit down quietly and wait until we have finished eating. We are not accustomed to being disturbed during breakfast. And remember, any threatening movement on your part, and this newly crowned Mir and this recently hatched general will lose their lives. After

: 410 :

I've eaten, I'll talk to them, and to you. But not before."

They looked at each other. This was something new to them. A thousand against five, but the five were fearless, and yet the Hadji was such a little fellow! Quietly, they counselled with each other. But their two leaders did not like having the dogs' powerful jaws directly before their eyes, and so the general commanded:

"Sit down and wait."

He hardly dared move his lips, and the "Panther," though certainly no coward, was just as scared.

"Don't do anything to these beasts. That's an order," he warned.

One of the officers grumbled:

"We should have shot them the moment we came in. Now, it's too late."

They looked for a place to sit down and wait for orders. The soldiers did likewise. The Mir had recovered his composure sufficiently to give in to my urgings to take some food. Otherwise, he might not stand up under the exertions that probably lay ahead. We took our time, and ate as slowly as if we were back in the castle in Ard. We also discussed our situation, but in subdued voices so that the "Panther" and his general would not hear us. It was obvious that we have been lured here to be dragged off and imprisoned somewhere. We did not know the place our captors had in mind, but assumed that it would be the "City of the Dead," a most suitable location for such a purpose. The Mir said:

"Should that be the 'Panther's' intention, we need have no fears. I know that 'City of the Dead,' not only the prisons but the place in its entirety. When I was a boy, I roamed it with my servants and guides, for it is the most interesting place in Ardistan and so many legends and tales are told about it that I did not leave my father in peace until he had given me permission to explore it. The two of you also know it, at least the part I had you assigned to."

These last few words had been addressed to the Ussul princes. They nodded, and the Mir went on:

"The person who knows the secret of the construction of the prisons cannot be kept confined there against his will. Naturally, there is only one such person, and that is myself, the ruler. Should they really take us there, it will be child's play to escape any time we choose. Here, we cannot defend ourselves. We would be crushed at the first attempt and it would do us no good to take the 'Panther' and his general prisoner. Someone would inevitably shoot the dogs, and then those two would be free, and we couldn't hold them."

"Then you think we should simply submit and let them take us to the 'City of the Dead?' " I asked.

"Yes," he answered. "I hope they will let us know what they plan."

"Perhaps they won't."

"Leave that to me," Halef said. "To speak to such bandits and rebels can only impair your dignity. But I would derive satisfaction from making them betray their secret, should they be unreasonable enough not to let us know their plans. Do you agree?"

He was right. And since he had acted with such circumspection before, the Mir permitted him to speak on our behalf. When we had finished eating, he picked up the leavings, placed them into a saddle pouch, and then addressed the "Panther" jovially:

"We have eaten now, and will ride on. A while ago, you asked where we were going. We weren't ready to answer then. But now that the situation in which you find yourself has demonstrated so convincingly that you really are the new Mir of Ardistan, we owe you an answer. Here it is: We will ride with you."

"With us?" the "Panther" asked in surprise. "What do you mean? Call your dogs away. It seems they are ready to bite if one so much as moves one's lips."

"Oh, no. You may move your lips, but that's all, remember that! So I must ask you to put up with the presence of these dear loyal animals a while longer. And I repeat that we especially came here to go riding with you."

"Where to?"

"Wherever you please. We have the time. Since you are the new Mir of Ardistan, the old one can go on vacation and rest from the labors of governing. And to what guide would we rather entrust ourselves than to his successor? Everyone knows that he is his most loyal friend and grateful disciple. So I ask you to decide where we will go."

The "Panther" was gnawing his lips, indignant at being the butt of a joke. He knew as well as we that we were powerless, although momentarily we seemed to have the upper hand. It infuriated him that we did not allow this to weigh us down but could treat our situation with irony. His surprise attack had not been a success, as he had hoped. He had been convinced that we would fall into his hands; instead, he had fallen into ours. Unable to gloat over his victory, he had to endure our laughter and contempt. Even worse, his fear of the dogs forced him to restrain his anger. He had to swallow his fury. The whole depth of his hatred sounded in his voice when he answered: "I certainly will take you wherever I please, and where the Erdjani preceded you."

This was an invaluable piece of information for us, yet Halef had enough self-control to answer with seeming equanimity.

"The Erdjani? It's foolish for you to attempt anything with him. There is more intelligence in the smallest part of his little finger than there is in your entire hollow body."

"Listen to me," the "Panther" snarled angrily. "It was easier to outwit him than you. He's been in the 'City of the Dead' for a few days. And my beloved brother with him."

"You mean the first-born prince of the Tshoban?"

"Yes."

"That's your brother?"

"Yes."

This second "yes" sounded almost triumphant.

"You betrayed him as well, and lured him to the 'City of the Dead'?"

"Especially that mangy cur, who turned my loyal Tshoban away from me! You will see both of them. I want you to see them. You'll have to go there, and when—"

"We have to?" Halef laughed. "We have to? No, we want to. We will even compel you to take us to them. Now we'll let you know our conditions. If you accept them, nothing will happen to you. But should you refuse, our dogs will tear you and your victorious general to pieces."

"Conditions? You will stipulate conditions? Of what sort?"

"The two of you will remain our prisoners. When we reach the 'City of the Dead,' we'll let you go."

"What else?"

"When are you leaving here?"

"This very moment. We meant to capture you and then ride there."

"Very well. The entire regiment will ride ahead. We don't want anyone behind us who might suddenly start shooting. We will follow at a short distance. Your hands and the general's will be tied. You will be riding between me and the Effendi, with two dogs following us, and the general will be flanked by the two Ussul princes and be followed by the other two dogs. Don't think that riders are safe from those dogs. They will jump on the horse and kill the man in the saddle. Don't get the idea you can get away from us."

"Well, you can't either. The moment the regiment sees that you are trying to escape, you will simply be ridden down."

"Your threat sounds as if you were ready to accept my conditions."

"Not at all. There are more than a thousand of us. We would be silly to turn ourselves over to you."

"You don't have to; you are prisoners already. In any case, you know us. We don't joke, and will make good our threats unless you do what we tell you."

"What threats?"

"Here they are: We will give you ten minutes to come to a decision. If you reject our proposal, we will take you between us and leave here. First, your soldiers have to withdraw far enough so we'll be out of range. The moment even a single one tries to come closer, we will shoot you down with your own pistols. So be quick!"

"And if we do what you ask, you will come with us?"

"Yes."

"And you will release us once we get to the 'City of the Dead'?"

"Yes."

"Right away?"

"Yes. There will be no tricks."

"Couldn't we go without having our hands tied, and without having to ride between you?"

"No."

"But we promise—"

"Be silent!" the Hadji broke in. "I don't wish to hear any promises from you. You are rebels, traitors, cheats, and liars. No one believes you. It's either yes or no. Hurry!"

They spoke softly with each other for a few moments, and then the general said to the others:

"I have never seen men of such recklessness. Their courage verges on madness."

Now the "Panther" informed us of his decision:

"We'll accept your proposal if you promise to stick to what you said."

"I promise in the name of all present."

"That you will not try to flee?"

"Yes."

"And that you will release us the moment we arrive?"

"Yes."

"And that you will remain our prisoners and ride to the prison that I picked out for you?"

"Yes," Halef answered, having covertly and quickly looked at the Mir.

"I demand that each of you swear an oath that he will keep this promise."

"An oath from everyone?" Halef asked angrily. "What are you saying? One more word from you, and it's all off. I gave my word on everyone's behalf, that's enough. If that doesn't suit you, we'll take you away. Your ten minutes are up. We are leaving here now and taking you back to Ard with us. We'll see if your brave cavalry will oblige us to shoot you."

He got up and walked over to the two to take their weapons, but the "Panther" quickly told him:

"Wait. I'll accept your word."

Nonetheless, the Hadji, carefully watched by the dogs, took their pistols, knives and sabres, brought them over to us, and told them:

"Call your officers together, but only close enough so they can hear you. Tell them what we decided, and order them to do precisely as we agreed. But don't move. The dogs won't tolerate that, and I notice that your pistols are loaded."

They obeyed. When the officers had come within fifteen paces, they were informed in precise detail how they had to conduct themselves during the ride to the "City of the Dead." They were disappointed, and some of them even grumbled loud enough for us to hear them. But their regard for the safety of our two prisoners forced them to comply. They left and the soldiers of the squadron followed so that we were now alone with our two captives. Then two soldiers returned to bring their horses, but immediately left again. We now made ready to leave. We watered and saddled the horses, tied up the "Panther" and his general, had them mount, tied their reins to ours, and sent the courageous Halef outside to see how things stood. Our demands had been met. The regiment had moved some distance away from the ruin and was waiting for the order to set out. When we emerged, it immediately got under way, and we followed at the same pace.

We felt both victorious and defeated. Halef was in excellent spirits, asking how he had done and accepting his well-deserved praise with a proud smile. None of us could have handled matters better. Our prisoners avoided looking at or talking to us. The "Panther" wanted to vent his suppressed fury on his horse while his fellow conspirator, the general, was calm and docile. The Mir was equally subdued. He preferred being the last in our group. Later, he admitted to me that he had felt as if he were dreaming. What was unusual was not that an Oriental despot had suddenly been stripped of all his power, for that has happened often and will presumably happen again. The circumstances surrounding this central event were what gave the impression that something curious, fantastic, even dumbfounding, was happening. The behavior of the two protagonists was difficult to understand. If a group of novelists was asked to write about the conspiracy of the "Panther" against the Mir, it is likely that every one of them would portray this first hostile encounter of two exceptionally volatile characters as vivid and jarring. Instead, there was an icy silence. Neither one had spoken a single word to the other. What was really at issue was passed over in silence, as if it did not exist. How curious that these two men had fallen into each other's hands! We were the "Panther's" and his general's prisoners, as they were ours, and I was wondering how it all would end.

The same problem preoccupied the Mir, although he was convinced that the answer was obvious. He really believed that after our arrival in the "City of the Dead," we would regain our freedom more quickly if we accepted our capture with docility. His anxiety was about something entirely different—water.

He said nothing about this as we rode along because he did not want our enemies to hear us. But when we stopped for a rest early in the afternoon, he took Halef and me aside to tell us what was worrying him.

5 : The City of the Dead

I should mention first that we were no longer travelling over tilled soil. We only saw an occasional meager field, and pastures also were rare. We had reached the steppe, and the part we had to cross was the most arid. From Ard in the north, we had been riding due south to reach the mosque. Now, we were going due west. Our destination, the "City of the Dead," lay on the dried-up river whose water, according to legend, had reversed its course and run back to its source. Where the long-uninhabited but well-preserved houses of the former capital lay, there was only desert now, and the steppe in which we found ourselves was gradually turning into that desert. The further we went, the less grass and forage we saw. Finally, there was no vegetation except those small, low-growing dry herbs which are rich in ethereal oil and therefore cannot be eaten by horses. As far as we were concerned, this was no cause for alarm, for we had taken ample rations for ourselves and our animals. Even our dogs carried water, and we had replenished our supply at the well by the mosque. The question was where the more than one thousand men and an equal number of horses would find the water they needed.

I was becoming increasingly concerned with this problem. When we saw that the regiment had stopped for a rest and we also had to come to a halt, there was no source, no puddle, not a single drop of water anywhere to be seen. We therefore took what we needed for ourselves and our prisoners from our skins, and also gave the dogs and horses enough to refresh them. It was then that the Mir gestured to Halef and me to come to him. To avoid all contact with the prisoners, he chose a spot some distance away from them. When we had sat down near him, my first question was about this water shortage. He answered:

"That is what I wanted to discuss with you. It is not pressing now, but will become so when we have made our escape and are ready to start on our way back."

"Then there is no water at all in the 'City of the Dead'?" I asked.

"Not a single drop."

"But what I heard from you and others suggests that people live there, exiles, prisoners, and presumably also officials who guard them. Surely they must get water from somewhere."

"They do, but not in the city. It is brought in from some distance away, from a small well which is several hundred feet deep. The water is laboriously drawn from it and runs into a cistern especially built to store it. Then it is poured into skins and transported on camels to the 'City of the Dead'."

"How far is the city from that well?"

"It takes the camels two full days to make the trip."

"So the round trips takes four?"

"Yes."

He was looking at me oddly, but I returned that look because a thought had suddenly occurred to me which made this lack of water appear not only in an ugly but a truly horrible light. To rid oneself of unpopular exiles or prisoners, all that was necessary was to stop the transport of water to the city for a few days. Man dies much more easily from thirst than from hunger. I did not mention this, however, but continued:

"Then we would have to get a four-day supply at this well if we don't want to die of thirst on the way back to it."

"That's correct."

"But that's going to be very difficult. Who is going to carry the amount we will need for that length of time? And even if that were no problem, the 'Panther' will make sure that we die."

"Do you think that's what he wants?"

"There is no doubt in my mind. He is obviously leading us to our death."

"Or the other way around. Let's wait and see. I did not trust him enough to tell him about the secrets of the 'City of the Dead.' He doesn't know them, and will die through that ignorance."

The break was over, and we resumed our march. Nothing remarkable happened along the way, and since all that can be said about the region we passed through is that it became ever more desolate, I shall be brief and merely mention that our goal that day was the well that had been discussed. But the ride was so long and strenuous that we had to rest repeatedly along the way and did not arrive at our destination until midnight. Because there was no moon when we got there, it was dark and we could not inspect the terrain.

The horses of the cavalrymen were so worn out that they could not have continued another hour, but ours had stood up extremely well. The order to camp was given. The circle that was formed around us was so tight that we protested. We suspected that an attempt might be made during the night to rescue the prisoners. Therefore we threatened that we would immediately kill them and continue on our way, should someone try to attack us. As a result, the soldiers withdrew far enough so that we could feel safe. Nonetheless, we took all necessary precautions. We did not all sleep at the same time. One of us was always awake and could rouse the rest in case of danger.

When it began to dawn, we saw that we were at the foot of a long chain of hills which consisted of pure, very hard rock of considerable depth. This was the reason that a water source had come into being, the general aridity notwithstanding. The rock ran from east to west, and thus held all the moisture seeping to the surface from the north where the mountains lay. Apart from this chain of hills, the region was a single uninterrupted plain as far as the eye could see. There was not the slightest depression or ridge anywhere. Wherever one looked, there was sand and more sand, of the sort which feels like finely ground pebbles and is called Raml el Hijawahn* by Arabic desert dwellers.

When we woke up, the troops were still sleeping. There were only the guards and a group of some twenty men who were working at the well and the cistern, unceasingly raising water and filling several hundred skins lying about. Not far from there, we saw stacks of dried fruit, various kinds of bread, and other provisions. There was even fresh meat from animals which must have been slaughtered the day before. It seemed that our capture had not been improvised but carefully planned. Certain tracks revealed that all horses except ours had been watered during the night. Now that our own supply was gone, we decided to give them as much water as they could drink, and also to fill our skins. This could be done conveniently and easily at the moment because the water was still clear and pure. It would quickly muddy when all the men came to get their share.

We could not simply walk to the well and leave the "Panther" and his general. They had to accompany us, but they refused to get up.

"What are we supposed to do? Where are we to go?" the prince of the Tshoban asked. "Do you plan to run away? You wouldn't succeed."

"Run away?" Halef laughed. "From whom? You, perhaps? What a silly idea! If anyone wants to run, it would be you. Except for you two, there is no one here

---

* Sands of horror.

that could be considered a prisoner. We want to wash and water the horses and also fill our empty skins."

"That's a waste of time."

"Why?"

"Water will be taken along for you."

"By whom?"

"The men that are accompanying us."

"You mean the entire regiment?"

"No. Only fifty will come with us. There wouldn't be enough water for more."

"Yes, and we are that 'more' for whom there won't be any water. So we have to get it here. Get up and come along. Otherwise I'll force you to."

He pulled the general up by his collar but the "Panther" required no such invitation. He considered it beneath his dignity to yield to force.

"You see, you can if you try," Halef praised him. "The longer you stay with us, the more useful you'll become. When are we setting out for the 'City of the Dead'?"

"The moment the fifty men are ready. You seem to be anxious to get there."

This was meant ironically but Halef pretended not to have understood and answered:

"Then we have to hurry so that we won't have to keep these important gentlemen waiting. Come along, new Mir of Ardistan."

He pushed the two forward and we followed, leading our horses by the reins. No one tried to interfere with us. Most of the men were still sleeping and all those who were awake knew that they could attempt nothing unless they wanted to get their leaders into trouble. When they had come to the well, they had to sit down again and watch Halef and the two Ussul water the horses. The Mir was standing nearby, silent and with a dark look on his face, watching the proceedings. In addition to his own, he had the loaded pistols of his enemies in his belt and I was convinced he would shoot them the moment they attempted to escape or defend themselves. This gave me a chance to move more freely. I walked over to the stacks of provisions to select what I considered necessary, and without asking for permission. When the "Panther" saw this, he was about to forbid it, but the little Hadji snapped at him:

"Be silent! Keep in your mouth whatever is inside it. It can't be anything good."

The "Panther" made no reply and I filled all our pouches and also picked up fodder for our horses. As I looked at the "Panther" and his general, I noticed their sarcastic expression and the clear message: "Do what you please. Go on and pick up your provisions; it's all useless. You are doomed whatever you do."

When I was finished I entered the shack housing the cistern. I had no special motive for this but merely wanted to be able to tell myself that I had done everything possible to orient myself thoroughly. The walls were bare, the building was empty. But there was a single man inside, sitting on the ground. He was no soldier. As I approached him, he almost devoured me with his wide open, fearful eyes, jumped up, and asked in the hasty, subdued tone of a person who wants to say something he is forbidden to:

"Who are you? Tell me quickly."

"A stranger."

"A stranger? You aren't from Ard?"

"I come from there but am not a native."

"Who is with you?"

"There are five of us. The others are friends of mine."

"Is one of them a very highly placed person?"

"Yes."

"Tell me quickly who he is."

When I hesitated, he went on:

"There is no reason you shouldn't. Is it perhaps the Mir of Ardistan?"

"Yes."

"Is he a prisoner?"

"Almost."

"And is he to be taken to the 'City of the Dead'?"

"Yes. And who are you?"

"I am the watchman here at the well. The Mir is my ruler. I served him loyally, and am still loyal to him. But I had to swear to keep silent. Is the Mir to die?"

"I assume so."

"He is meant to die of thirst and hunger. And not

only he but all those with him. Can't you get away?"

"Perhaps, but we don't wish to."

"I don't understand. You are facing certain death."

"Does it behoove the Mir to run from these rebellious traitors? Besides, we have other reasons for allowing ourselves to be taken to the 'City of the Dead'."

"Then I must remain silent. I can't save you, however much I'd like to. But I warned you. Do you have any idea what is awaiting you?"

"Yes. But we aren't afraid."

He looked at me searchingly, shook his head, and said:

"You seem confident, and I can guess the reason. The Mir believes he knows the secrets of the 'City' but he is mistaken. He knows some, but not all. Those secrets are the property of the clergy, or at least its highest dignitaries, and the rulers have always only been told what the spiritual leaders wanted them to know."

"What clergy do you mean?"

"The Moslem and the Lamaist."

"Not the Christian?"

"Oh, no! No effort was ever made to initiate them. The Christian clergy was not only not respected, it was suppressed. You are done for. Don't believe you will be able to escape. Only very few know the labyrinths in the City. The man who knew most about them was the Maha-Lama from Djunubistan, who now seems to be a prisoner of the Ussul. After him, the Maha-Lama of Ardistan and the Basch Islami are probably best informed. The latter was here a short while ago in the company of a small number of initiates. They rode to the 'City of the Dead' and remained there for several days. Whenever that happens, it means that important arrivals are expected, and that preparations are being made to have them disappear forever. It turns out that those people are you and your companions."

All this was very interesting. It meant that the old Basch Islami knew the secrets of the City better than the Mir himself. And since he believed that the "Panther" would take his daughter for his wife, he had told his future son-in-law as much as was necessary. This, in turn, explained the confidence with which the new Mir had let us know that we were doomed. There were some other questions I wanted to ask this watchman, but he pointed to an officer who was coming toward the shed. He said:

"We are being interrupted. That is the major who has been promoted to colonel because the colonel has become general. For heaven's sake, be careful. Do you have matches?"

"Yes."

"Lots of them?"

"No. Why do you ask?"

"Because you will probably need them to save yourselves. You will spend a long time in darkness. Make sure you have an ample supply. I was watching you when you were filling your pouches and bags. You only took things from the large stack where the provisions for the soldiers are. But there is another smaller one for the officers. There, you will probably find the candles and lamps you need."

He had spoken quickly to finish before the officer entered.

"Thank you," I whispered. "I won't forget what you have done and will tell the Mir about you when the time has come."

The "colonel" entered.

"What business do you have talking to this man?" he barked at me.

I would have liked to answer him in the same tone but told myself that this might cause the watchman trouble and would not benefit me. I therefore answered as nonchalantly as possible:

"I asked him how deep the well is and how the water is brought up, and he explained it."

"Do you know it now?"

"Yes."

"Then your business with him is over. You should be glad to have any water at all and needn't bother your head how it is procured. I wish to speak to the new Mir of Ardistan."

"Then you should ask the old one for permission."

"He's been deposed. It's not up to him to allow or forbid us anything whatever."

"Then why don't you try speaking to the traitor without his permission? But let me warn you: You are exposing the man to great danger."

"You can't be serious."

"But I am."

"You would actually stab or shoot him?"

"Certainly. And not just him and his general, but you as well."

We had left the cistern and were walking toward my companions. The officer stopped and asked:

"Me too?"

"Yes. Depend on it."

My tone was so serious and determined, and I wore such a threatening expression, that he changed his manner:

"But what am I to do then?"

"Whatever you please. Your life is in your hands. If you want to throw it away, we won't prevent you."

"But that would mean your death as well. Our troops would tear you apart."

"That's something you can really leave up to them, and to us."

"My instructions only cover the march up to this point. From here on, I need further orders."

"We don't object to that, provided we also hear the orders you are given."

"Impossible. They are for me, not for you."

"Then you should go back where you came from. You must be either mad or insolent to demand that we should allow you to talk to the 'Panther' in private. I see more officers coming. They apparently want to join you. Tell them not to approach any closer. We won't allow them to talk to our prisoners. Unless they stop right now, something you won't be able to answer for may happen. Look at the Mir. Do you see what he is doing?"

The Mir had also seen the men who were apparently intent on coming toward us. He had pulled the two pistols from his belt and was aiming them at the "Panther" and the general.

Promptly, the colonel gave the signal I had demanded, and was obeyed. Then he said:

"This is a disgrace. You are in our power, and yet

we must obey you who are our prisoners. Do you really think that we won't pay you back?"

"Yes, we do," I laughed.

"Then I should be talking of madness, not you. What makes you think you can go on treating our two highest officers as prisoners and using them as a shield?"

"Why not?"

"Today and tomorrow?"

"Today and tomorrow, until we arrive in the 'City of the Dead'."

"And then what?"

"Then we will let them go."

"And will you also keep all the other promises you made?"

"I know what you are thinking of. We promised you that we would release your two leaders and allow you to lock us up wherever you please. We promised that voluntarily; no one could have forced us to. And we will keep our word as freely as we gave it. If we wanted to break it, that wouldn't dishonor us in the slightest, considering the people we are dealing with. Shielded by our prisoners, we could ride away from here and you could do nothing to stop us. But it is not our custom to deceive anyone, not even scoundrels, and so—"

"Scoundrels?" he interrupted me. His eyes were flashing. He put his hand on his sabre and went on: "I should really kill you right here. Or I should order that a sabre be brought to you, and then fight with you until one of us falls down and dies. But you are a stranger here and do not know our motives. The Mir was a tyrant, worse than that, a cruel despot, a whip that hurt everyone that came near it. Not just a few thousand, thousands upon thousands were killed by that whip. The number of those he broke, whose peace and happiness he destroyed, whose misery he caused, is countless. There is no torture he did not invent, no pain he did not inflict, no fear he did not—"

I shall stop recounting his speech here. As he continued talking, he took me by the arm, pulling me along until we reached the Mir, into whose face he now hurled his accusations. He was a man of honor.

He spoke so loudly that his voice carried a considerable distance, and went on for some ten minutes. He did not spare him a single reproach and stood there all the while, erect and proud, steadily eyeing the target of his recriminations. When he had finished, he turned back to me.

"That's what I wanted to tell this unfeeling blood sucker and oppressor of his people. He sowed violence. All his thinking and acting has violence, and so was his entire life. So what could he harvest but violence? He was kind to you, Effendi, because you were a stranger, and you believe that you owe him gratitude. You tied your fate to his and will perish with him. I feel sorry about that, and would like to save you. I should advise you to ride away and to leave this country, never to—"

"Be silent! Don't talk so much," the "Panther" interrupted him. "This stranger has the same right bothering about the rights of others as the devil has bothering about Allah. He is ten, a hundred times worse than the Mir. They deserve each other, and I wouldn't dream of letting one of them get away and only punishing the other. Did you come here for further instructions?"

"Yes," the officer said.

"You already know that we will take only fifty cavalry with us. Pick them, for you will be in command. That is my reward for the frankness with which you told the tyrant what all of us think of him. Let him consider us his prisoners. When we reach our destination, that absurdity will end, and we will see if he is strong enough to stand up under its consequences as calmly as he did just now when he listened to you, unable to find a single word in his own defense. During the march, and while we camp, you and your men will stay far enough away so that you won't spoil the composure of the deposed Mir and his friends. You know that all of them become panic-stricken whenever one of you takes it into his head to approach us. We are going to Prison Number Five, where we will leave these men. I hope we will get there before tomorrow evening. Now you should see to it that we can leave here as quickly as possible. The new ruler of Ardistan has more important matters to attend to than to go riding around the desert with a Mir whom his own people threw out. That's all."

The colonel left to carry out the orders. Halef inspected the harness of our horses and I went to the small stack of provisions the cistern watchman had mentioned to me. It was covered by tarpaulin. When I folded it back, I saw that everything there was intended for the exclusive use of the officers. I did not wish to attract attention or spend much time, for I wanted no one to know what I took. Fortunately, I almost immediately spotted a number of boxes of matches and some bottled sesame oil, probably intended for use in preparing salads. Close by, there were several little Oriental coffee makers, and small burners with metal holders to go with them. Using pieces of linen and string, I quickly wrapped up all these things. Only the "Panther" had observed me. When I fastened the package to the saddle of one of our pack horses, he commented sarcastically:

"Do you really think you'll starve on the way? That's absurd. And there will be real delights awaiting you in Prison Number Five."

I did not answer. It was better if he thought I had only taken edibles.

After perhaps a quarter hour, we observed the colonel leaving the camp at the head of his fifty cavalry, and then stopping some distance away to wait for us. Followed by the glances of those remaining behind, we set out. What were they thinking? Did they know the fate that was awaiting us? Was there one among them who felt remorse at having deserted the legitimate ruler? As I turned around, I saw that the watchman had climbed on the roof of the cistern shed. Since the soldiers were looking at us, they failed to notice him. He raised his hands and folded them to indicate that he was praying for us. I gestured with my right arm to thank him. The soldiers thought this was meant for them and quickly, several hundred arms shot up into the air, returning what they took to be a gesture of farewell. They continued waving for some time. Since this was not meant for the "Panther" and his fellow prisoner, I concluded that many of the men did not share the feelings of those they had to obey.

Today, we rode in the same order as before. Again, the Mir trailed us. He had not said a word since the scene with the candid and wrathful major. Since he stayed by himself, I imagined that he did not wish to be disturbed, and therefore did not turn to look at him. The frank accusations of the officer had been like blows with a club, and I hoped that they had found their mark. It is impossible to come to terms quickly with something like this, for remorse, repentance, and a change of heart are related. They develop slowly but that makes their force all the more certain.

The "sands of horror" I mentioned before seemed endless when seen from the well. But as soon as we had covered the stretch visible from there, it became apparent that it constituted only a relatively narrow strip which originated in the mountain chain at whose foot the well lay. In the course of the morning we came to its edge, and then rode across terrain an uninformed person would have taken for desert but which actually was only soil which had not been irrigated. Occasionally, it sounded so hard and solid under the hooves of our horses that one would have thought we were riding across poured metal rather than earth or stone. But in the absence of water, even the mud of the Nile is infertile. Then, countless cracks open as if the soil were longing for moisture. Here, in this desolate region of Ardistan, that same situation must have prevailed for decades after everything had dried up. Gradually the winds which blew from all directions and encountered no obstacles had covered those cracks and turned the entire region into a smooth, iron-hard shell. It stared at us wherever we looked, and did not show the slightest trace of organic life.

Around noon, we noticed some points directly ahead of us. Their color differed from that of the soil; they were motionless and seemed to be waiting for us. As we drew closer, they turned out to be two men with pack camels. It had been their task to transport water to this point. There were several more outposts which formed a chain from the well to the City and back again. As I had expected, we were refused a share of this water. The "Panther" pointed out to us that we had our own, but we paid no attention to him and simply took what we needed. He wanted us to die quickly, but we did not propose dipping into our supply. We were determined to protect ourselves against a shortage for as long as we could.

In the evening, we again saw an outpost with an adequate supply of water at the place that had been chosen as the camp site. We were again refused, and again took what we needed without anyone attempting to prevent us. During the entire day, the Mir had trailed us and during the evening also, he stayed away. He had not eaten at noon, and did not do so now. I therefore got up and walked over to him. When I was standing in front of him, he looked up at me and said:

"Aren't you afraid of coming to see me?"

"Afraid? No."

"It would be natural for you to hesitate, to be afraid of me, to recoil."

"Not at all."

"Then you think that the major or colonel lied?"

"No."

"You believe him?"

"I think that what he said was substantially true. The facts are as he presented them, although they loom larger because he was angry."

My answer upset the Mir.

"How terribly sincere and honest all of you are! It's so sudden."

"I always mean what I say."

He looked at me again.

"Yes, you do. And you were perfectly frank the first time you talked to me." Then he pointed at the ground directly in front of him, and said: "Sit down, right here."

I did as he asked. Then he said:

"I ask you to believe that what I am now telling you is absolutely true. I never thought for a single moment that I was the heartless, cruel despot I now hear myself called. It was my feeling that I had never found love except the love of my mother, and even that love did not seem a virtue to be grateful for, but rather an instinct which she could not help but obey. My mother is the only person I really loved, and still love today. My father was a calculating, severe, even harsh man, and I am not inclined to consider it a crime that I acquired those characteristics from him. He also had the kind of cruelty that takes pleasure in torturing his fellow man. I see now that I also have the capacity for cruelty but only because I consider the ordinary, lowly-placed, and common person unfeeling and insensitive to pain that would be intolerable to us, who are men of a higher nature. Just as a boy will torture an insect, a butcher an animal, a hunter his game, or a porter his ass, because they are all convinced that that torture is not felt as such, it is my belief that my severity was mere severity, not cruelty, and I thought this because it would hurt me more than anyone else, were it to be inflicted on me. All these people that are so far below me I took for a herd of sheep whose wool protects them from the pain of the blows they suffer. If I caress them, they bleat; if I beat them, they also bleat; it's all the same. All they ask is that they be taken to pasture. At night, they must be protected so that they won't be devoured, for you are the only predator that may eat them when they are fat enough. They can be sheared as often as you please. After that, they are killed so that their soft skin can keep you warm. That's all they are there for, but you are their master, their ruler, the Mir. Do you understand, Effendi?"

"Of course I do. All of that would have been perfectly proper if your premises had been correct."

"What premises?"

"That the insect, the animal about to be slaughtered, the game, and the ass feel their pain less than you, that you are a different, more perfect, more sensitive, higher, and more valuable being than others. Believe me, if I slaughter you, your flesh will taste no better than other flesh, and your bones will not make a more delicate soup than other bones. Your hair is not even as useful, for it cannot be made into fur, and anyone who had the idea of making shoes, boots, saddles, or leather trousers of your skin would soon discover that any calf's or ox's hide is better suited for that purpose."

"Effendi, aren't you being presumptuous?"

"There is no presumption," I answered. "How can it be presumption that I should open your eyes? As soon as you understand, you will not be angry, but grateful. You considered yourself a 'higher human being,' and I proved to you that, physically, you are the same as any other, the same as those sheep whose master you claim to be. If you really are superior, it can only be intellectually or spiritually. But where have you ever done anything so outstanding intellectually that you would deserve to be called a 'spiritual' Mir, a 'spiritual' ruler, a prince of the intellect?"

I waited for his reply but he remained silent. I continued:

"Nowhere! You were no scholar, no poet, no artist, no theologian, no discoverer or inventor, no—"

"But I was more than all that," he interrupted. "I was a—prince."

"Yes, that's true. But what sort of prince? What did you do to deserve being one? Did you become one through your own efforts, or wasn't that title passed on to you like those shortcomings you admitted to a moment ago, your severity, your cold and calculating nature, your cruelty? What did you do when you were prince? Did you do more than other princes or even ordinary individuals to bring happiness to others? What laws did you promulgate to increase the well-being of your people? Where are the roads, the schools, the hospitals you built? What deserts did you turn into fields and pastures? How did you care for the poor among your subjects? Who gives them work, who gives them bread? Where are your granaries, your storehouses which you could open when the harvests are bad and hunger walks your streets? I know that the former rulers of Ardistan built gigantic structures where they stored huge quantities of grain and fruit. Did you do anything similar?"

I paused, and he persevered in his silence. He sat in front of me, huddled, his hands folded over his knees, his head lowered. I saw that the time had come for him to be forged and purified, and so I went on:

"And what did you do spiritually that would entitle you to claim to be better, more noble, or a superior person? Did you ever even attempt to do something good or extraordinary? What is the state of your own soul? And what of the soul of your wife, your children? Where was the ray of sunlight without which both wife and children wither and die? And the souls of those that surrounded you, your court, your residence? When I came to you, I saw you dressed in heavy, thick, flashy, ostentatious garments. They enveloped you so completely that they made you invisible. All I saw was flamboyance, trappings, ceremony, ritual, fancy dress, and masquerade, but no substance, no life within. And where such things existed, fear, lies, hypocrisy, rebellion, and treason existed also. And what did you do for the soul of your people? Did you win it over? Did you do anything to win its love, respect, confidence, or trust, or make it share your joys and suffering so that it would loyally and eagerly stand by your side whatever happened? Think of this poor, tormented, and tortured soul of a suppressed people which hourly and daily goes begging to its master's throne and is never heeded for even a moment. Consider—"

Suddenly, he jumped up, opened his arms wide, and said:

"Stop, stop, Effendi. You are going too far! I would like to strangle you with these two hands, like this." He pulled back his fingers as if to clutch my throat, moved his hands back and forth, and gnashed his teeth. Then he breathed deeply, and continued more calmly: "And yet I fear that I would weep for you if I killed you. You are the only one I respect and love, but also fear. You are a frightful human being. A horrible murderer. You have killed something within me that I believed of infinite value."

He slowly left and disappeared in the darkness to be alone with the thoughts assailing him. But the "Panther" shouted:

"Stop, stop! Anyone who gives us reason to believe

he intends to escape will be seized by my men."

Without deigning to answer, the Mir returned to his place.

"Effendi, try to sleep," he said. "I cannot. You opened a door within me, but you did not do it gently and considerately as one opens the doors of strangers, but violently, with kicking and beating. You smashed that door and it crumbled. Out there, on its other side, it is light. Thoughts and shapes enter of whose existence I was unaware before this day. I must scrutinize and test them; I must talk to them and ask what they want. And then I must tell them whether they may stay or not. Be patient until I am done. I will tell you everything tomorrow."

Using his saddle as a pillow, he lay down, took a deep breath, and stretched out. With his eyes turned toward the stars, he was immobile and I wished that the stars in his soul would also appear, for without them human life must always remain in darkness. I did not want to leave him, and went to get my own saddle. But I found it impossible to sleep. When a soul is struggling to be born, it must be given the reassurance that counsel and help are near.

"Effendi, are you asleep?" he asked when about an hour had gone by.

"No."

"Go to sleep. Do not concern yourself unduly. It was not for nothing that I witnessed Christmas and even participated in the celebration, not just mechanically but with conviction. May I tell you how I feel now?"

"Please do."

"That old, courageous major who accused me of such crimes today and offended me so grievously shall not just be a colonel but a general. As soon as we have returned safely and before I do anything else, I will inform him of his promotion. Are you content with me?"

"May God bless you," I answered. I was gratified that he had won this difficult victory over himself. "During the one hour you have been lying here, you have achieved more than during many a long year in the past."

During the second day of our journey, the region

through which we passed gradually took on a wholly different, and, for me, very interesting aspect. It was coming alive. If I express myself in this way, I realize that I am guilty of saying something illogical, for what it became alive with was death. First only occasionally, but then with increasing frequency, we detected signs that this repellent desolation had once been inhabited. Along our way, we saw corpses of houses and small groups of houses, and sometimes even entire extinct villages. At places where they clustered, it always turned out that a brook, a small river, or even stagnant water had once been nearby. These corpses were either partly or wholly preserved. We passed by many quarries which had furnished an exceptionally durable and resistant material. The villages with their stone walls, built of indestructible loam and with flat roofs, often looked as if they had only been abandoned recently rather than centuries ago. I only began to realize how long they had been deserted when hours passed without my seeing a single tree, shrub, or even blade of grass. There were trees, to be sure, in what had once been gardens and along what must once have been paths. But they also were corpses. These pale skeletons made a terribly sad, often horrible and ghostly impression. Wholly stripped of their bark and bent by storms, they raised their inaudible moans to the sky. Lifeless in their nakedness, they stared and almost seemed to grin at us. Only a few of those who had passed here had stopped long enough to obtain material for a fire, and everyone had hurried to leave this place of horror as quickly as possible.

The Mir was well acquainted with this curious region, this uninterrupted field of lifeless trees and empty dwellings. I mentioned before that, in the company of a tutor, he had often roamed the City of the Dead and its environs as a young man. Today, he was not riding behind us but had joined me to talk to me in private. He told me the names of the deserted places where no longer visible paths had once led, and what the life of the inhabitants had been. He also described the City of the Dead, but I omit his account because it would go far beyond the bounds of my narrative. He also spoke of its prisons where only military personnel and political prisoners were detained. Because he had wandered through them, also, he knew them well.

"Do you also know Prison Number Five where we are being taken?"

"As well as the rest."

"Does it have a secret?"

"Oh, no."

"Are you certain?"

"Quite."

"But the watchman at the cistern claimed that you did not know all there is to be known."

"He did? And who told him how much or how little I know? He was just guessing. He is a small, insignificant official who attends to the well, the cistern, the water carriers, and their camels. One doesn't take such people into one's confidence. What did he say to you?"

I repeated the entire conversation we had had. This seemed to give him pause.

"Up to now, he knew nothing. But now he has heard the soldiers and the officers talk. So the three he named know more than I do? The Maha-Lama of Djunubistan, the Maha-Lama of Ardistan, and the Bash Islami whom I freed because you forced me to? The first is not dangerous now. He is with the Ussul. And the second one can do me no harm either. I hope I will soon get my hands on the third. This time, he won't get away."

"Do you think you are right when you say that there is no danger? The fact is that these men know something you don't. And that means that there are secrets you are unaware of, and which may therefore become extremely dangerous to us."

"That danger is something you are responsible for, not I."

"What do you mean?"

"If you had not persuaded me to let the Bash Islami go, he could not have told the 'Panther' anything about the secrets of the City of the Dead."

"You are mistaken. I am convinced that those two had come to an agreement before that incident. You just reproached me twice for the same thing. For that reason, I am anxious to tell you what I think of the

Bash Islami. It is true he is a fanatic, but fundamentally he is a well-meaning and just person. Also, when I make a mistake, I always correct it. But first, we will have to see if what you call a mistake really is one. The danger we may be riding toward is not in me but in you, and by that I mean that there is the possibility that you do not know all the secrets. We must find out if this Prison Number Five is really as harmless as you say. Does it lie away from other buildings, or not?"

"It does, and it is not far from the bank of a dried-up river. It is built in a perfectly straightforward manner, is square, and consists of two stories with a flat roof, small cells above, and larger ones below. It is probably in the latter that they will put us. It lies in a walled-in courtyard but the wall is not much higher than a man."

"How large is that yard?"

"Quite large, for the apartment of the prison administrator also lies in it, and adjoining it there are some low depots and stables where our horses will be taken."

"Then the prison does not have double walls or anything of that sort which might hide a secret or danger which we cannot anticipate?"

"No. And there is no need for that sort of thing. The lack of water is enough to make an escape impossible. Anyone who tried would die of thirst along the way. That's why we have to save all we can, otherwise we are doomed, like all the rest. I hope all this reassures you."

Unfortunately, that was far from being the case. On the contrary! His confidence seemed unfounded and created an impression that was the opposite of the one he intended. I did not mention this but decided to be doubly cautious and not to take a single step without having considered it carefully.

On that day, we passed three water supply points and acted as we had the previous day. We saved our water and satisfied our needs at these posts. As we were coming closer to the former residence, signs of what had once been a vigorous civilization became more frequent. The land had once again become mountainous, and when, shortly before evening, we reached the crest of a gradually rising but very high elevation, we saw our destination ahead and far below us.

6 : On the Maha-Lama Lake

A more detailed description of this curious "City of the Dead" will be given elsewhere. For the moment, a few comments must suffice.

The valley of the vanished river ran in a straight line from north to south. The dried-out riverbed divided it into two unequal parts, one to the east, the other to the west. The former, which we saw first, was considerably wider than the other, and contained what may be called the residential quarter, while the section which lay beyond it could be referred to as the military town, or citadel. We saw hundreds of thoroughfares and streets with an abundance of temples, churches, mosques, palaces, houses, and hovels. All of this made an impression of utter desolation, of lifelessness and death. There was no trace of greenery, of human or animal life. Yet the terms "lifelessness" or "death" are not really quite accurate. Perhaps the word "sleep" would be more precise, but I am not certain. There is really no altogether correct term to describe my irresistible feeling as my astonished glance fell on this unusual, rigid, desolate, and empty sea of buildings standing exactly as they had centuries ago. There was almost no destruction. Only the distant hovels of the poor, which lay far out along the perimeter, had turned to ruins and amorphous heaps, although not of dust or earth. They were as hard as iron.

This former residence and capital of Ardistan had been beautiful. When I tried to imagine the curiously shaped heights between which it lay crowned with woods and green, blossoming gardens, I could think of no European metropolis I might have compared to it.

Now it was a corpse or, rather, it was like a winter without snow or ice, frost or cold, its life driven deep into the ground so that no traces of it remain visible. But at the first signs of spring, that life re-awakens and its blood begins to surge again. And "blood" was perhaps the most accurate word. This city lay before us like the unconscious body of a beautiful woman, her face drained, her limbs rigid and immobile. But the moment blood returns to the heart, the unconscious person will rise to her feet. Her eyes will sparkle again, her cheeks glow, and she will be more precious and lovely than before. And this would also be true of what had once been Ard. If the vanished water were to return, this emptiness would fill with people and a new, purer, and higher life would begin to pulsate through thoroughfares and passageways. The sun was about to disappear over the horizon and as its rays flickered across the sea of houses, it was as if the rigid lines were beginning to move and throngs of vanished souls were returning to greet us as we stood there in the dusk.

The commanding officer quickly put an end to these reflections. Not having stopped to look, he was now far ahead of us and called on us to come along, since it was still some distance to Prison Number Five and only half an hour remained before dark. We obeyed.

As we were riding down the ridge and I let my eye travel over the cyclopean walls of the citadel, fear about the outcome of our adventure crept over me. Those walls and towers were so tall that it seemed impossible for anyone behind or inside them to escape. I asked the Mir:

"Are we going to be locked up over there?"

"No," he answered. "But even if we were, there would be no grounds for worry. I know my way around here. I can recover my freedom whenever I choose."

"Where is our Number Five?"

"On this side of those strong walls that seem to disquiet you. Do you see that deep riverbed and the three stone bridges arching across it? The far bank has been raised. Do you also see that great wide opening in that wall, a little below the center bridge?"

"Yes. It seems to be the mouth of what was once a subterranean canal."

"Not a canal but a tributary which originally flowed directly into the main river but later had a vault built over it. Above the mouth, there is a large open area at whose western side you can see a square wall surrounding two buildings. The large one is our prison, the smaller the living quaters of the administrator I mentioned before."

"Hm. That prison doesn't seem terribly threatening."

"It isn't, not at all! No one can keep us there. Escape is not only not impossible, it's very easy, and only the fear of dying of thirst could keep us there. But all our skins are full."

"But we also need a lot. There are five of us, seven horses, and four large dogs. All of them need to drink. It's our lives that are at stake, so we must be very cautious. And it is important that we know whether this Prison Number Five contains trapdoors, double walls, or similar things, or is a perfectly straightforward building."

"You need not worry. When I was a boy, I stayed with the then superintendent and came to know every nook and cranny of that building. If there were such things as you mention, I could not have failed to discover them, or the superintendent would have shown them to me just as he showed me all the other things no one was supposed to know about."

"Then I have no reason to be disquieted?"

"None."

He sounded so sure of himself that I believed him. Besides, I would have offended him, had his assurances left me unsatisfied. We rode down the slope and straight through the town until we finally crossed the center bridge and then turned left into the open area I mentioned. Along its western side our prison lay. It certainly did not look like one. I have said before that the wall encircling this area was not much taller than a man. A child could have climbed it. As we passed close by it, I could easily look into the yard without raising myself in my stirrups. The entire main building did not have a single windowpane in it. The empty openings were staring at us. To be free, it was enough to scramble through them. To call this a prison seemed absurd. My worry of a while ago was disappearing.

The gate was not along the river but on the other side. As we stopped before it, the sun had disappeared and dusk was settling.

"We have arrived," the commanding officer called out, gesturing to his men to surround us.

The "Panther" breathed deeply with relief and said to us:

"Here we are. The fun is over. Things are going to take a serious turn now. Are we finally free?"

"Yes," I nodded because the Mir did not answer.

"And you submit to your fate?"

"With pleasure."

"Which means that you will ride through this gate into the prison yard without resistance?"

"Yes. That was our promise, and we will keep it."

Halef untied the "Panther" and the general. Then their weapons were returned to them and they jumped from their horses. The "Panther" was making a strange face. He looked at us, laughed sarcastically, and said:

"Actually, I was going to take your horses and dogs. But I know that those beasts are trained to perform tricks that may surprise me, and so I'll do without them. You keep them. And now we'll say goodbye."

He stepped up to the gate, picked up the hammer hanging down from it, and knocked. Someone opened immediately. It seemed that the knock had been expected, that our arrival had been observed. The gate was a double one, consisting of two outer and two inner wings, the former opening outward, the others in the opposite direction. Between them was an area where the prisoners were received and the appropriate formalities attended to. It was large enough to accommodate us, our horses, and dogs. The Mir had mentioned the wall but not this reception area, but perhaps that was no reason to become suspicious. There was no time for that in any event, for both the outer and the inner wings were opened simultaneously and a man, probably an official, called on us to enter. The Mir complied immediately, I followed him, and was followed by Halef and the two Ussul princes in turn.

"Give my regards to the Erdjani and my splendid

brother," we heard the "Panther" call after us. Then both wings closed abruptly and we found ourselves in total darkness.

"Allah kerim," Halef exclaimed. "What's the meaning of this? Is this a trap?"

"You may be sure," I answered.

"No," the Mir contradicted me. "The administrator will reopen the gate right away. The outer one will stay closed, of course."

"But who closed it? Not the 'Panther,' surely," I said. "It wasn't closed by a human hand."

"Then it was done by some mechanism. There are many of them in the prison complex."

"But you assured me that there were no hidden devices in Number Five. Let's dismount quickly and try to open the door."

But as I was still getting off my horse, there was a hoarse screeching as of unoiled wheels below us, and the floor began to descend. The Mir shouted, and so did everyone else. We did not go down very far, perhaps three or four times a man's height. Then the movement stopped, but only briefly. For now the floor tilted so steeply toward one side that we could not maintain ourselves on it and slid off. If our dogs had not been such well-trained thoroughbreds, the confusion would have been fearsome. As it was, we got away with a few jolts and superficial contusions.

"Light a match, quickly," the Mir ordered.

"No, we don't want light," I objected.

"Why not?"

"Wait! Listen!"

The screeching resumed. The floor was starting back up and at the same time, the voice of the "Panther" rang out above:

"You didn't expect that, did you, you scoundrels! That was the secret of the Maha-Lama of Djunubistan and my dear old Bash Islami."

"It doesn't matter," Halef answered with a laugh. "We'll be at your wedding when you and his daughter ascend the throne."

The tough little fellow couldn't restrain himself. He would rather have suffered God knows what punishment than be prevented from lashing out at the "Panther."

We could not understand the reply because the floor had returned to its original position above and the opening was closed.

"Why don't you want lights?" the Mir asked me.

"I do, but not now," I answered. "We will be observed for some time and I don't want them to know that we can have all the light we need. Do you have any idea where we are?"

"No. I could say that we are obviously below Prison Number Five, but that wouldn't be a very illuminating answer."

"It wouldn't. Our getting out of here depends on remaining coolheaded and not taking a single step without having oriented ourselves. Let everyone take his horse, and Halef and I will also take the dogs so they remain quiet."

When this had been done, I continued:

"First of all the compass points. In what direction did we slide off the platform?"

"West," Halef answered. "I was already facing west up there and have not turned since."

"That's right. The open area on which the prison stands lies above the mouth of the small tributary I mentioned to you when we were coming down the mountain. This river flows into the main stream from the west. I remember two things very clearly, where its mouth is, and where the prison is. The river passes directly under the prison yard and therefore I am convinced that we are in a canal which had a vault built over it. If we can follow this canal east, we get to its mouth and we'll be free. But I imagine that will be impossible. It has probably been filled up to prevent escapes. What do you know about that?"

This question had been addressed to the Mir.

"Nothing," he answered. "Go on."

"If we follow the canal west, that will take us under the citadel. Do you know perhaps where it emerges there?"

"No, I don't, unfortunately," the Mir said rather apologetically. "I am almost ashamed. I bragged about my extensive knowledge of the 'City of the Dead' and was convinced I had it. Yet here we are, barely arrived, and it turns out that my ignorance is greater than my knowledge."

"That doesn't matter," Halef consoled him. "Ignorance isn't such a terrible thing. Sometimes, it's more useful than knowledge. There only has to be a measure of belief, belief in Allah and the hosts He will send us when the danger is greatest. Often, when I thought I had acted intelligently, I had actually maneuvered myself into a hopeless impasse. And as my ignorance loomed up before me and I asked Allah for help, I had barely said 'Amen' when I was saved. My Effendi and I have extricated ourselves from much more precarious situations. We'll find a way out of this and our Effendi will tell us how we should go about it. Just listen to him."

Halef's humor was timely. The nonchalance with which he viewed our situation would probably free the others of their fear. So I agreed with him.

"Very well, I'll try to live up to your expectations. First, we'll determine if we can go east in this canal. If we can, we will come to the main river and be able to get out. But I assume that will not be possible. Surely the 'Panther' must have examined this entire area carefully before sending us down here. We have no choice but to turn west."

"Let's get started then, and light some candles," the Mir said impatiently.

"No, not yet! We are going to wait a little longer. I think they are listening up there. I don't want them to see that we have lights, that we are calmly reflecting instead of acting precipitously, that we are not as desperate as they probably believe."

The Mir had to give in, although he did so reluctantly. We waited for all of an hour, and it turned out that I had been right. During the time we waited, the movable platform was lowered twice and far enough so that one could see past its edges. We also heard barely audible voices. Perhaps it wasn't absolutely essential to spend all this time waiting but I wanted to lull my enemies into a sense of security. The more firmly convinced they were that we could not escape, the less they would bother about us. When an hour had passed without their having undertaken anything further, I opened my package and we lit some candles and lamps.

It immediately became apparent that it was impossible to go east. In that direction, the canal had not only been filled with earth but also closed by large rocks so heavy that our combined strength would not have sufficed to loosen or move a single one of them. We therefore had no choice but to turn west.

There, we could pass. The canal did not resemble a low, narrow tunnel, but was nearly four meters high and wide enough for a dozen persons to walk side by side without touching. In the center, a row of pillars supported the ceiling. The floor was completely level and smooth and had been worked on with some care. The air was fairly good, without a trace of moisture.

"That doesn't look like a canal or a riverbed," the Mir said.

"Then you don't know it?"

"No. I only know what I already told you, which is that the small tributary flowed into the main stream at the place I showed you, and that a vault was then built over it. It never occurred to me to go down into this canal. I wonder how long it is."

"We'll find out if we count our steps. And that's very important if we are to determine our position at a later time."

Because we had to husband our resources, only two lamps were filled with sesame oil and lit. We walked very slowly, for the small flames were so inadequate that we could not even see three steps ahead. At any moment, we might come to a break in the canal, a hole, some trap which could endanger or destroy us. But we encountered nothing of that sort. We had walked five hundred paces.

"This is getting boring," Halef said angrily.

"Do you think we were put here for our amusement?" I asked him.

"No. But if this continues, I'll sit down and go to sleep."

When we had counted six hundred paces, I figured we had done one kilometer. But we walked another one without reaching the end. We were leading the horses, and the dogs had been quietly following us. Now, they were becoming agitated and pressed forward. We had to leash them, but they accepted this unwillingly. Uucht suddenly stopped to sniff the ground. Then she raised her nose, inhaled the air with her neck stretched out, and tore loose. Howling with joy, she disappeared in the darkness that was yawning at us. The other three dogs immediately followed. We were unable to hold them back. In the long canal, their voices reverberated like the shouting and screaming of a legion of devils.

"The Erdjani?" the Mir asked.

"Probably," Halef answered. "The Erdjani and the prince of the Tshoban. Let's hurry."

Now we heard human voices but could not understand a word for the echo effect completely distorted the sound. We started to rush along as fast as we could; two men came toward us with equal speed. They were the Erdjani and Sadik, the firstborn prince of the Tshoban.

I shall not describe our reunion. The two had been lured into this trap the same way we had, having been convinced that they would be meeting the ruler of Ardistan to negotiate with him. But they had been less lucky. They had been seized, disarmed, and tied up. Not until their arrival at Prison Number Five had their feet been untied, and then they had suddenly been dropped, exactly as we had been. Once below, they had helped each other get their hands free. Having spent two entire days without food and water, and having been given nothing to drink during the transport, their thirst was considerable. We were about to give them water when they suggested it would be more convenient to move on to the end of the canal where there was more space and even some seats. They led the way, and we followed.

Two days before, they had carefully groped their way along the path by which we had also come until they had reached the end of the canal. It was blocked by huge boulders which had been hewn so skilfully that one might have taken their present shape to be their natural one. The thin, carefully cut edges where they were joined looked like natural cracks. At its end, the passage widened into a large, square room which resembled a hall and had seats of stone along its walls. We sat down.

Here, in this faintly illumined subterranean room, the Mir and the Erdjani saw each other for the first time. When the Erdjani and his companion had been given water, I lit some of the candles I had brought along so that we could see more clearly. The Mir took the Erdjani's hand, the Erdjani the Mir's. They looked at each other without speaking. Then the Mir sat down on one of the stone benches, and turned to me:

"This is not the place for princes and generals to greet one another. The 'Panther' lied when he told us that we would talk and negotiate. But that lie will become truth. Providence changes evil into good. That won't happen here, however. At this moment, we are not even the masters of our own destiny, so how could we have the audacity to guide the destiny of others? Here, we are merely human beings in distress who need help. Once this has passed, we will be what we were before. But now I am asking you, Effendi: What do you think of our situation? Is it hopeless?"

My answer was quick and incisive:

"I am sure that it is not."

"Thank you. That reassures me. But suppose we cannot find an exit here either?"

"Then we return to our starting point. Up to now, the fact that the floor of the reception area was movable was a disadvantage to us. I have no reason to believe that it might not also be an advantage. If the floor moves up and down, there must be weights, and a mechanism which controls them. If those weights were above ground, our situation would indeed be hopeless. But there was no room for them along the gate or the wall. So they must be below ground. I am sure we can find them. When we have, neither the 'Panther' nor anyone else can hold us."

"You sound optimistic. Who could have foreseen this? I relied on my knowledge of this place, and now have to rely on you. Is there something else you want to say?"

"Yes. As yet, it has not been demonstrated that we

must turn back. This room was made by men. But no one constructs a room which can only be reached by walking four thousand paces below ground. I am convinced there is a door here which will lead outside."

"I don't see any."

"Neither do I, but we will look. We won't find a wooden one, of course. If there is one, it will be of stone, one of those large rocks which are so carefully joined that the cracks between them seem natural. Such a stone door, however, would be much too heavy and cumbersome to be hinged. We must assume that it moves on wheels. If that is true, there should be visible tracks on this floor."

"Then you think that we only have to examine it to see if there is a door or not?"

"Yes."

"Let's look, then."

The lamps and candles had barely been lowered when Halef exclaimed:

"Sidi, I found it."

"How did you do it so quickly?"

"There's a track, no, there are two. Over here!"

He was right. Where he was standing, the floor consisted of a very hard, heavy stone slab which had two indentations running along it that could only be tracks. The slab was not completely horizontal but sloped, rising toward the wall and falling in the opposite direction. It adjoined a second slab of the same hard rock in which the two tracks continued. This second slab also rose. One could see clearly that the weight which had to roll along on these two stones first moved down, then up again. This meant that it was both propelled and stopped by its own mass.

The question now was which stone was the door. Obviously, it must be the one below which the tracks originated. We examined it but it would not move, which meant that it was anchored in some manner. If we succeeded in removing what kept it in place, our problem would be solved. We began examining the immediate surrounding area. Soon, we noticed two small spots whose coloration differed from that of the rocks. They lay somewhat below chest height to the right and the left of the door, along the edges of the adjoining stones. Scratching first with a finger nail and then with my knife, I exposed two small holes or cracks which looked exactly like the coin slots on vending machines. It struck me that they had been hidden under moist dust so that no one would see them, just as the cracks on the water angel near the Chatar defile had been masked.

"A hole, a keyhole," Halef said. "Isn't that right, Sidi?"

"It seems that way," I said.

"And there are probably some on the other side."

"Let's have a look."

When I had removed the dust, we saw an identical opening.

"Strange, very strange," the Mir said. "But what about the key? Where could it be? Perhaps it is hidden here somewhere."

"I don't think so," I answered. "An important object like that is not hidden at the place where one is most anxious to find it. But wait!"

At this very moment, I remembered the key knife of the Maha-Lama of Djunubistan which I had found where he had camped with the "highest minister." I had kept it safely tucked away in my saddle pouch. I took it out and moved the blade until it was in the position that had been described on that occasion. Then I inserted the point in the keyhole and turned. It worked. I felt like shouting with joy. I sensed that other, very important matters were connected with this knife.

"He's opening it," the Mir said.

"Oh, my Sidi can do anything, and so can I after he has shown the way," Halef said very proudly.

"I said he could rely on me and now I have to rely on him. Effendi, unlock the other opening, too."

"When you step aside, not before," I answered, for he was standing directly in the path of the stone. I added:

"The moment this heavy door opens, it will throw you down and crush you."

He quickly stepped aside. I inserted the point of the knife into this opening also and had barely turned it when the stone moved. Under its own weight, it left

: 449 :

its place, came away from the wall, rolled down across the first slab, then up the second, and stopped. In spite of what must have been a weight of hundreds of pounds, it would only require a small push to return it by the same path to its original position. Cool, pure air entered.

"We are saved," the Mir exclaimed.

"Are we?" Halef wondered.

"Not so loud," I warned them. "And quickly, put out the lights. We don't know what's on the other side. We aren't saved yet. The real danger is only beginning. Let's move cautiously. And most important, be absolutely quiet."

Outside, it was almost as dark as in the canal. Only after some time, when our eyes had adjusted to the darkness, did we perceive that we were standing under a kind of arcade which had been hewn out of the rock, so that there were only powerful pillars up ahead on which the rock rested. And that rock made it impossible to see the sky. As we moved forward, we could see the stars shining above. Yet we still could not make out our surroundings. Every contour dissolved and became indistinct. The Mir had led a life quite unlike Halef's and mine. His senses had never been trained. He claimed to be unable to see anything but the stars. But although everything was shadowy, we realized that we were standing in a very steep depression in whose center there seemed to be a pedestal supporting a tall, winged object, perhaps a figure.

"Do you have any idea where we are?" I asked the Mir.

"No."

"We are standing in an immense, circular, or oval basin with what seem to be perpendicular walls."

"There is no such thing," he said.

"Oh, yes. There must be, for I can see it. In the center of this basin, there is something like an island, and on it, a figure."

"A figure? What sort of figure?" he asked hastily.

"Probably an angel, for it has wings."

Abruptly, he shouted:

"May Allah protect us from—"

: 450 :

I interrupted him by taking him by the arm, and warned him:

"Not so loud, not so loud! We must be careful."

"May Allah protect us from the stone devil!" he completed his sentence more softly. "It seems we have come to the most horrible and sinister place on earth."

"What is that?"

"The Maha-Lama Lake."

"The Maha-Lama Lake? I've never heard of it."

"Because you are a foreigner, from far away. But in Asia, it's well known and anxiously avoided."

"Why?"

"Because cruelties, sins, and crimes were committed here which cry out to heaven and echo back again."

"By whom?"

"The Lama priests."

"Who were the victims?"

"All those who dared resist them. Actually, they weren't priests of the Lama but of the devil. It's difficult to believe that there should have been human beings capable of the things that are told about them."

"Then tell me. We are at the right place for stories of that sort, apparently. Sit down here. There are the same sort of benches here as in the room at the end of the canal."

I pulled him over to one of the stone benches, and he came with me, though reluctantly.

"One must not talk about these things," he said.

"Why not?"

"Because it is dangerous, particularly if it should really be true that this is the Maha-Lama Lake. It is said: Woe unto him who dares enter the site of the former lake, or even look down on it. It's impossible to get to it, and it would occur to no one to try to find it because people are convinced that that can only bring disaster. No one mentions it, no one even thinks about it. That's why I said just now that there was no such place. And that's also why I don't think we can be certain that we really are at the Maha-Lama Lake."

"That's very interesting. What is there so remarkable about this lake?"

"It's a legend, but people believe it."

"Do you believe it?"

"Why shouldn't I? Much of what is taken for fairy tales is true."

"I would put it differently. There is a grain of truth or a hint in most fairy tales and legends. To heed it, one must discover what it is. And that is probably the case here. So why don't you tell us?"

The Maha-Lama Lake

"At a time when the tributary had not yet been blocked, there lived a Maha-Lama that was the most famous of them all. His people loved him but the devil hated him. He had lived to be one hundred years old. On his birthday he was walking along the bank of the river, thinking to himself: 'If I could only live another hundred years! How happy I would make my subjects!' No sooner had he thought this than the devil appeared before him, and said: 'You can, if you want to.' He raised his hand. There was a horrible noise and the entire earth quaked and opened up before the Maha-Lama, creating a wide, deep crater into which the river disappeared immediately. At the same moment, precipitous rocks had risen from the ground. Far too tall for anyone to scale them, they formed a wall all around the crater. The Maha-Lama was frightened, but the devil told him: 'Calm yourself. Nothing will happen to you. I came to grant your wish, not to destroy you. You will live exactly one hundred years more and your people will be even happier than they are now. I only demand one thing in return.' The Maha-Lama asked what that was, and the devil answered: 'The water of this small river which now seems to be disappearing in this crater will rise again and form a lake. In this lake, you will drown all those who offend and insult you. That's all I ask.' The Maha-Lama laughed: 'I can accept that condition. No one offends or insults me; they all love me. Will I live another hundred years if I agree?' 'Yes, even longer. You will live until you have thrown so many into this lake that it will dry up and disappear again. If no one offends you, you need not drown anyone. But should someone offend you and you fail to drown him, you will die on the spot and your soul will be mine for all eternity.' Because of his desire to live another hundred years, the Maha-Lama signed the pact with his own blood, sure that he would not have to sacrifice a single person, for everyone had always loved him. But when people saw the suddenly risen, insuperable rock wall and became aware that the river that had nourished so many had disappeared behind it, there was one who accused the Maha-Lama because he had been there at the time of the disaster. The Maha-Lama wanted to forgive him. But the devil appeared, showed him the hidden path to the lake which only he could find, and gave him a single day to drown this man or else to die himself and lose his soul. The Maha-Lama obeyed. The man disappeared and was not seen again. This aroused suspicion against the Maha-Lama, and some expressed it, but they never returned home again. The suspicion now became certainty. First his followers and then his friends turned against him until finally he was as universally feared and hated as he had once been respected and loved. The water had long since become a lake and created a passage to what had been the mouth of the river, and the number of unfortunates who were tied to heavy stones and lowered into the depth increased. What had at first been an almost bottomless crater began to fill up. The lake became shallower and shallower. The hundred years were not nearly over yet, and already there was no room left for more corpses. From the completely filled lake, the small tributary carried the bodies out into the open, and that is how this mass murder became known. The Maha-Lama had become a despot, a hypocrite, a blasphemer and a criminal, and the people united to chastise him. But the devil got to him first and seized him because this was an insult the Maha-Lama did not punish. From the first day on, the rock walls the devil had caused to rise from the earth had been hated and avoided. But when it was learned what had happened behind it, this aversion deepened immeasurably. And later, when the small tributary and the large river disappeared, and death and desolation came to the city and the region, it was said that every night, the moment it had become dark, the spirit of the Maha-Lama appeared on the shore of his lake to wait for a helper to deliver him from his hellish torment."

"That is the old legend of the Maha-Lama Lake. What do you think, Effendi? Is it truth, or a lie?"

"Probably both, a truth behind a veil of lies. As long as it is dark, I can say nothing, but this mystery will probably be solved like all those other universal problems which appear in the garb of legend and fairy tale because they would be incomprehensible otherwise. If the figure standing over there really is an angel, you may be the man to deliver the Maha-Lama from his torment."

"Me?" he asked in surprise. "I don't know what you mean. I don't understand you."

"That isn't necessary at this time. You won't hear but see what I mean, but you cannot do that until it has become light."

"Then you aren't afraid of the Maha-Lama Lake, if that is where we really are? And what about the ghosts and spirits people talk about?"

"They don't exist as far as I am concerned. In all the cases where people spoke of 'spirits' or similar creatures, and I investigated the matter, I have always found that what was said to be supernatural was just as natural as all other natural phenomena. Where is this lake in relation to the other parts of the town?"

"You saw the citadel. Did you also see the high, strong walls around it?"

"Yes."

"But you did not see its western part, which is not surrounded by a wall but built directly against the ring of rock which circles the lake. Those rocks are the best, most natural protection and could never have been built by even the best builder of fortifications. The western chain which constitutes the outer city area is much further away. If you climb its highest point, you can see into the crater, although you would only be looking through a narrow gap and not all the way down to its bottom. But one can see the head and the upper part of the angel."

"So no one has ever entered the crater?"

"Not as far as I know. Of course, it has become apparent that I know less about the 'City of the Dead' than I thought. So it is not impossible that people have been there. But I don't think so."

"If someone had been here, we would probably find tracks, at least if it was visited recently. But for that investigation also we have to wait until daylight. We should eat now, and then sleep."

"Sleep?" the Mir asked. "With all this excitement?"

"You no longer have any reason to be excited. Halef can unpack. We haven't had any supper, and the horses and dogs also must be fed and watered. But we have to make sure to leave both water and fodder for tomorrow. I hope that we will find everything here we need, but—"

"Everything?" little Halef interrupted. "Water too?"

"Yes, even water. But caution demands that we keep some for an emergency."

While Halef and the two Ussul unpacked our provisions and fed the horses and dogs, I returned to the opening through which we had come so that I might have a look at it from the side on which we now found ourselves. I wanted to close it to protect myself against possible surprise moves from the canal. It would have been careless to light a lamp. Since I now knew the mechanism, I would probably no longer need my eyes but could rely on my sense of touch. It had to be possible to close this door not only from the inside, but from the outside as well. It could therefore be expected that I would find keyholes on this side. I assumed that they would be located at the same height and at the corresponding place, and this assumption was confirmed. My finger tips immediately identified two places to the right and the left of the opening. I used my knife to clear them of the accumulated dust and then tried the key. It fitted. There was a spring there which snapped back and forth. It was not difficult to lock the door; I merely had to take care not to be hit and thrown down by the heavy stone. Since it was now inside, I had to pull it, for I did not want to remain inside the canal. I thought that this might require a considerable effort because there was no handle of any sort, but the slope of the slab on which the stone rested at that moment had been calculated so

: 455 :

carefully that it required a mere touch and the colossus moved. I had to jump back quickly to avoid being pushed down. When it had returned to its position, it stopped and I heard the spring snap back into place.

7 : The Deserted City

The Mir had not remained with the others, but had come to the door with me. He explained to me that he could not eat, that he was not hungry. I checked his pulse. The man had a fever.

"Are you ill?" I asked.

"No," he answered.

"Just excited?"

"Very. I feel my blood pounding against my temples."

"Why? Feel my pulse."

"You are different, Effendi. You are a stranger here; the whole affair doesn't concern you. But I am deeply involved. Tell me, do we have to stand here?"

"Why are you asking?"

"Because I cannot sit or stand still. I have to run, to move. I don't know what's the matter. I have never been so restless, or so moved."

"Come along then. I think we can take the chance. Let's walk away from these columns and their roof of rock and out into the open, under the stars."

"Yes, Effendi, let's go outside. Out into the open! Under the stars! How terrible it was back there inside the canal, in that stagnant, immobile air, in that dead, lifeless darkness! I didn't say so but I really got frightened, terribly frightened there. Come along."

I placed his arm under mine. We left the arcade and walked slowly out into the night. But we were not alone. My two dogs abandoned their food and followed us. These faithful animals considered it their duty not to leave me unprotected in this darkness. We walked for a while without speaking. He did not know whether he should tell me what was moving him so profoundly. But I preferred to wait for him to begin because I probably would have frightened him into silence and made all communication impossible, had I said something. Thus we walked on and on. We did not see the entire firmament, for the tall rock walls limited our horizon, but some stars were sparkling above us. Just then the first quarter of the new moon appeared as a narrow, thin arc behind the highest, most precipitous rocky ledge, pouring a mysterious light over us and everything towering round about us. We saw that it was indeed an angel standing in the very center of the wide, deserted square at whose edge we found ourselves. Involuntarily, we walked toward it.

"Yes, we are at the Maha-Lama Lake," the Mir said. "There can be no doubt about it. That is the angel whose head I saw so often when I was standing on the western heights, looking over here with a youthful shudder. Perhaps we should turn and go back."

"Why? Are you afraid?"

"Almost. Yes. And yet it draws me there as if I had to discover something, as if I had unconsciously long yearned for it. Effendi, don't laugh! I am not talking nonsense, I am not raving; I am merely telling you how I feel."

"Why should I laugh? When a man's soul begins to speak, it is always a serious, sacred, momentous occasion. Listen to what it tells you. Don't interrupt it. Don't speak to me until it has become quiet again."

Thus silence returned. The large, wide, utterly level expanse across which we were walking had once been a lake, the Maha-Lama Lake. Looking back, we could see the arcade we had left. Being closer to us than anything else, it was fairly clearly visible and appeared to circle the entire area that had once been a lake. As we approached the angel, the figure kept increasing in size and distinctness. It was certainly twice as tall as the one we had discovered near the Chatar defile, but identical in shape. It seemed as if the one we were seeing was the original of the one we had discovered earlier, as if the latter were merely a smaller copy of the one we now had in front of us. What if I had guessed right, and it contained water?

Now Uucht suddenly stopped, raised her head and then one of her forefeet, stretched her neck as far as it would go, and sniffed. She raised her tail, moved it back and forth with increasing speed, and finally wagged it in the manner familiar to me, appearing eager and confident. Aacht followed suit. This reassured me. I was no longer worried about anything that might happen here. My dogs had discovered the first trace of water. The angel was a well angel, precisely like the one I mentioned earlier. Naturally, I did not hesitate to draw whatever inferences seemed logical. The myth of the Mir would necessarily reveal itself for what it was. In it, truth had not merely been disguised but turned into a lie.

As we walked on, the movements of the dogs became more animated. I forbade them to utter a sound. Surprised, their glances travelled back and forth between the angel and me. They assumed I had not understood them. I patted them to express my appreciation, and this calmed them immediately.

"What do your dogs want?" the Mir asked me.

"They are simply telling me something you will discover soon."

"Is it something evil?"

"No, something good. It is my hope that from now on we will experience nothing but good here. Do you know perhaps what the Maha-Lama gave his victims to eat and drink before they were thrown into the lake?"

"Nothing, of course."

"How do you know?"

"Surely that's obvious. People doomed to be thrown into the water the moment they were taken prisoner would hardly be given something to eat and drink beforehand."

"Are you convinced that all of them were killed immediately? That the Maha-Lama made no exceptions? Look at this arcade, these pillars. To hew them out of the rock and to hollow them out is a gigantic task which could hardly have been undertaken by corpses, let alone by spirits or ghosts, but only by living, healthy, strong, and vigorous human beings. And there weren't just five, ten, or twenty workers here but

: 458 :

hundreds, even thousands, and they were given good, ample food. And water was an even greater necessity. Where do you suppose all that came from?"

"The Lake, of course."

"Which was filled with dead bodies?"

This question gave him pause. He reflected for a few moments and then admitted:

"I cannot answer your question, Effendi. All that is known is that the Maha-Lama never had a single drop of water transported from the wells of the city to the lake."

"Are you absolutely sure of that?"

"Yes, for that is one of the principal reasons to believe that he did not let his victims live but killed them immediately."

"If it is true that he did not have drinking water brought from the city for the workers he employed here, he must have had a well here, and it must have been a very large one that would never dry up and could produce at least as much water as was needed, and perhaps much more."

"Do you really think so?"

"I do. And where was this well? Where is it now?"

"Who can tell?"

"Can't you?"

"No, certainly not."

"Come along then. I'll show it to you."

"You? A stranger? A European? A man who knows nothing about this place whatever?"

"Yes, the same. Come with me."

We had reached the angel. As before, I took the Mir by the arm and led him to the base, which differed from the one on which the angel near El Chatar rested. There, it consisted of natural rock, while here brick steps led to the feet of this angel. Every day, countless workers had been busy here, so a more convenient access had had to be constructed than at the other place in the middle of the desert. The steps were perhaps six or eight inches high; it was easy to mount them. As we walked up, it occurred to me that I should have waited until daybreak. Then it would have been easier to find the trapdoor and the stairs. Also, if I surprised the Mir while it was still dark, it might look as if I wanted to show up his ignorance. But that certainly wasn't the case. I was going ahead at this moment because I wished to take advantage of his mood, which was such that the effect would be twice as great as at a later time.

I assumed that the interior of this angel would be identical to the other I already knew, and to my great satisfaction it turned out that I had not been mistaken. When we had arrived at the top, I did not waste time looking for chinks or cracks which it would probably have been difficult to find in the dim moonlight, but headed straight for the fold in the garment to see if this point could be moved. I did not succeed immediately, for after such a long time the mechanism did not function right away. But when I applied some pressure on a section of the garment, it receded into the figure. This raised the trapdoor which had closed the stairway.

"What is this?" the Mir asked in astonishment. "The angel is hollow?"

"As you can see."

"There is a hole. Can one walk down there?"

"Yes. Down to the well that I want to show you."

"To the well?—the well?"

"Yes. Come down with me, follow me. There's no need to be afraid. Grope your way. If you place your hands firmly against the rock, you won't fall."

The dogs pushed their way in and down. I calmed them, for they would have to wait outside. Using the same procedure as before, I cautiously went down with the Mir, constantly keeping the angel at El Chatar in mind. Here also, the steps led from the right to the left. They were solid and well preserved. With my outstretched foot, I tested each one carefully. As inside the El Chatar angel, there were twenty of them, and the air was just as cool and contained as little moisture as at the other place. I did not ask myself if there really was water in this well, for if there was in the earlier one, there could be no question about this one. It was obvious to me that both had been constructed on the same bed of rock.

When I had reached the floor of the uppermost level, I immediately turned to the right to see if we would find light in the same way and at the corresponding place, and we did. I could feel a large, hollow cube of rock which was covered by a thin, light stone slab which could be moved. I pushed it aside, put my hand into the opening, and retrieved a long roll of sturdy leather which had been tied at both ends to protect its contents from dampness. There was a very well preserved wax candle inside which I lighted immediately. The Mir ws still halfway up the stairs. This great, Eastern aristocrat was not used to climbing about in dark places, and so he made his way only slowly.

"So you even have a light?" he asked. "Allah be praised. I'll be down right away."

I lit a second candle which I handed to him.

"Am I also getting one?" He looked at it in surprise. "Where did you get it ?"

"Here, in this stone container. There are many more inside. And also other useful things. All of this has been kept here for us."

"Yes. For whom else? We are the only ones here."

"What a person you are! a magician, a real sorcerer."

"Not at all! I am a perfectly ordinary person, no better and no worse, no smarter and no more stupid than thousands of others."

"But you know absolutely everything."

"Believe me, I'm not omniscient. I'm the same as anyone else. All I know is what I know from others, or heard, and saw. I should tell you that I've been inside the very same sort of water angel before, with my excellent Hadji Halef Omar. We investigated it from top to bottom. And while this one here is perhaps twice as tall, it was built in the very same way and has the identical interior. So there is no merit in my knowing this place better than you do, for you have never seen or searched through an angel like this. Do you see these moving wheels, the belt, the bowls, and the trough the water drips into? It is raised from one level to the next—"

"A miracle, a miracle," he interrupted me. "Who constructed it?"

"The Mir of Djinnistan."

"Impossible."

"Why should that be impossible?"

"Here, in the middle of my own country? In what was once the capital and residence of Ardistan?"

"Is that so difficult to understand?"

"Of course! And not just in the middle of the country and in the middle of the residence, but even right in the center of the Maha-Lama Lake, which was an unfathomable mystery to me and all my predecessors."

"Which means that it was a secret, the secret of the Mir of Djinnistan who lives right among you without you knowing it, who is active here without your permission and knows all of you inside out without your ever having seen him."

"You are joking, Effendi."

"Not at all. I am utterly serious."

"Then I don't understand you. I really don't understand you this time. Remember that it was precisely your opinion that only the Maha-Lama of whom I told you could have constructed this well."

"That is my opinion. But it was the Mir of Djinnistan who gave him the idea, and everything else besides."

"How can you prove that?"

"Look up there."

As I said this, I stepped on the edge of the stone container from which I had taken the candles and raised my arm so that the light fell on the sign of the Mir of Djinnistan engraved above the stairs. Directly below it, one could see the word "built" written in the old Brahmana dialect.

"It's his sign, his sign," the Mir called out. "And I have to see this! Someone dared do this! If only I could punish such an offense."

"Why punish?" I asked very calmly. "Did this well harm you?"

"No. But it is an insult to me, an insult which I will not tolerate—"

He stopped before finishing his angry words for I had quickly jumped off the container and stepped close to him. I raised the candle and gave him one of those glances which cannot be false because they come straight from the soul. He did not dare continue but looked down and remained silent. Barely audibly but quite distinctly, I asked him:

"The Mir of Djinnistan whom you feud against gave your poor 'City of the Dead' this saving well which can restore it to life. You, its master, only have to wish it. We will probably discover that he gave it even more, much more, than just this water. Tell me now, what did you give? What did you do to transform this death into life? This once so magnificent city, which today would be one of the most beautiful and famous of the entire Orient had your ancestors been worthy of it, declined through the cruelty and inhumanity of its rulers. When you were still a child, you looked on its corpse as a nightmare that frightened you and sent shudders down your spine. You were not taught to think higher thoughts. And when you had become a man and a ruler, this magnificent valley which loudly entreats you, its lord, asking for mercy and compassion, merely served you as a remorseless abyss of hatred and revenge. You did not cast a single warm glance at this city that had died. And now that you hear that he whom you cannot tolerate because he has compassion for all suffering and misfortune has come to do it good, to save it, you become indignant, claiming that he has offended you and that you cannot tolerate that. How petty you are, O Mir! And how harmful! Harmful to all of humanity, your people, and even yourself."

"Effendi, you are being rude."

He had said this more in reproach than in wrath. That meant that he felt not only smitten but also so depressed that he no longer had the heart to strike poses. But I did not allow this to affect me and continued as before:

"And consider what this wholly imappropriate pride of yours really means. You are a prisoner. You are meant to die of thirst and hunger. And it was your excessive self-confidence that got you into this position. You relied on your knowledge of this locality, which has proved to be wholly inadequate. A man such as yourself, a ruler, should be careful never to allow himself to fall into such impotence. Once respect is gone, it is never recovered as quickly as it was lost. For Halef and myself, you are now just a helpless child, nothing more. Not only do you find yourself in the realm of death but among living enemies as well. For surely you realize that those who are now your companions are not your friends but your adversaries?"

"What do you mean? It never occurred to me that you were my adversaries. On the contrary, I consider you my friends, real, genuine, noble friends. You will not abandon me."

"No, we won't. But remember that the Erdjani and his army are at the borders of your country and that we, Halef and I, are their comrades in arms. You made the prince of the Tshoban what he is. Not only because of his people but also because of his brother, he cannot help but be your enemy. And finally, consider that the two princes of the Ussul also have no reason to sacrifice themselves for you. In their country, every one knows perfectly well that you look on them merely as hostages, that you imprison them whenever you please, that you punish their troops and exile and humiliate them, whether deservedly or not. Only recently, these two honest, sincere young men were once again incarcerated in the 'City of the Dead.' Why? What crimes did they commit?"

"But I released them again," he objected.

"That only changes the consequences of what you did, not the act itself. They knew that their lives hung by a thread, a single word of yours. Now you are here yourself, a prisoner, helpless and doomed to die. How great, how glowing do you think their enthusiasm to sacrifice themselves for you will be? Do you believe they love you, or do you think they fear and hate you?"

He did not reply.

"You are silent. It's undeniable that you are surrounded by enemies. Yet you are grandiloquent like a ruler whose mere gesture will cost all of us our heads. You, who can save neither yourself nor any of us, feel offended by the water which alone can do that. You will owe your life and ours to the Mir of Djinnistan, and I expect you to speak of him with the respect and the calm that befits anyone who mentions him, at least in our presence. Follow me now. We will continue our descent."

He followed me without saying a word. I quite deliberately had spoken to him in this manner, and I hoped that the surroundings would deepen the impression my speech had made. In particular, I called his attention to the words that had been inscribed above the stairs and which, when put together, read as follows: BUILT FOR VICTORY IN THE STRUGGLE FOR PEACE. When we arrived at the bottom, we saw a veritable lake of the purest drinking water in front of us, which indicates the dimensions of the underground vault in which it had collected. He scooped up a handful and tasted it. Then he said:

"Stay."

Between the wall and the water, there was a circular stone walk. The vault itself, which was supported by a gigantic central pillar was circular in shape. The walk followed the circumference of the water. The Mir walked slowly along this line. Its radius was so large that the tiny flame of the candle disappeared in the impenetrable darkness after only a few moments. Only his steps could be heard. I could clearly tell that their echo was traveling up to the dome, but it could not return on the far side. This caused the sound waves created by the steps to collect up there, creating a thunderous roar which was no more than the mysterious rustling of a few, half-wilted leaves where I was standing. Then even that stopped. The Mir was no longer moving.

It was a curious, even an indescribable situation. After a while, the rustling returned, but only briefly. The Mir had made a movement, probably to sit down. There followed a very long pause, an hour perhaps, of utter stillness. Then I heard some curious hissing, almost snorting sounds. Was he crying perhaps? A short while later, beyond the water, there was a loud blustering that sounded like four individuals, angry thrusts interrupted by three short pauses. Forgetting that I could hear him, the Mir had probably uttered some excited exclamations which reached me not as words but as unintelligible noise. But in the dome, where all that confusion coalesced to articulate itself again, the laws of acoustics caused the individual sounds and words to return to a harmonious order. They came back down to me so softly, so intimately, and yet so clearly, that it reminded me of a cherished person bringing his lips close to my ears to tell me something welcome. There was a murmur: "He is right ... I want ... I want ..."

It was this insight, this decision, that he had struggled to achieve. Involuntarily, unguardedly, these words had risen from his heart and he probably wasn't considering whether I might have heard and understood them, or not. Now he returned, but from the other side. He had circled the basin.

Holding the candle in his hand, he walked past me without saying a word and mounted the stairs, absorbed in his thoughts. I followed him without anger at his inattentiveness. When we had come to the upper level, he did not stop but blew out his candle, replaced it in the container from which I had taken it, and ascended to the top. I followed him, but less hastily.

As I left the stairwell and stepped back out into the open, I was greeted by my dogs, whom I had left behind. They had been worried about me; they got up on their hind legs, and tenderly pressed their forelegs against me. The Mir had already gone down the steps, and was now standing on the lowest one, waiting for me. Since I had delivered my sermon, he had spoken only two words to me. Now, as I approached him, he asked:

"Effendi, what sort of person are you? What you desire, you accomplish, even if it hurts another person."

"Was it good or bad?"

"It was good."

"Then you should make it a habit, as I have done. One should accomplish the good whether it injures someone or not. Only an evil person reasons about the pain he causes."

"And it certainly was pain, and not a small one. When I was standing down there by the water, I thought I would have to jump into it to drown myself. But then I also thought of my mother, the only person who has ever loved me. It was as if she were standing by my side, helping me bear up under your serious accusation. And I saw that you were right in everything you said to me, and confessed it so as no longer to deceive myself. I called it out across the water; it was as if everything were to come tumbling down. You must have heard the noise that made. Are you now returning to your companions?"

"Yes."

"I shall stay here and wait. I request that you tell the Erdjani and the prince of the Tshoban that I will gladly talk to them, now, on this spot. Will you do that?"

"Gladly! May God bless you! And not only you but everything you discuss with them."

I left with my dogs. He stayed behind. But I had hardly gone some twenty paces when I heard his voice behind me:

"Effendi!"

"What is it?"

"I read what you showed me: 'Built for victory in the struggle for peace.' And I not only read it but also thought about it, down there, by the water. No one can give what he does not have. I cannot give my people peace unless I have it within me. Is that true?"

"Yes. This well lies within your own country, and it is through it that the Mir of Djinnistan took hold of what is within you. Think about that."

When I rejoined my companions, they had just finished eating. I had some food, and told the Erdjani and the prince of the Tshoban what the Mir wanted from them. Both of them were immediately willing to accede. "That will be a very important discussion," the Erdjani said. "A great deal depends on it, probably peace itself. But you, Effendi, have not yet told me your experiences after leaving me. It would be better if I could speak to you at some length before having this discussion with the Mir."

"Is it really true that you heard nothing?" I asked with a smile. "Did Halef really not say anything at all? That would be the first time."

"No, Sidi, I did not keep quiet," the little Hadji interrupted quickly. "I told everything, absolutely everything. The time before your return was short,

: 467 :

and so I hurried. But now they know everything and it is unnecessary for you to begin again at the beginning and to run through our adventures. And should I have forgotten something, I will get back to it, depend on it!"

"You don't have to reassure me, Halef," I laughed. "I am completely convinced that what you are telling me is true. It is not necessary to add your assurances."

When the Erdjani and the prince had left and I had finished my supper, I gave the horses and dogs all the remaining water. What they had been given before had not been enough because we had thought that we would have to be sparing. But now we no longer needed to economize. Halef, of course, immediately reminded me that the water would have to be saved for the following day.

"Or is there water here?" he asked.

"Yes."

"Where? In that angel?"

"Of course."

"What does it look like? How is it set up inside?"

"Precisely the same as the angel at El Chatar. But there is even more water in this one, much more."

"Hamdulillah! We have won, won! I'll leave right now to show our two companions the form and internal mechanism of the angel."

He rapidly rose and called on the two princes of the Ussul to follow him. They were quiet, genuinely good human beings who were happiest when left alone, and only spoke when spoken to. Neither one of them had ever initiated a conversation with me. They were less constrained with Halef. Now, as they were about to accompany him to the angel, they looked at me questioningly. Would I permit it? I shook my head.

"Please stay, Halef. You can't go there now."

"Why not?"

"Because the Mir is having a discussion with the Erdjani and his companion."

"We won't interfere. We'll walk quietly past them."

"Merely seeing you would be disturbing, for it would cause the Mir to discuss the internal mechanism of the angel and thus distract him from the main direction his thoughts should take."

"Main direction? Thoughts? Sidi, I don't understand you. When I have a thought, and it has a main direction, I should like to see the person that could divert me from it, or it from me, or the two of us from the main direction. But since I am your true friend and protector, I will do as you ask, as always. We'll stay; I won't leave you by yourself."

"I thank you for your protection, Halef. There is much to be done when the night is over. Let's sleep and gather the strength we'll need."

I walked up to Syrr, who lay down at my signal to serve me as a pillow. I stroked him affectionately and fell asleep, and I assume he did too. When I awoke, not only the night but the dawn had come and gone and daylight was spreading over what had once been the Maha-Lama Lake. Halef and the two Ussul were still sleeping, the Mir was nowhere to be seen, and the Erdjani and the prince of the Tshoban were sitting next to each other, talking softly. I got up, walked over to them, and sat down, having first scrutinized the area in which we found ourselves.

I can say that I was seized by a profound astonishment, a curious religious dread, or perhaps only religious in part, for this solemn solitude and quiet everywhere could not wholly mute the macabre thought that in the depth of this present, in the past, there lay hidden the uncanny, horrible sediment from which this deeply moving soundlessness had struggled free, and which was not like the stillness of death, but like that which settles after torment, torture, and suffering.

The area the lake had once occupied was so vast that we could just see across it. The perspective reduced everything on the far side to such an extent that what was one hundred and fifty or two hundred feet high where we were only seemed six or eight feet tall over there. The surface of the former depression was as level as a table top. One could not see the slightest rise, apart from the angel, of course, which stood in the very center. The rock walls, on the other hand, rose precipitously and without leaving even the smallest gap or opening, and had the appearance of the gigantic walls of a huge arena dating back to earliest antiquity. The stone seats were missing, but not the spatial dimensions large enough to accommodate the bloody massacres of human beings and animals for the amusement of the beast in man. I did not believe that unaided nature could have produced rock walls so similar to those created by men. Their vertical expanse did not show the slightest projection, the most minor irregularity. There could be no question that countless thousands of people have been at work here. And just as the attempt had been made to prevent anyone from climbing these walls on the inside, we saw later that the outside also had been smoothed down so completely that no one could have passed the tall, pointed battlements to cross over to the lake.

The first glance I cast over the enclosure showed me that human labor had been used here, on the inner as well as the outer wall. The outside had been hewn to a smooth, vertical wall, as I mentioned. Whatever gaps there may have been had been filled so perfectly that a keen eye was needed to distinguish what was natural creation, what human effort. Then a very high and wide hidden walk had been constructed which circled the entire lake at ground level. It was a more than astonishing achievement, and certainly a project that had required several centuries. At twenty-foot intervals, powerful pillars had been left standing whose arches, extending both laterally and backward, supported the masses of rock resting on them. Thus the miraculous structure, the arcade, had been built to look like an uninterrupted series of pillars circling the gigantic foot of the rocks. It was wide enough to allow twelve men to stand side by side without touching and had the height of two average stories. This meant that a distance of about ten yards separated the inner wall of the arcade from the main rock wall. There was not the slightest trace of any door. Yet doors there had to be, for there were windows, although they did not resemble what is ordinarily understood by that term. This leads me to the second type of gigantic labor which had been carried out on the inside of the rock.

I had reason to assume that this huge circular rock formation had an "inside," that it was not solid but hollow, and that the material that had been obtained in the hollowing-out process had been gradually used to fill the lake. Inside this rock formation, there were rooms, some perhaps very spacious and very high, some perhaps very long. I inferred this from the many openings which I called "windows." They resembled the long, narrow, vertical openings for air and light which can be seen in the walls of barns, haylofts, and other places of storage, and looked like embrasures rather than windows. There were any number of them, and they formed a regular pattern. Between any two columns or pillars I counted four, always arranged in pairs. One of the pairs was located in the wall of the arcade that had been set back, at the point where the arch of the ceiling began. The second pair was high up in the main or external wall, some twenty feet above the other. These embrasures were about two feet wide and five feet high. One could tell from the outside that they were not level but sloped down on the inside. Thus they permitted light to enter more readily than if they had been horizontal. In addition, an airhole large enough to accommodate a clenched fist was set between every two pillars, in the center of the arched ceiling. If some provision for internal circulation had been made, this was adequate to keep a fairly sizable room free of stuffiness or unbreathable air. For this and other reasons I imagined that there were many good-sized rooms, although I could not see a single door. But I was convinced that we would discover first one, then several, and finally a large number, once we decided to try to find them. At this moment, we did not have the time for such an investigation. I had to talk to the Erdjani and his companion to find out if something had been discussed with the Mir that I needed to know.

"Sahib, we just talked about you," the Erdjani told me. He preferred addressing me by that term. "It was an important, a beautiful, I would even say a sublime night."

"Did something important happen?" I asked.

"No, nothing really important. And yet something of enormous significance for Ardistan."

"May I hear what it was?"

"You already know," he smiled.

"Ah, you mean the change in the soul of the Mir."

"Yes. He told us everything, and it did not sound like what your Halef told us. How courageous, reckless, and daring a man you are."

"I simply think carefully, that's all. And if my reflections lead to a good decision, I act on it, even if I should appear rude and inconsiderate."

"That's a risk you've certainly incurred repeatedly lately."

"Did he complain?"

"Oh, no. Not a word. He had nothing but praise for you, and I believe it was sincere. You can rest assured about the way he speaks and thinks about you. He did not complain about anyone, not even his enemies and the rebels. Nor did he complain about himself. There was no trace of self-accusation or confession. We discussed belief, the religions of the world, the value of the sciences, the art of princes, which consists in making their people happy, the obligations man has toward his fellow man and all kinds of other matters which you refer to as 'universal human problems.' One could tell that he was warmly and sincerely desirous of orienting himself about these matters, about us, about himself. He strikes me as the first good and useful fruit of a previously useless, perhaps even poisonous tree. Your presence in Ard has had an excellent effect. Up to now, he had always hated and despised the Occident, but now he is beginning to value and cherish it."

When the Erdjani stopped, the firstborn of the Tshoban commented:

"Just think of this place! The sharply defined section of the starry heavens with the mysterious, growing moon over the legendary Maha-Lama Lake! Consider the thoughts, intimations, and feelings aroused by all this. And then think of the three of us, each one different, each one with his own particular temperament, each one placed in an extraordinary situation by Providence. We three men are together for the first time, doomed to die, yet certainly not in despair. We hope that we will be saved by a European whom we honor, love, and trust, for he did not come to exploit us but because he truly loves us. And consider also the sanctity, importance, and scope of the questions that were discussed here, and you will agree that the hours of the night just passed were truly sublime. The discussion was general; nothing specific was mentioned. In particular, every one of us avoided even remotely touching on the affairs and conditions that are of such urgent concern to us. That is still to come. And yet I have the feeling that the imminent destiny of the people here was decided in the course of our conversation, and that in a favorable, happy, peaceful sense."

"I believe it, although I did not have the chance to be one of you. Where is the Mir now? Did he not accompany you here?"

"At daybreak, when we separated, he said that he could not possibly go to sleep. He intended to walk around the lake and then to come here."

"How imprudent! It is possible that we may not be the only people here. How easily he could expose himself to some danger from which he would be unable to escape unaided! A Mir is no ordinary human being. He should consider his importance, not just for himself but for others. But I think I see him. Someone is approaching out there."

Far out, under the pillars, there was a point which was moving toward us. As it came closer, we saw that it was a human being and then recognized the Mir. His face had a distinctive cast that day, like that of someone suffering from hunger, a fakir, a penitent. His eyes were glowing, his cheeks sunken. His voice sounded almost hoarse, as if his tongue were coated. I could tell that he was feverish although he tried to hide it. When he reached us, we rose to greet him. He gave me his hand and said:

"A night like the one just passed is something I never experienced. And the morning is still more enigmatic and mysterious than the night. Give me something to drink. I am thirsty."

"There is no water left; we have to go to the angel," I answered. "You should also eat."

"I can't."

"You have to. All of us do. It's your duty."

He threatened me with his raised finger and answered with a pale smile:

"Not I but you seem to be the Mir of Ardistan."

"My intentions are good. But you are free to do as you please, and even become ill, precisely at a time when it is necessary to be as strong, healthy, and vigorous as possible. Your rule is at stake, even as you eat and drink."

"Very well, I'll eat."

"Then we shall ride first to the angel for water. You have been taking a walk, looking at things, but I imagine you only saw part of what is there."

"No, everything."

"What did you discover?"

"Nothing that could be called a find. The place is deserted and empty; there is no trace of animal or plant life. But I am struck, profoundly amazed by the buildings I see here. Who would have suspected that? Who would have thought it possible? Even you are probably astonished, Effendi, not about this architecture in rock or these columns, for you have often seen greater things, but about something altogether different, and by that I mean myself and my ignorance."

"How so?"

"I am the ruler of this country, yet knew nothing of these gigantic structures. Will people believe what you tell them when you return home? Won't they find it absurd and take you for a liar?"

"No. People will consider your development, your history, and local conditions. They will reflect that in Lamaist countries, there always were two rulers, a secular and a spiritual one. They always pursued their own interests in such a fashion that neither could find out what the other was doing. And here is the main thing: The desert encroached upon your country and engulfed the best and most beautiful part of it. I mean not just the real, the physical desert, but also the temporal, the historical one. You lack a history. All you have left is legend. Localities and structures which were swallowed by this physical and historical desert thousands of years ago have been so utterly forgotten that no one remembers them. And the devil's legend you told me contributed to wiping out whatever memory remained. When after prolonged and cruel struggles your ancestors succeeded in turning the

Maha-Lamas into feeble shadows, they also attempted to suppress the historical consciousness of their deeds. The devil that cheated the Maha-Lama is an invention. I am very much inclined to believe that it was the people that were cheated. They were cheated out of a blessing beyond compare which would have preserved the old Ard even when the river returned to its source, as legend has it. The ancient Maha-Lamas were friends of the Mir of Djinnistan who did not want Ardistan, his neighbor, to turn gradually into desert. Do you know the name of the Maha-Lama who, according to legend, concluded the pact with the devil?"

"Yes. His name was Abu Shalem."

"That means 'Father of Peace.' The name confirms my guess. The secular rulers were always for war, the spiritual ones for peace. You also favor war; the Mir of Djinnistan favors peace. You forced war upon this country. I would not be surprised if I were to learn after my return home that your once beautiful country had become all desert. Come, let's ride."

While we had been talking, we had saddled our horses. We mounted and rode to the angel. The others followed. The Erdjani and the prince of the Tshoban, whose horses had been taken from them, were given our pack animals. Now, as the Mir was riding alongside me, he said nothing further. I must confess that I felt unhappy. It is my constant endeavor to treat those I encounter with friendliness and love, yet here conditions obliged me to be severely objective, even ruthless and abrupt at times. I was sorry about that, it hurt me, but I could not help myself, for I had to do my duty, and that duty consisted in letting this man know without a shadow of a doubt that up to this time he had given no thought to fulfilling the obligations God had imposed on him, that he had failed both as a human being and a prince. Should this cost me the goodwill he had shown me up to this moment, that goodwill wasn't worth troubling myself about.

As we led the others who did not yet know about it inside the angel, and I attempted to explain its meaning to them, they began to suspect that the old legend about the lake was no legend, but a lie pure and simple, invented to mislead posterity. The wheels and gears were oiled and all the parts made of wood or leather were wetted. When this had been done, the machine that scooped up the water functioned almost flawlessly and it did not take long to fill all our troughs, buckets, and skins, and to give our horses and dogs all the fresh water they wanted. Then we breakfasted and could begin to explore the interior of this huge monument.

To obtain an overview, we rode slowly around the entire structure. We saw no blade of grass, not the smallest insect, and there was nothing to suggest that any human being had been here in the recent past or was here now. I became convinced that we were the first in centuries to find the way in. Then, when we had finished and dismounted, I had no doubt that even the "Panther" and his old Bash Islami were ignorant of this place. All they knew was the vaulted canal. We had been meant to die of hunger and thirst at the point where it widened. They had been unaware that there was a hidden door which led outside. Here, where the lake had once been, we could therefore move about without any fear that someone might interfere with us.

What was most important now was to find the hidden doors. If the locking mechanism here was the same as the one on the stone which closed the canal, we first had to look for keyholes and then see if my knife key fitted all of them. I've already mentioned that each pair of windows between any two pillars had been cut in the center of the wall, at a point where the ceiling began. Common sense told me that this would also be the place where the door could be found. It would be directly below the windows. We looked there and noticed cracks and fissures, and then the keyholes, covered with what had once been damp dust. Of course, this dust was now dry and hard but easy to remove. When we had done this, we unfortunately found that my key no longer fitted. It was too small. We tried another place. There also, we found the door and the keyholes, but again my key would not fit. This time, it was too big. My companions were growing impatient. They went from pillar to pillar, clearing the holes of the hardened dust, and yet got no further than

I, who had sat down to reflect calmly. My key was now too small, now too big, and fitted none of the holes. Little Halef was profoundly unhappy about this lack of success. And he was also furious with me.

"How can one sit down here and put one's hands in one's lap the way you are doing, Sidi?" he exclaimed. "Can't you see how hard we are trying?"

"Did I order you to?" I asked.

"No."

"Then reproach yourself, not me."

"But something has to be done. We are working. You are doing nothing."

"Oho," I laughed. "I am thinking."

He planted his hands on his hips.

"I see. You are thinking. And while you are doing it, you look so stupid that I'm really beginning to fear for you. Don't you see that it will get you nowhere, thinking with such a face? If thinking is to be successful, a person mustn't look like a sheep or a frog. I told you that thinking is your job, and that doing is mine, but if you don't at least look as intelligent while you think as I do when I act, it would be best if we swapped roles and I did the thinking, you the acting."

"Very well. I agree, dear Halef. Sit down right here where I've been, and start thinking! You will do it better and faster than I."

I took him by both arms and pushed him down where I had been sitting.

"But Sidi, you know that I am not as trained in thinking as in other things and that I—"

I walked to my horse and got into the saddle.

"Are you going to leave me, Sidi?" he asked, having so unexpectedly been taken at his word. "Have you considered the consequences?"

"No, thinking is no longer my job, it's yours now. Farewell."

I rode off.

"Allah, Wallah, Tallah! He's really leaving me! He has no sympathy for me and my torment. He takes me at my word, but there's nothing solid there, it's all air. He wants to revenge himself for having been called a sheep and a frog. He's not a great, noble, sublime person. And when he comes back, I'll—" I heard no more for by this time, I had covered some distance and his voice no longer reached me. But soon I heard another one behind me. When I turned, I saw the Mir following me on his marvellous white stallion. I stopped. When he had reached me, he began:

"That's a good lesson you gave the sheik of the Haddedihn. I wonder if he'll profit from it?"

"I hope so, although it really wasn't my intention to teach him a lesson."

"What else?"

"I simply wanted to be rid of all this, that's all. I wanted to get away from all these questions being addressed to me. Everyone demands that I think, that I find the solution to these mysteries, and yet they won't give me the time and tranquillity for it. Thoughts don't come like mosquitoes from a puddle, nor in such numbers. One has to allow things to affect one, otherwise they cannot be fathomed. And that's as true here as everywhere else. I can only grasp the peculiarities and enigmas if I have an imaginative understanding of the period and the men involved in the creation of this giant structure. And it's only natural that I cannot arrive at that if someone like Halef keeps talking at me."

This was not precisely mincing words, but unfortunately the desire I had expressed was not understood or observed by the Mir. It simply did not occur to him that I might also include him, the ruler. He continued alongside me.

"Are you going to ride around this place again?" he asked.

"Yes. When we circled this area for the first time, someone or other was always talking to me. I did not really look at what I saw, and did not have the concentration to reflect. I have to do that now."

"I wonder if you will find now what you didn't before. It would be regrettable not to understand a single one of these mysteries when we are right among them. You mentioned looking at things but also thinking about them, seeing them with both the physical and the inner eye. I only understand part of what you mean. But I imagine that your search would be easier if you knew more about the conditions under which these gigantic structures were built. I think I can help you there. I have to make a confession, a confession that refers to the implacable enmity between my ancestors and the old Maha-Lamas. The secular rulers, my ancestors, always were the victors in these bitter struggles and several of the spiritual leaders lost their lives as a result. Early this morning, when I was walking past these pillars, I asked myself whether I should tell you about it or not. You have become my conscience. You can burden but also relieve me. When I wish to understand my errors, I ask you, for you are true and just. You don't excuse a single one, and yet, with all your severity, you are also kind, for you always let me see the reason, the beneficial effect of your severity. And if I wish to comprehend the errors of my ancestors, I must tell you everything I know about them. Then you can tell me if there was also some praiseworthy purpose, some beneficial result in what they did, or not."

I answered:

"That purpose is too profound for our mortal eyes to fathom, and the result lies in your hands."

"In mine?"

"Yes, for you are the representative of your tribe. All that your ancestors did that remains hidden and obscure so far, the good as well as the evil, weighs you down. A single ruler who gains the necessary insight may bring the errors of his entire family to a good end and thereby transform the curse pronounced by the world tribunal into pardon and blessing."

"If only I could," he exclaimed, clapping his hands like one who wishes to underline the strength of his desire.

"You can if you have the will. What counts is the will, the will."

Now he raised himself in the saddle, stretched out his arm as if to swear an oath, and affirmed:

"I have the will. Effendi, I will tell you, I will confess to you. You shall hear all the sins that have been committed against the people of Ardistan. Right now, I shall tell you all I know. That's the reason I followed you. I heard all these things from my mother. She was the only one that loved me, as she was also the only one who never lied to me about the deeds of the rulers of Ardistan. I was still young when she died, but now the depths of my soul are stirring and the warnings and tales of the dear departed are rising from their slumber. You must hear all this. I shall begin with—"

"No, no," I quickly interrupted him. "Not now, not now."

"Why not? I feel a strong urge; these things have to come out. I only followed you to be alone with you, to be able to tell you without being disturbed."

I stopped my horse, forcing him to do likewise, looked laughingly into his excited face, and asked him:

"So you are riding here by my side to tell me something?"

"Yes. I have a confession to make. In my name, and the name of those that were my ancestors."

"And you want me to be wholly attentive as you confess?"

"Of course."

"And I am riding here. Why?"

"To—to find the keys to the many doors," he answered hesitantly. Gradually, he was beginning to realize that I was not precisely enthusiastic about his company.

"And you want me to find all those keys?"

"Very much."

"But then I will really have to concentrate and not be distracted by other matters. The choice is yours. Either you, or the keys."

"Why not the two at the same time?"

"Impossible. Each of these two things requires one's undivided attention."

"Then I'll wait until later. The most important thing is to get these doors open. But may I stay with you?"

"If you don't talk."

"I'll be silent."

"Come along then."

We rode on. The poor man had no idea that his mere presence was distracting even if he remained silent. The further we went without seeing anything that might serve as a clue, the more fearful I became that this time also all my efforts would be fruitless.

And this upset my inner equilibrium and made me less susceptible to the impressions I wanted to receive. Fortunately, the rocks had more insight than the Mir. They absorbed my attention. They began to speak secretly, faintly, not in words but only in numbers at first. In one of the pillars, a crack had appeared that extended from the upper left to the lower right. Because it was not deep, I might have overlooked it but here, even such an insignificant fissure was at least a break in the eternal, stony monotony. Involuntarily, without any specific intent, I stopped by the pillar to have a look at it. There was nothing, not even dust. And yet I did see something of great importance. It was not in the crack itself but alongside it. There were two depressions in the stone, one above the other. Far from being conspicuous, they were so small that it would have been easy to overlook them. They could only be spotted from very close up. They seemed to have been made by a small, pointed stylus, and they formed figures which certainly had to mean something. I jumped from my horse to determine their position more accurately. They had been made at eye level. One of them seemed to be a letter, an Arabic Dshim, but the other was certainly the Chinese character for Orh. I went to the next pillar. Again, there were two signs, at exactly the same height. One was the Arabic letter Dal, the other a Chinese Tshhi. On the third pillar, there was an Arabic Be and a Chinese Liu. What was the purpose, the meaning of this? These signs were not only letters or words, but also had a numerical value. But how were they to be interpreted here? As letters or numbers? I decided on the latter. In Arabic, the letter Dshim is a 3, the letter Dal a 4, and the letter Be a 2. The Chinese character Orh is a 2, Tshhi a 7, and Liu a 6. This yielded the following sequence on the three pillars I had looked at:

	Arabic	Chinese
First pillar	3	2
Second pillar	4	7
Third pillar	2	6

I did not try to work out the meaning of these numbers at that moment. First, I had to discover whether all the pillars along the entire circle had these double signs incised on them, or not. Naturally, the Mir had also dismounted and I showed him what I had found.

"Do you perhaps believe that these signs have some connection with the keys?" he asked.

"Yes, I do. Consider how many rooms there probably are. They must be numbered. And so the keys have to be, too."

"But why not just Arabic numerals? Why the Chinese ones? They are unknown in Ardistan."

"Precisely for that reason. Only certain officials were meant to understand them, not everybody."

"But why did they choose Chinese signs, of all things?"

"Because almost every educated Lamaist knows Chinese. But we mustn't waste our precious time with questions of that sort. What we have to do now is to examine all the pillars to see if every one of them has its two numbers. The rest will take care of itself. Let's hurry!"

We could not proceed as quickly as one might imagine, for now and then other matters arose which delayed our progress. To make the round took us two full hours and the result was that there were only two pillars which had not been numbered. They were facing each other, one of them in the very center of the northern, the other in the center of the southern circle of buildings. It followed that there was something special about these two. We also noted that two successive pillars frequently carried identical numbers. It could therefore be inferred that they led to the same room, and that this room was larger than the more common ones which merely extended over the area between two pillars.

As regards the unnumbered ones, the rock surfaces belonging to them were either not hollow or the rooms lying in back of them had served as what we would call administrative offices or "porter's lodges." Should the latter be the case, they probably contained everything we needed and were looking for. But however closely I scrutinized the surfaces, tapped and touched them, I could not find a keyhole. This suggested that the wall here was solid and that no rooms lay behind it. There was a second fact which pointed in that direction. Precisely in the center of the largest stone, I saw a relief of the sun with twenty-four rays. At each side, two letters had been engraved, an Arabic Ta on the left, an Arabic Rhain or Ghain on the right. These letters gave me pause. The picture of the sun might lead one to believe that there was no interior space, for why should the one relief to be found anywhere be on a door where it could most easily be damaged? Yet the two letters undoubtedly had a purpose that had some connection with this sun. I stepped close to the stone and knocked against it. Strange! It sounded odd. Almost as if it weren't stone. When I knocked more firmly, some very fine dust, which the wind must have blown in over many years, sifted from behind it. So I had been mistaken when I had assumed that the sun was part of the rock, that it had been hewn out of it. That had not been the case; instead, it had somehow been attached to it. As soon as I understood that, I used the point of my knife to scratch the image, and discovered that the sun consisted of metal, probably zinc and copper which had been worked and etched in such a fashion that it could be taken for stone. This discovery made me change my mind, particularly because I noticed upon closer examination that the stone had been polished smooth where the rays issued from the sun. This meant that at an earlier time the sun had moved, and moved very often. But how, in what direction, and for what purpose? Had the two letters perhaps been engraved here to provide an answer to these questions? Most probably. They were certainly the initials of words. I considered several possibilities but quickly rejected them until Tuluh and Ghorubb occurred to me. Tuluh esh Shems means the sun's rise, Ghorubb esh Shems its setting. The real sun rises and sets. Could this perhaps mean that this man-made bronze sun should be pushed or turned from the letter Ta toward the letter Ghain? I tried that, but it wouldn't work because of the dust which had collected between the rock and the metal. When I repeated the attempt by knocking and shaking more forcefully, the dust came loose and scattered. Now I could turn the sun like a wheel. I heard and felt that this movement pulled back a bolt. The huge, powerful, square stone changed its position in the very same way the stone at the end of the canal had, toward the inside, on tracks and with the aid of two surfaces, one of which came down, while the other rose to arrest the sliding stone.

"Mashallah—a divine miracle," the Mir exclaimed when the hidden door suddenly opened. "I almost got frightened. How did you find this? Are you omniscient, Effendi?"

"Hardly," I laughed, pleased with my success. "Omniscience merely means giving one's thoughts the proper direction. If that is done, the objective is attained. Let's enter."

I passed through the open door; the Mir followed. The room in which we found ourselves was fairly large. As we looked around, we saw that I had been right before when I had assumed that it would be something like an office, comparable to a porter's lodge. The room contained everything we needed in the way of tools, and luckily also the keys we had been trying to find. There were fifteen of them, hanging on one of the walls, and they were marked with Chinese numerals. They had the shape of knives whose handles could be adjusted so as to make them elbow-shaped. The bits were of bronze, narrowed toward the point, and had the hardness of steel. Since each bit had nine grooves running across it, there were ten wards, all of which were identified by Arabic numerals. And because these bits were all unlike each other in length and width, these fifteen keys could be used to open one hundred and fifty doors, provided one knew which key fitted which door and how far it would have to be inserted. As I realized this, I suddenly understood the purpose of the numbers we had seen on the pillars. The Chinese number referred to the number of the appropriate key, the Arabic one to the number on the ward having the profile to catch the one bolt for which it was intended. Every numbered pillar and the door following it belonged together. This discovery was of such enormous importance that I did not wait a moment to test it. I took the knife whose Chinese numeral was given on the next pillar outside, walked up to the door belonging to it, and removed the dust from the keyhole. The Arabic numeral was Arb'a, which means 4. I inserted the bit down to the fourth ward and turned. It worked. The moment I had completed the turn, the stone moved back so rapidly that it almost startled me. The Mir, who had followed me, exclaimed:

"Here, too, you can open doors. I am beginning to be afraid of you. And yet you are so quiet and say nothing."

It's true that I had been silent so that I could pursue my thoughts without intrusion. Nor did I answer now but went back into the room to continue my investigation. The tools were all in excellent repair. Drawn on Chinese rice paper, a detailed plan of the entire structure hung on the wall. At either side, there were two partial plans of the southern half where we found ourselves at that moment. Other maps, catalogues, and similar documents lay on a large table in the center of the room. But these and any number of other things did not interest me at this time. We left and mounted our horses to cross the open square. On the other side there were also two unnumbered pillars between which there might well lie a room similar to the one we had just discovered. Our assumption turned out to be correct. We found the very same sun and turned it as we had the first one. The stone receded and we entered a room of precisely the same size as on the opposite side. It also contained the same objects: the same tools, the same plans on the wall, and also the same keys, fifteen of them, with Chinese numerals and ten wards, each with an Arabic numeral. This meant that here, on the north side, there were also one hundred and fifty rooms. Their purpose was revealed by several larger and smaller plans which lay on the table. I was astonished to discover that there were many storage rooms for rice, beans, wheat, manna, leather, cloth, and other provisions. All that was indispensable for survival had been seen to, except weapons. Not war, only peace, had been planned for. There were apartments for higher and lower ranking officials, work rooms, sick bays, burial chambers, and even a temple. We also saw two counsel chambers which appeared to be quite large. They had been entered on the plan as "Djemmah of the Living" and "Djemmah of the Dead." By "Djemmah," the Bedouin means a tribunal or counsel of the elders of the tribe. It was impossible to determine just then what the expressions "Living" and "Dead" might refer to but we hoped to find out later. What we had to do now was to inform our companions and then make a tour of all the rooms so that we might acquaint ourselves with this unique structure. We therefore took one of the plans and the keys and rode back to the place where our comrades were waiting for us. When Halef saw us approach he called out:

"Sidi, I did some thinking but to no avail. Who's going to act on that? You or me? I think you'd better let me, because I—"

He stopped, jumped up, and continued in an entirely different tone:

"Hamdulillah! You found something. I can tell by the way you look; I know you. When there is that twitching around the corners of your eyes, one has reason to be content with you. I know you well."

"Yes, we can be satisfied with him," the Mir confirmed as we jumped from our horses. "Your Effendi is an incomprehensible human being, almost as incomprehensible as this huge structure that is so difficult to penetrate. But he found all the keys."

"Is that true, Sidi?"

I nodded and clanked the fifteen keys I had in my hands.

"You've got them with you? Formed like knives? Knife keys again? Will they unlock the doors?"

"We'll see right away."

I walked up to the first door we had discovered and tried the key whose number could be read on the pillar. The stone moved back into the interior of the room. As we went in, we saw that it had been filled from floor to ceiling with solidly made sacks of woven reed containing rice, the best, most beautiful rice one could desire. How many centuries had it been stored here? Should it not long since have rotted and become inedible? But the air was completely dry and remarkably pure. The ventilation I mentioned before had to be exceptionally well planned and efficient. And the rice gave off that curious, pleasant aroma it always has immediately after harvesting, and which is an infallible sign of quality. We were amazed. There must have been thousands of sacks, for, at the back of the room, a staircase went down a long way. When we walked up to it, we saw that the rooms below were just as full as the one we were standing in. The Mir had grown very grave. He placed his hand on my arm and said:

"Do you recall, Effendi, that you once asked me what I had done for my people? Whether I had put up buildings for storage?"

"Yes," I answered.

"I didn't. But the person who created this did. Don't laugh when I tell you that this abundance accuses me, this aroma of food and stilled hunger."

"I wonder if this rice is still edible?"

"I am sure of it. In antiquity, there was a period when people knew how to preserve grains for thousands of years. Such grain always retains the freshly harvested smell. I am convinced that this is rice of that sort. In those days, people knew of a moisture which made the bodies of the dead indestructible and preserved them in the very state that had been theirs during the last hours of life."

He was probably right. There are certain discoveries which were made in earlier times and which we must rediscover because they have been lost. Ruby glass would be an example, and so would the chemical composition of the liquid in which corpses were bathed to preserve them forever.

We went from room to room. In all cases, we managed to open the doors. There were more than twenty rooms that were filled with nothing but rice, and an equal number with manna, wheat, beans, lentils, and vegetables I did not know. I mentioned before that I would describe the "City of the Dead" elsewhere, and in some detail. This also holds for the gigantic structure at the former Maha-Lama Lake. Here, some brief, general observations will suffice.

Most important, I should mention that although we wasted no time, it took us two entire days to inspect every one of the three hundred rooms. We had our meals out in the open. There were enough pots, dishes, wood, and charcoal to cook, bake, and broil. It had not been our original intent to spend much time here. There were any number of reasons, especially political and military ones, which made it mandatory that we hurry. The country was without a ruler and the armies of the Ussul and the Tshoban without leaders. The flag of rebellion had been hoisted. Perhaps anarchy already prevailed. But the very people who had the most pressing reasons for concern, the Erdjani and the Mir, were so fascinated by the mysterious place in which we found ourselves that they stated they did not wish to leave before having at least superficially oriented themselves. They felt and recognized that their life paths had converged here at the doorway to a decision or a future which offered them infinitely more than they could lose to the "Panther" and his co-conspirators, even if worse came to worst. They always walked side by side, and always stood next to each other. They found pleasure in each other's company, and their relationship became ever more frank and beneficial. I interfered with them as little as possible, and since Sadik, the taciturn prince of the Tshoban, usually kept the two Ussul princes company, I asked Halef to stay close to me and to disturb them only when absolutely necessary. It was my belief that the association that was in the making here would last for the rest of their lives, and I wanted this development to occur at its own pace and without our direct influence.

In the course of one of the conversations between the Mir and the Erdjani, the latter began speaking of Abd el Fadl, the prince of Halihm. The Mir immediately interrupted him, and asked:

"The prince of Halihm? Do you know him, per-chance?"

"Yes."

"Does the Effendi know him, too?"

"Yes, he does."

"From where?"

"He is with our army. You must know him, too."

"How so?"

"I sent him to your capital, to Ard. He lives in your palace."

This was not a careless remark of the Erdjani's, but had been made quite deliberately, and I welcomed this openness. The Mir stepped back a few paces. With surprise, he looked first at the Erdjani and then at me.

"The prince of Halihm is called Abd el Fadl, his daughter Merhameh. Those are fairly common names and that's why they did not strike me. Do you mean to tell me that this singer Abd el Fadl and his daughter Merhameh are the prince and the princess of Halihm?"

"Yes, I certainly do," the Erdjani answered.

"Then you deceived me!"

"Deceived?"

"Yes, deceived. I was deceived, especially by you."

These last words had been directed to me. His brows contracted and his eyes flashed angrily. But I smiled at him calmly and asked:

"Do you feel you have been misled?"

"Yes," he maintained.

"Why? What is this deception I am guilty of?"

"It lies in the fact that these two names suddenly take on an entirely different meaning. The prince of Halihm is one of the staunchest supporters of the Mir of Djinnistan and that makes him one of my greatest enemies. And you send him into my country, my residence, my palace! Isn't that deception?"

"No, just cunning. Our intentions were good."

"Good? We'll have to see. At the moment, I am thinking that now everything that had been prophesied has been fulfilled: 'Peace' and 'compassion' raised their voices in my own house. Only because I believed that the minstrel and the girl were perfectly ordinary people did I fail to attribute to their names that significance which they have suddenly acquired. Now the most faithful adherent of my hereditary enemy finds himself in the palace which is my residence. Not only that, I also put special trust in him and thus was exposed to much greater dangers than I suspected up to now. You outsmarted me. Woe to you, should I decide to call you to account."

He was so angry that he left us. He went outside

: 489 :

and crossed the square toward the water angel where our horses were. We saw that he was busying himself with his, but did not allow his anger to spoil our good spirits. He would come back; there was nowhere else he could go. In the meantime, we continued our inspection of the locality. It wasn't long before he returned to inform us of a discovery he had made. He had wanted to water his horse again, and, while inside the angel, had heard a noise on the lowest level which we had not noticed before. Naturally, he lit a candle and descended. By its glow he saw that in the meantime the water had risen above the edge of the basin and was draining noisily through an auxiliary pipe installed for that purpose. This information was so important to us that we immediately went down inside the well to have a look. What he had told us was correct. The basin was overflowing and this overflow was so considerable that the pipe intended to accommodate it hardly sufficed. It sounded like the roar of a torrent and was the result of the volcanic eruptions in the sky-high mountains of Djinnistan. For months, and uninterruptedly, these mountains had been in flames. The snow- and ice-fields had melted. Before, when one looked up at the mountains from the south, they had looked white against the blue sky. Now, they were dark. The constantly radiating heat had devoured the ice of the glaciers. Masses of water had been created, and were still being created. New funnels were forming and where there were none, the abundant moisture penetrated the earth to find subterranean paths to the low-lying country and plain. I mentioned before that the angel wells lay along such subterranean waterways. Therefore, the effect was speediest and most noticeable inside them. This was no longer mere dampness but flowing, rustling water. I would not have been surprised had I discovered water in the dried-out river bed. As we continued our round, the Mir joined us without recurring to the matter that had aroused his wrath. He had understood that it would have been a great stupidity to be sulky with the only people who could extricate him from his predicament.

8 : Dreams

In the course of the afternoon, we went through the living quarters of the officials, where we found indications of the most happy family life. We also inspected many work rooms where all the crafts known in those days were represented. There were ateliers, and concert rooms for the performance of music. There were sick bays which seemed adequate even by present-day standards and, next to them, very large halls, some above, some below ground, which were burial sites. Toward evening, to round off the day, we visited the temple, which made a considerable impression on us, for it was of a rigorous and total simplicity. It constituted the inside of the tallest and most compact mountain of the entire circular layout, had been hewn out of the rock in its entirety, and given the form of a circular cone. There was not a single seat on its floor; that area was not designed for the community of believers. Instead, an unbroken spiral rose from the floor to the highest point of the structure, consisting of nothing but seats and forming a gradually ascending balcony with a solidly made balustrade. This balustrade was provided with hundreds of openings and a candle which had never been lit had been placed in each of them. It seemed that at some time in the very remote past, preparations for divine services had been made, but that before they took place it had been necessary to abandon the temple. At the very bottom where the spiral began, there stood a small, very simple pulpit. When I saw it, I wondered about the acoustic effect produced when the priest raised his voice to address the shining spiral above him. This may be a good place to say a few words about the illumination of all the interiors on the Maha-Lama Lake.

I have already mentioned the window openings that were located above each door. They were not horizontal but sloped down on the inside. This admitted more light but also dust, insects, and even animals, all of which might have an adverse effect on the supplies stored there. For this reason, these openings had been closed tightly from the inside. The result was that no air, though abundant light, was admitted. But how had this been done? It might be thought that glass of great purity and quality had been used, but that was impossible. Up to now, we had been unable to inspect the completely transparent, glass-like material more closely because the windows were too high to reach. But here, inside the temple, I could walk up the spiral balcony until I was level with the first window. I saw that it was a kind of muscovite which had probably been prepared in a manner unknown to me. It was quite as effective as the most transparent glass. But even during daylight hours, that wasn't enough to illuminate the huge, exceptionally high temple. This explained the abundance of candles.

It was only natural that we should want to ascend to the very top of the spiral balcony. And we did, or rather, the others did, while I remained behind to make some acoustic tests. After I had instructed my companions when and how to answer me, they started out on their slow circular path. I called it slow because they lit all the candles as they went along, one after the other. I spoke to them, and they answered. But the higher they got, the fainter their answers became. Finally, I no longer heard anything. Now I raised my voice to twice its former loudness and asked questions the answers to which I had asked them to memorize, but without result. They gave the answers but I did not hear them. This made a very curious impression on me. I saw the number of burning candles increase. Their line became longer and longer and mounted higher and higher until it reached the top of the temple. I later learned that my voice had penetrated there with the greatest possible clarity but their answers did not reach me. I was surrounded by a profound, total silence. Was this perhaps an intentional symbolism on the part of those who had once hewn this temple out of the dead rock? I am inclined to think so, for no one would undertake a difficult, time-consuming task without having given some thought to its effects. I was growing eager to get away from this oppressive sound-lessness, and hurried after my companions.

In the meantime, it had become evening, and thus not only total silence but utter darkness also sur-rounded me on the floor of the temple. Straight ahead of me, the line of lights rose up, describing an ever ascending, seemingly infinitely repeated, open-ended circle. That this circle became progressively smaller and narrower seemed, not real, but an optical illusion which doubled, decupled, indeed centupled the real height of the structure. It was as if it had been built straight into heaven, as if one could move from light to light and arrive directly before God's throne. And it was this path I now followed.

The higher I climbed, the greater the number of lights below me. But I deliberately refrained from looking down so as not to spoil the effect I would obtain later. Having arrived at the top, I noticed that there was an aperture leading to the outside, and as I stepped through it, I and my companions found our-selves on a platform of rock allowing a distant view which I noticed even then, though it was evening. The door which led from the top of the temple to this platform could not be locked. It consisted simply of a stone which could be pushed open and shut.

"You finally got here," Halef said when he saw me. "Did you hear what we called down?"

"No," I answered.

"But we roared! We understood every word you said. It sounded as loud and powerful as an organ or a trumpet. Don't you want to hear it? Would you like me to walk down and talk to you?"

"Yes, go ahead."

"Very well. I'll recite some passages from the Koran, something really solemn and serious as is fitting for this building."

But the Mir interrupted.

"From the Koran? Is your Effendi a Muslim? Let him hear something different. You stay here; I'll go down myself. I'll recite something which is more in keeping with this stirring site."

He left. There was a profound reason why he, the

highest ranking of us all, wanted to do me this service. This rock temple had affected him deeply and therefore he wished us to react strongly to it.

From the height of the platform, we could see the northern sky glowing and in flames, as I had seen it when I had sat atop the temple at Ussula. Here, where we were, in the midst of the desert and of death, it was even more stirring than it had been earlier. How intimate our connection was with these fires since they fed our well and were our saviors! Thus salutary threads in human life lead from the incomprehensible to the comprehensible, from heaven to earth, from the creator to the creature and back again to the creator if we only wish it. We now stepped back from the platform and into the temple so as not to miss the moment the Mir would begin to speak. We sat down and waited quietly. A very long time passed. He must have arrived at the bottom long since, and still he was not speaking. This made my companions impatient but I could understand his continuing silence. The sight of the temple was moving him even more deeply than it had before. He felt overwhelmed. What passed within him so totally absorbed his attention that we necessarily took second place. And it was a truly marvellous divine dispensation which had compelled the Mir to come to the "City of the Dead." I have already mentioned the "spirits' forge" of Kulub where human souls are wrought. The Mir now found himself in this psychic Kulub, this "spirits' forge," and I was intensely interested in finding out whether he would emerge successfully, or not. The spiral of flickering lights led down to him and he was standing where it began, looking up, but not seeing us. What was he going to say? Surely it would be something which conveyed what was stirring within him at that moment. Just as I was considering this, a voice resounded from the dark depth that seemed to be coming from wholly different worlds, addressing wholly different worlds, not our small, insignificant earth and our equally insignificant little group. Slowly, clearly, solemnly, and momentously, like bells or trumpets, his words rose up to us:

: 494 :

Whither shall I go then from thy Spirit?
Or whither shall I go then from thy presence?
If I climb up into heaven, thou art there;
If I go down to hell, thou art there also.
If I take the wings of the morning
and dwell in the uttermost parts of the sea,
Even there also shall thy hand lead me,
and thy right hand shall hold me.

The others sat still for a few moments. They also felt that this had been more than the sound of a voice, that something purely inward had occurred that must not be desecrated by trivial comments. They started to push the rock back in place and got ready to descend. They assumed that I would follow them, but I said:

"Go on ahead. I shall remain for a while and close this opening when I get ready to leave. Extinguish all the lights as you pass. Don't leave a single one burning."

"But when you come down, you'll need light. Otherwise you'll fall," Halef said with concern.

"Then leave one for me."

"But you mustn't stay too long. You must eat with us, Sidi. You know, today we will cook, really cook, roast, and fry. For we have everything we need. Countless delicacies. I will prepare them myself. And the others will help. We will have a supper that even the Shah of Teheran or the Sultan of Istanbul could not improve upon. Are you coming?"

"Yes."

"Then farewell for now. You are a poet and write books. So you like the heights where there is nothing to eat. But we, who are not poets and don't write books, we belong down there on level and safe ground, and prefer the aroma of a good roast to the juiciest rhymes and the fattest tomes."

"And I hope that your roast will turn out well, dear Halef."

"So do I. We are leaving."

They descended, extinguishing light after light as they went. I watched them for a time and saw the lighted spiral recede further and further. Then I stepped back outside and sat down to be finally, finally, alone with my thoughts, to examine everything that had happened, to infer what might still be awaiting us. But this beneficial solitude was not to last. I heard steps coming from inside. It was the Mir. He had a burning candle in his hand, blew it out, sat down next to me and apologized:

"Your Halef told me you wished to be alone. I have the same wish and yet cannot fulfill it. For in solitude I find no support. I had to come to you. Forgive me."

"I did want to be alone," I answered sincerely. "Events such as we are experiencing here demand concentration and undisturbed reflection if they are to have useful and salutary effects. But you are distressed and expect help. I do not know if I can provide it, but you are welcome."

"I know that, and that's why I come to you, Effendi. I must tell you a secret, a great, weighty secret which was passed on in my family from one generation to the next and guarded so carefully that not even all the members of my family, let alone strangers, heard of it. Only the ruler knew, and whenever he considered it necessary, he communicated it to the oldest prince, his successor, but never to anyone else. You are the first and only stranger who will hear it, and this will show you how fond I am of you and how important I think you are to me."

"I thank you. Secrets should be respected, particularly family secrets which the individual member is not free to deal with as he pleases. Do you feel it absolutely essential to tell me?"

"Yes, I do. As soon as you have heard, you will agree with me. For this affair has entered a precarious and difficult phase. The secret is about to become public, common property. I am too weak to prevent this. I need your help, and you can only give it to me if you know as much as I do."

"Then I must not prevent you from speaking frankly. But before you do, I ask you to tell me how you came to know the passages from our Bible which we heard you recite just now."

"They are a Christmas present."

"From whom?"

"From our common friend, the Bash Nasrani, the

high priest of all the Christians in my lands. He copied a great many important passages and brought them to me. He said that this was Christ's acknowledgment for my having permitted his followers to celebrate his birthday at Ard. The passages pleased me a great deal. I often read them. And when the Bash Nasrani was with me, he had to explain their meaning and content to me. It was his opinion that from them my own happiness and welfare, and also the happiness of my country, might grow. So I learned them by heart and meditated a great deal about them. When your Halef promised you verses from the Koran, I thought it would be better to give you sayings from this, my own treasure. I thought this would bring you joy."

"And so it did. It is no small, no ordinary joy you gave me. That's why it is my sincere wish to be able to be useful to you concerning your family secret. Please tell me about it now."

The Mir and I were facing north. The flaming masses shifting up and down in the distance were casting a gentle, warm, transfiguring light on his face. He began:

"What a year this is! Will it really be that great, long-since-prophesied year when the angels of paradise may announce that peace is approching and that the nations no longer hate but love and respect each other? Are you aware, Effendi, that every Mir of Djinnistan has always favored such peace, and that every Mir of Ardistan has opposed it?"

"I am."

"This explains the eternal enmity between these rulers. And this enmity was all the greater and more divisive because we, in Ardistan, believed we had to hate our enemies, while those from Djinnistan felt obliged to love us in spite of our hatred, and to show us benevolence. It outraged us; we considered it the greatest imaginable disgrace and insult to receive nothing but benefits and forgiveness from those we were incessantly warring against. Can you understand this wrath of ours?"

"Only too well, unfortunately."

"And can you imagine that for certain proud natures it is absolutely terrible to accept mercy and compassion when one is burning inside to encounter virile anger and an avenging strength, for once?"

"Yes, I understand that as well."

"And are you perhaps reasonable or unreasonable enough to see that because of their eternal, wearying love, kindness, mercy, patience, and forbearance, we thoroughly despised the Mir of Djinnistan and all his allies?"

"When one mistakes the greatest power and strength in heaven and earth, love, for incapacity and weakness, it is not difficult to feel this contempt. But tell me, do you still despise it?"

"Until a short time ago, I did. But then you appeared. You were absolutely fearless. There was Halef's all-conquering devotion and loyalty, the Bash Nasrani with his powerful quotations from the Bible. And then I heard the bells, an organ swelling, the cannons fired for the first time for a great, a peaceful purpose. The prince of Halihm and his daughter dared come into my own house to teach me to understand the kindness and compassion of the Mir of Djinnistan. Yes, that was a risk, a true risk they took, and I recognize its value as much as I recognize the Erdjani's boldness in sending you and Halef to me in Ard, into the lion's den. Now it seems to me as if love and kindness were infinitely more manly, courageous, and heroic than hatred which blindly and unthinkingly rushes into acts whose issue it doesn't know. That is not courage but recklessness and unscrupulous behavior. And after all that, there was the conspiracy, the disloyalty of my officers and civil servants, the ingratitude of the 'Panther' to whom I had given more of my heart than I kept for myself. Such were the fruits of Ardistan, the harvest of my deeds. Then followed the ride to the 'City of the Dead' where I was to die of thirst and hunger, the miraculous rescue here and the still more miraculous revelations from the Maha-Lama period which we despised but which was blessed by the people. Those I considered my friends have become my enemies, and those I considered so lowly and pathetic that I had to smile when I thought of them are now my only support. Only with their help can I get back on my feet and become once again what I was. But I swear to you, Effendi, that I will sit in judgment, that I will avenge myself, that I—"

"Stop! Don't go on," I interrupted him. "What you said and still want to say is correct. Your train of thought is right. But suddenly, you cut it short and abandon it. Your wrath has disturbed you. The thought of revenge is about to destroy the proper ending of your speech. You are not saved yet. You have not yet become the Mir again. Thousands of circumstances may still intervene which will destroy all your hopes and frustrate your plans. Most importantly, allow me to tell you that God will probably not help you to avenge yourself. I am neither your judge nor the judge of your enemies. You judged yourself and your entire dynasty when you said a while ago that you all had been the servants of hatred, not the servants of love. You confessed that you had only reaped the harvest of your own deeds. How can you wish to avenge yourself for something for which only you are to blame? I still hear one of the passages you quoted from the Bible and which you spoke to us from down there: 'My soul thirsts for the Lord, the strong, the living God.' Didn't the Bash Nasrani explain the meaning of these words to you? Do you believe that you can appear before God as a judge and avenger when you call yourself the truly guilty one? And even if you were innocent—"

"Forgive me," he interrupted. "You are right; my wrath unsettled me. The secret I wish to share with you is a confession, and someone who makes a confession should not be angry with others. I ask you now not to believe that it is evil deeds, crimes committed by me or my ancestors that I wish to confess. What I am talking about is a kind of inherited illness, though it is not actually an illness but something altogether different and completely incomprehensible. Do you believe dreams can be inherited?"

"Inherited? Hm. I think I can say that certain physical or psychic conditions which contribute to the origin of dreams may be inherited. In this general sense, it could perhaps be maintained that dreams may be passed on. But you surely have a particular sort of dream in mind?"

"Not only a particular sort, but a particular dream which is always the same. The father dreams a certain dream which his grandfather and his ancestors dreamt before him, and which his son and his grandson will dream again. This happened many years ago and will happen many years hence. It is a dream in which the very same moments, localities, situations, people, words, and acts recur."

"That's impossible, utterly impossible."

"No, it's real."

"Prove it!"

"It happened in my family, and still does."

"Then it can only be an illusion, not a fact."

"But there's proof of it. I ask you to believe me. During the entire time Ardistan has been governed by my ancestors, there has been a dream, a certain dream which all of them dreamt, down to the last ruler, and without a single exception. My father was the last one to dream it."

"What did they dream?"

"They dreamt of a 'Djemmah of the Living' and a 'Djemmah of the Dead.'"

"How strange."

"Isn't it? My father told me this dream in exact detail, in precisely the same way as it was told to him by my grandfather and as I will probably tell it to my son."

"Have you already dreamt it?"

"Not yet. But I know that I cannot escape it."

"Are you afraid of it?"

"Of course. Up to now, everyone has been afraid of it, but the fear disappeared because the horrible threat the dream conveyed to the dreamer has never yet materialized."

"What threat?"

"That he cannot die and be buried until there is a remorseful and courageous Mir of Ardistan who is ready to take upon himself the guilt and evil deeds of all his ancestors, and to expiate them."

"Now you are speaking of the misdeeds of your ancestors, yet you just admonished me not to believe that you would confess evil deeds or crimes they may have committed."

"Exactly. Am I confessing any? I am simply telling you that the dream talks about them, but I am not naming any. I am not enumerating them."

"And you want to tell me this dream?"

"Yes. Listen. The Mir dreams he is sitting in an age-old but very beautiful sedan chair such as was used thousands of years ago. He is being carried across a large, round plaza and then through many dimly lit rooms into a great hall above whose door there is the inscription 'Djemmah of the Dead.' All the Maha-Lamas and all the Emirs of Ardistan who ever lived are sitting there. But the Emirs who in life ranked high above the Maha-Lamas stand far below them in death. They are prisoners, their hands and feet are shackled, and they are about to be judged. They are expecting their sentence. But the Maha-Lamas are free. They are the judges who will pronounce sentence. At their head is the most famous, most just, and kindest of them, Abu Shalem, the Maha-Lama who drained the Maha-Lama Lake and erected these gigantic structures where the water had been. A book listing the misdeeds of all the Emirs, of the entire dynasty, lies before him. An abstract from this book lies before each shackled Emir. The content of this book and of these abstracts not only refers to all purely human sins that have been committed, but principally and especially to all the crimes and omissions of which the accused were guilty as rulers. But the principal question, the weightiest, is whether or not they respected the lives of their fellow men. Murder is punished most remorselessly, both that of individuals and the mass murder that is war. The Djemmah may take no pity on the one that plotted a war. Only God, the highest judge, can pardon that crime."

Here, he paused as if to reflect, and then went on:

"Those are the dead, and yet they aren't dead. Their flesh is warm and soft. They can see and hear; they can talk. They rise, leave and return, precisely like the living."

"But all this happens in the dream," I interrupted.

"Yes, in the dream. My father told me. He looked at everything carefully. His father, who had died several years before, was also there. He was as if alive. He left

: 501 :

his seat and went along into another room to participate in a counsel. Above the door to this second hall,
there was the inscription 'Djemmah of the Living.'
There, the judges were people who were still alive,
and whom my father knew. He even told me their
names. These living were joined by some of the dead
from the first hall, particularly my father's father and
the old, famous Maha-Lama Abu Shalem who presides
here as well."

"And what happened during these proceedings?" I
asked because I wanted him to finish as quickly as
possible.

"First, a coffin was opened. My father's dead body
was lying inside it. He was told that this was his
corpse and that he could save it and all his ancestors if
he assumed all their sins and guilt and made expiation.
Then the entire content of the great book of accounts
which the Maha-Lama Abu Shalem had brought in
was read out to him. He was asked whether he was
willing to absolve his ancestors from bondage, and to
take all their sins, their wars, and the blood they had
spilled upon himself. If he did, their souls would immediately go free, as would his. But if he refused, their
souls would remain shackled as heretofore and he himself would be unable either to die or be buried until a
later Mir of Ardistan should be courageous enough to
bring the sacrifice of deliverance to them all."

"And what did your father say?"

"What all his ancestors had said before him, that he
did not feel like paying debts he had not incurred, that
it was not his task to free ancestors who had had no
desire to save theirs. Should there be such a thing as a
life after death, every individual's sins had to be
atoned for by him."

"What happened when he said this?"

"He was returned to his costly sedan chair and carried away. When he woke up, he was lying in his
bedroom at home, on his pillows. He had been dreaming."

"Had he truly dreamt?"

"Yes. But there's something strange. He had been
lying on his bed and sleeping for six entire days without once waking up."

"Hadn't someone been concerned about him?"

"No. No one found out. The bodyguard kept the secret and saw to it that no one heard about it, not even I, until he told me everything himself."

"And now you are telling me. Why?"

"Because since yesterday, everything has been reminding me of this dream. Every Mir of Ardistan dreamt it, exactly like my father, and as I am repeating it. Everyone was asked the identical question, everyone gave the identical answer. So it is no ordinary dream. There is some truth connected with it which no one can fathom. Now reflect that here also, there is a 'Djemmah of the Dead' and a 'Djemmah of the Living.' Don't you see why this dream should preoccupy me so?"

"Oh, I understand it easily enough. I'm even thinking of things that haven't occurred to you. But surely you had reasons for confiding in me? What are they? What intent are you pursuing?"

"I want you to help, to support me. You must not leave my side, should it be my turn now. I fear the dream will not surprise me at home, but here. If so, I want it to remain a secret. I feel like a man who senses that he is about to become seriously ill. Before that happens, he turns to a physician and asks him for help. I trust you as one trusts a physician. You will give whatever happens to me a beneficial turn."

"A turn which will benefit not just you, but also your country, your entire people, provided I have a chance to intervene. I will be frank with you and tell you that I feel as you do. Not only do I sense it, I am convinced that you will not leave the site of the former Maha-Lama Lake without having dreamt the dream of your ancestors. With none of them, the necessity of this dream was as pronounced as it is in your case. The only question still to be discussed is also the most important: How will you act?"

"Do you imagine I know?"

"Yes."

"I wonder. No one can know what he will do and say in a dream."

"That's true for an ordinary dream, but things are different here. You will act just as you would when awake. Suppose you were in this strange Djemmah, not sleeping and dreaming, but fully conscious, acting deliberately and with a will of your own. What would you answer if you were asked whether you would take the sins of your ancestors upon yourself and expiate them?"

He jumped up and answered quickly and energetically:

"I would say yes. I would immediately be ready for everything that—"

He interrupted himself. He had allowed his emotions to master him. Immediately, what we normally call reason intervened and tore the golden thread about to be spun. The Mir made a slow, reluctant gesture and continued:

"Not so fast, not so prematurely! This matter is of enormous import. Up to now, none of my ancestors had the courage to burden himself with these mountains of guilt that have risen over the course of millennia. If there were no future life, I could confidently say 'yes,' for it would be mere sound, and meaningless. I have doubted that there is a future life, but am wholly convinced now that this doubt was foolishness. There is no question that this other life will come, and it will come directly after death, or perhaps even earlier. Perhaps it manifests itself already in our present existence. Whether I say 'yes' or 'no' to the question of the Djemmah will determine what happens to me after death, what I will have to regret, bear, do, and accomplish after death, in the life to come. So I must be careful, enormously careful. If I say 'yes' and assume all this guilt, I may call down upon myself eternal, unending damnation."

"And not eternal, never-ending blessedness as well?" I asked.

"Perhaps. Who can say? If I ask you to tell me sincerely what your answer would be if the Djemmah asked you whether you would take upon yourself and expiate the sins of your fathers, what would your answer be?"

"I would quickly and gladly agree."

"Really Effendi, really?"

"Yes, really."

"And why?"

"Because that is my nature, my character, my temperament. And also because I believe in eternal love. Surely you won't maintain that your ancestors, all of whom refused, can serve as guides either for you or for me."

"Effendi, they were rulers."

"What if they were? They could not even govern themselves, let alone others. They obeyed voices they heard far below them, not those that came from above. For me, the word 'ruler' means something altogether different. Abu Shalem, the 'most famous, and most just, and kindest' among the Maha-Lamas, was a ruler. He still rules today, even over you and me. Hundreds of years after his death, he is our savior. And I am convinced that the blessings which stemmed from him will extend further and save uncounted others who will come after us. Can you name a single one among your ancestors that even remotely resembles him? Do you know of one?"

He did not answer.

"Listen to what I am telling you, but don't be angered by my frankness. You say nothing when I ask you about their greatness as rulers. Now, let us consider their value as human beings. Tell me: Were they good human beings? Were they loved?"

"Some, perhaps," he answered hesitantly.

"Some, you say. And you say 'perhaps.' I tell you they were cowards! Cowards and egomaniacs, all of them, from the first to the last."

"Effendi, the last was my father."

"That does not change my judgment. On the contrary, it gives it more substance, more incisiveness. Did a single one of all these 'fathers' of yours ever once think of the well-being and the happiness of his children, his grandchildren, and those that would come later still? That's what I must tell you: You are blind; I have to open your eyes. You must not only view the cowardice and selfishness of your ancestors by going back in time, but also by going forward. Listen carefully: Your ancestors were too cowardly to shoulder the acts of their fathers. They were even too cowardly to save themselves by resolving to lead a different,

more noble, and better life. And they were so utterly
without honor and so indolent that they passed on
their guilt to their innocent descendants because they
did not want to expiate their acts themselves. Pusil-
lanimous as they were, they contented themselves with
waiting for the poor wretch who would be compassionate and strong enough to take all their filth upon
himself, and perhaps to suffocate under that weight.
What do you say to a person who can change, improve, rise to a higher level, become more noble and
enlightened, and yet rejects all this? What do you say
to one who prefers to pass all his weaknesses and
shortcomings on to his miserable children and grandchildren because he is too lazy, too cowardly, too ego-
tistic, and too infatuated with pleasure, to feel the
obligation to try by his own strength to rise to a higher
level, to be the last of his family rather than to wait for
a salvation he certainly does not deserve? Shame, I
say! As I say this, I am not only thinking of the long
succession of the Emirs of Ardistan but of every tribe,
every dynasty, every family everywhere, nobles and
commoners, old and young, famous or unknown.
Every person has ancestors and may expect to have descendants. Every single human being, whether prince
or beggar, has the task of saving both his ancestors
and himself by courageously and vigorously freeing
himself of the errors of upbringing and the shortcomings of heredity, thus creating for himself the great
happiness of participating in the ennoblement of all
mankind. That is what I had to tell you. Now be angry
if you can."

I turned away from him and looked down on the
large, circular expanse and the water angel in its center. The Emirs of Ardistan had been carried across this
open area in the "costly sedan chair" to be placed
before the Djemmah. I knew what their answers had
been. And now I also knew what the present Mir
would answer. I had intentionally spoken frankly and
bluntly. I had even been insulting. I felt that I could
take that chance, as I had done before without ever
having miscalculated. He was standing still. His face
was turned north where at that moment any number
of fiery pillars was rising from the restlessly churning

volcanoes. Due to the perspective, they seemed to coalesce and were rising so high that one might have thought they were meant to conquer the sky and to absorb the splendor of all the stars. He suddenly and energetically turned to me, embraced me, kissed me on the forehead, and said:

"My dear Effendi, you are a terrible, a really terrible man, and yet a truly good human being. Will you grant me a request? The same I ignored before?"

"Which one?"

"I wish to be alone. Here. I must try to see things clearly."

"Very well; I'll leave you."

I also kissed him on the forehead, left the platform, and entered the temple. There, I lit one of the candles and slowly walked down. The most difficult task had been accomplished: The Mir had been conquered. Whatever the future might have in store and however difficult that might be, it could only flow from this day which had been blessed by God. What would the morrow bring?

9 : In the Realm of the Dead

As I came down, Halef still had much to do to finish preparing the meal. He was working slowly. This supper was to be a culinary effort of the first order, and that is how it turned out. The Mir came much too late, but the best portion had been set aside for him. That evening, I did not see or talk to him further for when he finally joined us, I had long since gone to sleep.

That day we had gone through the first half of the structures. We started in on the second the following morning. Of all the things we saw, I shall only mention the library. It was very interesting, although the books it contained dealt only with the history and the diffusion of the humanitarian efforts of its founders. There were any number of clay tablets and cylinders covered with cuneiform, not so much Babylonian or

Assyrian but old Persian. In addition, there were countless wooden tablets with Chinese, Mongol, and Tibetan writing. We saw many books, notebooks, and papyri, and discovered maps and star atlases, drawings of human beings, animals, plants, minerals, and weapons. We also found paintings in all sizes and colors. Most interesting to us was a large, heavy, costly folder which bore the title: "The Djemmah, Its Judges and Accused." As we opened it, we saw two separate parcels of drawings in Chinese ink. One of them was entitled "Judges," the other "Accused." They contained surprisingly well done portraits. The first included those of the most important and eminent Maha-Lamas, the other all the Emirs who had ever ruled Ardistan. The best, most valuable drawing was certainly the portrait of the famous Abu Shalem, a man with unusually expressive features. The striking distribution of light and shade was such that the psychological qualities of this eminent personality emerged at least as clearly as the physical features of his kind and intelligent face.

While we were looking at this drawing with great interest, the Mir went rapidly through the contents of the second package to familiarize himself with the portraits of his ancestors. At one point, he exclaimed:

"Mashallah! My father! And here my father's father whom I remember. How marvellously life-like they are! Who was the artist? No one has ever seen this. Were they done secretly, I wonder, and why weren't we asked?"

The "ruler" was once again coming to the surface. I was about to answer, but the Erdjani was quicker.

"Do you mean that you should have been consulted?"

"Of course," the Mir answered.

"You are mistaken. Look at the inscription: 'The Accused.' Where would you find a judge who asks the accused for permission to place him in the dock, be it his person or his portrait? No Djemmah asks. It acts on its decisions, which means as it pleases."

The Mir had not expected such a rebuke, especially from a younger man who had been called "leper" and "madman," and whose behavior toward him had been so polite and considerate, indeed almost obedient, up to this moment. But now the young man was facing him, drawn up to his full height, and his usually friendly eyes expressed rebuff and repudiation. He looked so severe that the Mir's anger came up against a blank wall. As their glances met as if the deepest layers of the soul were being tested, the Erdjani seemed to tower above the Mir. He felt this, for he roughly and angrily put the portraits of his ancestors aside and said:

"Away with them! If those from whom joy, pride, and honor are demanded bring nothing but disappointment, disgrace, and distress, one loses one's patience and would prefer no longer being a son and a grandson."

He walked out. We followed, for we did not have the time to investigate the library more fully at that moment.

It was only in the course of the afternoon that we got to the two halls we had been so curious about for such a long time. Tensely, we stood in front of the side door above which we read the inscription "Djemmah of the Dead." Halef and I had experienced and seen a great deal, but now, as I am writing this, I can think of no situation where our inner tension was greater than before this door to a great and profound mystery.

For the sake of clarity, I should mention that these two halls did not have doors leading directly to the circular arcade. They could only be reached through the room adjoining them, which is why I referred to the entrance as a side door. From the "Djemmah of the Dead," another side door led into the "Djemmah of the Living." These doors could be opened like the others.

As we entered the "Djemmah of the Dead," we found ourselves in mystical semi-darkness. Only blurred shapes could be made out. The hall was very large and very high. Because the small windows did not admit enough light, candelabra with many candles had been placed on the floor. We lit them, and it became bright enough for us to see everything distinctly and to examine the hall carefully.

When this great room had been hewn out of the

rock, gigantic pillars had been left standing. The high
arch of the ceiling rested on them. Forming two rows
they created three sections of uneven width, the one in
the middle being more spacious than those that
flanked it. The Djemmah had gathered in the center
section while the other two contained seats for the
public and were empty, of course. Those who had
gathered in the center were all in their seats. These
seats were not all on the same level. The president sat
highest, as though on a throne. A table stood before
him, and on it lay a book, presumably the one containing the offenses of all the Emirs of Ardistan. Abu
Shalem was dressed in a very modest, unbleached
garment of hemp, had straw sandals on his feet, and a
simple, white cloth on his head under which unkempt
locks of silvery hair continued to grow in death. It was
parted in the middle and hung down to his belt in two
braids. The beard also was full and had the same silvery sheen. It covered his chest and stomach and disappeared under the table. His face looked as I had
always imagined the ancient Persians. Once, I had
seen a portrait of Cyrus the Great, showing him in the
full strength of his manhood and at the height of his
glory. Now, as I faced "the kindest, most famous, and
most just" of the Maha-Lamas and studied his magnificent head, I wanted to say: "Those are the features of
the Great King of the Persians. This is what he would
have looked like, had he reached the age at which this
Maha-Lama died."

I stepped up to him and touched his hands and
cheeks. They were cool and soft. Though almost feeling guilty of an act of desecration, I also inspected his
arms, legs, and body. Something like a plea for forgiveness welled up within me that I, an insignificant
creature, should dare speculate what thoughts might
once have dwelt in this body. The eyes consisted of
three different stones which formed the bluish white
cornea, the blue-black iris, and the coal black but
transparent pupil. The stones had been cut and joined
so successfully that one might have taken them for real
eyes if one had not known that this was the mummi-
fied body of someone who had died long ago. The
glance of these eyes was directed at the bench of the

accused, not at me. This increased the respectful timidity with which I examined the body of the president of the Djemmah.

To his right and left but three feet lower, other Maha-Lamas were sitting at similar, low, Oriental tables which stood so close together that they formed a quarter-circle on either side. These dead thus represented a semi-circle above whose center the highest judge was enthroned. Some of them were dressed even more modestly and unpretentiously than he was. All looked in the same direction. Not every Maha-Lama who had ever lived was represented here, but only the most important among them, all of them men who had died at a very advanced age and whose dull or shimmering white hair and beard had grown even in death. These figures certainly did not look like corpses. There was the temptation to believe that once upon a time when elves, fairies, and magicians still existed, a most important Djemmah had been held here and been surprised and hypnotized by a powerful sorcerer. It was as if every one of these judges might suddenly rise, move about, and speak. This impression gained strength from the total absence of any odor. The air was pure, as if it were constantly being renewed.

All the Emirs of Ardistan that had ever lived were sitting still further down the hall, poor accused sinners that they were. Not a single one was missing. Yet their seats were higher than those of their judges, for they were sitting on thrones decorated with an abundance of precious stones and metals. The former rulers were dressed in costly garments and wore marvellous rings, chains, and insignia of rank. But upon closer inspection, all these metals and stones proved to be imitation. Some of these men were old, others of middle age, and some young, depending on the time of their death. It was apparent that the preservation of their bodies had been as skillful as that of the Lamas, yet they made much less of an impression than their judges, and this despite all their ornaments, splendor, and jewels. They lacked the majesty of death. During their life, they had been so majestic that none was left, now that they were dead. They were looking down at a book or notebook lying on their knees, an abstract from the great black book of the entire dynasty they had belonged to and still did. Their hands and feet were shackled with rope and chains.

The loud voice of the Mir startled me out of my thoughts and reflections. The rest of us were silent. We felt we would desecrate our feelings if we articulated them. During the first few moments, that had been true of him as well. He had been standing in motionless astonishment. But now he suddenly shouted loudly:

"My father, my father!"

He ran up to him, stopped a few steps away, raised his arms, and repeated:

"My father! You, a prisoner, and chained!"

I could not see his face because he had his back turned to me, but the tone of his voice indicated profound agitation.

"And you too, you too!" he exclaimed, turning his head somewhat. "My father's father. What are you being reproached with, the two of you? Tell me, I have to know!"

He listened a few moments and then stepped closer to them as he continued:

"You are silent? Very well, you have no choice, since you are dead. You could not defend yourselves when the crime of bringing you here secretly was committed. I will look into that. And woe to the guilty if I find him. But right now I have to know what you are being accused of. Let's see."

He was very excited. He hastily picked up the notebooks lying before the two dead rulers and, going to the nearest candelabra, sat down there and began reading. But not for long. He glanced at the title of one of the notebooks, slowly leafed through, and only paid close attention to the last few pages. He repeated this procedure with the second notebook, and I observed him closely. I noticed that his excitement left him as quickly as it had seized him, receding by degrees until it turned into depression. He rose and returned the books to their place without saying a word, looking like someone who has fallen from the height of anger to the depth of shame, and cannot hide it. Then he went up to some other ancestors who were within easy reach, and glanced into their notebooks. Again, I saw that he only looked at the last pages. Now he walked up to Abu Shalem and inspected the principal book. I had not touched this during my previous investigation, but had gone down to the other Maha-Lamas for a closer look. At that moment, I was standing near the rulers of Ardistan whose names and reigns could easily be determined because that information was given on the cover of their notebooks. The behavior of the Mir made clear that the important information could be found on the final pages. I took the book belonging to the one at whose side I was standing. Its cover was made of white leather and it bore the following inscription in large, black letters: "Mir Burahda-i-Mihribani, during the years 102–112 of the Hidschra."

Burahda-i-Mihribani means "brother of kindness." Because this was an official title, the name suggested a man of good character. Besides, this ruler had governed for ten years, and so it could reasonably be expected that the account would not be unsatisfactory. But what did I find? I first looked at the last page which contained the summary. Eight of the ten years had been years of war. All the losses in human beings, animals, capital, and landed property caused by the war were listed there, as were other matters damaging to the well-being of the nation. More than fifty thousand had died, and the ruler had been called "brother of kindness!" The comments not only referred to the wars for which this man had been responsible, but also detailed all the harm mankind had suffered under his government. There was a list of executions, persons exiled, confiscations of property, illegal and unjust sentences, favoritism, overt and covert plunder by violence and cunning. Not only figures but also the names of the victims were given. There could be no doubt that here was proof of crime upon crime, countless inhuman acts, innumerable instances of foul play and deception. The subjects had only existed to—

"Effendi," the Mir called out to me, interrupting my reading.

I looked at him questioningly.

"You are reading?" he continued.

"Yes."

"Please put that book down."

"Why?"

"Isn't it enough that I ask you? Do I have to tell you that these are not your ancestors but mine? Come up here, there's something I want to show you. There is one thing you should find out, and that's all that is necessary. No one need know the rest, except myself, for I am the heir, the one who is saddled and burdened with all this, the beast crushed by everyone's sins. Come here, come here!"

This did not sound like an order but a request. The tone was imploring, tortured, and oppressed. I put down the account and walked up to the Mir. He had opened the large book to its last page.

"Read," he asked me, pointing at it.

I did. The lists were horrible, the figures frightening. My vision was becoming blurred. All this seemed incredible, yet it was true. "I've finished," I said, and closed the book.

"Already?" he asked.

"Yes. I think that's enough. No one could stand seeing any more of this."

"There is someone who wants to know more and has to know more, and that is myself. It's not for me to believe and be horrified. I have to examine without fear, though not now, but later, when we have discovered what the other rooms contain. Come, Effendi, we are leaving."

He walked back to where his ancestors were sitting, stopped in front of his father and grandfather, and addressed them:

"I am flesh of your flesh, blood of your blood. But if life is love, you did not give me life but death. But console yourselves, I will not seek revenge. Should I dream the dream that found you weak, all of you, from the first to the last, I will be the first not to succumb to it. How I wish it would come soon!"

He was about to leave the room, but stopped after having taken a few steps, turned to the throne of the president, raised his arm toward him, and said:

"And you, old man, tell me who permitted you to play the eternal judge, to play God whom even rulers have to obey? Where did you get these dead? I shall look for them in all the vaults and coffins and then tell you who and what you are. Take care! Should you go so far as to call me and my family to account, I shall do the same to all of you."

Having spoken these words, he called on Halef and the others:

"Put the candles out again and come with me; we are leaving."

When all the lights had been extinguished, we opened the door with the inscription "Djemmah of the Living" and entered the assembly room. It was not as large as the previous one. Its construction and appointments were identical, however, except that it was intended for a smaller number of people.

Here also, there were three sections, two for the public, and the one in the middle for the judges and the accused. The arrangement of the seats was also the same. The highest, in the center, was the throne-like chair of the president; somewhat further down, and forming a half circle, there were the seats of the judges, and again somewhat lower and extending the half circle, the places for the accused. All the chairs and seats were unoccupied. There were eight for the judges and three for the accused with room for more. Chairs and mats to accommodate additional persons were stored in an adjoining room and could easily be brought in. The illumination was similar to that in the larger hall. We saw candelabra with candles, though they were inaccessible. Readily visible even in the semi-darkness, an inscription in large letters was hanging from the table of the president. It said:

"Tomorrow, exactly at midnight, there will be a session of the 'Djemmah of the Living' against Shedid el Ghalabi, Mir of Ardistan. You are the judges. Those who fail to appear will be punished."

This sign had an extraordinary effect. We looked at each other in astonishment and dismay. Over in the large hall, only two of us had dared raise our voices, the Mir and I. The others had been silent, utterly absorbed by the enthralling scene. This silence was repeated now. There was no question that this announcement was addressed to us. But who had placed it here? Who could have known that we would be at this place on this particular day? Who had foreseen that one of us would succeed in penetrating the secrets of the Maha-Lama Lake, finding the keys and opening the rooms?

"Shedid el Ghalabi?" the Mir asked. "That's me! No one in my entire country would dare have the same name as I. So it follows that I am being addressed. Do you agree, Effendi?"

"Certainly," I answered.

"The 'Djemmah of the Living' against me! As early as tomorrow! Precisely at midnight! My wish is being granted more quickly than I had thought possible. I wanted the dream to come quickly."

As he said this, he was shaking with fear and I felt as if a cold breath were slowly blowing across my entire body. It was this sensation that made me say:

"But this dream will be no dream, but reality."

"You think so?"

"Of course."

"But perhaps I will really fall asleep, and merely dream."

"I hardly think so. Remember that we are supposed to be the judges."

"What the announcement means is that I will dream that."

"I very much doubt it. I see notes on all the seats. Let's light some candles so we can read them."

When this had been done, the Mir walked to the seat of the president and read the note lying before him.

"Abu Shalem, the Maha-Lama."

Again, we stood there, looking at each other. Finally, the Mir said:

"Isn't this strange? A corpse is to preside over the living. How is it going to get here to its seat from the hall next door? But let's read some more."

The paper on which these notes had been written was dark, the writing light as if white chalk had been used. Walking from one judge's seat to the next, the Mir read out the following names:

"The Erdjani, Kara Ben Nemsi, Hadji Halef Omar, Prince Sadik of the Tshoban, the two princes of the

Ussul, the sheik of the Tshoban, the Sheik el Beled of El Hadd."

Thus we had eight associate justices but two of them were absent. How were the sheik of the Tshoban and the ruler of El Hadd going to find this unknown place? But the Mir did not give us a chance to puzzle over this problem. He walked to the three seats for the accused, took the notes lying there, and read:

"Shedid el Ghalabi, Mir of Ardistan—his father—his father's father."

The notes had been placed so as to indicate that the Mir was to sit in the middle, his father to his left, his grandfather to his right. He shuddered like someone suffering from cold, returned the notes to their places, and said in a soft voice, as if speaking to himself:

"Between two corpses. And between these two, no less."

"Precisely at midnight," Halef added. It was the first time he had opened his mouth.

"Whether at midnight or at noon is a matter of indifference," the Mir rebuked him. "They are all God's hours. If I am found guilty at noon, that's just as bad as being sentenced by these judges at night. And these candles have to be lit, whether it's dark or light outside. But let's go on. There are two more seats over there."

Off to the side from the semi-circle of the associate justices, there stood two low, Oriental chairs, meant less to sit than to rest in. They were covered with soft blankets. Notes were also lying on them. The Mir picked them up and read out:

"Abd el Fadl, the prince of Halihm, and Merhameh, princess of Halihm, as defense counsels."

For the third time, we looked at each other in silence. Without saying a word, the Mir put the notes back, walked from candelabra to candelabra to blow out the candles and then to the adjoining room to go outside. We followed him. Outside the building, he said:

"It isn't evening yet. Do you wish to continue your investigation?"

"Yes," I answered. "We absolutely have to finish today to be ready for whatever may come tomorrow."

"Do you think something will happen tomorrow?"

"Yes."

"Such as the 'Djemmah of the Living?' "

"Absolutely."

"Do you also think Abd el Fadl and Merhameh will be here? And the sheik of the Tshoban and the Sheik el Beled?"

"I am almost convinced that they will all be here."

He took a deep breath.

"So am I. I can hardly tell how I feel. I would almost say: We are not alive, we are being lived. We do not think, we are being thought, we have no will of our own but obey that of another. It is as if there were someone high above us, leading us as the rider leads his obedient horse."

"Do you really think that's how it is? Or does it simply seem that way? I believe nothing is appearance here. Everything is certain and tangibly real. We are being led, and we are not alone."

"Do you mean there are other living beings here? Other persons?"

"Yes."

"Who could that be?"

"Think!"

"I will. May I be excused? Having been in these two halls, I don't care what else we may find. I have to be alone to collect myself. You will understand that. I shall be back in time for supper."

As the Mir slowly walked off, the rest of us turned toward the rooms still to be explored. Then I heard his voice behind me. He had stopped, and gestured. When I reached him, he asked:

"Do you know who controls all this?"

"Yes. The Mir of Djinnistan, of course. No one else."

"My enemy!"

"Your best, your most devoted friend. He will prove it to you. Unfortunately there are individuals who cannot believe and trust without tangible proof. And when they have been forced to acknowledge such proofs, they brag about their belief and demand that they be given credit for it."

"You are becoming severe again, Effendi, very severe. And I wanted to make a request which would call upon all your kindness."

"What request? I will gladly grant it if I can."

"Tonight, will you sleep inside the 'Djemmah of the Dead' instead of out here under the open sky?"

I knew immediately what he had in mind, and answered:

"Gladly."

"And you are not afraid?"

"Afraid? Of whom? Even if I were, I would not be alone, for you will be reading the black book of your ancestors."

"What makes you think that?"

"It's obvious. I will be sleeping while you struggle with words, figures, snakes, and monsters. But remember that you already sacrificed the last few nights. Don't overtax yourself. And should you need me, wake me so that I can help you."

"Only two can help me, God and myself. If I could only pray! I would give a great deal to be able to, for I feel that the heavenly judge will first settle accounts with me and my ancestors before the 'Djemmah of the Dead' or the 'Djemmah of the Living' can deal with us. The judgment the Djemmah will pronounce must first be discussed between God and myself, and the path to Him is the same today as it has always been. It is the path of prayer, and I do not yet know it. Now then, will you grant my request and sleep in the counsel hall?"

"Yes."

"I thank you. It is not the ordinary, foolish fear of corpses that makes me want not to be alone, but caution which I owe not only to myself but all of you as well. Wondrous things are happening here, and all of it has the greatest importance. No one knows how I will fare during the night I spend among the dead. It is not impossible that I may be forced into a quick, immediate decision which I cannot make unaided. Therefore I want you to be close by. But I ask that you keep this a secret. No one need know that we will not spend the night out here, with the others."

He gave me his hand and left, and I returned to my

companions. It had been difficult to feign indifference when he had expressed the desire to be able to pray. I had been deeply moved and was also joyful. When someone wishes that he could pray, he is close to having his wish granted for the mere wish is a prayer, a prayer that is more certain of fulfillment than any other.

We continued our inspection of the buildings and finished before evening. In the last room, which lay farthest west, we discovered a second door facing the one by which we had entered, and which could be opened with the same key. We unlocked it. When the powerful stone had slid back into the room and we passed through the doorway, we were amazed to find ourselves out in the open. We were no longer prisoners. While we had been certain that we would get out again, we breathed a sigh of relief when our expectation was confirmed.

We were far away from the city, on land which had crumbled away from the ring of mountains surrounding the Maha-Lama Lake. To get to the city and the river, one could pass either through the citadel or describe a wider arc through open country. But we decided against such a visit. It was enough for us to know that we were free at any moment to leave the prison in which we had been meant to die a miserable death. We went back inside, closed the aperture, and agreed that we had done enough work for one day. I would very much have liked to ride to the city to pay a visit to "Prison Number Five" to see how things stood there. But there was not enough time before dark and therefore we postponed that excursion until the following day. We went back to the place along the arcade which we had chosen for our camp and where Halef, our chief cook, was busily preparing a meal for us. To devote himself exclusively to this task, he asked me to see to his stallion as soon as I had watered and fed my own horse. As I was taking care of this, the Erdjani came up to me. Normally, he was serious, taciturn, and thoughtful. On this particular day, these qualities had been especially in evidence. Even now, as he was leaning against a pillar, looking on as the horses nuzzled me, he did not speak.

"Well?" I finally asked, smiling. "Do I also have to find the key to unlock you?"

"No. You have had it for a long time, ever since I first saw you."

"You wish to speak, and yet you remain silent."

"I am not clear in my own mind, and it is not my custom to say something confused. Ever since coming here, I find myself in a world which is utterly unknown to me, yet it seems as if I already knew it."

"Perhaps you were here before, with your father, when you were young."

"Oh, no."

"Or did you see old pictures of this area?"

"Not that either."

"You may have heard talk about it."

"Yes, that's it. But only in private."

"By whom?"

"My father and mother. No one was allowed to be present, and the only reason I could stay was that I was still a child. Yet certain words, names, expressions, and images have remained with me. They are hidden inside me but now they suddenly emerge and form a coherent whole. Today, it was as if I were dreaming. I was a child again. I saw my father and mother and was listening to them. They were speaking of the 'City of the Dead,' the Maha-Lama Lake, the giant angel in the center of the open area, the 'dream' of every Mir of Ardistan, the sedan chair, the 'Djemmah of the Living' and the 'Djemmah of the Dead,' of Abu Shalem, the 'most famous, the most just and the kindest' of all the Maha-Lamas, of—"

"You knew all that and never told me about it?" I interrupted.

"Knew?" he smiled. "If that were true, I would have told you long ago. It was inaccessible to me, wholly unconscious. Only when we came here did it rise, slowly and unnoticed at first, until today it confronted me and said to me: 'Here I am, you had forgotten me. Do you still know me?' Isn't that strange, sahib?"

"Strange? Oh no. I find it quite natural, and I ask that you also behave naturally. Allow these childhood images time to come gradually to the surface. Don't force them lest you destroy them. The soul yields what it holds of its own accord but will resist pressure. You must not rob yourself."

Had he heard what I said? He had raised his head and was quietly looking toward the West. The sun was setting. We could not see this but the sky above us began to take on the color of a blushing virgin's cheek, and this redness seemed to be reflected on the Erdjani's face. How much that face had changed in recent days! And how different his body, his movements had become! If I were to describe an appearance that was utterly informed by the soul, I would have to say that he was a tall and splendidly formed, virile, handsome young ascetic before the beginning of his fast. I had never seen his face look like this before. I felt that his features were entering my consciousness more and more to etch themselves there forever. He finally answered:

"I know what you mean, and am already disciplining myself so that I won't destroy anything. Just now, it was as if I saw my father as I so often saw him, playing the 'royal game' of chess. He always maintained that the game was a lie and to be wholly rejected as an image of war. In chess, the player is compelled to sacrifice pawns, bishops, rooks, and even much more valuable things to win. But at the end of the game, both sides are devastated, not only that of the vanquished, but that of the alleged victor as well. The warfare of the men of violence still resembles this old game which was suddenly arrested in its development. The man of grace, however, whom all of us expect, would wage every war that violence forced upon him in such a way that victory would not cost him a single sacrifice."

"You heard that when you were a child?" I asked cautiously.

"No. I was already a boy, playing chess myself. My mother told it to me and repeated it so often that it implanted itself firmly in my mind and I began thinking about it. The task of winning without sacrificing something is one of the most important in life, not only in a military sense, but in all others too. I meditated and reflected a great deal about this, but in vain. Then you and Hadji Halef appeared. At the Chatar defile where you defeated the Tshoban without spilling a drop of blood, the two of you showed us what my father had meant when he had condemned chess. Since that day, I have endeavored to put his and your teaching into practice and—"

He was interrupted by Halef calling us to supper. At the same time, the Mir was coming back from the well in whose interior he had sought solitude. He joined us. We hurried to comply with Halef's invitation, for he easily became angry when his preparations were not shown the respect he felt they deserved.

As we were eating, it grew dark. We had been walking about all day and were quite tired. Because neither the Mir nor I made the effort, no real conversation got started. There was no need for an immediate discussion of what we had seen and experienced that day. Such matters first have to be filtered and thought through before they can be expressed in ordinary language. Feeling no need to talk, we retired early. The Mir went some distance away from us and I joined him so that I would not be noticed when I left. About an hour later, when we could assume that all our companions were asleep, we took our blankets and went to the hall of the "Djemmah of the Dead."

It was sufficiently far from our camp so that the others would not be awakened by the sliding of the stone that served as a door. Inside, profound darkness reigned. We lit as many candles as the Mir needed for his purpose. Then he had to descend into the purgatory of this extraordinary place to study the black books of his ancestors. I prepared a bed on some seats in the left auditorium.

The light of the candelabra did not reach me. The curious illumination caused the immobile figures of the Djemmah to seem far away. This created an optical illusion; their size became gigantic. I had the feeling of looking from our world of darkness into a supernatural realm whose secrets were beginning to become visible. Such phantasms would make sleep impossible. I turned over and closed my eyes. I must have fallen asleep immediately. Some time later, I was awakened by a loud voice.

It was the Mir. At first, he had been standing near

Abu Shalem, starting with the main book. Now he was near his ancestors, had one of their account books in his hand, and was reading from it. He was facing the judges. Unfortunately, his position made it impossible for me to hear his words, for their sound was not reflected by the wall. He seemed to have forgotten reality, to have become totally absorbed by the fiction, taking the dead for living beings. He was reading aloud to them; sometimes, he would address them to provide a commentary, gesticulating like an accused, or a defense counsel for whom everything he is and has is at stake. Not for a single moment did I consider this behavior fantastic, let alone senseless, for while I could not really understand anything, I yet heard the sound of his words and was aware that he spoke from the most profound anguish and torment. But what was that?

Straight ahead of me, but in the farthest corner and the most impenetrable darkness, a tiny fluttering flame had appeared and was slowly coming toward me. As the distance decreased, I could make out the shape of the person carrying it. It was a woman who was wearing a white, ample garment that hung down to the ground and had long, wide sleeves. It fitted tightly around the neck. Face and head were uncovered. Her hair was arranged in simple braids. This being seemed to be very familiar with the hall. She paid no attention to the path she was taking but had her face turned to one side. She was looking at the Mir so that she did not see me when she passed at a distance of ten paces or so. Yet I made myself as small as possible to avoid being noticed, and closely scrutinized her face. Though I could only see part of it, I could tell that she was not a young girl, but a woman clearly over forty. She was as tall as an Ussula, her bearing erect, her walk proud although she took care to step lightly.

Having advanced somewhat further, she stopped and blew out the candle. She was now standing in darkness, listening. She wanted to hear what the Mir was saying. She raised her head so that her face, half in profile, half head-on, was illumined by the light from the candelabra. She was holding her head precisely as the Erdjani had when I had admired his beauty and expressive features shortly before dinner. Oddly enough, I had the impression that I was looking at the very same face, albeit in a female version. It did not suggest asceticism, but had the expression and the large, serious, receptive eyes of a visionary. There was no doubt that it was the Erdjani's face. I immediately thought of his mother. The age was right, and the figure and movements unmistakably the same. Physically a descendant of the Ussul but spiritually and intellectually from Djinnistan, she was standing there, drawn up to her full height, her entire attention riveted on the living person who was talking to the long-since dead as if they could hear, understand, and answer him. But she could not make out the individual words and sentences in the abundance of sound that was flooding us. The white-robed mysterious woman therefore moved on, softly and slowly approaching the Mir.

I stood up. It was possible that she might retrace her steps and I did not wish to be seen. I decided not to let her out of my sight and followed her as cautiously as I could.

She continued on, stopping occasionally to see if what she was hearing was becoming more distinct, but then advancing further until she reached the steps that led to the seat on which Abu Shalem, the highest judge, was sitting. She came to one of the great, strong pillars on which the high ceiling was resting and stopped behind it. I also advanced until I was level with her and the Mir, and then sat down so that the light would not fall on me. I wanted to wait for what was coming without being observed. And it came very quickly, much more quickly than I had expected, and in a wholly different form.

The Mir's voice was still ringing out. He was still reading, still interjecting what he felt compelled to, and still directing everything he read and said to the judges. While the white woman behind the pillar probably understood every word, I unfortunately did not. The distance was too great. Now I saw that he closed the book with a bang, threw it behind him with a violent gesture, and directed a demand to the dead which I also could understand because he had turned somewhat in my direction and was articulating every word so that they were no longer blurred by the acoustics.

"My soul is full of fear and misery. It did not address you as if you were dead but as it would speak to the living. It assumed that you also had once had souls, that you had not lost them but that they came down to you and were present whenever you believed yourself justified and worthy of pronouncing judgment on such enormous injustices. I have described my distress, my torment and misery to you. I directed my questions to you. But your tongues are paralyzed by death. I can expect no answers from lifeless bodies. But I do demand an answer from your souls. I demand it by everything they once held sacred, and still so hold. I demand it from them, now, here, at this very spot where I am standing! I cannot wait, for at midnight tomorrow, the decision about me and about you will be made. Yes, you! Not only the accused, the judges also will be judged, I assure you."

He paused to give greater emphasis to his closing words. He was in extreme agitation. He was trembling, his voice quivering. He continued:

"Let your souls speak to mine. It is inside me, waiting. I am receptive to what you have to say and ready to hear you."

He joined his hands, lowered his head, and stood for a very long time. Occasionally, he raised a hand to wipe the perspiration from his forehead. I was standing away from him, yet could see his chest heaving. This gave me the impression that I could also hear his heavy, fearful breathing. There was something struggling inside him in an effort to detach and free itself. I could not but think of the wish he had expressed toward evening: "I would give a great deal if I could pray." Finally, he thrust his arms forward as if he were throwing something, and exclaimed:

"I hear nothing. Not a single word, not a single syllable. Neither from outside, nor within. Where are the souls that are supposed to speak to me? Don't they wish to? Are they unable? Or did they perhaps never exist? What am I to do? Whom shall I turn to? Who is willing and ready to help me?"

He looked in all directions as if he really expected an answer. And there was a sound, almost as faint as a breath, yet audible throughout the large hall. It seemed to be coming from above:

"Pray!"

He twitched, then turned around timidly. Yet his expression became happier.

"Pray?" he asked. "Pray? I heard it, I heard it quite distinctly. Who spoke? Did it come from outside, or from within? Was it one of the souls that has been silent up to now? I, the unbeliever, the criminal, am I permitted to pray, a man burdened not only by his own sins but also by those of his entire family as he dares to face God to ask that they be forgiven—"

He sank down on his knees and continued in that position. But he did not speak loudly as he had heretofore but almost inaudibly. He was praying.

I turned away and folded my hands. The place where he was praying was sacred now. My profane, critical glance must not penetrate this shrine. I looked back at the white figure of the woman who was leaning forward so as not to lose a single one of the Mir's words. She had her hands raised but folded and was visibly and deeply moved. Now she left the pillar. Having reached the bottom step, she waited. Without really wanting to, I had to get up. I drew closer and closer to see the Mir's face clearly. He was so completely absorbed in his thoughts and feelings that he began expressing them. Toward the end of his prayer, his voice became louder and louder until finally, rising from his kneeling position, he exclaimed:

"And now I will no longer turn to the earth, the dead, and the souls of the departed, but raise my confidence heavenward, to the infinite, eternal life, to the nowhere absent, ever present spirit to whom I prayed and who will answer me in my soul when I ask him: 'Is my decision presumptuous? Is it forbidden to—' "

Surprised and perhaps startled, he stopped in midsentence and fell back. He had seen the white figure which now placed its foot on the first step and slowly ascended. Having arrived at the top, the woman went to Abu Shalem's side, rested her hand on the black book that lay open before him, and said in a clear, resonant voice:

"After midnight tomorrow, this book will be forever closed, if such is your wish. An answer will be given you, not only in your soul, but also from without. Put out all candles."

He immediately obeyed but did not stop looking at her. I could tell that he took her for a supernatural being. When the last candle had been put out and nothing could any longer be seen, the same deep, clear voice came through the darkness:

"What you decided is not presumptuous. You may shoulder the entire burden because your strength is the sum of theirs. Rely on kindness and compassion. They are already on their way."

It grew quiet. Nothing seemed to stir. Then there was a gentle rustling near me as if the hem of a soft garment were brushing the floor. A barely noticeable current of air wafted past me. A fine, sweet odor remained, similar to the scent of pussy willows at Easter. Much closer than before, the mysterious woman had walked past me. She had been wise to order the candles put out. In the darkness, no eye could follow her. I too felt it best to let her vanish unseen. A clear view would have destroyed much of the poetry of this event. As I wondered how I should now act toward the Mir, I decided to wait and see what he would tell me, what views he would express. I tiptoed back to my blankets and lay down. Some time later, I heard his steps. He stretched out his hands to touch me. I did not move immediately; I wanted him to think that I was asleep. He shook me. I pretended to wake up.

"You sleep very soundly," he said. "Did you fall asleep right away?"

"Yes." And that was true, though I did not mention that I had waked up again. "Have you finished already? Have you seen all the books?"

"I have. I know what I wanted to find out."

"And you put out all the candles?"

"We are leaving. We'll spend the rest of the night outside. Then no one will suspect that we were gone. Come along."

I got up, took my blankets, and followed him. We

let the stone slide back into place and went to where
we had lain down after supper. Until we got there, he
did not say a single word but when we had settled
down, he asked me:

"Effendi, do you believe in spirits?"

"Yes," I said. "God is spirit."

"I don't mean that. Do you believe in ghosts?"

"No."

"In saints?"

"Yes."

"In the blessed?"

"Yes."

"Then listen: I saw a blessed one."

"You are mistaken."

"No! I not only saw her; she talked to me."

"You are mistaken nonetheless. Did she tell you she
was one of the blessed?"

"No, but I am certain she is. She can't be anything
else."

"Don't you want to tell me—"

"Not now. I have to put everything in order before I
can talk about it. Good night."

"Good night."

He turned on his other side but I didn't. Experience
told me that he was not yet through. As expected, he
turned back toward me after a few minutes, and asked:

"Are you already asleep, Effendi?"

"Not yet."

"Are you convinced that the 'Djemmah of the Living' will take place tomorrow midnight?"

"Completely convinced."

"So am I. I even know that Abd el Fadl and Merhameh will come."

"How could you?"

"I just know. Let that suffice. Perhaps I'll tell you at
some later time who told me. I can rely on kindness
and compassion; the two are already on their way.
Good night."

After some moments, he began again:

"Are you sleeping now, Effendi?"

"Almost."

"Forgive me for disturbing you once more. I have
something very important to tell you."

"Is it something good?"

"Very good. Do you remember the heartfelt desire I expressed when during the late afternoon you were called from my side?"

"Yes, I remember."

"Well, what was it?"

"The desire to be able to pray."

"Yes, that's what it was. And just think, Effendi, I did pray."

"Is that really true?"

"Yes. I readily admit that it seems almost impossible, yet it happened. Can you imagine what it means that the Mir of Ardistan prayed? Do you realize how great a victory for God that is?"

"A victory for God? What do you mean?"

"A victory God won."

"Over whom?"

"Over whom, you ask? Over me, of course, and my disbelief."

"You poor fool," I said in a compassionate tone.

"Whom are you calling a poor fool?"

"You, of course."

"Why?"

"Because that's what you are, one of the poorest imaginable."

"I don't understand you. I feel rich, very rich. I say that with all sincerity. And instead of calling me lucky, you say I'm a poor fool. Why?"

"Because your happiness does not make you humble, but arrogant."

Now he sat up, bent down over me, and asked:

"Arrogant? How so? I'm not aware of it."

"You aren't? Didn't you just place yourself on the same level with God?"

"On the same level? Me? Are you out of your senses, Effendi?"

"Not at all. Didn't you just say that God overcame you?"

"Yes, I did."

"But isn't it true that a victory presupposes a battle?"

"Of course. Or isn't it true that I fought with God, that I did not want to acknowledge Him?"

"You poor fool, I say again. Do you really imagine that God was compelled to do battle with you? The cloud that must dissolve brags that it fought the sun! As a piece of wood burns to ashes, it boasts of the life and death struggle it is waging against the fire. On his death bed, the sick man exclaims grandiloquently that death has reason to be proud for having defeated such as himself. Do you want more examples, other comparisons? What reason do you have to pride yourself on finally having prayed? And consider this carefully: Even if you were to shoulder the sins of the entire world, there would be no reason for you to boast of it. Such pride is madness, nothing else. To sin, and to assume sins, is no honor. The more you assume, the less you may expect to be honored for it. Should you pray again, ask God for modesty! The most sincere friend you have gives you this advice. God does not do battle with any creature, not even the first of his angels. Good night."

He did not answer but lay back down, shifting from side to side for some time. Then all became quiet, and I fell asleep. When I woke up, he was lying next to me, breathing peacefully and smiling in his sleep. My companions had long since risen and washed, and were now having breakfast. I hurried to make up for lost time and the Mir followed that example when the noise woke him later.

10 : Toward Freedom

Our plan that day was comprehensive and turned out to be much more interesting than we had thought. It had been decided to return first through the canal by which we had come here, and to examine the trapdoor by which we had so unexpectedly been dropped from the upper to the nether world. Then we planned to investigate carefully to see whether the lock of this canal could perhaps be opened toward the river. It was my guess that the great rotunda of what had once been the Maha-Lama Lake was connected with the citadel by some secret passage. But this was something we could look into later. What was important now was to search through the city to find out if people lived there, who they were, and what connections they had with the rebels and our imprisonment. That our reconnaissance had to be circumspect need hardly be mentioned. We could not use our horses for we would have been too conspicuous. A man on foot can pass anywhere, a rider may encounter many and impassable obstacles. We would have to split up inside the town where each of us would reconnoiter in one district, but first the canal and our Prison Number Five had to be investigated. We set out to do this after breakfast. The two Ussul princes had agreed to stay with the horses. All the others had wanted to participate in our search. We opened the gate that led into the old canal. In the room that lay behind it and had seats all around, we lit small lamps which showed us the way to the spot that lay below the double gate of the prison.

At first, it seemed as if we would not find anything, but at the place where we had come up from below ground, I was struck by the fact that one corner of the floor of the shaft was not of stone but of earth, and this earth was loose, as if someone had been working there recently. I thrust my hand into it, and finally pulled out a key which had precisely the same shape as those we had found earlier. Now that we had it, and knew what kind of secret we were dealing with, the rest followed naturally. We knew at what level the keyholes had been made and therefore did not take long to discover what we were looking for. Having unlocked a door, we came into a narrow but very long room which contained the mechanism which raised and lowered the platform which had taken us down. Large stones weighing several hundred pounds each were fastened to ropes passing over rollers which raised or lowered the floor between the two gates. It would have required no more than a turn to move all of us above ground, but we decided against that since we did not know what was happening in the prison at this moment.

Almost more important was the second discovery we made. One of the walls of the room in which we found ourselves adjoined the very heavy, thick wall of the canal at the point where it ended. If a hidden exit to the river did exist, it would have to be looked for here. Repeatedly, I went outside and returned to look and compare. There was nothing conspicuous in the room that housed the mechanism except two wooden beam heads which projected from the rock along the wall. One of them was about three, the other some five feet above the floor. They were perhaps two feet in length and usually heavy. This made me wonder. What were they doing here? It seemed unlikely that they had been intended to support something, for in that case stone, not wood, would have been used. These beam heads therefore had to have a purpose which had no connection with the function of the room in which we were standing. And this purpose could only be discovered outside. What we had outside, and directly adjoining, was the wall which blocked the canal. If one of its huge stones was really a door that could be moved like those we had found on the Maha-Lama Lake, it had to be the one that abutted against the outer side of the wall whose inside we were facing. In that case, the purpose of the two head beams became obvious. And their unusual size suggested that they had to withstand an unusual amount of pressure. They must be the handles of the strong bolts by which the rock door was kept in place outside. Bolts are useless unless movable, but here it looked as if these beams had been bricked in. I tried to shake them. That wasn't easy but the mortar began to crumble. As I continued shaking, more mortar fell to the ground. My companions helped, and as we joined our efforts it became apparent that these bolts only seemed to have been bricked in. The mortar had merely been used to create a misleading appearance. As soon as it had crumbled, we managed to pull first one, then the second beam out of the wall. But although the bolts had now been removed, nothing happened outside. We went out there and started pushing. The large stone block yielded, slowly at first, and then more easily. Its placement was precisely the same as that of all the doors in the great Maha-Lama structure. When it had finished moving and was standing still once again, only a slight pressure was required to return it to the opening.

Pleased with this success, we quickly stepped outside and followed the canal under the prison and the open area to its end. When, at our arrival, we had come down from the mountain, we had seen where it opened into the river. As we reached that spot, a considerable surprise awaited us. There was water in the river. This was extraordinary when one considered that it had been dry for so many centuries. What is more, this return of the water coincided with our presence. There wasn't more than an occasional pool, but small channels were already being opened between them, and this meant that the earth contained much more moisture than the warmth of the sun, considerable that day, could evaporate. We were jubilant.

"That explains the loud rustling in the well of the angel," Halef said. "The water that drains there makes its reappearance here. Don't you agree, Sidi?"

"No," I answered. "The causes of this phenomenon must not be looked for in the well of the angel but in a region that lies very much higher. The gift we see here was entrusted to the earth of Djinnistan."

"Will this water disappear again, will it stay as it is, will it rise?" the prince of the Tshoban asked.

"As God wills. We cannot understand His counsels. There is divine intent in everything that happens."

"In this water, too?"

"Yes. Sooner than we think, we may discover why it was sent to us, and why at this precise moment."

"Why? Because the time has come," the Mir exclaimed. "If the gates of paradise up there open evening after evening, the time for the promised return of the river has come. When God returns to Ardistan, then—"

He stopped. He felt that what he was about to say would give the lie to all his earlier beliefs. But the Erdjani quickly walked up to him and challenged him: "Go on, go on. Or are you afraid to?"

"Afraid?" the Mir asked.

They looked at each other seriously and penetratingly. For a moment, it seemed the Mir would take offense, but he fought the temptation and overcame it. With a calm smile, he answered:

"At an earlier time, I would have been afraid. Now I know that it is no disgrace to become wiser, more reasonable, and clearer in one's perceptions. At an earlier time, my pride would have forbidden me to admit error, but now—now—"

He turned away from the Erdjani and addressed me:

"Effendi, you advised me to pray for modesty. I did, after you had fallen asleep. I was about to bring war to all of Djinnistan. I wanted to conquer those mountains from which the water flows, the water which my country lacks. I considered myself a great strategist. I wished to accomplish through blood, murder, and death what can never be achieved by the clenched fist. But today, I am saying to you: If God now came down the river to ask whether I wanted peace or war, I would tell Him that there would be peace from this time on, not just between the lands and the peoples of my state but also between us and Djinnistan, that blessed country whose citizens may claim that no blood was ever spilled among them. Are you content with my statement, Effendi?"

Cheerfully, I gave him my hand and answered:

"I thank you. Take the water which we are welcoming here with such joy as an external sign of the beneficial sources within us. There can be no question that God will come. And therefore it is good that all of us know how this question will be answered. Now, let us return to our investigation. We will close the door behind us, leave the river bed by the bridge and then walk to the prison. What is to be done next will depend on what happens there."

My companions agreed. We went back inside the canal and pushed the stone into the opening. Then we walked into the river bed and toward the bridge which we had crossed on our arrival. Steps led up to the bank.

Our return to freedom coincided with an event which was of no great import, yet pleased us greatly. For when we had come to the top of the steps and found ourselves at the bridge head, I wanted to go straight to the prison and therefore turned my back to the river. But Halef called out to me:

"Stop, Sidi. Look across the bridge!"

I saw six camels coming from the far side. They were carrying water and on the lead animal, there sat a man whose face could not yet be recognized clearly because he had pulled the hood of his haik far down over his forehead. When he came closer, I saw that it was the good cistern watchman who had done so much to help me. He recognized me at the same time. Without stopping his camel, he jumped down, hurried toward me and exclaimed joyously:

"Hamdulillah, how glad I am to see you! I had feared for you. How pleased I am that you and the others are still alive. I wanted to save you. I am bringing you water."

"Your loyalty has been great," I answered. Then I pointed toward the Mir:

"Your lord will thank you for it."

He knelt down before the Mir but was ordered to rise. The Mir told him:

"I only saw you briefly, yet recognize you. You gave us good advice and will not regret it. How was it possible for you to leave your post and your cistern to bring us water? Did no one try to prevent that?"

"No. No one was there to forbid it. And there is no one here who might catch me."

"No one?"

"No. All those who were in the 'City of the Dead' had to leave. They did not want anyone there who might see and talk to you, or try to save you and all those that were to be driven to certain death here."

"Whom do you mean?"

"The army of the Erdjani, the Ussul, and the Tshoban. All manner of force and cunning are being used to make them rush to the City of the Dead."

"Is that true? How do you know?" the Mir asked as he looked at us in consternation.

We were as surprised as he, but not frightened.

"Everyone knows," the watchman answered. "The rumor was spread deliberately so that everyone might see how great, bold, and wise the new ruler is. The

'Panther' has turned toward Ard, the Christians are being driven from the city, all the rest have taken his side, and those who are still loyal—"

"My wife, my children!" the Mir interrupted. "I must leave immediately."

He seemed about to act on his words but the Erdjani took him by the arm and warned:

"Where will you go, alone, without us, and without having taken the time to reflect?"

"But think, my wife, my children!"

"Mashallah! You want me to think, and will not think yourself? Your wife and children? Don't we also have much at stake? Haven't you heard that all the Ussul and Tshoban, and that means my entire army, are to be driven here to their certain death? The lives of thousands are in peril! But do you see me running off?"

Almost superhuman in his self-control, the Mir lowered his eyes in shame and calmly turned back to the watchman. "Let me hear what else you know."

"The 'Panther' will remain in Ard for only a few more days," the man answered. "Then, he will take all the troops which are still there and join those marching against Djinnistan. With a single, powerful thrust he means to end the war he is waging against the Mir of that country."

"Go on!"

"That's all I know."

"And how do you know all this? Surely the 'Panther' didn't tell you himself?"

"No, he didn't. I heard it from the soldiers he left by the well when he rode with you to the 'City of the Dead.' Other soldiers coming from elsewhere joined them. They were to block the edge of the desert along its entire length and to let no one pass until it could be assumed that you had died of hunger and thirst. No one can reach or save you. And the few that were here were taken along by the 'Panther' when he left the 'City of the Dead' with his 'general' and fifty horsemen."

"So there is absolutely no one here?"

"No one. I know that for certain, for I had to determine how much water there was, and supply some to everyone here. I also had to set up stations which would provide you and your escort with water along the way. I knew when and in what order those fifty men would return. When the first of them arrived and it was believed that the plot against the previous ruler of Ardistan had succeeded, I was chased away. I was told I was no longer needed, that I was free to go and should not come back."

"Did they know you were loyal to me?"

"They suspected it, and that was enough. I did go, but not the way they assumed. During the night, and unnoticed, I used my camels to transport as many provisions and as much water as I could here into the desert and returned with them to the well before day-break. Then, when I left in the morning with the six unladen camels and took the opposite direction, no one suspected that I would describe an arc and bring what I had hidden to this place. But now, I see to my surprise that you are free and cannot die of thirst since the river is carrying water. I would not believe such a miracle, had I not seen it with my own eyes."

The man had acted with devotion and intelligence. The Mir gave him his hand, and said:

"Be of good cheer! I shall think of everything you have done as if you actually had saved our lives. So you are convinced that there is no one here except us?"

"Yes."

"And that includes Prison Number Five?"

"Yes."

"We shall have a look nonetheless."

We made for the prison and the watchman followed with his camels. Because the gate was locked, Halef climbed over the wall and opened it from inside. We entered. The watchman was told to wait outside; there was no need for him to find out our secrets. The buildings were empty; they did not interest us. Our attention was wholly directed to the movable floor between the two gates. It consisted of wooden planks that had been covered by layers of earth and sand. To the left and the right of the inner gate, there were two wheels onto which ropes had been wound. Turning one of them lowered the floor; turning the other brought it

: 538 :

back up. That was all there was to this contrivance whose intended victims we had been. We cut both ropes, lowered them so that they were no longer visible, and buried the ends in a pile of earth lying in a corner of the yard. This way, the secret would remain hidden from those who did not know it and be useless to those who did. Then we called in the loyal watchman. For the time being, he was assigned an apartment and told to keep himself in readiness.

Because it was the "Panther's" plan to drive the Ussul and the Tshoban toward the "City of the Dead," we would soon see our friends again, should he be successful. But we had to ask ourselves where and how they should be housed. There was more than enough room in the large, spread-out town, but because we had to concentrate rather than disperse them, I felt that the citadel would be the best place. The Mir was willing to take us to it. He assured us that he knew its every nook and cranny and that we should believe him this time because he certainly was not mistaken. We accepted his offer.

As we ascended through any number of utterly deserted alleys, I tried to discover a connection between what I saw here and what had once been the Maha-Lama Lake. The upper part of the citadel had been built against the unbroken mountain chain that enclosed the former lake. We already knew that the rocks and mountains had been hollowed out to create the rooms we had seen. They could only be separated from the highest apartments of the citadel by relatively thin natural or artificial walls, and it therefore seemed plausible that some secret passage would connect the structures on the Maha-Lama Lake and the citadel. I could not rid myself of this notion as we continued our ascent, passed through the tall, wide, gateless entrance of the citadel, and then had the Mir show us through all the rooms he knew.

I have no intention of describing this citadel, however interesting such an account might be. Suffice it to say that it was admirably suited to the purpose we had in mind. But something happened that secretly amused me and that I should mention. We found ourselves in that part of the fortress which had probably been the quarters of the commanding officer. In one of these beautifully situated, high rooms, I saw something which immediately attracted my attention, although I kept it to myself. On one of the walls that faced the window and which was built of huge square stones, there was the same picture of a sun I had seen before on the door of the so-called porter's lodge or "administrative office." It was obvious to me that this had to be the entrance to the passageway to the Maha-Lama Lake whose existence I had merely suspected before.

The windows of the apartment offered a panoramic view of the town and its environs as they lay below us in the full light of the sun. But the many places along the river where water had appeared shone more brightly than anything else. It was only from up here that one could see how numerous and extensive these pools actually were. It was not stagnant but flowing water. We were standing side by side, looking down, pleased with the sight.

"If there is no change," the firstborn of the Tshoban said, "the desert will cease being one."

"There will be no change," the Erdjani said in a tone that suggested he could make that decision all by himself. The Mir's eyes had grown large and were shimmering with tears.

"Do you recall what you said a while ago, Effendi? Down there, by the end of the canal?"

"What are you thinking of?"

"You said: 'There is divine intent in everything that happens. Sooner than we think, we may discover why this water was sent for us, and at this precise moment.' Only a short time has passed since you made that remark, and it is already becoming reality. This water is here to save the army of the Ussul and Tshoban. They would perish if they found nothing to drink. The ways of Providence are marvellous. Didn't you fear for your troops when the cistern watchman was talking?"

The question had been addressed to the Erdjani, who answered:

"No. The sheik of the Tshoban is with my army and during my absence, my cautious, brave Irahd, the captain of the Hukara, is in command. He cannot be outwitted."

"Really? Didn't that happen to you?"

"No."

"But it did. Forgive me, but didn't the 'Panther' trap you into coming here?"

The Erdjani reached under his garment, pulled a folded piece of paper out of a pocket, and answered with a smile:

"I have been silent so far because it was sacred and important to me. But now at least the sahib shall see this so that he won't also believe that I am careless. I received this piece of paper from a messenger whom I did not know and who immediately disappeared again. But I do know the writing and the secret sign at the end. What I did, I did because of these lines, and for no other reason. And events will show that I can accept responsibility for it."

He unfolded the paper and handed it to me. It said:

"For the first time, I am greeting you with this note written by me personally. The 'Panther' will attempt to persuade you to go to the 'City of the Dead.' Let him! Then, when you are gone, the 'Panther' will try to drive your army there. Order your Irahd to yield to his pressure, not across the desert but up the river. He will find water and know how to keep the enemy away from it, and thirsty. Your father."

I folded the paper, returned it, and addressed not only the Mir but all the others as well:

"I wish to state that our friend, the Erdjani, did not act carelessly but very intelligently. I note that important events are about to occur. It is very likely that the Ussul and Tshoban will arrive today. I propose that, even if we don't ride out to meet them, we at least reconnoiter along the river, and that we do this immediately."

"Should we get our horses?" the Mir asked.

"Yes."

"Then we will have to go back down to the river and return by the canal."

"No."

"What else?"

"There is a shorter and much easier route and you will show us the way."

"But I don't know of any."

"You don't? But a while ago, you said that you knew this citadel inside out."

"Do you mean we can get there from here?"

"Yes, from this very room."

"You are speaking in enigmas."

"I will immediately clear up this enigma, although I have never been here before."

As I walked toward the stone I have mentioned, the others followed. A bare touch of the sun showed me that it was also of metal and could be moved. I turned it from the left to the right. Inside the wall, one could hear a faint, short click. Then the stone receded and we could enter. The room lying before us was windowless and dark. But now light fell into it from the outside, and we saw that it was narrow and formed a short walk or corridor. At the far end, there was another stone door with a key in its keyhole, as we noticed with satisfaction. I turned it. The stone also moved, but toward us so that we had to jump back quickly to avoid being knocked down. As we moved on, we came into a narrow room that received its light through windows shaped like firing slits. Because of its furnishings, we immediately recognized it, for we had seen all this before. It was the large sick bay in the Maha-Lama building. We only had to pass through its front door to find ourselves in the arcade. A few more steps took us to our horses. Halef seemed on the verge of launching into a long, enthusiastic speech about our great cleverness and ingenuity, but I gestured to him to remain silent, let my companions precede me, and locked both doors behind us. I also locked the outside door of the sick bay after we had stepped out into the arcade. The two Ussul princes were rather surprised to see us approach from this side rather than from the direction by which we had left. After they had been told everything we had seen and heard, we saddled and mounted our horses and rode through the western door which we had discovered the day before. I put the key to it into my pocket.

We rode around the citadel and followed the course

of the river toward the southern section of the town. The Mir and I were in the lead and as we were riding along, he said to me:

"Don't be surprised that I am so quiet, Effendi. It is a very difficult time for me. More and more, I am being pushed down from the elevated place on which I thought I was standing. I have to accept countless instructions, and time and again I am being made to see that—"

"You are not moving down, but up," I interrupted him. "That I discovered a door you knew nothing of is no reason to be downcast."

"Oh, yes. Everything that happens is not happening through me but through the agency of others. I feel ignorant, incapable, superfluous. It seems that everyone else is considerably better suited to be the Mir of Ardistan than I, and that makes me—"

"Thank God," I interrupted again.

"For what?"

"That you consider yourself incompetent. For that is proof that you have the highest possible qualifications to really become what you only appeared to be heretofore. God is shaking you. Persevere! Your former strength was weakness, but your present, supposed weakness will become your strength and glory. You should not believe that you have to know and do everything yourself. To rule means to guide, not to attend personally to every detail. And, most importantly, let the Lord think, care, and work for you. He does it gladly."

He smiled gratefully, and said:

"Effendi, that's the way you are! I only wish it were also the way I was."

"It will be. You may believe me."

"With difficulty. In my case, burden is being added to burden. Think of my wife, my children! I was indifferent to them, they were almost strangers to me. You reunited me with them, and this union has grown stronger day by day. I have come to love them dearly. And now they find themselves in Ard, unprotected, and in the power of this beast, the 'Panther.'"

"Unprotected, you say? If you had my belief and my confidence, you wouldn't feel that. Have you nothing but enemies in Ard? Believe me: Those you love are in good hands. The time will come when you tell me so yourself. I even think you may see them much sooner than you expect, much sooner."

"You are trying to console me, Effendi. And it is odd that your faith so often turns out to have been justified, that your hopes materialize with astonishing speed. Today, I still have to persevere, to wait, for at midnight the 'Djemmah of the Living' will take place. But tomorrow, I won't be able to hold out any longer unless I get some reassuring news about my wife and children. But look, aren't those people up there?"

He pointed across the city and at the heights from which we had come as prisoners of the 'Panther.' Something was moving up there. It was a line of men on horses and camels, which was not yet visible in its entirety because just then it was slowly emerging from behind some rocks. We all stopped and looked up. Now a sedan chair appeared, then a second and a third one, and they were followed by a number of pack animals with more men on horseback behind them. The distance was considerable, yet we could clearly make out the shape of the chairs. We could also see that the first had been decked out with fluttering ostrich feathers, the second with red, the third with blue yak hair. The Mir was jubilant.

"Those sedan chairs are mine, ours! They are coming from Ard. My wife! My children!"

He spurred his horse and rode toward the heights. We followed more slowly to give him time for a first greeting. At a suitable place, we stopped and waited.

It was a while until the group arrived. The Mir, his face radiant, was heading the procession. He had the smaller boy in front of him on his horse, the bigger one behind. Following this image of happiness, we saw two persons whom we knew very well, Abd el Fadl and Merhameh, both on horseback. They stopped and greeted us warmly, and the entire train had to come to a halt. The Mir's wife was sitting in the first sedan chair, the two girls in the second. Then we recognized the Sheik el Beled of El Hadd and his three companions by their tight-fitting garments which resembled knights' armor. Veils hid their faces. I shook

: 544 :

hands with all of them. The rest were loyal retainers of the Mir, chosen by his wife to accompany her. It was with sincere delight that I kissed this woman's hands. Her eyes were filled with tears of joy. Her only concern had been the life of her husband, the father of her children. Quite deliberately, the "Panther" had spread the rumor that the Mir had been captured and taken to the "City of the Dead" where he was to die the same miserable death as so many of his victims before him. When she had heard this, she had felt it to be her most sacred duty to save him or die at his side. She had wanted to join him with her own regiment, the Ussul Guards, but had been persuaded by the Christian bishop and the Sheik el Beled to abandon this plan and to proceed as she was doing now, for she had been unwilling to give it up altogether. The Guard regiment had remained behind to defend the castle and the cathedral to the last man, should the "Panther" attack. The old Bash Nasrani, as courageous as he was upright, a man who put his trust in God and was now the head of the priesthood in Ardistan, had volunteered to form a well-armed corps of Christians for use against the "Panther" whenever the Mir ordered. Those troops of the rebel that were keeping an eye on the desert so that no one could enter the "City of the Dead" had been seen from a distance, but it had been possible to cross their lines at night and without being noticed. In this undertaking, the Sheik el Beled had proven especially capable. The Mir's wife praised him as an exceptionally intelligent, circumspect, and courageous man. When he had heard that she wanted to ride to the "City of the Dead," he had immediately offered himself as her protector and companion, and had sworn the famous "oath of Djinnistan," on which one could unfailingly rely in any situation, even in great crisis and mortal danger.

"The oath of Djinnistan?" I asked. "What kind of oath is that?"

"It is an oath to veil one's face and not to let it be seen again until whatever has been sworn to has been accomplished. No inhabitant of El Hadd and Djinnistan would be capable of breaking it."

I had never heard it explained in this way. Most

probably, it was somehow connected with the fact that every citizen of Djinnistan is the secret helper, protector, and guardian angel of a human being who is well aware that he is being aided but does not know by whom. Such were the brief, preliminary communications the Mir's wife considered necessary, and the train resumed its march.

"Well?" I asked the Mir when I joined him at the head.

"It has been fulfilled, and so quickly," he rejoiced. "Effendi, I am prepared for whatever may come. You are absolutely right. God does not have to do battle with the likes of us. I am coming of my own accord."

The Sheik el Beled spurred his horse, joined us, and reported:

"Effendi, when we were riding along the crest of the mountain, we could see far south along the river valley. A large body of horsemen was coming up the river."

After these words, he fell back, leaving to the ruler and me whatever was to be done. This modesty impressed me.

"That is the Erdjani's army," the Mir said. "Tell him. Weren't we going to reconnoiter? Why don't you ride out to meet them? In the meantime, I'll conduct my people through the city and the back gate of the Maha-Lama palace. Please, give met he key. And tell the Ussul and the Tshoban that they will be assigned quarters in the citadel. Water and provisions will be brought to them through the doors we discovered today. You won't need the key when you get back. I will leave the doors open."

I did as he asked. He, his family, and its escort rode toward the bridge. But we remained on the left bank of the river, riding through the city at a walk. Once outside, we began to trot, and then gallop, to reach those toward whom we were riding as quickly as possible.

11 : The Battle at God's Mountain

What went on at the Maha-Lama Lake that evening was quite different from what had taken place there earlier or even in the most recent past. The ruler of Ardistan had established his residence in the "City of the Dead," which suddenly looked so much alive that one would have thought death had forever disappeared from it. The Mir, his wife and children, and the rest of us had moved into quarters appropriate to our rank. Because of the presence of the troops, we felt obliged not to act in the modest manner of refugees but to show by our conduct that we were unscathed by our recent experiences and had not renounced any of our rights.

The higher-ranking Ussul and Tshoban were also assigned quarters on the lake. Everything that would be referred to as headquarters, quartermaster, general staff, had been moved there. There was incessant bustle and stir. The storerooms had been opened and while the followers of the "Panther" believed that all of us were doomed to die of hunger and thirst, we enjoyed an abundance of food and as much water as we could possibly use.

Some troops had been assigned to the citadel, others to the upper part of the town. The horses of all these men were watered at the river whose level did not fall again but kept rising, as we noticed to our delight. Sentries were posted toward Ard and the desert. They were to remain invisible and had to report any approach from those directions. No one seemed to ask himself how order had been established so efficiently and without confusion. But a careful observer could have no doubt that the unassuming and reserved Sheik el Beled was responsible for this. It was not until later that I became aware of his guiding hand. But once I noticed how quietly and methodically he saw to everything, I examined his influence more closely and soon became convinced that his was a very superior intelligence, and that he probably had a greater share in events than he appeared to.

The Mir had been profoundly impressed by the fact that all the associate justices of the "Djemmah of the Living" designated on the pieces of black notepaper had actually arrived, for such an event had hardly seemed possible. He called them together and apprised them of what lay in store. Afterwards, they came with us to the two Djemmah halls to familiarize themselves with the locale. They were serious and calm, as befitted the occasion. Abd el Fadl, Merhameh, and the Sheik el Beled said nothing. But the sheik of the Tshoban asked all sorts of questions. He was anxious to do his duty. Yet he really had no conception of the great significance of the approaching midnight hour and probably looked at it as no more than a superstitious shaman game with corpses, although he didn't say so, of course. Nor did the others express their personal opinions. Whatever they might have thought or believed, however, they all agreed that the weal or woe of the Mir and the entire dynasty was at stake. Uncertain and tense about what that would do, none of them ate that night and only those that would not participate in the Djemmah satisfied their hunger.

Because almost all the Tshoban were Muslims and must not neglect their regular prayers, the hours were announced, and therefore it was possible to order everyone to turn in at precisely one hour before midnight.

I must confess that I also was unusually tense, which seems natural enough in view of our circumstances. At eleven o'clock, the most profound silence reigned. Half an hour later, the Mir and I went to the door of the antechamber by which one entered the "Djemmah of the Dead." He was calm and controlled. The others were already there, waiting for us. I opened the door. We entered and lit some candles to show us the way into the great hall of the Djemmah. There, and subsequently also in the "Djemmah of the Living," we lit all the candles in the candelabra. All the pieces of notepaper were still in place so that everyone knew where to sit. The seats were all empty. We returned to the "Djemmah of the Dead" where Abu Shalem and the father and grandfather of the Mir were sitting. They would take part in the proceedings. We were extremely curious by whom and in what manner these three bodies would be moved. Now, the hour of midnight was announced outside, and the half-chanting voice of the Muezzin could be heard:

"It is midnight. The sixth and the twelfth hour for all mortals. Darkness on earth; light above the stars. Man must be just. But God is merciful."

The moment this voice fell silent, Halef, the liveliest and most impatient among us, could no longer restrain himself. He took a deep breath, and said:

"Now the great mystery of life will be revealed. The time has come for the dead to return to life, at least for three of them, so that—"

He was interrupted. Something wholly unexpected, indeed miraculous, happened, for at this moment, Abu Shalem, the kindest, most famous and most just of all the Maha-Lamas, rose from his seat, and said:

"They are returning to life. Darkness on earth; light above the stars. I shall precede you. Come with me, all of you."

He took the large book of accounts from the table and slowly and solemnly walked down the steps. His long, braided, silvery hair stirred as he moved. His beard, whose tip had been invisible under the table, flowed to his knees and his large, wide-open eyes were turned toward us as if to penetrate us with their glance. He walked past the other Maha-Lamas who had remained seated and immobile and then through the entire group of accused Ardistan rulers. Having come to the last two, the father and grandfather of the present Mir, he stopped, raised his hand, and told them: "You will accompany your son."

"We are coming," the grandfather answered, and rose.

"We are coming," the father echoed.

They flanked the Mir and followed the president to the hall of the "Djemmah of the Living." There, Abu

Shalem walked up to his high seat, placed the account book before him on the table, and sat down. As though in a dream, the Mir had obeyed his ancestors. He had allowed himself to be led to the three places of the accused. He sat down as if utterly absent in spirit. And the rest of us who were the judges? I can only speak for myself, and must confess that I did not feel in the least like a judge, but like a human being who had no inkling what the present situation demanded or what his task really was. I almost think I would have remained outside, had Merhameh not taken me by the arm and whispered:

"Are you forgetting yourself, Effendi? Come, collect yourself."

She accompanied me from one hall to the other and did not release me until I was standing before the seat where the piece of paper bearing my name was lying. Then she joined her father. I do not believe that any of the persons there was any less bewildered. It was essential to discover how three persons long since dead could return to life. That was the only thought I had, and it required an enormous effort to set it aside so that I might satisfy the demands of the moment. So I pulled myself together and told myself to look on the presiding judge as a person whose present conduct rather than former life had to be dealt with.

He was now sitting in exactly the same position as in the other hall, utterly immobile, his eyes fixing the three accused. When it could be assumed that our agitation had subsided somewhat, he looked at all of us in turn, indicated that he wanted our attention, and said:

"The 'Djemmah of the Living' is now in session. May it practice justice! God will grant us mercy."

He paused, and then continued:

"The accused is Shedid el Ghalabi, the present Mir of Ardistan. His fellow accused are his two ancestors. These men are the last three rulers of Ardistan. Abd el Fadl, prince of Halihm and Merhameh, princess of Halihm, are the counsels for the defense. Every time a Mir of Ardistan has been the accused in this chamber, there has always been an Abd el Fadl and a Merhameh to defend him, as is the case today."

Again he paused, again he looked at all of us in turn, and then went on:

"And whenever a tribunal was called to sit in judgment on a Mir of Ardistan, one of the judges had to declare himself willing to be the prosecutor. So I ask you today: Who of you will take that office upon himself?"

All of us remained silent.

"I am asking a second time," Abu Shalem said.

Now the Erdjani rose and said:

"None of us will volunteer to prosecute. We also are sinners. Only those without sin may accuse."

He sat back down. Something like a ray of warm sunlight passed over the face of the presiding judge, yet the tone of his voice was very grave:

"If no accuser can be found, the Djemmah is dissolved and our fate remains undecided. I may only ask three times, and this is the last: Who among you will be the accuser?"

Now someone rose from his seat. It was the Mir himself.

"I cannot permit my fate and yours to remain undecided. There is an accuser, the strictest possible."

"Who?" Abu Shalem asked.

"Myself, Shedid el Ghalabi, Mir of Ardistan. I hope I shall not be rejected although I am not one of the invited judges. But no one knows my sins as I do."

Something like a second, warmer ray of sunlight passed over the face of the presiding judge. He answered:

"Self-accusation is a human ideal. None of those who ever sat in your seat understood that. You are the first. I will not reject you; I thank you. Of what do you accuse yourself and your ancestors?"

"Of all the sins listed in the book here. All of them, without a single exception."

"And you demand punishment?"

"I do."

"Of what sort?"

"Whatever punishment will be imposed by this Djemmah."

He sat down. Abu Shalem said:

"The accusation has been stated. Listen to all that is written here. I will read it to you."

He opened the book, but the Mir quickly rose from his seat, and protested:

"That is unnecessary. I am no longer speaking as prosecutor but as accused. I admit everything, every page, every line, every word."

"You can only confess your own acts, not those committed by others. You are not the only accused."

"I am. For I am stating now that I will take upon myself the sins of my entire family."

Abu Shalem placed both his hands on the table, and rose very slowly, inch by inch as it were, pushed his upper body far forward, and asked:

"Do you realize what you are saying and doing?"

"I do," the Mir assured him.

"Then repeat it. You have to utter this important, difficult, momentous word three times."

"I state for the second and the third time that I shoulder the sins of my ancestors. Let them go free. I alone am the guilty one."

"And you accept not only the sins but also the punishment?"

"I do."

The tension in the face and bearing of the presiding judge decreased. His body straightened. His eyes and face were shining as if they were flooded by sunlight. He exclaimed:

"We have never had a Djemmah such as this. I ask you once again: Have you carefully considered what you are saying? Just think of the wars, the bloodshed, the unceasing murder of human beings. That alone deserves the death sentence a thousand times over. Do you abide by what you said?"

"I do."

"Then you are the only accused. The others may leave."

Now father and grandfather rose from their seats and walked out, unhurried, without saying a word. The Mir himself remained where he was. Abu Shalem sat down again and continued in a cheerful tone:

"Every time a Mir of Ardistan has stood before us

here, he had to be asked three times if he wanted to take the sins of his fathers upon himself. None had the faith, the charity, and the courage to do so. But Shedid el Ghalabi, the present Mir, did not wait for this question but anticipated it like a man, indeed a hero, who can bear a heavy burden and accomplish difficult things. He will therefore be treated like a man and a hero whom we, his judges, trust. I must ask him: Do you regret what was done by all your ancestors against God and man?"

"I do."

When the Mir gave this assurance, one could see and hear that he was utterly serious. Abu Shalem continued:

"And are you ready to expiate and to have all those that will come after you do likewise, before God and man?"

"I am ready."

"Will you promise yourself and us that from this day forward you will work for peace as persistently as your ancestors violated it?"

"I will."

Now the kindest, most famous, and most just of all the Maha-Lamas rose quickly and vigorously, raised his hand as if he were about to pronounce a blessing, and called out:

"I hereby absolve you of all the guilt and punishment you have assumed. I place this entire burden in the hands of the Highest Judge. May it fall on that successor of yours who violates the promise you gave us today. Do you consent, you judges, who also called yourselves 'sinners'?"

This question was addressed to us. Immediately, we stood up to express our agreement.

"I do," everyone called out. Now Abu Shalem turned to Abd el Fadl and Merhameh:

"Has Kindness or Compassion any questions to ask, or anything further to mention or add?"

"No," they answered.

"Then my judgment has been approved and becomes the judgment of the Djemmah. This book is yours. Take it, but do not destroy it. Keep it as something sacred for yourself and your family so that everyone of them may know the huge burden he assumes when he acts against you and violates your promise, for that means that he will be acting against God and mankind. Midnight has passed. There is light not only above the stars but also here, on earth. Not only God is merciful; man also has that obligation. The Djemmah is dissolved. I salute you."

He took the book, came down from his raised seat, walked past us toward the Mir, gave it to him, and then passed on, slowly and solemnly, without turning. For perhaps a minute, we stood where we were to collect ourselves. Then we followed him out of the hall of the "Djemmah of the Dead." Outside, it was dark; the candles had gone out. But from the raised seat of Abu Shalem, we could hear his voice:

"You cannot see without candles. Go and light some."

We obeyed, but a few did not suffice and it was only when many were burning that he became visible. In their flickering light it seemed as if he were still moving, but then he sat as still and immobile as ever. The rest of us would have liked to look at his body more closely, but a readily comprehensible awe restrained us. But the Mir, who was the most important person here, and certainly had more right to do so than any of us, touched his father and grandfather who were sitting in their places precisely as they had before. He tried to move their hands and arms. Then he said:

"They are dead, quite dead, also cool, almost cold. But when they were sitting next to me, I felt their warmth quite distinctly."

He now stepped up to Abu Shalem to touch him as well. The result was the same. "He's also dead. There is no trace of life in him," he reported. "The way he's sitting there, he cannot possibly have presided over the Djemmah and uttered such well-conceived, profound things. It's altogether impossible."

"And yet it was he," the sheik of the Tshoban maintained. "I saw him very clearly standing where you are now, and then slowly sit down. He was alive and now is dead again. I am sure. I could testify to it."

At this moment, the hour was called out and we heard the Muezzin's chanting voice:

"Past midnight. The seventh and the first hour for

all mortals. Suffering on earth; bliss in heaven. Man seeks to console himself with hope, but only God can bring fulfillment."

The Mir came down and picked up the account book. We put out the candles and left. From our arrival to our departure, exactly one hour had passed. We were all silent, barely wished each other good night, and separated.

The following morning, Halef and I were invited to breakfast with the Mir and his family. The Erdjani was also there. When we were done, the Sheik el Beled came to ask us to accompany him to the top of the temple because he had something very important to show us. We climbed the spiral stairs. When we pushed the stone from the opening to step out on the platform, we were greeted by floods of warm, golden, morning light. The "City of the Dead" lay at our feet in a living, surging splendor, as if it had been allowed to celebrate its resurrection by the master of life and death who governs all suns and guides their light.

As was his custom, the Sheik el Beled had veiled his face. We only heard his voice. He first pointed down to the river:

"You can see the water coming. The stream is returning. Perhaps the time promised us is approaching. Perhaps God is returning to Ardistan to proclaim our salvation. The water has already begun to flow."

We were delighted to see he was right. The scattered pools were beginning to form a single surface, were flowing into each other and now constituted a steady current that had the width of a sizeable brook, following the course of the dry riverbed like a shimmering, winding ribbon.

Then the sheik pointed northwest, and asked:

"Who is coming there?"

As we turned our eyes in that direction, we saw a second and even brighter stream, almost like silver crossed by golden lightning, which also formed numerous twists and bends. It was coming from the precipitous rocky heights into the deep valley below. It could therefore not be water, which would have formed rapidly descending cascades but not such calm turns, and would have been flowing without interruption, while this moving, shining band showed occasional dark gaps.

"Those are human beings," Halef said.

"Horsemen," the Erdjani added. "They are coming in troops, in individual sections, one behind the other, in regular order. And the horses are all white. There is not a single dark one among them."

"Yes, nothing but white horses," Halef confirmed. "The riders are also white, entirely white. But with sparkling helmets, it seems."

"And armed with lances whose points refract the morning sun. I have been told that the hosts of the Mir of Djinnistan have such snow-white horses and such light coats. I wonder if that is true?"

The Sheik el Beled answered:

"Those you see approaching are the lancers of El Hadd."

"So they are yours?" the Mir asked. "And how did they get to Ardistan, to the 'City of the Dead,' when everyone knows that no one can find enough water there for himself, let alone for an entire army?"

"I ordered them to. I knew that the water would come."

"You ordered them? I should have thought that only I can give orders here?" This was said rather sharply. "Are your troops permitted to cross the borders of Ardistan without my consent?"

"I hope so, for it was done for your sake," the sheik answered calmly.

"For my sake? What do you mean?"

"I heard of the rebellion against you. Indeed, I was even asked to join the conspirators, so I travelled to Ardistan and ordered my troops to follow me on a certain day if no counter order was given. There they are. I place them at your disposal against the 'Panther' and all those who abandoned you. If you don't need them, a mere signal will suffice, and they will immediately return home."

That sounded simple, modest, and honest. The Mir saw that his outburst had not only been unjustified but even absurd under prevailing conditions. He answered in a completely different, heartfelt way:

"Oh, no. They are not to turn back. They are very

welcome. Contrary to our expectations, there is enough water for them, and they will also find whatever food they need. We'll gladly give it to them."

I had briefly looked at the sheik. When I turned back in the direction from which the lancers were coming, they had disappeared.

"Where did they go so suddenly?" the Erdjani wondered. "Can so many soldiers hide so quickly? That's impossible."

"They are still where they were," the sheik answered, "but they made themselves invisible."

"How?"

"By using their wide coats which are light on the outside, dark on the inside."

"Was there any reason for that?"

"I should think so. They must have seen something suspicious."

"What could that be? They cannot yet have seen us and our troops in the 'City of the Dead.' Their view is blocked by the heights lying between them and the city. So whatever made them cautious must be outside the city, in the direction they were facing as we saw them approach."

"That would be east," Halef said. "Could someone be coming from the capital and the well? But he would be seen by our sentries, and there are fifty of them up there on the heights from which we came on our arrival. I think—Mashallah! Look, Sidi! You see, I was right. There's one of them, running as quickly as he can. So our guards noticed the same thing as the lancers, and are sending this messenger to report it. Someone should ride out to meet him! There is not a moment to be lost."

We shared that view. By the time the messenger had arrived and found us, half an hour might pass. Halef and I had the fastest horses, and we left immediately. When we reached the messenger, he reported that soldiers on horses and camels were coming from the capital of Ard and approaching the "City of the Dead." He did not know how many. Having received orders to report such movements without delay, he had not had the time to count them. After I had indicated to him where the Mir could be found, and ordered him to tell him what he had told us, Halef and I continued on in the same direction as before.

When we arrived on the heights, we could see far east. The cavalry troop had come close enough for its members to be distinguished. It consisted of ten persons on horseback and three who headed a line of camels that were carrying water. Our posts were thus numerically far superior. They were Ussul and Tshoban and had been stationed behind the wall of a large building to which, thousands of years ago, the inhabitants of the residence had walked to enjoy the magnificent view. We joined them.

When the mounted troops had approached closely enough so that we could distinguish the features of the men, I recognized their leader, for he was the major whom the "Panther" had promoted to colonel and who had come to me and the guard in the cistern shack and then made a long, sincere speech to the Mir. At that moment, he had been the commanding officer of the unit that had taken us to the "City of the Dead." What was he doing here? When he had reached the building behind which we were waiting for him, I left our hiding place. The others remained under cover.

"Mashallah!" he exclaimed in surprise as he saw me. Then he stopped and added: "You are the foreigner from Djermanistan. You should be in Prison Number Five. How did you get here?"

"On horseback," I answered.

"Where is your horse?"

"In there," I answered, pointing to the building.

"Bring it out here. I am arresting you. I'll have to take you back. You'll have to show me how you escaped. Where are the others?"

"Still down there."

"All of them?"

"Yes, except for Hadji Halef. He is with me."

"Where? I don't see him."

"He's in there with the horses."

"Then he'll have to come out and go back with you. What's more important: Is the Mir still there?"

"Yes."

"And the two Ussul princes?"

"They are there as well."

"Did you see the Erdjani and the oldest Tshoban prince in the canal?"

"Yes."

"Are they still alive?"

"They aren't quite dead yet."

"How did you and Halef manage to escape?"

"We found a hole and crawled through it."

"You'll show me that hole. It will be bricked up. Did you ride through the town after your escape?"

"Yes."

"Did you see anyone?"

"A great many."

"Whom?"

"The Ussul and the Tshoban."

"The entire army of the Erdjani?"

"Yes."

"That's good, very good. Then all of them are trapped."

He had said this to his men. Then he turned back to me.

"Did you see anyone else? Women?"

"The Mir's wife and his servants."

"And what about Merhameh, the princess of Halihm?"

"Her too."

"And her father?"

"Yes."

"Do you know where those two are now?"

"Yes."

"Then tell me! Where?"

I had deliberately stopped a few paces away from him so that he had to raise his voice to talk to me. I had wanted Halef and the guards to hear what he was saying. They apparently had, for Halef now came out and answered in my place:

"You claim to have been a major and now you've even been promoted to colonel. Can't you think more clearly and ask your questions more coherently? You should be ashamed of yourself. If the two of us are free, the others must be, too."

"But the Effendi says they are still down there."

"Yes, down there, in the town, but not in the canal. You want to lock us up again. Didn't you hear that the Erdjani's entire army is here?"

"Most of them have probably died by now," the officer defended himself.

"Even if that were true, you couldn't do as you please. You are like a big stupid sheep running straight into the butcher's hands. I'll show you how hungry and thirsty the Ussul and Tshoban are. Pay attention!"

He gestured and those he'd mentioned came out on their horses and quickly surrounded the few men and their camels. The colonel was about to draw his sabre, but Halef cautioned him:

"Leave it where it is. You are our prisoner. If you resist, we'll shoot you. It's no joke to fall into the hands of the first sheik of the Haddedihn. Turn over your weapons quickly if you don't want us to prod you."

They obeyed without resistance when they saw that we outnumbered them. But the officer was worried about his honor. In spite of Halef's warning, he drew his sabre, made his horse rise on its hind legs, and raised his weapon. I jumped toward him and pulled him from the saddle. He fell on the ground and was disarmed before he could get back on his feet.

"Allah does not wish me to escape you," he shouted. "But you will regret this. And you, Effendi, you will testify that I did not surrender without a struggle."

"With pleasure," I answered. "You did what duty and honor required and need not fear facing your ruler."

"Which one?"

"The Mir, of course."

"The Mir? There is only one Mir, the new one."

"You are mistaken. There is only one Mir, that's true, but he's the old one, and I am taking you to him."

"I don't want to see him."

"Whom did you wish to see?"

"Abd el Fadl, the prince of Halihm."

"Are you being sent to him?"

"Yes."

"By whom?"

"By the new Mir of Ardistan."

"There is no such person. You must mean the younger prince of the Tshoban who is now called the 'Panther.' Where is he now?"

"I was not ordered to tell you that."

"Then you will tell someone else. You are an honorable, courageous man, but there is also such a thing as reason. Your plans were unreasonable, and the 'Panther' is acting like a madman. Could you not find someone better suited to replace the former Mir than this foreign, unruly, and inexperienced boy? How could you trust this most ungrateful of all ungrateful men after he had so unscrupulously abused the confidence the Mir had shown him—"

"He will not misuse us," the colonel interrupted.

"He already has."

"What do you mean?"

"You'll hear soon enough. Every people deserves the ruler it has. If you did not care for the Mir, you can be certain that he didn't care for you either. It would certainly have been better if you had met each other halfway, if you had schooled each other, and not dethroned him and entrusted your fate to the 'Panther'."

He laughed sceptically.

"The Mir could never have been schooled or made a better person."

"More easily than any of you. You don't really know him. I'll take you to him."

"But I don't wish to go."

"It doesn't matter what you want. He is the supreme commander in the 'City of the Dead' and it is my duty to turn you over to him and to no one else."

"Supreme commander? 'City of the Dead'?" the officer laughed again, but almost sarcastically now. "The title sounds good, but there is no water, and it can't be a pleasure to command dead and dying men. In any event, it is my duty to turn this water here over to the prince of Halihm. I hope no one will prevent me from doing so."

"Why should anyone want to?"

"Because you are dying of thirst."

Now Halef broke in:

"You really are a sheep, a big, foolish sheep. Have a look at us! Do we look like dying men? And what

: 561 :

about these fat, round Ussul horses? Anyone who would call those dying must be dying himself, but up here, in the brain. What's the use of talking? Sidi, I suggest we go back. How large an escort do we take along?"

"Escort? What for?"

"To guard these prisoners."

"They won't run away. Their weapons will be kept here. Bring our two horses, that's enough."

Our horses had remained behind the wall and after Halef had brought them, we mounted, took the colonel between us, and rode off. His men followed without fuss. They were tired and had no will of their own. But as long as he clung to his belief that we were in dire straits, their leader could not be trusted. When we reached the edge of the heights and looked down on the city, he saw the river and the people moving about in the streets and alleys. He was dumbfounded.

"May Allah protect me," he exclaimed. "That's water."

We said nothing. After a few moments, he continued softly, as if talking to himself:

"Water—lots of water."

He drew his hand across his forehead several times as if he had to put his thoughts in order, and then turned to me.

"Tell me, Effendi, is that really water?"

"Yes."

"Then I have to believe it. I would not trust my own eyes. But if that is real water, all our plans concerning the 'City of the Dead' are worthless."

"Correct."

"You have more than enough water, so you won't die of thirst. But hunger will kill you."

"No, we have more food than we can use."

"Where?"

"You'll see soon enough."

When we reached the open area on the Maha-Lama Lake, the Mir and the others were standing there to see whom we were bringing. He was surprised when he saw the officer.

"Allah, Wallah, Tallah. Our benefactor. The man who brought us here to die, who was so well intentioned toward us. We owe him a great deal. And we will show our gratitude."

The poor devil found himself in a very embarrassing situation. He was staring at the ground, not daring to raise his eyes. The Mir had spoken ironically, but now he sounded severe and commanding:

"Why were you sent here?"

"I was sent to Abd el Fadl, the ruler of Halihm."

"By whom?"

"The—the Mir."

"The Mir! You dare call this liar and traitor by that title, and in my presence at that?"

The man did not answer. The Mir went on:

"Why were you sent to Abd el Fadl?"

"To give him a document."

"What else?"

"To escort him and his daughter Merhameh to the capital."

"Just those two? No one else?"

"Yes."

"So they were to be saved, and no one else was supposed to find out about it?"

"Yes."

"Do you know what is in the letter?"

"Not word for word, just the general content."

"Give it to me!"

The Mir stretched out his hand, but the officer shook his head and said:

"Forgive me, but I won't do that. It is my duty to turn this letter over to Abd el Fadl, and if I cannot do that, I'll take it back to the man who wrote it."

"I can have you shot on the spot if you refuse."

"You can. I promised my loyalty to the new Mir of Ardistan and as long as you have not proven to me that he is a liar and a cheat, I will obey him."

The Mir stepped up close to the officer, placed his hand on his shoulder, and said:

"I expected that answer. Woe to you if you had acted differently. There's Abd el Fadl and his daughter. Give him the letter."

The officer complied. Abd el Fadl took the letter and then handed it to the Mir without having opened it. He said:

"You read it. I have no secrets from you."

One could tell that the letter had not been written in the capital but on the road, on crumpled, perhaps even dirty paper such as every officer carries in his saddle pouch. The Mir opened and read it. He read it a second time and then returned it to the prince of Halihm who quickly skimmed it and then read it out loud so that all of us could hear what it said. The "Panther" reminded Abd el Fadl of the final moment at the Chatar defile when he had stated that he considered Merhameh his bride. He was now demanding her for his wife, stating that there was no reason to refuse her to him since he was now the Mir of Ardistan and not just Abd el Fadl's equal but far above him. He went on to say that Abd el Fadl could save himself and his daughter from death by writing his consent on the unused portion of the letter and by following the messenger secretly to freedom from the "City of the Dead."

"Then you knew all this?" I asked the officer.

"I did."

"And would you have done it?"

He nodded. Because it was important to me to win him quickly to our side, I asked:

"Didn't you know the agreement the 'Panther' made with your Bash Islami?"

"What agreement? I have never heard of any."

"The Basch Islami is to make the 'Panther' Mir of Ardistan. The moment that has been done, the 'Panther' will become the Basch Islami's son-in-law. In that way, both will govern."

Astonished, the officer looked first at me, then at the others.

"If that were true—" He was so startled, he was stammering.

"It is," I assured him, and the Mir and the rest repeated that affirmation.

"Forgive me," the officer said. "It's enough if just one of you tells me."

He pointed at me, and then continued addressing me:

"Effendi, are you certain that things are as you say?"

"Quite certain. The Bash Islami told me in my own

apartment in Ard that the Mir of Ardistan would be dethroned. The Mir was there, unseen. He heard these words. He could have had the Basch Islami arrested on the spot but let him go because I asked him to."

"Is that true?" the officer asked, looking at the Mir as if he were seeing him for the first time.

"It is," the Mir nodded. "I heard everything the Basch Islami said but let him escape."

"In that case—then you are—"

He did not continue but hurried over to the Mir, sank on one knee before him, took his hand, kissed it, and exclaimed:

"Then you are a better person than we thought. You are kinder, more noble than you appeared. Forgive me, lord, forgive me."

"Rise," the Mir ordered him. "You just finished saying that you owed allegiance to the new Mir."

"I did not know any of the things I just heard from the Effendi. But now I realize that the 'Panther' is unworthy and deceives his friends for his own advantage. And I will not place myself and my arms at the disposal of such a man."

"Are you abandoning the 'Panther' then?"

"Yes. For I believe the Effendi. What he says is true. The 'Panther' lied to you and deceived you. That only concerns you. But he also lied to the Basch Islami, his highest-ranking and best ally. And that does concern me because I am the friend and confident of the Basch Islami."

"If you are, I am surprised you did not know that his daughter is to become the 'Panther's' wife," I interrupted.

"That must have been a secret clause in their agreement, so the Basch Islami felt obliged not to mention it to me," the officer answered. Then he turned to the Mir:

"Grant me a few moments' time to reflect. I must consult my conscience whether I may tell you what I know, or not. Then you can do with me whatever justice demands. I rebelled against you, and that is punishable by death."

The Mir answered in a serious tone:

"You may take that time. I will turn you over to our

: 565 :

friend Hadji Halef, the sheik of the Haddedihn. He can show you this place and you will see that we need die neither of thirst nor of hunger. In two hours, you will let me know if there is something you wish to tell me, or not."

No one could have been more adept at changing the officer's mind than Halef. He took him by the hand and walked off with him. At this very moment, a deep, sustained sound, which seemed to float high above the Maha-Lama Lake, rose from the highest point of the citadel. It came from the military trumpets of the Ussul.

"That is the signal that the lancers of El Hadd are close," the ruler told me. "While you and Halef were gone, I saw to it that they would be properly received and assigned quarters. Let us go back to the top of the temple to have a better view of their arrival."

All of us who were standing together climbed up to the platform of the cathedral. Our assumption had been correct. The lancers had seen the small caravan of the colonel and immediately made themselves invisible because they had been uncertain whether this was a hostile or a friendly force. Now they had turned their coats again. They came directly from the north, rode around the western section of the city along the foot of the heights, and then turned left toward the exit we had been using. It was a curious, moving spectacle. We were in the midst of a desolate area, a large grave in which cities and peoples had been buried and in whose depth we also had been meant to disappear. Death had been grinning at us from all sides but, when we had looked at it more closely, it had turned into a herald of life. We had burst open the grave. The moment we had shown the will to emerge from it, help had come from the mountains rising high into the sky. That help was the clear, pure, brightly shining water and this cavalry whose milky white contrasted with the rock walls as their helmets and lances sent us golden rays. The appearance of these troops at this place and on this sunny morning had something unearthly, supernatural about it. It called to mind the "heavenly hosts" which are mentioned in so many old, sacred books.

When the head of the train reached the point which was only separated by a depression from the entrance we used, it stopped. We saw trumpets and trombones sparkle. They had the form of instruments used in the early centuries. They played a long, solemn fanfare that could be heard far away and sounded as if higher beings were requesting permission to enter. From the highest point of the citadel, the huge horns of the Ussul answered in a joyous welcome. Then the procession of white horsemen resumed its march into the wide expanse of the Maha-Lama Lake.

All of them were dressed exactly like the Sheik el Beled, in tightly fitting suits of braided leather straps which looked like armor from a distance. These straps were tanned but not dyed. The magnificent helmets were of a light metal that had a golden shimmer. They had pieces of cloth attached in back which could be pulled forward to make them invisible to a distant observer. I have already mentioned the coats. Their weapons consisted of very long, dangerous looking lances, and knives that were attached to their belts and encased in leather sheaths. There were no other arms of any sort and even the lances and daggers seemed to be intended for peaceful rather than warlike uses. The horses were all white, of noble breed, wearing Persian saddle and harness, and with long, flowing tails and manes. At the head, there rode a strong, proud, silver-bearded giant who did not cast a single questioning glance anywhere and conducted himself like one perfectly familiar with the locality and everything that had ever happened there or was still to come. He was followed by a group of four officers, perhaps his staff. The soldiers, riding four abreast and in sections of one hundred men each, came next. As they slowly and impressively passed through the gate and, following the circular expanse, rode along the northern arcade, we saw behind them a long but orderly train of mules carrying tents and other baggage.

But we also noticed that there was another troop following the mules. Again, the men rode nothing but white horses and were equipped exactly like the first group except that their leather suits were not in natural color, but blue, a deep, soothing, slightly purplish blue, the color of the sky when one looks up from a deep, narrow ravine and can only see a strip of it.

"A second army!" the Mir exclaimed. "Who could that be?"

"Those are the lancers of Halihm," Abd el Fadl answered.

"Yours?"

"Yes. I place them at your disposal for use against all your enemies."

"You too! What helpers and saviors you and the Sheik el Beled are! I thank you, I accept your aid. But permit me one question: Where is your infantry, your artillery, your rifles, sabres, and cannons?"

"We do without all that."

"Why?"

"Because we consider them superfluous up there in the mountains where the battle will be decided."

"Why up there? I am determined not to fight Djinnistan. I am only concerned with putting down the rebellion, and that can be done down here."

"No. That also will be settled up there where all your weapons are entirely useless. We'll discuss that later. Now we have to pay attention to what goes on down here. I suggest that we go down to welcome our men, and I also request your permission to present them to you."

They left the platform of the temple. Only I remained. I observed that when they arrived below, they mounted their horses and rode toward the officers of El Hadd who had just reached the easternmost point of the huge open area when the last troops entered the western gate. The lancers of the Sheik el Beled thus formed an unbroken line of four men abreast which was exactly as long as the northern balustrade. The mules which carried the baggage remained outside, veering toward the left and the slopes where a camp was set up.

The Halihm cavalry followed immediately. They also sounded a fanfare which was answered by the deep horns of the Ussul. I saw Merhameh gallop toward the gate and take up a position at the head as her army appeared. She wanted to present it to the Mir herself. She turned toward the south side of the open area. Facing in the same direction, I could not follow the movements of the new arrivals, so I left the platform to find a more suitable place below. I only saw that the Halihm cavalry, too, had many mules with them which also remained outside, looking for a site toward the right.

When I came down, the Mir and the Erdjani, Abd el Fadl, and the others were standing at the foot of the steps leading to the water angel. I jumped to the saddle of my horse and rode over to them. Halef also joined us. The officer that had been entrusted to him was still with him but there was no time to deal with him now.

It turned out that the host from Halihm and the one from El Hadd were of identical size. When the leading elements of these two were closing the gap between them at the eastern end of the open area, the last troops were entering from the west so that these men who had come to save us formed two adjoining semi-circles of four men abreast, the northern one having come from El Hadd, the southern one from Halihm. In the middle, there stood the man and his friends to whose succor they had come although he had neither deserved nor requested them.

When Merhameh reached the officers from Halihm at the head of her troops, she greeted them and then galloped to the water angel to join us. It was only now that I became aware that she was not dressed as she usually was but was wearing the purplish blue of her cavalry. It was only natural that I should ask myself how everything could match and harmonize so perfectly. Without attracting his attention, I scrutinized the Sheik el Beled closely and began to realize that it was he who knew and ordered everything, that everyone took his cue from him.

At the moment the two armed units had joined in the west and the east and the circle had been closed, I saw that he put his horse through some curvets for which there was no apparent reason. Was this a signal, perhaps? Apparently so, for when it was seen, the trumpets and trombones on both sides began to sound, and at the same time the Ussul band, mounted on the sturdiest of their horses, came toward us. I looked questioningly at the Erdjani who answered with a smile:

"The Sheik el Beled requested this, and I consented. The Mir is to review the troops to the sound of music."

The other two bands joined with the Ussul in the center of the open area and continued playing until we had completed our round, which took considerable time. Then they posted themselves at the exit to play a fanfare as the troops moved out in the same order in which they had entered. The large numbers of men were now housed and fed. The Sheik el Beled attended to all of this without any help from us.

While all this went on, the time granted the colonel to come to a decision had long since passed. It was noon, and the Mir invited all those who deserved that distinction to a noon meal. Halef brought his charge to me and asked whether he might approach the Mir now.

"He will be very surprised when he hears what the colonel told me. Can you guess where the 'Panther' is at this moment?"

"He's no longer in Ard? Or not yet there?" I asked.

"He's no longer there. He only stayed one day. He was less interested in the city than in Merhameh whom he wanted to capture with her father. When he returned victorious, the town would be his, or so he thought. The connection with the dynasty was more important to him. The colonel had to accompany him from the well in the desert to Ard. Along the way, they heard that the Mir's wife had escaped to the 'City of the Dead' and that Abd el Fadl had accompanied her with his daughter. Then—"

"I can guess the rest," I interrupted.

"No, not yet. For he heard at the same time that the Mir of Djinnistan had responded to the declaration of war by the Mir of Ardistan by invading that country, attempting to take the capital by surprise. To hesitate was impossible. Troops had to be sent out against him so that his forces might be defeated on the march before he could deploy them for battle. That's why the 'Panther' went to Ard for only a few hours. He wanted to collect all the soldiers still there and hurry after the troops that had already been sent ahead."

"And what about the city? Does he think it is secure?"

"Yes, he's certain of it. He is leaving the old Basch Islami there as commandant. While the 'Panther' is in the field, he is to set up the new government, organize reinforcements, supplies, munitions, and everything else."

"Did he tell you that himself?" I asked the colonel.

"Yes, he told me, and no one else was present."

"And do you think that he will stick to this plan?"

"I am absolutely certain. He developed it for me in all its details. There was enough time for that during the lonely ride back through the desert."

"Do you know where the troops he sent ahead are now, and which route he will take from Ard to reach them?"

"Yes. Moving north, he means to keep as far away from the riverbed as possible, for there is the danger of dying of thirst if he stays close to it. He has no idea that enough water has appeared in the meantime to supply entire armies."

"That's very important. We must see the Mir right away. A council should be held immediately, before lunch. One more question: What do you intend to do? To whom will you be loyal, the old Mir or the one you call the new one?"

"The old, of course. Don't I have eyes to see that a new, hopeful future is developing here in a wholly unexpected way, and ears to hear what Hadji Halef told me? He changed my mind. I am ready to tell the Mir everything I know. Then he can do with me as he pleases."

"Come along, then. There is no time to be lost. We'll go to him."

The ruler was quickly found. He paid very close attention to what the colonel reported and agreed with me that a council would have to be held immediately. The result would be communicated to all the officers present during the noon meal. I shall pass over both. It is sufficient to say what was decided.

That day was going to be a day of rest, but on the morrow, we would leave the "City of the Dead." We had a two-fold strategic task. First, we had to seize the capital as quickly as possible to return it to the Mir and to obtain a base for further operations. This would mean that the "Panther" would lose the solid ground under his feet and be floating, as it were. Then, we had to drive the "Panther" and his followers toward the north, so that he would find himself between our troops and those of the Mir of Djinnistan and be forced to surrender unless he wished to be destroyed. The Sheik el Beled and Abd el Fadl and Merhameh solemnly assured us that the Mir of Djinnistan had not come down across his borders to help the rebels. We believed this because we knew that these two men, the lord of El Hadd and the prince of Halihm, would not have come to our aid unless the Mir of Djinnistan had given his consent. They were much better informed than we and certainly knew much more than they were allowed to tell us.

In addition, we had to split up our army into three parts, a center and a right and left wing. The center would be commanded by the Erdjani and be made up of the Ussul and Tshoban, a solid, heavy, compact mass which would have the task of pushing the "Panther" forward by its sheer weight. The right wing would be made up of the lancers from Halihm. Under the command of their prince, Abd el Fadl, they were to keep the "Panther" from deviating from his precise northern direction, and to prevent his breaking out toward the fertile and well-watered eastern territory where he might recuperate and provision himself. The left wing consisted of the lancers of El Hadd under their incomparable Sheik el Beled. They would keep the army of the rebel away from the river and deny it any room to maneuver. The principal weapons with which we were to defeat the enemy were hunger and, more important, thirst. The supreme commander of these three contingents was the Mir of Ardistan, of course, for it was his country, his people, and his rule whose weal and woe were at stake.

To execute the first part of our plan, the two wings had to be sent out ahead of the main body. They were faster and more mobile than the heavy cavalry in the center, and it was necessary to act as rapidly as possible. They were therefore to move out early the following day, at dawn. The Erdjani would follow them directly. We calculated that he would reach Ard an entire day later but this was acceptable because we required at least that much time to secure the capital. The Mir's wife and children were also entrusted to them for they could not be asked to undergo the hardship of a forced march. Merhameh, who had been requested by the Mir's wife to stay with her, objected that she could not possibly comply. Her duty lay with her father and his troops.

That evening I had an experience which was so curious that I do not want to omit it. Because the troops would leave at daybreak, the order had been given to turn in early and to be as quiet as possible. It was therefore very calm in the large open area of the Maha-Lama Lake the moment the evening meal was over. Halef and I retired promptly. We soon fell asleep, for the events of that day had rushed in on us and worn us out. Just as the Muezzin was calling out midnight, I woke up. I felt as if I had slept enough, and though I had my eyes closed, I remained awake. Later I got up and walked outside. The first quarter of the moon had grown in size during the last few days. It cast a clear but mysterious light on the giant angel which rose before me, almost seeming to move its hand in a gesture of farewell. To impress its shape on my memory, I took some further steps outside. At that very moment someone scurried softly past, like an enigma that refused to be solved. If I had not quickly moved back half a pace, we would have collided. The shape uttered a suppressed cry of terror and slipped to the next pillar to hide behind it. I sensed a delicate, sweet fragrance, similar to that of pussy willows at Easter, the same I had noticed in the "Djemmah of the Dead." I started to follow the figure to the pillar but decided against it, reminding myself that this was a woman and therefore it would be in questionable taste to intrude on her secrets. I turned to go back to my room but had not yet entered it when I heard the command:

"Stop, stay where you are."

I turned around. A voice said: "I cannot recognize you, but you seem to be the foreigner from Djermanistan."

"Yes, I am."

"You saw me and would have let me pass without stopping me?"

"Yes, I am your friend."

"My friend?"

She said that slowly, questioningly, and then came out from behind the pillar and slowly advanced toward me.

"Do you know me?" she asked.

"I am not certain, but I have a feeling."

"What is that feeling?"

"That I stood by your empty grave."

"What else?"

"That the Sheik el Beled is the father of your son."

Now she was standing in front of me, raising her arms as if to rebuff me.

"Stop! Don't go on. Your feelings are telling you things that are true, but they must not yet be uttered. I have to maintain silence and I know that you also can keep a secret. That's why I called out to you although no one should see me."

"But I saw you before."

"Where?"

"In the 'Djemmah of the Dead,' when you instructed the Mir."

"Whom did you tell about that?"

"No one, so far."

"You did right. I know you. Marah Durimeh recommended you to us. You will see her again, sooner than you think. I must go now, but not without thanking you."

She took my hand, raised it to her face, placed her cheek against it, kept it there for a few moments so that I clearly felt its warmth, and said:

"I feel your pulse. We should feel the heartbeat of all mortals, of all of humanity, just like that. I love you, for you are a true human being. Farewell! But not for long. We shall meet again."

She released my hand and walked away. I looked after her until she had disappeared in the darkness of the arcade. Then I went back into my room, lay down, and immediately went to sleep. It was as if I had awakened merely to see and talk to this person who was allegedly dead.

Shortly before daybreak, I was roused by Halef. We fed and watered our horses and dogs, breakfasted and filled our saddle pouches with whatever we had to take along. In the meantime, reveille was sounded. The time had come to depart from this mysterious, unforgettable place. We also had to take leave of the two Ussul princes and the two Tshoban because they were joining the troops of the Erdjani. After we had bidden the Mir's wife and children farewell and passed through the gate, we discovered that the lancers of El Hadd and Halihm had already set out. We hurried after them across the bridge and rejoined the Sheik el Beled, Abd el Fadl, and Merhameh at the head.

The distance to the well, for which the camels had needed two days, was covered in exactly twenty-four hours. Day was about to break when we arrived. At that place, we came upon a small troop of sleeping horsemen. They were soldiers of the "Panther" who had been ordered to block the route to the "City of the Dead." We took them prisoner and had them guarded by a small unit of El Hadd that would turn them over to the Erdjani and then follow us.

Those who were thirsty drank their fill, and we gave ourselves and the horses a chance to rest so that we could expect them to continue until evening. At first, our march took us through the steppe where human habitations were rare. But when the steppe turned into grassland, and fields were becoming increasingly frequent, we passed more and more huts and houses. When we came to small villages, we could not continue in a single formation. Because it was our plan to attack the city from the north and the south simultaneously, the Sheik el Beled and his cavalry took the northern route to cut communications between the "Panther" and the city, and then to move into the town at an agreed-upon time. The rest of us would come from the south and rejoin him at the castle.

Now the villages became more frequent. Those who

saw us were surprised and startled; some even fled. That part of the population that lived farther away from the capital had not been involved in politics and not participated in the rebellion. But the closer we came to Ard, the more uncertain people felt when they saw us, and the more frequently they took flight at our approach. Partly, this may have been due to the fact that horsemen such as the Halihm were completely unknown here. Their tightly fitting, rhomboidally braided leather garments looked like armor of bluish steel. Helmets such as they wore had never been seen here before, nor had horses of the breed and color they rode.

Once, however, people did not flee before us. This was late on the second afternoon, about six hours away from the capital, on a plain dominated by a single, tall, tower-like rock from which our approach had apparently been spotted. There were people up there who quickly came down and hurried toward us. When the first of them reached us, I recognized him as the altar boy of our good and venerable Basch Nasrani, the Christian bishop. The others were craftsmen. Even before he was close, the boy called out cheerfully:

"God be praised that you chose this route where we were waiting. Of course, you could not have passed unnoticed anywhere. All routes are under surveillance."

"By friends?" the Mir asked.

"Yes. The enemy doesn't know, because we have been unobserved."

"Who gave that order?"

"My God-fearing, venerable master, the Basch Nasrani. He knew you would come. And he wanted you to find out what is happening in the city before you reach it. So he posted guards. Please dismount and rest. This place is well suited for that purpose. It is out of the way and no one will see you."

"But that would mean wasting time. We must hurry on."

"And so you shall, but not now. You probably wanted to continue until it was dark, then camp, and set out again early tomorrow?"

"Of course."

"That would be a mistake, for then you wouldn't get there before noon. But the right time is just after dawn."

"Why?"

"Because that's what the conspirators decided."

"The conspirators?"

"There is no need to be alarmed. All of the Christians have conspired against the 'Panther' to restore you to the throne. All of them, both inside the city and throughout the country, will proclaim their allegiance to you at an agreed-upon moment. There will be no bloodshed. This plan has been kept so secret that no one we don't trust even suspects it. We know that only the rabble sides with the 'Panther,' by which I mean all those who want to enrich themselves by rebelling against you. We are convinced that all the others will join us the moment we begin to act. When it became known that you had been lured to the 'City of the Dead,' all those who have some decency left began to feel compassion for you. Then it was learned that your wife had fled with her children to die at your side, and that fact also won you the hearts of many that had been your enemies. All this means that you will be welcomed by large numbers when you enter Ard tomorrow."

The boy had spoken enthusiastically, wholly absorbed in what preoccupied him. The lips of the Mir twitched; his eyes filled with tears he could not hold back. He had to control himself before he could answer.

"So it's early tomorrow morning?" he asked. "How could you set the time so precisely? Even though you may have believed that I would not perish in the 'City of the Dead,' how could you predict the exact hour of my return?"

"There was no question about the hour, though the day was uncertain. It didn't matter whether you came today, tomorrow, or the day after. But you must enter the city to the ringing of bells, and early, when the sun rises above the eastern mountains."

"Who gave those orders?" I asked.

"The Mir of Djinnistan."

: 577 :

"How do you know that?" he was asked by the ruler of Ardistan.

"The Basch Nasrani told us."

"Are those two communicating with each other?"

"They have been for a very long time. The Basch Nasrani loves and worships the Mir of Djinnistan and undertakes nothing of consequence before first consulting this lord who is the best friend you will ever have. To conspire against the 'Panther' was not our idea, but his. He says he wants no one to rule Ardistan but you—that you are the right one."

Fixedly and without expression, the Mir was staring into the distance, though in reality he was looking into his soul. Then the rigidity disappeared. A faint, almost embarrassed smile spread over his features. Turning to Abd el Fadl, Merhameh, Halef and me, he said:

"Did you hear? The head of my priesthood does not obey me; he obeys the man I considered my greatest and most remorseless enemy. Yet he is right. For this man whom I had taken for my enemy never intended anything but my happiness, and the happiness of my people. I was a fool, a senseless and thoughtless monster. His magnanimity is a much more severe punishment than defeat by his army would have been. This is a lesson I shall not forget."

"That lesson is not just for you, but for all your descendants," the prince of Halihm, who usually preferred to remain silent, said in an almost imploring tone. "Think of the 'Djemmah of the Dead' and the 'Living.' And remember the promises made that are binding not only on you but on all your successors as well."

"I am always conscious of them. I shall never forget that scene or those promises."

He dismounted and continued:

"So we shall obey the Mir of Djinnistan. We will remain here and camp. We will comply."

He did not say this ironically or sarcastically but as someone who has genuinely mastered himself. He did not suspect how profoundly he impressed us with his humility, his greatness of soul. The moment he dismounted, Halef, who had more skill in practical matters than in psychological reflection, asked the altar boy:

"Tell me, why is it that we are to camp and wait precisely at this spot? Why not somewhere else?"

"Because it is out of the way, so you are safer here than elsewhere. And because this is the appointed place which is constantly being observed from the city and the other stations."

"What stations?"

"For communicating at a distance. As soon as it is dark, we will report your arrival to the bishop in the city. He wants you to wait for his answer until midnight, for the moment he receives our signal, our revolution will start. That simply means that we will lock up all those important persons and officials who have taken the 'Panther's' side. The police you organized is still functioning and has been enlarged. They have quietly made all necessary preparations. The city will end this day as the residence of the new Mir and wake up tomorrow as that of the old one. It will be surprised but it is our hope that it will react calmly to this sudden and peaceful changeover."

"And the Bash Islami? Is he really the commander in chief in the city?"

"Yes. But he will be the first to be arrested."

"And what about the castle?"

"Things there are the same. The 'Panther' did not dare enter it or make any changes there. The loyal Ussul Guard has been occupying it and would have resisted any intervention, weapons in hand. The 'Panther' did not have the time to force them out. The Bash Islami has probably been told to get them out by cunning."

"These peope are so reckless that they must be mad," the Mir exclaimed. "What I first took to be a very serious, real revolution, a thorough upheaval, now strikes me as a farce, as the acrobatics of a bunch of monkeys. I'm afraid it will nauseate us. The first man I'll have to talk to is the Basch Islami. The letter in which the 'Panther' asks for the hand of the princess of Halihm will have a quicker, more certain, and more profound effect on him than anything else. Is the station from which you send your signals up there on the rock?"

"Yes," the altar boy answered. "Would you like me to show it to you?"

"Later. Accept my thanks for now."

He held out his hand. For this modest, loyal man, this was a greater reward than any gift.

The area where we had stopped was large and covered with fresh, nourishing grass. A small but brimming brook rippled across it. It was a good place for our horses to graze and rest, and we gladly gave them this chance to recover, since it would take us another six hours to reach the city.

When it began to get dark, we had the altar boy take us to the top of the rock which he had called a telegraph station and which offered a panoramic view. The apparatus he showed us consisted of a pole that had been hammered into the ground and a number of rockets which carried different charges, depending on the message to be sent. In those regions, dusk is of very short duration. Soon, it was completely dark, and the first rocket was set off. Ard lay directly east. When we looked toward it, we saw an identical flash barely a minute later. After another minute, we noticed a second sheaf of fire. It was so far away that it seemed quite small and would have been overlooked, had we not been still staring in the same direction. The message was continuing.

"In a quarter hour, the Basch Nasrani will know that you have arrived," the altar boy told us. "Fifteen minutes after that, the Basch Islami will already be a prisoner. We will be told sometime between now and eleven whether you should continue on, or not."

"We certainly will ride on," the Mir told him. "If the city doesn't open its gates as you say it will, I shall use force. Do you always keep a careful watch here?"

"Yes. We don't miss any signals."

"Then we can go to sleep without worrying?"

"Yes. We will wake you when the time has come."

We went down, ate supper, and turned in. I felt great confidence in this curious, almost childlike "counterrevolution" of the courageous bishop. Even if it did not accomplish its objective, we had a large army and enough men to impose our will on the enemy. With nothing to preoccupy me, I slept soundly and did not wake until Halef roused me.

"Get up, Sidi," he said. "The signals have been given."

"Which one?"

"I don't know that yet. But the people up there on the rock were jubilant when they saw them. It must have been favorable. Look, they are answering."

The altar boy fired three rockets in succession, and then called down to us:

"Wake up! Get up! We have won! Things turned out better than we had expected."

After watering our horses, we set out with the altar boy as our guide and reached the environs of Ard when the sun was about to rise.

When Halef and I had seen the city for the first time, we had come from the south. Today, we were approaching it from the west. Yet the terrain was the same. Riding up a ridge, we saw the city lying below us as we had once before. But in one respect, things were very different. A large compact crowd had gathered here to welcome the Mir with loud shouts of joy. In spite of this mass of people, the main road leading down the slope was unobstructed, although the edges were densely packed by other crowds. The officers of the castle garrison and the most eminent Christian officials and delegates of the community had stationed themselves among them. At their head was the venerable Basch Nasrani on a white mule, ready to lead the procession. He rode up to the Mir and bade him welcome in a loud, cheerful voice. At this very moment, the sun suddenly rose in a quick, joyous leap from behind the mountains. Millions of golden rays flooded the town, the people burst into seemingly unending shouts of joy, and from the high dome, bells could be heard ringing. A sunny, warm light was shining in the eyes of the Mir, the first prophetic shimmer of a new and happy time.

12 : Into Battle

Nothing had interfered with the Mir's entry although we had been prepared for sporadic expressions and outbursts of discontent or even of hatred. It was odd. A revolution had taken place; one ruler had been deposed, another installed, yet nothing inside the castle had been touched. The corner of my rug was still turned up, the dish containing the water for my dogs at the precise place I had left it. The Mir's quarters were equally undisturbed. One had the impression that nothing irregular or extraordinary had occurred during our absence.

Unfortunately, this was not the case outside the castle. Inside, the bodyguard had prevented all disturbance. Happily, there had also been someone in the city who had acted with intelligence and foresight so that the inevitable confusion was brief and problems did not go unresolved. That was the bishop, and the Mir had much to thank him for. In spite of his ecclesiastical office, he was therefore appointed town commander, as the "Panther" had appointed the Basch Islami.

Until the night before, the latter had been the highest-ranking individual in the residence, and had believed he would continue in that position, for he looked upon the "Panther" as his puppet. Now, he had been locked up in a basement room of the castle and was being brought up to be interrogated. He had been arrested in his home, had received no answers to his questions, and was therefore unaware that things had taken a disastrous turn for him. It was the Mir's wish that I be present during this interrogation and that Halef conduct it. He took pleasure in the little Hadji's unceremonious manner when he dealt with people he did not care for, and felt that the Basch Islami was the sort of person that deserved such curtness.

The Basch Nasrani was not present. Being the "first Christian" of the country, he had been sensitive enough not to wish to witness the humiliation of the "first Muslim." But Abd el Fadl had to be there, as did the major the "Panther" had promoted to colonel; he was being kept next door for the moment.

The conspirator was brought in by two huge Ussul who remained at either side of him. He entered with his head held high, looking as if he were about to remonstrate and demand an accounting. But the moment he saw us, he hesitated as if confronted with something altogether unbelievable, and then withdrew into himself. He must have been quite terrified. He seemed to have become an old man and could no longer stand straight. Looking for support, he stretched out his arms and bent his knee as if his weakness forced him to sit down. But the two guards quickly took hold of him and kept him upright. I have described him as fanatical and bigoted, though fundamentally benevolent and just. Because of these qualities, I had persuaded the Mir to let him go. Because he was also a fair-minded man, his present situation must have seemed doubly embarrassing to him.

To give Halef his due, he quickly gave up his plan to torment this man remorselessly. As he saw him collapse, he shook his head and exclaimed:

"May Allah protect me from the misfortune of ever looking as pathetic as this greatest of all wretches and sinners in Ardistan. I was about to humiliate him, but he's done that himself. I wanted to enjoy his torment, but who can take pleasure in the sight of such feebleness? I wanted to crush him with proofs, but he is trembling all over. I therefore request permission to cut this short. There is no glory for you or me in employing all our strength to bring down a man who is so fearful that he is breaking down under his own weight. I think a small push is all that is needed."

He took the "Panther's" letter which was lying on a table in front of the Mir, handed it to the Basch Islami, and told him:

"Read this!"

The Muslim approached slowly, took the document, unfolded it, and began to read. His eyes grew bigger and bigger, the blood drained from his face, he took a step backward and staggered. He seemed about to fall. But he was not the only one to be unsure of his footing. Suddenly, the floor had begun moving under our feet. A tremor was passing through the castle and through our bodies. We could feel it to the very tips of our fingers. A curious, faint, but extremely disquieting sound, similar to a distant, hissing wind came through the walls.

"An earthquake," the Mir shouted and jumped from his seat.

"An earthquake, may Allah protect us," said Halef and seized my arm.

At this moment, the curtain hanging over the entrance was pulled aside to reveal the Sheik el Beled standing in the opening, looking like a portrait by a master painter, framed to give it relief. His face was veiled and he did not speak or salute but gestured to all of us to ignore him. Only the Bash Islami did not see him because he had his back to the door, his hands raised like someone in great fear. He called out:

"One."

We didn't know what he meant. His head was inclined to one side as if listening. Listening for what? Involuntarily, we strained our hearing. Suddenly, we had the sensation of standing on gently flowing water. To support ourselves, we took each other by the hand. Then it was as if we were on a cart which had no springs and was being pulled by galloping horses over poorly maintained roads, but this only lasted a moment. Had it continued, we would all have been lost. Everything would have come crashing down.

"Two," the Bash Islami exclaimed with an expression of terror.

He sank down on one knee but continued listening. From the distance, a sharp hissing and crunching came closer, then passed under our feet and beyond as if the earth had taken a deep breath of relief. We were almost thrown to the ground. Only the Sheik el Beled stood firm and immobile. For him, the trembling and shaking of the earth seemed an ordinary event.

"Three shocks," the Bash Islami shouted and jumped to his feet. "Now the danger is past, but only the small one. The great one, which is foreseen only by those who know of it, is still to come. For the last three months, the glaciers have been melting and now three tremors are passing through the earth to prepare mankind for what is in store. That's what the legend says. The legend of the river that returns, of paradise that opens its gates every hundred years, of the archangels' question whether peace has finally come, of the appearance of the angels among men, the return of the river, and the return of God to Ardistan and Ard."

His cheeks had reddened, his eyes were sparkling. Was this the look of madness or enthusiasm with which he was eyeing us, one after the other? "You don't know what I know," he continued. "I thought you had been destroyed but you were saved and have come here to judge me. I am in your power. But not through your doing but through that of a higher power which I must obey. I am prepared to die for what I did, but I ask you to answer the questions I will put to you. You were in the 'City of the Dead.' Is the river there still dry?"

"No," the Mir answered. "It has received a great deal of water. It is already flowing."

"Since you escaped from the canal, you must be familiar with the door. Were you at the Maha-Lama Lake?"

"Yes."

"And at the 'Djemmah of the Dead' and the 'Living'?"

"Yes."

The Muslim was silent for some time. He looked at the ground as if in despair and moved his hands as though compelled by an inner urge to wring them. Then he turned to Abd el Fadl who was wearing the blue dress of the lancers, and asked him:

"You are Abd el Fadl who with his daughter Merhameh pleaded for kindness and compassion?"

"I am."

"And are you perhaps the prince of Halihm?"

"I am."

"Allah, Allah. What a calamity! Who could have guessed it? You saw that I became frightened when I entered this room. It was because I saw you here, for I had believed you were dead. But I was even more disturbed at the dress of Halihm because it immediately put me in mind of the fate which will overtake those of us who are resisting with the sword. Please tell me, are your lancers here?"

"They are. The Mir of Ardistan entered the city with them. The bells rang out, and the people rejoiced when they saw him."

"Mashallah! Have the Ussul and the Tshoban also been saved—the Erdjani's entire army?"

"Yes."

"Woe to us! All that has to happen now is that the lancers of El Hadd appear and—"

He was interrupted.

"They have arrived," came from the door.

He turned and saw the sheik. The effect was extraordinary. Uttering a loud shout, he drew back to the wall, supported himself against it, and called out:

"The 'Oath of Djinnistan'! No one can resist it. Who are you with the veiled face? Are you the Sheik el Beled, the Mir of Djinnistan, or both? Where are your hosts?"

"Wherever they are needed," the sheik answered as he slowly advanced into the room. "Today they are with the man you betrayed. Tomorrow, they will pursue the 'Panther' until he collapses."

"Then he is lost," the Bash Islami said. "And it was precisely the Mir of Djinnistan he had relied on."

"What madness! How could he dare?"

"The Mir of Ardistan had declared war on the Mir of Djinnistan, who immediately sent his hosts across the border. This could only be aimed at the Mir of Ardistan, and therefore we hoped to have an ally in the ruler of Djinnistan."

"And what if he did not do as you wished?"

"Then we had planned to treat him as an enemy and to crush him."

"To look on him as an enemy! To crush him!"

It was a curious, laughing, yet also plaintive tone in which the Sheik el Beled said these words. Then he went on:

"You fools! Because you are so weak and shortsighted as to return enmity for enmity, you think the Mir of Djinnistan does likewise? I tell you, your thoughts are not his thoughts, your ways are not his ways. His victories come on the wings of love, not those of hatred and violence. He sent his hosts across the border to protect the enemy, not to destroy him. His victory does not lie in defeating the adversary but in assuring his triumph. Learn that from him, you who are endeavoring to renounce violence and become men of grace. Only baseness and brutality succumb, the animal in man, the beast, the 'Panther' that rages against its own brother and always lies in ambush to disembowel its benefactor."

"How true, how true," the Bash Islami agreed. "He is the enemy of his own brother, his own father. He prowled around the Mir of Ardistan who had shown him nothing but love and then leaped at him to tear him to pieces. And he also prowled around me. He promised to make my child the ruler's wife, and we believed him. But he was after the princess of Halihm. Later, he would have disposed of us, as the Mir was meant to perish in the 'City of the Dead.' I utterly renounce him."

"Do you believe you can escape punishment so easily?" the Sheik el Beled asked.

"No. I was not thinking of that. I am indignant about his treason and rascality, and I only say what this indignation demands. There is no calculation. I am your prisoner and know the fate that awaits me. The Mir allowed me to escape once; he won't do it a second time, for I rewarded him ill. Nonetheless, I should like to make a request, not for my sake, but for yours. It may sound insane but it is carefully considered, and has its reasons."

"Go on," the Mir told him.

"I am the head of the Muslim clergy, what is called the 'Sheik ul Islam' in other countries. What I order and do is binding on all those below me. I ordered the rebellion against the ruler. I can therefore countermand it, and am willing to do so this minute. Give me pen and paper so that I may write the orders which those below me will pass on. And have my seal brought so that these documents may be validated. Are you willing?"

"What you ask is not unreasonable," the Mir answered. "But according to local law, what is merely written, even though stamped with a seal, is useless unless you publicly and personally announce and con-firm it in the principal mosque of the country."

"That is my request. And that is what I meant when I said that it may sound insane. Call the believers to the mosque and then take me there so that I may speak to them and tell all Muslims that the 'Panther' is a liar and traitor and that the former Mir is the true ruler approved by Allah. But I know that it is vain for me to utter this wish. You cannot grant it."

"You are a prisoner and would have to remain one, should it be granted," the Sheik el Beled said.

"I am willing. Take me back to my dungeon, let me write my orders there, and then take me to the mosque with my hands tied. I shall announce what I must and then return to prison voluntarily."

"What is your decision?" the sheik asked the Mir.

The Mir was standing by the window, looking west. He did not answer immediately. When he did, he pointed in that direction:

"That's the road to the 'City of the Dead.' I am thinking of it now, and also of everything I promised there. I shall keep my word."

He turned to the Basch Islami and continued:

"You shall not be a prisoner but completely free until tonight. You are not to write in the dungeon but in your own home, with your child who was so grievously misled by your side. And you will enter the mosque as a free man and at the head of your clergy, and address the believers. The dignity of your office demands it. No one, neither police nor guard, will watch you during that time. But precisely three hours before midnight, you will come back here, report to me, and then return to prison. You may go."

The Bash Islami was so surprised, he was rigid. Then he flew toward the Mir, knelt down, kissed both his hands and shouted fervently:

"Hamdulillah! Allah be praised for he suddenly opened my eyes and made me recognize how blind I have been. Today, I see you for the first time as you truly are. I no longer accuse you but myself and all of us. We were the slaves of our errors and learned prejudices. But you are a ruler who will only be satis-fied with subjects that are free men. That's why you despised us. I accept your kindness and grace and will go now to act on your behalf and for your welfare, and then return to imprisonment. I would be better able to perform the task I take on today if I knew what happened during the last days in the 'City of the Dead' while you were there. But I suppose I must not find that out?"

"We have no secrets from you," the Mir answered. "The Erdjani, who will arrive here tomorrow at the latest, closed the Maha-Lama Lake again when he departed and left a garrison in the citadel. For the time being, the loyal cistern watchman has been appointed river master. He will regularly report the water level. Anyone who was there with us can tell you what you wish to know. But our Hadji Halef Omar would be the best person to inform you, for the sheik of the Haddedihn witnessed everything that happened. I hope he will accept, should you invite him to go with you and instruct you. And there is someone else who may be able to answer your questions. You already know him. Here he is. Take him with you."

He went to the door of the adjoining room, pushed back the curtain, and signalled to the colonel to enter.

The Bash Islami knew this man well. He showed no embarrassment, however, but was very pleased to have this former confidant of the "Panther" assigned to him.

Through the choice of this officer and Halef, the Mir gave evidence of diplomatic talent. No one would be better able than these two to influence the Bash Islami. Halef was particularly delighted that he had been chosen.

"Yes, I'll go with you," he said. "But first I must attend to my horse." The three men left.

When we had separated from the Sheik el Beled and his cavalry, we had agreed that we would all enter the city at the same time, three hours after noon, and then rendezvous at the castle. We had not known that we would be expected and persuaded to do in the early morning what had been planned for the afternoon. The Mir was therefore surprised that the Sheik el Beled was already there. But Abd el Fadl and I were not. It is true that Abd knew much more than I, but I was aware that the omniscient and omnipotent Sheik el Beled had arranged everything in advance. While he may not have been responsible for the Bash Nasrani's plan, he had certainly known of it and endorsed it. He informed us that he had executed the first part of his task and cut the "Panther" off from the city. A continuous chain of military posts, stretching from the bed of the dried-out river in the west to the eastern highlands, had been set up to intercept all messages coming from or going to the enemy. During the night and the following morning, he had arrested a number of persons who had hurried out of town to seek safety with the "Panther" when they had heard of the sudden counterrevolution, the rescue of the Mir, and his planned return early that day. It was obvious that these were persons with a bad conscience who had to be interrogated closely to discover which of their accomplices had remained behind. For since the capital was the organizational hub, it was important to clear it of all suspect individuals. It was decided to transport all these people to the "City of the Dead" and to isolate them in the citadel there.

It proved necessary to stay longer in Ard than anticipated. It would have been irresponsible recklessness to only stay one day and to chance leaving chaotic conditions behind. The march north would therefore begin the following day but only the El Hadd and Halihm cavalry would set out. The Ussul and Tshoban would not follow until two days later. They deserved a day's rest. The Mir decided to remain a few additional days to arrange for the administration of the city and the country by loyal and dependable personnel during his absence.

Leaving the Ussul and Tshoban army in the city for an extra day also served the purpose of impressing the population and making our dear old Bash Nasranr credible as town commandant. That was also why the El Hadd units entered the town in the afternoon although this was neither a strategic nor tactical necessity. The splendid, serious-looking lancers did not fail to awe the populace. When they left the next morning to be replaced by the Ussul and Tshoban, we could be sure that the Mir would be properly respected.

The Bash Islami seemed transformed. I had not been mistaken about him. Fundamentally, he was a just man and now that he had understood the profound change in the ruler, he championed his cause as vigorously as he had once opposed it. We read his orders and quickly distributed them to the entire Muslim clergy. I went to the mosque myself to hear his speech. He entered the town at the head of his clergy. The mosque was so crowded that one could barely see the stone floor. Halef had once again done well. Our enthusiastic Bash Nasrani could not have spoken more persuasively on behalf of the Mir than the Bash Islami, and when the ceremony was over, all the Muslims streamed out of the building into the streets and alleys of the town praising the returned ruler.

In the evening, the Muslim dignitary returned to the Mir with his escort and stated his willingness to return to his prison. But the Mir said:

"From now on, you are my personal prisoner. You will accompany me on the campaign and into battle so that I may benefit from your advice whenever necessary. In this way, you will be tied to me until you can prove to me that I do not need such advice. Then I shall release you. Go home in Allah's name, and speak to me again tomorrow morning. I want your help to return to law and order all those the 'Panther' has led astray."

I shall not describe the effect this unexpected decision had on the Bash Islami. He had been won back and would not waver again.

The Erdjani, who had once set out to defeat him, moved into the Mir's castle as his guest after he had entered the town with his troops. Because he did not know Ard, we rode through the city. This would almost have turned into a triumphal procession, had we not taken pains to elude our enthusiastic wellwishers. In the evening, we had a princely meal to which all the eminent Ussul, Tshoban, and Ardistani who deserved such preferential treatment were invited.

The following day, the Erdjani left with his army to take up his position in the center. The Mir stayed another three days, and Halef and I with him. He did not wish to be separated from us, and this showed good judgment. Since he was at the heart of the entire enterprise, we would be kept posted more readily than anywhere else.

First the Erdjani, then the Sheik el Beled reported that messengers the "Panther" had sent to the Bash Islami in Ard had been intercepted. The two men were interrogated by the Mir. The first reported that the "Panther" had rejoined his army without mishap and would immediately begin operations. He was still in Shimalistan province where provisioning his troops posed no problems. But later, when he had penetrated beyond this area and into the high-lying, wholly arid, grassless mountain country, he would have to rely on being promptly supplied, according to arrangements he had made with the Bash Islami. The second messenger was to inform the Bash Islami that scouts had discovered that the Mir of Djinnistan and his hosts in black armor had already come down across the Djebel Allah and would not ally themselves with the "Panther," but were rushing to the aid of the old Mir of Ardistan. This could actually be advantageous to the new government because a quick victory over Djinnistan would win it the confidence and gratitude of all of Ardistan. Absurd though it seemed, the Mir of Djinnistan apparently had nothing but light cavalry whereas Ardistan's superiority lay in its heavily armed troops, particularly its artillery which would simply knock down the flimsy Djinnistan cavalry. The enemy was to be pushed back to the foot of the Djebel without further delay, and annihilated there.

Hearing this, I asked the Mir about this important mountain. He told me:

"The Djebel Allah is the southernmost of the Djinnistan volcanoes, but it is part of them only geologically. It does not lie in Djinnistan but on the border of El Hadd and Ardistan. It has not erupted within living memory. But this year, it also glows though its light is peaceful. Three flames rise from it, which spread a calm, intense light but not a trace of smoke or ash. In earlier times, when the main river of our country still carried water, trees grew halfway up its slope; higher up, there were green meadows and pastures. But now it is barren like the surrounding countryside. It forms a single, compact mass of rocks which divides into three tall domes at the point where the treeline used to be. Each of the domes has a crater at its crest which is glowing this year.

"These three domes are called the father, the mother, and the son. The son lies between the other two. A wide path leads up the mountain, and where the mountain divides, this path does also. It forms two trails, one leading to the right, the other to the left. The one on the right passes between the father and the son, the other between the mother and the son. Behind the son, they rejoin and form a large plateau from which one descends into the first valley of El Hadd. There is room for thousands on this plateau. It is said that in remote antiquity, services were held up there, and that the three domes glowed at those times. The path leading down into the valley is wide, yet dangerous. Ravines and abysses yawn on either side and anyone falling would be lost. People say that the Djebel Allah never spewed ash or slag but always gave a pure, peaceful light. But at considerable intervals, when the filth from the other volcanoes settled on it and collected there, it became angry, shook to its very foundations and discharged boiling water to free itself of these impurities. What do you think about this fairy tale, Effendi?"

"It is no fairy tale. It has a much deeper meaning than you imagine."

"It is even said," the Mir continued, "that to cross from Ardistan into El Hadd and Djinnistan via the Djebel Allah is possible only for those that are good. When an evil person attempts to force his way across, or uses cunning to accomplish that purpose, he is certain to die. He either disappears in the abysses along the border area or drowns in the waterfalls of El Hadd."

"I have heard of those falls. Do they come down from Djinnistan?"

"Yes. They are the largest on earth. They come crashing down from high-lying Djinnistan and form a huge lake whose depth has never been plumbed. On this lake lies the castle of the Sheik el Beled of El Hadd. But no one who does not belong in El Hadd has ever been allowed to enter it. If everything people say is true, the 'Panther' has every reason to fear the Djebel Allah."

This is what I was told at the time. When we were on the road to catch up with the Ussul and Tshoban, a third messenger reached us. He had been sent by the prince of Halihm to tell us that the "Panther" was hurrying north in forced marches and seemed to believe that he was driving the hosts of Djinnistan ahead of him while they were actually luring him on.

When we reached the camp of the Erdjani, another messenger sent by the "Panther" had just been caught. He was to report to the Bash Islami that the army would cross the Djebel Allah and invade El Hadd to punish the Sheik el Beled for having allied himself with the Mir of Djinnistan to depose the new Mir. But large new supplies were required for this undertaking, and the Bash Islami was ordered to send them forthwith.

On the evening of that day, the commanding officers of the wings visited us to greet the Mir and to counsel with him although a council was really unnecessary. The "Panther" was senselessly marching toward his own destruction; all we had to do was follow him. As though blind, he was hurrying straight ahead without making the slightest attempt to swerve to the right or the left. He was therefore quickly overtaken by our two wings, and Abd el Fadl and the Sheik el Beled had established contact with the calvary "in black armor" of the Mir of Djinnistan before the "Panther" suspected what was going on behind him.

During this discussion with our two allies, we heard that there was not only the "wide" path which led up the Djebel Allah and down again on the other side. There were two other routes but they were known only to a few. While the "wide" path runs between the father and the son and the mother and the son after it divides, thus enclosing the son on either side, the two that were kept secret pass toward El Hadd along the outer edges of the father and the mother, so that the three domes lie between them. Because they lay higher than the known path, it could be observed from them. Along these two hidden trails, which a person who did not know of them would not even see, our wings were to follow the "Panther," while the center would remain on the "wide" path and push him ahead of it. These trails could be travelled by light cavalry but were impassable for heavy vehicles or cannons. The "black-armored hosts" of the Mir of Djinnistan which the "Panther" had mentioned only appeared to be wearing armor when seen from a distance. Actually, theirs was a leather dress, the same as that of the Halihm and El Hadd lancers, except that it was not in natural color or blue, but black. This dark color was best suited to their purpose, which was to mislead the enemy.

After several days' march we had left Ardistan behind us and were passing through Shimalistan. Just as a plow sweeps the masses of snow toward both sides where they remain after it has passed, the "Panther" had driven the inhabitants out of his way. Our wings found them where they had fled and persuaded them to return home. Before us, war was raging, but peace returned the moment we had passed.

Without a break, Shimalistan rises toward the north. It had once been exceptionally fertile but when the river which forms its western border had run dry, it became desolate in the course of the centuries. Only in its eastern part were there some fairly large rivers which irrigated it and Ardistan. But they became smaller and smaller in Djunubistan and dried up altogether in the desert of the Tshoban. It was through this eastern part of the country that the "Panther" had moved and spread terror about him. Our coming brought only joy; when we made known that the river was carrying water once again, the people rejoiced.

Up to this time, we had been careful not to let the "Panther" know that he was being pursued, and this had been easy because he had considered a rear guard unnecessary. Now, this changed. Contact of a sort was being established. Stragglers and malcontents appeared. Shortages were becoming noticeable; supplies were being exhausted. The only water there was were widely scattered pools which lay along dried-out and completely silted riverbeds where after centuries of drought some moisture was suddenly beginning to reappear. Because he needed water, the "Panther" was forced to search out such spots and this was the reason we saw men he had sent to look for them. But we avoided taking these men or the stragglers prisoner, for that would merely have relieved him. They would have been a burden to us. Instead, we simply chased them back to increase his worries and tribulations. This meant, of course, that he became aware that there were troops behind him, but this did not matter for the time had come to make him feel our presence. After we had repeatedly driven deserters and stragglers back toward him, three horsemen approached our lines. The one in the middle had a white cloth attached to his lance. He had come to our outposts and asked to be taken to the commander in chief. He had been disarmed and given two Tshoban as an escort. The Mir did not wish to be recognized, for it was not in our interest to have the "Panther" discover how things stood at that moment. It was therefore decided that I would interrogate the emissary myself. He was a fairly old, strong-boned man with a full beard and a face which did not inspire much confidence. He scrutinized me closely as he came toward me, saluted, and asked:

"Who are you? I've never seen you before."

"Nor have I seen you, yet I don't ask you who you are," I answered. "Dismount."

"Why shouldn't I stay in the saddle?"

"Because I don't like being talked down to," I answered. Because we had set up camp, I was not on horseback. "Were you promised safe conduct?"

"Yes. What are you going to do if I don't get down?"

"I would shoot you off the horse if you had not been promised freedom and safety. As it is, I'll shoot your horse. Now then, are you coming down, or not?"

He got off his horse slowly, mumbled a curse, and said:

"I have to know who the people are that dare follow us—"

"Be silent!" I interrupted. "I'm going to ask the questions here, and no one else, least of all you. Who is sending you?"

"The new Mir of Ardistan."

"That's not so."

"Are you telling me I am lying?"

"Yes. The new Mir of Ardistan is with us, not you. Are you perhaps referring to the so-called 'Panther,' the younger of the Tshoban princes?"

"I am."

"The rebel! You should know that he is doomed, and all of you with him. You may have liked him, but the Christians didn't. So they turned the country over to another Mir who was confirmed by all of Ard and Ardistan. This true Mir is pursuing the 'Panther' to crush him."

The man looked at me uncertainly, his eyes flickering.

"Is that true?"

"Are you telling me that I am lying?" I answered him with his own words.

"Then take me to him," he demanded. "I insist on seeing your commander in chief."

"It's not for you to insist on anything. He charged me to talk to you. If that doesn't suit you, get back on your horse right now and I'll have you returned where you came from."

The man had obviously expected matters to take a different turn and was telling himself that it was now his job to find out as much as he could and to report it to the "Panther." He wouldn't accomplish that purpose if he persisted in his manner, and therefore he was more polite. "Excuse me. If you had told me who you were, I would have given you no cause to deal with me in this way."

"Then be modest and brief. What does the 'Panther' wish to tell us?"

"That he wants to talk to the commander of this army."

"When?"

"Right away."

"Where?"

"In his tent."

"Our commander is to come to him? Into your camp?"

"Yes."

"Run after that traitor, that liar? That's out of the

question. We'll grant him a parley because we are compassionate and merciful, and for no other reason. It should be up to him to come to us, but he is so foul that one cannot bear speaking to him inside a tent. We will see him halfway between your camp and ours. Our Mir will come unarmed and with an escort of fifty unarmed cavalry. The 'Panther' may do likewise. If we see a single weapon, he will fare badly. I am warning you, and him. It is now late morning. Precisely three hours after noon, our Mir will be at the appointed place. If the 'Panther' isn't there, the Mir will immediately turn back and the fate that is awaiting you will overtake you without delay. Now get back on your horse and follow me. I will point out the spot where the 'Panther' is to go."

"So I am to leave now?" he asked.

"Yes."

"But I have many other questions."

"Keep them to yourself."

I went to the nearest Tshoban unit and asked for a horse. I could not use my own for, if the envoy had described it to the "Panther," he would have identified me immediately. I did not take the man directly to the spot I had designated but made a detour to impress him with the strength and disposition of our forces. When we had reached the place that seemed suitable for the meeting, and he had stuck his lance into the ground to mark it, the Tshoban took him back. I returned to the Mir. The Erdjani and Halef were with him. After I had informed them who the man had been and what message I had given him, the Mir said:

"I will gladly go along with your decision. The 'Panther' will come, but it nauseates me to show him my face."

"You won't," I said.

"Who else?"

"Halef."

"Me?" the little fellow exclaimed. "What do you mean, Sidi?"

"You will ride the magnificent white horse of the Mir, receive the 'Panther' or greet him in your own fashion, and tell him that you have been elected ruler of Ardistan, and accepted that honor. Then you'll demand his immediate surrender."

Halef jumped up from his seat, seemed about to leap into the air, but restrained himself.

"Allah be praised! I was about to jump into the air with joy but reconsidered in time. That isn't suitable behavior for a Mir of Ardistan and that's what you just made me. I thank you, Sidi, with all my heart. I am finally being given a fitting task. I shall play this role to your unending praise. If there is something I should tell the 'Panther,' let me hear it."

"We cannot now decide what you should say," I explained to him. "We don't know what the 'Panther' may propose. You know our situation and plans. The 'Panther' is not crafty; he's too excitable and careless for that. But I think we can rely on your judgment." Halef gestured his appreciation of this compliment, but the Mir asked:

"Why are you joking? Don't we have every reason to be serious?"

"There are jokes which we only make because we are serious," I answered. "I have long since stopped feeling that the 'Panther' should be taken seriously. The Bash Islami absurdly overestimated this self-willed, extravagant buffoon. To enter into real negotiations with him would be an unpardonable error. He must be treated as the fool he is. When we are done with him, he should be completely in the dark."

"You are right," the Mir admitted. "Let Halef play his role. That way, the 'Panther' won't see me. But I would like to be there and hear what is said."

"So would I," the Erdjani said.

"And I, too. All we have to do is join the escort. I have noticed that the lancers are carrying extra uniforms. Two of us will dress as El Hadd, the others as Halihm lancers. And we can use the same blue veil as the Sheik el Beled."

"Why four?" the Mir asked. "There are only three of us, and Halef."

"I am going to take the Bash Islami along."

"Why?"

"Because I think he should get to know his former

favorite and ally for the person he really is. It's not impossible that he still feels some of his former confidence and trust in that man, and this is a way of destroying it."

"You are right again. Let's get the uniforms and change."

Some time later, the "Panther's" envoy came back to make some changes in our agreement, but I refused. He returned a third time, but his proposals were rejected again. When he recognized that he could not get the better of me, he finally condescended to inform me that the "Panther" would do precisely as I had stipulated.

13 : On the Djebel Allah

When it was past two, we changed and put on the blue veils. We also took horses from the lancers so that we would not be recognized by ours. Halef was given the magnificent white steed of the Mir. When we came to the meeting place, we saw that the "Panther" and his men had already arrived. He was sitting off by himself, his soldiers forming a half-circle behind him. Halef would not have been true to himself, had he made his arrival brief and simple. He had told us what he wanted, and we followed his instructions. Arriving at a gallop, we placed ourselves as if we were going to ride down our enemies but pulled up at the last moment. We repeated this maneuver twice, and then distributed ourselves so that Halef was facing the "Panther" at five paces' distance, the Mir and the Bash Islami to his right, myself and the Erdjani to his left.

For a while, nothing was said. The two principal actors had not even greeted each other. It did not occur to Halef to be the first to open his mouth. If need be, he would have remained silent all day and longer so that he could then reproach his vis-à-vis for being talkative and hasty. But the "Panther" was much too impatient to wait. After a bare two minutes, he called out:

"How long is this silence to last? Let's begin. I am the Mir of Ardistan."

Halef said nothing.

"Did you hear?" the "Panther" asked. "I am the Mir of Ardistan."

Halef maintained his silence.

"Are you deaf?" the other continued. "I told you that I am the Mir."

Now Halef finally shook his gigantic turban, raised his arms slowly, and answered:

"Oh, Allah, how long will there be people who cannot remain silent but are so loquacious and in such a hurry that they cannot refrain from announcing to all the world that they are raving mad. I came here from Ard with 163,000 infantry, 290,000 cavalry, and 385,000 cannons to blast a pathetic liar, cheat, and rebel. I was elected Mir, placed on the throne, and proclaimed the sole ruler of Ardistan. Now a frog is squatting in front of me, croaking into my ears that it is not I but he that is the Mir."

When Halef had begun speaking, the "Panther" had pricked up his ears, for the Hadji was making no effort to disguise his voice. The rebel's hand shot to his belt, but he had no weapons. He asked:

"Whom are you calling a frog?"

"You," Halef answered quietly and very sincerely.

The "Panther" jumped to his feet, shook his clenched fists at him, and started shouting:

"Dog! Consider yourself lucky that we are unarmed. Otherwise, I'd shoot you down like a mangy jackal or a stinking hyena. I find you nauseating. You have the voice and figure of someone I know, the dumbest of the dumb. Be careful! Or you will fare as he did!"

"What happened to him?" Halef asked.

"I had him locked up. He died of hunger and thirst, and in great torment. Do you wish to suffer the same fate?"

"Yes, I do. It's not possible for me to suffer a fate different from his. And I am satisfied with that fate.

He doesn't look as starved as you imagine, and has become Mir of Ardistan besides. He'll show you who and what you are. Look!"

He raised his veil and threw it back over the turban. The "Panther" had been about to sit down again, but leaped up a second time:

"The Haddedihn, the cursed Hadd—"

He interrupted himself, too frightened to continue. He sat down slowly, lowered his head, placed his hands in front of his face, and remained silent. Halef did not understand such profound inner turmoil. He turned to us and said:

"Wasn't I right when I called him a frog? First he jumps up, then he jumps down, he puffs himself up only to collapse again. And what impudence to call himself the Mir of Ardistan!"

I gestured to him and he fell silent. The "Panther" pretended not to have heard the Hadji's words. Perhaps he had really been oblivious to them. But after a few moments, he let his hands sink, raised his head, looked at us one after the other, and then directed his gaze at Halef. In spite of his sunburnt skin, one could see that his face had grown pale. But his fear was gone. His face changed. Gradually, it took on a stealthy expression, something truly panther-like. And when he began speaking again, his voice did not betray a trace of excitement but such uncanny control that it seemed he had only withdrawn into himself to rush at us even more vehemently and threateningly.

"The Haddedihn lives," he said. "The fool, the blatherer. And if he lives, the others must, too. They got away. The Mir had inhuman luck. He returned to Ard and joined forces with the Erdjani. I can tell from this cavalry here which isn't part of the old Ussul Guard but belongs to his army. So that fellow also escaped from the 'City of the Dead.' Probably with the help of that vile individual from Djermanistan whom I will crush between my fists, like this."

He rubbed them to demonstrate his meaning, and continued:

"Then the Mir, the old Mir, began pursuing me. The Mir of Djinnistan took pity on him and sent him help.

: 602 :

For shame! And the Sheik el Beled also joined up with him, as did the prince of Halihm—"

"Whose daughter you want for your wife," Halef quickly interrupted.

"How do you know?" the "Panther" burst out.

"I read your letter."

"Which letter?"

"The one you had your colonel take to Abd el Fadl."

"Liar! The prince of Halihm would never give you such letters to read."

"Are you going to deny it?" the Bash Islami shouted, unable to suppress his bitterness any longer.

"Who are you? What business do you have interfering?"

"Who am I? Have a look! We all read your letter, all of us, including me."

He removed his veil, but this did not have the result he had expected. The "Panther" hesitated a moment, and then said with a sarcastic laugh:

"Fools, all of you! Pathetic, miserable fools, whoever you may be. You wanted to put on a show. The crazy Haddedihn had to represent the Mir, the ruler. You must have an absurd idea of the man who has to preserve law and order in Ardistan."

He was roaring with laughter and because he turned to his escort, they joined in. Then he went on:

"Yes, quackery, imposture, and lies. We really believed that we had the lancers of El Hadd and Halihm before us. We were even convinced that your veils meant the 'oath of Djinnistan.' But now that this old man who imagines he's the father of the future wife of the ruler has given away your masquerade, I know what I am dealing with. I will go along with this joke, but I'll make short shrift of you, much shorter than you think."

He again rose, crossed his arms over his chest to assume the imposing stance of a strategist, and asked Halef: "So you are the Mir of Ardistan?"

"Yes."

"Very well. Since I make that same claim, one of us has to die, either you or I. You understand that?"

"So it's going to be a duel? Between you and me?"

"Yes."

"I am willing. Right now. Shall they bring us weapons, or shall we use our fists? That would be acceptable also."

The little Hadji knew that he was the "Panther's" equal and felt no fear. On the contrary, he was delighted to have a chance to defeat this man in combat. But the "Panther" quickly interrupted:

"Not like that. I wouldn't dream of tussling with someone like you. If you really are the Mir, we both have our armies. I am talking about a battle between the two armies, not between you and me. I won't fight dwarfs. I invite you to a battle. Tomorrow morning. It will begin at dawn. Do you consent?"

As he asked this question, he cast an extremely disdainful glance at the Hadji, who didn't immediately respond. He felt so profoundly offended by the reference to his stature that he was temporarily at a loss for words.

Besides, our attention was distracted as the sky suddenly darkened, although we could see no clouds passing across the sun. At the same moment, a strong wind rose which did not seem to come from an identifiable direction and was whirling sand and dust everywhere.

"Mount your horses," I called out. "Quickly! Keep the reins tight. And see that they stay away from each other so they can't kick. The earth is about to quake."

Our men immediately jumped up and obeyed my order, but the "Panther's" escort stayed where it was. He laughed sarcastically and called out:

"Earthquake! When one offers cowards a real battle they refuse, and talk about earthquakes. You should be ashamed of yourselves."

After this even more serious insult, Halef was about to reply, but the real Mir told him:

"I ask you to remain silent. The word battle has been spoken, and this changes everything we thought and wanted. From now on, I'll do the talking." He removed the veil from his face, confronted the "Panther," and asked:

"Were you serious? Are you prepared for battle?"

The man stepped back a few paces. Though he may have suspected our identity, he was afraid at that moment. The rest of us also took off our veils. In his rage at seeing who we were, he gnashed his teeth. "They all got away," he said. He stepped back further, looked at us with hatred in his eyes, contracted like a cat about to jump, and addressed the Mir:

"Will you tell me the truth if I ask you something?"

"One doesn't lie to people of your sort," the ruler answered proudly.

At that moment, it began to rumble but I could not tell whether it came from above or below.

"Are the El Hadd lancers really with you?" the "Panther" asked.

"Yes."

"How many?"

"Count them during the battle."

"And the Halihm lancers?"

"Yes."

"Do you have enough water for so many men?"

"We have water for many more."

"May Allah curse you. And you want to defeat me through hunger and thirst?"

"Yes."

"I have been cut off from all supplies. I have no water. You are thinking that I will die a miserable death, just as I wanted you to die in the 'City of the Dead.' But you are mistaken. You don't know me. I will get water; I will get food. And do you know where? From you! Though I was being ironic before when I mentioned a battle, I am serious now. I invite you to battle, a battle of desperation between you and me. Do you accept?"

"Yes."

"Tomorrow?"

"Yes."

"Where?"

"Wherever I come upon you."

It was thundering now. It sounded as if it were not just coming from the sky but also from below ground. The enemy's horses snorted and became restless. The "Panther" pointed north where the three domes of the Djebel Allah were towering high into the sky, and went on:

"This battle which will decide between you and me will take place over there, at the foot of the Djebel

Allah. Tomorrow, at dawn. Do you agree?"

"Yes."

Now, a thin, sharp noise passed over us with lightning speed, like a running crack travelling across a frozen surface. At the same time, we felt as if we were standing on a swing about to be set in motion. The horses were frightened.

"Then we have an agreement," the "Panther" went on. "Tomorrow morning, the moment there is enough light to tell friend from foe." And with indescribable sarcasm, he added: "I hope you will be there. It wasn't precisely heroic to want to defeat me through hunger and thirst. It's not your water that will decide, but the sword."

"No, neither water nor the sword, neither you nor I, but someone higher than both of us," the Mir answered him.

"Someone higher? Who?"

"God."

"God?" the "Panther" laughed disdainfully. "I don't need the sort of help only the weak and incompetent long for. I shall win through my own strength, but not—"

He could not finish his sentence. There was a noise at this moment as if heaven and earth were to end, and the ground began to shake. The "Panther" fell. He started to get up quickly, but further shocks followed which kept knocking him down. The horses of his escort neighed with terror and rushed off. His men roared as they chased after them, and then he too shouted:

"Away, away! The devil has a hand in this. I hope he gets all of you. Away, away!"

Taking great leaps, he dashed after the others. The earth had become still once more.

The sky had darkened very suddenly and became light again with the same abruptness. As the "Panther" was scurrying away, it cleared and the sun shone as before. The tremors did not affect us as they had the "Panther." We all had the feeling that a higher power, an invisible being stood at our side, that He had wanted to show us through the tremors that only He

: 606 :

could be relied upon, that only His help, not human plans, could bear fruit.

How quickly my plan to ridicule the "Panther" had collapsed, how promptly the Mir had had to renounce his intent to remain incognito! We had wanted to put on a show, and now were standing there, looking at each other. What had we accomplished?

"Sidi, I'll never impersonate the Mir again," Halef said. "I did it so badly that even the earth was trembling with anger. I'll remain the sheik of the Haddedihn of the Shamar tribe. A person who pretends to be more than he is or can be will have the ground pulled from under his feet, and I have no wish to go through that again. The 'Panther' offered to do battle with us, just as great heroes did in early times. Perhaps the time will come when we shall talk about the 'Battle on the Djebel Allah.' Do you think he'll keep his word?"

"No," I answered.

"For what reasons?"

"Very weighty ones."

"I wonder if you aren't mistaken. He is obliged to fight. He'll die of thirst if he doesn't get water, and he can only get it from us. He said so himself."

"That's precisely why I don't believe him. There is water, and it isn't even far from here."

"Where?"

"Directly on the other side of the Djebel Allah. All these mountains which seem barren to us are desolate only on the southern side where they were exposed to the destructive influences from Ardistan. I was told that by Marah Durimeh herself. In the gorges on the far side, there is flowing water but it cannot pass into this dried-out, parched land. I would be surprised if the 'Panther' didn't know that as well or better than I, a foreigner."

"He knows it," the Bash Islami interrupted. "I myself pointed it out to him."

"Then he will cross. First, to get water and to save his life. But there are also other reasons. He thinks that the hosts of the Mir of Djinnistan are fleeing, so he must pursue them if he wants to punish them. He knows that the lancers of El Hadd and Halihm are with us, and thinks that their country is therefore stripped of defenders. He believes he can quickly conquer it."

"Very true," the Erdjani agreed. "If he can occupy El Hadd, he thinks he'll be safe, while we are stopped here along the bare Djebel Allah and cannot cross because he will place artillery along the only route he knows of. That is the reason he inquired whether the lancers were with us. I also believe that he only talked about a battle to avoid it. Let's return to camp, send for the Sheik el Beled and Abd el Fadl, and counsel with them."

We followed this suggestion. The two men arrived toward evening. As we told them what had happened, it became apparent that they shared our views. After a lengthy and detailed discussion, we knew what steps to take in any contingency, and they departed.

The tremors had left me with a curious sensation. Let the reader imagine a hollow, light rubber ball, bobbing on gently moving water. A fly is sitting on this ball and feels this movement. The ball was the earth, and I was the fly. It was as if something might capsize or burst under me at any moment. My little Hadji felt the same way, and came to tell me about it:

"You wait and see, Sidi," he said. "Something is going to happen here at the Djebel Allah. Even if the 'Panther' tries his best to outwit us and to get away, there is someone whom he cannot outsmart, from whom he cannot escape. That is the Emir es Salsale,* who will not be mocked. I don't know whether he was serious about a battle on the Djebel Allah or only trying to trick us, but he was reckless enough to demand it, and he will get it, though not the way he thinks."

There was something prophetic in these words. From this moment on, events began moving toward a climax. Providence, which stands high above all merely human calculations, seemed to have decided: The "Panther" wants a battle, and he shall have it.

---

* Lord of the earth, i.e., God.

The two armies were facing each other along the border of El Hadd, which was formed by a high, precipitous mountain chain running straight from east to west, utterly impassable except at the Djebel Allah. There was no road except the wide path I mentioned which divided at the top, and the two secret trails which went up and came down along the two outer sides of the Djebel and ran parallel to the path but could not be seen from it. Until early that morning, the "men in black armor" of the Mir of Djinnistan had been stationed at the foot of the Djebel. But they had moved back up the mountain when they had seen the army of the "Panther" approach. The Djebel Allah is so wide that it takes several hours to ride from one end to the other. Because the "Panther" was heading straight for the wide path, it was easy for our two wings to move along the sides of the mountain without being noticed. Our center remained stationary because we knew it was being observed. It was a good hour's ride from the enemy, though our outposts were naturally much closer. The advance elements of our wings had reached the foot of the mountains and the trails by which they were to proceed. Because in the south the "Panther" was completely closed in by the half-circle we had formed, and had the mountains facing him in the north, his only escape route was the Djebel Allah pass. But there, the lancers of El Hadd and Halihm had established contact with the "men in black armor," and this contact was maintained when the latter withdrew before the "Panther." We were consequently informed of everything that was happening on the heights. All attempts of the enemy to conceal his movements were thus frustrated.

Shortly after darkness had set in, a messenger from the "Panther" was brought to us. He handed us a note with the words: "Challenge to battle on the Djebel Allah." This man had barely been taken away again by his guards when our lancers reported that the enemy was about to cross the pass under cover of darkness, and that the "troops in black armor" would not try to deny him access to the plateau. It was not certain as yet whether it would also be advisable to allow him to come down on the far side. Two hours later, another messenger arrived. He delivered a piece of paper with exactly the same words as before. The "Panther" probably did not realize how childishly he was behaving, but his motives were obvious. It was not even to dawn on us that he intended to try to escape. He also wanted to find out whether we were still at the same spot or had begun moving. And he was already looking forward to ridiculing us, should we let ourselves be taken in by him.

At two-hour intervals, two more messengers with the identical message arrived. But there were also further reports from the El Hadd and Halihm, informing us that the crossing had begun. The "Panther" had sent a sizeable cavalry detachment ahead to reconnoiter and then ordered the artillery forward. It was important for him to get it to a safe place and to cover the pass with cannons so that only a few rounds would suffice to repulse any advance we might make. The other troops followed his artillery at such speed that his camp had been completely evacuated by the time his last messenger arrived. It was now between two and three o'clock in the morning. We were still where we had been during the day, having no intention of undertaking something in darkness that we could accomplish more safely and easily when it was light. But there was another reason for our caution and delay which had nothing to do with the tactical situation, but lay in the surrounding landscape.

The moon was in its last quarter. During the early evening, it had shone brightly in the sky, and the stars were so clearly visible that we could have counted them. This gradually changed. The stars disappeared or, rather, they were still there but could no longer be told apart. The moon also became less distinct, losing its well-defined contour. Its haziness became so pronounced that around midnight it could no longer be seen at all, although we could still tell where it was.

The horses of the Tshoban were getting restless, and the troops also were overtaken by a curious sense of uncertainty. The air had changed. It wasn't that it had become more difficult to breathe, but one also seemed to breathe in a feeling of oppression. This did not subside but became more intense. We were in the general area of the volcanoes whose eruptions we had earlier observed from a distance. During the entire journey from the country of the Ussul to this place, we had seen them shine and glow every evening, sometimes more, sometimes less distinctly and impressively. All those who believed the legends of the river and peace had thought that the present year was the well-known hundredth year during which the gates of paradise would open and the question of the archangel would resound over the entire earth to all mankind. Very often it had seemed to us that the earth was quaking gently, almost hesitantly. These tremors had been so faint that we had not really paid much attention to them. But lately, these isolated movements had been superseded by what I previously described as a swimming, swaying, and floating, and the sense that something under our feet was about to turn over or burst. And that evening, we were so absorbed by this presentiment that I should have to call the psychological result a constriction, an uneasiness.

That day, also, we saw a glow coming from the mountains, particularly from the one furthest away, in the highest region of Djinnistan. Those closer to us did not seem to be active. The nearest one, the Djebel Allah, was acting more strangely than the rest. Its center dome, the "son," was rising silently and darkly into the sky as though dead, as if it could no longer be vitalized by the fires in the interior of the earth. But the other two, the "father" and the "mother," were breathing feebly, like someone choking. It began with a faint rolling. If one stretched out on the ground and placed one's ear against it, one could hear it distinctly. At first, I had thought it was the rolling of cannon wheels but soon realized that it had nothing to do with that. This rolling was succeeded by an exhalation of one of the domes which passed through the air like the hissing breath of fear being forced through the lungs of a dying person. From one hour to the next, this rolling became louder and more palpable. Forces gathered inside the earth seemed vainly to be seeking release. All my companions felt this, although it was my belief that these forces would not be discharged from the right or the left dome, but from the one in the center, the "son." But I could not prove this.

About three o'clock, the Sheik el Beled arrived. When he inquired what had happened during his absence, we showed him the pieces of paper the "Panther" had sent.

"How imprudent he is, and what a blasphemer," the Sheik said. "Hasn't he understood yet that a man is held to his word? He will be made to feel the weight of his. What he promises in words he has to pay in deeds. And since he promised a 'battle on the Djebel Allah,' he will have to wage it, no question! He will have to fight us or the One for whom all of us fight, and against Whom he rebels. That is the reason I am coming to you now, in this frightful night of truth. I want to be with you. My cavalry is used to such nights, while you shudder as the laws of Heaven enter into force because the laws of earth do not suffice to bring justice."

"What do you mean to say?" the Mir asked. "You are hinting at something extraordinary."

"I am saying that the Djebel Allah will finish what the 'Panther' has begun."

"Finish what? And when?"

"At dawn. The 'Panther' said so."

"I still don't understand."

"An eruption of the Djebel Allah is imminent. Look up at him and listen to the rumbling under your feet. This is something new to you, but I am familiar with it. I know every one of these strange mountains, not only its name, but its temperament, its character. And I know the Djebel Allah especially well. The 'father' and the 'mother' are breathing, albeit laboriously. They do not threaten us. But look at the son! I was up there early this morning. I was sitting at his feet and heard him rumble. And I felt the wrath inside him. His time has come, the great time when the boiling floods will erupt from his chest and hips so that he may cleanse and purify himself of the filth, of the ashes and dust which cover him. He wants to turn green, as he once was when God still walked through Ardistan. He wants to put on the dress of life, of happiness, of bliss, not only for those of us who live in these mountains, but for all of you and all those who think he is dead, barren, desolate, and extinct. Harken and behold!"

He raised his arm and pointed at the heights. There was a clanging and rolling inside the earth as if scythed chariots were rattling past below us, sharpening their metal weapons. A biting wind suddenly whistled round about us, and the next moment a glowing sheaf rose from the craters of the "father" and the "mother." This was accompanied by sounds reminiscent of millions of files passing over steel and iron. The Sheik el Beled stood before us in his fluttering coat and veil, his arm raised toward the mountain. In the light of the blazing crater, it would have been impossible to say whether he was a natural or a supernatural being. We could not see his face because it was veiled but in his voice there sounded the profound, sacred seriousness which dwelt in him and also seized us.

"Did you see and hear?" he asked. "Can you feel the cold wind being irresistibly pulled up toward the heat? God tells us, in the powerful sermon His nature preaches, what must happen in the lives and souls of peoples and individuals if the decrees of Heaven are to be fulfilled. I know the 'son' and his way. The forces under his foot are already stirring. Soon there will come a moment when all the domes which are glowing now will be extinguished as though by a single breath. Then his time will have come, then he alone will act, he who gathers the waters of Djinnistan under his throne to guide them far below ground to the angels of the 'City of the Dead' and the Chatar defile."

"Did the water that saved us come from here?" I asked.

"Yes, from here, from the Djebel Allah."

"Are you convinced this mountain will erupt?"

"It may happen in a few moments."

With fear in his voice, Halef exclaimed:

"Then the 'Panther' and his entire army are doomed. May Allah show them mercy, and us as well. We must save them!"

"Yes, we must save, or at least warn them," I agreed. "Our two horses are the fastest. We will immediately—"

"Stop! Don't be foolish!" the Sheik el Beled interrupted me. The Erdjani held on to the Hadji, who had been about to run off without waiting for me. "It is already too late. You would only rush to certain destruction. Do you feel it? No one can ride to that mountain now."

The earth was trembling under our feet. But Halef shouted:

"I'll go nonetheless. Sidi, help me! I want to leave."

He was struggling with the Erdjani who was holding him with his giant's strength.

"Let him go," I told him. "We must go up there to warn them. That is our human duty."

"Human duty?" he asked. "Sahib, I respect and love you, but here I must contradict you. You are being weak and shortsighted. When God pronounces judgment, is it really human duty to resist Him and save the guilty?"

"Not all those being threatened by destruction are guilty," I objected.

"Yes, they are," he insisted. "Think of the 'City of the Dead.' Here is your Halef. Will you struggle against fate and go to your certain death for the sake of a person such as the 'Panther'? You may, of course, but I shall remain."

He had released Halef and stepped up to the Sheik el Beled who pressed his hand and said:

"You spoke well. I am glad to hear you say this, you of all people. Love of mankind must never become weakness of heart. The more nobly man thinks, the more remorselessly he should deal with all that is harmful and vile. Pay heed! The highest domes are already darkening."

He did not let go of the Erdjani's hand. Clothed in identical garments, the two were standing next to each other. The Sheik el Beled was somewhat shorter and less broad-shouldered, and yet it seemed as if they belonged together. I did not have the time to pursue this notion, however, or to join Halef in warning the enemy as we had intended. The sheik had been right; it was much too late. The voice of the heart had to remain silent because the voices that now began to speak were too powerful for our weak human speech to prevail. The pillars, domes, and battlements to the north had been glowing uninterruptedly up to this moment; now, they faded one after the other. It was becoming dark up there. The wind which had risen some time before had subsided again, and a profound, uncanny silence reigned.

"Are the Tshoban in control of their horses?" the Sheik el Beled asked.

"Yes," the Mir answered. "I gave strict orders. Listen! What was that?"

A shot had been fired in the distance.

"A cannon," the Erdjani exclaimed. We heard a second, and then another and still another. The Sheik el Beled, who had been listening attentively, turned to us:

"Yes, those are cannons. The 'Panther's' announcement of triumph. When his advance guard went up the mountain to prepare the way for the artillery, the 'troops in black armor' retreated slowly, so that they might see and hear as much as possible. They found out that the 'Panther' had given the order to fire three salvos of ten shots each when the retreat had been successfully completed."

"For what purpose?" the Mir asked.

"Probably to mock us," Halef said.

"Or to make us believe that he was still down below and that the battle was about to begin," the Erdjani said.

"That's right," the Sheik el Beled agreed. "It is dawn, the time that had been set for the beginning of the battle. And those whom we overheard said we would be misled by these shots and assume that the battle had begun, and they ridiculed us for it. We are expected to act foolishly, and to be embarrassed and annoyed about it. What a clown! Neither here below nor up there is there a single person that would be deceived by him. He'll find that out soon enough. Let's be quiet now until the thirty shots have been fired. I don't think we'll have to respond."

As we waited, it was becoming utterly dark in the direction of Djinnistan. Above us, the sky had been the color of lead and looked heavy, oppressive, as if about to collapse. Now the darkness increased and soon became so impenetrable that it could only be called blackness. I held my hand some twelve inches away from my eyes and couldn't see it. That was unnatural. Halef's horse and mine were neighing faintly, asking us for permission to come closer. They lay down near us and remained quiet during the following terrible hour, requiring no more than a friendly word or pat to calm them.

We had barely taken care of these irreplaceable animals when the catastrophe erupted. The impious, repeated call to "battle at the Djebel Allah" was bearing fruit. Like the approach of certain, deliberate fate, a deafening rolling slowly came from the distance. It passed below us. It was as if a giant tortoise several miles in length was creeping along under our feet. When it reached us, it lifted us in the air, pushing its remorselessly solid shell on and on, and finally letting us drop behind it. I felt it quiet distinctly, for when this destructive tremor came, Halef and I quickly lay down next to our horses to let them know they had nothing to fear. The Mir and the Bash Islami fell to the ground, but the Sheik el Beled stood erect, still holding the Erdjani's hand, and called out:

"Do you still hear the shots? No! They suddenly stopped although there were less than thirty. When He whose voice we are about to hear speaks, everyone else must be silent. This one tremor sufficed to destroy the 'Panther's' artillery, and perhaps his entire army. Listen to the crashing."

In spite of the distance, we heard the noise of rocks detaching themselves and rolling down. Then thousands of animal and human voices seemed to unite in a single, loud, dreadful death cry which rose to the sky, but we only felt its distant vibrations.

"Horrible, horrible," the Mir called out. "They are all dead. They are—"

The rest of his remark was swallowed by a shot, a noise of such loudness that it seemed my inner ear had burst. For a few minutes, I could not hear. I saw the Sheik el Beled pointing to the mountain, saying something, but did not understand a word. This shot had come from the crater of the "son." He had disgorged what was inside him. The rubble and debris were not scattered outside but fell back. Now the giant tortoise seemed to be coming back, moving in the opposite direction, toward the mountain. What it had not ground and crushed before would certainly be destroyed now. There was a blow as if a giant fist had knocked violently against the inner crust of the earth to bring everything crashing down, and at that precise moment, something indescribably beautiful rose from the crater of the "son."

It came so quickly and suddenly that we had not had the chance to see it emerge and develop. It resembled a bright, immaculately ground chalice filled to overflowing with sparkling champagne. At the bottom, this chalice had a diameter of perhaps twenty meters, but at the top it must have been at least one hundred. I could not estimate its height. As it was rising toward the rim, the frothing champagne was of a light gold at the bottom which changed first to light silver, then bright green, and an indescribably delicate blue at the top. These various colors had a metallic shimmer. They were not clearly set off from each other but gradually merged. At times, the gold flashed to the top, the blue to the bottom. The foam that bubbled over had the color of peach blossoms shot through with golden and silver sparks. In the black night lying upon us, the almost supernatural appearance of this fountain united all the qualities and effects of the miraculous within itself. The froth which crowned it did not overflow but could be seen evaporating. Sparks and flashes carried it in all directions into the night, even toward us. We could feel it. It was warm, coming down as an incredibly fine, gentle rain and enveloping us in a veil which became increasingly dense until it gradually obscured the view of its origin and finally made it invisible.

"The 'son' is giving us water, the long yearned-for water," the Sheik el Beled exclaimed. "And what he gives, he will not take away again. We may keep it."

I heard these words. Thank God I had not become deaf. The sheik continued:

"For us, this is a blessing, but it will have sealed the

enemy's fate. Here, it is warm, but it will be burning hot where he is. Who would want to be in his place and—"

He was interrupted by a clap of thunder, real thunder this time, not a subterranean rumble. Lightning flashed, and more thunder followed. The damp veil which had enveloped us condensed. It began to rain, but the thundering and lightning did not cease. How extraordinary! A thunderstorm here, where it had not rained in centuries! It frightened the horses more than the earlier tremors. We heard them becoming noisier behind us in the camp. Efforts were made to calm them. But with several of them, that proved impossible. They broke away, came running toward us, and shot past. One of them not only neighed and snorted, but roared, howled, and whined to rival the thunder in loudness, pulling down the Mir and the Basch Islami as it rushed across our lines.

"Mashallah," Halef marvelled. "Did you see that horse, Sidi?"

"Yes, but not clearly."

"It was huge."

"An Ussul nag."

"The fattest I've ever seen. And what a voice! This howling and roaring, this elephant-like trumpeting. Haven't we heard that before?"

"Hm."

"It must have been our old friend Smikh."

"It certainly sounded like him. But what would he be doing here? He's home now, in the homeland of all Ussul nags."

"Who knows what happened there, or what—Oh, Allah, help!"

He had interrupted himself with this cry of terror because at that moment a series of flashes of lightning and claps of thunder followed each other with such rapidity that they merged. These lights and sounds had barely ceased when the rain stopped abruptly. It had not lasted more than two minutes. The moist veil had also disappeared and the Djebel Allah and the surrounding country again lay before our eyes. But they did not look as they had before. We did not see them in the light of the moon and the stars but in the brilliance of a dawn that rose over the heads of the "father," the "mother," and the "son," and slowly spread down to envelop us.

All of us uttered exclamations of relief and admiration. It was a morning of extraordinary beauty. Both the mountains and the plain which had been chosen as the field of battle lay before us as though wholly unchanged. The peaks shone in the peaceful light of the resurrected day. There was no trace of volcanic fire, rising smoke, or flying ashes. Nor did anything seem to have changed on or about the Djebel Allah. It was as if we had dreamt. But as this soothing sight emerged during the last, powerful clap of thunder, that thunder and lightning proved to have created greater confusion among our horses than we had believed while it had still been dark. Many had torn loose. They were scattering in all directions, snorting and neighing, kicking about them, now stopping and hesitating, now dashing aimlessly on. The task of recapturing got under way. The gigantic nag that had run down the Mir and the Bash Islami was the wildest. The final, enormous clap had brought it to a halt. Struck with terror, it had turned and was coming toward us once more, howling and screaming even louder than before.

"Sidi, it's coming back," Halef called out. "Don't let it knock you down! It's beside itself with fear, exactly like—"

"Exactly like Smikh," I finished his sentence. "It's he, it really is."

"Allah w'Allah! How did he get here?"

"That's unimportant. But how are we going to stop him?"

"As we always have. He knows your voice, and he can also see you. Surely his fear can't have blinded him?"

I spread out my arms and stepped in the path of the onrushing colossus.

"Smikh, Smikh," I called. And "Smikh, Smikh," Halef joined in.

"Not you," I ordered. "He must only hear my voice."

The horse was coming toward me. He saw me, and yet he didn't. He did not recognize me because I was wearing the leather garment of the El Hadd. I had to jump out of his way to avoid being thrown to the ground. But when the chubby animal had me directly before his eyes, I roared at least as loud as he, and finally got results. He couldn't stop as quickly as he wanted to, but described an arc and turned back toward me at a slower pace. Then he stopped at a distance of some ten or twelve feet to have a closer look.

"Smikh, my dear fellow," I said as I went toward him with outstretched arms. A twitching passed through his body. He had recognized me. He raised his head as high as he could, opened his mouth, and gave a roar that startled everyone present. Then he took two or three jumps toward me, sniffed me, and wiped my face with his tongue.

"That's the monster that knocked us down," the Mir said. "He seems to know you. Whose is it?"

"It belongs to our friend Amihn, the Ussul sheik."

"Who is riding him here?"

"Probably no one. That horse is his favorite and he lets no one else sit on him. If Smikh is here, his master must be, too."

"I didn't know Amihn was here."

"Nor did I. But we'll soon find out why this horse has suddenly turned up. Look at those two riders. I think it's the prince of Halihm and his daughter."

It was indeed Abd el Fadl and Merhameh. They came from the east and quickly reached us. Both were dressed in their blue, braided leather garments, their light coats billowing behind them. On their snow-white horses that were barely touching the ground in their gliding movement, they seemed like messengers from another world. Their cheeks were suffused with color, their eyes shining when they dismounted.

"That was the battle at the Djebel Allah that was intended to mislead us," Abd el Fadl said. "Sham has become truth. Someone who cannot be deceived took our place, and now it is over. The cannons crashed into the ravines and abysses, and those who did not have a chance to escape are lying crushed under rocks or smashed in the depths. But from the Djebel Allah, warm, healing water is gushing forth, and at the feet of the 'son,' a newborn stream is rushing down the mountain to irrigate the parched steppe. Such is the punishment of a higher justice; thus the kindness of heaven transforms the punishment into a blessing."

"Does only heavenly kindness accomplish that?" Merhameh asked. "Isn't there also kindness among men? My name is Merhameh, compassion, and I want that to be not only my name, but also my nature. I am turning to you, the Mir of Ardistan, and to you, the Mir of—" she stopped to correct herself "—the Sheik el Beled of El Hadd. The border between your two lands runs across the battlefield of this night. I therefore turn to both of you to say that there has been enough severity, that the time for kindness, humanity, and compassion has come. Give me and my father the suffering and the wounded. The hosts of the Halihm not only fight but also heal, not only destroy but also restore. Permit us to take them to the place of devastation so that we may also follow the commands of the heart after the voice of retribution has spoken."

"As regards my territory, I gladly give that permission," the Mir answered.

"And so do I," the Sheik el Beled consented. "Here is Irahd, the leader of your Hukara. What does he have to report?"

Irahd, who commanded the Ussul, had a second Ussul with him who had just arrived from the capital. He had been riding so rapidly that his horse was steaming in the cool morning air. When he noticed Smikh, he laughed.

"There he is, the clamorer, the runaway, the noise-maker. He must have come here in a straight line and without stopping, for I left Amihn and Taldsha directly after he had disappeared."

"Then Amihn and Taldsha are nearby?" the Erdjani asked.

"Yes. They and their company will arrive in half an hour. I was sent ahead to tell you this."

"What company?"

"The nurses the Bash Nasrani is sending."

"How curious! And yet, how welcome! But we knew nothing about it, and gave no such order. How did he happen to think of it?"

"He is advising you through me that this thought occurred to him after a conversation with Merhameh, and that he did not wish to burden you with worries and preparations. He asks your pardon for acting on his own."

"It is granted. And Amihn and Taldsha are among them? How did they get to Ard, and why?"

"They heard that the 'Panther' had lured their two sons to the 'City of the Dead' so that they would die there with the Mir of Ardistan, the Erdjani, Kara ben Nemsi, Hadji Halef, and the entire army. It was their fear that drove them from home. They hurried to Ard as quickly as they could. They rejoiced when they found that those who had been doomed to a miserable death had not only been saved but had already set out to pursue and punish the rebels and murderers. They immediately joined the march of the 'compassionate ones' that had been organized by the bishop and which was about to follow the army on fast mules. They continued receiving favorable reports as they moved from outpost to outpost. They had hoped to arrive here toward evening. But when we were within an hour's ride from here, we saw the approach of the terrible catastrophe, and had to camp. It wasn't the earthquake but the screaming of the mules that terrified our horses. Smikh became especially furious, and began screaming himself. Nothing would calm him, and he ran away. Now I see where to."

"Will he be missed?"

"No. We know what he's like. And he is comfortable here, now that he has found his favorite."

The messenger wanted to continue his report but just then a second horseman, an El Hadd, was seen arriving from the northwest. At the same moment, Halef pointed south where the head of a line had appeared on a low hill.

"A very long caravan seems to be approaching," he said. "Who could they be?"

"It's they," the Ussul answered. "They got here more quickly than I thought."

"I am pleased," Merhameh exclaimed, clapping her small hands joyfully. "There you have the 'human kindness' I spoke of just now. That is a law in the realm of love: No sooner does one wish for something good than it is already on its way. Come, father, we will ride toward them. I want to be the first to welcome them."

Both of them left. Meanwhile, the El Hadd had arrived and reported to his sheik:

"The 'Panther' seems to have got away. It is still uncertain how many are with him. He probably managed to escape during those moments when we also had to retreat to avoid destruction. The Djinnistan cavalry is returning to the plateau and we are establishing contact with them. The route is being carefully looked over so that nothing can happen to you. What is awaiting you there is only for stout hearts and strong nerves. A shot will be the signal that you may move forward."

"How are you going to shoot?" the sheik asked.

"We'll use the only cannon that has been found so far. The rest have disappeared. Only one was not smashed to pieces."

"Then I shall go alone. Kara ben Nemsi and Halef will accompany me. The others will wait here until the 'compassionate ones' arrive. Then they will follow us and camp at the foot of the Djebel Allah. If the 'Panther' really did get away, it will be merely a reprieve. If he lets his last chance pass, he will be shown no mercy."

"Was that possible up to now?" the Bash Islami asked.

"Yes, if he had really waged the battle he announced to us. I don't mean the battle against us, but against himself, and the dark hosts of his soul. When he came to negotiate with us, all those he wanted to destroy were facing him. At that moment, he should have searched the depth of his nature to overcome himself. Had he done so, he could have counted on our pardon. But he was too blind and cowardly to turn against himself. And thus he went to his doom when he left us."

We were facing the Djebel Allah and saw a tiny cloud at the foot of the "son." It dissolved again, and a detonation followed.

"There's the shot I just mentioned," the El Hadd pointed out. "Now, this last cannon will also be thrown into the abyss. Not a single one will be left intact. Such murderous instruments must not be seen in El Hadd and Djinnistan."

When the smoke had dissolved, three white, contracting lines could be seen where the dome of the "son" rose from the base of the Djebel. At the same time, there was a flash in the east. It was the sun. It was not rising gradually but suddenly stood above the horizon. Now not only the domes and peaks lay in the morning light, but that light changed into liquid gold which seemed to flow from the sky. The entire mountain, the entire visible world lay in bright, happy sunlight. As this light fell on the Djebel Allah, the white lines became so distinct that we could see them for what they were, the three armies that had come to our aid. In the middle were the "troops in black armor" from Djinnistan, to the left the lancers of El Hadd, to the right the blue squadrons of Halihm. The points of their lances were sparkling, their helmets reflected flashing shafts of light. To the right and the left of their white horses and white coats, we saw hot water gushing from the rock and crashing into the depth in steaming cascades. And at the foot of the mountain, a small river meandered in countless, uncertain turns to find the way that gravity prescribed for it. As I saw this, my eye was drawn to the mountain. The same fist that had dealt out punishment during the night had become a helping, saving hand during this morning of love. I returned Smikh to the Ussul and mounted my Syrr. Halef, impatient as he was, had already swung himself on his horse, and the Sheik el Beled followed suit. Pointing first to the sun and then to the Djebel Allah, he called out to us:

"Onward! This is a new day, and a new time. The mountains are giving water once more. The desert has become habitable, and peace is approaching from wide-open gates. Let us ride toward it."

He spurred his horse. We followed him, riding first at a walking pace, then at a trot, and finally at a gallop.

14 : Toward the Border

El Hadd should be thought of as a constantly rising mountainous landscape which borders on Ardistan in the south and on Djinnistan in the north. In earlier times, it had been possible to travel through El Hadd and to Djinnistan either by an overland route or a waterway. The southern border region lying between El Hadd and Ardistan could be entered at only two points, the road across the Djebel Allah in the east, and by way of the river Suhl in the west. It was this river which had later become completely dry and given rise to the legend that its water had reversed its course and returned to Djinnistan. In earlier days, commerce between Ardistan and Djinnistan along both routes had been lively. But later, as the rulers of Ardistan had become ever more unjust and violent, both river and overland traffic had gradually decreased and finally stopped altogether. In the end, no water had been left in the river, and the overland route had only remained open for traffic between El Hadd and Djinnistan, so that the rumor began to spread that no inhabitant of Ardistan was allowed to cross the Djebel Allah.

Once, the border area of El Hadd had been fairly well known, but this was no longer the case. Those who had visited it were long since dead and old accounts could not be relied upon because it was said that much had changed in the mountains in the recent past, although these changes were not known in the lowlands. The intention of the Mir of Ardistan to wage war against Djinnistan had therefore been a foolishness whose extent he now clearly recognized. For the same reasons, it was not brave but reckless when the "Panther" compounded this foolishness by making it his own, and finally even came to believe he could extricate himself from his very difficult situation by persisting in it.

Except for about a thousand men whom he had saved with himself, his army had been destroyed. His escape had been possible only because the "troops in black armor" had been obliged to let him pass to avoid being destroyed themselves. At daybreak, when it became known that he had got away, cavalry had been sent after him to observe his movements. Then, a regular pursuit was organized. The advance guard for this action consisted of a unit of the "troops in black armor," followed in the center by the Ussul regiment from Ard under the command of the Erdjani. The Erdjani would proceed on the wide road as long as the "Panther" did so. On both sides the lancers of El Hadd advanced along the hidden trails. The Sheik el Beled was both the commander in chief and the commander of this unit, for the action had now shifted to his homeland. Because he had not felt that additional troops would be required, the rest had remained in camp at the Djebel Allah where the prince of Halihm was in command and his daughter in charge of caring for the wounded and all those who might need help. The Mir of Ardistan, Amihn, the sheik of the Ussul, Hadji Halef, and myself had been allowed to join in the pursuit of the "Panther." In view of the whole nature of the situation, none of us had any doubt as to its eventual outcome. Beyond that, the Sheik el Beled had assured us that a defense had been prepared against attacks on El Hadd, a trap which no enemy, however enterprising and well equipped, would escape. Because of the name of his enemy, he called it the "Panther trap."

Because he had been forced to flee precipitously, it could be assumed that the enemy was no longer well equipped or adequately supplied. He therefore had to obtain what he needed from the inhabitants of the country and it was obvious that he could not count on their good will. Already on the second day of the pursuit, we had proof of this. We found the first large El Hadd village devastated. The "Panther" had not confined himself to requisitioning but had burned and looted. The buildings were in ashes, provisions he had been unable to take with him had been burned, and those who had not immediately surrendered their possessions had been mistreated and tortured. Several had been killed. When the Sheik el Beled saw and heard this, he decided to pursue the enemy more rapidly and in a different manner. The "Panther" had to be deprived of the chance to repeat such misdeeds; he had to be driven into an uninhabited region. That was the western part of the country which had turned into a desert when the river had run dry. While the water had returned there by now, it was also the area where the trap to capture and punish the enemy had been set, as the sheik told us.

The villagers had hidden because they had been told that more enemy units would arrive shortly. But when they recognized their own lancers, they gathered and told us what had happened. They had been interrogated. From the questions they had been asked, we could infer the "Panther's" plan and what he expected from it. His objective was the "watershed" and the "watercastle" of El Hadd, famous since time immemorial, and the seizure of the castle. Possession of it, he thought, would give him control of the entire country, whose ruler he would then depose. Should he succeed, this would constitute the basis for an agreement with Djinnistan and a renewed, victorious offensive against Ardistan. But it was apparent from the kinds of questions he had asked that he had no clear conception either of the "watershed" or of the "watercastle" of the Sheik el Beled. He only knew what legend reported about them, and that was totally insufficient as a basis for a campaign.

Toward evening of the following day, we again came to a village that had been sacked. But already during the next afternoon, we saw that the enemy had changed direction. The "Panther" had taken some prisoners, men we had sent ahead precisely for the purpose of letting themselves be captured, and forced them to show him the way to the "watershed" and the "watercastle."

This meant that he would have to cross the western part of the country. Although this was not a fertile region, it impressed me with a prosperity I had not expected. Throughout Ardistan, this border area was believed to be desolate and barren, its inhabitants impoverished. The simple, modest appearance of the Sheik el Beled and his companions had also inclined me to believe that their country was not rich. But now I saw that this had been a great error. Only along the side facing Ardistan did these mountains look arid; along the border with Djinnistan, they were exceptionally well irrigated. There were countless canals which carried moisture wherever it was needed. In the mountains from which these ditches and channels came there must be an inexhaustible supply of water. For hours we rode through woods whose growth would not have been possible without it. High up on these mountains, we saw green meadows and pastures. The houses were clean, with well-tended gardens and fields, and there were mines where gold, silver, copper, iron, and other metals were found in large quantities. The country road we were now following did not pass through large settlements but every mountain, every valley, every nook and cranny was inhabited, tilled and put to use. Quiet industry greeted us everywhere, and the people lived in concord and contentment. But the moment the "Panther" and his band approached, they fled. Along his path, the roads were deserted and the dwellings empty, for terror spread before him.

I noticed that the Mir of Ardistan showed the Sheik el Beled a respect, almost a deference, which one would hardly have thought possible in a man who had been so unscrupulous and haughty.

They almost always rode side by side, discussing questions of interest to any prince who is well intentioned toward his people. The rest of us kept away from them as much as possible for we saw that the sheik had become the Mir's teacher, and were sincerely glad about this development.

The Erdjani had his hands full, commanding and provisioning his Ussul. When he was free, he also sought out the sheik. He did this in his reserved, modest manner, and was content just to listen to this man for whom he felt an unusual sympathy.

"I am very fond of him," he told me. "I often feel as if I had to embrace him. But I worship him so profoundly that it seems offensive to approach him in such a purely physical manner. When he speaks, I sometimes think I am hearing my father's voice. This is probably due to the veil, which gives the voice that intimate quality I remember from my childhood."

It was with considerable satisfaction that I observed this developing affection, this ever more compelling intuition and recognition. Nor did I fail to notice that these sentiments were reciprocated. The sheik also listened whenever he heard the Erdjani speak. And much of what he appeared to be telling the Mir or others was meant for him as well. One could see that the sheik was always trying to draw the Erdjani to him, and that he was genuinely pleased when he succeeded. The result of this could easily be foreseen. When, where, and in what manner it would come about was unimportant.

Late one afternoon, we reached the Bab Allah.* This was the name of the high, wide opening in the rocks through which the waters of the Suhl had once flowed. Where the river had forced its way through, then to fall precipitously, there were indications that the "Panther" had stopped and evaluated his situation before deciding to entrust himself to the not very tempting riverbed. Because it carried water now, he had probably given in to the advice of his officers.

"He went down there," the Sheik el Beled told us. "But he won't get back up again."

"Is this the trap?" I asked.

"No, we won't get there until later. But the path to it begins here. For the next two days, the banks will be so high and steep that the enemy won't be able to leave the riverbed. We will spend the night up here and follow him down there tomorrow morning."

It was the sheik's opinion that we should leave a fairly sizeable contingent at the place where we went down into the riverbed, and it later turned out that he had been right. The bed was filled with rocks and sand and there was no trace of vegetation, not a single blade of grass. Our earlier smooth progress became a laborious stumbling and climbing. In addition, the rocks reflected an intense heat. But the horses of our allies were used to such terrain, and the Ussul nags were too good-natured to lose patience, provided we occasionally gave them a chance to rest. Most impor-

---

* God's gate.

tant, there was water, and we had enough provisions for ourselves and the horses. When we did run short, supplies could quickly be brought up, for we had set up a chain of outposts along the entire route. The "Panther," on the other hand, was short of food and supplies even before he had entered the riverbed, and while he might have been persuaded that this would soon change, this was a miscalculation whose consequences we could expect to make themselves felt very shortly.

As early as the afternoon of the first day we had spent riding up the riverbed, we overtook stragglers and horses, men and beasts who either were unable or unwilling to continue the march. Toward evening, some of the soldiers who were moving parallel to us along the banks reported that the men we had sent ahead for the "Panther" to capture and who had served him as guides had succeeded in escaping his revenge. Because they knew the way, he had sent them ahead to arrange for provisions to be supplied from the "watercastle," promising bloody retribution upon his arrival there, should they fail him. This threat revealed in what situation he found himself.

The next morning, we encountered a unit of over one hundred men who had deserted, and a second, larger one toward noon. Both of them had turned back but been unable to make much headway because they were too hungry and exhausted. We took them prisoner, disarmed them and sent them back under escort. The man in charge of this transport was told by the Sheik el Beled to hurry and not to be gone for more than two days, because by that time there would be enough flowing water to engulf everything between these precipitous banks. We did not understand the meaning of this warning, but the man he was addressing answered that he had no intention of dying the death of the "Panther" and would no longer be in the riverbed with his men once the water appeared.

During the afternoon, the sheik ordered us to fill our waterskins because the water would disappear and not return until we had reached our destination. Everyone obeyed and no one inquired how he could know that the river would be drying up again. His prediction proved correct. Before evening had fallen, the river bed was completely dry once more. The sheik explained himself more fully:

"The 'Panther' will again suffer from a lack of water and all the more surely be driven into the trap."

"Is it within your power to have the riverbed full or empty?" Halef asked.

"Yes," he answered simply. "You'll see. Everything has been carefully thought out and arranged in advance."

Before darkness set in, we came upon the cadavers of twelve horses. A cavalry troop that deprived itself of its mounts to avoid starvation had to be in an unfortunate state.

On the third day, the appearance of the river bed changed completely. There were fewer rocks and less rubble in it, and finally there was no more debris at all. The huge channel still led through a compact bed of granite but the bottom was now as smooth as the walls, the result of the friction created by the moving rocks pushed along by what must have been an enormous water pressure. When I mentioned this to the sheik, he said:

"That force comes from above, like any other. Precisely from where, you will see tomorrow."

In this desolate, huge, rocky depression, there was no drop of water anywhere. The heat was stifling. We were fortunte to have enough drinking water but the "Panther" and his men must have been suffering terribly. Their trail showed where they had camped during the night. And here a stampede had taken place which had turned the cavalry into infantry. When we wondered why the horses had torn loose and run off, the sheik said:

"It's the lack of water. They were almost dead with thirst. Then, during the night, cool damp air moved toward them. The horses sensed that there was a great deal of water ahead of them. They could not be restrained and started to bolt."

From the way my Syrr was behaving, I could tell that this was correct. He had begun carrying his handsome, delicate head quite differently from the way he had before. As we were riding along, I observed the soil carefully. We only saw the tracks left by galloping horses, which meant that all had fled and none remained behind.

The chubby Ussul nags were especially sensitive to the dampness and began moving at a much more rapid pace. We noticed that the high banks also had changed in appearance. First, there was grass, later shrubs and trees. After some time, we even saw paths. People appeared above us, looking down at us with interest, but silently.

Some time later, we saw houses. Scattered at first, the intervals between them gradually became shorter and turned into shaded, flower-filled gardens strung out along both banks. Behind them, the countryside became hilly, the slopes being dotted by light-colored dwellings sitting in orchards. Were we perhaps drawing close to the capital of the country? Could we hope that we would soon reach the "watercastle" of El Hadd? The sheik was silent and we did not ask. What questions we had were answered so suddenly that we were speechless with surprise and could not even express ourselves in exclamations.

We were heading directly north. Abruptly, the river bed widened enormously. All around us, we were facing something like an arena that seemed to have been built for giants. It was a deep basin of huge dimensions. At its bottom where we found ourselves, it would have taken at least an hour to ride across, but it was much wider at the top. We had stopped at its southernmost point where the rocky walls surrounding it were lower than anywhere else. As the two sides followed a semi-circular course toward the north, they rose more and more, and receded further and further the higher they became, forming a sequence of steps and terraces on which garden followed garden, with country houses, built in different architectural styles, standing in each one. This remarkable basin was of bare rock but only up to the level of the banks. At that height, a wide road with houses on it led all around. The opening the river had made in this circular expanse was bridged by arches of rock which consisted of such large and heavy stones that one wondered how it could have been possible to raise and move them. At an earlier time, the water had almost reached the road and the houses. But where had it come from? Even today, after so many centuries, one could still see that the Suhl, the "river of peace," had emerged from this basin full-blown. In the southern Rocky Mountains, there are also rivers which are already full-sized when they come out of the rocks, but they are small, and their sudden appearance can be explained easily enough. The Ssul, however, was not a small river but a stream which could not originate in some subterranean source.

As I reflected about this and looked up, I saw an aqueduct at the northeastern end of the basin, and another at its northwestern end. It seemed that they might hold the answer to my question. They were not man-made but works of nature and arched two huge openings which yawned like black abysses at the foot of the mountain. Were those perhaps the places from which the water had once come and from which it would probably come again? And was there perhaps some connection with this return and the large barges or riverboats we saw at the southeastern and southwestern points of the basin? For there were harbor-like inlets there on whose bottom these vessels were lying. Each one of them had a name, but I could only read one of them, "Marah Durimeh."

As one let one's eyes travel upward from one terrace to the next, one could see open, circular spaces on each of them. Sizeable buildings stood there which presumably served public functions. High above all this and directly facing us, an angel was towering into the sky. It had the very same shape as the water angels in the "City of the Dead" and at the Chatar defile, but was much taller than they. It formed the highest point and climax of the magnificent panorama that had opened before us, and was flanked by buildings with balconies, towers, and battlements. Those closest to it were very tall, their height decreasing with their distance from it.

This sight made a curious impression. One felt poor, weak, and small, and yet uplifted. Below, there was the bare rock of what had once been the riverbed. As if to document that the soul of this rock had no other desire than water, not a single blade of grass grew there. And yet, built on this foundation rose all the levels and steps of earthly existence which finally terminated in the image of the angel towering high into the clouds, which not only regulated but bestowed the longed-for water. For between the two, the seemingly lifeless rock and the angel which art had created from it, we saw a varied, multiform life milling up and down, back and forth on all the streets and open areas. Everywhere, people were standing, looking down on us. They appeared as festive and happy as the magnificent surroundings in which they lived. We could see that they had been told of our arrival, that we were expected. The appearance of our lancers on both banks had indicated that the Sheik el Beled was near. And as he appeared now, the first to ride out of the riverbed, the powerful surge of shouts of jubilation rose like the thundering swell of the sea, travelling from terrace to terrace until it finally reached the angel and seemed to fade away into the sky.

The sheik turned to us and said:

"This is the 'watercastle' of El Hadd, and that is the angel of the 'watershed' which legend talks of. Down there is the 'Panther' who was presumptuous enough to want to be lord and master here."

Halfway between the center of the basin and its highest wall, there lay a kind of island with bushes and trees on it. There had to be water there. While it would have taken us three quarters of an hour to reach it, its distance from the northern edge was only a quarter hour. From the road along the high bank, wide stone stairs led down to the bottom of the river, and from there a path ran directly to the island where the "Panther" was camped with his band.

"That is the 'Panther trap' into which he walked because there was no other way," the sheik explained. "The island is merely the protective cover of a cistern which reaches far down to the natural route leading from here to the Djebel Allah and from there to all the water angels. Abu Shalem, the great Maha-Lama, built it. There are more of these angels that you know. The cistern is the place one has to go to see whether they have water in them. It was thirst that drove the

'Panther' there. You can see that the entire edge of the basin is occupied. There is no other place from which one can get down from or up to the bank except that staircase there on the northern rim. His horses probably got here earlier. They were watered and then taken up those stairs. We will follow the same route. When the 'Panther' arrived here, he must have seen immediately that he knew nothing about our country and its inhabitants. It was impossible for him to scale these walls, and access by the stairs was denied him. It would have been madness to try to force his way. Now he is camping by the cistern. The river will return; it has to, for the promised time has arrived. It will rise and flood the island and everything on it. We will now ride across the basin and stop by the cistern. We shall ask the 'Panther' if he wants to surrender. If he does, he may still find mercy; if not, the neck he will not bend will be broken through his own doing. So we—"

He stopped, for first one, then many shots had been fired on the island. What was shouting and screaming at first became the furious howl of battle. We saw that our enemies had engaged in a deadly fight at close quarters. It had been our intention to ride quickly to the island but now we slowed our advance. With the "troops in black armor" in the lead, we formed a long line to encircle the "Panther's" refuge. When the enemy saw this, the battle became more furious. Shots were fired in more rapid succession, and the howling doubled in intensity. Then it suddenly became quiet. A loud, commanding voice rang out, another answered. Someone emerged from the trees with a sabre in his fist. A goodly number of soldiers followed him and began rushing toward us. Some fell and did not rise again. The man in the lead stopped when he had come close enough to be heard:

"We surrender. The 'Panther' has gone mad. He is shooting his own men."

The Sheik el Beled gestured to the man to march his soldiers to the staircase, take the wounded with him, and await a decision there. He obeyed. His example had its effect on those who had remained behind. A good many more abandoned their leader and marched toward the stairs. The "Panther" was now roaring like a madman. When we had surrounded the island, we sent Irahd ahead to ask whether he would surrender. It became quiet and some time passed until an answer was given. The "Panther" seemed to be deliberating and finally consented to a short parley with the sheik.

Each of the two was allowed a two-man, unarmed escort. The parley would take place between the island and our position. The sheik chose the Mir of Ardistan and me to accompany him. The "Panther" arrived with two men known to me, the "Sword of the Prince" and the "Pen of the Prince," the two Tshoban who had been our prisoners with him. It had been my impression that we would meet halfway between our respective positions, and it therefore struck me that the "Panther" and his two companions stopped short of that point. That he should want us as close to the island as possible aroused my suspicion. I communicated this to the sheik and the Mir. We therefore went no further than we were obliged to, and thus forced the "Panther" to come closer. His face was an immobile mask, but his eyes were glowing. He must have been furious that he had not been able to trick us into moving further away from our troops. He stopped but did not sit down while I carefully scrutinized him and his companions to make sure they had no weapons hidden on their person. Then I was struck by the position and movements of the three men. They avoided placing themselves between us and the island. To see if I was right, I repeatedly moved about during the parley and noticed that they acted correspondingly, always taking care not to stand before us. It followed that someone was going to shoot at us from the island and I now began scanning it closely.

"What do you want?" he hissed at us when we met. I answered:

"To ask you if—"

"To ask me!" he interrupted. "I am the one that will ask the questions, not you. What do you want here? What business do you have? And why are you looking at me? If you cannot answer my questions, I'll do it for you. Your fate has driven you into our hands. You are about to die, and you amply deserve to. The same goes for the Mir. The Sheik el Beled will be taken prisoner.

I'll force him to resign and to put me in his place. He will be compelled to give that order to save his life, and his people will obey him."

Was this madness or a plan he had quickly decided on? Or both? A restless, dangerous light was flickering in his eyes. He went on:

"I am asking you: Will you surrender voluntarily, or not?"

"We surrender to you, or you to us?" I asked.

"We should surrender?" he thundered. "Have you lost your mind? Do you think we are afraid of you, or of this naked rock? Or of the people standing up there? They can do nothing to us. I am telling you that you are in my power. You miscalculated when you thought I would die of thirst. There is more water in this cistern than I can use. And those people who are so proudly looking down on me will receive me with cheers tomorrow."

He spoke like a man firmly convinced of his hallucinations. Was this due to the night of horror at the Djebel Allah? Or was it a natural psychological event that the delusion that had governed his entire life and made him want to become a great ruler should suddenly have brought on this madness?

"You are mistaken," I told him. "You won't die from a lack of water but from an abundance of it. You are about to drown."

"Where? When?"

"Now. Here. The river is coming, and will rise. And so will the water in the cistern. Together, they will flood the island and engulf you."

"Engulf me?" he exclaimed with an incredibly ugly, repulsive laugh. "Do you really think those threats will make me commit the stupidity of surrendering to you? I am telling you that I would rather die a thousand times and rather suffer the worst tortures than turn myself over to you. Even now, I don't fear death. I scorn it. But you—Now, now."

"No, we won't be harmed but you will be seized as I am seizing you."

I had been very attentive, and I had noticed that several of his men had stepped behind some trees. When he gave them the signal by shouting "Now,

now" they aimed their rifles at us, ready to fire. I quickly seized him, pulled him toward me, and pressed him so hard that he could not move. Then I called to the sheik and the Mir:

"Quickly, get behind me. You'll be covered there."

"Why should I seek cover?" the sheik asked. "Who is there to be afraid of?"

He clenched his fist and struck. Two blows, and the "Sword of the Prince" and the "Pen of the Prince" crashed to the ground as though felled by an axe.

"The Sheik el Beled never seeks protection behind someone's back," he added. "He has no need of that. Look over there!"

He was pointing at the "men in black armor" who were rushing toward us to form a wall around us. Some ran toward the island where hand-to-hand fighting had begun again between those the "Panther" had told of his plan and those who had been unaware of it. The fight gave us the opportunity to withdraw. I had taken the "Panther" by the neck and was pushing him ahead of me until we were out of range. Then I shook him vigorously and asked:

"Are you surrendering, or not?"

"No," he breathed although both his arms were limp and my grip was driving blood into his eyes.

"You'll drown miserably."

"Gladly." He tried to laugh sarcastically, but couldn't manage.

"If you surrender, you'll be forgiven."

"May Allah damn you and your forgiveness. It's not for dogs to forgive. Let me go!"

"Go on then, be free!"

I pushed him so hard, he hit the ground and somersaulted. He quickly picked himself up, did not stop to curse and threaten, but ran quickly toward the island. We rode away, indifferent to what would happen there. We noticed that the shooting had started again but did not concern ourselves with it until we saw that a number of the "Panther's" followers were running after us. Some of the soldiers in black armor were ordered to wait for them and bring them to us. Of the thousand men that had escaped with him from the Djebel Allah, the rebel now had at most two hundred left. We heard from those that had followed us that the Mir and I were to have been shot. The "Panther" then had intended to seize the sheik and take him to the island. Once he was in his power, he could force him to let him escape or perhaps even ally himself with him. What is more, Ardistan would once again be without a ruler and the intrigues and confusion could begin anew. It was not a stupid plan for a person who seemed to have utterly taken leave of his senses.

15 : The Oath of Djinnistan

When we had reached the stone stairs, the sheik was received by profound, respectful silence. When a ruler of El Hadd veils his face, it means that he has sworn the "oath of Djinnistan." He is considered taboo until he has fulfilled that oath and removes the veil. This was the reason for the silence that greeted us wherever we went.

We walked up all the superimposed terraces until we had reached the highest one and only the top of the mountain remained. At least, that had been my assumption, but I soon discovered that there was no mountain. The basin that now lay below us was nothing more than the carefully terraced edge of a plateau whose southern side sloped upward toward Djinnistan. The foot of every mountain we could see was covered by water whose extent and depth had never been determined. Once, it had flowed into the valleys and plains of the countries bordering Djinnistan on the east, the west, and the south. As the river Sulh, it flowed through El Hadd to Ardistan and poured into the sea in the country of the Ussul. Why it had dried up, turning the regions watered by it into desert, is something a legend attempts to explain. But the time will come when an exact science tries to solve this problem. All that has been established so far is that the Sulh is fed by those waters which flow from Djinnistan to the castle of El Hadd, and that its water is regulated by the mysterious and extensive structures built by Abu Shalem.

As we were leaving the basin, I did not know any of this, but thought that I would again see deep valleys when we had reached the heights. The Sheik el Beled, who knew better, said nothing to correct this misapprehension. The town which lay below the castle did not extend all the way up to it. Four terraces lay above its highest houses, and this was also the height of the base on which the angel rested. The foundations of the castle, to its right and left, were only two terraces deep but also built on solid rock. The impressively strong structures enclosed spacious rooms at ground level. They had a southern exposure and offered not only healthy quarters but superlative views. Here, the Ussul were housed. Higher up, other quarters had been set aside for the lancers and the "troops in black armor."

When we reached the plateau and emerged from a grove of splendid, millennia-old cedars, a wholly unexpected sight came into view. What we had before us was not a mountain peak but a huge lake. Toward the east and the west, no shores were visible, but in the north the mountains of Djinnistan rose from its waters. Shrouded in light veils, they resembled prophetesses that had turned to stone. They almost seemed to be raising their heads to see if what the depth below had been promising for thousands of years was about to become reality. At the south side of the lake where we were, there stood the almost supernaturally tall statue of the angel, raising its hand as if in blessing and looking from the plateau across the border. Behind it, there lay an inexhaustible supply of water for which men down below had been thirsting for centuries. On its eastern and western side, this angel was flanked by the tall, far-flung buildings of the castle. Solidly constructed, yet gracefully articulated, their style did not show the slightest trace of western architecture. In front of the castle, there were a number of blossoming, fragrant gardens, separated from each other by deep canals, which formed a uniquely landscaped park of unrivalled beauty. The purpose of these fan-shaped gardens, stretching from the castle far out into the lake, was to disguise a network of rock walls which projected out into the water and served to reduce the enormous pressure while yet permitting the waves to reach the castle.

This curious complex of rocks, walls, openings, and canals had a second purpose, however, which was related to the interior of the angel. There was another pressure there whose effect was regulated precisely and whose potential danger was turned to beneficial ends. For these rock formations constituted the famous and legendary "watershed of El Hadd," and inside the angel there was the key that would unlock this secret if one of a small number of initiates turned it.

We had stopped our horses to take in this splendid picture. The sun was sinking and about to disappear in the lake. Sparks were beginning to flash across the clear, immobile crystal of its surface. A boat with two white sails was coming from the northwest, moving calmly and inclined slightly to one side. We could not determine its size or the number of passengers but both bow and stern were oddly raised and the sails were immaculate and showed no trace of a seam.

We had been silent with amazement and admiration. Now, the Sheik el Beled pointed toward the boat and said:

"How punctual she is!"

"Who?" Halef asked.

"You will be surprised," the sheik said without mentioning a name. But his voice was joyful. "The horses are being brought. Her arrival has been observed. Both of them like riding."

Two magnificent white horses with sidesaddles were being led from the castle.

"We will go and receive them," the sheik told us. We rode to the center of the castle yard from where the wide path leading through the park formed a straight line to the wharf. The boat lowered its sails and we saw two men and two women. The men secured the sails and began to row. One of the women steered while the other stood erect at the bow and gave the instructions necessary to guide the boat past the rocks and cliffs. She was dressed in dark clothes but wore a white veil. Her hair, in two long tresses, almost touched the ground.

"Mashallah," Halef exclaimed. "Is this a vision, or is it reality? Sidi, do you see her?"

"Marah Durimeh," I answered.

"And Shakara is at the helm. Do you recognize her?"

"Yes."

The boat arrived and the passengers disembarked. The Sheik el Beled took Marah Durimeh's hand to support her, and I assisted Shakara.

"Did we arrive in time?" she asked me.

"You did if you intended to come here when we did."

She was very grave, yet amiable, and her good, gentle eyes were like those of a child still unaware of fate and Providence. Marah Durimeh gave me her hand, kissed me on the forehead, and said:

"If you find my appearance here mysterious, you will soon have the answer. We are going directly to the angel."

The Mir of Ardistan was immobile, his eyes not leaving her for a moment. He was so deeply moved by the sight of my queenly friend that he barely dared breathe. Only when she went toward the horse that had been chosen for her did he hurry up to her, kneeling down and offering his hand and shoulder to raise her into the saddle. With youthful grace, she swung herself on the horse and said to him:

"I thank you. You and the sheik will ride by my side. We will take a turn along the water while you report to me." The Sheik el Beled was brief and to the point. We were facing west, and, as he finished, the sun was setting, the radiant gold turning to a glowing red and the purplish tints one sees just before darkness falls. Marah Durimeh guided her horse toward the castle and said:

"Now I know what happened, and it could all have been foreseen. The times of such men are past. They are disappearing as the sun disappeared, as the last colors of this sky will fade. The earth yearns for quiet, mankind for peace, and history will no longer record acts of violence and hatred, but acts of love. It is becoming ashamed of the crude and bloody heroism of the past and is forging new, golden, and diamond crowns for the heroes of science and art, of true faith and noble humanity, of honest work and decent citizenship. Violence will not rule beyond this day. The coming night still belongs to it. It will terrify and torment the souls of men. But early tomorrow, these men will exult as God's word in the Bible exults."

We rode to the castle, passed its western wing, and stopped before the tall, broad base of the angel. The lancers had posted themselves along both sides of the stairs leading up to it. On the highest step stood a woman in white who was wearing the same blue veil as the Sheik el Beled.

"The chatelaine," Shakara told me.

"We are coming quickly and with great pleasure. I salute you," Marah Durimeh called out.

The Mir quickly jumped from his horse and took her hand as she walked up the stairs with youthful ease and yet with the customary dignity of a ruler. We followed her. The women embraced. When we had reached the top and were facing the chatelaine, the Sheik el Beled told her our names. She took us by the hand and spoke a few brief and friendly words. She exuded a delicate, sweet scent, not unlike the fragrance of pussy willows at Easter. When the Erdjani perceived this, he started. He seemed to be about to kneel down at her feet but Marah Durimeh quickly stopped him. She took the chatelaine by the hand, walked to the front of the angel with her, and said:

"Come, let us look toward the plains and all those who expect peace and blessings from us. There is still enough light to see the help the angel of the watershed is lavishing upon them. Meanwhile, the officers of the lancers can open the stairs."

The place where one descended into the interior of the base was opened by the same kind of mechanism which gave access to the angel in the "City of the Dead" and at the Chatar defile. Marah Durimeh led the way, and we followed. The upper chamber was furnished precisely like those in the other two angels. There was the same machinery except that it was much larger and more powerful. There were also two doors to the right and the left which seemed to lead into the castle. The floor projected beyond the wall to form a wide, spacious balcony with a strong railing to protect those standing on it. Marah Durimeh seemed to be familiar with this room. She touched the handle of the wheel and nodded seriously. Then she stepped out on the balcony. We followed her.

We were at a dizzying height. Below us, the depth of the basin yawned. But all fear was quickly allayed by the sight of the houses and gardens. On the streets and open areas of the town, there was a festive bustle. Seen from where we were standing, the "Panther trap" looked no larger than a few bushes. Some of the "Panther's" men, standing apart from the trees, were only small dots, about to be swept away. As far as the eye could reach, the country sloped down toward the south. It seemed a paradise, and yet it was waiting to be saved from the drought. Dusk was about to pass into night.

The bells of a church began pealing, and those of others followed. Marah Durimeh folded her hands.

"Let us pray," she said to us. "Grant us peace, Lord, grant peace to this earth, these beings, and to all of us. The river of Your peace and Your blessings has awakened again. Let it pour its floods over all that live and are still to be born so that when your paradise opens its gates and the angel asks the question that is asked once every hundred years, we may answer: Yes, there is peace on earth. Praise to be God."

The bells continued ringing and Marah Durimeh's prayer did its work within us. We prayed silently, each of us taking stock of himself, of mankind, of life. Then Marah Durimeh addressed the Sheik el Beled:

"You and the Mir of Ardistan, go to the wheel."

Both obeyed, the sheik quickly and deliberately, the Mir slowly, as though in a dream.

"No spoke of this wheel may be turned without the permission of the Mir of Djinnistan," she continued. "Does he know what is happening today?"

"He knows everything, and approves," the sheik answered. He sounded as if he were smiling.

"Then begin! The Mir will help you."

The wheel was turned easily and noiselessly.

"Come and look," Shakara whispered to me.

She took me by the hand and led me out to the balcony. I looked down and saw a miracle. At the very bottom of the basin, foaming masses of water suddenly erupted under the aqueducts. As the wheel was being turned, these masses swelled. The bells were still ringing but were being drowned by the thunderous rejoicing of the inhabitants of El Hadd.

"There is still time to stop," Marah Durimeh said, "but later that will no longer be possible. Have warnings been given? If not, this river will bring destruction, not blessings."

"All have been warned," the sheik answered. "I already gave the order at the Djebel Allah. More quickly than the water flows, our soldiers carried the news as far as the land of the Ussul. Here in El Hadd, everyone knows what is about to happen today and tomorrow. Only the 'Panther' knows nothing."

"Then finish what you are doing."

The wheel continued turning and the stream which poured into the rock basin became ever more powerful. A deep, monotonous roar reached all the way to the balcony. Half an hour had passed when the sheik announced:

"It is done. The wheel is standing still."

"And thus it shall stand for all eternity," Marah Durimeh said. "At this moment, the oath of Djinnistan has been fulfilled. The parents may show themselves to the son. Rejoice and raise your veils."

I was still looking down into the depth when I heard these words. The water could no longer be seen but its roar was still audible. The darkness of evening was rising from below.

"Come with me to the castle," Shakara said. "We should not be here now. These sacred moments are not for us to share."

She took me by the hand again and led me from the balcony through the room to one of the doors. As I passed, I saw the chatelaine unveiling her face and recognized the woman I had seen in the "Djemmah of the Dead."

"Mother!" the Erdjani exclaimed as he spread out his arms to rush toward her.

She pointed to the Sheik el Beled who was also removing his veil at that moment.

"Father, my father!" the Erdjani exulted.

That was all I heard or saw, for Shakara pulled me with her, through two covered walks, up some stairs, and along another corridor where some servants showed us the way. The Sheik el Beled had earlier sent a messenger to the castle to announce our arrival and to have rooms prepared for us. Hadji Halef had been given an apartment next to mine. The furniture was Oriental, opulent, and comfortable. When a servant came to ask if I wanted to eat, I did not hesitate to say I was hungry, and I also ordered food for Halef. I told myself that this was not the time for a long, formal supper with our companions. Everyone had his own affairs to attend to. The parents who had just been permitted to reveal themselves to their son could not be expected to share this evening with others.

Before the food was brought, I attended to our horses. As I was sitting down to eat, Halef came in. He was all happiness and joy.

"Sidi," he said, "this is one of the most beautiful days of my life."

After supper, we went out to the balcony of my apartment and sat down. The roaring of the water had abated somewhat. It had covered the bottom of the basin and was quietly rising. The sky looked like a black cloth hanging down on the roofs of the castle, and the lights of the city were small, barely visible points. A servant entered to let us know where our companions were awaiting us.

It was a fairly large, brightly lit hall. We found the Mir of Ardistan, the sheik of the Ussul, his courageous Irahd and some high-ranking officers of the "troops in black armor" and the lancers. Cold food was being served. We did not see any women. Occasionally, though briefly, the sheik or the Erdjani would join us.

Some time later, the sheik took us to another hall whose size and appearance we could not determine because it was completely dark. But opposite the door by which we had entered, there was an open gallery where the women and the Erdjani had just sat down. What looked like a bright strip as we entered turned out to be the lake. Toward that side, the sky was clear.

One could see the outlines of the volcanoes of Djinnistan. They were bright and they gradually broadened, turning into surfaces, domes, and peaks which were beginning to redden and glow.

"Sit down by us and watch the old paradise legend taking leave of us," Marah Durimeh said. "Reality is taking its place. Midnight is past, a new day is dawning. I feel that today the Djebel Muchallis will raise its inaudible voice, that it will glow to tell us that what was begun has been completed, that what had been hoped for is being fulfilled. It is said that the mountain glows only once, from midnight till morning. For everyone who sees it, it will signal peace on earth."

Now those optical phenomena appeared that I had first seen from the Ussul temple. They developed in precisely the same sequence and in precisely the same manner, proving that the forces and laws responsible for their creation were always the same. But suddenly, it became utterly dark in all directions.

"Now the decision will come," Marah Durimeh said with a tremulous voice as she folded her hands. "Will he show himself, or not?"

Long minutes passed. Our eyes were turned expectantly toward the north, but we saw nothing. Yet Marah Durimeh exclaimed:

"He is coming, he is coming! There he is!"

"Where?" we asked, for we still could not see anything.

Above our heads, the peak of a mountain, dark at first, then radiating brightly, became visible. Its golden contours slowly extended downward and then branched out like falling threads to outline the entire shape of the mountain and set it off against the dark background. What had at first been the invisible areas between these golden outlines gradually filled with colors descending from above. They did not seem to come from this earth but from a wholly different world.

Marah Durimeh whispered: "There he is, the magnificent Djebel Muchallis, the dream of my youth, the hope of my years, the final step from which I wish to pass to join the blessed of other divine worlds. He appears at midnight and will glow till morning. Thus legend tells us, and so it will happen today. Let us sit here in silence."

We sat for almost two hours. Only occasionally, someone got up and walked into the dark hall to rest his eyes and mind. It was no longer dark outside. As far as one could see, a colored glow was spreading as if daylight were being refracted by ruby red glass. It was almost light enough to read. Then a servant entered and announced that the time had come, that the river would flood the island in half an hour.

The Erdjani got up, kissed his father's and his mother's hands and told the sheik:

"I thank you for giving me this permission."

"But remember my conditions," the sheik admonished him. "Take Kara ben Nemsi, the sheik of the Ussul, and Irahd with you. Then I know you will be safe from danger."

Marah Durimeh said:

"The dawning day is a day of thanksgiving. When the sun rises, the horns of the Ussul will resound from the battlements of this house, and the trumpets of El Hadd will answer. The priests will lead the inhabitants of this town up here to celebrate the peace which will flow into all lands. But you will perform the first act of this peace: Love your enemies, do good to those that hate you. Go and save them. There is only one true victory, and that is the victory of love. Go down to them and forgive. And may God's blessings precede you."

"And come back to us unharmed," his mother requested. "I would not wish to have you restored to me in the evening only to lose you again in the morning."

Those of us who had been named by the sheik left the castle with the Erdjani. Four saddled Ussul nags were waiting for us in front of the gate. One of them was the chubby Smikh. The other three mounted, but I waited. I asked the Erdjani:

"First, I want you to tell me how you think these men can be saved. There are no boats."

"But there are the horses of the Ussul that do not fear the water. Two hundred of us will swim across and each one will take a second horse with him. That will be sufficient for those that are left on the island."

We rode down to the quarters of his countrymen. Two hundred of them with an equal number of riderless horses were awaiting us. In the subdued, mystical red light of the Djebel Muchallis, our train had an unearthly appearance. When we reached the stairs, we could clearly see the island although it must have been around three o'clock in the morning and there was no moonlight. The entire gigantic basin was already filled with water. And while the stairs were not yet entirely submerged, the flood was beginning to sweep across the island. The "Panther's" men were crying for help and whining with fear.

Our undertaking would pose no danger if we took care not to be swept into the countless eddies beyond the island. To be caught there and propelled into the riverbed was certain doom. The Erdjani was the first to enter the water. The rest of us were to remain on the bank, but this did not suit me. When about one hundred men had been saved and the Erdjani still had not returned, I asked Amihn for Smikh, took the four dogs with me, and went into the water. The "Panther's" men claimed that the thunderstorm had driven him out of his mind, and that he was raving. This proved to be true. He had refused to allow himself to be saved until I arrived, but the moment he recognized Smikh, he called out to me:

"I know this horse. On it, the emperor of the Ussul rides into battle, and so it is worthy of me. I shall entrust myself to it. Dismount!"

To get him to safety as quickly as possible, I obeyed this order and took another horse.

"And you are my prisoner and must follow me," the "Panther" bellowed at the Erdjani.

Like me, the Erdjani feigned compliance with this command and followed Smikh as he entered the water and began swimming back to the bank.

"Stop," the "Panther" called out. "Not over there. I must go down the river, to the Djebel Allah where my army is awaiting me."

He wanted to guide Smikh downstream, but the horse didn't obey, and so he started belaboring it with spurs and knife. They were approaching the eddies.

Smikh recognized this and began to rebel against the stabs and spurs which were driving him to his death. He roared, dived, and somersaulted to throw his rider, and succeeded. Howling triumphantly, he returned to us, riderless. No one ever saw the "Panther" again.

Meanwhile, the red light of the Djebel Muchallis had faded; it was dawning. As we emerged from the cedars on the plateau, the sun was rising and the deep, powerful voices of the long trumpets of the Ussul were resounding from the battlements of the castle, the ancient trumpets of the lancers blared, and from the city, others answered. The day of "thanksgiving" had begun.

A week later, the Mir of Ardistan returned with Amihn and the Ussul to the Djebel Allah. From there, he and the entire army went to Ard. Everlasting peace had been concluded.

Some months later, the first ship sailed down the river. It was called *Marah Durimeh* and established connections between El Hadd and the regions downstream. The link thus created would never be broken again. But we had another goal to which we turned. Our path would lead us across the mountains and passes, toward Djinnistan.

Editor's Note

Karl May wrote the two volumes of *Ardistan and Djinnistan* in 1907 and 1908 at a time of great personal distress as a justification of his own life and as an impassioned plea for religious and ethnic tolerance. Indeed, he hoped, perhaps naïvely, that Kaiser Wilhelm II and other politicians might read his books and thus be converted to a peaceful foreign policy. However, just as his previous pacifist novel . . . *And Peace On Earth!* (1901–1904) and his religious drama *Babylon and Bible* (1906), his visionary new work proved to be out of step with the increasingly materialistic and jingoistic spirit of the times. Still, the author had the satisfaction of attracting some high-minded new admirers, among them Bertha von Suttner, the first woman to win the Nobel Peace Prize. Yet it is only today, after the tragedy of two World Wars, that Karl May's later novels have gained some wider critical and popular recognition. Indeed, they are now often seen as his most enduring literary contribution.

Ardistan and Djinnistan has the outward simplicity of a fairy tale and thus is easily accessible even to young readers. A closer examination reveals, however, that the book's scope is quite ambitious. What, at first glance, seems to be nothing more than a romantic adventure in some obscure Asian country, is actually an allegory on the development of the human soul and the ultimate destiny of mankind. The colorful, fantastic, and occasionally even surrealistic action illustrates May's belief in the eventual transformation of human beings from "men of violence" into "men of grace":

"Mankind's question," Kara Ben Nemsi, is sent to Ardistan, land of violence, by Marah Durimeh, "mankind's soul." The mission is conceived inside the womb—the city and port of Ikbal (place of promise)—from where the hero sets sail in the ship Wilahde (birth) and, by way of a narrow canal, is delivered into the open sea. He is accompanied by his friend and *alter ego* Hadji Halef Omar who represents man's innocent, but irrepressible and often inconvenient urge for sensual gratification.

Soon the ship lands at the coast of the Ussul (people of origin), archetypical hunters, where Kara Ben Nemsi discovers that he has forgotten to bring along the maps and notes that he had prepared for the trip. This means that, in the act of entering the world, he has lost all memory of a former life and cannot profit from previous experience. Thus, he has to begin his journey without guidance. Among the Ussul he finds the first traces of the developing "man of grace" in the Djirbani (leper or deviant). Kara Ben Nemsi frees him from the power of the Sahahr (sorcerer) who represents the obscurantism of primitive religion. Traveling further, Kara Ben Nemsi meets the Tshoban (desert dwellers), archetypical nomads. Among them he encounters Palang (the panther) representing blind passion and the "beast" in human nature. However, he also receives the first message from the Mir of Djinnistan (ruler of the land of grace—God).

Finally, Kara Ben Nemsi arrives in Ardistan, finding a highly civilized people representing the refined "men of violence," i.e. representatives of our own contemporary civilizaton. However, the slowly approaching state of grace is resisted by the still violent passions. The "Panther" abducts the Mir of Ardistan and then abandons him in the City of the Dead which represents the untapped sources of the human spirit. Any further progress on life's journey is impossible until the Mir of Ardistan has searched and tested his own heart. Confronted by the reanimated victims of his ancestors, he accepts responsibility for the past and thus expiates his own guilt. It is then that the Mir of Djinnistan sends help. Sulh (peace), the great river of Ardistan, which had long been dry, begins to flow again, and the ancient treasure buried in the unconscious is rediscovered. In the meantime, the "Panther" had seized and occupied the capital city Ard (the body), but now he is driven out and pursued further and further, until he drowns in the waters flowing down from Djinnistan. The newly irrigated Ardistan is transformed into a green and fertile land. Lasting peace is established. Kara Ben Nemsi is reunited with Marah Durimeh. "Mankind's question" has returned to "mankind's soul."

The cover illustration shows "The Chodem", a work by the symbolist painter Sascha Schneider who, in close collaboration with the author, designed a series of book covers for the first comprehensive edition of May's novels. However, "The Chodem" was painted independently for May's private art collection. The picture represents man's confrontation with his own conscience or better self.

E. J. H.

Glossary

Aacht: Brother
Amihn: faithful
Bash Islami: leader of Islam
Bash Nasrani: leader of Christians
Chatar: danger
Ed-Din: faith
Djirbani: the leper
Djunub: South
Gharb: West
El-Hadd: border
Halihm: wise
Hi: she
Hu: he
Hukara: the despised
Ikbal: place of promise
Irahd: honorable
Madaris Lake: lake of science
Djebel Muchallis: mountain of Salvation
Sahahr: sorcerer
Sadik: friend
Shark: East
Shimal: North
Sitara: star
Sulh: peace
Syrr: secret
Tshoban: desert dweller
Ussul: pl. of Asl: "origin"
Uucht: sister
Wilahde: birth